Acclaim for Nancy Clark's

The Hills at Home

"Like a jumbo-sized Shakespearean comedy . . . leisurely in its pace and lavish in its detail, with a humor that ranges from arch to zany." —*The Seattle Times*

"Imbued with a sweet intelligence that brings each member of the title family to vivid life. . . . Clark has created each character with a unique, stubbornly individualistic voice and parcels the narrative among them as deftly as Becky divides the after-dinner pies." —*Houston Chronicle*

"Delightful. . . . Sets a new standard for modern family novels, a twentieth-century Trollope. . . . Offers a harvest ground of subtle, smile-out-loud hilarity." —*BookPage*

"Witty. . . . Charming, old-fashioned, and leisurely, reminiscent of Elizabeth Bowen or Muriel Spark, with petty strifes rendered truly as both comic (in their pettiness) and poignant (in their strife)." —*Kirkus Reviews*

"A warm, amusing and sparkling domestic comedy of manners. . . . Colorful and lively." —*Publishers Weekly*

"Narrated with great intelligence and subtle humor . . . accomplished, invigorating. . . . Clark has a keen eye and an outrageous gift for wry understatement." —*Bookforum*

Nancy Clark

The Hills at Home

Nancy Clark is a native of Massachusetts and a graduate of Trinity College. This is her first novel, and she is currently at work on her next novel about the Hill family. Clark lives in West Wilton, New Hampshire.

The Hills at Home

The Hills at Home

A NOVEL BY

Nancy Clark

ANCHOR BOOKS

A DIVISION OF RANDOM HOUSE, INC.

NEW YORK

FIRST ANCHOR BOOKS EDITION, JUNE 2004

The Library of Congress has cataloged the Pantheon edition as follows:
Clark, Nancy, 1952–
The Hills at home / Nancy Clark.
p.   cm.
1. Family reunions—Fiction.   2. New England—Fiction.
3. Recessions—Fiction.   I. Title.
PS3603.L368 H55 2003
813'.6—dc21
2002072314

Anchor ISBN: 1-4000-3096-X

Book design by M. Kristen Bearse

www. anchorbooks.com

Printed in the United States of America
10 9 8 7 6 5 4 3 2 1

For my father and my mother

"I should have called it
Something you somehow haven't to deserve."

ROBERT FROST,
"The Death of the Hired Man"

Contents

The Hills at Home

Chapter One The Hills Come Home

Outside, the night blew perfectly foul and all of the Hills had stayed home. Rain flung itself by the fistful against the clapboards, rain spangled the windowpanes, and the rain bore down so hard against the roof that shots bounced up from the slates and rained down again in shattery shards and splinters. The wind wheeled round and the startled rain skidded sideways. The rain sought, the rain battered, the rain invaded. This was an extravagant rain, as if somewhere, somehow, someone, miserly and profligate in turn, had been amassing rain until he possessed enough to hurl down fiercely and decisively upon the helplessly spinning earth.

The house stood alone out in the relative countryside of what used to be known as an old Yankee town, no longer situated so very far to the north of Boston. The house, whose rows of windows were goldenly, blurrily alight against the ragings of the night, could only be half seen through the tattered last of the October leaves, from a high point on the River Road which was, at present, mildly flooding along its low point. Drivers-by, the few drivers-by taking the windy route easy over the shimmery beech-leaf litter lying like slippery minnows across the pavement, thought the house resembled nothing so much as an ocean liner caught in elegant passage gliding toward a farther horizon. To enhance the passers'-by fancies, a sea-salt and sea-creature whiff of mudflats was conveyed upon the east wind as it soughed through an opened dashboard vent, conversational fog having whitened the windshield of a dark sedan nosing up the road.

"I understand Lily has her hands full," said its driver, a woman who knew a little of the Hills' situation, "with that crew she's got there with her these days."

"Oh?" asked her companions, encouragingly.

3

But if this was not a night to be out, this was not necessarily a night to be in. As the rain hardened, basins and pots were fetched from the closets where they were stored between storms and positioned beneath the usual roof leaks. The telephones kept ringing themselves, blurting or bewailingly pealing, and the electricity flickered off and on to add another element to everyone's measure of unease. There had been a single daybright bolt of lightning and one warning growl of thunder earlier and no one in the house quite yet dared to run the risk of making toast.

THEY, THAT CREW, Lily's family, had all come for visits the summer past and none of them had gone away again in the fall. The weekend stretched into a week, the week became weeks, the weeks accumulated into a month, the months made up a season, and then the season changed. Oh, Lily ought to have been warier. Their suitcases ought to have struck her as having been very thoroughly packed as she bumped their luggage up the stairs and hefted the ornery, strapped-shut grips onto the foots of their freshly made-up beds. She ought to have let their bags languish in the front hall wherever they had dropped them, however underfoot their effects might have remained, there where they were, crumpling the carpet pattern and nicking the shaky old legs of the deacon's bench and tripping up the careless returnees who would be too excitedly chattering and ranging about all at once on sorties of rediscovery and reclamation to mind their ways.

Surely, Lily should have made them bide their time on the terrace flagstones and finish the tall glasses of iced tea she had carried outside on an overburdened tole-ware tray. They ought to have been required to give good accounts of themselves and to stand close questions concerning the glossed-over parts of their narratives. At the very least, Lily should have let them ask which rooms were to be theirs. She ought to have leaned back on a terrace chaise and obliged them to campaign obliquely or openly, according to temperament, for assignment to the bedroom remembered as a favorite one—with a view of the river; with the framed print rendering of a nearly nude Squanto welcoming Miles Standish, overdressed in his flimsy jeweler's-art armor, to a rather too tropically fruited and plumed New World; or, best, the big square front-facing chamber containing the electrified invalid's bed, which, shuddering and creaking at the really determined press of a handheld button, closed up like a clamshell. They'd been sorry to learn the invalid's bed had been rented and returned after the last wave of old people's illnesses and deaths back in the mid-seventies. Sorry to hear, and surprised as well by Lily's owning to the fact of a rented deathbed in a house where, as Alden said, even the fused clump of peppermint drops kept in the domed dish on the big parlor mantelpiece was, surely, the original fused clump.

Yes, there was a footing Lily ought to have established at the outset but that had never been the family's way, for all of the Hills had been raised to regard the old house in Towne as home whether they had been reared there or in some other place. The Hills lived, if not in exile, then as self-perceived expatriates in midwestern suburbs and at New York addresses where they could be tiresome on the subject of Towne. No one else quite understood the unswerving attraction, even after they'd been shown photos of the graceful Towne green and the view from the River Road bridge, and been told about the deep-voiced frogs who lived in the swamps, and who, the Hills said, said, *Mud, mud, mud.* Some salmon urge to return must have been encoded in their DNA, non-Hills privately decided, but Lily, even as she grumbled to herself, even as she paid the property taxes year after year and continued to worry about the roof and ran her vacuum cleaner once a week back and forth over the floorboards and carpets and stair treads, might have answered back to the mutters of outsiders, No, not salmon urge but *soul,* were she less reluctant to speak the word outside of Morning Prayer at All Saints'— a word which, of late, Lily had been less frequently speaking in that venue, having lapsed in her regular attendance. She liked the new rector. He spoke the General Confession like someone with a clear but not complacent conscience. He did not need watching.

And so Lily had, according to custom, arranged welcoming vases of narcissi, and then iris, and later, roses, to set upon their bureau tops on the days of their arrivals. She had greeted them at the door or the top of the driveway, smilingly enough. She hoped on their behalves for fair weather. She pepped up the first-night supper menus with piccalilli and cottage cheese spread on Ritz crackers for before, and she baked batches of Congo Bars for after, a lavishing of hospitality, really, which must have given them all the idea that Lily was delighted to have them, a sentiment to which, in the long run, they were bound to hold her.

Her brother Harvey had been the first to return, on a cold day in May. "Lily?" Harvey was abrupt on the telephone. "Be there Thursday," he had said and then dropped the receiver as if from a height. He had been living on his own for a while now and Lily guessed he had already held a conversation with her in his head during which he had gone into the pertinent details.

On that Thursday, Harvey had barged through the front door without knocking, and he planted himself on the threshold of the big parlor inhaling its still, chilly air as if he meant to acclimatize himself before taking on the high-rising staircase. Lily had followed behind as he made a beeline for his boyhood bedroom which, like Thebes, was much altered but remained a place on his mind's map. The brand-new wallpaper, at long last made necessary by a pipe-burst the previous January, was not very nice, its pattern a drift of lavender daisies and skimming butterflies with elderly faces and horns on their heads, and Lily heard herself apologizing for the new paper but Harvey said he had never much cared for the old stuff which had been a marshy scene of ducks who looked too fat to fly and knickerbockered hunters standing elegantly about and nipping from their flasks of whiskey. Poor Marjorie had had to improvise an eyeshade, he said, last time, on their last visit, last year. There had been something malign about those ducks, Marjorie had felt.

"Think she must have been spoiling for something even then," Harvey said.

He leaned against his boyhood window, one knee levered onto the wide sill, his nose bent and blowing smoke upon a pane of glass. Slim saplings had turned into sturdy trees and a loose line of faux-colonial homes and lawn-service green lawns had advanced beyond the village limits, and even a bit of Boston showed now, or, at any rate, evidence of the city, a browny-yellow smudging of the southern sky, which may have been just as well; the way Boston was going he'd need to keep an eye on the place.

"You've let everything go," he told Lily, as if the shaggy trees and the march of houses had been her doing, as if, somehow, she had failed to resist, the lone figure pushing back the raised blade of a bulldozer. He would have heard, had Lily made the effort. She would have been in the papers as a matter of human interest.

He turned from Lily as she frowned at him and he fiddled at his bureau top, strewing a shoehorn, spare change, a pocketknife plucked from his pocket across the drawn-thread bureau scarf. Lily wouldn't have given him such a nice one had she known he'd become such a clutterer. He unfolded the standing triptych frame of his wives' photos, the late Amy, and later Naomi, and his latest, Marjorie, as he referred to them when, occasionally, he recalled one or another's ability to perform some necessary task—sewing on a last-minute replacement button while he remained inside his shirt (Amy) or speaking French to the French people in France (Marjorie). Naomi, the middle wife, like a middle child had been the least remarkable but quite the nicest (Naomi could bake), Lily thought as she studied the three similarly sweet and palely pretty faces. Amy, the prototype, seeming to age in portraiture as she had failed to age in life.

Then Lily, extra bath towels folded over her arm, watched Harvey as he tested the bed by kicking a post and lifting up an edge of the quilt investigatively. Lily had made a lumpy job of putting Harvey's bed together. As she thumped the old mattress, perhaps with some idea of tenderizing it, she had conducted her own half of the terse telephone call—What time shall I expect you? Will you require lunch? How long will you stay? Must I buy a tub of special margarine? Saltless salt? Shall I call someone in to install Stedi-Bars above the bathtub? Can you manage the stairs? These intimations of infirmities would have acted upon Harvey as a stick prodding the ribs of a bear curled round his rumbling slumber. Unwise, such questions would have been, yet resented, of course—a failure to anticipate his needs. Lily had split a too-small pillowcase stuffing it with a king-size pillow, and she had snatched a twin-size top sheet from the linen cupboard which she had used anyway as she argued at Harvey, in absentia.

"Short-sheeted my bed? Because I warn you, I'll break my hip and then you'll be sorry," Harvey told Lily.

Lily wondered whether Harvey wasn't becoming childish. He was a rosy-skinned and fluffy-headed old man, with a teary glint in his eye—some temporary duct trouble. She hadn't attended as he told her all about it, his mystified and impressed doctors, the useless prescription drops he was using, instead, on his hangnails. His trousers stopped too short of his ankles, as if once again he was outgrowing his clothes. His walk was springy; his new Air Jordans had been a successful impulse buy. And he seemed excessively cheerful for someone who had lost as much as he had. Amy, at the last, had clutched her head, and Naomi her heart, and Marjorie clung to the steering wheel of a careering car. (Lily could not stop thinking about them. She had been startled by the sudden unfolding of the triptych frame, for she had expected to view happy and similarly sweet grandchildren's faces.) That none of Harvey's wives had, at the last, reached for Harvey was at once an indictment and an acquittal, perhaps. None had chosen to take any essential part of Harvey with her, and Lily supposed that was how Harvey had managed to carry on—and how Harvey carried on, Lily reflected privately.

"Lily, you've let the old place go shockingly," Harvey stated. The crystal knob of his closet door spun off in his hand as he wrenched it open to check whether Lily had supplied him with the wooden clothes hangers he knew Lily knew he required. She had given him a sound dozen, all filched from good hotels in the days before even good hotels welded their hangers to the closet rods. Nevertheless, the hangers were no more than he was due, if Lily was expecting thanks. He shot her a look from the cover of the closet door, but she was only trying to push a sprung-loose thread back into the warp of one of the bath towels. She wet her fingertip and prodded.

"There can be such an old lady look to a house," Harvey told Lily. "I can always tell just driving by a place and I could tell driving up here. The window shades are all unevenly drawn because you can't remember from one room to the next whether the shades go halfway down or three-quarters of the way up, and you've let the shrubs run so wild and swooping across the doors that you can't get in or out and you'll have to call the Fire Department and they'll come roaring up in their truck and you'll be very embarrassed. And the paint, no matter what color it was originally supposed to be, looks like you went to the store and asked for a gallon of, a gallon of bilge-water grey."

"The shades are drawn in reference to house plants and certain upholstery fabrics I do not wish to fade," Lily said. "To fade further," she amended, lest Harvey take it in mind to collect specimen cushions to demonstrate that the damage had already been done.

Harvey scraped bureau drawers open and shut. He removed a wizened pomander from the bottom drawer, an apple stuck and studded with cloves and looped with red ribbon secured to a flimsy stem. Uttering oaths, he reached deeper and extracted a dozen or more shrunken and rather evilly dead-appearing objects, no, not heads as first he feared but only Seckel pears. Lily had left them in the drawer last fall to ripen undisturbed in the dark and she'd forgotten them, at least until she remembered last February and couldn't face what she knew she'd find. The pomander had masked the sequence of odors emanating from the tall old chest of drawers, such a fortunate set of circumstances, Lily had thought at the time.

"I suppose she keeps her hankies in the vegetable bin," Harvey addressed the air.

As he shoved the drawer shut, the triptych frame of wives' pictures fell flat onto the bureau scarf. Lily set them upright again, and were she feeling fonder of Harvey at the moment, she would not have positioned the faces so that their six similarly gazing eyes would meet Harvey's own as he awoke in the morning, yawning and scrubbing away the accumulated salt of his automatic tears.

"But what are you looking for?" she had asked, as Harvey ruffled through a stack of *Woman's Day* magazines Lily was keeping in a neat pile beside the radiator for their fresh-sounding recipes and clever craft ideas should a particular need arise to produce a Bizzy-Daze Peanut Butter Supreme Torte or create Muppet-character sock puppets for disadvantaged children, even as she recalled the days when the children of the poor had required only the socks themselves to wear on their feet.

"What am I looking for?" Harvey asked. "I am looking for my pair of paint pants that I left behind here, and I'm counting on having those paint pants because it came to me as I observed your flaking trim and your peeling clapboarding that the reason I've come home is to paint the house. I'm going to start in on the shudders."

Lily was caught between self-defense and self-justification.

"Harvey," she said, "you left home fifty years ago and on subsequent visits you haven't lifted a finger to help except that one time, I do recall, when you took a hammer to a cellar step because you trod upon a risen nail and you resented having a tetanus shot."

"Didn't want to get lockjaw," Harvey said.

"Well, no one wanted you to get lockjaw," Lily agreed. How he would have kept them hopping with the jaw-locked and angry issuance of memoranda, at the worst specifying his funeral hymns and coffin wood, followed by a long, crankily conversational convalescence.

" 'Course not, would have been very serious," Harvey allowed, mollified.

"And you won't fit into those old work pants without a crowbar."

Nevertheless, Lily had been collecting estimates from painters for the past few years and when she got around to calling on the least alarming figure, she had learned there was a statute of limitations on estimates. State law, Miss Hill, she'd been told by a former student who seemed to relish knowing better than she. She had had no further will to interview a second round of paint contractors, those whose advertising cards on the TrueValue notice board she had passed over the first time because of hard-to-read handwriting and the speckled and untidy appearance of having been pinned there too long and too unavailingly appealing for work.

"Very well, you may paint the shutters," Lily told Harvey. "But you may not choose the color." The shutter color was always the same, anyway, that deep shade of true green which surprises you when you prise open the can's lid by not smelling of a northern pine forest but only and oilily of paint.

"Hope you have a high enough latter," Harvey warned. "Otherwise I'm driving straight down to the TrueValue and I'll charge a fifty-footer to your account."

"There's a tall ladder in the barn," Lily said. "I think it still works."

"Still works? What aspect of a latter can there possibly be that works or not?" he wanted to know, a point he and Lily had discussed off and on throughout the late afternoon and the pepped up first-night supper, a ruffly bubble pancake with cherry jam, and the martinis that had been Harvey's idea. They had discussed ladders further during an otherwise quiet evening spent in the little parlor in front of the television set there, watching the nothing (they were united on this point) that was on.

LILY'S NIECE AND GRANDNIECE arrived one night toward the end of June: Ginger Hill Lowe Tuckerman and her daughter, Betsy. The local taxi, a long station wagon with rocket-age fins and writing on its side, dropped off Ginger and Betsy and their gypsyish and disheveled bundles and satchels in a confusion of lamplight and opening doors and asking and answering voices. Somehow, as Ginger, her hands burdened, leaned into and rattled the bellpull with her shoulder blade and whirled into the front hall, and Betsy flew like a wraith behind, pleading with Ginger not to cry, not to cry now, it had been left to Lily to pay the driver and to calculate a tip to compensate for the bundles and the inconvenience, and as well, for the really very unnecessary display of weeping on Ginger's part, springing from her eager, tired eyes as she caught her first glimpse by the rake of the taxi-wagon headlights of someplace she remembered well, the roadside shack where they used to walk to buy apples, where an apple-cheeked old-timer had always been so kind to the young and happy, then, Ginger, singling her out every time to hand her a peach from a newspaper-covered basket beside the old tin cash box.

Doris, the Towne Taxi Service night driver, didn't think any of this was worth crying over, peaches instead of apples. Peaches were better than apples in Doris's experience of their relative merits. She had eaten far fewer fine peaches than apples in her lifetime, and she said as much to Lily who had no idea what Doris was going on about, but she agreed, "Yes, I like peaches," as she and Doris tugged and pulled Ginger and Betsy's many bundles from the back of the taxi wagon. Eleven, Lily counted under her breath, an amount she factored into the figuring of Doris's tip.

"Because I've had my own troubles too, Miss Hill," Doris said, in blame or in sympathy. Even Doris wasn't sure where she stood. She only knew she too had tasted tears.

"Yes. Yes, I know you have, Doris," Lily said.

Unusually decisive that night, Lily had sent the emotional Ginger upstairs to bed at once, and presently she carried up a tray set with tea steeped in a tiny china pot and poured into a porcelain cup, and a square of Angel Gingerbread centered on one of the special dessert plates shaped and painted like an ivy leaf. Ginger, who, if consulted, would have said she was in the mood for Thai take-out and a robust Burgundy, recalled that this presentation of tea (of hot water tinted with tea) and the morsel of something not too sweet was exquisitely typical of her maiden Aunt Lily, and she decided to cherish this delicate handling of herself and her situation.

"We'll speak tomorrow," Lily had said, edging all the while toward the door. "If you feel up to talking," she added sagely, for she was in no particular hurry to hear what Ginger had to say for herself. (Husband trouble, Doris had predicted to Lily at the last.)

Ginger slid between cool, rose geranium–scented sheets and she picked up a small, brown-covered bedside volume of Elizabeth Barrett Browning (so very thoughtfully provided) and was not unconsoled by the Sonnets to which she turned, so familiar to her she did not read them but only recalled certain lines she loved and which she might have written herself, they so applied. Besides, she had lost track of her reading glasses' whereabouts among her suitcases and she needed her reading glasses to read now.

She was refreshed by the tea and cake, swiftly consumed, crumbs daubed from the darling (and she remembered it now) ivy leaf plate and she found herself, frankly, not a little bored, for it was not yet ten and she had been put to bed for the night. Lily had told her not to come popping back downstairs, which, stated that way, sounded too undignified an action to take, and so Ginger was stuck. She slid off the bedsheets which had been polished smooth by wear and washing, and she snooped through her bedroom's closet. Several well-stuffed garment bags with rusted-shut zippers did not yield to her first impetuous tugs that night and she resolved to tackle the problem with pliers in the morning. Still restless, she rucked up her window shade and gazed upon the unmoonlit terrace below, at the further end of which she momentarily mistook a tall, leaning ladder for a man she had once known. Man and ladder were of a height, it seemed to her, and she had been thinking of him. He had lingered on the edge of her thoughts for years, never insistently but always reliably there. Had she summoned him to her side, had her powerful wish to see him again drawn him here, he knew not why, to tarry until her voice called to him from a high window and reminded him? Ginger would not have denied she could be a bit of a mystic, even if her vision had fizzled when she narrowed her treacherously failing eyes (her far sight, her near sight, going, gone) for a confirming, more focused look.

But I'm working on him, Ginger told herself as she settled back among her pillows and lay dozily awake. Dear Lily, she had placed Ginger in the perfect bedroom. Lily had known without being told that the heartsick and loveworn Ginger required this lace- and chintz-rich, uncommonly easeful room with its skirted dressing table and silly tuft of dressing-table chair tucked into the voluminous skirt, and the rows of pretty silver boxes set across the mirrored top to contain her cotton puffs and her eyebrow pencils and her many, many shades of rouge, which blushed from the least to the deepest of reds. Yes, yes, this room, Ginger sighed, and picked up her bedside Barrett Browning and she mused, then, along other lines . . . "If I leave all for thee, wilt thou exchange and be all to me?" . . . as sleep stole slowly upon her.

That first night, Lily had sat up late in the little parlor with young Betsy (so this was Betsy). They shared a larger pot of tea and finished off the gingerbread batch, dolloped with vanilla-extract-spiked and not-quite-whipped-enough cream, while Betsy talked and talked. In shock, Lily diagnosed, spooning extra sugar into Betsy's teacup. The girl was thin as thread and shivery on such a summer night, whereas Ginger, vivid Ginger, would become stout if she didn't take care, for her long loose linen traveling jacket had not fit her as loosely as Ginger chose to believe. Lily had noted the strained buttonholes as she retrieved the tossed-off jacket from the deacon's bench and drooped it from a spindle of the coatrack.

So this was Great-Aunt Lily, Betsy had thought that night. Her grandmother, called Olive, had been Lily's sister. Betsy wondered what it would be like to have a sister. She wondered what it would be like to have a sister who died.

"You need not call me Great," Lily said, and Betsy didn't think Aunt Lily meant to be funny. Betsy hoped not, because she had not smiled, but earnestly agreed "All right" to this, the first mandate issued here. *This* was Aunt Lily, who had always sent them a Christmas card back home in Kansas which had always been the first card to arrive, as if the distant aunt caught Christmas spirit a week or two too early back there in the mysterious East where she lived and where, at the precipitate start of each Christmas season, reminded and recalled by the cards (Chickadees, holly; a fir tree, a fawn), Ginger told Betsy that she must always remember she too had come from. The East is our Oz, she used to say, that green and spired land.

No, Betsy had thought back, I do not come from that place, but, she had known the house as the bumpy old taxi wagon quit the road that had taken them this far and labored up the worse surface of a long, wandering drive. The unlopped boughs of guardian trees clumped against the windshield, scrawled scrapily along the car top, and snatched at them through the open windows. How very dark, this domain beneath the trees. She battled a branch, she tore at leaves. She and Ginger shrank from their separate, invaded windows and met in the middle of the backseat. Ginger clung and Betsy allowed her. Doris stopped at a spot. Oh, they must be there, and the darker against the dark shapes of a large dwelling, outbuildings, assembled as they tried to make out—there, but where? A single carriage light switched on in expectation drew them in a straight line toward itself. They blundered down a lavender border snapping old growth when just to the left lay the path. The front door blinked abruptly alight at the sounds of them, and Betsy had known that door in the flash for she had seen it again and again, featured (nearly *the* feature) in photographs her grandmother had kept and which her mother now possessed of all the family brides on their long ago and not so long ago wedding days. Every bride had stood before that beautiful broad and raised panel door, with tall side lights and an overarching fanlight, and the single, great, natural stone step sitting as solid as the earth itself underfoot, the transition from the past into a future perhaps not deemed official, or, at least, not real, until the white slipper or white pump or white sandal glided over the very threshold. Betsy half believed, then, that her lost grandmother had arranged for the familiar door to receive her, since she herself could not be there to meet Betsy, to say simply (for there was nothing else to say, nothing that could help), *Oh, Betsy, honey* . . .

By then, as she sat in the little parlor, a teacup atremble on one knee, a plate just balanced on the other, Betsy was beginning to flag. Nevertheless, she resisted the idea of again climbing the curving staircase and undressing and brushing her teeth and occupying one of the humped and shadowy beds she had glimpsed through ajar doors in this familiar stranger's house where family feelings flickered on and off disconcertingly. Betsy was afraid these family feelings might flare up and consume her while her T-shirt was pulled over her head or her eyes were shut against the lather of her complexion soap or she was entangled in an ancient quilt, every finicking stitch of which had been sewn by someone who held a counterclaim to her loyalties and affections. She had been shown to the room which was to be hers, and as she had unzipped a carry-all bag containing the present for Aunt Lily, an already used copy of *Northbridge Rectory* (unobtainable except used, Ginger had said), Betsy had been routed by the smell of burning. Emanations rose from the old and never used lightbulb of her switched-on desk lamp as the element heated and charred the dead dust and insect corpses coating the bulb—a distinct odor of cooking protein, of roasting meat, of scorching flesh which Betsy had fled.

So, postponingly, Betsy told Lily the complete tale of their travels to Towne as Lily sat with her excellent posture in her Boston rocker, noticing now the wearing patch on the old Afghani carpet just where Harvey had taken to sitting every evening, overreacting to the six o'clock news. (Harvey himself happened to be out for the night. Several local widows had fallen into the habit of calling him with an extra Music Theater ticket to give away or with circumstantial tales about having a spare lobster on their hands, as Lily pictured a grim pincer gripping a manicured widowed fingertip.

("Ought to stay home and greet the gals," Harvey had said, consulting Lily before he accepted a just-tendered invitation, holding the telephone receiver to his rumbly chest. "Lily, Lily," he had boomed for her until she came to tell him to stop booming, but he knew had he called to her in normal voice she would have stayed where she was at the dining room table critically consulting a major delphinium article in the *Gar-dener's Monthly*.

("Go, go," Lily had urged him with a shooing motion he didn't much care for. "I suspect Ginger and Betsy will be a bit worked up when they get here."

("Ah," said Harvey. "Worked up?" He had decided not to stick around for that.)

Mummy said one has to undertake such a long, sad journey on a long, slow train, Betsy explained to Lily. Otherwise, she and her mother might just as well have driven across country from Kansas, and then Betsy would have been able to fit her twenty-one-speed bike in the trunk of the car. They could have visited the Smithsonian en route to look at the moon rocks and the first ladies' Inaugural Ball gowns, as well as stop at certain excellent outlet malls in Pennsylvania she had clipped an arti-cle about. There might even have been a Benetton outlet. Did Aunt Lily think they'd have a Benetton outlet in Pennsylvania? Lily wasn't sure. Perhaps, she said. She hoped so, if Betsy wanted to find one there.

But her mother, Betsy continued, had, with deliberate ceremony, requiring Betsy as wide-eyed witness, lowered her car keys and her credit cards and her wedding ring into the Pawnee basket on the tele-phone table in the front hall for Betsy's father to discover when he came home from work. Every night, he flung his own car keys into the basket and called out, How are my girls?, to which Betsy, if she was home, always answered, Fine, while Ginger, if she was home, and she often had not been home lately, always bristled and haughtily refrained from saying.

On that last day in Wichita, as Ginger was rampaging through rooms streamering clothes into and out of suitcases and attempting to cram in her bonnet hair dryer, her interdental-plaque-removal system, her per-sonal air ionizer, and the rainfall showerhead removed from the master bathroom shower, Betsy had taken the cordless phone out to the pool-house and called her father at his office to tell him what was about to happen.

"She's taking me with her," Betsy said. "She said I have to go too. Do I have to go too?"

"You must look after your mother," her father had said after a very long pause as other voices ghosted indistinctly along their airwaves, other people who were able to say what needed to be said to one another.

"Daddy?" she asked.

"Try to enjoy your trip," he said.

"Betrayer," Ginger had accused Betsy. Then she had asked, "What did he say?"

"Daddy said to enjoy our trip."

That had resonated.

Betsy had boarded the train wearing her plain and everyday striped-cotton boxer shorts, her T-shirt with the sunflowers stenciled on the front and back, her Roman espadrilles laced up to her knees, and a knapsack slung over her back, its canvas sides strained by her Dante and Beatrice bookends, her alabaster horse, and her treasure box, plus a stone she had grubbed from the foundation landscaping as her mother was hustling her out to the taxi waiting at the curb in front of their house.

"Oh, is this what we're wearing?" asked Ginger who had made a major effort with a new suit, scarf, earrings, stockings, heels, Ivoire, clouds of Ivoire.

Betsy had become separated from her shoes in the club car where she had retreated with her book, *Wuthering Heights*—which was not turning out to be what she had expected based upon the artwork on the cover. She curled up in a club chair, barefoot. She had had to move twice, once when a man with a smoldering cigar sat across from her and studied the cover of her book and asked her what she was reading even though *Wuthering Heights* was clearly spelled out above the tousle- and tumble-haired heads of the passionately embracing couple depicted there, and Betsy had changed places again when the two women beside her began to discuss their problematic ovaries.

"Oh dear," said Lily, when Betsy spoke the word.

And then a young man stood for a while swaying in the doorway, surveying. He had taken a shine to her, Betsy could always tell. He stared at her. She glanced up at him from behind lowered lashes. She had been relieved when he disappeared but he had returned and approached her carrying two tall shiny plastic tumblers of beer. Help, help, he had appealed to her, indicating an urgent need to scratch his nose, and Betsy had been obliged to relieve him of one of the tumblers, and, at his bid-

ding, to sip politely even though she was underage no matter how progressive a state they were currently rolling across—Missouri by then,
or maybe Illinois. After every bitter taste, her plastic cup only seemed
fuller but that must have been due to the frothy head melting down,
Betsy had finally figured out. The young man had swung into the swivel
seat beside her. His name was Stefan. He was a Dutch exchange student.
He loved rodeos. He loved seeing cows on their backs with their legs
tied. He prised Betsy's story from her with careful English questioning,
although Betsy would have said inexpertise in a language should lead to
vagueness and inexactitudes, but Stefan had, with his direct and unnu-
anced questions, interrogated her thoroughly.

"Finish up the whipped cream left in the bowl with your spoon, don't
let it go to waste," Lily told Betsy.

Well, Stefan had become very foolish. He had fetched Betsy's espadrilles from beneath the first of the club car seats she had been forced to
abandon and he knelt before her and fitted them onto her feet, handling
and caressing her ankles and insteps. She could not bat him away. She
was holding his and her own beer cups and had she leaned forward to set
them down upon the floor, she would have fallen into Stefan's arms. He
wound the lacings up to her knees, and above her knees even as she told
him not to, and he had cinched the ends too tightly round her thighs and
tied them in impossible knots. He declared she was his Cinderella. He
seemed keen to carry their acquaintance to the next level. Betsy would
have quit the club car then and there, only she was keeping an eye on her
mother, for Ginger had found her way into the club car and sat with the
ovary ladies, contributing to their by then very technical conversation
with close details of a troubling case which, enjoying excellent health
herself, fortunately was not her own. Stefan rose from his knees and
took back his beer—actually, Betsy gave him her beer cup, which was
fuller.

The train lurched and shuddered across the darkened plains. Betsy
leaned into the arms of her chair at every switch and swerve. They had
just finished a unit in junior year Social Studies on "Our Crumbling
National Infrastructure" and she wished again her mother had opted to
drive instead of trusting the hurtling, unstoppable train bearing down
along its single undermined track carrying her farther and farther away

from everyone and everything she knew and loved and counted on. She pictured her parents reunited after the derailment beside her hospital bed as life-support sounds eeked and pat-pattered on her behalf and she heard her mother's voice speak bravely of pulling the plug.

At last, Ginger had risen and declared the time had come to retire to their luggage-heaped roomette, for the night was well advanced and the roomette had been an expensive option which they ought to enjoy—and their upper and lower bed-ettes and the sink-ette supplied for the dainty dipping of one's fingertips, Ginger's commentary had run on and on. Enjoying our trip? she had asked Betsy as Betsy pulled a pillow-ette over her ear. The pillow-ette, tough as a Chiclet, only covered an ear.

Stefan had seized Betsy's hand to kiss as she said good night and, meaningfully, good-bye to him. Good night?, Good-bye?, his face objected tragically and he had bent over and twisted her wrist and licked her palm secretly as Ginger watched, unsteady on her feet, flushed and exclaiming how continental the young man's manners were. Betsy pulled, Stefan held on to her hand. Betsy whispered, I shall scream. Stefan said, regretfully, No, you won't, and his sport concluded, he released her.

"And now Mummy says she's going to write a book, Aunt Lily. That's her big new plan, she says she's come here to write a book," Betsy said. "And it's going to be all about her life experiences and what she's learned in life and what she thinks about, I don't know, life and everything else that occurs to her. She's brought a stack of notebooks and file cards and a package of Roller-Rite pens and a drifty kimono to wrap herself in while she's writing. Still, I don't think we have to worry because I'm sure nobody will ever want to read a book like hers, only then she'll be so disappointed and unhappy again. You cannot imagine how upset she'll be."

"But there's nothing we can do about that tonight," Lily said sensibly, and she refrained from telling Betsy that, indeed, she had a very good idea of the intensity and reach of Ginger's borne griefs and disappointments. She had, in her time, been treated to a performance or two.

LILY'S NEPHEW AND GINGER'S BROTHER Alden Hill Lowe and his family came to Towne later in July. They drove up from New York in their boxy old green Volvo station wagon. The back compartment was packed solid with suitcases and sealed cartons, weighing the chassis down low over the rear wheels. The dragging tailpipe struck sparks along unimproved patches of the Connecticut Turnpike and they had been honked out of the way by salesman types, young men in company subcompacts who were beginning to feel the pinch themselves, Alden said. The last pinch had occurred before their time, but something in their bones told them they didn't like the looks of the Lowe family car beating its retreat from the city and, evidently, going down in flames.

There was a faded card taped to the inside of the windshield. NO RADIO, it read.

"You know, Alden," Alden's wife, Becky, had said, reaching up and smoothing a curled edge of the faded card, "someone smart should manufacture NO RADIO signs using a picture of a radio with one of those international NO symbols superimposed over it, that red circle with the crossbar, for all the thieves who don't read English. It would be more considerate for everyone. And for the people who still have radios, I suppose there could be plates with trompe l'oeil pictures of empty recesses that you could fit over your dashboard. Somehow."

Becky enjoyed thinking up businesses. She had never really had to work, apart from an early, undemanding cultural kind of job when her slight salary had been consumed by taxes and taxis. Alden had given up reminding her that a mere idea was the least of launching a business, but now he asked her, "How would you hide car phones?" for the trip had been too silent so far. They missed the missing radio and even Becky had not been inclined to chatter on as she usually did at the start of a family trip, anticipating what she would do first when they got to wherever they were going—swim in the pool, order a room service rum punch, stroll down to the shops, stake their claim to a spot on the beach, call on local acquaintances, arrange theater tickets for the week (in London), or maybe just sleep until dinnertime. So many choices, the exercise seemed almost onerous, settling on just one.

"I suppose I'd hide car phones with mirrors, the way that high-haired magician fellow made the Statue of Liberty disappear that time," Becky said.

"Harvey said it should have stayed disappeared," Alden remembered. "He thinks that chiseled verse about the huddled masses and the tired and the poor always spoke to the wrong sort."

"Oh dear, oh well, Harvey. Still, those poor people were all just yearning to be free, so how can one criticize?" she answered, vaguely. She was gazing upon the tinted windows of a passing limousine, too blackened to see through. She wondered how the driver managed to see out.

"That's only a rental," Alden said. "See, there's a fleet number on the bumper."

"Oh," said Becky, no longer very interested in who might be inside, although if they were newlyweds on their big day she was, of course, happy for them.

She reached up, then, and peeled the NO RADIO sign from the windshield and folded it into the litter bag, for it had just struck her as a rather peevish declaration, and Towne, she decided, was the sort of place where an anonymous well-wisher might very well leave a new car radio in a basket upon one's fender. One would not know whom to thank and ever after be burdened with a sense of obligation to nearly everyone, on the off chance.

"But you know," Becky mentioned after another while, "if I were a magnate riding around in my limousine, I think I'd trade it in for a Winnebago. Then you could get up and stretch and make a pot of coffee and iron your sat-upon trousers before important meetings. There's a business idea for someone, converting executive Winnebagos. I'd paint them dark grey with pinstripes on the outside and the interiors could be wood-paneled and clublike with oriental carpets, leather chairs, and of course all the office accoutrements, a desk, a fax, an assistant. People would think the first few they saw were peculiar, but then, everyone would want one after an article appeared in the SundayStyles section, say. I'd offer a sophisticated Gucci model, and a sportier Arnold Palmer version."

"You'd need a very large capital investment to start up a business like that," Alden said.

"Oh?" asked Becky. She questioned his profile. "How much? A lot?"

"A whole lot," Alden assured her.

"Well," Becky supposed, "all right. But I'd like one for myself if I were ever in a position to need chauffeuring about." She interrupted herself. "Please stop squirming, Little Becky. The car is crowded for all of us."

"No, it's more crowded for me," Little Becky answered back. This was her usual complaint. She always had to sit between her parents on these long car trips, and her psychical space was invaded, she explained loudly.

"What's psychical space?" asked Alden.

"My *mind*. I can't *think*. I'm so boxed *in*," Little Becky complained. "You won't even let me *think*."

"When you think, you fidget," Alden said. "Why is that?"

"I *don't*. I don't *know*."

"Encourage her to think, Alden. Don't tease her," Becky said. "We encourage you to think, dear. Think all you want," she said generously, "and use words like *psychical*, only try to use them correctly."

"I used *psychical* correctly. I said what I meant," Little Becky insisted.

"We can look up its meaning. Lily will have a dictionary," Alden said. "She'll be happy to let you borrow it. Remember, the P is silent."

"I know," shouted Little Becky, and then she subsided. These sessions with her parents wearied her.

The three boys inhabited the backseat. Brooks and Rollins had wisely brought books, hard-worn paperbacks, and when Brooks abruptly came to the end of his tale, he blinked at the blank endpaper and tossed the volume to the floor. He kicked Rollins's shin.

"What?" Rollins asked, his eyes fixed on his page. He was at a good part.

Brooks displayed his empty hands, held hinged like the leaves of a book, and Rollins tore his own paperback down the middle, another slab-thick something by Stephen King, and flipped his brother the front half.

"They're wrecking books," Little Becky reported. She reached and tilted the rearview mirror so she could spy down into the backseat upon her brothers. Becky glimpsed, as well, the two collapsed and lolling younger boys, and Glover, the eldest, erect but leaning into the window, such large boys, such solid boys, such unanimated boys, and she thought, suddenly, of the colossi of Easter Island, another of Creation's mysteries.

"But they're wrecking books," Little Becky insisted. "Was that my book?" she demanded as an awful thought occurred to her.

"Never mind if it is. I'm sure Aunt Lily will have Scotch tape," Becky said.

"Absolutely, Lily will have tape," Alden said. "She'll have a diction-ary, Scotch tape, and aspirin."

"Headache?" asked Becky. "Shall I drive?"

"No, *I* don't have the headache," Alden answered.

Glover had been out late the night before, his last night in the city, effecting farewells at his various haunts. He had not returned until morning, until the not so early hour named for departure. Alden had spotted him as he was loading the car, Glover, the dissolute figure on the corner, hesitating, and then forming an eventual decision to approach, or, more likely, realizing he had no other place to go but away with his family.

Glover was sleeping through the trip, retreating to an aloof and dig-nified slumber, sitting upright, his chin tucked into his chest. A hand loosely gripped each knee. He resembled some cryogenic pioneer hold-ing out in a frosty limbo until a better era dawned, one in which a cure had been found for whatever it was that had been killing him in his own day. Alden couldn't identify the nature of his eldest son's hangover, but he was convinced Glover wasn't suffering enough from whatever it was he had indulged in the previous evening. Alcohol, of course—they had thrashed out that subject in his freshman year at the Stoddardt School when Glover had carried home a pamphlet called "How to Talk to Your Parents About Alcohol" and he had told them what they could expect of him. He would not drink and drive, he swore. But you don't drive, Alden had reminded him. When I drive, I won't drink and drive, Glover had promised virtuously and Becky had hugged him as Alden reread the shifty little pamphlet to determine what, in fact, had been agreed to. But they had all signed some sort of sham pledge on the back cover and, as Becky said at the time, felt better. Alden also guessed at drug use in moderation, though electronic amusements seemed to provide all of his sons with their oblivion of choice and, at any rate, Glover only partied on weekends and designated school holidays which, in Alden's opinion, was best a lesson learned early, this partitioning of one's priorities.

Besides, Glover's grades were not nearly as bad as they might have been, and he scored off the charts on the standardized tests although Glover, reluctant to be corralled into ever more advanced studies, protested the standard tests were pitched unfairly easy.

"Hi," said Alden. "Brooks or Rollins, nudge your brother awake. Glover, look to your right at that spire, those towers. That's a college. Your mother and I want you to consider applying there."

"Huh? Spires? Yuh, right. Sure," Glover said.

"Seriously," said Alden. "Tell him, Becky, tell him seriously."

"Seriously, what?" asked Becky, who had been thinking her own thoughts about designing Winnebagos for women executives, but all of her ideas so far seemed more suited for the traveling buses of country and western singers—bright colors, large lighted makeup mirrors, closet rods set high enough to hang a floor-length evening gown for the days when work slid into play and maybe a rugged bus driver with stubble on his chin and a way about him who would turn up as the you ("You stole my Visa card, you broke my heart") in one of those sadder-but-wiser ballads no one ever seemed to learn from.

"Why did she have to call them the *wretched* huddled masses in that poem?" Alden spoke into the silence. "I mean to say, frankly, if I'd shown up on Ellis Island with my bunched belongings and hope in my heart, I'd have been so offended to be called that I'd have turned around and gone home."

"Well, darling, no one was expressing official U.S. policy."

Lily heard the car chugging up the driveway. She set aside her jar of soapy water. She had been killing Japanese beetles by tapping them, engorged and sluggish, from her rosebushes into an agitated froth in which they were trapped and then drowned with each fresh sudsing shake of her old mayonnaise jar. Such fun, as Ginger said. She had requested and been given her own death jar.

Lily walked across the lawn to greet the arrivals. Alden, who had the sun in his eyes, steered over the grass toward his aunt, and he parked where their paths converged at the edge of the remains of an orchard beneath the low-boughed apple trees. Lily regarded the Aldens—her sister's boy, his Becky, and his brood—through a fringe of green leaves and the tough green beginnings of apples. Alden grinned at Lily through his cranked-down window and Becky leaned across Little Becky and assured Lily, and perhaps herself as well, "Here we all are, safe and sound."

They had been riding steadily, not even getting out of the car for a lunch break. (Becky had packed chopped ham sandwiches, warmish Cokes, and Pecan Sandies, distributed over her shoulder to the boys. She held Alden's Coke, handing him the bottle for swigs as Little Becky complained of being reached over.) It took a moment before it occurred to any of them that a family reunion, unlike toll plazas and gas stations, could not be negotiated through a cranked-down window. But they were, just then, thoroughly enervated by the cessation of forward motion and they had to muster themselves before committing fresh effort to the incidents of arrival. Becky folded the map into the glove compartment, reluctant to part with its, thus far, direct and reliable information, and Alden patted his shirt pocket for his sunglasses case. Little Becky gazed up at her Aunt Lily, fallen too shy to work on the first impression she had planned to make, a sort of Sarah Bernhardt and Sara Crewe pastiche, standing injured yet indomitable in the face of adversity. Although she had yet to identify the precise nature of the woes that awaited her here, she was confident that they would manifest themselves soon enough and she would, of course, be on the alert lookout for those pending offenses.

The boys only gradually became aware that the car had stopped. Brooks perceived the monotonous highway iteration of weedy verges and dusty, wind-shimmying trees was no longer unscrolling itself beyond the margins of his book. He punched Rollins who punched him back, then understood as Brooks pointed outside. They glanced at the dormant Glover who thought he was so superior. Stealthily, Brooks unlatched the door handle and he and Rollins executed paratrooper drops onto the spiky grass. They scrambled to their feet and confronted the summer-rich woods, the rounded rise of the meadow, a red barn, and a very large house. They headed there, stopped short of entering through a side door, and disappeared around the back, drawn by the thwacks and thuds of a hammer pounding so irregularly it sounded to them as if someone was chasing a moving target.

"Boys," Alden called after them. "Say hello to your Aunt Lily first."

Lily said there would be time enough to get to know one another again. Again, she said, for Alden and Becky and the boys had last visited some years ago when the boys were very small and Little Becky had just not yet been born. Becky had not felt well at the time. Rollins had swallowed the lump of beeswax Lily kept in her sewing box for stiffening thread. Brooks had stuck a steak knife deep into an undefended electrical socket. These several highlights of their previous trip here were resummoned by Lily's *again*, though she had spoken the word quite naturally, if not very warmly.

Alden and the Beckys climbed out of the car, ducking beneath the apple branches and plucking at the seats of their cotton trousers which stuck to their skin after all their sitting down. All at once describing their journey here, they followed Lily, who had retreated to a corner of the flagstone terrace. She had noticed a pretty striped snake essing through the grass and Little Becky looked like a screecher at snakes. Lily pointed to an ordinary goldfinch fluttering at the echinacea as a further diversion.

"Those boys are in their own little worlds," Becky said, and as she heard her own voice apply the old formula to their current circumstances, she realized she was long overdue to amend her traditional excuse.

Glover, roused at last by the silence, or by the birdcalls and cricket chirps and hammer falls which composed a country silence, recalled, after a blank, blurred minute, who and where and why he was. He wandered over to the terrace edge. He retained some rudimentary manners; Alden and Becky had started out with such high child-rearing ideals.

"Aunt Lily," he informed Lily, and Lily accepted his extended, written upon (with last-call names and addresses of friends) hand which had a feverish feel. Glover endured the sensation of touching Lily's osseous old saint's relic fingers. But his parents were pleased with him and Lily had only said, "How nice to see you, Glover," simply and unfussily and left it at that. Glover stood there and found he remembered, in a tumbling rush of images, having once been trundled in a wooden wheelbarrow very fast across a rollicking field. He remembered the jouncing he took. He remembered catching splinters. He remembered resolving not to cry. He remembered being amazed to discover that he didn't have to cry if he really would rather not. So. He had learned that here.

"You know Harvey is with me," Lily said as raised voices reached them. Brooks and Rollins had discovered Harvey behind the house where he was wresting off the first-floor shutters as the slats clattered and collapsed when certain vital balances and tensions were disturbed. Harvey was beginning to wish he'd never started in on the damn things.

"Yes, poor Harvey," Becky said. "And poor, poor Marjorie. You know we missed the funeral last winter. We were out West skiing and we didn't even hear until two days later. We were so sorry. We sent a note and we sent him flowers. I ought to go give him a big hug, I really ought to."

"He'll enjoy that," said Lily.

"And I ought to propitiate my sister dear," Alden said. "Where's Ginger hiding herself? Where's she hiding Betsy? I understand she's brought Betsy with her, poor kid. Well, we can all be poor together."

(But Ginger had absented herself for the day. She had driven Lily's car, with Lily's not very happily granted permission, up to Ogunquit, where she ate a fried haddock platter beside the ocean and bought a box of saltwater taffy intended as a gift of welcome for her brother and his family and of which she consumed more than a few pieces, the wintergreen ones, and the molasses, and the rum-flavored ones, as she sat swinging her legs over the side of a cliff face and staring off across the swelling, glinting waters. The sea was calm all the way to Spain. Ginger heard a maritime report on a tinny portable radio playing on the counter at the roadside stand in York where she stopped for a pistachio ice cream cone.

(And Betsy had spent the morning vacuuming the house from top to bottom. Her uncle and aunt and cousins were going to take over the attic, which was partitioned into rooms—such interesting rooms had been fitted beneath the roof. The dividing walls were single widths of wide pine boards standing upright and once painted creamy white and pocked with spyholes where knots had long since dried and popped. The wide board floors had once been painted red and were covered with coming-apart sisal rugs which Lily hadn't realized were so shabby until she pictured the Aldens treading on them. Lily had rolled the rugs loosely and fed them through an open attic window, the rugs unfurling and skimming impressively to earth. A defenestration, Harvey came up with the word for it, and he and Betsy and Lily had taken turns launching rugs and standing below to watch rugs float and fall.

"Who's going to go in which room?" Betsy had asked Lily. Lily had put Betsy in charge of bureau-top bouquets and Betsy did not think her boy cousins would care for big arrangements of Miss Lingard phlox and gladioli and baby's breath although they might not notice a few Shasta daisies in a jam jar enough to be bothered by them.

"Where do you think?" Lily asked. She sat upon the reliable lid of an old army footlocker, reflecting upon bath towels and pillowcases and water carafes and coat hangers and extension cords—she understood the boys were bringing some sort of computer with them.

"I don't know. I don't think I know them well enough to say. There was only that one week we all went to Bermuda together, but Little Becky was too young to be anybody yet, she was just three, wow, that was ten years ago. And the boys never came out of the ocean. They were just heads bobbing in the water. Since then, it's been pretty much just phone calls and pictures between us. I know Glover's my age, we have that in common. Brooks and Rollins aren't really twins, are they? They look so alike, only I know Mummy has to send them birthday presents on different birthdays. She's always late and it's always video games."

"The younger boys are a year apart but Rollins received a double promotion after the third grade so they're together in school," Lily said.

"Rollins is smart?" Betsy and the daisy in her hand snapped upright.

"I recall everyone was very excited when he made a battery out of vinegar and zinc and paperclips and powered a lightbulb. A psychologist weighed in as well when they assessed him."

"Rollins made it past a psychologist?")

Then, at two o'clock, Betsy had borrowed a three-speed bike from the tangle of bikes left behind in the barn by a hundred years of Hills who had always meant to send for them, and she coasted off down the driveway to a babysitting job in one of the new houses in the planned community which had arisen a mile or so down the road.

"You're going to have a houseful with all of us here," Alden said to Lily. He placed his hand on Little Becky's head as if he would condense her if only he could.

"We'll be fine," Lily assured him, because Alden had been such a decent little boy. He had, on his successive summer holidays here, neatly put his dirty laundry in the hamper, and he had always given in to his younger sister when she howled for the last cupcake or the first ride on the rope swing. And years later, Alden's intended, Becky, had come downstairs with her hair in curlers and a mud mask on her face and washed and put away the breakfast dishes on the morning she married Alden, from her husband-to-be's grandparents' house, Becky's own parents having died so sadly, so early, of separate illnesses. Very little in the way of thoughtfulness and good behavior earned one a great deal of subsequent goodwill and obligation. At least, things worked that way with Lily. She sighed and went so far as to pat the elder Becky's sturdy shoulder.

"But just smell the air here," Alden declared. "I tell you, I'm going to work in the garden. I'm going to plow the field. I'm going to walk in the woods every day. I'm going to split wood. I'm going to tap the maples. I'd like to learn smithying, or maybe I'll try my hand at stone masonry." New England had so many spare rocks left lying about, he'd always noticed that.

Glover stared at his altered father and he sniffed tentatively—was this loco air? he wondered. A cluster of intensely sweet climbing roses hung beside his ear. He'd been backed into the prickly bushes by his mother who had been trying to tuck his T-shirt into his jeans to conceal at least a part of its message, Roses are red, Violets are blue, You're attractive, Let's—— which she hadn't noticed back in New York even as she ironed the thing, at the time being more mindful not to crease the sleeves—for Glover had strong feelings about creased sleeves—than to critique the coarse doggerel.

"Don't tell Glover the air is good for him," she said. "He'll wear a clothespin on his nose."

"Ha," Little Becky yipped, but Glover only allowed, "I might just have to." He was not sure. He remembered, as well, having once been read a falling-apart book here about naughty creatures called Goops.

(Are you a Goop? he'd been asked. No! he had piped back.) For now, he was going to proceed slowly. He was going to stay cool.

"Shall we move inside?" Lily suggested. "The mosquitoes seem to have found us." She brushed her own pale face at the spot where Little Becky's scarlet cheek was being fed upon.

They all carried mosquitoes into the little parlor, attached to their skin and caught in the folds of their clothing. Harvey, shedding paint chips over Betsy's careful vacuuming, had hustled inside to make certain none of them tried to move into his bedroom (he had not listened as Lily described the arrangements) and to explain his evening news-watching schedule, which was sacrosanct because somebody had to stay on top of the world's vagaries and in particular, CBS's weird skew. Brooks and Rollins entered on Harvey's heels, mocking his gait, his mien, his shallow, dry cough. They began to swat at the pestering mosquitoes, chasing them down and crushing them against lampshades, sofa cushions, Lily's nice walls, smearing and flecking blood all over.

"No, no." Harvey was disgusted with them. "Not like that. Hold out your arm and let the mosquito come to you and then tense the muscle just as she bites. You trap her by her burrowed snoot and grind her firmly out with your thumb." He demonstrated. The boys, whom he seemed to have fascinated temporarily, sat at his feet, staring at their raised, bared forearms, cooing coaxingly.

Lily led Becky up the grand, curving staircase and a second lesser, twisting flight of stairs to the attic. Oven air roiled over them as Lily suggested Becky look around and decide whom to fit where in the jumble of rooms. The attic was cooler at night, the upper windows caught what breezes there were, Lily said, and Becky had moved to a window to wait for the first faint stir of relief to finger the gauzy stuff of the curtains.

Little Becky, trailing her mother's and her great-aunt's voices, had become lost. There were doors and doors and doors in this house. She entered, after opening every door twice, Ginger's room, where such an interesting disorder dominated, and instinct told Little Becky her own encroachment would not be detected until too long after the event for any blame to fall. She lay upon the bed just to see how soft—for the bed looked very soft, pillows and pillows were piled—and she remained there reading extremely high fashion magazines lifted from a heap on the nightstand.

Alden surprised himself and fell deeply asleep out on the lawn where he had sat beneath the greatest of the ancient maples, clasped between the prongs of its risen roots, until Harvey found and fetched him in for supper, which, planned by Lily with pleasing the young people in mind, turned out to be individual English muffin cheese pizzas, baked French fries, and raspberry Zarex and lime sherbet floats, plus a grated carrot and raisin salad nobody touched.

LAST OF ALL, that summer, Harvey's grandson arrived one night when the aurora borealis arced and bowed, lambent and eerie, high overhead across the deep indigo northern sky. The family was sitting outside on the terrace, marveling at and entranced by the phenomenon. They stubbed out mosquitoes and fanned away the powdery wingbeats of moths and sipped from ice-filled glasses and held the cold, sweating glasses against their faces and breastbones and stomachs. They spoke aloud at intervals, *Oh, look,* lest any member of the group fail to look, or look away and miss the show. They were still, in those early days, making efforts. Ginger had just asked, brightly, generally, "Gin? Tonic? Anyone?" before finishing the bottles, and Harvey helpfully inquired, "Ice?" as he rattled the last cubes from the tray during the after-supper pre-aurora scramble for the dash of something that would hit the spot.

When particles of headlights quizzed between the trees and, swinging round the driveway curve, consolidated and homed in on the terrace sitters, heads swiveled toward the breakaway beam, the falling star, what was it? Dazzled, the Hills gazed. They set their glasses down upon the terrace stones and rose from their chaise longues, the swinging settee, the hammock hitched between posts, and approached. (And had this been a real thunderbolt headed their way, they would all have been killed, as Alden remarked later.)

"Why, it's young Arthur," Harvey said. "Young Arthur," he hailed the lanky figure angling out of an open-sided Jeep. "What are you doing here?" he asked. He did not embrace his grandson. Nevertheless, he stood close enough to him to catch him and hold him, or, alternatively, shake him. Arthur hesitated, then briefly leaned against the old man.

"There's been a change of plans," Arthur said. "And anyhow, meet Phoebe first," he added. "Phoebe?" he said, and a young woman emerged not very gracefully from the driver's side of the Jeep, her attention incompletely called away from some other situation within the vehicle.

"Hey," spoke Phoebe, with some sort of accent. "Hey," she spoke more sharply, her hand raised and pointed toward the Jeep's interior, holding on to, invisible in the gloom, a string. Her hand slid down the invisible string and vanished through the Jeep's side. She struggled, then lifted out a striped kitten. She swiftly set it down. The kitten rared and hissed and leaped on wire legs behind a mud-caked Jeep wheel. The Hills, except for Harvey, Lily, Ginger, and Glover, knelt and clucked and chuckled at the kitten who could flee no further, held by the length of twine looped around its waist.

"Change of plans?" Harvey asked Arthur coldly.

"Listen, toiling at the Huff and Sparks Agency was never my idea," Arthur said.

"Damn right, that was my idea, since somebody had to have an idea," Harvey said.

"I don't care about advertising. I don't want to name after-dinner mints. It took a team of us two months to come up with The Admiral's Assortment, which frankly, sounds more like Victorian pornography to me," Arthur said. "So I've given them their shot—"

"No, no, you've got that backward, sonny. They were giving you the shot," Harvey said.

"Okay, so it was a duel at twenty paces and, bang, everybody missed," Arthur said. "No harm done."

"Well," said Harvey. "Well. And now you've taken on, you've taken on . . ." He waved at the little cat.

"We only just found the kitten," said Phoebe. She had moved to Arthur's side. They had rehearsed this interview with Arthur's grandfather. She had advised against the Victorian pornography remark, but Arthur had said his people were nothing like her own Baptist kin, and Arthur had worked in the dueling metaphor beautifully, in her opinion, like a speech in a play. The kitten was just a plus. "We heard mewing under a mess of leaves and Dixie Cups and all that at a rest stop on the New Jersey Turnpike, that's where we were," Phoebe explained. "All its little littermates were gone."

"Gone? Gone where?" Little Becky wanted to know. Perhaps the other kittens were friendlier ones who didn't flex their common-pin claws and bare their icicle-chip fangs.

"Arthur's friend means they were gone gone," Alden said. "To heaven."

"God, that's sad," said Ginger, and she sent Betsy back to the terrace to fetch her drink.

"Anyway, that's a girl cat, Phoebe sexed it," Arthur said.

"I'm from West Virginia," Phoebe explained as the family regarded her consideringly.

"Does she have a name, the little mite?" asked Becky.

"Not yet."

"Arthur's all named out."

They were arguing over names for the kitten when Lily slipped away to the kitchen where she poured milk into a saucepan. She did not care for cats. They killed birds and they had such an undoglike way of switching their tails while counting the ways in which one had displeased them, but Lily had to feel sorry for this one, for the dead siblings, for the Dixie Cups, for the girdle of string tightening around its scrawny torso. Lily dipped a knuckle into the warming milk and she opened a can of white tuna packed in spring water and spooned half, and then the other half, into a saucer, and she tipped the warm-enough milk into a bowl. The kitten could have the saucer and the bowl to keep for its own. Lily also slipped a pair of scissors into her skirt pocket. She planned to quietly confiscate the string.

When Lily returned to the terrace bearing the cat snack on a toleware tray, with Diet Sprite and peanut butter on celery sticks and vanilla creme-filled wafers for young Arthur and his—for Phoebe, Harvey had already pronounced that the young couple could stay in the barn even though Lily had decided, as she pulled fibers from the rather too tough celery stalks, that Phoebe would have to take the small green-on-green-striped wallpaper bedroom across the hall from Betsy's room, and Arthur could double up with Glover on a trundle bed in the off-kitchen chamber Glover had moved into after a hornet stung him up in his attic bedroom and his throat swelled shut, which Glover had very much minded.

"In the barn?" Lily asked, which meant she did not think much of the barn scheme. She lofted the tray. The creme-filled wafers were not intended for Ginger whose hand reached up from a chaise and sought.

"In the barn," Harvey stated. "In that little flat under the barn. Hired man used to live there. There's a pipe for running water and a thunderbox and some old electricity. Woodstove's chucked its chimbley, still, 's summer yet, you don't need the woodstove." For Arthur wasn't going to be let off entirely easily for having forsaken Huff and Sparks, although in Harvey's private opinion, they were a la-di-dah outfit. Nevertheless, he'd been told young Arthur was creative. Though all this making up of things was not, in Harvey's further opinion, particularly a man's job of work. Indeed, Harvey was glad to see Arthur had a girlfriend even if she wasn't a very pretty one. Girls tended not to be these days, or if girls were still pretty, then Harvey was no longer any judge.

"All right, the barn it'll be," said Arthur after allowing a pause long enough to permit an alternative offer to be thought of and presented, but Lily understood that her plan would not be an improvement. "I'll just fetch our stuff," Arthur said.

"Sounds tremendous fun," Ginger drawled at Phoebe from her comfortable chaise. "You'll look back, as one finds one does and you'll see these romantic adventures resonate a lifetime. They have to," she added darkly.

"You can drive that jalopy of yours up to but not into the barn because Lily has let the floor joists go so badly," said Harvey.

"Wait," said Becky. "Before you start up the engine, where's the kitten?"

"I have her," Lily said. "And I think she'll be better off in the house. At her size, one of the barn owls could snatch her or that fox who's been hanging around, or even a coyote, although I didn't believe that horror story about a coyote grabbing a toddler in Byfield. And I think that was just a roving pack of feral dogs who savaged the sheep over on the Lawrence Road last week."

"That was people from Lawrence, I heard," Harvey said. "Diabolists or dope fiends or carnival workers or some such. Senior Village got the word. Of course, it's all been hushed up to avert widespread panic."

"Cool," said Brooks, or Rollins.

"My goodness, how awful," said Becky.

"Nonsense," said Lily even as she cradled the kitten in her two hands and peered uneasily toward the woods. "Still, the barn won't be a very nice place for the kitten," she said.

"Darling kitten, don't be eaten," Little Becky cried.

"Well, the Senior Village version, I'm not sure I'd put much credence in what all those folks with hearing aids imagine they hear," Alden told Arthur and Phoebe.

"You missed supper," Harvey mentioned to his grandson. "We had green beans and fish sticks."

THEIR CHANGE OF STATUS from guests to residents could be charted through the cessation of Lily's services. By the end of August, she had stopped changing their bedsheets for them. She drove down to the village without conveying their dry cleaning or their dry cleaning tickets, even when shirts and silk summer dresses were left in soft heaps on the seat of the deacon's bench and dated receipts were slipped beneath her morning cup of coffee, marked with additional notes—*Make sure that the butter stain on the sleeve is really gone this time.* Lily no longer called their attention to the early-evening pheasant strut past the French doors. She did not encourage them to watch exceptional sunsets from the west-facing viewing spot along the upper ridge. She began to begrudge them their armfuls of cut hollyhocks for their bureau-top bouquets as they depleted her gardens. She mentioned it when one of them broke the door of her toaster oven, and she also remarked upon the melted cheddar cheese seared to orange leather around the perimeter of her broiler pan, which even Ajax and an overnight soaking could not budge.

She no longer provided individual bars of specific and premium bath soaps, nor water-softening bath salts, fresh gourd loofahs, tartar control toothpastes, minted mouthwashes, waxed dental floss, whitening and brightening laundry detergents, fabric softener, spray starch, Woolite

Gentle Wash, 100-watt lightbulbs, AA batteries, out-of-town news-papers, *People* magazine issues featuring junior members of the royal House of Windsor on the cover, the *TV Guide*, postage stamps, business-size envelopes, safety pins, sewing needles, ant cups, OFF Spray, Calamine lotion, Vaseline, Bag Balm ointment, ear swabs, cotton balls, Bufferin, Anacin, Tylenol, Alka-Seltzer, Contac, nose drops, Immodium capsules, Vitamin A, Vitamin B, Vitamin C, Kleenex, Tampax, cream sherry, sin-gle malt Scotch, Tanqueray gin, dry vermouth, microbrewed beers, cer-tain very specific wines spelled out phonetically on slips of paper clipped, with borrowed paper clips, to Lily's shopping list so she wouldn't be misunderstood when she inquired at Towne Line Spirits. Recently Lily had taken to rereading her shopping lists and crossing off addenda items—Froot Loops, herbed Boursin, Evian water, Oreos not Hydrox, cocktail onions, lamb chops, those good crackers that come in the blue box from Sweden. One of the family had become adept at forging her handwriting so Lily had to read her list very carefully lest she be duped into buying a box of Funny-Bones. Harvey was her chief suspect in the handwriting caper because he and she were products of the same elementary school, but it seemed unlikely that Harvey hankered after Funny-Bones. So Lily guessed at a conspiracy.

Their mail began to arrive readdressed to the River Road. They had their own house keys turned, down at the TrueValue. Transcripts were transferred and Betsy, Glover, Brooks, Rollins, and Little Becky were registered for fall enrollment at the Towne High School in twelfth, eleventh, and ninth grades. Phoebe found a job in the admissions depart-ment at the Towne Community Hospital and Arthur began to make the rounds. Betsy was so in demand for babysitting that she was seldom home. Alden oiled and sharpened an ax found out in the barn heaved into a beam and he bought a gas-run chain saw down at the Co-Op, and ropes and pulleys and cleats to fit over the soles of his new steel-toed work boots.

Harvey, on his own initiative, erected a TV antenna that resembled a young airplane skidded to a stop against the central chimney pile on the rooftop. He propped his tallest ladder against the back of the house. He climbed, his feet executing sudden dance steps as the rungs spun. He tramped across the roof slates and fed a whipping wire over the precipitous edge and drilled a hole through a window sash to snake the wire through to the little-parlor television set, and after all that effort, reception still wasn't too good. He had to watch his Red Sox games with the television's volume turned down and a radio tuned to the play-by-play broadcast as shadow figures leaped on a shifting field and he thought of other rosters and other years.

Ginger fell in with some old friends joyously recalled from long-ago summers. She hauled them home for coffee. She used the Sèvres service which had been placed out of harm's way on the highest shelf of the china cupboard, but she stood on a tapestry chair cover in her muddy huaraches (she and her guests had first toured the plundered gardens) to lift it down. Dust, long settled at the bottoms of the seldom-used cups, floated to the surface of the coffee, but Ginger had been too vividly transported to the past to notice this rather regrettable presentation, and her old acquaintances made a great point of not noticing even as they sieved their coffee through their gritted front teeth. They were never, however, to be available for a follow-up picnic on the river using an historic Hill hamper outfitted with clever collapsible cups and a pie compartment, all the while adrift in an ancient Hill canoe Ginger had discovered in the barn beneath a pile of old window screens and which, she said, would be sure to float once the water swelled the gaps in the seams.

Becky, who hoped she wasn't hurting Lily's feelings, asked if she might prepare dinner from time to time. There were certain favorites the children missed—her crispy-skin duckling, her cold veal roast with homemade tarragon mayonnaise. Lily told Becky to pick all the tarragon she needed from the herb patch which at that time of year burgeoned with wasteful plenty. The younger boys found a favorite place to swim in cold deep pools in the river scooped by the current below the stanchions of the old railroad bridge and they were happily away for the remainder of the summer's days. Glover met a girl (down at the IGA magazine rack, he revealed under questioning), although there may have been two girls involved, no one was sure, for she, or they, looked same-ish but never quite the same when glimpsed, in Glover's company— never introduced, of course, as she waited in her car while Glover charged into the house to grab a flashlight, a blanket, the OFF Spray. Has anyone noticed if it's the same car? Harvey asked sensibly.

Lily made a vet appointment for the kitten's checkup and shots. Lily had no cat carrier so, on the day of the visit, she placed the kitten in the big oven roaster pan and fastened the lid with a bungee cord so she could prop the lid open an inch or two to admit fresh air. Little Becky, at loose ends as usual, tagged along and afterward wished she hadn't.

"We got looks," Little Becky reported back to the several late-afternoon sitters she tracked down in the little parlor. "We waited in the waiting room and everybody looked at the roasting pan and whispered."

Ginger set down the crooked piece of cross-stitch she was playing at working and remarked, " 'They wait to hang the cobwebs of their gossip out and catch a fly.' "

"Huh?" asked Little Becky. "What?" She was in no mood for Aunt Gingerisms.

"You heard me," Ginger said.

The family agreed, Lily's specific services had, all along, been imperfectly performed. She was a dreamy one, was Lily, drifting into their rooms carrying clean towels and then forgetting why she had knocked on their doors in the first place, after she swept a handful of spent blossoms from a bureau scarf and collected a scraped-clean cake plate from a bedside table and placed scrap-paper bookmarks in splayed-open library books, wandering off with the towels still creased over her arm. The family was forced, soaking wet after their baths, to clasp their damp-marked dressing gowns around themselves and embark on towel hunts, finding them draped over the balustrade, folded on a window ledge, or shoved inside the blanket chest at the top of the landing. However had Lily managed all on her own, living alone and looking after that great big ark of a house, the family wondered, when even the simple distribution of bath towels was beyond her? Harvey mentioned, as well, having discovered decayed fruit in his sock drawer, and Little Becky recalled then that on the same humiliating vet visit Aunt Lily had not even known what the cat's name was when the receptionist asked.

"I thought it was Puff," said Alden.

"Smoky," said Becky.

"No, she's Agnes," said Betsy, for the kitten was a grey.

"Well, you'd better tell Aunt Lily that," said Little Becky.

· · ·

BY OCTOBER, by that rain-wrecked night two-thirds of the way into
October, the Hills had retreated to their separate precincts. Supper had
been gotten over with early in deference to their various announced
plans for the Saturday night which the sudden storm had caused to be
canceled or postponed or independently judged just not worth the effort
of digging in the back hall closet for the same size rubber boots and a
functioning umbrella and a hooded slicker with a zipper that would ride
down as willingly as it rode up. They had not, after all, departed for the
movies, a mall crawl, bridge night at Senior Village, babysitting, the
Divorce Dynamics Workshop in the Unitarian Meeting Hall, a date.
They were peckish again, the simple supper long since bolted and regarded
in retrospect as a very late afternoon snack composed of uninspiring
elements not of their own choosing—tuna wiggle, cucumber slices in
vinegar, and brownies, a Becky effort. (She had swiftly lowered her
sights, catering for a dozen.) They thought of toast and hot cocoa and
the little Revere ware bowl of pale pineapple rings macerating in sugar
and their own juices.

They poked and stirred their wood fires, those who were lucky
enough to possess fireplaces in their bedrooms, averting their faces from
the oily, ashy surges of smoke the surly wind chased back down the
chimney stacks. They all wished Lily would switch on the furnace but
she had explained it was too early in the season to take that step. She
doled out extra blankets. She asked, reasonably, haven't you a sweater?,
and then she asked, impassively, haven't you a heavier sweater? as they
made shows of pulling on pullovers and shivering, regardless. But sincere shivering was involuntary and their versions seemed willed, in
Lily's opinion. Haven't you a scarf? Lily asked. Haven't you a pair of
house gloves? she asked, which unlikely item of innerware they all suspected Lily had just invented but they did not challenge her for Lily may
well have presented them with clumsy knit mitts which they would have
been bound to wear.

Alden speculated that Lily was obliged to wait for some late autumnal
sunset to align itself exactly with the rusty croquet hoops atilt in the side

yard before she could touch the thermostat. Towne was a very ancient and tradition-plagued enclave, he said. On the Fourth of July, half the householders raised thirteen-star flags by their front doors and the Ben Franklin Store still sold penny candy for a penny, though only as a loss leader to draw in the new people and the few knowledgeable tourists who came for the architecture—there was a late-Elizabethan domestic remnant tucked away behind the town tennis courts, which had been written about in books.

"Eat green Jell-O, Dad," Glover had said, which must have been very rude. Brooks and Rollins laughed so hard they had to lie down, rolling and overlapping, on the little-parlor sofa.

But on this particular stormy October night, deprived of other diversions, the Hills, for all their differences, were similarly occupied. They were writing. They wrote because they had a great deal to say for themselves and they had wearied of saying it to one another. Their old friends and former associates lived far away now. The eight pages of the latest NYNEX bill had been taped sequentially across the refrigerator door. They had rung a dozen states and chatted over three time zones. Harvey and Ginger had repeatedly called a 900 number to cancel one another's vote as they registered their contrary says in a nationwide poll, Should the U.S. Congress Bail Out the Failed S.&L.'s? It took the pleasure out of visiting the refrigerator, facing those eight pages of toll calls taped across the door. Initials had been inked beside charges, all claimed and accounted for except the solid, shameful tattletale block of Teen Talk Line tariffs occupying three of the NYNEX bill's pages. Becky, after a sad and disappointed appraisal of her eye-evading, foot-shuffling brood called upon the Missoni carpet in Becky and Alden's attic sitting room, said she was going to write a letter of protest to the FCC complaining of the exploitation of witless children, and it may have been this assertion of Becky's that put the idea in everyone else's heads, this option of taking up the pen.

HARVEY HAD COMMANDEERED the dining room with its broad polished cherry-wood table and proximity to the sherry decanter. He lifted up a table leaf, secured the leg, and pushed aside the drawn threadwork runner and the cut-glass bowl full of dried poppy heads, not raised in display but clumped face downward in the bowl. He dug his slippered heels into the sculpted pattern of the red Chinese rug and he buttoned his woolly cardigan up and over his chin. His posture telegraphed belligerence or he may have just been hunched against the cold. He had a mingy fire banked in a corner of the dining room's—originally kitchen's—great maw of a fireplace. Lily had told him not to get carried away. She was drying bristly bunches of rosemary suspended from the great old iron arm from which a great old iron pot used to swing back in the days when the Hills had been cannibals, Hill children were always told.

The chandelier, the wall sconces, the lamp on the sideboard, were all alight, but Harvey cast his own darkening shadow across his writing paper. His trifocal glasses slipped down the bone of his very straight nose and stopped at the knob on the end as he peered through the uppermost portion of the lenses. All surfaces, the grain of the table's wood, the bond of the paper, the brown freckles and silver hairs on the back of his hand, blinked into sharp focus but were imbued with a floating quality which he didn't mind, actually. He was, he concluded, coming to the disembodied stage which he did not doubt offered its own possibilities and pleasures to explore. Indeed, he had noticed he had to drink less now, which was a boon, considering the quality of Lily's cidery and oddly particled sherry. Besides, the scientists had just come out alleging the lead in leaded glass decanters seeped into any long-sitting liquor, although Harvey chose not to worry overmuch, the harm having long since been done in his case, he didn't wonder. Harvey chose to make the most of any predicament in which he found himself. He maintained a healthy rooting interest in his own happiness and well-being and even now, even at his age, he was keen to get on with whatever was going to occur to him next.

He flattened and reread a brief, typed letter. Receiving it earlier in the week, he had acted upon his immediate impulse to consign the letter to the wastepaper basket but second thoughts had told him it might provide better sport to answer the thing. Besides, he seemed to recall he was under some kind of contractual obligation to respond.

He picked up his pen after attempting, first, to scrabble up a pen-shaped bar of shadow that lay upon the tabletop. He'd torn a piece of lined paper from a school notebook left lying on the kitchen counter, never minding the algebraic equation homework written on the back of the scavenged page except to register a general impression that the solution surely was not correct. Lily had failed to respond to his request for a sheet or two of the best household stationery, which she had hidden away from him, otherwise he'd have fetched a hunk of it himself. He had yet to ascertain whether she had a hearing or merely a listening problem. Someday he'd have to slide up behind her in his house slippers and shrill into his London Bobby souvenir whistle, just as an experiment.

He wrote in a rush.

Listen, Archie, tell your "buyers" where they can get off. Never in my life have I been so insulted. The "Offer" is unacceptable. It is a Bay of Pigs of an offer. I suggest your "buyers" will be happier living in a cardboard box beneath an I-86 underpass. They seem that sort of people. I AM NOT SUGGESTING 750,000 DOLLARS FOR MY HOUSE, I AM DEMANDING. I can outwait any "regional recession." Just look at the plumbing, every inch of it copper, for God's sake, parquet floors, stained-glass casement windows, those beams in the Great Room came from Shakespeare's friend's birthplace before Parliament put its foot down on that sort of thing. I am beginning to wonder whether you could sell a paper poke to a one-armed man carrying three oranges and may be obliged to take my business elsewhere. Very cordially yours, H.R.H. P.S. You are aware the rose garden does not convey? My sister is a devout rosarian and I have promised her first pick.

GINGER LANGUISHED in her bedroom behind a firmly shut door. She lay like a Henry Moore lady upon her sloping sleigh bed, lolling against the half-dozen pillows whose support she required behind her neck, beneath her elbows, propping her knees. She had covered herself with a rose-pink shirred-satin bed puff she had come across folded in its original tissue, all the tags, except the price, attached, some ancestress having determined decades before that such a bed puff was far too nice ever to be used. Oh, Ginger could just picture the stern Hill aunt presiding at her sixtieth birthday dinner, only eventually consenting to unwrap her special gift, unknotting ribbons and peeling back tape so she could reuse the ribbon and the wrapping paper and, if at all possible, the tape. She reacted, when at last the gift was revealed, with the Hill Aunt variation. One was disappointed not by receiving too little, but displeased at having been handed so much. *But you shouldn't have,* had been spoken by the aunt, as if you had strangled one of the barn cats and worn the carcass wound around your bloodied hands like a tiger-striped muff.

Ginger mused upon her ancestresses who had left behind, in bureau drawers and standing chests, bars of petrified gardenia soap and cylinders of solid bath crystals and long-necked carafes of bath oils, their contents separated like salad dressing but which could yet be shaken and poured. Their kid leather clutch bags stuffed with crumpled 1955 newsprint, and their morocco-leather-covered diaries with gold-leafed, onionskin pages, remained unopened, unconfided in—well, they had had nothing to confide, for their emotional lives had been as stinted of the luxuries of passion and personal dramas as their cool and shallow bathwater had been bereft of emollients and scents. Ginger would have responded to the pathos of it all—such self-denying, unactualized, essentially lost women—were she not so distracted by seeking out and availing herself of the buried acorns they had squirreled away in all the corners of the house, indeed, craftily concealed, Ginger could not help but suspect, from someone very like herself whom they had anticipated with their sharp if squandered intelligences. The bed puff had been hidden in a box hand-labeled Useful Clean Jars, which had not rattled when Ginger aimed a kick against the nagging detail, Useful.

That the rose pink of the bedspread flattered her skin tones, Ginger was aware. She'd recently read an article reminding women that their bedclothes should be as sensitively selected as their makeup and daytime attire. Yellow sallowed, green could be ghastly, and pure white was not entirely kind to more mature skin tones. She did not care to be reminded that her skin was, perhaps, less youthful than it once had been. Oh, where was her hand mirror? She didn't like to look, but she had to.

There, the mirror had slithered down the satin smoothness of her bed puff, landing lightly atop a tangle of discarded underwear, lying just out of her reach for, arranged in bed, Ginger had no wish to upset her arrangements. Proper pillow positioning was such an art.

Ginger sighed heavily. She could see her breath hanging briefly in the air. How could that be? Her room was one of the warmer ones. A wood fire flared away in her fireplace. The silk flowers of her mantelpiece bouquet were beginning to curl and ruddy cinders launched themselves over the screen and dropped onto the hearth bricks as aglow nuggets. Ginger was keeping an eye on that situation. She huffed in further demonstration and wondered whether it was possible to blow a human smoke ring. She pursed her lips and puffed. Apparently not. She felt her brow. She wondered if she was running the opposite of a fever. Whatever ailment did that signify? She would not mind contracting a mildish illness requiring trays in bed and the little-parlor TV wrestled up the stairs and set upon her bedside table.

She wore a pair of her husband's plaid flannel pajamas snatched as her own (speaking of inattention to boudoir fashions) the day she had packed and left home. She was further wrapped in her grandfather's plaid—a different plaid—wool bathrobe. She had been sliding around in Alden's warmest pair of Ragg wool socks until he had spotted them on her feet and requested their return. His wife and his children might raid his sock drawer, Alden had said, but he drew the line at his grown-up, divorcing sister, which was not very brotherly of him. Ginger could only suppose Becky had gotten to him at some point over the past twenty-odd years of their marriage.

Which observation led to another insight for her book. She seized a 3 × 5 card. They were tucked everywhere, in her bathrobe pockets, between her layered pillows, beneath her wineglass. Her wine. She reached and sipped and plucked a pencil, speared into her hair helping to secure her knotted hair, and she began to write rapidly—Adult siblings—marriage of???—L. L. Bean sleepwear, footwear, etc. outlasting life, love, loyalties???!!!—concluding etc., etc.???? to remind herself she'd have far more to say on the subject as further examples occurred to her, for occur to her they would. Her mind was well seeded with these incipient pearls developing cool and smooth and glowing against her brain.

But enough of scholarship. She tossed the file card toward the old shortbread tin that contained a clutter of other cards, and she plunged the pencil again into her uncoiling hair. She burrowed down deeper among her bedclothes. She drained her wine and poured herself half a glass more, tipping the bottle empty. She tilted back the fringed shade of her porcelain shepherdess in a panniered skirt holding a crook and a lambikin lamp to shed more light upon her lapboard, extracted from Lily's very complete invalid's supply cupboard and leaning now against her pillow-bolstered knees. She had come across her grandfather's old Waterman fountain pen in his secretary desk's secret drawer, and one day while Lily was busy in the garden dispatching Japanese beetles by that amusing method she employed, Ginger had helped herself to a stack of his writing paper as well, a very heavy bond and creamy with age which was seldom used lest it be used up, a practice for which Ginger was grateful even as she was bound not to observe it herself.

She centered a sheet of the paper upon her writing board. She pointed her pen. It scratched effectlessly, and she shook the pen down in hard strokes as if it were a near-empty tube of moisturizer. *My darling*, she wrote then, in large, looping letters. The pen, subtly cracked along its agate barrel, seeped black ink onto her fingers. She flicked them clean against the dark lapel of her robe and poised her pen again. How far had she gotten? *My darling*, she read approvingly. *Oscar*, she added thoughtfully. A ruddy cinder launched itself over the fire screen. Ginger was keeping an eye on that situation.

BETSY WROTE TO her father once a week. She had set aside a certain hour several months ago when she and her mother first arrived here in Towne. Betsy had, in the beginning, approached the hour eagerly, she had so much to tell him and of course she very much missed him. But lately, the letter writing had become a chore to which she sat down dutifully. She possessed a picture of her father, kept in her desk drawer beneath a box of colored pencils (for her Advanced Biology homework, diagramming realistic hearts and such). Her mother would have had dramatics had she spotted a picture of Louis on Betsy's bureau top, but Ginger would have run even wilder riot had she happened upon Louis concealed in a drawer. Betsy had slid the photo under the lining of her suitcase that last, very terrible day at home in Kansas. It was the official portrait he had affixed to his campaign literature when he had stood, sadly not very successfully, for the Kansas state legislature.

(When Betsy and Ginger had accompanied Louis on the stump, Ginger sat on the edge of Grange Hall stagings, swinging her attractive legs and shredding the red, white, and blue bunting with her three-inch heels, all the while complaining of the rigors of political wifehood and wondering whether she was going to end up with her own ritzy rehab clinic someday, just like Betty Ford.)

Betsy recovered the photograph from the bottom of her drawer and propped it against the base of her wobbly old tole desk lamp. She had long since dusted off the bulb with Pledge and now, when switched on, it threw off a scent of singed, synthetic sweetness, an effect she had come to like. She replenished the Pledge coating at intervals. She guessed in years to come (and she yearned for the years to come) the same scent would carry her back to this time and place, though who besides herself would ever think to polish a lightbulb with Pledge Betsy couldn't imagine so she guessed she would not live in danger of suffering intense bouts of retrospection as long as she refrained from the practice.

As she met her father's photographed eyes, she realized how remote he had become. She had not anticipated that the fierce and raw missing of someone could fade into a mild pain when reminded of it and this not always convenient tug to her desk to compose that week's letter. And she was afraid her father, who must at first have minded very much and then had come to mind less, had perhaps by now learned to count on returning home every night to a dark and peaceful house instead of stepping into the full, accusing spotlight glare as Ginger sat, slightly atilt at the kitchen alcove table, presiding tragically over a baked-away casserole, sipping vermouth and twisting her rings. This was another picture Betsy had carried with her from home.

Betsy was glad she had packed her Wintersilks last summer. Massachusetts had sounded like a cold place, or, at any rate, the first mention of Massachusetts had made the hairs stand on the back of her neck. At present she was comfortable enough dressed in her Wintersilks and corduroy jeans, a heavy jersey, boiled-wool slippers, and a felt beret pulled down over her ears, although an irritating persistence of draft curled around that susceptible nape of her neck. She endured the cold breaths of air for she had learned to be an excessively tolerant girl and she believed the wind had a right to whistle where it would. It was not the wind's fault someone had built a house in its path although Uncle Alden had told her the main part of the house had been built well over two hundred years ago so perhaps one might reasonably expect the wind to have made other arrangements by now. Nevertheless, Betsy felt sympathy for the draft which was probably just coming inside out of the rain to get warm, although if warmth was what the wind was after, it had come to the wrong house. Betsy's thoughts rambled, disengaged. Perhaps moving her desk to a different corner of her room would help.

She leaned back and regarded the small chamber she had been given, the last bedroom on the right where they must have had floor left over when they finished putting up interior walls in the new (1830, Uncle Alden said) three-story kitchen ell. Betsy inhabited a wedge of space. She used a wedge of closet. Her skirts and dresses hung hunched and sideways as if furtively loitering behind the closed door. The wallpaper was a clothy feeling coffee-with-cream-colored gingham print. The curtains were made of papery-feeling gingham of the same coffee-and-cream color, but there the effort had ended. The bedspread was white chenille. She had to remember not to sit down when she wore a dark skirt. Betsy could not describe the furniture with her eyes closed, so ordinary it was. And her small desk, really meant for a child, had been fitted into the only corner that could take it, Betsy decided, as, in her mind's eye, she shifted the desk from wall to wall. Hopeless.

She stood, then, and scuffed in her slipper socks toward the window, her feet entangling with the oval of scatter rug placed in the middle of the floor to indicate, if not to serve as, floor covering. The inadequate rug, which was brown, reminded Betsy of the small brownie on the large plate she had been served for dessert earlier in the evening, crumbs of chocolate adhering to shards of walnut. Betsy was not being critical of the brownie. She was not a great eater at the best of times, but she was struck by the way in which life at Aunt Lily's house had been pared down to mere essences, like the four inches of warmish bathwater, the forty-watt lightbulbs, the good-night kisses addressed to the air and not to her cheek.

The wind may have had something to do with this, historically shuddering through the house, picking the Hills' existences clean to the very bone. Enough was enough, Betsy concluded. She hardened her heart and she thrust a rolled-up bandana between the windowsill and the sash.

She sat again at her desk and picked up her pen. She tapped the end of her nose which was so chilled that the tap stung the delicately molded cartilage. She had noticed since summer's end that a stubbed toe, a jammed finger, hurt worse when one was very cold. She wondered why that was. She thought the cold was supposed to numb the senses. She had read that freezing to death was an easy end, although who, she wondered, now, had ever truly died of the cold and then come back to report on the experience? She tapped her pen across her desktop. The problem was, she had less to say to her father when she didn't see him every day. She would have thought the opposite to be true, but whatever or whomever she mentioned in her letters had to be situated and described and explained, and none of it could possibly interest him. The commonplace details of her days here hardly interested her.

Dear Daddy [Betsy began], Thank you very much for the check. I deposited it in the bank they have down in the village. You have to call it the village, not downtown, not downtown Towne, I think they'd get confused. Anyway, the usual teller knows me now and always says hello. She says to say hello to Aunt Lily, too. I don't have to show I.D. anymore, though I don't know why they had to know me for putting *in* money. Anyway, I paid Aunt Lily for Mum's and my fair share of the groceries this month, telephone, and electricity. The water is free from a well. It tastes funny, that is, it has a taste but Aunt Lily says it's been tested. Plus, I gave Mum $200 just to have. I put it in her wallet without saying. I think she should have her own spending money, she's so used to finding money in her purse. She must know it comes from you, but I know not to say and she can pretend it's from the same $800 she ran away with, although that was used up I don't know when, our train tickets and all that, only I think she charged those over the telephone. We picked them up at the station. At first they couldn't find them. I wish they hadn't found them.

I've made $145 babysitting so far this month. Actually, sometimes it's not really babysitting. Mrs. Snowdon, my exclusive client now, is often quite tired and she has to rest in her bedroom while I play quietly with the children until Mr. Snowdon comes home from work. I like the hushedness of their house, only I hope Mrs. Snowdon isn't ill, but I don't think I'm meant to ask.

ALDEN AND BECKY SAT up in their own high-mattressed bed. They had retired to the largest of the several attic bedrooms. The low, slanting ceiling made them uncommonly aware of the roof over their heads. They agreed, the sound of the rain on the roof was pleasant, the regular thrumming so lulling and familiar, although they couldn't say where the sense of familiarity had come from. They had never before dwelt in an actual garret. Even their very first apartment had been a suite of rooms on the ground floor of a Victorian manse almost in Chestnut Hill where they had enjoyed the use of an orangery. Alden said perhaps the sound carried one back to one's time in the womb which was not the sort of remark he usually made. Becky only answered, Huh, in a tone pitched neither to encourage nor to quell him. Poor fellow, she found herself thinking of her own husband.

Their New York furniture had arrived just that week. Lily's house had been hard for the movers to find. A thicket of ornamental bamboo had overgrown the sign for the River Road and Lily would not display a name or a number on her pitted and oxidized mailbox. Everyone who needed to know knew where to find her, or, if not, should possess the sense to arrive at the unmarked mailbox on the unspecified road by a process of elimination. Lily, the former teacher, seemed not to be able to help herself as she set this test.

The movers, after driving past the same dog on the same lawn three times, stopped and asked directions of a jogger. Harvey, late for a luncheon appointment and stepping briskly, greeted the movers on Alden and Becky's behalf, for they had driven off to search for the overdue van. Harvey hustled the movers inside and marched them up the two flights of stairs to the attic, which rose particularly steeply and sharply turned three treads down from the top, although there was an accommodating sheared-off angle of plaster wall worn smooth by two centuries of shoulders rubbing past.

"That's an authentic colonial coffin corner," spoke up Ginger, who knew everything and who had emerged from her room at the trampling of footsteps. She was very curious about the New York furniture. She stood by her conviction that they, the muttering movers, could perfectly well ease her brother's fat Chesterfield sofa from New York around the coffin corner. Smitty, the veteran mover, thought not. Becky and Alden, whose business it actually was, had by then returned and were stationed by the front door intercepting certain cartons that didn't look familiar and rummaging through their contents and failing to recognize lamps that had been wrapped in sheets of the *New York Post* instead of the *Wall Street Journal*, which would have been enough to dispose them against the alien lamps even had they not proved to be highly colored examples of amateur ceramics. So Ginger, unchecked on the attic stairs, had her compelling way and the sofa jammed just where Smitty had expertly predicted it would. Russ and Stevie sat on the atilt sofa and smoked several inspirational cigarettes and remarked several times, for they'd grown fond of the remark, that they weren't surprised people had died up there in that attic, and then they heave-hoed the sofa decisively as wood snapped and leather cracked and plaster sifted and it slid through the door. Success.

There was a mix-up concerning the Aldens' dining room table and chairs and sideboard which made it up to the second-floor landing before Lily, though she had vowed to stay out of the fray, advised the men the dining room furniture was meant to be stored in a dry corner of the barn set upon and beneath fresh tarpaulins which she would supply.

The attic was such a repository, Lily explained. She feared for the floor joists even if the dining room furniture could find room up there.

Well it's quite a cozy attic, Smitty allowed.

Still, the day ended well enough for all the wrong boxes turned out to be surplus boxes and the Aldens could say they had come out ahead. Lily suggested they donate the ugly lamps to All Saints' next White Elephant table with a note stressing the complete mystery of their provenance and explaining how they had been foisted upon the Hills. Lily had some idea that the lamps would appeal to the new people in Towne even though she had never set foot inside a new person's house so she really wasn't in a position to say but she had her doubts.

"Lily knows of a man who can possibly repair the sofa on site," Becky mentioned now to Alden as they lay on their own comfortable bed beneath the low, strummed-upon roof.

"Have to be on site," Alden said. "That sofa's never going anywhere again. In a hundred years, people will wonder how the sofa ever came to be up here, just like Mike Mulligan's steam shovel down in its cellar." He had spent the afternoon browsing through a box of the children's old books and he had been reminded of a tiny universe of tidy accommodations and solutions.

"I'm just glad we're settled. I like looking at our own pictures," Becky said.

"I like that picture," Alden said.

"Lily doesn't."

"Well, no, not square blue apples such as are not to be found in nature."

"She didn't actually say she didn't like it. She looked and she didn't say anything at all."

"Lily often doesn't say. She observes in silence and you're glad of her silences."

"Is that bucket going to overflow onto the rug?"

"Not yet. I'm keeping an eye on."

The blue rug that had long been the rug underfoot in their bedroom lay upon the attic floor. Pond-sized, Alden said, as it lapped up and against the walls. Becky had studied the effect and decided if she were an interior designer she'd specialize in downsizing. She'd move her clients' original overstuffed furniture from the big place they'd had to give up into the little place they had retreated to and call the result Style— twelve-foot-long drapes puddling at the bottoms of windows, sofas stranded like whales in a swimming pool, home entertainment centers rising like the Hawaiian Islands. As one's horizons shrank, psychologically one would still feel mighty, Becky theorized. You think? asked Alden.

The heated bricks of a chimney stack rose through the floorboards and bled some warmth into the room. Their heaviest down comforter was billowed over them. Their excellent angle-poise reading lamps craned from their bedside tables, aimed at the clipboards and sheets of writing paper leaning against their knees. Becky thawed her fingertips on her lightbulb and picked up her pen. Alden, conscious of Becky as another source of warmth, shifted closer to her and leaned back among the pillows. His pen, slowly tracing across a sheet of paper, scrawled to a stop and he read over Becky's cashmere sleeve as she wrote, Dear William.

Becky, whose elbow he had jarred as he repositioned himself, disregarded Alden and she wrote steadily and calmly on, which was her way. Alden, who had been struggling, resolved to plunge in at the deep end and get his letter over with as well.

Dear Dexter, You've heard of last winter's showdown when heads rolled, including your's truly.

Or would that be yours truly's? He wrote that down and neither version looked quite right the more he stared at them.

"Which is correct?" he asked Becky. "Or neither?"

Becky considered. The *Fowler*'s was still thoroughly packed since Alden had frittered away the afternoon reading *Make Way for Ducklings* and *The Little Engine That Could* after she had asked him to organize their books. She had thought he would enjoy deciding about their books.

"Say, among them my own. Heads rolled, among them my own," she suggested. "If that's what you really choose to say about yourself, representing yourself to Dexter as somehow having lost your head over all that business, last winter."

"I'm trying to strike the right casual note, but you have a point," Alden said. "Particularly as I'm going to him hat in hand. Yes, yes, let's x out that mental image." Alden sketched hashmarks over what he'd written. "I mean to say, I'd look like a Halloween prank."

Dear William [Becky continued], I am writing to let you know how the Big Move has gone. We cleared out everything, every nook and cranny, which took some doing but all has been left in good order.

The professional cleaners are scheduled. I interviewed prospects the two days I was back in NYC packing—such talk of Q-Tips and tooth-picks probing. I detected an obsession with unclogging the crosshairs in the heads of Phillip's screws and I hired a nut but he'll be going nuts for us with his Q-Tip so that's all right. As we have said, please feel free to rent the apartment before the end of the quarter if you wish. We were always happy there and hope you were happy with us! I'll miss the butler's pantry, I confess! But best of luck with any new ten-ants, unless you plan to move in yourself? After so many years abroad, I don't know, can you go home again? A question for many of us, these days. At any rate, I hope we weren't preventing you. You have always been so thoughtful, William.

Yes, William had always been so thoughtful, whereas Alden had always been so full of ideas. Becky permitted herself to consider the dif-ference between the two men for a moment. After all these years, she was still coming up with Alden *this* and William *that* constructions, which wasn't fair to Alden and wasn't fair to herself but was, however, always very fair to William.

Dear Dexter [Alden began again], Sorry not to find you at the reunion. I found myself not far away and so looked in. It so happened that I found myself not far away having come back to the family homestead this past summer. We have gone native. In the evenings, we swing in the hammock and wait for the first firefly to arise.

Which didn't strike the proper note, either, settling himself too con-tentedly and immovably out to pasture in the country with a blade of hay clamped between his teeth. Besides, the firefly watch had lasted a week. Alden wasn't keen on fireflies. They shimmered into the house and sparked off and on above his head just as he was trying to fall asleep and impressed swirls of bacteria-shaped motes across his shut-tered eyelids.

—so thoughtful. [Becky's pen glided across one of her last hoarded sheets of good stationery. Alden had already spoiled two pieces.] We are now here with Alden's Aunt Lily who has always been good to us, to me, but I still worry whether we aren't a handful, and it happens we aren't the only ones here. Alden's sister Ginger, painfully divorce bound, is here with her lovely girl, and Lily's brother Harvey, the widower (thrice, poor man) has come for a stay. And there's Harvey's grandson as well, with his girlfriend, another very nice girl, different, but I like her. Arthur is trying to become a professional comedian. Well, he's an amusing young man so why not seek an interesting career? Lily's a good scout, but we must all be a handful. But of course, you've met Lily, twenty years ago—can it be that long?—at our wedding. Lily's much the same but older, as indeed, we all are. I may have to get reading glasses, I have just been told, either that or grow longer arms, as the old joke goes. Perhaps Arthur can use that in his act. Alden's future plans are still pending. We both agree, he must be selective. Of course, he has so many irons in the fire but I think his heart may really lie in doing something with the land. The land here hasn't been seriously farmed since the Civil War when, they say, one of the forebears got grumpy over the price of cotton and planted his own. Oh, I can picture that scene! Alden is contemplating berries—strawberries, raspberries, high bush blueberries—in a pick-your-own operation, and eventually we could expand into jams and pies, I have so many good recipes and so many people are succeeding these days, Ben and Jerry, those two, why not us? From micro to macro economics, which is all the trend, Alden says. Cross your fingers and hope General Mills comes along and eats you up. Well, until that happy day, we'll be well away from the epicenter when the Crash comes which Alden says *is* coming. Really, that's what was behind his dismissal last winter. He said some things no one wanted to hear, just like Cassandra—

Becky was fairly certain Cassandra was whom she meant. The *Collins Dictionary* was also lost in some box and she didn't want William to catch her in an error, because even now, even after all these years, she wanted William to think well of her. She admitted that much to herself. She needn't deny it, now that she was severing her last tie to him, one, perhaps, which she ought never to have allowed to continue, so many years ago agreeing to sublet, not really very legally, his large, prewar, parkside, rent-controlled apartment when William was first sent overseas. Why not? Alden and everyone else had asked at the time as she hesitated to accept William's offer. Why ever not, Becky?

A thump and a bump and a crash and a shudder broke into her thoughts.

"Remind the boys," she nudged Alden. "They won't listen to me."

"Boys," thundered Alden, glaring over the top of his clipboard as if he could see them through the wall. Well, he almost could—those popped knotholes.

Dear Dexter, What's the situation out there on the Left Coast?

"I wonder what fell," Becky said.

"Shall I go look?"

"No, no, the damage is done. Finish your letter and I'll finish mine, though, oh dear, I've come to the awkward part," Becky said.

"Which part?"

"First we broke our lease with William and now I have to tell him his sister's boy can't come here," Becky said.

"Oh, that. Don't feel bad. They just wanted a place to stash him for the winter. They're just being opportunistic, having heard of the setup here. The nephew sounds like the classic aging problem child," Alden said.

"Oh dear," said Becky.

Oh dear, [she wrote] after all your considerateness toward us, I'm afraid it's not the best of ideas for your nephew to come here to work on his thesis. I'm afraid I don't quite understand, his study subject is to be a family, an old, established sort of family? Really, we are not all that interesting. Why doesn't he look to the Cabots or Lodges, with all sorts of archival material available? Not that I can speak *as* a Hill or even as a Lowe, but when I married into the family, I recall how relieved I was by their ordinariness, in the nicest, most reassuring, and special sense, of course. Frankly, I didn't even ask Lily about your nephew. As I've indicated, we are so full up here. But, at any rate, I trust Andy has fallen back on alternative plans when you didn't hear from me. Your last letter was so long in coming—ten weeks. All that upset and Revolution in your part of the world! The Post Offices must be overwhelmed. Alden says they'll have to rename all the streets. He suggests Lennon (John) for all the Lenin Roads, and the People's Squares and People's Palaces can accept corporate sponsorships, i.e., IBM Square. Well, I'm just being silly. Nevertheless, I am responding promptly, please believe me, and please, please, forgive me, dear William.

Dear Dexter, I'd appreciate it if you'd keep your ear to the ground, out there where you are.

LITTLE BECKY ROLLED onto her stomach and hung over the side of her very own canopied bed which had come from New York at last. (Aunt Lily's lumpy old beds had all been shoved under the eaves. Good.) There had been a real question, a cliffhanger, whether they would have to shorten the posts to make her bed slide under the low ceiling of the attic. Well, they hadn't had to. The movers had figured a way to angle the bed into the room, and Aunt Lily had given her a night-light so she wouldn't bump her shins if she had to get up in the dark, for all of Little Becky's furniture had had to be angled to fit, and when Aunt Lily climbed up the attic steps to see for herself how nice Little Becky's new bedroom was, she had had to shut her eyes, the effect was so unsettling to her.

Moving was unsettling. So many items, long lost, had turned up as closets and drawers were turned out, items long lost on purpose—old report cards, sweaters she hated, books dropped into the bath. The other day as her mother was searching for some music (Becky sang) she had come across the clothbound Little Becky Book.

"Little B., come here, look at this," her mother had called her. "When you were tiny and you first noticed shadows, do you know what you said? You said, 'The sun is a good drawer,' when you saw the exactly etched lines of a wrought-iron café table cast across a sidewalk."

"I did?" asked Little Becky. Was she to be blamed for this or had her observation been held to be precious?

"Yes, and we wrote it down in this book we bought especially to note all your little sayings," Becky said. Yes, they had for months afterward waited for more gems, the book, a pencil kept at the ready. A friend in publishing had rather thought there might be something there—a slender volume, exquisitely illustrated. (The friend in publishing had anticipated the trend in hurried children.)

"And what else did I say?" Little Becky asked.

"Well," Becky ruffled through the book. "That's what you said, the sun is a good drawer. So insightful, so sweet, so dear. And I do recall, although we didn't put it in the book, how you used to sing 'Twinkle, twinkle, little star,' at the first streetlight you saw every night. So cutely," Becky assured her. "What if I give you the book and you can jot down all your current thoughts?"

"My current thoughts?" Little Becky asked. She hefted the book. So many empty pages. Her current thoughts? She thought Aunt Lily should turn on the heat. She could only wear two sweaters at a time before her arms stopped bending at the elbows.

Little Becky dropped the book, a pen, upon her bedroom floor. She would not have said that an empty book could speak of so much, for what the blankness told her, what the white pages expressed, was a tale of disappointment from the first. Even as a three-year-old she had failed to measure up. Well, she had not asked to be a disappointment, just as she had not asked to be disappointed.

A few nights before she had been watching the evening news over Uncle Harvey's shoulder until he told her to stop hovering and to sit down. *Life*, the news reader had announced, may have been discovered on a moon of Saturn. And how she had wanted to go there at once, to that round circle of moon just to the left of Saturn on the big TV news space map. She wanted to fly there immediately and meet a planetful of beings who wouldn't have *opinions* about the way she looked, the way she talked, the way she thought or failed to have thoughts. These beings, having no better prior information, would conclude that she was perfectly all right, that she was perfectly normal, that she was perfectly nice. She might have a chance if only she could get to Saturn's moon first. And, oh, she had been so very let down, she had felt so very stupid, when she understood that the Life being spoken of was no more than a wriggling molecule. She had gotten all excited planning how she was going to race to Saturn's moon *first* to impress a wriggling molecule. She ought to write all that down in her Little Becky Book.

Her hand swept under her bed (*dust*, already—dust was sloughed-off skin, Glover said—okay, okay, she wanted to lose weight). She pulled up her Walkman by its headphones and she jammed the headphones over her ears. Her fingers spun the volume knob up, up, and pure sound flowed into her ears and met in the middle of her head and whirled and danced down into her throat and moved all through her body to her fingertips, to her toes. The New Kids were singing "Step by Step" to her and when they were through, she stabbed the rewind button and they sang it to her again. Then, Little Becky flipped open the cloth-covered book and tore a page from the middle—less noticeable there—upon which she began to write in violent, no, *violet* ink, *Dear Jordan, I love you so much, you are my favorite one.*

"RAIN BUCKET'S FULL," Brooks said to Rollins. "It's sloshing."

They stared for a while as displaced drops scaled slowly down the silvery metal sides. The situation was not urgent.

"Open the window and pour it all out," was Rollins's advice.

"What?" asked Brooks after another while. "What? You said?"

"Open the window and pour out the bucket."

"Okay," Brooks said. The window scraped up, then thumped down.

"Now my sleeve's wet," Brooks announced. The flung water had not flown forward but fallen backward into the room—that's the way the house tilted.

Brooks and Rollins shared a narrow chamber with a single window set just knee-high overlooking the treetops and an irregularly red-blinking radio tower to the north. Their beds were pushed headboard to headboard so they could talk quietly at night and toss a Nerf ball back and forth between them in the dark to develop their sonar capabilities. Brooks had lately advanced a theory that modern man had lost his nighttime sonar capability since the discovery of fire and the subsequent illumination of the night, or at least, Brooks supposed, something of the sort might very well have happened back at the beginning of time.

"Why do you think Uncle Harvey told us if we ever flew from New Delhi to Kathmandu to sit on the left-hand side of the plane so we can see the mountains?" Rollins asked his brother.

"I think he had this mental picture of us sitting on the wrong side of the plane," Brooks said, "and it made him mad."

"Cool," said Rollins. How effortlessly they could rile Uncle Harvey. "When we go there, even if we sit on the left side, we'll tell him we were on the right. Remember to send him a postcard. 'Dear Uncle Harvey, We sat on the right side and we looked at . . .' What would we be looking at, on the wrong side?"

"I don't know. The flat part? We'll just write, we looked at the flat part."

They lay on their backs and listened to the sighs of the wind and the rattlings of the rain and the animated scrabblings of the mice in the walls.

"Where's that cat?" asked Brooks. "She eats mice. I saw her with one."

"Agnes doesn't like us, she avoids us," said Rollins. "I don't know why, I think something in her previous life ill-disposed her toward us."

"Hey," said Brooks. "Go find that ad, you know, that *ad*. We can fill it out now when we're not busy."

"Where is it?"

"Oh, you know. I can't look. My sleeve's all wet."

So Rollins slid from his bed and swung open the door of their closet and rummaged through a slipping, sliding heap of magazines they kept semisecretly on the floor beneath a jumble of cast-off clothing. On laundry days when their mother told them to fetch whatever needed to be washed, they withheld the Oxford cloth tab-collar shirts they had brought to Towne from their previous lives at their old prep school. They went to a public school now where they would be frowned at for wearing those shirts with crests woven into the breast pockets. They had learned this the hard way.

"It's near the back," Brooks said. He could hear Rollins rustling through the front of a magazine.

"But in which one?" Rollins asked.

"The Azerbaijani rebels one, the Stinger missiles one, the guy who had his face blown off, the face guy one," Brooks recalled. They read *Soldier of Fortune* because their father had told them he wished they wouldn't, besides, it was an interesting magazine in its own right.

"Here it is, okay, here it is," Rollins said. He rapidly turned pages and then tore.

"Okay," Brooks said. "Read it. No, read it out loud."

"Okay, it says, 'Enroll now in the Royal Peking Kung Fu Club. At no expense, Lesson Number One, *Mastering the Art,* will be sent for your delighted approval. If not fully satisfied, return to the Royal Kung Fu Club of Peking. But we believe you will be one hundred per cent satisfied, and every month an additional Martial Arts tape will be sent to you for just $29.95 until you attain supreme and ultimate mastery of—' "

"Yeah, yeah, that part," Brooks dismissed it.

"Right, this part," Rollins agreed.

"So, we've got our VCR here now and we have Aunt Lily's, and we'll just copy the tape they send us and then send it back and tell them it sucked," Brooks reviewed the plan, even though it had been half Rollins's idea. "We don't need to know any more. *Mastering the Art,* that should serve us, it's not like we're still in New York. Plus, plus, I just had this other idea, it's brilliant, plus, we can make more copies of the tape and then we can sell them around."

"Okay, here I am," Rollins said. "I'm filling in the order form. I'm putting my name."

"Your name?"

"My pen."

"My idea."

"Our both's idea."

They wrestled for the pen. Brooks sprang from his bed and lunged at Rollins. He struck at and scrambled for Rollins's wrist. He squeezed until Rollins's hand flared open and the pen launched across the room. Brooks rolled off Rollins and bumped him away with his hip and scrambled over the floorboards and dived under the bed where the flying pen had skidded. Rollins, panting and tasting blood on his tongue, threw himself onto Brooks's kicking feet and pulled. Brooks clutched a leg of the bed. He and the bed began to scrape over the floor.

"Boys," their father's voice warned them through the wall.

"Put both names down," Rollins said. "Put R. & B. R. & B. sounds cool."

"Pen's bent. But it works. All right, all right, I'm putting R. & B."

DOWNSTAIRS, IN HIS ROOM off the kitchen, Glover slouched at his desk. He cradled his head in his arms and a moan escaped him. Glover listened as the moan resonated off the cooking pots hanging from a kitchen wall. He had left his door open. The stove had expelled welcome heat while his mother was cooking supper. Glover decided he liked the sound of his hollowly echoing moans, so he moaned again. Uncle Harvey, hunkered down in the dining room, barked at him to button up. Glover's boot shot out and he kicked his door shut.

He turned on his radio. Very loud. The stamp of a slippered foot addressed him through the ceiling. That was Betsy, notifying him, but she had stamped more remindingly than blamingly. Glover plugged in his earphones and straddled them over his ears and he began to sing along. He supplied low harmonies. He moaned.

After twenty minutes or so, as a bank of commercials for Diet Pepsi, the Mass. State Lottery, and Stridex Medicated Pads intruded, he slid open his desk drawer and searched among matchbooks, gum foils, drifts of homework red-slashed and returned to him for emendation. There was a girl in New York to whom he did not write because she could not read, otherwise, on that long, lost, drear, drizzling non-night of a night, he might have had something to say to her. He thought about her, he thought about her fully half the time, and just thinking seemed to help and so, Glover figured, there might have been an extra charge in writing her a big, long, roundabout, philosophical, and sexy letter. But then, he wouldn't be able to sit back and think of her reading it and thinking big, roundabout, philosophical, and sexy thoughts back at him, let alone write him a letter in return. Too bad. He wouldn't have minded receiving a note from her (because even if she could write, she would most likely be brief), a testimonial to his abilities to carry around in his back pocket. He'd have to have it plasticined, eventually.

He had planned to go out that night to take his chances with Meredith, a strawberry-smelling and -tasting and -looking local girl, but she had called to warn him her parents were going to stay home after all. Meredith had known better than to suggest Glover come over to watch the video her parents had rented, *Harry and The Hendersons,* with an eye to entertaining the young people.

And the televisions here in the house were all airing the Snow Show, as his father called the rainy-night nonreception on their sets featuring the Snow Show Chorus singing Ssssss and the Snow Show Players performing in Sssssss, and that was how Glover had come, on a Saturday night, to search for his assignment book in his desk drawer and prepare to pick away at a history essay about Abraham Lincoln and The Military Strategy Behind His Issuance of the Emancipation Proclamation in 1864 After the Bloody Battle of Antietam (Glover read on his Am. His. syllabus). He thumped through the Life of Lincoln book Aunt Lily had let him borrow from her bookshelves when she heard he was studying the old killed guy, and after a while, after he looked up Lincoln, Death of, in the index and read the pages and pages detailing his end, such slow old bullets, poor old guy, Glover settled down and he began to make a fairly creditable job of his essay after all, after his interest and imagination and energy, stimulated in one area (Cosima, Meredith) translated into an extra measure of engagement in another.

ARTHUR AND PHOEBE SAT cross-legged at opposite ends of their mattress. A candle twisted upright into the earthen floor threw unsteady light onto a writing tablet that lay beside Phoebe's knee. She tip-tapped, then forced herself to cease tapping, a sharpened yellow pencil against her protuberant front teeth. A second glowing candle was stuck, jutting at an angle, from a crevice in the granite ledge just behind Arthur's head, looking, Phoebe decided, as though Wile E. Coyote had stuck a sizzling stick of dynamite into Arthur's cup-shaped ear. They had a small electric heater running, and they stayed comfortable enough within the cone shape of its fanned-forth warmth. But they would not be able to stick it out much longer in the barn when the real cold began. Arthur had recently said they could move into the house whenever they wanted.

Phoebe had been astounded. You mean we didn't have to live like this in a virtual cave? she had asked. No, not after a week or so, Arthur said, Gramps was only making a point. Becky says there's a nice room free in the attic, but I thought you liked the barn, I was staying in the barn for *you*.

Phoebe smoothed her heavy dark bangs across her forehead, a habitual gesture, for her hair waved in the direction of her swipe. Arthur massaged a plug of warm candle wax between his thumb and forefinger. Lost in his thoughts, Phoebe could only wish as she watched his vacant face, lost, but perhaps even now in the process of finding himself. The ancient rocks, the dancing candlelight, a howling, troubled night— surely they ought to amount to something significant. Why couldn't tonight be the night for Arthur to thrash matters out, to delve into his psyche and emerge reformed at last in the guise of his long-sought and elusive comic persona?

Arthur had courted laughter in many forms these last few months and he had been met with automatic laughter, polite laughter, nervous, scattered, and derisive laughter, and by the mocking laughter of naysayers who were more amusing than Arthur, so that the restless audience pivoted in their chairs and attended the alternative performance. Phoebe had endured dark, late nights stuck at an unsteady round of table at the far end of a murky-aired room in venues called HaHa and Risibility, located in tough, third-string cities. Most of the clubs had lately failed as discos, and occasionally the wrong, retired switch was flicked and odd exclamations of multicolored, swirly, swimmy lighting effects bathed the trembly, temporary squares of stage and the mottle-spotted, delighted audience. "Elvis has left the planet," Arthur informed the ether whenever this occurred. Phoebe slowly sipped her limit, one Grasshopper, and tried to appear unimplicated when Arthur began to tell his crazy girlfriend stories.

On the long rides home after those raucous, or silent, evenings, Arthur would tick off what had not worked. "Nobody laughed when I said, 'If the Arabs can kill Salman Rushdie for writing that book, why can't *we* do something about Shirley MacLaine?' What do you think, Phoebe, would 'Why can't we shoot Shirley MacLaine?' be funnier?"

Arthur's failures seemed to exhilarate him, going head to head with humor and losing, for some nights he lost less badly and one night he figured out that if he stepped away from the microphone and lifted one uneven eyebrow and stared back at the audience until they were chastened yet intrigued—Arthur was not pleased with *them, they* were not getting it—he could control his audience until the end of his set if he went real fast and finished before the effect of the Look wore off.

Now, Arthur spoke in his real voice, not his brash and baiting performance voice. He said, "Okay, here Phoebe, take this one down. I've just thought of this time from my childhood. It's true, which doesn't seem right, I mean, I'm supposed to make this stuff up, right?"

"Not necessarily. I think your childhood is a rich seam," Phoebe said. Oh, his childhood stories were heartbreaking to her because she loved him so much, but, really, it would not be good for Arthur's career were all eyes turned to him in tenderness and charity and trust.

"Because," Arthur said, "I was thinking about the time my mother lost her yardstick and she used me to measure for curtains because she knew I was exactly five feet tall, only her problem was, how was she going to work out the inches?"

Phoebe held her pencil above the writing tablet. Overhead, the wind prodded and tried every loose board and shingle and shutter and door of the barn. Her several good new work suits hanging from an iron pipe running between two worm-riddled beams swayed and swelled with the crisscrossing drafts as if another aspect of herself, the responsible, workaday Phoebe, was standing by. In one dim corner, water trickled down the rough stone wall and seeped through the iron-covered drain around which last summer's toads had dwelt, those abiding, alive lumps. The zigzag of lightning, that discharge of thunder earlier, had encouraged Phoebe in her hope that Arthur might undergo his metamorphosis that very night. All the elements seemed to have aligned to assist and effect a transformation.

She smiled encouragingly at him. Her pencil sketched a Roman numeral I at the top of the tablet. She knew shorthand, but at Arthur's pace of dictation, a monk in his medieval cell could have turned out a verbatim transcript illuminated with gargoyles and grotesques—that would be a record of very old jokes, of course, Phoebe told herself.

Sometimes she was glad her thoughts were her own and did not bubble up in cartoon captions above the top of her head.

LILY HAD AN excellent fruity fire crackling in her bedroom fireplace, apple wood, and the smoke smelled sweet. She had stacked the apple wood separately after Hurricane Gloria, on her last legs, had huffed and puffed through the orchard, also on its last legs. She had waited four years.

The kitten had entered an unattractive adolescent phase, a contagious state in her house these days, Lily reflected. It was sparring with her slippered foot, raking the Indian beading from her soft old moccasin. That the kitten had specifically sought her company, Lily didn't flatter herself. Agnes had gravitated to the warmest corner. She was a sliding creature, shadowy, and in and out of sight, forever finding herself on the wrong side of a closed door where she mewed rather too childlike until she was released. Then she darted off into more difficulties.

"Stop, you," Lily said and toed away the kitten. She had worked her tensile claws through the leather of the moccasin and Lily's cotton sock down to the skin and now Lily's skin seemed to present the next challenge. The kitten flounced off and began to battle the fringe of a Turkish rug, the tangled fringes of several thicknesses of woven and patterned rugs. Lately, Lily had rolled and carried some of the more fragile carpets up to her room for safer keeping, laying one atop the other. Alden's boys walked around on such tremendous, clumping feet. Lily could only picture andirons strapped to the ends of their legs, and their previous existence in the paved-over world of New York's asphalt and concrete chasms—where even the grass in the parks surely had to sit as perdurable as cement upon the earth—had not made the boys sensitive to the undesirableness of muck tracked into a house. And because Lily had been passing so much more time now in her room, out of the hullabaloo, she had asked the Aldens' moving men if they would kindly mind shifting one or two items of furniture up to her room—a wing chair from the big parlor, and the square hassock, and a small worktable to hold her projects, and the lamp that sat upon the table, and a club chair marooned in a corner when the table and lamp were removed, and a cabinet containing board games and jigsaw puzzles, and the framed print that had always hung on the staircase landing and which careless and hurried elbows and shoulders had been knocking too often askew, as well as the extremely old Chinese dragon vase into which someone had started to pitch his spare pennies, chipping the rim.

"No," Lily said. The kitten had hopped into a basket of unironed laundry where she kneaded a tatted border to bits along the hem of a hankie. "I shall send you outside in the rain," Lily threatened (no, she wouldn't) and she chucked a skein of embroidery thread at Agnes, who slunk under the standing wardrobe to sulk and to worry the skein of thread into a useless clot.

Perhaps she was worked up enough to begin her letter, Lily decided. A vein was throbbing beneath her parchment-colored temple and she had just noticed a new damp patch widening in the shape of a pair of spectacles across her ceiling. Her writing board had vanished from the invalid's supply cupboard and Lily had to rest her writing paper upon the back of *The Big Book of the World's Greatest Gardens,* which was another source of irritation for the book lay too heavily upon her lap. Her agitated pen seemed to assume a life of its own as its point wrote in firm strokes, *Mr. Avalon.*

Lily could not bring herself to address Mr. Avalon as Dear. She could not imagine anyone ever holding him dear.

Please cease sending me brochures concerning—

She stopped and retrieved the prospectus she had pushed out of sight beneath the cushion of the wing chair. Restport, she read, An Adult Living/Rest/Care Facility.

The prospectus featured more pictures than text, photographs of a chandelier in a foyer, of a tap dance company entertaining in the Recreation Center, a sea of white heads attending, some of the heads bent too far to one side, surely more a matter for medical concern than an indication of engrossed attendance to the performance. There was a shot of a Common Room with its windows heavily curtained against a view of a highway breakdown lane but one had to be local to know that. The dimensions of a representative Resident's Room were distorted by a fisheye lens. The colors in the photographs were intense, too orange, too blue, too deeply shadowed, and calculated to appeal to dulled and dimming eyes—Lily was aroused enough to form this insight into canny marketing practices. And the stampeding tap dancers would rattle that ersatz foyer chandelier which looked like it came from Sears, in Lily's opinion. The crystal prisms wouldn't ping, they would plunk. For which the old people would be expected to be happy and grateful, grateful for their suppers of stewed tomatoes. The very paper of the brochure gave off a whiff of stewed tomatoes. Lily didn't doubt that at Restport one would come to feel taken in, in every sense.

—your establishment. You most incorrectly assume I have, or shall ever have, any interest whatsoever in residing at your "Adult Community." I ask to be removed from your files, or whatever it is you keep on elderly people.

Ought she to threaten him with a lawyer? Lily was used to consulting a friend, a lawyer's widow, but May seemed lately to have retired from giving emphatic advice, and Lily didn't wish to approach her real attorney down in the village who handled her few interests and who had for some years been reminding her she had promised to think about making her will. Harris could be rather a pest on the subject.

Besides, the likes of Mr. Avalon, with his illegible signature signing off on his covering letter at which he might peer and indignantly disown in court, most likely retained an officeful of sharks. He would have to, wouldn't he, being one of those people who wouldn't take no for an answer. Mr. Avalon had been sending Lily a prospectus once a month for the past year and a half. He was proving to be as patient with Lily as Lily had been with her hurricane apple wood, and this worried her. Patience was Lily's coin, but could Mr. Avalon outspend her?

She became aware of a light rapping against her door, a fan of knuckles ruffling across the wood which did not sound like Harvey's full-fisted pound, nor was it Ginger's peremptory tattoo, so Lily decided to risk a response.

"Yes," she said.

Alden's head appeared around the door. His eyes swept the room. So this was where Lily had hidden the framed print of the wreck of the White Star steamer *Atlantic* off Nova Scotia recently gone missing from the front hall, never a comfortable picture but an oddly reassuring one, for the few survivors had been clinging to the hull of an overturned life raft for as long as Alden could remember, and if their plight had not improved, neither had their peril worsened.

He spied Lily and he made his way through the crowd of furnishings. The several layers of rug cushioned his tread, and he felt like he was walking on clouds, which must make Lily God, he supposed.

"Would you care for some tea?" he asked. "Or cocoa?"

Lily shook her head. She wasn't about to go into the reasons why she didn't drink liquid just before bedtime.

"How about toast? Cinnamon toast? We think the thunder's long enough gone now so we're running the risk. No? Toasty in here, anyway," Alden said. He sank into the club chair and swiveled to prop his slippers on the plump, tapestry-covered hassock (so this was where the hassock and the chairs and the table and lamp and cabinet had disappeared to from the big parlor—he was not the most noticing of men but he had just caught himself, the other evening, before he threw himself down where the chair no longer was as his hand simultaneously reached to switch on the vanished lamp). "Are you certain you can't be tempted by French toast? I'm thinking of rising to French toast if I can stimulate enough interest."

"Thank you, Alden, no. I have a letter to write." She indicated dismally with her pen.

"A difficult letter," Alden said understandingly. "May I help?"

"Oh, no. Well, no. It's just that I don't like receiving these," Lily said, tossing him the brochure. "They come rather often, as if they're planning to wear me down eventually. As if the one time I don't read their appeal and send back a refusal, somehow they'll hold me to some implicit yes."

"Yes. I see what you mean. Events can overwhelm a person," Alden agreed. He read aloud, "'Restport.' It's always a name like that, Restport or Havenholm, or some such. Although do you remember what

Grandfather Hill called the old folks' home in Cambridge where he used to visit his pals? Remember? Mt. Auburn Prep?"

Good, he'd made Lily laugh.

"Listen, write down what I say," Alden said. "Start a new letter." He crumpled and flung Lily's initial effort over the fireplace screen. The wad of paper bounced off bricks and dropped among the embers where its quick flare and abrupt consumption struck Lily as being rather marvelous. "Write what I say, Lily," Alden urged. "Here goes—Dear Mr. Havenport, Thank you for sending me your splendid brochure. How I would adore to live at your Home, if only I could afford to, if only I could afford to join your happy company—"

"I can't say that," Lily protested.

"No, no, believe me," Alden said.

"Well, go slowly then," Lily advised against her better judgment, but Alden was so happily energized at the moment when he had been sloping around the house so dispiritedly for weeks even as he acted at keeping busy making plans and rummaging in the barn for agrarian implements to polish and sharpen and balance, that Lily could not bring herself to discourage him now.

Alden grinned and continued, ". . . if only I could join your happy company but, alas, my home has been mortgaged to the rafters to pay off the complainants in the class-action suit after the incident. (Make that a capital-I Incident, Lily.)"

"What incident?" Lily wondered. "There was no incident."

"I know there wasn't but we'll let Mr. Restholm's imagination invent the details which will be worse than anything we could come up with," Alden said.

"Oh dear," Lily said. She frowned and shook her hand. Her hasty writing slanted across the sheet of paper in as mad a scrawl as a very hopeless-case student's science essay on "Nickel Is My Favorite Element Because I Can Buy Gum With It" had once so memorably deviated across its page.

Alden continued, "I am, as well, bound to pay the fines and penalties levied by the unconscionable and illegitimate usurpers of liberty who dwell in occupied Washington currently holding the American people hostage to the IMF and G7 and CIA. I am skint. I am stony broke. I am impounded."

"Really, Alden," Lily murmured as she scribbled.

"New paragraph. But, exclamation mark, I have just had a brainstorm. (Illustrate with lightning bolts.) Perhaps your Home would be willing to provide a scholarship opportunity for the particularly deserving elderly candidate. I, for my part, am willing and able to educate and instruct my fellow inmates in areas of my expertise, to wit, marksmanship, survivalism techniques, and my set lecture subject 'Are We the Dreamers or Merely the Dreamed Of, and In Either Case What Does It Matter If We Pee in the Sink?' Hoping to hear from you soon, Sic Semper Tyrannis, Yours Most Sincerely . . . Got all that?"

"Yes, barely, but . . ." Lily scanned the letter. She had not written pee. Her scrambling pen had automatically substituted *peer*, and Lily found it interesting and not a small consolation to know that even were she to lose her mind entirely someday she would still remain proper down, it seemed, to her fingertips.

"The claim of poverty will scare them off more than the fanaticism. We just put that in for fun," Alden said. "Here, I'll stick a stamp on the envelope and set it on the piecrust table with the rest of our letters."

And so Lily allowed the letter to be sent as it was rather than waste the twenty-five cent stamp, although were she less weary (and were the night less rainy and her joints rubbing less stiffly against one another in their sockets) she might have worked off the stuck-on stamp with careful prying to affix with a finger-skimmed clot of glue to a different envelope containing a more usual and a more sensible letter. Besides, her bottle of Elmer's Glue had recently gone missing from the kitchen drawer where it was always supposed to be kept and Lily seemed to recall Becky had mentioned that one of the alien lamps required a small repair before being fobbed off on All Saints'. An ear had detached from a ceramic rabbit and Lily guessed that the delicate reconnecting of such disparate planes, the sliver of ear rejoined to the rounded skull, the meeting edges of both pieces roughened and chipped after their recent rattlings round a moving carton, would devolve into a lengthy and not guaranteedly successful operation. If necessary, Lily would lend Becky her small and veteran tube of the infinitely more grasping and tenacious substance called Miracle Glue, which she stored for safekeeping wrapped in a cotton rag and placed in an old shortbread tin stashed at the back of the spare mitten shelf of the out-of-season coat closet, a precaution taken because, from time to time, one heard of accidental and undesired adhesions involving heedless misapplications of the clearly and sternly labeled stuff. Take great care in the use and conservation of, the manufacturers sagely counseled, and Lily believed them.

Chapter Two The Hills in View

ALL THAT FALL the leaves drifted down. They swirled unswept along the walks and ranged with restless, tattered trespass across the lawns. Leaves clogged the twisting systems of low, branching shrubbery and choked the frost-gotten garden plots which were brownly mounded over, dead now, and buried. Leaves lapped up the foundation of the house and, rising individually in the snatches of suddenly spun winds, seemed to be seeking impossible reattachments to the surrendering trees. Bright golden, scarlet, bitter orange, nothing so became them as their leaving.

Lily only glanced at the brilliantly assembling day as she tugged up the shade of her bedroom window, the day as yet muted by mists and unbuffed by the touch of the sun which was itself just akindle in the eastern sky. She crossed the room and tugged up the shade of the opposing window and she regarded the wan disk suspended above the pointed tops of the pines. A wedge of Canadian geese flew across its pale face, spelling out *V* for their vanishing. The sun seemed a very local occurrence these early mornings even though they said (on an episode of *Nova*, an emphatic scientist from England surely maintaining) that the Universe was expanding. Lately, however, this had not been Lily's experience.

Look, now, how her universe was filling up with dead leaves. It was, Lily thought, a plain nuisance that people in Towne were no longer permitted to burn them. The old and now officiously outlawed method had been to start a dozen or more fires scattered across the lawns and lining the driveway and edging the woods, the leaves raked into long and spreading heaps. A slosh of accelerant, lawn mower gasoline from a battered can, was spilled over each pile and a wooden kitchen match scratched alight was tossed among the leaves. After several seconds the

72

air hissed and caught its breath and shuddered and flashed into flames erupting unpredictably underfoot or spiraling upward along gasoline fumes to strike at a face or a hand, but lashing out harmlessly, for the fire was so suddenly there and as suddenly not there. Somebody's hair, the hair on their heads or the down along their arms, might be singed and stink like kippers for a while, but no real damage had ever been done. The Hills had been fireproof in those days and, evidently, they still were.

For, just a few nights ago at supper, Ginger had been talking about her firewalking seminar, one of those exercises she put herself through when she was still trying to save that marriage of hers—or had it, in the end, given her the impetus to leave Louis? Lily, listening carefully for once because it all sounded so unlikely, hadn't caught her point as Ginger seemed to claim that her personal firewalk across a glowing pit dug behind a Ramada Inn on the outskirts of Wichita had led her both toward and yet away from poor Louis. He had become poor Louis in Lily's mind, although not for having lost Ginger—rather, frankly, for having won her in the first place.

"So all this firewalking enabled you to face Louis before you turned your back on him?" Alden had asked Ginger. As to whether he was politely or wickedly inquiring, opinion was divided around the dining room table, although in either instance his impulse could only be sighed at, for now, one way or another, they would be told.

"Swami Nehru said . . ." Ginger began to explain in that aggrieved National Public Radio hostess voice she employed when she was obliged, yet again, to set them all straight on still another nuanced and intricate aspect of the case she was constructing.

"A Nehru, was he? That's a good old Indian name, at least," Harvey spoke up. He kept track of the good old names of every major country and culture. He could, he said, travel most anywhere with every confidence.

"Swami Nehru said that Louis was my pit of hot coals and our marriage vows were my asbestos shoes," Ginger said, firmly steering the topic back to herself.

A piece of lasagna slipped the wrong way down Arthur's windpipe. His coat hanger shoulders heaved, his face flushed terra-cotta fusing his freckles. Phoebe thumped his back and held a glass of reconstituted grape juice to his sputtering lips. The rest of the Hills gravely observed the couple, their forks raised or lowered in the contrary direction from an original intent as they wondered, What next?

"A crusty bit," Arthur explained when he could speak again although Ginger regarded him darkly, suspecting she had fed him a line and if so, she was glad he'd choked on it.

"Oh, that oven," Becky apologized. "I never know."

They glanced at Lily whose oven it was and Lily shrugged, indicating her own long history of mystification concerning the heating element.

Nevertheless, this had been one of Becky's better suppers. They had had lasagna and broiled grapefruit halves and two squash pies were cooling in the serving hatch. Becky was putting to use her big recipes, as Ginger characterized them. "Serves eight to twelve," she had read aloud, flipping through Becky's file box searching for something elegant to try for a change. "Serves eight to twelve, that sounds like a prison sentence," she observed, and she had wondered, then, whether she might not have happened upon another chapter for her book, a correlation of the commonly held vocabularies of housewifery and incarceration. She had yet to come up with many more examples to note upon her 3×5 cards. Might one also cite servitude in a "Big House"? Yes, one very well might.

"I can only hope, Ginger, that someone responsible was standing by with a hose when you took your firewalk," Lily said.

"No, no, cold water would have been the worst thing," Harvey said. "She'd have been steamed to death like a clam."

"Oh, Mummy, I said it was dangerous, didn't I?" Betsy cried as Ginger shot her a wince of boredom.

"Can we have her pie?" Brooks and Rollins asked. They had learned to identify the moment when Betsy lost her appetite entirely.

Then Lily had braced herself for Little Becky's shriek of objection but Little Becky had sat serenely unconcerned at her crumb-strewn end of the long table. Her hectic face was disfigured by a shadowy grape juice mustache and her purple tongue greedily flicked away at the residual flavor. Little Becky had recently worked out that when Betsy refused dessert, her mother would slice slightly bigger pieces all around and not leave an extra portion for everybody to call dibs on. Simple.

BUT LILY DIDN'T HAVE all morning to waste at her window thinking about the family. It was just after six o'clock and she had forced herself out of bed in order to claim the bathroom first before the mirror steamed and the towels sagged wetly and sour-smelling from their racks and the Dial soap turned to lemon marmalade in its china dish which was not a real soap dish with drainage holes but only a pretty orphan saucer so one had to be mindful and swipe the soap dish dry with a tissue. The odd hairs and mite-like whiskers collecting in the sink (Lily's further thoughts propelled her down the hushed corridor with its closed doors and fraying islands of bright old carpets), the stained twists of tissues flung at but not into the wastebasket, the hamper lid ajar above an overload of castoff nightwear, someone's long-toed, high-arched naked footprint, not unlike that of a fleeing ape, preserved in the drift of talcum powder spilled beside the reluctantly draining bathtub, the window curtain blindly snatched and used as a towel with the guilty faceprint nearly identifiable in damp relief, the tumbler cloudy with toothpaste and lip prints and replicating bacteria were all so unlovely to behold, first thing.

Lily tapped upon then pushed through the bathroom door and she caught at the string of the overhead fluorescent bar light which performed its lightning imitation, flashing on and off and on before settling into its customary glare, revealing a pedestal sink with stiffly turning china faucets, a deep-sided freestanding bathtub resting on the clawed feet of some giant, mythical bird, and an oak-seated chain-pull commode sitting by itself in the corner. This was known, rather famously in some circles, as the oldest bathroom in Towne, but Lily had never been convinced that agedness was an asset in the arena of plumbing. Very early pearly grey linoleum curling up around its edges covered the aslope floor. Dropped tubes of lipstick inevitably rolled beneath the bathtub and then one sank to one's knees and reached on faith and felt around and roused red-eyed spiders. The plaster walls and ceiling were painted a denser grey. A blue, flocky rug hung over the side of the bathtub and a rack of polished looking blue towels were rather too precisely aligned to encourage their casual use. The muslin curtains breathed in and out. The same thoughtful someone who had tidied the bathroom had left the window open a hygienic inch overnight. The air was clean and sharp and cold, an old-fashioned climate for an old-fashioned bathroom.

Back in her own room Lily dressed quickly. She put on a navy blue cotton divided skirt, a blue-and-white-checked cotton blouse and a pair of flesh-colored over-the-knee cotton stockings. The manufacturer stamped Flesh-Colored on the box but Lily didn't know whose flesh they were thinking of. Becky and Ginger had been filling out an "Is Your Foundation Right For You?" questionnaire in one of Ginger's magazines and they had concluded Lily's underlying skin tone was blue which wasn't one of the options acknowledged by the article's author, who had a Ph.D. (though in *what* discipline, they wondered). Becky had worried that Lily might be suffering from a medical rather than a fashion difficulty and Lily had admitted that her ankles tended to swell up by evening, though that may have been because the elastic tops of her over-the-knee stockings fit a bit tight—she strengthened the elastics on each newly opened pair so that she wouldn't be seen fumbling beneath the hem of her divided skirt all the time hitching and adjusting against the downward creep. Her ankles paid the price, Lily guessed; nevertheless, in life one faced one's choices and made them.

The stairs were solidly built and didn't betray her early-morning prowl by creaking beneath her feet as she descended. She lifted her barn jacket from among the many other garments adhering now to the coat-rack, which had grown bulky over the past weeks of colder weather, assuming an utterly different personality as it stood in the front hall-way, turning into someone whom she didn't like as well as she had in the days when it was sparer of shape and steadier on its feet, dressed in the shapeless hats and dim-colored woolens and tweeds of her own wardrobe. Lily wrapped a scarf around her neck for good measure, one of Harvey's, who made such a fetish of bundling up. It was handknit in red, white, and royal blue stripes, and ruthlessly well executed in Lily's opinion, the stitches as tight as the kernels in an early ear of sweet corn.

The scarf had been a gift from one of Harvey's admiring widow ladies. Lily, despite all her knitting projects, did not knit at all well. She was always being detained by wrought-iron palings and doorknobs when she wore her own loosely put together sweaters. A woman who could knit as competently as Harvey's new lady friend might, if very determined, just as skillfully entangle Harvey in the threads of her own life, Lily decided.

The loud, dousing rain of the night before had sluiced the clouds from the sky which, at present as morning had truly dawned, arched overhead tinted so brightly azure that Lily was reminded of the old color photographs in the *National Geographic,* the very earliest issues, when color itself seemed so shiny and new. The wide puddle that had formed with last night's rain across the dip in the driveway held a shimmering and ideal version of the surrounding scene within its clear waters, enhancing the beauty of the New England autumn to more effect than Lily felt capable of responding to as it struck her that this could be a too-showing-off world. For hers was a long driveway and by the time Lily reached the road and her scarred, oxidized mailbox strapped with fortified tape to a leaning post entwined with bittersweet and poison ivy vines blazing at their brightest this time of year, she felt her perceptions had been lifted quite high enough by the insistent display, and one final sycamore bush burning beside a telephone pole was not a revelation to her but just another contribution to the hot air that surrounded her these days. She extracted the wedged-in bulk of the *Sunday Globe* from the mailbox and glanced at the headlines, more news about freedom breaking out in Eastern Europe as the Soviets could only avert their eyes.

Lily let herself back inside the sleeping house and made her way to the kitchen. A calendar swung against the back of the door and slid to the floor as she pushed through. Lily knelt and searched for the thumbtack Little Becky had failed to jab firmly enough into the wood, for this was Little Becky's calendar, devoted to some singing group she adored. Significant days in the life histories of the group's members were outlined in red as if the birthday of someone named Donny were a national holiday. Once or twice when consulting the calendar, Lily had been caught short, imagining she had forgotten some occasion for which she ought to have sent out greeting cards or roasted a Butterball or displayed the Flag. There, the thumbtack had tumbled under the radiator where Lily would let it remain. Her only concern was for damage to bare feet—not her own, of course, but Ginger padded around the house like a South Sea Islander on vacation at the beach. As for the calendar, Lily propped that against Becky's looming microwave oven from New York. Boiling water in ninety seconds, Becky claimed on her oven's behalf but when they had a race, Lily's old electric kettle won, which Lily had been sorry about for Becky had been so sure and then been so let down.

The kitchen had been painted egg-yolk yellow, a free-range hen's fresh egg-yolk yellow, back in the days when everyone painted their kitchens yellow, although as Ginger informed her (Ginger seemed always to be informing Lily about something) colorologists had discovered that yellow was a highly unsettling color. Prisoners in yellow-painted cells rioted more often than those held in pink-walled cells, she said. "And what does *pink* make the prisoners do?" asked Harvey, as the boys snorted, which only encouraged him. There was more of the early pearly grey linoleum covering the kitchen floor, worn through to the original boards in front of the sink and refrigerator and counter. The boards were wide pine cut from trees that must have been growing when the Pilgrims landed, Alden had estimated after he pried up a corner of the linoleum to determine what lay underneath, and he wanted to pull off all of the linoleum and refinish the original wood with linseed oil and beeswax and take a picture of the results to send to the Letters column in *Old House Journal*.

We'll see, Lily said.

A long table occupied the center of the kitchen. A variety of styles of chairs, the age and distinction of several hiding below a dozen layers of slapped-on paint, sat around the table. A lazy Susan stood in the middle of the table, so crowded now with jars and bottles and cruets and sifters containing all their particular fads in condiments and seasonings that the twirling platform stalled out mid-circuit beneath the burden it bore. Lily was convinced Ginger's encrusted little pot of Ja Chai pickles was present only because Ginger liked the idea of liking Ja Chai pickles.

Lily filled the electric kettle and plugged the cord into a booster outlet. She dropped three tea bags into the brown teapot and shook two slices of bread from the loaf and inserted them in the toaster's slots. She remembered before it was too late to reset the dial from the highest setting to a medium one. Harvey doted on charred toast and she had told him, "You can always toast your toast more. I cannot toast mine less." Harvey had wandered off, so intrigued by the concept of reverse-toasting, he overlooked her primary point. Lily hoped some of the apricot jam remained. She rummaged through the refrigerator and could only find the stemmy wild blueberry preserves Becky had made as an adventure last summer.

The kettle steamed, then whistled. Lily snatched the cord from the socket before the spout could wail. She glanced at Glover's door. She didn't want to rouse him and be obliged to offer to make him toast or share the newspaper with him. She would surrender Sports if she had to—the Red Sox weren't in the Series—but she supposed Glover would really prefer the Sex section, if one was to be had.

GINGER FLUNG HARVEY'S soft-sided old Aquascutum raincoat selected from the front-hall coatrack over Louis's plaid flannel pajamas, the legs of which had to be rolled over several times above her ankles so she could walk about. She had scuffed on the pair of her grandfather's cloud-stepping shearling slippers she had come across stuffed in a paper bag and forgotten behind an accordion folder file containing an assortment of somebody's long-solved crossword puzzles confidently worked in ink. She had to clutch the flapping cuffs of her pajama sleeves as she thrust her arms down the raincoat sleeves and the material now hung below her fingertips, so she turned the excess flannel back up and over the coat cuffs and secured it there, tucked and strapped beneath the complication of tabs and buckles that lurk around the apertures of superior English-made raingear.

"Betsy?" Ginger inquired up Lily's elegant staircase which curved back on itself as it rose like a section of chambered nautilus shell broken open and beautifully revealed. Ginger pitched her voice low lest she awaken the others whom she found hard to take first thing in the morning, the speaking to and stepping aside for and sharing of her coffee with. Nevertheless, her summons resonated along the mother-daughter frequency to which Betsy's porcelain-shard ears must surely be attuned after seventeen years of finding out how little Ginger liked to be kept waiting. Cold air bled down the staircase, buffeting Ginger's upturned face in tumbling drafts redolent of unquarried stone and dead, dead chrysanthemums. God, this crypt of a house.

She distracted herself for a moment, riffling through the stack of letters waiting on the piecrust table for someone to become organized and drive down to the village to post them. Restport, read Ginger, pausing. Whatever did Lily imagine she was up to, communicating with that red brick and stucco establishment over on the Boston Road where, Ginger had heard, the old folks whooped it up at crowded and rancorous séances, everyone present heatedly insisting that a spectral "Eleanor" had come through specifically to advise *them* that "Mother" was "all right" and happy "here" with the "others." No, no, Lily had family enough surrounding her these days. She didn't need to seek out shades.

The Royal Kung Fu Club of Peking? Oh, those moronic boys—and they'd better not thump and crash in martial violence over her head and crack her ceiling plaster into ever more spider casts which would scuttle across the corners of her eyes as dusk fell and she grew weary over her manuscript. And what was Becky doing, writing so thickly (Ginger hefted the missive) to her great friend William Baskett who had been so long immured in one or another of those murky little potato-fed, crease-of-the-map crossroads of horrific history countries and doing his diplomatic best on America's behalf, whatever *that* entailed—arranging for fireworks on the Fourth and the reading aloud of "Concord Hymn" by a voice-y, out-of-luck-actor type?—Ginger, immured in Towne, could only suppose. She examined a scrawled-upon cerise-pink envelope containing Little Becky's pestering appeal to a film star or teen idol or whoever it was. Ginger no longer kept very close track of the popular scene. When Fleetwood Mac first dissolved in disarray, that had spelled the end of all true caring for her. She tossed aside yet another approach by Alden to still another former classmate, throwing his net wider and wider, all the way to California this time, that languid land of poolside negotiations where, indeed, he might be slotted in nicely, for he had revealed, of late, his own aptitude for doing nothing. She dismissed

Harvey's further happy and energetic harassment of his Connecticut realtor, whom he really ought not to have addressed as the Land Pirate of Old Saybrook, and she slipped her own letter to Oscar into the center of the pile, concealed from prying eyes. It was nobody's business to inspect the outgoing mail. (Betsy, for her part, knew better than to leave out a letter to her father, and when she received a letter from Kansas, Lily, who always fetched the mail, left it in Betsy's desk drawer, indicated and weighted by a condoling Mystic Mint cookie laid on top.)

"Betsy," Ginger called again. "Betsy," she spoke too forbearingly. Ginger had raised herself from the haven of her warm bed on this wretched Sunday morning solely on Betsy's behalf. She had been dreaming when her shrill alarm rioted and dispersed the dream, but shreds of significance had clung. In her dream, Ginger was being admired, although for what she wasn't quite sure and she had been keen to find out.

She turned on her soft heel and caught sight of herself in the glass of the front-hall secretary desk, her own much considered face floating across the silver sides of the vases, pitchers, bowls, and candlesticks crammed inside. I would make a terribly interesting photograph, Ginger thought. Such a pity there was no one to photograph her, yet another opportunity to chronicle the work in progress that was herself, lost. "Lost," she spoke aloud in her drowned voice and she peered harder into her own, accidental image to memorize how very sad she looked and to determine how she had achieved such a telling manifestation of her great inner grief. Her hand strayed toward her hair. Other women her age would have tried to subdue its electric excesses but she encouraged her hair's exuberances, pulling long strands out higher and wider, the chestnut strands, the silver-white strands which shot through the dark hair wirier and more springingly uplifting than ever as if even at this veteran stage her always interesting hair had worked out a way to defy time's sly compact with gravity. (As Alden said, one would not care to sit behind Ginger at the theater. 'Spect she'd hiss warnings to the villain that the authorities were on to him, added Harvey, wandering off subject but staying on target nonetheless.)

Ginger sank to the bottom tread of the stairway, her plaid knee jammed under the point of her chin. Morning sun filtered through the fanlight in apportioned patches. Ginger shifted, seeking her warmer share, and she subsided into reverie, trying to slip back into that delightful dream.

"Mummy? I've been waiting for you," Betsy was speaking to her. "I was outside, waiting." She knelt beside Ginger and she sniffed delicately—for alcohol or for some more animal reason?

"Outside?" queried Ginger as if she'd never heard of such a place. She tried to rise. Betsy held out an automatically helping hand which Ginger spurned. She was only having difficulties rising because she was stepping on the spreading hem of Harvey's long-skirted raincoat, not as the result of some incapacity as Betsy seemed so quick and so keen to assume.

"It's nice outside," Betsy stated wistfully.

"But I've been in here," Ginger said.

"Yes," Betsy allowed.

Oh, but how could one scold one's child merely for agreeing with one? Maddening, maddening Betsy.

Ginger fumbled under her coat and hitched up the waistband of her pajama bottoms and she swept past Betsy and strode out the door. A djinn-like dance of leaves swirled inside in her wake and scattered across the rugs. Betsy chased and stamped after them for they seemed alive and when the leaves lay crushed and senseless on the floor, she lingered, pitying them.

"Come *on*, Betsy."

"Yes, Mummy."

Betsy closed the front door after herself, quietly, because the household lay asleep, but firmly as well for there was so much within that burglars would find well worth their while to steal. She didn't want to return to discover all the family tied to kitchen chairs with silk neckties and electrical extension cords coldly discussing back and forth whom to blame for the outrage as their white-tipped fingers twitched and tried at their bonds. She would, of course, be obliged to confess her responsibility for the ill-closed door which they would probably have figured out for themselves eventually and Ginger certainly would have shopped Betsy while strenuously exonerating herself. Betsy would be sorry were thieves to carry off Aunt Lily's chest of sterling flatware. She had come to like the feel of the smooth round bowl shape of one of the big old soup spoons sliding between her lips and clicking against her teeth—the rich spoon itself seemed sustenance enough. She almost looked forward to another one of Aunt Becky's simple soup suppers.

"Betsy, are you serious about—"

Betsy chased the purposefully striding Ginger across the lawn. The heels of her pumps kept planting themselves in the spongy earth and she had to pull them up with every step so that she looked like a much younger girl much less successfully playing at lady. She was wearing a short-brimmed fedora hat she had found in an Empire Store box and which Lily recognized as having been her own. Betsy had rewired the hat's drooping plume so that it arced forward and up and down, just not brushing her cheek. She had also come across a very stiff pair of very white gloves in a bureau drawer (Lily couldn't think whose they might have been) which smelled of the drawer's interior, of translucent face powder and a secret store of cinnamon drops. Betsy's dress was her own, indigo-colored, corduroy, with a sash that tied in a bow in the front or the back, depending. She wore a locket round her neck. The locket opened into two hinged halves and there was space inside for two tiny pictures of the people who, she supposed conventionally, she most loved. She had snipped apart her parents' last passport proofs, the unchosen poses. Two eyes, two eyebrows, a nose apiece were all that remained after she trimmed them down to size. At the click of the clasp her parents were locked within the golden disc. She wanted to imagine the interior was golden and not black inside, and that her parents gazed into one another's eyes in an eternity of calm communion but she more truly believed that they were bitterly arguing there where they lay just above her heart, even though she had not included their mouths.

"Betsy, I swear—"

Betsy broke into a slow run, pulling her embedded heels out of the sod and kicking up clods. Her hair, which was secretly as thick and as long and as ungovernable as her mother's, hung in its usual tight, pale yellow mono-braid that lashed her back as she ran. She caught up with Ginger at the top of the driveway bowl beside the swaybacked barn. The cars were parked huddled at one edge of the driveway sweep as if keeping clear of the barn should it collapse, although as Alden pointed out, if the barn hadn't collapsed by now, it was never going to, much like the Brazilian economy, he said.

Ginger fished in the deep pockets of Harvey's raincoat. She withdrew a linen handkerchief, a tape measure, some twopenny nails twisted in a paper bag, a white chiffon scarf smudged with dark orange makeup, and last, the keys to his car.

"I hope he's left us enough gas," Ginger said as she switched on the engine and readjusted the mirrors.

"We can stop at the Mill Road Texaco, we go right by. I have money," Betsy said. "Look, the arrow is on E."

"Harvey can buy his own gas. We'll coast along on fumes. But I wonder, whose scarf is this? Can you picture anyone whose skin is that peculiar shade of orange? I don't know, Wilma Flintstone, do you think? How d'you suppose that would work? How would they interact, I mean to say, personally?"

"*I* don't know, Mummy. I don't wish to know."

Ginger glanced at Betsy's stern profile.

"But what if you run out of gas?" Betsy asked. She wished her mother would fasten her seat belt because if there was an accident what an uproar a wounded Ginger would raise as she shouted and shouted for a plastic surgeon.

"Like a dog with a bone," Ginger remarked.

"What if you have to walk a long way for gas in just your slippers and your, you know, just pajamas and all?" Betsy asked.

"Oh, you're embarrassed by my ensemble? Is that it?" Ginger asked. "I'll tell you what, I'll hide in the woods until dark or I'll swim underwater through the swamps with a reed up my nose, that's what I'll do if I run out of gas. Huh? How's that?" She had warmed to the notion of herself as a swift and secretive suburban guerrilla, lean, brown, sinewy, strong. One would become, necessarily, terribly fit living on the run, wouldn't one? Or one could, less radically, join the local little steamy-windowed, ivy-covered Y. She wondered if Becky would go halvsies on a family membership.

"No, Mummy. That's not what I—I meant, if you have to walk a long way in slippers, you'll hurt your feet." Those same feet that had not burned on a pit of flaming coals.

"Or perhaps," Ginger said, "you don't want me to embarrass my-self."

Oh, is there a distinction where my embarrassment ends and yours begins? Betsy wondered but did not ask aloud.

As they came to the outskirts of the village, Ginger watched for faces she knew or had known years ago and whom she might fill in on the sub-sequent story of her life over cappuccino and a croissant at Peddocks' General Store, but there were few people abroad on a shuttered Sunday morning for Ginger to spot and swerve toward and honk at and hail by an ancient nickname. Betsy had guessed her mother wasn't seeking just anyone. No, she was on the alert for a specific someone, so instantly uninterested was Ginger in the few candidates they passed, a woman, the paperboy, an elderly gentleman walking his collie dog. None was the specific someone Ginger sought, which was probably just as well, Betsy decided. She knew her mother was up to something. The signs were there. Why, for instance, had Ginger allowed herself to be persuaded to act as chauffeur this early morning?

They arrived at All Saints'. Ginger nosed across two curbside park-ing spaces as she read aloud the bumper sticker of a passing minivan. "Visualize Whirled Peas? Visualize Whirled Peas?" she repeated, mys-tified. "I don't want to visualize . . ." She twisted in her seat, delving once again in Harvey's raincoat pockets. She required money for a *New York Times* and a cappuccino and a croissant at dear old Peddocks' Store which hadn't changed a whit since she was a girl except in all good ways such as the *Times* and cappuccino and croissants now being available.

"If you were your Uncle Harvey, where would you keep your emer-gency twenty-dollar bill? Look in the glove compartment. Pick up the owner's manual and shake out the pages. Harvey's subtle," Ginger said.

"No, remember, you borrowed his emergency twenty last week from his golf jacket's inner zipper pocket," Betsy said.

"He should have replaced it by now."

"Maybe he hasn't noticed yet because he hasn't had an emergency. Because I'm pretty sure he would have mentioned an emergency and no emergency twenty."

"You have a point," Ginger conceded.

Betsy, who had laid her morocco-covered Book of Common Prayer and her own and Aunt Lily's sealed-shut offertory envelopes neatly on her corduroy lap, gathered them in one gloved hand. Ginger eyed the envelopes but even she could not suggest and Betsy had no intention of volunteering.

"You mentioned you had money for gas?" Ginger recalled, then.

"Oh, right. I forgot," Betsy said. She had only been intent on preserving the Lord's mite. She tipped her purse so Ginger couldn't twig the unlikely place where she concealed her own emergency funds inside an old codeine vial (prescribed for the terrible pain of her wisdom teeth extraction last winter) but Ginger guessed, for future foragings, that Betsy's cache had to be someplace like a vial for the two ten-dollar bills Betsy handed her were curled in cylinder shapes.

"Oh my God," Ginger declared unprayerfully.

"What, Mummy?" Betsy asked. "Isn't that enough?"

Ginger crouched behind the steering wheel staring through the windshield. The lowered sun visor threw a bar of shadow across her unsentimental eyes which were screwed into a fiercely focusing squint. She leaned into the horn. She rolled down her window and reached out and up and slapped the roof of the car.

"I'm late," Betsy said. "I think I hear the processional starting." She opened her door and slid out.

Ginger threw herself across the seat and rolled down the passenger-side window (all this very necessary rolling down of windows—she grunted) and called after Betsy, "No, no, wait up. Meet Goody, Mr. Palmer, my very dearest, oldest friend in Towne."

Betsy, who supposed it would be undignified to flee as her mother squalled after her, stood obediently if unenthusiastically beside the car. Mr. Palmer, startled by the blat of a horn churchside on a Sunday morning, peered alertly to discern any situation requiring his assistance. A Mrs. Palmer trailed a few steps behind her husband. She had paused to compose a note to the driver of a car parked with a rear tire rolled over the edge of the brick sidewalk. Babe Palmer didn't think cars should be parked with their rear tires rolled over the edges of the frangible brick sidewalks which were such a lovely feature of the village. She walked along making a further note of the offending vehicle's license plate number for her files, and, intent upon her notebook page, checking to see whether this car was a repeat offender, she bumped flat into Goody who had been stopped in his tracks.

"My word," Goody was saying. "My word," he turned and informed Babe.

"Your word what?" snapped Babe. She adjusted her hat, an open velveteen circlet clogged with stiff net veiling, which had been spun askew by the collision with her husband. "Your word this young girl?" she asked, indicating Betsy. Babe stared at Betsy's hat about which Betsy herself was having second thoughts. After all, she was wearing one of Lily's discarded hats and one could hardly enjoy supreme confidence in a hat which at some point had failed even to live up to Aunt Lily's standards. Betsy had heard that Aunt Lily had been known to button a cardigan over her storm coat.

The so cleverly accomplished resurrection of the elderly plume had not lasted the not long journey. The golden locket that lay so heavily against her breast, the prayer book and offerings on her knee, the borrowed hat atop her fair head, young Betsy herself had been severely jounced as Ginger oversteered Harvey's overengineered American mid-luxury car around the worst curve on Winding Road. Whoops, said Ginger who, weighing in rather heavier these days, had absorbed the jolt like a dashboard Buddha. Now, the fallen feather scraped Betsy's jawbone but it was a question of character not to scrub the spot even as her too-thin skin pinkened and prickled and Mrs. Palmer's sharp eyes exacerbated the itch.

"No, Babe. No, look. It's Ginger Hill Lowe of all people," Goody said. He ducked down to grin through the car window. Ginger sprawled across the seat. She stretched and hooked her fingers around Goody's starched shirt collar and drew him down to place a generous kiss of hello upon his mouth.

"Yes, it's me," cried Ginger, releasing him as he began to pull away from her, pretty sure she had meant to kiss his cheek and that their awkward angles of approach had caused the excessive contact he had not wished to call undue attention to by jumping back from Ginger's embrace as if scalded. Besides, he had not felt particularly scalded. Indeed, he had for a second or two quite entirely failed to mind what was happening to him.

"I've come home," Ginger said. "I was going to call you but then I decided no. No, I must wait for kismet to cause our paths to converge because, frankly, I'm very interested to find out what fate has in store for me and thus far, fate has counseled be patient, which wisdom I have accepted."

"Oh, but I knew all along that you were up at Miss Hill's place." Babe crimped her knees. Not at all tall, she made herself smaller and she addressed Ginger through the car window. "Because Doris broadcast the fact all over Towne as soon as she deposited you that night." Babe spoke of "that night" as if she had heard of details not to Ginger's credit—of her noisy tears, of her bundled belongings, of Lily's having to pay the fare from the train stop in Hamilton out of her retirement fixed-income personal funds.

"Well, I had no idea, no clue at all," Goody confessed as if a happy plot to surprise him had been carried off successfully by the women's coordinated efforts.

"*Fata obstant,*" murmured Ginger as she leveled a look at Babe who knew enough English to work out what Ginger was driving at with her smattering of Latin.

"So, you're visiting," said Goody. "Are you here for the foliage?" he asked as a churchyard maple stirred and released a bright flight of radiant leaves.

"Now is not the time to go into Ginger's situation," Babe advised Goody in an aside.

"Yes, I'll tell you all about it later," Ginger promised smoothly, and then because Babe seemed to be trying to work out what Ginger had worn downtown beneath her raincoat on this sunny Sunday morning, Ginger mentioned, "My daughter, Betsy."

"Your daughter? Imagine," marveled Goody. "You're very like your mother, very like," he told Betsy, smilingly.

"Oh. Am I?" uttered Betsy.

"Are you?" asked Babe meaningfully.

"Isn't she," stated Ginger.

"Mummy, that really is the processional I hear now," Betsy said. She didn't like to trail into church, as she so often had to for she so often arrived late, behind the crucifix and the choir and the acolytes and the curate and the Rector, as if the march of music and the episcopal banners and the berobed personages were conducting her to the forward pew she favored beside the square of stained-glass window which could be pushed out and propped open so that the dour St. Jerome depicted there seemed to be kicking up his heels. All Saints' could be stuffy. On Communion Sundays, you could almost count on one of the fasters to faint, slumping like an unstrung marionette onto a kneeler during the General Thanksgiving as if an awful recollection crushed her.

"Then scoot," directed Ginger. "Remember me in your prayers," she added irresistibly. She might even have joined them but for her attire, although, really, this proxy arrangement suited her better for there was the very real risk that one or another of the Lessons would hit a nerve (or more accurately, strike the side of the barn where her misdeeds were posted on multicolored hoardings) and she would have to sit there in the sepia-tinted gloom, fixed as an unfavorable photograph of herself, and then be obliged to endorse her own chastisement by speaking at intervals, Amen.

ALDEN HAD DUG a seasoned crewneck sweater and a pair of very old corduroy trousers out from one of the as yet to be unpacked boxes pushed beneath their bed. His resurrected clothes smelled strongly of moth crystals and were creased where they had been so long folded across the chest and elbows and at the thighs and ankles and knees. As he stepped outside squinting, nearly blinded by the hard and dazzling sun of autumn, he rather looked as if he himself had been retrieved from long storage. It was a usual remark about Alden that they had broken the mold after they made him although whether Alden was being considered a special limited edition or a flawed and discontinued specimen depended upon the remarker's usual experience of him. This morning Alden had stepped down from whichever shelf he had been consigned to feeling stiff in every joint after the previous night's dank incursions into his bones' very marrows. He had winced through the business of kneeling and reaching and dragging forth boxes searching for the one marked OUTER–ALDEN to which Becky had directed him. He had not thought to ask her where she had stowed the inner Alden.

But he loved the fall. He had declared his enthusiasm at breakfast although he had not won any reciprocal confessions from his wary confidants, his several sons who were slumped over their cereal bowls excising the edible inches from browning bananas.

"I love this time of year, boys," Alden said as he slapped a pair of leather gloves down onto the table beside his mug of coffee. He began to stoke himself with a great mound of Corn Flakes.

For the boys sensed work was in the offing. The leather of the gloves was stiff and scarred and Alden was eating like a lumberjack. He nudged the lazy Susan round and helped himself from the canister of maple sugar one of his Senior Village widows had given Harvey for his waffles. Harvey would mind Alden's theft, but Harvey wasn't there.

"Any juice?" asked Alden.

The boys shrugged and shook their heads. Out of juice.

"Pity," said Alden. "But what an inspiring day this is," he stated leadingly.

Inspiring, Dad?

Glover slouched, his chin so sunk onto his chest he had to breathe out to allow his mouth to sag open to receive a nugget of pared banana. Brooks hopped to rinse his bowl and his spoon at the sink. Rollins rose as well and jammed a banana peel into the wastebasket, and he and Brooks slipped away through the back-hall door not wishing to be recruited into Alden's work corps or to be forced to invent an extricating excuse. An expressed alternative intention to walk down to the river to see how high the water had risen with last night's rain would commit them to spending an inconvenient half hour doing exactly that. Alden would be sure to ask for a report. Were the arches of the stone bridge clogged with debris? he would want to know. They could, of course, invent—Yes, clogged, very clogged—but they would be sandbagged by further interrogation. Had any of the claw-footed bankside willows finally toppled in the storm? Yes, would say Rollins as Brooks volunteered, No. The two saw eye to eye, but sometimes they saw as in a mirror.

Glover, to whom Alden turned expectantly, had signaled his intention to observe a quiet Sabbath by picking up and reading the small print on the side of a box of Grape Nuts.

Now, Alden kicked through the leaves with his hands in his pockets. His cheeks, rounded by a big uncomplicated smile, took on color. The scratch of his wool sweater and whiffs of naphthalene energized him. The wales of his cords scraped to the swings of his strides. He forgot his earlier aches as he strolled across the lawns estimating all the while how *many* leaves had fallen, for he could measure and apportion and run large figures in his head. All problems are quantifiable and the very large number he arrived at, the formidable leaf count, presented him with a welcome challenge for the day. He needed to keep busy and he preferred to know how busy, for when his task was completed he would be able to tally what had been accomplished. Somewhere, a great recording ledger lay open atop a rat-gnawed ambo beside a guttering tallow candle. Alden's mind's eye had not upgraded the information-integrating system but he supposed the conscience's basic furnishings had not been much altered over the aeons, aside from a few pictures of various beauties and those brave heroes once and then no longer held ideal, nailed up in display and eventually turned to face the wall.

Alden entered the barn through the pulled-apart doors that had been leaning open all summer after they'd fallen off their runners. Lily had called out *Careful!* too late as the boys, told by Harvey there might be a motorcycle, had rushed the barn and battered the doors. It was going to be a project to remount the two wide-board constructions before winter blew in. Alden foresaw all the stinging splinters and crushed toes and resentful boys surging left when he ordered them to move to their rights. He did not think he would be able to manage the job on his own although he would at first make the futile attempt. Then Harvey would come upon him pinned beneath a fallen door or brooding over a shattered finger and Harvey would bellow for the boys to come at once. The boys did not quite dare not answer Harvey's summonses. Harvey had been known to charge up the attic stairs and seize the disobedient boys from their lazy beds when he required them, a direct tactic that had never occurred to their parents to employ, and the boys were bound not to let them learn by their elder's tough example. As it was, Alden and Becky were rather touched by their sons' respectful attendance upon their old uncle and they chose to view this most proper behavior as a validation of their child-rearing methods insofar as method had ever applied.

Leaves scuttled into the barn around Alden's duck boots and a dozen sparrows left abruptly but temporarily. They alit reproachfully in the forsythia bushes clamped to the too thin branches that bowed beneath their very slight and impatient weights. He was going to have to organize the door-repairing party soon or this really could spell the beginning of the end of the barn. Nature was keen to push back the line. Lily's woods, so lush in the canopy, so tangled on the floor, were crossed and crossed again by stone walls almost unseeable, almost lost, until one started to spot and to find them everywhere. Why who would squish a wall in *here?*, Little Becky had wanted to know last summer as she slip-sloppily balanced along rolly rocks and squeezed between the trunks of two high-reaching and rough-ribbed tamaracks grown up on either side of a boulder. No way, she had said when Alden explained that the walls had described the open agricultural fields of only a century or two ago. So, what happened to the poor farmers? Little Becky had wanted to know. I guess they turned into us, Alden had suddenly understood.

Alden didn't know where they would pitch a bale of hay these days should the need arise nor where they would fit the cow who would necessitate the hay. The barn's first stall held a rugged, rusted snowplow blade, angled in to fit, that had broken through brittle slats into the second stall which contained the Aldens' dining room furniture, the table, the chairs tucked under the table, and the upended sideboard, all covered with sheets and tarps tied on tightly with twine. The tabletop was strewn with dried brown hollyhock stalks, the puckered purses of flowerheads spilling their seeds like careless coins across the rough cloth. Ancient to modern Mass. license plates ran up and down a central wooden support post. Primitive shelving put up anyhow and anywhere supported paper bags bristling with nails and rinsed-out pickle jars full of nuts and bolts and screws and washers and casters and hinges and springs. Oily ropes looped over beams and lopped the unwary in the temple with knotted ends. Tennis and badminton rackets and snowshoes sagged from hooks. Wooden skis and poles leaned. Lawn mowers lay in pieces. There were bicycles and bicycles and Harvey had remembered right about the motorcycle even though it was only the Vespa an anything-Italian-mad cousin had acquired after he saw *Roman Holiday.* The boys had tried to coax a kick from its sewing machine motor. They had rubbed the spark plugs with rags and they had polished the chrome, so far to no effect. Apply some sewing machine oil, had been Becky's suggestion for such an unserious motor. Lily, drawn into the discussion, wondered if tapping out the dent in the scooter's tiny, tinny fender would be of any help. The dent was her fault, she confessed. She had dropped a clay flowerpot on it when she'd been startled by a strange bat, that is, a bat who had not been one of the regular bats who roosted in the loft and knew not to swoop at her when her hands were full of flowerpots and she was thinking where to put them.

Piece of junk, Alden dismissed the Vespa. He ought to load it onto the back of the station wagon and drive down to the dump but he didn't doubt he'd be made to drive back to the dump to retrieve it, recovered in a sorrier state than ever after a day or two left lying upside down in a great snarl of cast-off machinery, for the Towne Dump featured thematic disposal stations—plastic, paper, aluminum leavings. But much of the barn's contents would be unclassifiable. There would have to be conferences binside with the assembled refuse engineers, the guys who hung out at the dump, prodding much-altered objects and pronouncing them formerly animal, vegetable, or mineral. Perhaps it was just as well that the Hills found it so impossible to throw anything away—except lately their marriages and careers, Alden reflected.

He tested rakes lifted from the museum of rake history, crammed in a cobwebby corner and representing four or five generations of the family's tastes in rakes—short- and long-tined versions, bamboo- and steel-toothed, wooden- or steel-handled, heads wider or narrower. He gripped hafts and swiped the floor and selected two examples that felt good, a broad bamboo fan of long, flexible teeth for clearing the lawns and a short, sturdy metal-tusked model for routing round beneath the shrubbery.

HARVEY, CARRYING a coffee mug and holding the Sunday-morning cigar he was allowed (by his own edict and in his own scheme of things),

strolled toward the driveway. He conveyed his mug and his cigar delicately lest he spill coffee or ash. He sipped and puffed. His coffee had
been poured hot and his cigar had been rolled strong. Smooth smoke
scented his general vicinity. If dispatched to fetch Harvey one would
locate him easily and in the process perhaps come to appreciate how
a hound holds his nose to the air and gets his man. Alden, becoming
aware of a rich aroma (Cuban, he would not put it past Harvey to have
secured a source), retreated back into the barn preferring not to be
hounded himself by Harvey, who would be sure to ask him, indicating
the double-barreled rakes Alden was bearing, Signed on as a lawn boy,
have you? Good fellow, make yourself useful. The boys quit tossing a
deflated football in a three-sided game of Gotcha. They sniffed alertly
and stepped behind the giant sugar maple, which rendered them invisible like some enchanted tree in a magic tale.

Harvey's feelings would not have been hurt had he noticed how his
kinsmen scattered at his approach. He preferred a clear shot at the day,
the fine Sunday morning which was very likely the last fine Sunday
morning of the year. He paused and drained rainwater from the pot of
yellow pom-pom chrysanthemums Lily had carted home from somewhere and plunked down on a bench. He snatched a sluggish hornet as it
veered at him and cracked it to death between his fingernails. He plotted
a zigzag course down the driveway stepping on as much of its surface as
he could, testing it for weak spots. He groomed bits of gravel from here
to there with the side of his shoe. He kicked a footful of gravel into the
wide puddle that had collected overnight in the dip and he resolved to
kick gravel into the dip on a regular basis and eventually fill in the
depression, another project that required his attention. Throw a little
paint on the shutters, kick a little gravel at the driveway dip. He would
pace himself. Wise to.

Some woman waved at him as she sailed past out on the River Road.
Harvey lifted his coffee mug and fluttered his cigar and smiled his
crowded-cocktail-party smile at her. Who was she? Lily should know,
a woman, in a blue car, heading toward Topsfield, waving, at him,
friendlily. He clamped his cigar between his teeth and set his mug down
on top of one of the concrete posts that were holding up the mailbox

these days and with two hands he tugged at the ill-fitting mailbox flap, wrenching it open. The paper, where was his newspaper? Extracted, stolen, gone. He glared up and down the too quiet road on the off chance the thief lingered in the woods reading and approving the *Globe*'s editorial pages at some illicit and contaminated gypsy encampment.

As Harvey turned to pace back up the long driveway another car flew at him, rocketing from out of nowhere and frantically tooting. He leaped, landing knee-deep in the weedy verge, as the car swept up the drive in an unholy rush. It was his own car. Harvey recognized the vehicle racing crazy-wild away from him in a seemingly driverless condition, for at the instant of tooting and turning and, mistakenly, accelerating (her slippered foot had slipped on the gas pedal) Ginger had knocked her Styrofoam cup full of Peddocks' good mocha blend from the dashboard onto her stack of fresh magazines and the bulk of the *Times*. She had lunged and grabbed for the cup—luckily the lid held. Oh, that was Harvey who'd been standing there in her way by the side of the road. She observed him in the rearview mirror. She honked again and waved her thanks for the use of his car. But ought Uncle Harvey run? Ought he run and smoke? Studying him not without concern, she hit the sudden driveway dip fast and hard. Silvery marlin fins of froth and spray washed up and along and over the fenders, and the hood latch popped itself ajar. Ought Harvey to run and smoke and shout?

"HARVEY, IT'S KIND of you to want to help but why don't you rake over there while I work right here," Alden suggested. Harvey, in a fume, had presented himself with a steel-shafted, sharp steel-toothed rake grasped in his fist. He had attached himself to Alden, matching Alden's every steady stroke with a slashing one. Harvey did not speak of his fury. He vibrated with it. Alden began to breathe in concert with Harvey's growls and gusts and he felt as if he had been assigned his own doppelgänger, one whose weird mission on earth was to deposit a new flurry of leaves onto every patch Alden had cleared. Ginger had, just before, hustled past Alden, huddled inside a flowing raincoat and scuffing in and out of a pair of flapping slippers. She had informed him,

"You haven't seen me." *She* was playing at phantom. Alden decided he'd be the man who minded his own business until the natural law and order was reinstated.

He knelt and began to winnow leaves by hand from Lily's tangled lavender border. Lily tapped on her bedroom window. She was well pleased Alden was being so careful although it required some minutes of tiresome charades, Alden squinting up into the glary glass of Lily's sunnyside window, to establish that this had been a rap of approbation. Harvey helped to interpret, which took his mind off his recent upset as the satisfaction of solving Lily's mimery fell to him.

"She approves. She appreciates. She says carry on, she says," Harvey reported.

"Ah. Good. I'm glad." Alden signaled a simple okay to Lily.

Harvey sat upon the front stone-slab step, his legs elegantly crossed at the ankles, his feet, in effect, deactivated. He had dropped his rake— somewhere. The leaves had swallowed it up. Clever of the leaves not to want to be confiscated or whatever young Alden had in mind for effecting their ultimate dispatch.

"Hi. Alden," Harvey spoke up. "What's to be the plan for today? For all this." He motioned widely.

"The plan is to draw all the leaves out into the driveway in rows and to load them onto the wheelbarrow and cart them further out into the woods and throw them into the swamp," Alden said.

"Oh no," said Harvey. "No, no, no. Cart them? In that wobbly wheel-barrel? No, no. You have to burn the leaves. We've always burned the leaves. They'll give you a permit down at the police place. Ask them. Tell them who you are."

"The permits are only for burning brush. No one's allowed to burn leaves these days," Alden said. "What they really want for us to do is to stuff them into biodegradable bags which they'll accept them at the dump on the first and third Saturdays in November."

"Absurd," uttered Harvey. "That's fine for the tract-house dwellers who only have a weedy poplar and an ornamental cherry growing up inside a white-painted tire to worry about."

"Nevertheless," Alden said. He pulled off a work glove and pried at a fresh blister doming and stinging across his palm. The glove had given him the blister, that unlined, horn-hard, metamorphosing, barn-found discard glove.

"Nonsense," stated Harvey. "Rubbish."

"If I get a permit from the police?" Alden asked.

"Run fetch one just for a smoke screen and we'll take it from there," Harvey recommended. "Because I can only blame the so-called ecologists and their gassing on about carbon dioxides and whatnot, because has it never occurred to anyone else except me that this may just be part of the Great Plan for humankind to have evolved to the point where we can spray fluorocarbonated air fresheners hither and yon to offset the next scheduled Ice Age? I believe it's up to God *and* science now, like a joint NASA–Lockheed project to get us up to Mars someday. We'll just be subcontracting our own small contribution. Not on the Mars thing, I mean on the warming-earth-up end of the equation." Harvey's cheeks had flushed a slapped-looking pink. He leaned and scooped up a loose handful of the planet and let soil and pebbles sift through his fingers proprietarily but not unlovingly.

"Well, I've got this blister coming on," Alden admitted.

"Then go run fetch the say-so," advised Harvey.

ALL SAINTS' WAS STONE-BUILT and English-looking. The set-in cornerstone was chiseled A.D. 1916 but the church seemed to Betsy to be an even more ancient structure. Random corners jutted while taking unmodern, inefficient detours around interior second thoughts like the vestry robing closet and the kindergartners' two-thirds-scale bathroom which, if one had to use it, made one feel as awkward as Alice in an altered state.

All Saints' embraced a courtyard. A serpentine brick walk and a shade garden of fleshy, falling-over perennials were contained within the walls where a statue of Jesus himself was featured. The statue was a modern work cast in dull bronze going streaky in the climate. He was not, in the opinion of some, a very nice Jesus, but he was generally held, as a piece of sculpture, to be a very good one. A wanderer's rough cloak fell from his sharp, starved shoulders and his skin and hair and beard were ridged by deep, gouging pulls of the—acclaimed—artist's thumbs. What the angles and edges, assembled with such art, expressed depended upon the quality of the light and the viewer's susceptibilities. At the moment, Betsy decided, Jesus was withholding his usual tough judgment. A shadow struck off the rise of the cloister roof eclipsed his face and head and, anyway, church and church matters were finished for the week.

Betsy sat upon a carved stone courtyard bench to wait as she waited every Sunday for someone to remember to come for her. The figure of Betsy had become a fixture among the tent-folding details of the post-service stir—the coffee urn being wrestled from the Hall and down the cloister and through a storeroom door; the stanchions and chains and sign marking off NO PARKING DURING WORSHIP dragged from the driveway and stuck behind a juniper bush; the lower limbs of St. Jerome on the stained-glass window wrenched downright by an impatient hand; the altar flowers, wrapped in paper, borne away to be delivered to the hospital sick. Betsy listened for the gush of water to fall from an exterior wall spout directly connected to the drain of the sink in the Altar Guild's cupboard. Water, tipped from the vases of the altar flowers, seeped as it had seeped every Sunday since 1916 into the roots of a house-high rhododendron. Aunt Lily said there was something different about the altar flower water and she would like a bucketful for her roses but, apparently, there was a Rule against such secular usage. Betsy wasn't convinced that any kind of water so faithfully applied on a regular basis would not have worked just as well on the sturdy rhododendron, and as for Aunt Lily's roses, they already bloomed so beautiful it almost passed human understanding.

In truth, Betsy did not pay all that much attention during the service. So much of what was professed seemed so very unlikely, although Mr. Penworthy had been doing his best with an educational series of sermons tracking back what the words had really said in the Aramaic or the ancient Greek before an opinionated Victorian injected a nuance. That morning he spoke of a Cambodian refugee family new to the area and seeking work, any work, but Betsy could not help them. Her eyelids drooped as the Rector offered prayers softly, almost privately reciting them, and as the lay readers rendered the Lessons too swiftly or too slowly but always marble-mouthedly. The congregation muttered the responses. The choir dirged on about heaven and hosts. The air, even the air circulating through Betsy's pushed-open window, wafted an infectious lassitude one breathed into one's lungs with every floating mote of dust.

But occasionally she could be engaged by a seemingly direct address to herself from the Bible as grimoire. Today, as Mr. Penworthy read the Psalter for the 22nd Sunday after Trinity, he had stated, " 'The hills stand about Jerusalem,' " and Betsy had blinked herself awake again. Oh, she could picture that scene—the Hills and née Hills lagging far behind an exasperated Tour Guide in the sun-fried Old Town, yes, all of the Hills standing about Jerusalem in their fashions—Uncle Alden mildly contemplating a sad ruin, Aunt Becky frowning back and forth between her Baedeker page and the discrepancies between those things described and those things not seen. Her cousins scattered stones at feral cats and then slouched off to buy T-shirts imprinted with rude hieroglyphics at a junky tourist shop. She guessed Arthur and Phoebe had elected to stay behind by the hotel's swimming pool where Uncle Harvey remained as well, updating the names in his address book. But her mother, her mother at large in Jerusalem, confronted the Muslim ladies tilting like laundry baskets under their chadors, demanding of them, "Aren't you hot?" and complaining at them how it made her hot just to gaze upon them in all their swathedness, until Aunt Lily led Ginger off to help tap flyaway seeds from the wildflowers spearing up through the cracked eternal pavement into labeled glassine envelopes. For Aunt Lily had once mentioned that the Crusaders had propagated the ancient species of the Holy Land throughout Europe, returning home with husks and grains suspended in the mud clodded to the hems of their garments. If she had been a Crusader, Aunt Lily would have enacted a more systematic and deliberate dissemination and here now would be her great chance.

Just why she had been vouchsafed such a vision, Betsy could not say. Perhaps she had been shown what clearsightedness she possessed about her family and their situation. She was quite sure she had their numbers and, by having their numbers, would know how to deal with them in the months to come. (Betsy no longer pretended there would not be months to come here.) Then again, another thought struck her hard. She may

just have been sent an object lesson on the folly and the danger of falling
into hubris, for she had not described herself to herself as she too stood
about the city, as she trekked down into every damp, disputed tomb,
pausing to pray before every tatty icon with un-Protestant emotionality,
these willed acts of devotion all performed, of course, to reproach and
to burden and to madden her mother who only longed to retreat to the
hotel and the air-conditioning and the drink that awaited her at the bar.

"Betsy! Dear! All on your lonesome ownsome?" Mrs. Nicholls
popped herself down on the bench beside Betsy as she searched in her
woven Kenyan bag for her car keys. "Listen, I'm so glad I caught you,
honey, I wanted to ask you—" Mrs. Nicholls paused as she saw she
would have to empty her bag. She always had to empty her bag to get to
her keys which sunk like wacke to the cluttered depths. She really
should keep her keys clipped and jangling remindingly to a belt, but she
never wore belts—one might as well cinch a belt around a sack of flour.
Therefore, she endured this nonsense. She extracted and lay upon the
bench between them the whistle swinging from a plaited gimp cord
which she roped round her neck the one night a week she volunteered at
the Inter-Faith Elder Abuse Hotline located in a rehabbed mill building
over in Lawrence. For afterward, brooding on the tales she'd been told,
she had to walk alone across a wasteland an hour past midnight to get
to her car. On those nights, of course, she had her keys well in hand,
her longest and spikiest key to the front door of her Senior Village
condo held pointed outward between her middle and index fingers,
poised to strike at the throat or the temple or the eyes of a rapist. Then,
as he lay sprawled and writhing on the wasteground she would summon
aid with her whistle, blowing in pips short and long the internationally
recognized signal of distress. If only all elders were as well defended
as she.

A Nile-green leotard was tossed onto the bench, an individual-
serving-size packet of salted oyster crackers, her large, stuffed wallet, a
coupon file, unfiled coupons, curtain fabric swatches, a Kleenex blotted
with very orange makeup matching the shade on the stained chiffon
scarf discovered in Uncle Harvey's raincoat pocket, which gave the not
very interesting answer to a not very interesting mystery.

". . . to ask you, please," resumed Mrs. Nicholls, whose mind was as fully occupied but much better ordered than her satchel, "to remind your Uncle Harvey I expect him with bells on for supper Tuesday night at 5:30 in my unit before we go to the Senior Fun-Tasia Bazaar."

"Yes, I'll tell him," Betsy said as she wondered whether she was obliged to mention the part about Uncle Harvey having his bells on. She supposed she would have to repeat the message verbatim but she would recite it expressionlessly. She had come, in her last months at home, not to like having to convey coded information in all innocence, which may or may not—oh, probably not—be the case here. She wished Mrs. Nicholls wouldn't peer at her so alertly.

"How's Mother?" Mrs. Nicholls asked brightly.

"Well . . ." Betsy began.

"Oh, good," said Mrs. Nicholls. "Here they are," she announced. She was referring to her keys at last retrieved and tossed into the air and captured; however, the approaching Palmers, whom Babe had routed round the serpentine courtyard path in order to keep the adamantine Jesus between themselves and Betsy, mistook Mrs. Nicholls's exclamation for a summons.

Goody, smiling on his own and on Babe's behalf, stepped over a bed of flattened hostas and said hello. He had not particularly wished to cut the young girl, or that decent soul Penny Nicholls, who was Babe's mother's cousin, although Babe must have her reasons for whatever avoidance measures she undertook and doubtless in all good time he would be told them. Babe trailed after Goody carrying the folded altar cloths which she had been washing and ironing at home ever since the big argument at Briter-Ways Cleansers in 1977.

"Have you been waiting all this time? Do you need a ride home?" Goody asked Betsy. He had noticed that a tendril of groundcover ivy clung, now, curled round her thin ankle.

"We came on foot this morning," Babe reminded him.

"I'll get the car and come back."

"Oh, no, really," said Betsy.

"No," said Babe.

"My mother is coming and if I'm not here she'll . . ."

"Worry about you dreadfully," Mrs. Nicholls clucked approvingly at Ginger's natural concern, whatever else people had to say about Ginger.

Rampage, Betsy had been about to say but she had long since trained herself not to blurt.

"Yes, she'll wonder," confirmed Betsy.

"If you're sure," Goody said.

"She's sure. Don't upset best-laid plans. You don't want Ginger coming after you, do you? Do you?" Babe required an answer.

"No," supposed Goody.

"I must fly myself," said Mrs. Nicholls. "It's Cambodian can-drive day down at the Village and I'm chairperson."

"Cans? Cans of what? What kinds of cans of what?" Babe asked Penny as they moved on. "Because what do those people eat? Because I heard they can't eat wheat, they can't digest . . ."

By then, Betsy knew her mother would not be coming. Distracted by the curbside meeting with those Palmer people, Betsy had not at the last impressed upon Ginger that she would need a ride home from church as well. A promise to reappear had not been exacted. Betsy, Ginger would argue, had simply assumed. Betsy had taken for granted. Ginger was not a chauffeur. She was not a doormat. Betsy was being taught a lesson.

She glanced apologetically at the stern Jesus. She imagined he'd like to have the garden to himself again. Perhaps he would even sit down on the edge of his plinth and read some small devotional volume he kept tucked up his sleeve. It occurred to her that the All Saints' Jesus was going to look very cold in the snow.

Betsy felt conspicuous in her dress and gloves and heels and hat once she left the leafy brick sidewalks of the village. The high-flung, winter-turning sun cast off heat, and surviving, or mistimedly hatched, midges swarmed in atomized clouds and settled, sipping, in the corners of her eyes. Every widely spaced yard contained a dog and every dog charged at her yapping and circling, tail wagging or slashing. They yelped as they blundered into the force fields of invisible fencing and withdrew until next time as someone sent from the house to see what now, looked and saw Betsy. A match of pure white geese dashed on stiff mechanical legs from a graveled driveway and followed her, very stupidly, up the road. Betsy spun and waved her white gloved hands like a policewoman and ordered them, "Home." They fell back, knocking against one another, impressed, and continued to pace after her when her back was turned. One of them honked, irresistibly. Betsy spun and waved and ordered, "Home." They glinted at her, wholly enchanted. They were highly unintelligent creatures but somebody must have thought they loved them for they wore green gingham bows tied around their long white S-pipe throats. Foolish. Half a dozen times more resisting Betsy's spin, her wave, her order, "Home," they pursued her as far as the River Road and the bent arm of the river. There, they tumbled over a vertical embankment and launched themselves into the water, unsteadily paddling out into the smoother cord of faster current, where they capsized.

HARVEY HAD RAISED the junior troops while Alden was away, with the promise of fireworks to come. Lily and Becky had more responsibly presented themselves, rakes in hand, and as Alden pulled up to the top of the driveway bowl, he found his wife and children and uncle and aunt outside in bright wool sweaters, each engaged in a kind of formal dance of approach and retreat, guiding and gliding their stick-thin, flare-skirted partners by the shoulder and waist. Alden would not have put it past Harvey to have assigned plats. The boys seemed to have been spaced and sited out of mutual antagonism and roughhousing range. Little Becky, combing the lower lawn, could not quite see whose pile of leaves was growing higher than hers, whose grass plot was clearer than her own. Arthur and Phoebe had taken on the meadow where they were twisting and lifting sheaves of brown vegetable tangles, flinging them into a heap.

"Got the permit?" Harvey yollered from the terrace.

Alden held up a slip of paper and Harvey trotted off to the barn.

"What's all this?" Alden asked Becky and Lily, who were working from opposite ends of the front garden intending to meet in the middle, although Becky, by extra exertion, planned to clear more than her fair share of the leaves and so spare Lily at least a little effort without alerting Lily that this courtesy was being accomplished.

"The boys are looking forward to the fires. Anything destructive," Becky explained. "But I'm not so sure."

"We'll keep an eye on," Alden promised.

Harvey emerged from the barn carrying two mislabeled cans of old lawn mower gasoline and he had last Tuesday's *Globe* wedged and flapping between his upper chest and arm. He visited each boy and Little Becky. He motioned them away, so magisterially gesturing they obeyed him with only token truculence. He dispensed liquid from a can. He rolled a peeled-off sheet of newsprint into a taper, ignited an end with a kitchen match, and held his torch aloft to catch in the breeze. Then he plunged each disintegrating wand into the leaves. Flames reared skyward in a pillar, subsided, and the leaf piles blustered smoke. Harvey sprinkled on more gasoline, watchful as a chef flambéing tableside.

"Oh my," said Becky every time.

Lily's rake had dislodged a rich strand of earthworm. She knelt and replanted him and sent him on his way with a firm but encouraging nudge. Rising on Alden's offered arm, she remembered that they had always kept a sputtering relay of all the garden hoses, connected and spraying prismy mists at the joints, ready to douse any rogue licks of fire that might escape underground and run for the woods, igniting tiny pines like sparklers and scorching the moss carpets and attacking the oaks at their risen roots. In the event, one must be alert to a change in the smell of the smoke, Lily advised.

"You mean less cannabis-y?" asked Alden, sniffing a sweetish undertone in the developing haze. No wonder the kids were so keen to cooperate.

Presently, Ginger emerged from the house. She had mused over her magazines and eaten three raised doughnuts and lolled about in a hot, deep, scented bath and then dressed for what remained of the day in her navy-blue palazzo pants and a creamy silk sailor blouse and the Egyptian beads that clicked like knucklebones as she walked. She dragged a soft lambswool shawl to shrug on and off, she ran so cold and hot. She carried a notebook into which she meant to enter her Sunday thoughts. Several pencils secured her hair.

She stepped outside. Well, she was glad they were seeing to the yard. She'd been wondering when they'd realize it was rather too casual to have so many leaves left lying about, the sight of which, massing and matting outside every window, only oppressed certain already lowered sensibilities. She spoke aloud to the sky above, " 'What time that yellow leaf was green, My days were gladder.' " She may have been putting the universe on notice.

She wandered round to the cleared terrace where one could once again locate one's particular favored chaise released from its rustling shroud of tattery tree litter. She settled back among musty and not entirely dry cushions and she fanned away smoke with her notebook. A little red-hearted volcano puffed at terrace edge which she wished had not been placed quite there. Why oh why was nothing ever right? She sighed and tented her shawl above her head.

"Betsy," Becky's voice accused her. "Shouldn't Betsy have been picked up from church?"

Ginger's sherry-colored eyes snapped open and she stirred, just displacing her back from its points of perfect alignment against the cushion bumps.

"And now no one can get down the driveway to go for her because there's a line of fire blazing away across it," Becky said. The wall of fire had been Harvey's big brainstorm to repel any Nosy Parkering inspectors sent from town.

"Then I guess I can't get down the driveway to fetch her because of the fire, I guess," Ginger replied.

Becky sat on a tipsy aluminum tubing and mesh webbing chair, tiresomely prepared to discuss the matter with earnest and futile concern. "But what will Betsy do then?" Becky wanted to know.

"The sensible thing," Ginger predicted, because the obvious course for Betsy was to ask that nice Mr. Palmer, now met as an approved friend of the family, for a ride home. And Goody would just have to battle a way through the flames to arrive at her side. His ordeal—his tires melted into taffy twists, the gas cap catapulted into eternity—would become one of those memories to laugh at later when they were in a laughing mood and at quieter times they would more solemnly marvel at all they had passed through, together and apart.

BETSY STOOD ABOVE the riverbank watching the geese as they spun and flustered out of view around the bend. The current was carrying them back to the riverfront gentleman's farm where she had first met them and she guessed she had provided their midday's amusement, or perhaps she had just hindered them in their pursuit of their daily stroll.

She decided to carry her hat. She placed her prayerbook inside the hat. Her shoes pinched and the left heel wobbled. She thought it might be nice to wade in the shallows, but the embankment was steep along this stretch of the river and it was pocked with burrow holes smooth-sided from use. The local otters seemed charming creatures when at frolic but she wasn't sure you could trust them not to turn nasty if you got in their way.

She heard the car before she saw it. She had time to move from the crown of the road onto which she had strayed—rather a satisfying feeling to take an entire road for herself. She paused on the sandy verge and followed the progress of a VW Beetle as it rounded the curve. She nearly waved, for Towne was a wave-y place. *Well, I saw you only you didn't wave,* people went out of their way to mention. But Betsy stayed her hand because she saw that the driver was male and young and good-looking, at least as far as she could tell from where she stood. To wave at the likes of him would be something her mother would do. Betsy walked on. The car passed her, slowed as if musing over something, stopped, and backed up alongside her.

"Can you help me? I'm looking for an address along River Road," the young man leaned across the passenger seat and asked through the cranked-down window. "If this is River Road? I have every hope it might be, being next to the river, but I haven't seen a sign."

Betsy nodded. "There is a sign that's overgrown, and anyway, some-body's taped a YARD SALE TODAY sign atop it, only I believe the yard sale was yesterday. My mother and my aunt went to it."

"So that explains. And now I'm looking for some people called Lowe although they live with someone called Hill. I've no number to go by and I haven't seen either name on a mailbox. There's been no one else to ask except some horseback riders but they just stared through me as if they were centaurs and I was an Aeolian peasant. You don't know them, those people, the Lowe-Hills, do you?" he asked.

"Yes, actually, I live there too, I'm on my way . . ."

"Do you? I'm in luck. So, are you the one called Little Becky? There are two Beckys and one is called Little Becky, I gather."

"No, no, no, I'm not," Betsy set him straight. "I'm Betsy Tuckerman?"

"Betsy," he confirmed. (How did a Betsy fit into the household?) "And you must have guessed I'm Andy Happening," he said after a beat, after she failed to name him. "I expect you've all been expecting me?" he prompted.

"No, I don't think so. But I don't know. I am seldom confided in," Betsy allowed.

"Why don't I drive you and you can show me the way," Andy Happening said. "I'll have to make room, first," he said, as he opened the passenger door and shifted a carton, a tweed jacket, a tumble of heavy, unjacketed books from the front seat to the carton- and garment- and book-filled backseat. Betsy knew at once she didn't like the looks of his obviously earthly possessions all in transit. She did not wish to understand what had occasioned the cataclysm that had thrown up crammed cartons like boulders to weigh down his put-puttering car. Still, she had never ridden in one of those old VW Beetles. She sat in the cleared front seat. The pavement, as they drove off, flew up at her suddenly beyond the snub snout of the hood. She let the sensation dazzle her.

"Turn here," she spoke up. She herself had nearly overlooked the narrow gap between the trees. They started up the rutted track which looped back on itself as it climbed.

"I would never have found this," Andy said.

Betsy smelled the smoke before it enveloped the car. She pressed gloved fingertips to her nose as Andy hit the yellow and acrid cloud and braked abruptly. He swerved into bushes. He reversed. His rear chassis rose up and over a stump. He crept forward and halted before a wall of fire. He reversed. He stalled out in a deep puddle.

"This is unusual," Betsy informed Andy as she slipped off her pumps.

"BUT NO ONE told me not to come. My Uncle William assured me he would arrange everything. That he had arranged everything," Andy said.

He and Betsy had walked the rest of the way through the fumy woods. Betsy had blindly borne off in a direction. She skimmed over the hulks of logs and rushed at impossible coverts and rematerialized on the other sides of thick spruces or so it seemed to Andy, who kept her, just, in sight. She was acting a bit will-o'-the-wisp for his tastes; then again, if the rest of them proved as oddball as she, he was going to find himself standing knee-deep in research clover once he cleared this aftermath of a Mohawk massacre brew of ash and burn and as soon as he presented his credentials here. He had brought a great globed jar of marron glacés for Mrs. Lowe which remained in his stranded Bug and he dared not turn back for them. His coughed-out calls to please slow down, to please stop, failed to reach Betsy.

They broke free of the woods and crossed a sloping lawn, skirting smoldering barrows of leaves, and approached a very large, very old, very white, and very wooden house. They swerved past a front door he was not invited to enter and they tramped down a pathway and came, at last, upon the Hills as they stood about a side terrace. They were consuming black and blistered hotdogs slipped between folded-over slices of mustard-spread oatmeal bread and drinking paper cups of pale ginger ale, empty bottles of which were impaled on the branches of a spirea as if being made examples of for being empty. The people were soot-streaked and scarlet-faced beneath the soot, one, two, three, eleven of them arranged across chaises, sitting on overturned stone planters, propped against a low retaining wall, all regarding Andy with their remarkably alike eyes, alike, at any rate, in their wary and wondering expressions. Now that he, whoever he was, had returned Betsy, he should go away. Why was he not going away? Did he require a hotdog? They were surprisingly good hotdogs, stuck on sticks and charred over the fires. Harvey had buried a dozen foil-wrapped baking potatoes in the coals although he could not locate them at present. Alden said Harvey's potatoes must have burst but Harvey said potatoes had never used to burst.

"How did you get up the driveway?" Alden asked Betsy.

"We didn't."

"I expected to be expected," Andy was saying.

"Oh, dear, yes, but William's letter about you didn't even arrive until this very week. That Revolution, you know, Andy, one of the ones in the news, must have interfered with the mail. Of course we're all delighted for those poor people over there, or we shall be once things have calmed down," Mrs. Lowe, the primary Becky, tried to tell him. An excellent interviewee, Andy anticipated. She was an overexplainer. "But, I must confess, we assumed you had made other plans, because, because, isn't it late in the semester to begin?" This was diffidently asked. Becky was not a scholar herself.

"My Dean is very enthusiastic about this project," Andy announced. The Dean would protest had he heard himself so described, for Andy had felt himself tumbled here and landed in a heap on the downdraft of the Dean's deep sighs for the decline of his Department.

"And one never likes to disappoint a Dean," a chaise-longuing woman cried gaily. So she was on his side, Andy guessed, but that would not necessarily advance his cause with the rest of them. Those alike eyes flickered over her, narrowly dismissive. An elderly woman detached herself from the rest and moved to the edge of the terrace to confer with an as elderly gentleman who was prodding purposefully among a pile of cinders with the wrong end of a rake. The old lady removed the rake from his grasp, and she held the darkened end over the misting spray of a sputtering hose connection.

"Do you mean *he's* still in school?" asked Brooks. He and Rollins sincerely sought information. Based upon this fresh datum, they might have to amend their academic exit strategy.

"Yes, yes, you can languish in school for . . ." Alden began.

"And how is William?" Becky asked. "You saw him, I gather, last summer?"

"Donkey's years," concluded Alden.

"I've met your Uncle William," Ginger spoke up from her chaise. "Tell me, does he still have that marvelous higher-life-form wrinkle-crinkled brow?"

The Hills pictured versions, real and imagined, of Andy's uncle and Andy seemed to rise in their estimations for his linkage to such a personage.

"Kindly crinkling," Ginger entirely invented. Betsy hovered behind her mother's chaise as if she meant to intercept any further remarks by sweeping them into her church hat and smothering them with the prayerbook.

"Yes," Andy answered Becky. "I saw William last August, but he was on such a fleeting visit he said he wasn't really home at all." Which had made the occasion seem all the more unreal in retrospect. Andy and William had had lunch at a Chichi's, Andy's not at all successful choice, although he had only been following William's orders. Andy was to pick him up at his hotel and drive him to the airport, stopping for lunch en route at a convenient restaurant that served speedy but not fast food and which was not a fish place because the oceans were sewers, William knew, he had been to an international conference. Nevertheless, Andy had noticed that William's plummy accent had relocated itself somewhere in the vicinity of the mid-Atlantic. Syou-ahs, he had denounced seventy percent of the earth's surface.

But it had long been Andy's wish to cultivate this always absent uncle, for William was known to possess contacts and to wield a degree of influence. Indeed, he possessed a sizable stock of influence, he had been so seldom persuaded to part with any. The extended Baskett-Happening clan charged that William had not been inconvenienced enough by family concerns, choosing, as he had, to remain wifeless and childless and abroad for so much of his life. They surged around him in airport arrivals lounges, unfurling documentary evidence of tax audits and divorce decrees and car-leasing contracts. Then, falsely consulting his pockets, which his tailor forbade him ever to fill, William would regretfully reveal he had left his reading glasses behind in some Old World corner. Wear mine, his grown-crafty family offered, passing over their own spectacles. But William claimed his presbyopia was of a special order, not easily compensated for.

Still, William had called Andy one day last summer and proposed they meet to talk about that future of Andy's from which William had theretofore been content to hold himself aloof. Andy, upon receiving his summons, had felt himself chosen, not unlike one of the ancient kings of Calicut who had their throats cut after enjoying a brief, prescribed term of reign, although here Andy, as a student of the human condition, posited too darkly what William may or may not have had in mind.

"Sociology," William had spoken across the restaurant table at Andy, denying the discipline one of its syllables—sosology. He ordered chimichangas with a shrug, hurting the feelings of the very young waitress who was new that day and keen.

"I've heard you're floundering," William observed, dredging a bowl of greenish and flecked dip with a bright blue corn chip. He sniffed warily and held the corn chip at knee level as if he hoped a voracious mongrel or hungry urchin would swoop and snatch the regretted savory. But he was not in Mexico for all the serapes and sombreros flung casually about the banquettes as if by local patrons.

"I argued—your mother was my informant, by the way—I argued on your behalf that I could not believe you were in over your head with Sociology, those undeeps," William said, and then paused to regard with disbelief the neighboring table where a birthday was being celebrated.

"*Gag* gifts," uttered William, and Andy had explained that the giant pair of sunglasses just torn from its wrappings was in fact a useful and serious item. Parked-car windshields wore them to keep the hot sun off front seats which were a torment to sit upon particularly if one was wearing shorts.

"Good God, America, America," William said, sipping at a cloudy margarita poured into a too-wide glass in which he wet the tip of his nose. He signaled to the forlorn waitress to bring two more drinks and he pointed to his watch and pantomime-scribbled, Check, please, and he indicated his spoon was not clean by scrabbling at dried Mexican gravy with his thumbnail and he revealed his plan to redeem Andy's fortunes. He had the solution to Andy's thesis dilemma. Yes, even he had been apprised of Andy's problem a quarter turn of the world away. The family cries had penetrated the sound- and surveillance- and bomb-proofed chamber locked with a secret key and guarded by upright Marines where William spent his days working at what he was not at liberty to say.

"I know just the people for you to study and write about and so produce whatever it is you're supposed to produce. At any rate, you will live among them and probe and observe and theorize and at last, to everyone's great relief, finish your formal education once and for all, after all, you are almost thirty . . ."

"I'm twenty-six," clarified Andy.

". . . you're already in your late twenties (all this hairsplitting, you won't split hairs when they're grey). As I was about to say, these people are in crisis to boot, so everything will rise to the surface. They'll be recalling and reviewing and regretting every corner and turn of their lives. You will live among them, move among them, find out what you can find out about them.

"Sensible fellow," William added almost fondly, for Andy must have agreed to his proposition. He had accepted and pocketed the square of envelope William slid across the table surface, containing particulars and an address. "Wise of you not to want to thrash around some jungle eating hallucinogenic grubs and being ritually tattooed on your whatsis to gain your subjects' confidence."

"You're confusing me with an . . ."

"Mind you," William warned, "these people will expect you to play contract bridge and listen to Mantovani recordings and subscribe to certain revisionist accounts of the Nixon years and to be in bed by ten with the windows flung open after you've performed two hundred standing jumping jacks. I am describing him, the husband, of course. And a word to the wise about the children who are, I'm sorry to say, modern children."

William had promised to see to the arrangements. Andy was told to stand by for further instructions and he returned to his off-campus apartment furnished with a double futon, stacks of books, and his girl-friend's pottery dishes. Renata had said William's scheme sounded more than a little peculiar to her. Andy disagreed, but disagreements rose automatically between them by then. "What do you suppose modern children are?" he had asked her, and Renata expressed, instead, an opinion of modern men.

"It's September," she had said significantly as the new month began. "October," she announced more ominously, and Andy came home one day after assuring his Dean, once again, of all that he intended, to dis-cover Renata had uncoupled the individually owned components of their conjoined stereo systems. A modern woman, she possessed and could employ a set of utility tools. Laura Nyro, not heard from lately at Andy's request, was singing less richly from diminished-capacity speak-ers, but the weakened cries of a woman's wroth nevertheless more truly communicated just how one felt, Renata told Andy. They effected an awkward parting. They had never, expressedly, been in love and with the cessation of this uncharacterized affair they were left with mere disaffection to demonstrate. To linger would be—it had been—undignified. Andy drove away as if he knew where he was headed and then, suddenly, he had known.

"WILLIAM IS the same as ever," Andy told Becky.

"Oh, I'm glad to hear," Becky said as Andy glanced at her and saw she was sincere.

The wind switched and a charge of smoke scattered them all from the terrace. They bore their hotdogs and paper cups and rakes onto the lawn where the muttering and seething mounds of ash had a geothermal look about them, as if they provided a link between this and the infernal world, Andy thought, but the others no more shared this apprehension with him than they had shared their lunch. His pants leg was soaked by a hissing hose as he slowly registered the sensation, disliked it, and hopped clear of the mist. The several boys laughed. A large girl (Little Becky?) stared at him and walked backward and blundered into the wandy branches of a mock orange. Ginger, a step behind the others— having had to enact a more encumbered retreat, her shawl having snagged on the arm of her chaise—clutched a crammed notebook to her breast. She shed file cards which the breezes snatched and wheeled inevitably into the muttering mounds. She tottered after several aflight and erratic cards, stepping out of her step-in mules.

"Rescue them, rescue them, rescue them," she shrieked.

"Rescue what? What?" asked Harvey, annoyed. "What am I supposed to rescue now? If I'm going to gad about rescuing something, first I have to know what it is." He sat upon the granite outcropping toward which he'd been heading. "Alden, attend to your sister," he ordered.

"Not I," answered Alden.

Betsy slipped on a glove and lifted aflame cards by their nonburning ends and placed them on the grass where she stepped them out, and then, kneeling down, gently brushed away scorch marks and tried to read the writing that remained. A less thoughtful daughter might have burned her fingers lightly just to show Ginger. Betsy, however, had considered and been unable to determine, show Ginger *what*, precisely?

"Careful, careful, careful," Ginger exhorted her. "Careful."

"You've caught us at a moment," Becky told Andy.

"Well," said Andy.

Wasn't anyone going to assist Ginger, Betsy? Ginger berated, Betsy forbore. And 3 × 5 cards were incinerated.

"They can hear you in Chelsea," Lily approached Ginger and informed her.

Andy decided it would not violate his mandate not to interfere if he collected a card lodged in the yoke of a tree trunk. He swiped off sticky pitch against his wet pants leg and swiftly read, A CONFESSION: WHEN MY DAUGHTER WAS FOUR YEARS OLD I SCOOPED UP ANY OLD ALPHA-BET SOUP LETTERS WITH A SPOON AND TOLD HER THEY SPELLED B-E-T-S-Y. He passed the card to Ginger who thanked him extravagantly.

"Glover, go see to that," Alden directed his eldest son to deal with a line of flames making a run for the woods. Glover loped off and beat the fire to death with a flat-headed shovel.

"So," said Andy, detaching his arm from Ginger's confiding arm.

Harvey motioned to Andy to come sit beside him on the ledge and he explained that the ledge formed a long, rising throne upon which to sit and gaze off into the meadow and think one's meadow-inspired thoughts. He liked to think about being a bee, for example.

"Yes," said Andy.

"But isn't it late in the semester to start a project?" Alden asked the question again. The family had reclustered around Andy. These people gathered like pouty pigeons, jostling to the front of the flock as the flock kept switching direction.

"I had preliminary research to complete," Andy said.

"On us? Are we on file somewhere?" worried Becky. "The boys aren't, are they?" Because certain documents were supposed to have been sealed.

"How fascinating. I must read your notes sometime, because as you can see, I'm something of a researcher-writer myself," Ginger said.

"It was just, you know, general background, procedural, demo-graphical, methodological information I was compiling," Andy said.

"Yes, we have a lot of, you know, background," Harvey said.

"And just what do you mean to accomplish, Mr. Happening?" Lily asked sensibly. She brushed aside a clutter of acorn shells a squirrel had cracked open and she sat on the stone outcropping to await his reply. The cluster of family nodded and fell quiet because they hoped they were about to be enlightened about themselves.

And Andy explained that while he had not discovered the Middle Class, he would, like Columbus, return with word of the great, theretofore unexploited mass he had encountered. He would, with their cooperation, reconstruct their history and their ethos from the unextraordinary siftings of their unexceptional lives, from their letters, from their living memories, from their photo albums, check stubs, Bible entries, school records . . .

"Hey," objected Brooks, or Rollins.

Andy meant to trace the straight and steady lines across the charts of the lives of utterly ordinary people who came home from World Wars without a scratch on them to marry the daughters of bankers and enjoy long, fruitful unions and peaceful deaths at an advanced old age.

"That wasn't one of us," Harvey said. "Sounds like a Bartlett. Think you may want to see the Bartletts. Tell you how to find their place."

"The exalted have been done and the unfortunates as well, those peaks and valleys. I believe I want to explore the Hills," Andy said. The Hills acknowledged his graceful remark. "It is very seldom that anyone has ventured from the Groves of Academe into the surrounding suburbs," Andy resumed. "I shall provide a map. This could well prove to be as important as Margaret Mead's field work in Samoa."

Lily had never cared for Dr. Mead. In her opinion, a lady, even a lady enarmored in scholarship, ought at times to have averted her eyes.

"Or Oscar Lewis and *The Children of Sánchez*," Andy added.

"Oh dear, those poor people," Becky said.

"Upper-middle class, surely we're upper-middle class," protested Ginger.

"It's very middle class to want to be upper-middle class," Alden told her.

"I don't know, it all makes sense to me, having a resident sociologist around here," Arthur said.

"Rather have a cook," Harvey said, "and a groundskeeper and one of those all-around handyman old-time jiggery tinkerers."

"Well, I think it's perfectly marvelous of Andy to take such an interest," Ginger exclaimed.

Becky spoke softly to Alden. "I wrote to William as soon as I could, but what can we do, here he is landed right in our laps? He doesn't look very robust. Where else can he go? How can he go, through the fire? How did he even get here?"

"I don't know, but is any of that our responsibility?" asked Alden.

"Yes, I rather think it is now," Becky said.

"So," said Andy. They were an obstinate bunch. They leaned on their rakes and threw their paper cups onto pyres and watched the wax coatings melt into strange configurations more interesting to consider than Andy's proposal. Nevertheless, Andy had hardened himself to pose pressing questions and they had made him walk through fire to get here. "So," said Andy, "my boxes and bags are in the Bug, if I can just organize my rooms?"

"Room," Lily corrected him quickly, and thus she committed herself to letting him have one.

"I say," Alden remarked. The cunning of the construction—he stepped between the confident young man and his aged, outflanked aunt. "Hi, Glover," Alden said then. "Run fetch this fellow's car for him since he funked driving through the fire. You do it for him."

Eventually, after more quadraphonic chatter by the clustering family, restating all that had just been expressed and confirming what had just been decided, and after Andy had been informed, as well, about Harvey's plans to paint the shutters that very green shade of green, and of Alden's idea of growing an agricultural crop of some sort in the meadow, and of Ginger's slowly going but very exciting work in progress, and after Becky apologized because William's letter had been so long and so late in coming, and Arthur told a newly minted joke about the California earthquake which was pretty funny even though sixty people had just been killed so suddenly and so violently on a warm autumn evening, eventually, then, Andy was conducted inside. Brooks and Rollins toted his effects inside like sulky native porters. An unsmiling Lily led Andy up the floating staircase and he followed her down a long hallway stepping from fraying rug to fraying rug. Standing aside, her arm barred against an opened door, Lily bade him enter a dim and airless chamber covered with green-on-green-striped wallpaper and containing too many large pieces of dark, carved furniture. Andy sidled to the window and peremptorily yanked apart the curtains. Cool October sunlight washed through the room which now looked less sinister but very much sadder. Andy asked, without thinking, "Did someone die in here, or what?"

Downstairs in the kitchen, Alden was prudently and persistently calling Andy's university, and the Dean, disturbed at home on a Sunday, pronounced Andy bona fide. Becky collected her letter to William from the stack of letters on the piecrust table (two trips to the village today and no one had thought to mail them) and she sat down to write again to William to inform him of his nephew's safe and welcome arrival.

Andy crouched before his boxes which the complaint-speaking boys had tumbled onto the floor just inside the door. Lily lingered just inside the door as well—such edginess here—and Andy was very conscious of the hem of her blue cotton culotte skirt hanging too near to his face. He breathed shallowly, not wishing to breathe upon her which would be construed as rude, he was certain. He forgot what he had been seeking among his belongings, rummaging for reassurance among his books and folded sweaters. He stood and began to clear dusty and contaminated-looking prescription bottles from the desktop where he wished to plunk down and plug in his Apple as soon as possible so that he might sit resolutely before its familiar screen. He glanced at the bottles as he ousted the insomniac, heartsick, deeply in pain invalid who had preceded him here. He filled an emptied shoe box.

Meanwhile, hovering with hops of agitation, Harvey had pounced upon Alden and detained him in the attic stairwell which was adjacent to Andy's room.

"That Andy fellow doesn't look like to you he could be up to very much, do you think?" Harvey's unmodulated old man's voice bore through the wall. "Not robbin' us? Not killin' us?"

Alden's voice murmured back with better information.

"What? You called that school of his? What school? Not a *top* school."

Lily slipped from the doorway and Andy listened frankly through the plaster to a lively session of whispers and hushes and the rumble of ascending footsteps. He became aware of a cat sniffing among his boxes. It sneezed fastidiously and minced off with its tail raised. Andy shrugged and searched along the baseboard, head thrust under the bed, the desk, the bureau, for an electrical outlet. He found none and he became certain that if there was an outlet, it was hidden behind a massive wardrobe. Reluctantly, he put his shoulder to a sharp corner and shoved as effectlessly as if he were trying to push a mountain up another mountain.

Lily reappeared in the doorway, pinker-skinned and with brighter eyes after settling Harvey. She supposed Andy had heard himself being speculated upon, and she felt obliged to say something pleasant to him even though the young man seemed to have dedicated himself to dismantling the room he had tricked her into giving him. She scooped up the shoe box, a-rattle with medicine vials, incidentally wondering if any of it might do her any good. She cleared her throat, almost wishing that what ailed her these days could be done away with by taking a simple pill, although these pills must be ten years old now and probably pure poison. Harvey had picked up a cautionary brochure on the dangers of aged prescription medicine at the Senior Village Health Fair.

Andy responded to Lily with an uncertain but politely prompting throat clearing of his own, which reminded Lily that the intrusive young man was still there and she had yet to be nice to him.

"Yes," she told Andy, "somebody did die in here but I have, of course, since changed the sheets."

Chapter Three · The Hills and History

T HAT MORNING HAD NOT gotten off to a very good start. Becky stood in a corner of the kitchen trying to iron her challis skirt and a wool-blend lace-collared blouse recovered from a box wedged beneath their bed. Choral practice began at nine o'clock down at the Congregational Church basement and she thought she'd contrive to look smart for a change if only to hearten herself when she glimpsed her passing reflection captured in chrome plating or advancing, hand outstretched to greet herself from every polished glass door surface. For Becky had awakened reluctantly, more tired than when she'd dropped into bed and read a page of her library book and switched off the light, brushing her bedside box of Kleenex, her reading glasses, and her tube of Replenishment Formula Eye Creme, which slid down and wedged between her night table and the wall, the fact of their not quite having fallen making it seem not worth the effort to lean on her elbow and reach over to retrieve them. Nevertheless, her sleep had not been unaffected. She believed she may have dreamed of an avalanche, which had not been restful, muffled voices implored her to "do something" and as she shivered helplessly, feeling a great weight pressing down on her from above.

Now she was sipping determinedly from a tumbler of honey and lemon juice, attempting to fend off the head cold that had been making the rounds. The children had suffered from, or perhaps enjoyed, their recent bouts lying aswoon in their rooms, missing a day or two of school and inhaling lime sherbet floats, all they claimed they were able to swallow, through flexible straws. And Ginger had taken to her bed for the better part of a week reading the decidedly unimproving *Dancing in the Light* and dragooning passers-by into running downstairs for her to fetch fresh orange juice and ice cubes. Ginger's remedy of choice was to chip away at her head cold with strong screwdrivers.

Becky pressed the green paisley pleats of her skirt and she swigged a shot of honey and lemon. A deep cough welled and she sputtered honey and lemon droplets over the ironing board. Her racing iron seared honey and lemon into the challis which didn't seem to show on the busy pattern and which, indeed, smelled rather pleasant even to her becoming-congested nose, not unlike the first breath of a heated Greek isle as one stepped off the steamer although a sharper note of thyme or tarragon was lacking. She studied the spice rack nailed to the end of an upper cupboard as it occurred to her to wonder whether there mightn't be a niche in the fashion world for prescented clothing. One wouldn't search the shops for a red dress, but instead close one's eyes and sniff for just the right warm tone of cinnamon or cayenne. Someday she really ought to write down her ideas, Becky decided, when no one was around to explain to her very patiently why a mere notion was the very least of any successful new business undertaking.

"Have you seen the car keys?" Alden came into the kitchen to ask her although she knew no more than he where the keys could be were they not where they should be. She was moved to make suggestions, however, as he hopelessly searched in the clean apron drawer, in the short-bread tin, beneath the frying pan lid, down along the dusty mopboards. He scraped open the clean apron drawer again and turned out apron pockets and sighed.

"Not hanging from the hook?" Becky asked. "Not tossed on the piecrust table? Not left in the ignition? Then I can't say, unless, didn't Ginger have to drive herself to her divorce support group last night? I know her usual ride called to say she had unexpectedly reconciled with her husband, although Ginger was trying to talk her out of it. She advised her to remember the bad times, which she was going into graphically, chapter and verse. They must be encouraged not to leave out a single detail down at that group. I can only imagine they vie to provide the awfulest account," Becky added, not unintrigued by the dynamics of such a gathering.

Ginger, who happened to be up and about uncommonly early that morning, overheard herself being accused as she stood darkening the kitchen doorway. She rummaged haughtily in a capacious satchel resting on her jutting hip and she flung a rattling bunch of keys toward

Alden. They glanced off the top of Harvey's head as, uninvolved in the key quest, he sat at the kitchen table stooped over his coffee cup and glaring down upon his Connecticut realtor's latest letter, conveying nagging news about tile slippage in the master bathroom shower, which, in Harvey's opinion only showed what came of cavalierly power-scrubbing away the very necessary grout mold as the realtor had mandated. Harvey daubed at his watery eyes with the still warm linen handkerchief Becky had kindly pressed for him. She had ironed two handkerchiefs, one for mopping himself with and the other for producing in a gallant and timely manner for any of his several lady friends, who were an unusually weepy lot. Any small courtesy could set them off and at this point he was laying on treats like traps just to test the waters, so to speak. They cried at the presentation of a spare carrot and coconut and raisin muffin left over from his second-stage breakfast at the Do-Nut Hole preserved in a paper napkin, and even Penny Nicholls had turned on the waterworks when he saved a cautionary clipping from the *Towne Crier* concerning a locally operating burglary ring that kept their unsuspecting elderly victims occupied at the front door answering a presidential preference poll (to which the only correct answer was, I prefer the one we have) while accomplices slipped in through the back door and looted the sterling flatware chest and the liquor cupboard.

At any rate, Becky seemed to understand how necessary a fresh supply of presentable hankies was to Harvey without his having to go into details about the carrot muffins and the burglars and the Niagara fall of gratified tears. Becky was a good egg, unlike that other one, his niece by blood, Ginger, whom he was not at all accustomed to encountering before he effected his getaway, scheduled early enough on a normal morning to escape her premier performance of the day. At present, Harvey reckoned, Ginger was up for something and more than likely up to something.

"Whoa," he barked at her and touched the top of his head carefully as if probing a sticky wound. Ginger peered and informed him he was fine.

"Boys. Little Becky. You'll miss the bus," Alden called up the back stairs. "It's not convenient to drive you to school today. I have plans of my own." This he stated with satisfaction. He met Becky's eye and she smiled at him encouragingly.

"Betsy?" Ginger generally inquired as well. She emptied the coffee-pot into her personal mug which sat in its own spot on its own shelf, the other mugs huddled out of its way. She failed to start another pot which was the general practice, though Ginger would argue in her own defense that her version of coffee was so criticized—bitter, she said they said, bitterly—she could only default. She slid the coffeepot out of sight, barricaded behind a box of Cheerios and the milk carton, and she sat across the table from Harvey, bravely or belligerently staring him down. He swiveled, displaying his late Roman emperor profile, motion-less as on a coin and as hard-edged. Ginger twirled the lazy Susan, snatching three packets of Equal sweetener and a long-handled spoon plucked from the spoon jar in transit, and she squinted at the heat-activated message as letters materialized on the side of her mug. BEAM ME UP, SCOTTY, she read. She lifted soulful eyes toward the ceiling and she communed with the hovering Mother Ship, receiving her orders for the day. This morning the command came down as the single whispered word, *Persist*.

Harvey spun the lazy Susan back around so that his bottle of buffered aspirin and flask of rhubarb syrup and earthenware pot of Tasmanian honey were facing him, even though he had already swallowed and dosed and sweetened, because, because, that's how the lazy Susan "went."

Becky set down her iron so she could give her full attention to a coughing fit. She ruffed the collar of her bathrobe around her throat as Lily, who had been outside feeding the nuthatches, admitted a funnel of frigid air. She had come in to refill her seed scoop from the fifty-pound bag of Northeast Songbird Mixture left leaning against the pantry wall, slumping and much bumped into and spilling out seeds, which only encouraged some mice to whom Lily referred as a nice little family whenever Ginger overreacted to the sudden sight of a tiny tuft of crea-ture skimming across the vastness of the pantry floor. Now Lily, locked into a more mouse-tolerating attitude than even she would normally have held, toed a scattering of unmistakably mouse droppings down through the gap between the linoleum and a rising radiator pipe so that Ginger could not point to them and exclaim further.

Phoebe clipped down the back stairs then. She and Arthur had moved into the available attic chamber Glover had vacated, back when the hornet stung him, before any other Andys could arrive and claim the space, and after many thousands of glossy brown beetles had lethargically winged into the barn one evening. They had crawled into every crevice and deposited pale powdery strands of eggs and then they had died or gone to sleep, riveted to stone, to beams, crackling and cracking under touch. Even Arthur had minded, for the bugs had gotten into his files and obeyed various biological imperatives across the pages of his screenplay, which Phoebe had had to retype during her lunch hour at work. But everybody at work, everybody at the Towne Community Hospital offices, had said they would go see Arthur's movie if it ever became a movie, so that was positive.

She bade a pleasant good morning to Arthur's people. She lifted her jar of Taster's Choice from the lazy Susan and made a mug of coffee using hot water direct from the faucet. She stirred vigorously, crushing afloat coffee crystals against the side of her mug. The Hills braced themselves as Phoebe took her first sip and did not instantly die of it.

"Did you call me, Mummy?" Betsy asked, having taken her own time to answer Ginger's earlier summons which had not sounded urgent. Then again, with her mother everything turned urgent eventually. Betsy had been in the little parlor updating her babysitting appointment book. She was expected at the Snowdons' that afternoon after school. She was going to help Mrs. Snowdon dress the children in rational little outfits, in bright, happy colors that matched, no stripes disagreeing with plaids, no unsanctioned dress-up boas and diamond tiaras and space-gear stun guns strapped to pipe-cleaner hips. Betsy was going to drive with the Snowdons to Therapists' Row behind the Freedomway Mall, making sure none of the children fell from the back hatch of the station wagon en route. There, the three small children disappeared through three tall doors and Betsy and Mrs. Snowdon retired to the Food Court in the Mall for ice waters and nervous cigarettes on Mrs. Snowdon's part as she talked to Betsy as if Betsy were yet another therapist, defending the undisputed rationalness of the children's outfits (the girls dressed as girls, the boy as a boy) and pointing out that at least they had all arrived at their therapists' in one piece which surely must count in her favor.

Betsy received four dollars an hour for this. She wished she had held out for five at the initial interview.

"What, Betsy?" asked Ginger. "What is it? Why are you looking at me? What do you want?"

"You called me," Betsy reminded her.

"Oh, yes. Don't you miss the school bus, I wanted to tell you," Ginger said.

"I haven't missed it yet. I mean I haven't missed it today and I haven't missed it so far this year," Betsy answered.

"Well, fine, only don't start today because I can't deal with your little problems today. I've got my own business to see to," Ginger declared. "So run along with you," she advised as Betsy leaned against the refrigerator door, the back of her neck and the knot there, manipulated by the thubdub of the cranking motor. For now that Ginger herself had admitted to having plans, Betsy hoped she might ask a further question concerning them without being accused by Ginger of interrogating her like a secret policeman. Oh, why didn't they just implant a tracking device in her rib cage? Ginger had been quite fierce in forcing this point of her nonaccessibility and her nonaccountability during her late dalliance, and Betsy had long since learned the lesson that, on the whole, she would rather not know just where her mother went when she went out. Betsy had noted, however, this early morning, that Ginger had saturated her hair with Jazzi-Jel and slicked the thick curls up and back, tightly twisting and pinning them in place so that a stiff shock sprouted and wilted on the top of her head very noticeably. She had on a black silk-and-cashmere knit turtleneck, her big colliding pieces of turquoise jewelry, and a pair of pleated and cuffed grey flannel trousers she could still zip and button on. She had discovered her grandmother's Autumn Haze mink coat left behind inside the garment bag at the back of her bedroom closet, and had been trailing about in it at every opportunity since the weather had worsened, the shawl collar turned up to frame her face, the drooping hem kicked forward by her striding steps and sweeping the pavement behind her. Grandmama Hill had been a tall old girl, thank goodness. Ginger didn't have to hunch beneath some shrunken munchkin fur that didn't reach her wrists, her knees. Ginger swanned inside the coat even now at the breakfast table, quite content within its soft, wide embrace as she clicked apart a tube of Red Surrender and accurately thickened the color on her lips without consulting the shiny side of the toaster, impressing Becky and Phoebe, who appreciated how unsuccessful such blind repairs could be.

But Betsy only knew she had cause for concern when her mother made such an effort. Ginger had been inspired to glue on faux fingernails and to paint them rose-violet and, presumably, sensibly, before she had fitted on the fingernails she had feathered on her false eyelashes which Betsy really didn't think you were supposed to wear during the daylight hours but doubtless Ginger had risen and commenced dressing before dawn broke so she would argue she had discovered the exemption should anyone, should Betsy, raise an objection.

"What are you doing today, Mummy?" Betsy asked as she half turned and began to move about refrigerator magnets so that she would seem rather more interested in aligning the smiley face and the plasticined twist of real pretzel and the tester magnet handed out at the dump to check whether recyclable cans went in the tin or aluminum bin, than in pinning Ginger down to a particular statement of her intentions.

"I'm taking a well-deserved day off," Ginger announced. She wished Betsy wouldn't fidget. She wished Betsy would listen.

"A day off from what?" wondered Harvey. "A day off from lying about like Queen Cleopatra?"

"I'm going to Boston for a day of shopping, museums, lunch, and lawyers," Ginger continued. She wished Harvey wouldn't share his picturesque opinions about her activities. "Because, Alden, because Alden," she addressed her brother severely, "because that local shyster Lily put me onto is utterly hopeless, the exquisite Harris Desmaris. He'd have had me in the public stocks with a great scarlet letter safety-pinned onto my smock, I declare, so *your* fellow, Alden, your candidate, this great old legal-brained chum of yours, had better be up to snuff." She sniffed.

"Oh, is it today you're seeing Ron?" Alden asked. "Just listen to what he tells you. Don't you try to tell him. It's a tremendous favor he's seeing you at all and only then in an advisory capacity. He's not a divorce attorney. For one thing, his taste in suits is too sober."

"Yes, yes, yes, yes, I'll listen to him," Ginger impatiently waved away the very idea that she would not. "But first I have to get in to Boston. Where are you headed, anyway? Not Boston, I daresay, you're dressed like Paul Bunyan. Are you going in to Cambridge? That'll do just as well. I'll start off at the Fogg. I adore the Fogg."

"No, sorry, I'm not going anywhere near there," Alden said, not sounding at all sorry.

"Well, at least you can drive me down to Peddocks' and I'll find someone to take me in. Towne has turned into such a bedroom suburb. I'll hitch a ride. I'll hold up a sign like one of those pale parolee hitch-hikers along the Interstate," Ginger said as she batted her way through the contents of her satchel searching for her notebook and a marking pen. The checkbook for the joint local account she held with Betsy flipped out and fell to the floor. Ginger bent and retrieved the Luxe Leatherette folder swiftly and glanced up to glower back at Betsy's inevitable look of reproach, for they were set on a sensible budget of Betsy's reckoning, to which Ginger had only grudgingly assented and with absolutely no intention of abiding by. Nevertheless, the designated figure served as a posted speed limit to the hurtling vehicle of Ginger's overspending, a limit to exceed, of course, but only by so much and no further without exacting a stiffish penalty, for Betsy had promised to take away her mother's "privileges" should she offend too grievously. Betsy, however, had slipped away when Ginger first mentioned lawyers. Betsy had no wish to hear of attorneys and stratagems. She had not been able to decide whether she was honor bound to inform her father of legal developments or to keep Ginger's counsel and so she tried not to know anything at all.

"Boys, Little Becky," Becky set down her iron and called up the back stairs. She turned to Alden, who was hovering by the stove watching over two frying eggs. "Rap on Glover's door, dear. He's awake. I can hear him prowling around in there."

Harvey, who by now required more coffee, rose and slid the pot from Ginger's hiding place and started, fussily and in a martyred manner, to measure and grind beans and run clear, cold water through the faucet and filch a paper filter from the stuck-together stack.

Arthur clattered down the back stairs. "Sorry to delay you, Phoebe," he said. "I just had this idea, this memory. It must have come to me in a dream or something and I had to write it down right off. About the Halloween I went out as a chicken pot pie. Mama wrapped me all up in silver foil and she stuck feathers in my hair and hung a carrot and a celery from my ears and she wrote 'Heat at three thousand degrees for twelve hours' across my forehead. You know, I'm real lucky I didn't run into one of those psychopaths because I think he would have had a defense, don't you know."

"That's great, honey, only it's elective-surgery day today and I really can't be late. I've got to admit a crowd and those procedures are scheduled to the minute." She had found an unclaimed toasted English muffin lying on the drainboard and she held it up to him inquiringly.

Arthur shook his head. "Are these Rice Krispies?" he asked, picking up the Rice Krispies box.

"Yes, but the milk is iffy," Becky warned him.

Ginger set her mug down sharply on the table, sloshing coffee onto her sign and dissolving the ink into streaks so it now appeared she required a ride to some hick town in Hunan province.

"Boo-tang?" Harvey questioned in a squeaky-pitched Chinese secret policeman interrogator voice.

Arthur unpeeled a banana and rolled it in a bowl of dry cereal. "Any caramel sauce?" he asked. "If I dunked a banana in caramel sauce and rolled it in cereal, I'd really have something. No? No caramel sauce?" He sat and helped himself to the Tasmanian honey, hunching his shoulders so Harvey couldn't see what he was up to.

Phoebe nibbled at the English muffin which was cold and tough and even, perhaps, dish soap—soaked from its time on the drainboard, and she answered Ginger and Becky's questions about the most popular elective surgeries.

"You're up and at it early for a showbiz type," Alden observed to Arthur. "Boys, Little Becky," he called up the stairs. He threw a rolled-up pair of socks from the clean laundry basket at Glover's door. Glover thumped back from the other side.

"I'm driving to work with Phoebe," Arthur explained. "She got me this gig cheerying up the sick kids. Well, I'm glad to do it." He shrugged. "Only I don't think my stuff on how to tell who's gonna die first in a Freddy Krueger movie will work with sick kids, and I've got twenty minutes on stuff about how *Adler* isn't a real good name for a psychoanalyst which is kind of medical but over their heads, probably, so I'm thinking I'll give them clown stuff, you know. Kids, clowns. That'll be, what's the word Aunt Lily likes so much, that'll be more appropriate."

"How lovely to entertain those poor children," Becky said. "Phoebe, I should talk to you about Women's Chorus arranging a Christmas concert for them."

"Actually, we're booked through St. Patrick's Day with programs for the kids," Phoebe said.

"Oh?"

"I've always despised clowns," Ginger said. "I don't know why, but I just do. I particularly don't like sad clowns, and I really can't stand those foreign art clowns and I hate female clowns with the single wilted daisy in their hats—"

"Yes, well, clowning is just a sideline," Arthur said.

"Didn't know you had a front line," Harvey muttered.

"Aunt Lily, do you like clowns?" Ginger asked.

Lily had gone out and come in again. Her loose cheeks and long nose were mottled yellow and scarlet from the cold. She fished a Kleenex from her coat pocket and blew into it. "If I feel like laughing," she said. "I need my suet now," Lily added, pulling open the refrigerator door.

"Look behind the six-pack of Pepsi," Becky said. She carried a map of the refrigerator in her mind.

"And the bird peanut butter?" Lily asked.

"*Bird* peanut butter?" Ginger asked. "Have I been eating bird peanut butter and raspberry jam sandwiches?"

"In the butter hatch," Becky said.

The coffee perked and Lily departed and Alden threw a second pair of socks at Glover's door.

"Amazing events happening in East Germany at the moment," Alden said, leaning over the counter and working the dials of the radio searching for a weather report. He had an outdoor day planned.

"You think so?" asked Harvey.

"Well, I think it's perfectly marvelous, throwing off the yoke of tyranny. One so empathizes," Ginger cried, flexing her furry back.

"The kids have missed the bus," Becky announced, consulting the clock on the stove.

"Betsy?" Ginger asked. "Betsy?" she called. When Betsy didn't answer she assumed Betsy had made her own way, somehow.

The kitchen wall phone rang just then. Alden answered it, said, Hold on, and tossed the receiver to Becky which she caught one-handedly. She set down her iron.

"Yes?" she spoke into the mouthpiece. She listened. "What?" she asked. "Well, I really have no idea. Guess? Yes, all right, I'll guess. I'll just say Vincent Van Gogh. Yes, the sunflower guy, as you say. No? Not Van Gogh? Oh dear. Well, that's perfectly all right. Good morning to you too, and thank you."

Above their heads, Little Becky began to scream, No, no! The sound, emanating from the attic, began as an eerily thin wail, fading and strengthening, the sound picking its way down two flights of stairs and seeking out the conduits of water and radiator pipes. Little Becky thundered down the attic steps and her howling loudened. She pitched herself off the last tread of the back stairs and slammed into the kitchen, incoherently shouting.

"Always strive to be dainty, darling," Becky reminded her, lifting the hot iron out of her daughter's way as Little Becky fell upon her, but not to seek the solace of a motherly embrace as Becky anticipated. Rather, Little Becky meant to strike.

"Steady on," Alden said, pulling her away. Little Becky, energetically enraged, flailed at the kitchen air.

Glover's door shot open and he tottered cockily across the linoleum. "Ah-ha," he jeered at his sister.

"Shut up, shut up, shut up!" she shrieked and she kicked out hard at his shin but he was wearing the pair of tough-skinned riding boots he'd found in the barn and imbued with saddle soap and vaseline and canola oil over the past weeks until today they were—almost—wearable. Her foot connected, then skidded sideways and she clipped Harvey's arm with her heel.

He flinched out of harm's way. "You know, I believe this constitutes elder abuse," he said. "Penny Nicholls has a brochure, I shall consult it." He kneaded his elbow. He unbuttoned his shirt cuff and rolled up his sleeve to display an existing callus which, nevertheless, presented as a fresh welt. Phoebe, inured to such demonstrations down at the hospital, looked and tsked.

Brooks and Rollins spilled from the stairwell laughing in shrill whoops.

"Ma, that was so cool," Brooks said.

"Wicked excellent," Rollins said.

"Real smooth, Ma, you on the radio pretending to be Little Becky," Brooks said.

Little Becky, her fury spent and not unremorseful that she'd injured Uncle Harvey even though it wasn't her fault, it was Glover's, resolved to weep and to weep copiously now, and she turned with a roil of misery to permit her mother to comfort her after all. She jammed her head against Becky's shoulder and Becky set down her iron and unplugged the cord just to be on the safe side. She folded Little Becky in her arms.

"The radio wanted to talk to *me*. I sent in the postcard and they called *me*," she sobbed into Becky's flannel bathrobe which absorbed the hot tears. Becky shifted. She was half dressed beneath her robe and she didn't want her slip straps to lay damp against her skin all day.

"Well, I'm mystified," Alden admitted.

"Ma, didn't you know you were on the radio, on WROC 99.99 FM and they asked you for the artist of the day and you said that guy, you know, Vango, only the artist of the day was White Snake," Glover explained.

"White Snake," Little Becky moaned. "I knew it, I knew it. I always listen. I always know. It isn't fair. It's never fair. Why can't you all just be fair? To *me*."

"Actually, who ever calls you on the telephone, Little B.?" Ginger asked. "I can't recall a single time, so why should one think to inquire, Which Becky?"

"We meant to find you a nickname," Alden recalled, "but nothing ever really suggested itself. Still, a nickname for you was definitely the original plan."

Everyone considered, then, and even the boys couldn't come up with suitably derisive recommendations so early in the day, besides, Alden indicated he would not tolerate unkindness as he gripped Brooks's and

Rollins's shoulders and dug in sharp fingers. They writhed away from him and lolled, loggishly, on the back-stair treads.

"I know you must be disappointed, sweet pea, honeybunch, muffin tin. I'm sorry for the mix-up," Becky said, detaching Little Becky from her side. She picked up the dish sponge and swabbed at Little Becky's cheek where misapplied mascara seeped down in dark streams. "So, what would you have won?" she asked. "A nice sweatshirt? A nice CD?"

The boys snickered and Little Becky resumed weeping and she sputtered, "Just before he called *me*, the Super Siren blew and Manfred in the Morning said he was feeling real generous on of account of the Berlind Wall and all, so he was going to give away nine *thousand* nine hundred and ninety-nine Big Deal Dollars this morning on the Super Cash Call."

"Oh dear," said Becky, and she meant it. "Still, your name is going to be placed in the consolation bin. They mentioned something about a consolation bin. Is that good?"

"For a Ford Escort," Brooks said.

"For a sucky Ford Escort," Rollins said.

"I can't drive," Little Becky hollered.

"First dibs on the car then," Ginger spoke up.

"Yeah, I've heard that Manfred guy," Arthur said. "He moves the decimal point around. Usually, you'd just have won ninety-nine dollars and ninety-nine cents. Really tough break, Little Becky."

"Van Gogh," Ginger uttered better-knowingly. She would have guessed Frida Kahlo just to expand the tired old male-centric, Euro-centric, beauty-centric aesthetics of the listening public.

"Vango? Vango? That's not a group. Everybody at school will think I don't know a group, everybody will think I'm such a loser," Little Becky fretted. She had whirled away from her mother's scrubbing motions and she was rooting beneath the sink behind a box of Brillo pads where the previous evening she had stashed the last packet of Swiss Miss Cocoa Mix.

"That's no problem, everybody already thinks you're —" Glover started to say but Alden yanked at his recently attempted pigtail sprouting from the back of his head. Glover was wearing his EAT ME T-shirt today. Alden wondered why they permitted Glover to go to school dressed like that. He wondered why the school permitted it. Perhaps he and the school could get together and object in concert.

He observed, "All your little pals will have been on the school bus where you should have been as well. So technically, Little Becky, you weren't even home to take the Cash Call, so let's not dwell on it. Tough luck, too bad, just drop it. And now I'm going to have to drive you all to school and I have an appointment of my own so let's get cracking. Stir your stumps. No, no breakfasts for any of you, you missed it. You'll know better next time to get up when you're called."

"Dad's just mega-bummed because Ma lost us ten thousand dollars," Glover said.

"*My* money. I wrote the postcard," Little Becky said. She had slipped the opened envelope of Swiss Miss in her jeans pocket. Secretly, she licked her forefinger and dredged it through the chocolate powder and stuck the finger in her mouth.

"But Dad really should have asked which Becky they wanted," Brooks said.

"Yeah, I have to blame Dad," Rollins said. "Definitely, this is all Dad's fault."

They surged into the front hall and grabbed their parkas from the coatrack and jostling and complaining at one another they arrayed themselves for the out-of-doors, slinging knapsacks over their backs, jamming gloves onto their hands, winding and knotting scarves. Brooks tipped on his Yankees cap which was routinely snatched from his head and flung onto the field house girders. The visor was strapped on with duct tape. The logo was fraying. The janitor was tired of snagging the thing down with a twenty-foot drunkenly wobbling bamboo pole.

"Nest of vipers you've got there," Harvey remarked to Becky. "We should all have been listening to the news from Europe. It's history happening all over again in front of our eyes."

"Yes, how wonderful," Becky responded vaguely.

"Don't forget me," Ginger called, rising. She hoisted up her satchel and hunkered down into her coat. She swept off. A drooping sleeve clouted the upstanding sugar spoon. Sugar crystals flashed from the bowl and sparked across the tabletop.

"Well, it never ceases to astound me, the variety of ways a day can go awry," Alden said, kissing Becky dryly good-bye.

"Oh, I don't know, it makes me feel quite splendidly extravagant to have squandered ten thousand dollars before eight a.m.," she told him as she replugged her iron and sawed the reheating press up and down the sleeve of her lace-collared blouse forming a sharp crease which she believed lent a slimming effect. Still, she could not help asking herself why Glover hadn't bolted from his room and seized the telephone receiver and shouted, White Snake, White Snake, White Snake, at the chit-chattering DJ. But to rise to such exertion, to display such enthusiasm, doubtless lay beneath his dignity, or his vision of his dignity. Alden should have a serious talk with the boy. Then again, she wasn't certain Alden was the best one to plead the case for the sometimes necessary sacrifice of dignity to a merely (merely!) economic imperative. No, Alden was not the person to plead that particular case at the moment.

LILY SAT UPON a flat-topped rock hidden from sight by a stand of shaggy spruces but with her own viewing line to the back of the house worked out through the branches. Her table knife scraped the side of the jar as she spread peanut butter upon pine cones which she had been finding on the ground all fall and collecting in bushel baskets. She rolled the coated cones in Northeast Songbird Mixture and laid them end to end upon an old cookie sheet to cure a bit before she hung them availably from the privet hedge and the clothesline with Christmas ornament hooks. The scavenging squirrels were too heavy to climb and sit upon the privet—they swayed, they swooped—but they had learned to cling to and inch along the clothesline, perilously upside down yet agile as French Riviera diamond thieves, to attain the prize.

The cat had followed Lily outside and weaved herself, now, between Lily's shins, but this adoration was a calculated effect. Agnes meant to turn Lily and herself into a predatory team. She glanced at Lily knowingly and gleamed her serrate teeth but Lily wasn't buying. She had already steeled herself not to strew millet across the terrace bricks for the mourning doves who had come to expect to be fed in the winter. Lily could only hope that the disappointed birds who plumply paced and ill-temperedly peered through the French doors (and pecked sharply on the glass, Ginger claimed) would wander off elsewhere. Perhaps some of the new people in one of the new houses understood about strewing millet.

Lily shooed the cat away. Agnes withdrew stiff-backed, flicking her skinny bandicoot tail, and shimmered out of sight between barnboards.

The exodus from the house commenced then. Alden herded the boys and Little Becky who was bleating about her latest tragedy. Broken syllables expressive of misery traveled toward Lily—the wind gusted this way and that, this morning. Ginger lagged behind, luxuriating in her appropriated fur. Alden detoured to the barn. Making several journeys, he piled two new and bright chain saws, a safety can of gasoline, a coil of rope, into the back of the station wagon as Ginger and Little Becky sparred for the front seat. Ginger, impatient with the nattering, suddenly hip-checked Little Becky out of contention. Little Becky shook off the bump and flung herself into the backseat and fell heavily over the front, feigning unconsciousness, which was her special talent, an ability to collapse as completely as a meringue. Ginger, weighed and breathed upon, balanced on the edge of the seat, hugging her satchel, her neck crooked, persisting. The boys tumbled through the back hatch and tossed the saws and gasoline can and ropes into the backseat beside their sister, who would have yelped were she not so committed to maintaining her swoon.

Then Arthur and Phoebe hurried into view and jumped into the Jeep, which tinnily turned on and jounced down the drive. A pause, and Harvey appeared rebuttoning his overcoat and honking into his handkerchief. He also visited the barn. He emerged, hefting a hammer in either hand. He determined he preferred one and pitched the other through the barn door. It landed hard and skidded. The cat streaked from the barn as if set alight.

Harvey eased himself into his car and waited as the motor quietly idled and his heater kicked in. He glared through the windshield in search of Lily whom he only wished to ask if she needed an errand run down in the village, although he would have greeted any request she made of him with amazed challenge—African violet food? African violet *food?* So onerous, so absurd, Lily's commissions. Still, poor old Lily, deficient old bat, things can't have been easy.

Becky left the house last, clutching a stack of sheet music which she attempted to organize as she bustled along. She had asked last night if she could borrow Lily's car and Lily had said, Yes, at once (as Ginger drew a sharp breath because whenever *she* asked, Lily only ever told her, Yes, eventually). Becky stopped and waved in several directions endeavoring to say good-bye to Lily, wherever Lily was hiding. Becky was aware that Lily sometimes hid and she was sorry that Lily felt the need to hide. Then Becky was gone, too, carefully steering down the driveway taking the hump and the subsequent dip as cautiously as Lily herself would have.

She was alone. Lily savored the sensation. She would be unobserved and unrequired for the next few hours. If she wished, she could watch the *Learn to Paint* show on Channel 2 which was really quite interesting. The bearded and energetic host demonstrated how to paint pine trees and the setting sun and ocean waves according to a foolproof method he had worked out. One need not possess any artistic ability at all in order to produce a perfectly adequate landscape or seascape or sunset, and Lily was tempted to try her hand at a sunset. Then again, suppose her painting revealed what she sometimes felt after watching a particularly violent sunset all the way through to its final fingerings of that red that contained so much black smudging the sky, when she asked herself, Is this it, is this the end? No, her morning would be more usefully spent in washing windows while no one was around to pry the bottle of ammonia from her hand and order her off the step stool, saying they'd wash the windows when they got around to it, around the turn of the century, Lily reckoned. In the meanwhile, they were all very hard on her windows. They gazed through them excessively, watching for what or for whom to come up the drive. They huffed upon the panes, leaning their noses and cheeks and chins against the cool glass and laying down their handprints where they remained, long-fingered and beseeching tracings.

Her sister, Olive, had been like that, always at the window, back when Frank Lowe had first wandered into the picture and Olive had so swiftly made up her mind. She had dragged a chair and an ottoman into an attic dormer. In those days the trees weren't so tall and you could see all the way down to the road and the river. She had supplied herself with Lorna Doones and the new *McCall's* to see her through her vigil. Why had Olive been so set on Frank Lowe? She had been very clear in her mind. She must have had a very clear picture of what she wanted out of life and whom she wanted to be there beside her, but it must have been rather a paint-by-number picture if Frank was anything to go by, Lily decided. Nothing about Frank had ever been very inspiring.

As Lily so critically regarded her windows, an upper one was flung open. *Andy,* whom she'd not forgotten, such an insinuating young man. She had, however, shuttered that agitated corner of her mind where he probed so assiduously.

Andy stood at the window, wrapped in his woolen Black Watch plaid robe, a perfectly sober garment, yet he wore it in such a negligent manner, loosely tied at the waist with his bare chest exposed. Lily had to wonder what his pajama situation could be. Sunlight dazzled off his polished glasses lenses as he hauled up the string bag suspended from a nail driven without her permission into the sill. He kept his milk, butter, cheeses, and navel oranges outside in the cold. Several times over the two and a half weeks that Andy had been in residence, Becky had sent Little Becky to borrow his milk—Little Becky had gleefully spurted up the stairs to knock, thrillingly, upon Andy's personal door.

Andy seemed to be searching as he lingered holding his window wide open. Lily could see the heat pouring out in that liquid swirliness of the atmosphere where domestic air met the wilder stuff, and she lodged a mental note to inform him what heating oil was costing her these days since he was so curious about her finances. Percentages of her budget, that was Andy's hobbyhorse—What percentage of your budget do you expend on leisure-time activities, Miss Hill, bingo, movies, pottery classes?

Lily shrank into the prickly softness of the surrounding fir trees knowing herself to be invisible, protectively colored in the grey-and-brown landscape, just another craggy feature of the woods. Lily had always been overlookable, which once she had minded but not for many years now. Andy, however, keensighted and elevated, zeroed in on her position like a hungry hawk. He hailed her and raised the wrist which would bear his watch, reminding her that the hour of her promised interview approached.

. . .

GINGER, IN HER bulky animal coat, sat on a swivel stool at the soda fountain counter in Peddocks'. She sipped a cup of coffee and nibbled a raspberry-jam-filled croissant, too hot from a minute in the microwave, as she slowly turned round and round on the stool alternately carrying the coffee for one circuit and the croissant for the next, all the while inspecting everyone who entered the premises. Females were given short shrift, working women with wash-and-wear haircuts and boringly tailored suits with rigid shoulder pads jutting out shelflike to signify their willingness to bear the weight of the corporate world upon their backs. It occurred to Ginger that this was what was wrong with the corporate world, because why didn't Brooks Brothers sew breast pads into the fronts of their button-down-collar men's shirts to demonstrate a compensatory male solidarity with the female virtues of nurturing and compassion? Another insight for her book which she must write down at once before she forgot. Her mind felt such a fragile vessel this cold, early weekday morning. She spun around to the counter and plucked a pencil from her hair and grabbed a paper napkin from the metal dispenser. She scrawled, then scratched several question marks—another trail to investigate even though she was taking the day off from scholarship. She stuffed the napkin into her satchel and picked up her croissant and rotated again and she spotted Goody Palmer, who had entered while her back was turned and was on his way out, the newspaper he'd come in to buy tucked under his arm like a rudder. He was in a rush. He jostled the Rev. Penworthy who automatically cried "Oopsa-daisy." The Rev. was the father of four under five. Busy Rev., Ginger thought.

She snatched her satchel and her coffee cup and she pursued Goody. He had slammed his car door but couldn't back out of his parking slot having been cut off by a double-parked Jeep Wagoneer. Ginger tapped on his passenger-side window until Goody could not pretend he didn't hear her. He released the lock and she slipped in beside him exclaiming a triumphant syllable. "I was watching for you," she said. She exuded strong perfume, a stronger fur scent. She loomed close to Goody, tilting to fumble for the seat belt, strapping herself in as if preparing for takeoff. She settled back in an intimate, long-distance way, reclining her seat and fiddling with the heat vents, training them toward her feet which were shod in tight, shiny, high-heeled boots which had made treacherous her run across the almost icy pavement to reach him.

"I didn't see you," Goody too instantly denied.

"Then it's very lucky I saw you because I desperately need a ride into Boston. Let me out anywhere as nearish to Newbury Street as possible. Otherwise . . ." She began to mention other corners where she might be left. She mentioned some unlikely corners.

The Wagoneer's owner returned, ducking down to shoot Goody a wince of apology, and Goody found himself on the road with Ginger. Ginger waved widely at Anna Webster who was standing at the end of her driveway Dust-Bustering her mailbox. Anna stared, unable to determine who was with Goody whose car, of course, she knew. She'd have to call Babe to ask so she could apologize to whomever she had inadvertently snubbed, some wild-headed woman swathed in fur.

"Anna Webster just cold-shouldered me," Ginger announced. She seemed grimly pleased for Anna Webster was famously softhearted. She had even appeared in court as a character witness for her burglar who had not, after all, urinated on her carpets or killed her big, barky Eskimo dog.

"Oh no, I hardly think Anna meant—" Goody began to protest but he wasn't going to be tricked into defending Ginger's mysterious midwestern sins against small-minded locals' righteous or not demonstrations against her. He switched on the radio and tuned into a traffic report. His mind darted down alternate routes as the familiar ride in turned labyrinthine.

Ginger swigged the last of her coffee and planted the lipstick-stained cup in the glove compartment tucked out of casual sight behind an unfolding road map of the Canadian Maritimes annotated with yellow highlighting pen.

"Do you remember—" Ginger started to ask.

Goody automatically asserted his memory wasn't what it used to be. Indeed, Babe was going to try him on a vitamin supplement.

"Then I shall remind you of that summer," Ginger said.

"Summer?" Goody denied all knowledge and experience of summer.

He smashed hollyhocks, drained swimming pools, and dimmed the wattage of the sun.

"Our summer," Ginger spoke of it softly. She smoothed out the green folds and fragrant hours of summer gently, although one had to suspect she had removed summer's lawns and balms from the drawer and examined them often, so often that her thumbprints lay everywhere upon them now.

"Right, that summer," Goody said. If it was unbecoming of Ginger to have recalled the time, it would be caddish of him to repudiate the memory.

"When you said, when you said to me, remember how you said to me that you didn't think it would matter if we didn't make love but that it would be terribly important if we did," Ginger said.

Goody wasn't even sure what that was supposed to mean and he very sincerely had to doubt he had ever pressed such a point. Surely, he would never have spoken so complex a sentence and certainly not one which was as slipperily allusive, so deftly placing the ball in her court, if he understood the construction. For, primarily in Goody's recollection, 1969 had been his tennis summer. The Websters had risen to the expense and upkeep of a clay court in an effort to launch a dowdy daughter.

"We were important, weren't we?" Ginger murmured.

No, that was not at all the sort of proposition Goody would have posed. For in that situation, he had not attempted any argument at all. He had not really had to. Women, the few women before Babe, had been the instigators, silkily sliding across sofa cushions, placing a hand upon his arm, and very solemnly regarding him before lifting a kiss from his lips. They excused themselves. He sat in fragrant chambers, picking up and putting down magazines. The women returned wearing loose, light robes and their diaphragms. His sentimental history, such as it was, had been a mild one involving treaties, not battles, and until the present moment there had never been a flare-up from any long quiescent quarter. He had not been untruthful when he told Ginger he did not remember, but, more accurately, as unexercised feelings began to stretch and push behind his rib cage, he realized how very thoroughly his memories of Ginger had been suppressed. Babe, whom he had married the winter after Ginger went away to Chicago at summer's end, had scoured Gin-

ger from every corner of his life, banishing the six declarative letters
Ginger had sent, her glamorous photograph framed in silver, and the
beach sarong found kicked beneath a car seat and which had to have
been hers for who but Ginger would have possessed a beach sarong and
one so strongly colored crimson?

"OH, MR. SPENCER, we all think the world of Dr. Dunlop," Phoebe
reassured a nervous admittee, although she was not supposed to dis-
pense medical opinions. But Harvey had heard Senior Village thought
highly of Phoebe. She flew through the Medicare forms and kept her
voice discreetly low when she was obliged to mention what ailment it
was that had brought the patient to the hospital, which was often some
not very pleasant condition. She had her nice Southern sayings for
symptoms. Are you backed up? Are you coming up? she'd ask softly.
Have you slowed down? Did you just come over all queer-like? She had
revived a little vogue in suffering from palpitations among the more
susceptible ladies, just a finicky sensation of fluttering that could be
fanned away with an Osteoporosis Information brochure, and which
kept the ladies' minds off their other pangs and panics about cancer.

Phoebe tapped out Mr. Spencer's data on her keyboard, his answers
to her gentle questions dealt with as he fished for a flavor he liked in her
lollipop jar. He was forbidden sweets, of course, but he was going to
save the lollipop for later when his grandson came to visit, that is, if
Grandpa survived the day.

And up in the bright and cheerful children's ward decorated with
Mylar balloons and a ceiling mural depicting delighted children swinging between crutches and flying up and down ramps in wheelchairs,
Arthur pulled a shiny quarter from the bandaged head of one wan
little boy who had mistaken Arthur, dressed in scrubs and wearing a
false mustache, for yet another doctor who had found another something alarming to extract from his skull. The nurses, the other sick kids
(though none so sick as he) had clustered round to observe the impromptu operation and to laugh as the tall skinny new doctor held up
the quarter, flipped it between his fingers, and made it vanish. The wan
little boy supposed his condition *was* becoming ridiculous, nevertheless

he was quite sure he would not have laughed at any of them, were they in his shoes.

ALDEN HAD NOTICED a need as he drove around Towne and he had set about supplying a service. He ran an ad in the *Towne Crier* on the back page below the Citizens' Forum column, MY SAY, where Babe Palmer was that week's Guest Voice questioning the need for handicapped parking spaces in package store parking lots because she didn't think crippled people should drink and become even more unsteady on their feet. Alden had been so astonished by Babe's assertions, he had nearly overlooked his own advertisement printed in italic type contained within a black-lined box.

> *Some boy been bending your birches?*
> *Has time oer-topped your mighty oak?*
> *Painless tree extraction and prompt,*
> *expert timber removal by an M.B.A. . . .*
> *. . . hewn down and cast into the fire.*
> *Call for a quote.*

This appeal had set him back seventy-five cents a word, still, Alden had enjoyed the act of composition and he had received not a few calls. The ad had generated confessions concerning giant problem pines that dropped their needles onto the surfaces of reflecting pools and loomed over rooftops shading the new solar panels, or which had taken to swaying distressingly loose at the roots when the north wind rose. There were diseased trees, leafless and gaunt and sprouting contagious-looking boles on their trunks, and there were the unsanctioned scrub oaks the landscape architect had disparaged, and pear trees whose fruit progressed from unripe on the limb to rotten on the ground in a single night and then harbored wasps in the holes in their seepy, sticky sides. Desirable and expensively acquired views were blocked, branches rapped at windows like escapees from asylums on stormy nights, and buckling roots rippled pavements, crumpling and creasing imported tile and kiln-fired patio bricks. Trees, as Alden had surmised, were becoming just another variety of enormous weed to be removed as humans hacked suburbia out of the countryside.

This early November morning Alden had contracted a biggish job at the young Fairweathers who lived in a Tudor split level on an inner cul-de-sac in the executive neighborhood that had grown up down the road at the edge of Lily's property—or the former executive neighborhood, as Towneites had started to call the area after a long bad summer for corporate downsizing and the selling of real estate. Alden drove past the FOR SALE signs still pitched on the front lawns of the French chateau, the saltbox with diamond-paned windows, the stucco Southwestern ranch, the modern place all jutting angles and plate glass. A traditional garrison Colonial wasn't for sale but the powerboat was, trucked home from the Marina and parked in the drive with a sign slung over the gun-wale. Becky and Ginger had gone down to these people's yard sale a few weeks earlier and reported they wanted $25,000 for their dining room set, not an antique but one so recently acquired that the white linen seat pads showed pristinely clean in the brilliant autumn sunshine when set out on the ill-tended lawn (for they had quite obviously canceled the service).

"Not to my taste," Becky had said as if, otherwise, she might have been interested, as if her own much nicer dining room furniture were not stacked in the barn bundled beneath tarpaulins. Ginger had stalked the sale muttering, M.M.T.T., which was her code for More Money Than Taste, a charge so manifest that Becky had been convinced everyone within earshot had cracked the cypher for themselves. Because Ginger had been so indiscreet, Becky had bought a set of chrome and cylindrical Old-Fashioned glasses for which she paid the asking price and expressed far more liking than she felt, spending M.M.T.T.W.W., More Money Than They Were Worth, her sister-in-law had whispered in her ear.

Alden had pulled up in front of 117 King Arthur's Court for the initial interview with the Fairweathers. He had suppressed a smile as he mounted their marble steps and located the doorbell button concealed in the finial of a fleur de lys. He had read the book featured on their coffee table, the solid block of *Foucault's Pendulum*. "The next big effort," Alden had said, tolerantly. He wore a clan scarf with an air of entitlement. Some-how, in the course of their preliminary chitchat (he had spotted the brochure) the subject of Caneel Bay had come up and Alden allowed he and his family had enjoyed their first five visits, but not the sixth, irrationally so, he admitted, holding the management responsible for some very foul weather. They had vacationed next in the Seychelles but the children had not cared for the spicy food and the great circling sharks in the Indian Ocean who were keen to devour the spicy people.

Alison Fairweather's eyes had met Glen's. They had had such bad luck with an ex-hippie carpenter and again with an ex-priest marriage counselor that they had vowed not to hire anyone else who had an ax to grind as the result of a midlife crisis and collapse, although in the case of a prospective lumberjack ax-grinding was not necessarily a negative quality (Alison had made a private joke).

Adjourning outside, they had tramped around the grounds. Glen revealed his anxieties, pointing out, if felled incorrectly, his trees (see the doomed one pre-tied around with red ribbons) would crash onto the gazebo roof or slice through power lines or crush the new struggling plantings of the Home Grow-A-Maze kit (a second-wedding present to the Fairweathers). Alden had jotted with a yellow pencil stub on the back of the forwarded envelope in which his latest Platinum Card statement had arrived. The Fairweathers had stamped their feet and blown into their hands in the chilling shade their trees cast across the earth but would not cast much longer, evidently, for Alden's estimate seemed reasonable even though he was going to have to hire another man, as Alden had heard himself explaining.

Now, this morning, they both had early meetings but the Fairweathers waited for Alden and his assistant to show up. Alden's proposed eightish E.T.A. proved to be eight twenty-one. Someone—the Fairweathers didn't know about Ginger—had written FREE JEAN HARRIS in the dust of Alden's station wagon's rear window. Alden introduced Gee Weeden, his helper. Gee, a tongue-tied bachelor in his forties, tugged the bill of his Patriot Rebuilt Motors cap and commenced hauling the ropes and saws out of the car as Alden and Glen cleared up a misunderstanding concerning stumps, stump removal being another matter altogether from tree cutting.

"I'll leave low stumps," Alden said.

"And then what? Then what am I supposed to do?" Glen could suddenly turn combative. The ex-priest marriage counselor had been no help at all, advising him to picture his anger heaped upon a raft floating away down a mountain river and out of his life forever, but Glen's raft always capsized in the rapids and his anger, wet and sputtering, washed back to shore.

"You can bore holes in the stumps and fill them with buttermilk," Alden said, "and they rot right away from a fungus. After a while."

Glen said that sounded highly unlikely but Alden knew he'd read or heard of the method somewhere and they argued the point rather tentatively.

Alison startled Gee by speaking to him, asking him if he had been following the remarkable news from Berlin. (She always had to be the pleasant one.) Gee dropped a handsaw which struck a boulder and emitted a cautionary and distressed two-tonal ping which was to resonate in Alden's mind as the day's cautionary leitmotif. For he was beginning to wonder whether some of the red ribbons hadn't been retied around around taller and bulkier and more treacherously sited trees. Furthermore, Glen didn't seem to remember having agreed to leave cash in the mailbox for Alden to pick up on his way home. Glen now required an itemized bill for his accountant. Alden was beginning to understand why Gee looked so old for his age and why he started when spoken to and answered back warily, keeping his seamed face expressionless. Gee, who was wifeless and childless and who spent his days out-of-doors handily repairing, painting, and puttering around, or sitting snugly by the woodstove in the Co-Op's back storeroom usefully recalling where the spare box of ice scrapers had been stashed the previous May—Gee was on his second pacemaker. He'd worn out the first one from the beating it took.

ANDY SHUT HIS WINDOW after Lily, choosing to believe herself invisible, failed to return his wave. The window escaped his grip and slammed itself down. The casing was missing its ropes and weights and had to be propped open in warmer weather with a notched stick. Shortly after he moved in, Miss Hill had confiscated the stick. He trusted it would be returned in the spring and he had almost resolved to perch here until spring, if only to test this thesis.

The Hills were not warm and openhearted people, he had decided. They had not filled in his preliminary questionnaires in the natural course of rising to a usual standard of a willingness to please. He had not, in the past few weeks, been made welcome among the Hills so much as become lost in the crowd. Harvey Hill, the antic old uncle, kept calling him by the names of the resident boys although Andy did not in the least resemble any of that crew with their wide, dough-colored faces in which too small features had settled too close together in the middles of their half-baked heads while cooling. They had such an unrisen look, dull raisin eyes, pinched plugs of dough for their noses, rounded plugs of dough for their assertive chins. It had been a while since he himself had been a boy or had been among boys, but he was not yet far enough removed from the experience to remain unaffected by the cracks in their voices and the tight longings that distracted and distorted them.

Andy wished he could shake the contents of their brains into a burlap bag to sort through at his leisure with gloves on.

However, he further recalled as he sat on a needlepoint cushion, a Skye terrier depicted in fraying stiches, raising him up on his short-legged desk chair, he was supposed to leave personal descriptions out of his work. He riffled through a stack of 3 × 5 cards bearing blackly inked notes in his private shorthand—no vowels, verbs, or connectives. At first glance, his notes resembled personal ads in an alternative weekly which only those compelled by loneliness or lust could bother to decipher. When the family was more used to him, perhaps he would ask to measure their noses and the distances between their eyes and the lengths and angles of their jaws and thus objectively chart and account for that phenomenon known as a family resemblance. But then he would have to go out and graph a selection of random faces to demonstrate variant general population characteristics because, he supposed, all he would prove would be the existence of ordinary, not remarkable (except in the case of Betsy and Ginger, and Ginger was fading) looks all around which was not the sort of discovery the examination committee expected its candidates to bring before them. Professor Janacek's standing order was, "*Frighten* me, my students." He leaned back in his endowed swivel chair and commanded, "Knock me out." It had been a temptation not to shoot out a foot and tip him over.

For Andy had, in his extended academic past, been labeled a Romantic. He had been warned against employing too novelistic an approach. Reality was not shapely. Data did not develop along the lines of character, theme, plot, conflict, and resolution. His various mentors called for more statistics, most of them in the Eastern European accents of refugees who had been cast adrift from their own anecdotal pasts and so begrudged him his familiarity with his own native culture, or so Andy believed. Perhaps now, if the morning's news on his radio was anything to go by, they could all go back to their soon-to-be-free history-trampled little homelands, although he doubted they would return except, perhaps, for big emotional visits, their expandable luggage stuffed with bottles of Kentucky bourbon rolled in Banana Republic T-shirts and stonewashed denim jackets.

Andy had been accused of inserting too much of himself into his research. He had given money to a colony of street people he was studying. He had bought them sandwiches, found them winter coats, and got them into shelters, those who agreed to go. He had signed on one of the more mentally able derelicts at a computer training school. Andy was about to be failed for the semester when the local news heard about his efforts. (Renata, who had been on his side then, had made a few calls.) Andy was featured in a "Special Report: Making a Difference, Everyday Heroes" segment on the local Channel 6. Whereupon Andy had asked for an extension and turned his senior-term project into a study of The Further Effects of Media Attention upon an Average Citizen's Life (his own). His colony of street people had accused him of exploiting them and demanded money, their fair share of the money they assumed he had earned for being famous. The Mayor had sent Andy a congratulatory letter which Andy had deconstructed to prove that the Mayor resented Andy for calling attention to the problems on the Mayor's streets.

After this incident, Professor Janacek had suggested Andy remove the letter I from his word processor keyboard.

"Sir?" asked Andy, mentally spelling *sr*. "What do you mean?"

"This will rechannel your emphasis."

"Rechannel, you say?"

"In my country, all typewriting and information reproducing machines must be registered with the authorities." One of Professor Janacek's wandering observations.

"Sir? Well, power to the people." Andy believed that was what they used to say back in the olden days.

Now, Andy switched on his desk lamp. He had bought his own 100-watt long-life soft-light G.E. bulb which, nevertheless, flickered and stuttered and strained in the socket of the rickety old tole lamp that had been provided him. He was leery of the lamp, which dealt out sporadic shocks. And he had learned not to touch the lamp and his computer at the same time for electric impulses shot from hand to hand tracing a route across his shoulder blades causing the computer screen to blurt out ancient data like the draft of one last conciliatory letter to Renata he thought he had dumped. The shock activity seemed only to happen when he was barefoot and there may have been more causes but he was not keen to explore them, and as a result of those early jolts he approached his desk, when he approached his desk, warily.

The plane of the desktop struck his ribs as Andy leaned over his work. He needed to rise upon another cushion. The chair legs had lost their casters although he doubted the casters were truly lost. He would bet they had been preserved somewhere, in some corner he had yet to discover down in the cluttered cellar or out in the crowded barn or under the attic's overstressed eaves, or at the bottom of a rattling tin receptacle shoved to the back of a stuck-shut drawer. Then again, were he to refit the casters to the legs of his chair (rods slotted into drilled holes—he had upended the chair to see how) he might be inconvenienced by instability. His floorboards sloped noticeably northward and he pictured himself rolling slowly backward until he was caught by the opposite wall.

He reviewed the notes of the conversation he had held last night with Harvey outside the bathroom door, which Andy was finding a useful venue for striking up the odd conversation. If he lingered, a towel over his arm and his soapdish in hand, the Hills tended to chat divertingly at him as they edged themselves between him and the bolted bathroom

door. They favored him with a passing observation or a small recollection and then, as the bathroom fell free, they swiftly seized it first, breaking off midsentence, shortly informing him over their shoulders, Shan't
be half a mo'. This was considered fair trade by all.

Last night, Glover had been locked in the bathroom, endlessly show-
ering. It may have been the plash and gurgle of vigorously running
water, it may have been his own remark that young Glover was going to
grow gills, that caused Harvey suddenly to think of the frogs in the
swamps who said, Mud, mud, mud. *We* learned the word from *them*,
Harvey had informed Andy, way back in the shadowy mists of time.
Frogs have always spoken English? Andy had asked. This was *pre*-
Babel, Harvey informed him. Ah, said Andy.

In the spring, Andy determined, once his notched stick was returned
to him, he would prop open his window and listen out toward the
swamps to hear for himself these unlikely creatures calling.

HARVEY MADE the rounds of Senior Village enjoying another breakfast
and midmorning coffee and an early lunch on the strength of his shelf-
hanging abilities and his report of that morning's Cash Call fiasco and
further revelations concerning the latest Pearl Harbor of an offer on his
house in Connecticut. Everyone at Senior Village was a veteran of the
house wars, when they had all been told they should bite the bullet and
allow some nice young family, whose turn it was now, to buy their house
for a song. *That* was Communism right here and now in America, talk
about the Berlin Wall falling down.

"I mean to keep the chandelier," Harvey said. "After all, it's mine and
I want it. Venetian, you know, Venetian glass. Here?" He was holding a
nail against Penny Nicholls's buff-colored wall.

"Now, you have to be reasonable," Penny said. "Where would you
put it? Lower." She meant the nail should be placed lower on the wall.
"Because," she went on, "from your description, your chandelier would
be far too grand and big to hang just anywhere. In an ordinary house
everyone'd be bumping their heads. They'd get up in the middle of the
night with other matters in mind, and thump. And let me tell you from
personal experience it's very freeing to get rid of your old junk. Just

make them pay you a fair market price and walk away with your head held high."

"I can keep the chandelier in a box, if it comes to that. But *if* I sell it, I'll want top dollar. Tip top dollar," he declared as he struck the nail for emphasis. The nail bent into a U and the hammer bounced from his hand landing on a sofa cushion and jouncing onto the carpet just missing the kidney-shaped mahogany coffee table with the glass top that covered a gallery of grandchildren pictures from first grade through law and business school, the same faces losing their chubbiness and gaining wisdom. It made Penny so blue to look at them that she kept them covered most of the time with Pops albums and her current to-do list. She wouldn't have minded had a randomly flying hammer shattered her own wedding portrait, however, as it sat propped on an end table, not that her marriage hadn't been exceptionally happy but she had not been a pretty bride and she had never cared for the picture of record. She'd been a much better bargain than she seemed in the photograph.

"I'm pure brick beneath the plaster here," she told Harvey, recommending her construction. Senior Village occupied the old Towne Elementary School building, which had been replaced by a modern structure with a natatorium and an atrium and a Snapple dispenser in the cafeteria.

"Ah," Harvey regarded the wall. "You know, I think I went to the second grade in this apartment. I used to sit in your kitchenette, as it wasn't at the time. I was set in the back because I was tall, and up front in your dinette area was a row of the nearsighted ones, squinting, and Ben Elliott who was deaf as a pike, he could have sat on the teacher's lap and he wouldn't have heard anything. Weren't we primitive? But happy," he stated stoutly.

"Life is but a dream," Penny remarked as she always remarked whenever Harvey reminded her of days past. She knew, she knew. Sometimes when she was alone late at night she heard children's voices. She heard laughter and recitations which was lovely but nothing she was prepared to tell anyone about. They would explain it away or put her away, she told herself tartly.

"So this wall shouldn't give *me* trouble, bearing in mind our long-standing relationship." Harvey hammered again at a nail selected as sturdier. The tip penetrated a quarter inch, then that spike fell to the floor into the loopy wall-to-wall carpet.

"Rat crap," Harvey said and he and Penny lowered themselves stiffly to their knees and searched, dapping their fingertips across the floor. Penny didn't want to vacuum up a nail by mistake and puncture her vacuum cleaner hose because they had long since discontinued her model and subsequently its parts and she was devoted to her original Electrolux. Harvey, for his part, wished to find the nail so he could bash at it again with more science.

"Because," Penny said (like all women she could not let a subject just drop), "when you listed your house with the Land Pirate, did you say whether the chandelier would convey or not?"

"Convey or not?" Harvey mocked. "Convey or not?"

"Otherwise, your chandelier has to go with the house, anything that's actually attached remains with the house," Penny said.

"You mean all my paintings and the hunting prints in the library and the Coca-Cola bottle cap opener screwed to the end of the kitchen counter and even the plaster plaque thing young Arthur made me at summer camp when he was seven, displaying all his saved baby teeth arranged in a grin? I'm not sure I could trust eventual buyers to be fastidious about young Arthur's old teeth," Harvey said.

"No, no, decorative objects are different from actual fixtures," Penny said.

"I was an actual fixture in my leather lounger chair in the den, if that's the definition," Harvey told her. "I'll go with the house, shall I? That's what I really need, live-in help, somebody to be there should I step on soap in the bathtub or go rigid listening to the evening news or walk off and forget the teakettle's on. Found it," he added, and brandished the nail. He scrambled to his feet and offered assistance to Penny who still knelt, at a loss.

"Bum knee from all those power lunges at Joy of Movement," Penny explained.

"Bum knee," Harvey barked. "Now that's a physical impossibility."

. . .

DOWN IN THE DEEP BASEMENT of the First Congregational Church, Becky sat a bit apart from the others on a numbered (18) folding chair enjoying the luxury of thinking her own thoughts. She came to Women's Chorus to sing, not to socialize, and she had no wish to add her oar to the topic currently under discussion, deciding the final content of their Christmas program. There were factions forming roughly along the lines of traditionalists versus sophisticates. The sophisticates smiled encouragingly at Becky who had admitted to having had vocal training in the past (she'd been forced to, her ability had been too in evidence on the a capella numbers: she could always find her note). From time to time over the last weeks she'd been coming to chorus Becky had seemed to be on the verge of suggesting some embellishment or adventurous touch before recalling she was no longer in New York. Besides, she truly didn't care whether they sang the "Hallelujah Chorus" or merely "Joy to the World." She just went with the flow.

"What about trying 'Do They Know It's Christmas?,' the starving-Ethiopian song all the rock stars cooperated together and recorded?" asked Cindy Peck, who was very young.

"Of course they don't know it's Christmas. They're all Muslims over there in that part of Africa," Rosalie Chubb said. "Really, it's a very ignorant song and intellectually imperialistic to boot."

"No, no, I see that, but the sentiment is to share our happy spirit of generosity with them," Cindy said.

"Well, you don't see them coming over here offering to share Ramadan with us or whatever their big do is," Rosalie said.

"I shouldn't care for Ramadan. That's the one where you don't eat for a month, isn't it?" asked Anna Webster.

"Well, then, if *not* eating is such a virtue with them, I don't know what the problem is," Rosalie said. "Just call all hunger spells Ramadan. Make it a movable feast like Easter, or in their case, a movable fast. Ha."

The ladies stirred because Rosalie, while being so ungenerous was, nevertheless, almost making sense. But then, Rosalie was a real old Yankee, even for Towne. She was so practical she rinsed and reused her tinfoil until it caught fire in the oven and disflavored the re-reheated casseroles it covered. This was known.

There was a faded Civil Defense Fallout Shelter poster thumbtacked to the pale, paneled wall and child-drawn pictures of sunlit Christian days where houses, people, birds, and flowers were all of an equal size. A Sunday School attendance chart was posted for all the world to see. One distressingly blank week someone explained parenthetically in red ink—*flu bug rampant*. If it were the Middle Ages they would have written the message upside down so God could look down from His cloud and read it, Becky reflected, remembering her Art History. She hoped she wasn't coming down with the flu. When she was feverish, her mind raced and she remembered schooly facts. The honey and lemon hadn't helped. It never did, except for the seconds the mixture took to pass through her clogged throat affording a moment of clarity which seemed to make the reclogging worse.

She harrumphed testily. There was a full feeling and a scratchy roughness down there, and a sense of discomfort was forging a passage toward her ears.

"Yes, Mrs. Lowe? You have a suggestion?" Trinka Benson asked.

She had, thus far, failed to become Becky here which was how she wished matters to remain. As Mrs. Lowe, she could be less easily asked to Xerox sheet music or chauffeur stranded members, or bake cakes for Sales or sew concert robes or create nametags or centerpieces or otherwise be volunteered to perform those time-consuming and innately female tasks which prettified or cushioned or diverted, which perhaps might even be said to civilize, but really, these days it hardly seemed important to her to spend several evenings making fifty holiday ribbon nametag rosettes to hand out to the audience at the Restport Nursing Home concert. How very nice nice women strove to be. And then the Restport residents would be left with some crumpled clutter of ribbon which they themselves were too nice to throw away even though they had no space to spare in their tiny assigned rooms. The rosettes would be discovered crammed among their effects after they had died and, at last, be discarded by a niece or daughter steeled to be unsentimental. Then the niece or daughter would drive home swiping her eyes.

"I'm sorry," Becky said. "I was clearing my throat." Becky harrumphed again in demonstration and felt as if she had swallowed an angry hornet.

Viv Harricott said, "I think we should demonstrate by song our support of German reunification."

"Not necessarily," Naomi Liebenthal spoke up, and everyone murmured at her strong assertion.

Yes, her ears were going to be involved. It was as if she were listening through damp cotton balls and Becky prodded her temple where the faint crease of a headache was setting in behind her eyes. What she really needed was to lie upon a tropical beach and bake out her head cold. Rum punches wouldn't hurt, and a stack of best-sellers to pick up and put down between naps and treks to the buffet table. The children could be signed up for sailing lessons, daylong sailing lessons, overnight sailing lessons that involved trips to uninhabited islands where they would be left for three days with an iron pot and a book of matches and a jug of fresh water and be told to find their own ways home. Alden could go snorkeling or something. He could visit the local Institute of Seashells and return enthusiastic about seashells.

It occurred to Becky that, had she answered that morning's WROC Cash Call correctly, she could have afforded to fly off to a sun-stunned island. But first, had she $10,000 to throw around, she'd buy the kids five pairs of Levi's apiece which would take a bite of $400 or so, and then she'd have that jangly situation underneath the car's carriage dealt with which Alden said the mechanic said sounded like $1,200 to him, and then they'd siphoned $3,000 from Little Becky's college trust to pay an unexpected tax bill, vowing to replace the money as soon as possible, and besides, a big quarterly medical insurance bill was looming.

Anna Webster whispered at Becky, "I want to apologize to your sister-in-law for not waving to her just a while ago as she drove past my house. I couldn't imagine who that could be with Goody Palmer so I called Babe and we worked it out after I described the woman's hair which is what I best caught a glimpse of. Babe knew her right away from my description of her hair and her general, oh, you know, aura."

Oh dear, thought Becky. Ginger has an aura now.

Cindy Peck spoke up. "I still feel we should sing about *something* to acknowledge our appreciation of these exciting times."

"The times don't need the likes of us to acknowledge they may be exciting," Rosalie Chubb said. "I vote we leave well enough alone."

"Oh, all right, we'll have a vote," Trinka Benson said. Women's Chorus was a highly democratic institution. "Shall we acknowledge these exciting times or leave well enough alone is the question on the table," Trinka said.

"MEET YOU HERE at five-thirty, so I can fill you in on all the details," Ginger had told Goody as he let her off on Devonshire Street. "Thank you, thank you for all your assistance. I'd have been utterly lost without you. I'm so terribly encurged now that you've taken up my cause." She bumped the door shut, mislatched, and was gone. Traffic lurched as she stepped in front of fenders and Goody was unable to protest why he could not possibly pick her up at 5:30, that he did not require her thanks; moreover, he sincerely doubted she would be lost, utterly, without him, and indeed, he had not taken up her cause, he was not at all sure what her cause might be. An alerting buzz trilled at him from the dashboard. Goody stretched across the seat and yanked the door handle, secured. He drove on. But of course there could be no question that, having brought her here, Ginger must continue to be his responsibility. If he did not collect her at day's end she would be stranded in the darkening, emptying city creating and encountering uniquely, peculiarly Gingerish travails in the rain. He knew there would be rain, a drear drizzle heavily dripping down from the black cloud which she would claim had settled, inevitably, over her poor, bowed, humbled head for good, nay, that it had settled there for ill, Ginger would claim.

All that day, dire images of Ginger were to float across Goody's activated mind's eye—his imagination had been powerfully, unprecedentedly stimulated by her presence, and her imminence. His left thumb twitched vainly at the channel-changing button of a ghost remote. He was not accustomed to witnessing such dramatic goings-on in real life or, for that matter, as entertainment. Babe always brought Ealing Studio comedies home from Video 2000, except on his literacy volunteer night at the high school when she treated herself to something black and white and tragic. Then she sat by herself in the den with the shades pulled down talking back to the screen, always knowing better than the straying, sinning, beautiful actor-people what they ought to have

done, or, as was more often to the point, those things they ought not to
have done.

THE MECHANISM OF a crystal-encased clock on the big-parlor mantelpiece prepared to strike. The apparatus hitched, ratcheted, whirred, a
small brass hammer soundlessly tilted like a tomahawk. Andy had come
to the parlor fifteen minutes beforehand to dwell unchallenged in its
atmosphere of agedness and unaired graces, for he had not been encouraged to frequent this room. A pair of tall raised-panel doors between the
parlor and the front hall were always pulled closed and were one door
or the other to be found to have been left ajar, Lily or Harvey or Alden
or even Ginger would seek out any intruder among the formidable
ranks of armchairs and the pale and slightly a-bobble lampshades.

Andy wondered whether they were all caught under the sway of some
long gone but powerful personality, perhaps the very one who had caused
antimacassar to be piled upon antimacassar. For there were three doilies
placed on either arm of the wing chair upon which he had sat to declare
his right to sit there. He plucked at the dainty heap beneath his elbow
and to his inexpert eye it appeared that the finest piece of crocheting was
sandwiched between two lesser examples of the art. Andy wasn't sure
what to make of this, but not too much, he cautioned himself. Perhaps
the practice was simply a common and a "good" one. There was so
much he did not yet know about these people.

He balanced his notebook on the jut of his knee and he wrote swiftly,
"Every surface is barnacled with belongings." He picked up and examined and catalogued the items present upon an adjacent tabletop—a
porcelain plate, 12" round, fluted edge, floral pattern, Bristol imprint; an
embossed silver box containing safety pins and a button; the china figurine of a dapple-backed fawn; a small, stopped carriage clock; a tall
wooden Beefeater nutcracker perpetually choking on a well-stuck Brazil
nut; a length of maroon cording detached from the hem of a window curtain coiled inside an art pottery bowl. None of these objects had been
very recently dusted, but they were not not ever dusted, Andy estimated.

The small brass hammer fell and the clock struck a single, purely
pretty note. Lily drifted into the big parlor on the fading resonance of

the chime. She stuck her hand into the Delft basin full of dried lavender florettes sitting on the radiator cover and she churned them briefly. Motes huffed along a shaft of sunlight and flyaway specks of petal sifted down onto the several squares and oblongs of patterned carpets. Lily swiped her hand against her navy-blue wool-blend flank. Lavender debris was caught beneath her short fingernails and she didn't know why she had reached into the basin unless the act represented some deep-rooted impulse to clear the air of Andy, for she knew the action had been aimed against him. But Andy was not daunted. He remarked, "Very fragrant."

"Well, not really," Lily said. She ought to have added a few drops of lavender oil to the dried florettes last July but she'd been so distracted by the press of family events that spiking the potpourri had not been uppermost in her mind.

"Are we going to remain in here?" she asked, lifting her eyebrows, to suggest that Andy also rise.

"We'll be undisturbed in here," Andy said firmly.

They sat, at Lily's alternate invitation, at the large round table pushed into the bulge of a bay window. Lily tugged at the chain of a lamp to no avail and she tilted back the shade—bulbless. Andy was peered at— responsible?—for the thin line of light that burned around his door-jamb and sill late at night shone suspiciously bright. Lily reached and tugged apart heavy lined curtains exposing the light-diffusing sheers beneath, with the husk of some summer's dragonfly pinned between the folds. The table was clothed in maroon velvet edged with dull bullion fringe and topped by a lace runner made lacier by moths. The table supported a gallery of photographs in picture frames propped or standing in any order. Faces filled the frames, faces that staringly resented the picture-taking process, faces smiling at an off-camera individual, faces looking forward to the future, faces gazing backward toward the past. There were as well views of snow-covered mountainsides being conquered by tiny splinters of skiers, and of misty lakes upon which floated tiny, leaf-like canoes. A mustached man sat upon a biplane as delicate as the dragonfly. An aproned woman stood beside the back door with a crow at her feet.

Lily followed Andy's eye.

"Occasionally," she explained, "you come across a friendly crow."

"Who are they all?" Andy asked.

"Oh," Lily looked. "Us. You know." She puzzled at a skier. "Possibly Harvey," she identified him.

"Ah," said Andy.

Lily scraped her fingernails across the horsehair underside of the unsteady little side chair on which she sat. The rough fabric served as an emery board and scoured the lavender grit caught beneath her nails. A satisfied exhalation escaped her and Andy took heart.

"The Eskimos have over three hundred words in their vocabulary to describe snow, Miss Hill. Tell me, how many words do you have for vase?" he asked.

A flush of alarm crossed her face when Andy mentioned Eskimos. Lily would have read up on them in the family Britannica had she known they were going to be a subject for discussion. But she felt herself to be on firmer ground when Andy mentioned vase although he spoke the word in that curious out-of-state accent of his. Vaze, he'd said, rather oilily.

"Just vase," Lily supposed. "Vaze," she tried to say for Andy's benefit. "Unless, do you mean, cut glass or pressed glass or Depression glass or Sandwich glass or cranberry glass vases? Are you interested in bud vases? There's a piece of my grandmother's Meissen, or that lusterware amphora. But then, I often throw flowers into drinking glasses or the lemonade pitcher when it's not being used for lemonade, just because they're at hand. But that Wedgwood ewer on the mantel is lovely except it has an invisible crack so I can't use it, it seeps. Then there's all that Hull Art pottery, not my favorite thing but people gave it to teachers at one time. I confess, I can be confused by the shapes and what's called what. My sister, Olive, was up on all that but then she collected. Delft. All the Delft you see was hers." And which would have, should have, gone to Ginger but Ginger had once made a face and uttered, "Not more Delft, Mother?" as another posset pot was lifted from tissue wrappings. Ginger had refused to apologize to Olive, so that was that.

Lily indicated the basin full of dried lavender. This was going quite well. Andy hadn't asked her anything impertinent or upsetting, and she decided she would also be prepared to discuss silverware patterns and he might even wish to hear about her garden and her efforts to locate authentic plants.

Andy, writing rapidly, said, Whoa, and Lily subsided, easily quietened, because she didn't after all trust this talking business, chattering on and on about her own concerns. But she could see how one could come to make a habit of monologizing. One's own thoughts were not uninteresting to oneself and one did not necessarily even know what was occupying one's mind until a view was given voice. Nearly everyone she knew had long since fallen into the practice; everybody talked. Nobody listened at Eastern Star meetings; Patsy Parker had to flicker the lights for silence so they could induct new members and even then inductions degenerated into free-for-alls of private conversations. Lily blamed television. Her own family kept up a discourse during every program—*Is that a wig? Well, I hope his hair isn't real, a wig can be returned, a wig can be complained of. Is he married? Still? To her? Hush, he's about to unmask the true murderer. Yes, yes, I know the landlord did it. The concert pianist was his illegitimate son and he was avenging the hand accident.*

"Well, just vase," Lily supposed again, and she scrubbed her fingernails across her navy-blue wool-blend-covered knee. She had exchanged the lavender grit beneath her nails for horsehair fiber shreds. She flicked her thumb against her index finger and then, aware she was fidgeting, she willed herself to bear all in stillness just as she had been taught as a girl.

Andy had caught up with her, his pen tapping out his private shorthand. "And Delft?" he prodded, but Lily only nodded and noticed a curl of loose wallpaper lifting up from the wall behind Andy's left ear. The paper was maroon and printed with gold medallions which began to swim as she stared into them, recalling the circumstances of the paper's selection—in stock at Towne Decorating, ordered by someone else who had unfurled a bolt and experienced second thoughts. Well, it wasn't a very remarkable wallcovering but Lily had gotten such a good buy on it—eleven years later she remembered the seventy-two dollars she had saved below list price. Besides, she'd gone into Towne Decorating that day with her mind made up to special-order the Roman Holiday Stripes in peacock green and carousel yellow with a Tropical Fruit and Nesting Birds Swag border because she had thought she wanted a change from the eternal beige-on-beige rosettes she was replacing. A lucky escape, even though Ginger claimed the small gold medallions reminded her of trilobites and made her think of her own mortality, which was only an added attribute of the wallcovering, in Lily's opinion.

This is like wildlife photography, Andy decided. The antelopes are all lined up at the water hole and they scatter at the click of the shutter. He decided the time was right to admire something else in the room and he sought a likely object.

"Great table," he said. There were eleven of them distributed about the chamber, he quickly counted.

"Thank you," Lily said, not to be drawn out. She did not ask if he meant the drum table, the piecrust table, the old gateleg table, the carved mahogany marble-topped table, or the Queen Anne end tables positioned at either end of the camelback sofa. She nearly called his attention to the small Sheraton-style sewing table very like the one she had seen in the sitting room at Ash Lawn when she visited there but Lily was overcome by an awful insight that perhaps she liked her things too much and was recommending them too highly, for she ought to have mentioned her grandmother's vase just *might* be Meissen.

"They are only objects," Lily reminded herself.

"Indeed, only objects," agreed Andy and he ruffled to another notebook page. He had not hoped to draw out Miss Hill on a big wandering concept at this initial interview but as she had declared herself to be above the merely material, he decided to ask, "Do you find yourself becoming more and more adrift as the nineteenth century floats further and further away from you, Miss Hill?"

"How old do you think I am?" Lily asked in genuinely amazed challenge and as Andy had estimated she stood somewhere between seventy-five and the end, he bent his head over his notebook page.

"Can you complete this sentence for me, Miss Hill? 'The highest good that man can attain is—' " he read.

Lily noticed that the antimacassars on the arm of the wing chair in which Andy had been sitting when she entered the big parlor had been picked up and put down.

"Fill in the blank," Andy prompted.

"Yes, I understand," Lily said. "Do you want me to say something along the lines of saving a life, or killing an evil tyrant, or painting a masterpiece, or planting enough wheat in Africa, or curing diseases, or nursing the dying?" That was all she could come up with off the top of her head.

"*I* don't want you to say anything in particular. Say what *you* think," Andy said.

"And did you mean the highest good a *man* can attain, or mankind which would include women, who I personally believe possess many different abilities from men, in which case I might have to answer that raising decent and successful children is a very great good," Lily said.

"Let's say humankind," Andy suggested.

"Humankind," Lily repeated and she frowned for in her mind's eye all of humankind suddenly appeared en masse whom she saw as naked yet genderless, and milling about on a grassy plain very early on in the history of the world, at considerable risk from the gathering elements and perhaps from one another as they began to notice and then to heft rocks and sticks in a meaningful manner. She wished Andy hadn't mentioned humankind. She had had no idea she felt this way about humankind.

"There is no right answer," Andy said.

"But your statement is posed as if there were," Lily said. "Besides, I think there must be a correct answer, and I wouldn't be surprised if the correct answer turned out to be something simple and surprisingly practical like maintaining the money supply and the free market and encouraging capitalism, though perhaps that concept is just in the air today." She gestured in the general direction of Germany. "But Harvey could explain better than I and expand upon the reasons."

"Indeed," said Andy. "Still, why don't you tell me the answer that is right for *you*."

"Then I think I may be leaning toward the wheat," Lily allowed, "in East Africa, that is, if the climate and soil are suitable for wheat."

Andy didn't know. "Wheat, potatoes, manioc," he shrugged.

"But I'm also very much in favor of children being successfully launched as well," Lily added. "No, let's stick with the wheat. You can't learn much if you're hungry," she said as Andy sagged over his notebook, erasing her answer. His alert interviewer's expression had momentarily slipped sideways. He reminded Lily of several of her acquaintances who had lately suffered strokes and were not doing well.

"We'll ask Harvey later about the highest good because in his working life he sometimes had a role in things that actually mattered, you know," advised Andy almost kindly. She saw now she was going to have to be kind to Andy. She wished he would go away, but she gathered he had nowhere else to go and nothing else to do but inflict himself upon near strangers who were in no position to help anyone for they could not even help themselves at the moment; nevertheless, Andy was counting on them all to make his thesis possible and thus, she supposed, the rest of his life. Some old teacher's instinct had kicked in. Youth must be served, she concluded with a sigh.

"I'll tell you one thing I have always found to be true," Lily said. "I've never had a rug taken up that I haven't found a penny underneath, slid far beneath the rug and the pad."

"Indeed?" asked Andy, and he wrote upon a fresh notebook page and highlighted what he had written by inscribing a box around the words and starring it with an anemone-like asterisk.

They both relaxed. Lily touched her snowy cloud of hair and resettled her hands in her lap and Andy asked a string of harmless questions then which did not tax and sometimes tickled her.

GINGER HAD PLANNED a busy day for herself in Boston. Shopping came first. She squirmed in and out of cocktail dresses at Bonwit's fancy frocks department and then she had a long consultation at the Chanel counter, gravely discussing her options and ultimately agreeing to give their foundation one more chance, but in a darker shade. She decided she couldn't say no to a pair of kid gloves she spied on her way out the door. She examined bracelets at Shreve, Crump, and Lowe and said she would have to think about the emerald one but she purchased a sterling silver key chain curled in the shape of a question mark because she had left her old key case back in Kansas dropped into the Pawnee basket on the Pembroke table in the front hall and she'd been making do with the one Lily had given her to hold her single house key, an orange plastic disk, bearing the message, COMPLIMENTS OF NORCO FUEL, SNUGGLE UP WITH US THIS WINTER. She bought a paisley shawl at Burberry's after trying on their raincoats and a walking suit that, frankly, looked like something the second Mrs. de Winter would have worn, Ginger declared to all within hearing. She rummaged through their handbags and sprayed their perfumes on her wrist and found nothing to tempt her on the condiments shelf. Nor did she care for the specially advertised holiday dresses at Lord & Taylor, too fussy and froufrou, she complained, although the very young salesgirl answered back that they were gala dresses, young and gala dresses. At Laura Ashley, after flipping through a basket of ruffly-edged place mats, Ginger announced, in her carrying voice, she was afraid she just wasn't the Laura Ashley type, she was not afflicted by a deep nostalgia for all the pale chintz cushions and Blue Willowware china and manicured cricket lawns that had never been in the first place. She marched back to Burberry's and returned the paisley shawl she had just bought there, suddenly going off English goods, she told them as her reason, because Burberry's had rather insisted on being told one before giving her her refund. She thoughtfully leafed through the travel books at Rizzoli's and she bought a Blue Guide to France. The clerk assumed she was about to embark on a lovely trip to Paris and he told Ginger he envied her. Ginger didn't set him straight. She regarded him as if she were already far away. Then she headed for Filene's Basement where she recognized all the silk and cashmere sweaters with the labels sliced out as having come from last year's Anne Klein collection and she bought herself a cardigan in every color, plus a terribly sweet needlepoint cushion that read "If you have nothing nice to say, come sit by me" which had been misplaced among the sweaters, otherwise she would not have come across it. She also bought a pair of knee-high cashmere socks for Alden. They cost only ninety-five cents but there didn't seem to be anything very wrong with them, at least as far as she could tell when she held them together, heels to toes.

Ginger had been keeping up a brisk pace, and she searched for and rediscovered a Brigham's, where she ordered a strawberry sundae. She sat at the counter with her shopping bags clenched between her feet so she wouldn't forget them when she left. A tear touched her eye as she thought of her mother (a sweet thought, for once, about her mother) who always sought out a Brigham's after a buying spree. They had always tried to order something different, convincing themselves that this time they were really going to order something else up to the instant they heard their own voices asking for a strawberry sundae, after all, and coffee ice cream with marshmallow sauce and chopped walnuts, and a single glass of ice water to share between them since her mother had seemed to think ice water was such an "extra."

Ginger was heartened to recall what decent stock she had sprung from and how aspects of that native goodness had infused her when she had lived and moved among her kinfolks. She had been simple, then, susceptible, sweet. She must make a mantra of her positive qualities to fortify herself for her upcoming consultation. She was worthy, deserving, beloved. She must remember that she was someone who could not possibly be the villainess in a heated divorce action. She looked at her watch. She would have to dash if she was going to be not too late for her afternoon appointment at Rowe's Wharf where she had a meeting scheduled with that attorney friend of Alden's, an old school connection to whom, Alden had told her, he had once given valuable investment advice of a negative nature. "I'd steer clear of those particular boys were it my hard-earned dollar I was risking," Alden had said, which was really more than he should have said at the time.

Ginger had not met Ron Revenaux at Alden's wedding. This was an ancient grudge because Ginger had been unmarried and Ron had been available and one's brother's wedding was supposed to be an occasion for encountering very possible prospects. That was written in stone, or, possibly, blood. But Ron, in an early-on career coup, had been too busy prosecuting some ungrammatical but noteworthy Mafiosi at the time to meet friend's sisters, however lovely they were promised to be. Ron had, however, been one of those people whom Ginger had filed away for one purpose or another and lately she had pressured Alden for this belated introduction, letting him know that if her future happiness and security were compromised by inadequate legal representation the bitter blame would be heaped on his head.

"If you can find any room left up there, my head is yours to saber dance on," Alden had told her; nevertheless he called Ron on Ginger's behalf and incidentally mentioned his own situation which seemed a more graceful way of getting the word out in that particular quarter, just as an afterthought, nothing urgent about Alden's circumstances, but about his *sister*, his admittedly rather headstrong sister . . .

Ron Revenaux, who had been such a tantalizing mystery for so many years proved after all not to be her type, Ginger saw at once as she was wafted into his office by a fragrant assistant wearing an ultrasuede ensemble. (Saks had been swelling with ultrasuede and Ginger had to admit it looked well on.) Ron wore a dark blue suit with a just too wide and wide apart chalky stripe which struck her as rather gangster-ish, a bit of bravado left over from his crime-busting days. He was a little man (Alden ought to have mentioned that back in 1969 and saved her years of fretting over Ron). He sat behind a desk the dimensions of a billiard table. Its broad polished surface seemed to billow, a trick of the light. He compensated with the costume and the desk, Ginger adjudged him automatically as she shrugged her fur coat from her shoulders and arranged her shopping bags around her slender crossed ankles. It occurred to her that her shopping paraphernalia with the expensive logos on display (she had hung on to the Burberry bag) cast her in a less forlorn role than she had meant to act out that day, but as she gazed upon burnished tropical hardwood paneling—which winked back—and listened to the low, expensive humming of some remote appa-ratus that provided perfect air at a perfect degree and which fluttered almost alive across one's cheek, she realized that the prevailing sympa-thies hereabouts would lie with someone who did not deny herself. And was that not a small Hockney on the wall, a swimming pool scene? Hockney was always swimming pools, wasn't he? Ginger regretted she hadn't indulged herself after all at Shreve's, where she had very much desired a silver-barreled Mont Blanc pen for book-writing purposes.

A light pulsed on the beautiful face of his sleek telephone system. Forgive him. Ron had to take this call.

Oh, why hadn't Louis become this kind of attorney? Ginger thought of Louis in his shirtsleeves with his half glasses sliding down his nose answering his own noisy telephone as he sat beneath a blown-up photo-graph he had taken himself of a domestic sunset. Ginger eyed the Bachrach portrait of Ron's eventually acquired family, a tall, blond wife with a pretty but insipid face, two dainty fair daughters, a tall dark son . . .

Ginger, not openly listening to Ron, who had swiveled round in his deep leather chair, nevertheless overheard words that at once soothed

and excited her. "... go easy on deutsche marks ... must reposition ourselves now ... what's the last word from Geneva?"

"Forgive me," Ron said, swinging round again to face her with, Ginger noted, a reassumed expression of compassionate patience; when a
minute before, upon seizing the telephone receiver, his look had sharpened and grinned into one of wolfish animation. But this was, Ginger
thought, precisely the range of emotion one should wish for in one's
attorney.

"I don't know what Alden has told you about my situation," Ginger
said. She was sure wicked Alden had offered a version, and an opinion,
and a caveat.

"Why don't you tell me in your own words," Ron offered.

So Ginger explained and expressed herself articulately and com-
pellingly as was her way. Ron tented his hands and balanced his chin
upon the ridgepole.

"So you see. So you do see," Ginger concluded, smilingly inviting
him to—see, and to inform her precisely what sort of picture she had
limned. Besides, one rather needed to be told how one was viewed.
Then, necessary adjustments could be tweaked and twitched.

Ron's face slipped behind his tented hands. He pinched the bridge of
his nose between his thumbs and he passed his hands back and forth as if
dispersing a cloud, these choreographed tics signaling his sincere concentration upon the facts of the case at hand, Ginger decided. Oh, she
was such a student of men she found her knowledge distracting.

Ron pointed out, "You resided in Kansas for the majority of your
marriage. Have you come to Massachusetts for a no-fault divorce?
Don't you have no-fault in Kansas? This is not, as Alden must have told
you, my area of expertise."

"But it's not a no-fault divorce I'm after. I want Louis to—" Ginger
stopped herself before she uttered the word pay, or she may have been
about to blurt (most irretrievably) suffer. She might even have meant to
say, I just want Louis to sit up and take notice. Ginger herself wasn't
sure why she had stalled on the very brink, it seemed, of a revelation,
but, best to let Ron tell her what she ought to want, what she should
realistically want.

"And as I understand you, there was fault and the fault lay on your side," Ron observed, across his broad desk.

"Ah, but you see, if we examine the roots of the estrangement, you'll realize that Louis's neglect and indifference and absences, particularly during that disastrous political campaign of his, all of that drove me to do what I did," Ginger explained. "Possibly as a cry for help."

"Yes, well," Ron said, "to be perfectly frank and I'm not doing you any favors by not being perfectly frank, that's not the best argument for you to make, that that devil Louis made you do it."

"It's an excellent argument," Ginger declared, "because I know it's the truth and I always face up to the truth regardless and soldier on bravely from there."

"Yes, you certainly strike me as a self-sufficient woman, exceedingly able and strong and independent, who knows her own mind and is in charge of her own destiny," Ron said.

"Yes, I am. I am in charge of my own . . ." Ginger began eagerly to agree before she stumbled smack into his trap. What a pitiless cross-examiner Ron must be. Somebody remind her not to run numbers for the mob, should she ever sink so low.

Ron suppressed a smile behind retented hands. He said, "I think, in a case like yours, when a woman, particularly a woman past her first youth, is contemplating leaving her marriage, she ought to ask herself this question—what shall I be doing a year from now?"

"What shall I be doing a year from now?" Ginger repeated. Well, she'd be a published authoress frantically busy on a book tour, having lost twenty-five pounds. She would be living in some charming old brick Back Bay building with a roof terrace where she sincerely hoped there would be someone waiting to greet her with a glass of wine and exclamations of delight. Perhaps he was someone she had yet to meet. Yes, this was going to be a busy year and she was keen to get started.

"At any rate, bearing in mind your ideal image of a year hence, let me tell you off the top of my head what you can expect by way of a settlement here in the Commonwealth in your general situation," Ron said.

It was all very well and good for Ron, fiddling now with a valuable old green-and-white-cane Clichy globe paperweight (symbolically holding her world and her fate in his hands, Ginger understood) to lecture her about the need to downscale her lifestyle (Ginger rustled shopping bags) and to recommend petitioning for additional funds to retrain her for a suitable occupation (a computer course, he suggested, just off the top of that legal-brained head of his), although significant employment opportunities were not abundant for women her age. Furthermore, she would have to plan for her retirement years which were not, if one did the math, so incalculably far off.

Ginger, who was not hearing what she had come to hear, ceased listening. She studied Ron's daily view of the harbor through his several vast windows—lead-grey wintry waves bumping and jostling as if there weren't enough room for them all in all the Atlantic Ocean, gulls skidding backwards, caught on drafts. Planes landed and took off from Logan, climbing and coming down so low over a water-route flight path one could almost make out faces at the windows. A tanker so large and so long that it seemed not to be moving at all was pointed toward the open sea. Only by tracking the tanker's central superstructure's position relative to a building on a harbor island could she tell any headway was being made.

". . . and child support," Ron was saying, "will be in effect for a few months more since the child in question will soon turn eighteen, although should she remain in school, the period will be extended."

"She's school mad, that one," Ginger spoke up.

"And there needn't be a custody question," Ron concluded. "At least, I should hope not," he warned.

"My good friend Bonnie in Kansas who was married to an utter fiend got the house in town and the time-share in Telluride, the stock portfolio, a clothing allowance, and alimony and a restraining order," Ginger roused herself to inform him.

"Perhaps there was a prenuptial agreement in that case," Ron suggested.

"Not in our day, there wasn't. We didn't know what they were, we were so naïve," Ginger remembered.

"And is there a time-share in Telluride among your assets?"

"No, not actually."

"Then we needn't concern ourselves . . ."

"Oh, needn't we?" Ginger asked, with acid on her tongue.

SINCE HIS ARRIVAL, since his begrudged yet strangely unopposed and perhaps even more weird, his scarcely acknowledged admittance to the house, Andy had embarked upon a conscientious campaign of ingratiation. He paid particular attention to Mrs. Lowe, whom he had spotted from the first as a likely source to cultivate—a middle-aged, middle-class woman burdened with a distracted husband and truculent children, and stranded high and dry in the underequipped kitchen of an aunt by marriage as a bleak Northeastern winter lowered beyond every smudged and draft-flowing window where dispirited curtains sullenly flipped. Becky's loneliness, her thwarted sociability, and her natural niceness as well wanted an outlet and, Andy figured, he and Mrs. Lowe could only be of assistance to one another in the months to come.

He had shifted unpacked boxes for Becky up in her overstuffed attic without questioning why the shifting had been necessary. He had helped Becky find her madeleine pans, lost at the bottom of the last box he looked in. He had assisted, holding apart the flaps of a carton, when Becky decided to put away Alden and the boys' summer seersucker suits. When she needed to lay her hands on her annotated Schubert *Schwanengesang* for Women's Chorus, Andy had slapped through bundled stacks of music as Becky told him how, when she was singing at her best, her voice took on an amethyst-colored presence that enveloped her listeners and herself. Andy, crouched beside a carton, thought, How much these cartons contain.

He routinely carried Becky's grocery bags in from the back of the station wagon. He had asked if he might track how often she had to replace laundry detergent, mayonnaise, grape jelly, mustard. He calculated the ratio of fresh to prepared food that Becky brought home, and they discussed how to categorize fresh-frozen vegetables. They counted as prepared food, Becky thought, for she bought frozen broccoli spears for their convenience. But Andy maintained that nutritionally, fresh and fresh-frozen must be almost the same and Becky had conceded the point for, of course, she hoped the statistical balance would tip in favor of freshness even though none of this was a contest, Andy had assured her.

After the satisfactory conclusion of his session with Lily—at the end she had offered him a peppermint from a domed dish on the mantelpiece and he had taken three (he had had to, they were fused)—Andy had listened for the sound of the Buick nosing up the driveway as Becky returned from choral practice and a run of errands. He met her by the barn and carried in her grocery bag, dry cleaning, library books, and the six empty beer cans she had noticed tossed out around the base of the mailbox for which she hoped her boys were not responsible. She didn't think the boys would drink Miller Lite by their druthers but she planned to set the cans conspicuously upon the lid of the aluminum recycling bin in the pantry and keep a weather eye out for any unnatural reactions, for, say, a striking avowal (though never an act) endorsing some universal and uncontroversial virtue, pronounced in the vicinity of the reproachful cans.

"I bought a gallon of two percent milk, bread, hamburger, and Granny Smith apples for two pies, one pie really isn't enough for all of us," Becky reported as she shed her coat and put on the kettle. "I have a Molly Keane from the library, I like her, plus *How to Build Your Own Stone House Using the Easy Slipform Method* which Alden requested, why I can't imagine. And the cleaners couldn't get the pine pitch from the front of Alden's jacket and his best tweed pants. I wish he'd pay more attention when he's out fooling with trees, he's ruined more good clothes. Oh, I forgot to put away the ironing board! You know, my cold suddenly felt better at the library, I suppose because my mind was better occupied, but I was croaking at Chorus. Has anyone called? Did you hear about the Cash Call this morning? The more I've thought about that, the more I'm inclined to agree that Alden really ought to have asked which Becky did they want? Oh, I'm sorry Andy, did you have a question?"

"Do you mind if I weigh all the grocery bags before you unpack them from here on? I've decided to document the accumulated tonnage of the average family's haul home from the supermarket," Andy said.

"Of course," Becky said. "Look, there's Ginger's scale right next to the refrigerator. It's digital and accurate. It's driving her crazy because she can't shade where an arrow is pointing." Becky considered. "But will that be useful to know, the accumulated weight of our groceries?"

"Oh yes," said Andy. "I need to know for my own records and then there may be other applications, for instance, as collateral data in a kinesiological study of the lifelong expenditure of muscular effort by the average American woman. Ben Gay might like to know."

"Huh," said Becky. "But are *we* an average family?" she asked, in hope, it seemed.

"It's this sort of inquiry that establishes a norm," Andy said.

"Can norms be *a* norm? Shouldn't they be *the* norm?" Becky asked.

"*The* norm is more and more becoming abnormal," Andy said.

"Oh dear," Becky said. "Still, hamburger, apple pie, Wonder Bread, milk," she repeated, reassured as Andy lowered the bag of groceries to the scale.

"Eight pounds," Andy said.

"Glover weighed eight pounds when he was born," Becky remembered.

"Ah," said Andy as he wrote in his notebook, Mlly Kn, Stn Hs Slp Frm? Pn Ptch, Csh Cll.

"And your William sent roses," Becky said. She piled apples in a wooden bowl, the prettiest, least marked, placed on top.

"What? William? Roses?" Andy asked, setting down his pen.

"When Glover was born, William sent red roses, such masses of them, I'd never seen so many outside of the Kentucky Derby," Becky said. She opened and closed cupboard doors and she began to consolidate the contents of several nearly empty cereal boxes into one—Rice Chex, Cheerios, and Raisin Bran poured into the Cap'n Crunch box to trick Little Becky into eating them because there was a strict rule, no one could unpour cereal no matter what slid into one's bowl.

"William always sent me savings bonds for my boyhood birthdays and Mother still receives baskets of crumpets and strawberry jam from some outfit in the Midwest. I think he placed a standing order twenty years ago."

"So thoughtful," Becky sighed.

Andy didn't agree. The standing order absolved William of all further thought, but he played the William card carefully around Becky.

"Yes, William's all right," Andy said.

"If only he'd settle down," Becky said, as she had said before, and Andy replied, as he had replied before, "Mother thinks he's carrying a torch." He used his mother's archaic term for what must be a rather old flame by now.

"Oh dear, isn't that a shame," Becky said as she always said in what had become a ritual exchange with Andy, when she invoked William and alluded to his mysterious romantic past and concluded on this comfortable note of regret. Andy privately theorized Becky had played some peripheral part in the long-ago drama. Perhaps she had lent William's true love an important pair of pearl earrings on the evening a declaration was made. Andy could picture Becky being generous with her jewelry and happy to help.

Becky handed Andy the register tape (he collected them) which was grisly with streaks of blood although Becky referred to the smears as hamburger juice. Andy made a note of that usage as well for his Hill lexicon. He was compiling a word list in which such niceties of idiom figured. He asked Becky why she was disinclined to speak the word *blood* and to acknowledge that butchered and processed livestock continued to bleed into the polystyrene and plastic wrap of its commercial packaging material.

"Oh my," said Becky. "I don't know. Why am I reluctant to say the word?"

Which was not for Andy to say in his strictly adhered-to role of observer and recorder, and he wandered back to his room to order his notes. Becky remained in the kitchen to roll out piecrusts and to think her own thoughts about unstanchable wounds ceaselessly seeping and weeping.

LAST-PERIOD CLASSES had been canceled and the school population trampled into the field house and swarmed the pull-out bleachers, rumbling and speculating on the reason for the unscheduled assembly. But it was too late in the afternoon of the dying school day for the airing and exercising of thought, and the student body shrugged and slumped as one large resistless organism. The heat was tropical under the bright, switched-on lights, the atmosphere was thick with paste wax and expended efforts, and everyone knew it was about to rain boredom in metal buckets.

Brooks and Rollins peeled off their MegaDeath and Slayer (respectively) sweatshirts down to their Iron Maiden and Question Authority T-shirts. They had chased their great desire to sit on the top row of the bleachers up to the top row and now they rocked and swayed the tiered benches from high above. They heaved their backs against the cement-block wall and kicked at the bleacher seats as, below them, clambering students stumbled and lurched with every shudder of the apparatus.

Little Becky was bounced off her feet as the bleachers pitched, and she sat abruptly in the front row. She was jabbed in the lower back by the sharp and careless knees belonging to a popular Senior girl who drove her own car, so Little Becky couldn't say anything to her. But what if, Little Becky thought, what if she had won the $10,000 that morning. She could have bought her own red Ford Mustang, the very same car and color as Missy DeStefano's which she would park in the student lot right next to Missy's own and Missy would see how much they had in common, a red Mustang with an I BRAKE FOR UNICORNS bumper sticker. If only she had won $10,000. If only her father had asked, which Becky? If only she could drive.

Betsy appeared in front of Little Becky as a blur of blond hair and teal mohair and the scent of the Lily of the Valley powder she kept on the bathroom shelf and which Little Becky routinely sneaked after one of her shallow and cool and hurried-along-by-a-thump-on-the-bathroom-door baths. Little Becky sniffed. Lily of the Valley smelled different on Betsy which was just as well. Otherwise, Betsy would suspect.

"Is anyone sitting next to you?" Betsy asked, when it was perfectly obvious that people would balance on hot stove tops rather than sit beside Little Becky. Taking no answer for a no, Betsy gracefully settled beside her cousin and arranged her dainty effects. Her textbooks were covered in Gordon Fraser wrapping-paper patterns and her pencil case was a needlepoint sheath covered with a scene inspired by the Bayeux tapestry which, Betsy had to explain, she had designed and worked herself when the local girls asked her where she had bought her pencil case and which, somehow, did not seem to be the right answer. But *where* can I *buy* one? the local girls still wanted to know.

Little Becky could only gloom at Betsy. Then she shrugged and began to paint her fingernails blue with her nylon tip pen. Her pen skidded and she winced extravagantly as Missy, gesturing energetically to friends, again bore her pointy knees into Little Becky's back. Betsy, observing, casually dropped her shoulder bag onto Missy's foot.

"Oh. God. So sorry, Betsy," Missy said.

"That's okay," Betsy said. "Do you know my cousin Becky?" She dropped the little, which in Betsy's opinion only seemed to call attention to how *not* little Little Becky was.

Little Becky swiveled round with a terrible grin stretched across her hectic face.

"Really? She's *your* cousin, Betsy? You're, like, related? Really?" Missy asked, prepared to ally with Betsy against such an unfortunate connection. Missy's pert features creased into a complicit smile.

But Betsy informed Missy, "Becky's from New York City, you know. She's lived there all her life," and even Little Becky appreciated that this arresting information stumped the oh-so-certain Missy, for what if, what if Little Becky were to prove to be secretly, subtly cool in some utterly avant garde and unsuspected New York City way which would only become known in stuck-in-a-rut Towne months after the trend had fallen fatally dead and over everywhere else and Missy, flashing and enjoying her shiny new nail transfers (say) in all pathetic innocence unaware, turned out to be the tragically incorrect one?

"New York? So, do you know any Ramones then?" Missy asked Little Becky warily.

"Yes, she does," Betsy answered before Little Becky could blunder in. "They all worked out at the same fashionable health club," Betsy smoothly invented as Little Becky stared at her paragon cousin whom she was always, always being told to be more like and she filed away the fascinating fact that Betsy was a fluent and spontaneous and big liar, though no one would believe *her* if she said so about Betsy.

"Really?" asked Missy. "Really. So The Ramones exercise. *You* exercise?" she questioned Little Becky. "But what are they really like? Come on, you can tell me." She switched her sharp knees sideways as a gesture.

"Nice?" Little Becky ventured. "Really nice?" she added, as Betsy lifted fair eyebrows to express, Good answer.

"Yes, I could see they might be nice," Missy said. "Like underneath."

"Like, I mean, so way nice," Little Becky expanded, fain to prolong such an interesting conversation with such an estimable individual from the Senior class.

"Uh huh," Missy said then.

Glover, late, last, swung into the field house. He'd been routed from the third-floor custodians' closet where there was a collapsing armchair and an ashtray. His long arms were slung over the shoulders of two sophomore girls who notably dogged him and whom he appeared to be using now as a set of crutches, for his reconstituted riding boots, pointed as a pair of peg legs, were killing him. His long, lax hands dropped slackly, brushing over the tops of their breasts which the girls permitted by pretending not to know where his hands lay and his fingers felt until, as if suddenly cured, Glover threw them off (the girls scuttled to the bleachers) and he rambled over the field house floor grinding his boot heels into the Towne Fightin' Titan logo stenciled on the center line of the basketball court—a highly suspect depiction, Glover happened to think, of an overdeveloped giant guy wrapped in a loincloth grasping a puny opponent around his scrawny waist. Glover traversed the field house, his back turned to the bleachers, and he came to rest on the top of a stack of tumbling mats, reclining there like a potentate, propped on an elbow. He waved generally—all eyes had followed his progress. Benevolently, he indicated, Very well, I'm here, let's begin. Missy sighed. Little Becky felt breath on the back of her neck.

And then the theme music from that old-timey space-voyage, homicidal-computer, vast floating cosmic-embryo movie everyone's parents thought was so great spouted over the P.A. system. The student body tensed, guarded and alert. The program was going to be Inspirational. Damn. They were going to be exhorted to get high on life instead of drugs and alcohol and video games. They were going to be given sunflower seeds to plant in barren corners of the earth. They were going to be assigned old people.

A banner, unfurled by the release of a rope from the beam high above the climbing ropes, was read with difficulty. As-yet-wet lettering (this was a very suddenly called assembly) had imprinted itself like batik during the furling. "THE DEFEAT OF COMMUNISM — THE TRIUMPH OF THE WEST — A CELEBRATION OF U.S." was made out eventually, but no one knew quite what to make of the assertion. The school waited for a second banner to fall, one more fairmindedly pointing out Defeated Communism's view of the matter. Perhaps they were going to be assigned Russians to make it all up to, somehow.

Ginevra Platt-Willey, the school actress, effected a quiet entrance from a side door. She wore a grey sweater that hung down to her knees, a grey skirt that drooped to her ankles, and a grey scarf knotted behind her head. Nevertheless, the outfit worked. Missy tapped Betsy's arm and they conferred. Betsy said the Look would have been all off had Ginevra tied the scarf under her chin. Missy said Ginevra was wearing a Vassarette body shaper. She'd seen it hanging in her locker and who did Ginevra think she was fooling? Betsy said *Vogue* said grey was the new black this winter. Missy said she could wear grey if she wore something pink between the grey and her face but she generously allowed that Betsy could carry off grey next to her face because Betsy herself was pink. *So* pink, Missy had to say.

Ginevra, locating herself in the vicinity of the Titan and his victim, indicated through evocative miming that she was standing in a line and had been standing in a line and would continue to stand in a line to obtain, after an eternity of standing in line, a shriveled potato. During that eternity, as Ginevra frowned at her sluggish Soviet wristwatch and tapped her shabbily shod foot on the broken pavement and seized and berated a queue-jumper, Brooks and Rollins became restive. They understood all of this had something to do with Russians whom, of course, they conventionally disliked, and long-nurtured instincts caused them to mutter automatic gunfire noises back and forth which rapidly escalated into a carpet-bombing run above the Kremlin. Dr. James, the assistant principal, clambered up three steps of the trembly bleachers and hissed at them to report to his office at once.

"Who? Him?"

"No. You."

"Huh?"

"You."

"Us?"

Brooks and Rollins disruptively descended, maintaining an air of insouciance which would have been admired were they, indeed, downed American pilots appearing in gritty documentary footage of the show trial and they were quietly cheered because Dr. James was very much disliked. He coached the Math-A-Letes and encouraged known favorites.

Ginevra, jealous of her audience, won back the house by singing a traditional folk tune softly to herself in a lost and dreamy voice as she walked along carrying her precious potato now, down Old World streets. She passed over a graceful arched bridge and turned down a grand avenue which, after a long mile, debouched into a blighted hinterland of People's Housing and overheating nuclear power plants. She climbed to her apartment on the twenty-ninth floor of a disintegrating high-rise with laundry flapping from every condemned balcony. She opened her stiff, stuck door with a dungeon key and after throwing a shabby shoe at a scampering rat, she set the potato to boil in a tin cup held over a red cellophane flame. She gazed into the cup, so intent upon her one-potato dinner to come that everyone leaned forward intrigued, willing the water to boil. Ginevra, or her Russian character, must know some really good way to fix a potato.

Then, in staging borrowed from the cemetery scene in *Our Town* (which was produced in quadrennial rotation with *The Sound of Music, The Crucible,* and *Pippin*) the rest of the Drama Club assembled bearing highly desirable examples of portable electronic items—a small television, a CD player, speakers, a cell phone, a food processor. They carried, as well, in-line skates, a leather coat, a motorcycle helmet, a six-pack of Classic Coke. They sat on folding chairs and pronounced their lines in carrying voices, painting a pastiche of highlights from American history and culture—the Pilgrims, Cowboys, the Moon Landing—no one was listening. They were all watching Ginevra as she heard snatches of the faraway voices and their long-ago stories reaching her through the thin apartment walls, above the tinny hubbub of stalled Moscow traffic, across the European continent, over the cold, wide ocean. She was intrigued yet not convinced, attracted yet uncertain of the tale being told her. At last, bravely choosing, she set down her tin cup with a relinquishing motion and Harold Post, wearing his Eagle

Scout uniform, rose and took Ginevra gently by the hand and led her to the seated panel of American high consumers, and in a solemn ceremony, she was presented with a toaster oven and a frozen Tostino pizza, although everyone was still thinking about her potato. Dylan Grant was so overcome by the moment that he handed Ginevra the portable CD player he was holding, which was too much for Ginevra to carry so she had to set it down upon the floor.

Betsy didn't think the toaster oven was a very practical gift because they had different electricity in foreign countries which would cause the toaster oven to explode, an indication that perhaps we were still at odds with the Russians in many unacknowledged and unanticipated areas. Nor was Betsy certain that it might not be better to be sincerely thrilled with just a potato than to enter into all the complications of creating and operating a state-of-the-art sound system because you were never through replacing parts made obsolete by the next technological breakthrough. Otherwise, you began to feel deprived. And could you even buy CDs in the Soviet Union? What if the poor Russian girl only possessed one CD which she was forced to play over and over again? And Betsy had heard Soviet pop music on a PBS special which had been very terrible music, worse even than the French version, which was sinking pretty low.

Little Becky only knew that it wasn't fair that even Communist girls were going to be happier than she was and get more stuff and have more fun and friends and everything else. She could not bring herself to clap for Ginevra and company as they took their bows and the school stomped and hooted at them and Ginevra and company stomped and hooted right back.

Dr. James waded into their midst and thanked everyone for their fine efforts and he was about to bid the assemblage to rise and sing Our National Anthem while Visual Arts recorded the heart-filling moment on their camcorder, which he planned to present as irrefutable evidence of what a tight ship he was running the next time the School Committee started making noises about declining S.A.T. scores. But Glover had had enough. He slithered from his high pile of tumbling mats and he tipped on his sharp-toed boots across the field house floor, nodding at Dr. James in passing, signaling to all with negligent wave of his hand, Dismissed.

"Listen, tell Ma I'm going to be late tonight, okay?" Glover stood over Little Becky, rising on his stalk-like dusty blackclad legs. He smelled, in a heated way, of pepper and cinnamon.

"Why?" Little Becky asked. "Why are you going to be late?"

"None of your business why. Just tell her, late, okay?"

"Well, Ma'll ask *me* why."

"Is *he* her brother?" Missy tapped Betsy on the arm and asked. "Is *he* your brother?" she asked Little Becky. "He doesn't look like your brother. Are you adopted? I think you may be adopted, they don't always tell you. So *he*'s your brother. I'll drive you home and you can show me where you live and you can tell me about your brother."

"SO HOW LARGE IS a cord of wood, technically? I suppose I ought to know," Alden asked Gee.

The big trees had come tearing and toppling down. They lay at broken angles. Gee unnimbly walked their lengths, kicking at the rubbish of ancient squirrels' nests, whacking at jutting branches with a sturdy ax. Alden, standing amidst the woodsy litter rubbing gummy pitch into his blackening fingertips, experienced a twinge of regret. He knelt and counted the rings of the roundest fallen trunk and he came up with seventy-five years which was not nearly as great an age as he had imagined. This tree had not been standing since the Revolution. It was not even a contemporary of Lincoln—rather, of Wilson. Men were already driving cars and flying planes and talking on the telephone and playing ragtime on the parlor piano by the time the seed of this tree had split and sprouted and shouldered its way up in the woods. Alden supposed this tree should consider itself fortunate that it had survived as long as it had the exigencies of the twentieth century and, indeed, all of the trees seemed not uncontent to lay themselves down at long last, stretching thirty feet or more across the Earth, measuring themselves against their own shadows.

Well, this must lead to philosophical considerations, this spending the day out-of-doors in the bracing air revising the landscape because some up-and-coming couple had been inconvenienced by the tap of a twig against their roof, Alden decided, and he resolved to keep his thoughts to himself. Otherwise, people would learn to cross the road when they spotted him approaching with a lively step and a glitter in his eye, denoting the formulation of still another wizard concept culled from yet another bout of contemplating the obvious.

"A cord of wood. How big is it?" he again asked Gee. Gee had a good ear and a bad ear and he wore a wax plug in his good ear to save his hearing for Bible Church on Sunday and nightly reruns of *Sanford and Son*.

"Hey? They'll be four by four by eight to fix a cord," Gee said.

"In feet? Really? That much?" Alden asked. He had pictured something that could be tied with twine and toted away like a weekend brunch order for twelve from Dean and DeLuca's.

"Gotta get this pile of wood all busted up," Gee reminded him as Alden just stood there tugging at a loosening cuff button.

They passed the next several hours slicing the trunks into movable parts which they stacked by the side of the road but they were left with a sprawling mess of branches and boughs strewn across the lawn. Alden didn't bother to hope that Glen Fairweather would be willing to overlook this by-product of the day's activity. Perhaps he and Gee could drag the detritus deeper into the woods and fling it naturalistically about. Whatever did one do under the circumstances? Surely he was not the first to experience this problem.

For in his previous life, Alden had delegated the clearing up of these incidental details. Research filled in the blanks, legal looked at the small print, marketing got the word out, accounting cut the checks. Alden had presided. Now, he sat upon a stump (he was sure he'd been right about the buttermilk-fungus stump-eradication method) and as he unwrapped a Mars bar saved from lunch he contemplated the view from his new rung on the food chain. He was, he declared to himself, the sort of visionary who had overlooked the forest for the trees, apparently. He uttered, Shoot, dismally and realized he'd never been so tired. How did workingmen get up every morning after the day before and pull themselves through their paces all over again? Alden hoped he would never drive past another highway construction crew and remark how many of the men were just leaning on their shovels.

Gee, plucking the plug from his better ear, eased himself down onto another stump and smoked a menthol cigarette and mentioned, "The chipper should be here any time.

"Ya wanted one, didn't ya?" Gee asked as Alden puzzled at him.

"To clear up this here brush and all that," Gee said. "A woodchipper. The guys from Tiptop Tree Service are in the area today and they said they'd stop by on the way home. Half hour, it'll take them, tops. I told them you were good for fifty bucks. Don't let them gyp you for more. It's their boss's rig and they'll sell the mulch on the side. Probably turn around and sell it to these people."

"Great," Alden said. "Great. Thank you, Gee."

Later, near dark, Gee's nephew Spaz came by with his Loadstar to cart away the logs. Gee had requested his pay in wood, which he claimed to trust more than money.

"Money don't come by the truckload," as Spaz observed, although Alden could remember the days when it had, when some of the guys at First Manhattan had worked out how large a heap a billion dollars in one-hundred-dollar bills would make. (They'd been attempting to recapture a sense of just how much a billion dollars was—they'd become too cavalier about risking immense sums, a personnel consultant had warned them, hence the exercise.)

"This guy pay ya?" Spaz asked, pointing his long, local nose at the Fairweathers' front door.

"Well, he was supposed to up front, but he decided he needs an item-ized bill first," Alden confessed.

Spaz and Gee communicated with a look, and Gee spat thoughtfully onto a pile of sawdust and massaged a mass with his boot toe into a kind of puck which he kicked back into dust.

"That's why come they all have so much money at this end of town. Seldom known to part with any," Gee said.

"Not to the likes of us anyways," Spaz muttered.

RON HAD NOT SUGGESTED meeting for a friendly drink at the Ritz-Carlton after their chat as Ginger had rather counted on, Ron turn-ing relaxed and confidential and coming round to her side. She knew there was always the real story behind the official story and she refused to be told she couldn't procure an advantageous divorce settlement if only she knew the secret handshake or the magic words. But it struck her that lawyers would look out for one another and she was beginning to despair of finding anyone who would take on Louis unless she hired herself a feminist attorney who would possess a very different set of loyalties. But then, a feminist attorney might not support Ginger's desire to leave the marriage with as many of the family assets as she could carry away in an interstate moving van.

And then she considered that child, that callow associate with curiously yellow fingernails (as if he'd been carving pumpkins) whom Ron had attempted to fob off on her, pleading pressures of time and his own lack of knowledge on the subject, to handle her divorce. Quaking in his loafers when Ron called him into his corner office—anticipating a reprimand? expecting to receive the heave-ho?—his was not a demeanor to inspire confidence, that of this young Simon (his name was) who found himself in the unhappy position of having to be happy to take what was given him.

Unless—Ginger was by now hurriedly walking down State Street in her furry coat, embracing her day's shopping, caught up and carried along by the grey crush of homeward-headed office workers among whom she knew herself to be a vivid and separate creature, a woman who, within the year, would be relishing that entirely new life she had just thought of and having thought of had as good as achieved—unless Simon, who had, she could not help noticing, regarded her admiringly and flushed when she turned the full wattage of her best smile on him just on the off chance she would require his assistance—unless Simon came to take a special, zealous interest in her case and made up with diligence what he lacked in spark as he labored on her behalf. But it further occurred to Ginger that whenever she wished to cite her personal legal authority she would have to preface her remarks with the phrase, "Simon says," and she would be obliged to wait for the inevitable smile to smooth from a face before she could proceed to make her point.

No, she'd have to keep looking, but truly, how hard could it be to break away from Louis? She refused to be discouraged, for freedom frolicked in the very air today of all days. The oppressed peoples of the planet were crawling out from under the dark and heavy sways of every startled brute and tyrant. Ginger looked to the sky as if searching for an answer generally spelled out for all to understand.

And then Goody's car miraculously pulled up to the curb beside her. "Perfect timing!" she exclaimed as she slid in beside him, filling the enclosed space with fur and crackling paper bags spilling tissue wrappings and scents. Goody didn't attempt to tell her he'd been circling the area for the past forty-five minutes, uselessly arguing with himself all the while. Yet, he had to concede, after completing three (in forty-five minutes) snarled tight circuits, caught in the near-solid blockage of traffic which bumped along like platelets moving through a vein in magnified film footage of a heart attack under way—he had spied Ginger suddenly standing out among the sidewalk crowd, the taller, more attractive, more glidingly moving woman whom he sought among all the rest, and his annoyance had vanished. Success, he had thought. At last, he spoke aloud, leaning forward and darting toward the curb.

ANDY TURNED TO A PAGE of his Hill lexicon. *Vase*, he wrote, *varieties of*. . . . *Mud (mud, mud)*, he entered. *Hamburger juice*, he noted. He returned the notebook to its place in a stack of other bound and labeled volumes and he slid William's recent letter from beneath his blotter pad. He thought it might help to order his thoughts and impressions to date as he constructed a likely account of his progress for William's particular consumption. For any approach to William worked a tonic effect on Andy, and now that he had become William's protégé (after all, William sponsored him here) Andy must undertake to rise even higher in an estimation he had, frankly, not been conscious was being made. Heretofore, if Andy had stood unaware as a candidate—his previous efforts, such as they were, had only been pitched to cause his difficult Uncle William not to dislike him excessively—now that he had gotten the job (so to speak) he was constrained to provide William with more of the same. Whatever that same had been.

Dear Uncle William [Andy wrote], Here I am, in situ, and grateful for your advice to "head for the Hills" where, to answer the first of several questions you put to me in your last letter let me assure you I am taking pains not to "overburden the family with my hovering presence." I observe the fieldwork techniques sanctioned by my discipline, i.e., I do not eat with the family. I sit in the kitchen on a high stool topped with a small round of braided rug and eat cheese and granola and fruit and observe the family at table in the dining room through the open serving hatch. I have concluded that food does not represent love to the Hills; food affords them an opportunity to bite and chew consideringly while thinking up a sharp comeback to a previous pointed remark. I have never come across this phenomenon in the literature. This may be significant.

To answer your next question, Mr. and Mrs. Lowe seem to be adjusting to their new circumstances, although their relationship, their "famous marriage" as you term it, is not without strain as is to be expected during a transitional time. Mrs. Lowe seems to focus on the damage done to Mr. Lowe's expensive sportswear in the pursuit of his bucolic schemes, his stained jackets, torn shirts, ruined shoes. How swiftly even the most civilized among us (and Mrs. Lowe is very most civilized) revert to taking out their unacknowledged and dangerous impulses on an effigy as it were.

But events are far more stirring in your part of the globe. Such a triumph for you. We, that is, the family and I shall watch events unfold tonight across the television screen as has swiftly become the custom in this linked and shrinkening world, to cluster round the cathode-ray tube. But this will give me an opportunity to assess attitudes—political, social, historical—for I believe that in some cases the family talk a wider view than they vote. Their votes are, I daresay, cast in stone though not stones, *their* Revolution having happened so long ago although it is still remembered hereabouts with great satisfaction and often with the proprietary *We*.

THIS WAS BETSY'S NIGHT to wash the supper dishes. Lily didn't believe in automatic dishwashers. She had noticed how they left mysterious encrustations between the tines of her dishwasher-owning friends' forks, although Ginger argued those were just the pioneer models such as her circle of biddies would possess, heaving and regurgitating antiques.

Still, Lily could not be persuaded to invest in a Silent-Flo Dishmaster System with an onboard computer that detected fork encrustations and aimed powerful expunging water jets at them. Ginger had collected the literature from Towne Line Appliances and left the brochure and a favorable rating index from *Consumer Reports* in Lily's knitting bag to no avail.

Betsy didn't mind washing the dishes. At least she knew they would be properly soaped and rinsed when it was her turn which she couldn't be sure of on Brooks's and Rollins's attempts, or with her mother's resented efforts, and Little Becky's concept of a clean plate left much to be desired. And they all replaced the salad bowls on the cupboard shelf where the dessert saucers were supposed to be and seldom-used implements like the melon baller and the nutmeg grater would be very illogically stowed underneath the sink or in the clean apron drawer, tucked between clean aprons as if someone had panicked over them. Uncle Harvey was a surprisingly good dishwasher. Every surface had to pass his squeaky thumb test but the bathwater tended to flow rather tepid after his stints for he emptied and refilled the sink separately for glasses, cutlery, plates, and pots and pans, in that order. He frothed Ivory Soap suds with an old hand-turned eggbeater (Lily's well water was very hard) as he sang songs from *Oklahoma* and *South Pacific* and *Pal Joey* and he encouraged family participation as he played the eggbeater, faster, slower, higher, lower, among the soapsuds. It sounded like a very hoarse ukelele. Harvey's dishwashing duties ran on well into the evening snack runs and he washed the snack dishes as well if they were slipped onto the sideboard to mingle with the yet to be dealt with supper dishes, although he noticed when a tumbler, a cocoa mug, a cake knife, appeared out of order and was puzzled.

Tonight, Andy lingered in the kitchen with Betsy. He was musing upon the spoons rising from the spoon jar set upon the laden lazy Susan. The variety, yet the essential sameness of the spoons, reminded him of all the thin and tapering and luminous women he had known or wished to have known, yes, just like those smooth and oval faces in which he had sometimes seen his own soul reflected and answered back, or so he always thought at the time.

He sat upon his high stool beside the serving hatch consuming Concord grapes, slicing them in half with his sharp front teeth and flicking out the seeds with his index finger onto the lid of a pot of yogurt he had just finished. He blinked away from his contemplation of the lovely spoon maidens (that reverie was getting him nowhere) and he began to read aloud from Little Becky's new cork notice board crookedly slung from a hook specially hammered into the wall beside the telephone. She had worked on this project all afternoon in response to the morning's Cash Call disaster. The board was festooned with thumbtacked 3 × 5 cards laboriously printed on—For Thursday, Nov. 9, 1989, The Magic Word on MROC is THRILLER. The Mystery Amount in the QHIT Cash Jar is $86. NOTICE TO EVERYBODY PLEASE!!! Whenever you answer the phone between 2 and 6 in the afternoon always say BARRY B. PLAYS THE HITS FOR ME, FROM COAST TO COAST I LOVE HIM MOST. This is for to win a trip to DISNEY-WORLD. And remember, remember, remember, always ask *which* Becky they want. Remember!!!

Andy said, "I can't quite see Ms. Hill answering the telephone with Barry B. plays the hits for me."

Betsy smiled. Andy watched her expression caught in the night-filled window above the sink, her expression softened and saddened by a haze of steam. She had tucked her braid out of the way down the back of her sweater, the teal tunic she had been wearing all day. She had been almost late for supper and had not had time to change. Babysitting at the Snowdons' had run on long. Mr. Snowdon was staying at his office even later these days and Mrs. Snowdon didn't like Betsy to leave until he came home. Betsy wondered who she was supposed to be looking after, who it was at the Snowdon household who could not be left alone with the sharp steak knives and the harsh cleaning compounds stored under the kitchen sink. Mr. Snowdon had told Betsy he relied on her, and so far he was the only husband who had not pulled to a stop alongside the River Road on the late ride back to Aunt Lily's and, leaning close on a pretext—to recover an envelope from the glove compartment, to adjust the whistling seal between her window and the window frame—attempted to kiss her by chance, on the off chance she would not mind. Mr. Snowdon had not tried that. He drove his expensive car in a straight shot across Towne as Mrs. Snowdon waited at home, alone. But, while the other husbands practiced silence and sidelong looks in which Betsy, having to do all the work (after all, she had been hired for the evening) was expected to find the meaning, Mr. Snowdon talked to Betsy. He remembered his long-ago days, a time he pronounced as his "carefree youth" with Uncle Aldenish articulation. The presence of Betsy in the front seat seemed to set him off, to spin him back to that pre–Mrs. Snowdon past where Betsy was invited to wander with him, through Williamstown as it had once been, through certain corners of London which were all changed now and not for the better. Very little had not turned for the worse since . . . Mr. Snowdon never said since when. He didn't really have to.

"Not that Barry B. will ever call," Andy was saying.

"I don't know. Maybe he will. She sends in all those postcards," Betsy said. "She has stacks of tropical vacation postcards she must never have sent to her friends."

Betsy reached down and scoured the bottom of the big frying pan. Aunt Becky tended to burn the onions (they'd had hamburgers with onions and green beans and fruit cup and pie for supper) because she was cutting back on oil—she'd read an article about cutting back on oil—and she was always being called away from the stove at critical moments to hunt down a lost glove or to dictate, meaninglessly, that no one could watch TV if the boys and Little Becky could not agree on a program. Andy's intelligent fox's face floated against the black and steam of the window glass and as she leaned back and forth scrubbing the seared-on crust of carbonized onion, Andy's reflection and Betsy's merged and parted rather like a movie special effect, as if they were dreaming of one another or one of them was dead or one of them was missing in action but trying to get a message through. The plot would determine the particulars of their apparitions' raison d'être, Betsy supposed, although the reason would be a romantic one, of course. She sifted more Ajax powder down into the frying pan. Aunt Lily always bought the Ajax brand because, she said, she had liked him in the *Iliad*. So even Aunt Lily must have a romantic streak in her somewhere, which rendered this business of romantic streaks surely quite harmless, Betsy concluded.

"Like a grape?" Andy was asking her.

"No thank you. My hands are sudsy," Betsy said.

"They're quite good. They're very sweet. They're just beginning to ferment in their skins," Andy said.

"Ferment in their skins?" Betsy asked.

Andy slipped from his high chair and came to her side. "Here," he said, holding a grape to her lips. Betsy's mouth opened to a startled O and Andy deposited the grape. So this was the taste Andy experienced as sweetness. Betsy, for her part, bit down upon a strong flavor, and she swallowed an even more bitter after-grit of crushed seeds which Andy had not removed with an incision of tooth and a flick of thumb. He had acted impulsively and imperfectly.

"Going to watch the big news on the tube tonight?" he asked her.

"In a bit," Betsy said. They had been assigned to watch the Berlin Wall coming down in Current Events class, except for Ginevra Platt-Willey whose family did not believe in television. Mr. Patrick had said she could monitor local German coverage on her shortwave radio. Perhaps, Mr. Patrick said, Ginevra would hear what the Germans didn't want the rest of us to hear, at the prospect of which third-period C.E. had not felt privileged but oppressed. Was there going to be a test, not of the multiple choice and essay variety, but some greater challenge to their hopes and their futures?

Andy left her, mentioning some notes that needed ordering, and Betsy decided to let the big frying pan soak although usually she didn't approve of leaving any dish undone. Tonight that could not be avoided. She had to inspect her mother's day-in-Boston-worth of shopping before Ginger could conceal or alter or destroy the sales slips. Betsy wanted to be able to balance the checkbook without tears, disavowals, and deceit.

She ran, not lightly but noiselessly, up the back stairs and she tapped on her mother's bedroom door. There was no response, no too peevish, no too alert, no too studiedly exhausted answering, *Yes?* Betsy put her ear to the jamb and she detected no interior rustling of paper bags and tissue, no clink of glass against bottle and of a bottom bureau drawer opening and closing, nor did she hear any sequence of breaths raggedly withheld and expelled in shuddering sighs. Glancing over her shoulder, Betsy sidled through the smallest possible wedge of opened door. She crept over boots, the fur coat, a tumble of shiny clothing and accessory catalogues, a rucked-up needlepoint rug. She skirted a tottery pillar of books with dark covers and long, explanatory titles and she was careful not to tread on that morning's range of rejected outfits lying in several color-coordinated heaps just where Ginger had stepped into and out of them. Betsy half feared that the outfits, which all so looked like her mother with the air let out, would rise up and carry on like an army of her mothers if provoked.

The bed had been hastily made up. The beautiful shirred pink satin spread Ginger had discovered in its secret box and which was now marked with a spilled coffee stain shaped like an eighth continent, had been flung sideways rather than lengthwise atop the bed, covering a cache of shopping bags. Her mother's methods never varied. Ginger thought if she made the effort to conceal, seekers should play the game and make the effort not to find. But then, her mother lived life on a very emblematic plane.

Betsy twitched back the bedspread. The clutter of fine shopping bags piled upon the mattress was not as formidable as she had feared. She winnowed aside scented tissues and extracted sales slips, adding figures loosely in her head. Ginger had not spent two hundred dollars, a very modest total after she had spent (so often literally spent) a day alone and unhappy in a big city. Betsy ruffled through the Blue Guide to France. She hoped her mother wasn't pinning her hopes on a big trip to Europe. Had she gone so far as to purchase an airline ticket, piling on options as she went—oh, why *not* the Concorde, well, why *not* the George V, yes, why *not* a suite? Betsy could just hear her mother being knowledge-able and expansive in a travel agent's office as coffee was poured and totted up from a nip-sized bottle of inflight (already!) brandy. Betsy had to locate the checkbook. She spied her mother's satchel hanging inertly from the closet doorknob and even though to delve into some-one else's handbag was very impolite, she reached inside and carefully not looking but feeling identified by touch the simulated-leather folder of the checkbook. She scanned the stubs. No, her mother had not writ-ten an additional exorbitant check, yet. Betsy pocketed the checkbook and she replaced the bedspread as negligently as she was able—her neatness genie militated against such slatternliness. She resisted a great wish to hang up the poor fur coat which looked so recently deceased sprawled across the floor, outstretched arms imploring life to return to its embrace.

Betsy slipped from her mother's room. She glanced up and down the hallway. Downstairs, a discussion and the television were holding and distracting the family and she was free to act. Using her pocketknife (she had planned for and supplied this part of her expedition) she pried up the screwdriver attachment of the knife and quickly unfastened a tole-ware plaque (black background, pink Chinese peonies design) which covered over a decommissioned heating duct opening. She balanced the checkbook upon a narrow slice of ledge made by interior wall and pipe, and she reattached the plaque. She needed the checkbook to remain thoroughly lost at least until the latest deposit cleared. Surely, her mother wouldn't think of searching inside the walls unless this Berlin situation gave Ginger ideas about seizing and swinging some emblematic sledgehammer.

ALDEN DECLARED THIS a most shameful business, two of his sons getting themselves conspicuously expelled from a school assembly celebrating the defeat of Communism and the evident triumph of the West. Alden read, he read aloud from Dr. James's passionately scrawled note home of complaint and indictment. Celebrate appeared more like calibrate as Alden tried to make out the emotional script but he cottoned to the gist several paragraphs on as Dr. James warmed to his theme. Alden wondered whether this James fellow possessed the appropriate temperament to work with exuberant young people year in and year out.

"What does the school want this time?" Becky asked. "Have the boys been suspended? Do we have to escort them back and fall to our knees to beg forgiveness? Shall we have to pay for damages? What is it this time?" She held out her hand and snapped her fingers for the letter. Startled, Alden relinquished page one.

Brooks and Rollins regarded their mother warily. She was being uncommonly impatient with their father while she had yet to turn upon them to demand to know their version of events although, of late, she had not allowed them to express more than a token protest of their outraged innocence before she shook her head in sorrow and retreated to the attic with a library book and a mug of coffee. On these several recent occasions, dinner had been uncharacteristically late. The family gathered hopefully in the dining room. They sat at their unset places. Against all evidence they reached for their napkins, scrabbling at the shiny tabletop. They listened through the open serving hatch to pots and pans just beginning to rattle and scrape. Ginger, who was boldest and hungriest, ran a swift cheese and cracker raid on the pantry, returning short of breath and clutching provisions enough to tide them over until Becky, whom no one blamed, could become organized.

So Brooks and Rollins had withheld the note from school until after dinner, not wishing to spoil dinner they protested virtuously, as the square of envelope was lifted from Rollins's back pocket and handed round across a sweep of crumbs and the fallen-over saltshaker.

"You decided to ruin our after-dinner, then?" Alden unreasonably asked as he rolled up his sleeve. For a heartbeat, the boys asked themselves if their father was thinking of beating them, not that he ever had but they were aware they had not, theretofore, sinned against such a moment of consequence. This had been their first opportunity, really, for they had been born into such unremarkable times.

But Alden was only seeking relief from the scratch of his plaid wool shirt against a long gash laid down along his forearm, the wound rendered even more vivid by the slash of an iodine paint job.

"What happened, Dad?" Brooks asked.

"Don't change the subject," Alden said.

"No, Dad, really what happened?" Brooks asked.

"Dad, really," Rollins echoed.

"A tree fell on your father today," Becky looked up from the letter to speak, sounding more displeased with Alden than with the tree.

"No. *I* fell on the tree," Alden said—at the end, in the dark, when he and Gee and the crew from Tiptop were flying, flinging branches into the maw of the chipper. The crew chief had been in a rush. He had tango lessons at the Y that evening.

"Stupid tree," said Brooks.

"Stupid," muttered Rollins.

"It's not the tree that's . . ." Becky allowed herself to observe so far, and no further.

An atmosphere had developed, a cloud of grey and lowering feelings that followed them as the discussion continued, amidst the rub of chair feet across carpet and a sharp whiff of snuffed-out candle smoke. They rambled from the dining room into the hallway where Alden halted and rummaged in a drawer of the Governor Winthrop desk for the house-hold address embosser, an elegant object that left an elegant impression. He collected writing paper, an ink pen, a bottle of India ink and a ruler, as well, from the desk's several other drawers and cubicles and niches.

"Everything is all entirely my fault," Alden conceded wearily as he carried his utensils into the little parlor, and a not very great weight was lifted from Brooks's and Rollins's backs. Their father's announce-ment obviously took the heat off them and their mother only said, "No more sound effects, all right? Brooks? Rollins? All right? Because no one is interested. You are very tiresome boys." They accepted the rebuke. Of course they were tiresome. The wearing down of authority was the linchpin of their strategy.

Becky sighed and sank down onto a corner of the sofa beside Little Becky who had hustled into the little parlor to establish the evening's rights to the sofa's center cushion where the springs were still sound and did not uncoil disconcertingly underneath one. She had had a wretched day. Bagging the center cushion was the sole bright spot. Missy De-Stefano had suddenly not been able to drive her home from school as she had offered to, having rapidly hatched the far better plan of driving Glover himself where he wanted to go, and the pair of them had driven off together on Glover's unstated errand. And Little Becky was pretty sure her mother had just become an alcoholic because there had been six empty beer cans lined up on top of the aluminum recycling bin which Little Becky had pitched into the bin so no one else would guess but then her mother had gone around asking, Who threw away those cans?, very vexedly asking—perhaps she'd been desperate to swallow the dribbly dregs.

Little Becky wrapped herself in the scrap yarn afghan and stuck her legs out over the big round ottoman, jamming her heels into the plush top. The television channel changer was concealed on her person, pushed up a droopy sweater sleeve, and she was sitting upon a private Hershey bar which she hoped she would be able to eat secretly if she draped the afghan over her head. She could still watch TV (currently a M*A*S*H rerun) through the afghan's loose stitches. Her mother, even though she had plunked herself down right beside Little Becky, was all snuffly with her head cold so she couldn't smell chocolate tonight.

Becky shivered and drew an edge of the afghan across her knees as Little Becky sounded an affronted squeally note of protest and hauled back at the blanket and reshrouded her head.

Harvey entered bearing an armload of oak logs which he arranged in the fireplace grate and stuffed in the wood basket and he stoked a fire quickly and without fuss using the pine cones he had soaked in rubbing alcohol and kerosene and dried last summer in the barn rafters. The glass eyes of ornamental owl andirons glowed a fierce flickering orange as the wood caught. Ginger had seen not nearly as nice a pair of andirons on sale for $375 at Lydia Spofford Antiques, down in the village. Oh, that place, Lily had said when informed of this and she refused to allow Marilyn Rathbone, the proprietress, into the house to give an opinion on the value of her glimmer-eyed owls. The woman had previously exercised mind control over several of Lily's acquaintances, walking off with a Derby dessert service, a Lowestoft teapot, two precious samplers, and a mahogany stick barometer after she had invited herself over on the pretext of a little chat about a question of local provenance concerning a stoneware jug which may or may not have come from the shop of a rum importer who had once lived in Towne. But even the oldest residents weren't old enough to remember the eighteenth century however hard they tried at Marilyn's urging. No, Lily wasn't about to fall into that trap, while she was off time-traveling through a lost century and being robbed blind in this one, as she signed binding legal documents in a trance.

Harvey dealt the fire a last sparky jab with the iron poker and he pointed a sooty finger at Rollins who knew better than to sit in Harvey's reclining lounger. Rollins rolled off and settled next to Brooks upon the central motif of the Indian rug. The Kung Fu tape had come in yesterday's mail and they had passed the previous evening mastering the Basic Survival Kick. Their leg muscles, or where they hoped to have leg muscles someday, felt unsolid and disconnected, they noticed now. They sprawled and laughed at something Radar said. They laughed automatically, prompted by the laugh track. Ginger had to step over the two great outstretched boys. She dragged a Hudson Bay blanket behind her, trailing like downcrest plumage and she had brought her new pillow to stuff behind her back after making sure everyone had read it. She gazed significantly at the owl andirons and narrowed her eyes at Harvey who had supported Lily in her assertion that Marilyn Rathbone was a real Salem witch, and Ginger mistakenly trod upon the back of Brooks's knee, suffering as she did so the nasty sensation of having a large, strenuous lizard writhing underfoot. Ginger yelped. Brooks hollered. Becky told him, "Hush. No one is interested."

Ginger toppled onto the sofa on the other side of Little Becky. She hooked the ottoman with strong toes and drew it toward herself as Little Becky clamped down her heels and exclaimed, "Hey."

"Oh, all right, we'll share," Ginger allowed ungraciously, billowing her blanket up to her chin.

Little Becky didn't want to share with Ginger. Auntie Ginger wasn't a sharer, she was a hogger. And it really wasn't fair because Ginger could sniff out a chocolate stash like she worked for the FBI or something, for the Chocolate BI. Oh misery. Little Becky collapsed. Her head plunged into her mother's lap. Jolted, Becky, who had been trying not to, sneezed and hacked and gargled the phlegm in her throat. Little Becky sat up and retreated beneath the lofted afghan. "Ma-ha," she objected.

"Cold sufferers are at their most contagious before they're symptomatic," Harvey said, but he held his handkerchief over his nose and mouth.

"Are you taking anything?" inquired Ginger.

"I thought there was some Contac in the medicine cupboard," Becky said.

"I took 'em," Harvey said. "Felt stuffly, one day. Knocked the cold right out. Knocked *me* right out. Best thing, just go dormant like a carp under ice when you're feeling low."

"Could you have sinuses?" Ginger asked. "Because I suffer so from sinuses."

"No, this is just a cold," Becky said. She wasn't about to be lured into a discussion of comparative ailments. She never won and tonight she rather thought she deserved to prevail.

"Because I have some Vitamin B-complex tablets if they'd help although vita-therapy is preventative and not really curative," Ginger said.

"Oh, thank you, that's all right," Becky said resignedly, reflecting that Ginger's vitamins *would* be complex.

"I'll drive down to the Rexall and get you something," Alden spoke up from the kneehole desk in the corner where he had settled to prepare a bill, an ironic mockery of a bill, composed, calligraphic, embossed, for Glen Fairweather's "records." He had spread out paper, the embosser, pen, ink, ruler, pocket calculator, and several replacement Band-Aids for his fingers which were rasped raw along the knuckles by the rough scrape of bark and which bled as he flexed his joints. Alden considered allowing a bit of his life's blood to streak across his effort, but everyone was being so odd about blood these days so he wrapped his handkerchief around his hand.

"No, you just finish what you're doing," Becky ordered Alden.

Ginger did not bother to conceal her grin. She glanced between Alden and Becky, taking her own experienced measure of the two of them. She observed their body language, of which she was a keen interpreter. Alden twisted round in his chair, his shoulders hunched against further suggestions. Becky lifted mending from a basket, a white cotton undershirt fraying beneath the arm. Her needle struck and stabbed as she rewove the fabric.

"Oh, are we all watching *M*A*S*H?*" Ginger asked. She meant she did not wish to watch *M*A*S*H*. "Lily!" Ginger greeted her. "Do *you* want to watch *M*A*S*H?*"

Lily was making her way across the lolling boys whom she viewed through an awkward spot in her bifocal lenses. They were bifurcated boys over whom she stepped with exaggerated care, nevertheless, her shoe came down upon Brooks's hand. He hollered. Becky said, "I've told you and I've told you to hush."

"Ought to rise for your old Aunt," Harvey said, straightening his recliner and lowering the foot rest to allow Lily clear passage. He operated his chair skillfully, punching the correct sequence of cloth-covered buttons concealed in an arm.

Lily sat in her Boston rocker. She leaned back and gazed toward the window instead of at the television screen. She could see the television screen in the glass, however, several sets of images reflected in several panes, and additional colors and movements were more ghostily sketched upon the outer storm window. Lily preferred this method of viewing. She was, she would have explained, less assailed by what she saw there.

"Because," Ginger said, "there are far more important things on tonight than a silly *M*A*S*H* rerun."

Glover hovered in the doorway. He had just swallowed a red which he trusted would ease him through this enforced evening with the family. In fact, he had been asked over to Missy's house—after she'd run him on his not so mysterious errand in her Mustang (scoring reds in a McDonald's parking lot—Missy had acted all scared they'd be arrested and she had required comforting). He would have gone— Missy said they had a fifty-four-inch screen and Surround Sound—but then Missy had gone and mentioned she had a little sister at home and that the little sister had a new baby which, according to Missy, was so far proving to be loads of fun to dress and decorate. Well, Glover wasn't falling for any of that, but it depressed him that he'd had another offer for tonight and not a better one because his current standard for better offers was such a pitifully low one.

"Glover, you're blocking my light standing there," Alden said. "Either sit down or go away, why don't you?" He seemed to favor that second option.

"Where?" Glover asked.

"What?" Alden asked.

"Go, sit, where?" Glover asked.

"Oh, anywhere," Alden said.

"Here?" Glover asked.

"*I* don't care," Alden said.

Glover wedged himself between the wall and the end of the sofa, his stiff leather boots crackling and popping as he folded and receded into his recess. Becky reached and dropped snipped-off threads onto his head. She was used to having a wastepaper basket beside the sofa but Lily had brought it up to her room, the Victorian papier-mâché wastepaper basket into which someone had taken to tossing apple cores and plum stones, and which had begun to disintegrate from the inside out.

"Hey," said Glover. "I have to watch the, you know. Where's the like, clicker thing? I really have to watch the wall, the wall thing, for, you know, school."

The family, unalert, ignored him.

"Where's the thing?" Glover persisted.

"It's never to be found," Ginger complained helpfully.

"Where's the clicker?" Glover clarified.

"Get up and change the channel manually," Alden said.

"Huh?" Glover asked.

"Get up and change the channel manually," Alden said.

"Huh?"

"My God, you kids. Brooks, you're closest. Reach up and put on Channel Four or Five. Not Seven, though, that's CBS," Alden said.

"Not Seven, no, not Seven," Harvey said. "Don't even speed past Seven. Go round it otherways lest I be unwittingly influenced by a subliminal image." He closed his eyes against this possibility.

Brooks fumbled and twisted a knob and Tom Brokaw's face briefly materialized before the picture reverted to a *M*A*S*H* surgical tent.

"Well, someone of us has the channel changer," Harvey deduced.

Little Becky squealed, squealing on herself.

"Give the changer to me," Becky said. "Now."

"No," said Little Becky. "I'm in charge. I was here first."

"So were the Injuns," Harvey said. "And do you see any Injuns?"

One of Ginger's ring-covered hands crawled out from beneath her Hudson Bay blanket and sought and slid beneath the afghan. Excited as a spider, the hand probed and investigated along Little Becky's leg. "Don't," Little Becky objected and she relinquished the channel changer to her mother's custody. She slapped away Ginger's hand which seemed to sense the presence of candy and began to scrabble against Little Becky's thigh.

Tom Brokaw's fratboy face bounced off a satellite circling high in the sky and tumbled down into the little parlor. He was advantageously placed above Berlin with an alight and important building standing behind his shoulder where it seemed to be whispering semiofficially into his ear. For he recited, fluently and certainly, the names of apparatchiks, the dates and details of wars and treaties, and the particulars of the political machinations which had brought events to the boil, and anchorpeople were all hired for their looks, Harvey said. Brokaw uttered on in his easy manner as live footage of celebrators filled the little parlor TV screen. People jostled, shouting and waving in paroxysms of sheer happiness. They ran, they danced, they surged irresistibly from one crowded corner to another as if everyone had suddenly been struck by the same conviction that that other corner was an even more giddily blessed spot on which to stand and cheer.

"They've been drinking there tonight," Harvey said.

"Did you catch *her?*" Ginger asked as the camera darted and picked out a woman with hair spiked into horns and eyes lined with the blackest kohl who was beating upon a section of wall with a serpentine boa as others flailed away with picks and hammers. "She's like something out of *Cabaret,*" Ginger said, and she began to hum, "What good is sitting alone in your room?" as Becky forgot herself so far as to mutter, No hope of that.

"What have we missed?" Arthur and Phoebe wanted to know. They had dragged their beanbag chair down from the attic and they plumped it on the floor just in front of the hearth. They subsided into the chair and settled into one another's contours. The occasional launched ember landed and melted through the beanbag's malleable plastic covering, through to the Styrofoam pellet innards which spilled onto the rug where they would resist being vacuumed up. Instead, the pellets would bounce and hop in front of her old beater head, Lily knew, but she didn't mention this because her difficulty seemed trivial when one considered the cleanup job they were going to face in Berlin as the next day dawned.

"You haven't missed anything. This seems to be an ongoing spectacle," Ginger told Arthur and Phoebe.

"But I don't know how that *M*A*S*H* turned out," Little Becky protested as a bank of commercials began to run: Kentucky Fried Chicken, Ford Trucks, which were built to last, and a Public Service spot endorsing the benefits of reading aloud to one's children.

"Everybody dies," Rollins said.

"That time the Communists won and they killed everyone," Brooks said.

"No sir," said Little Becky.

"Yes sir, that was the very last *M*A*S*H*," Brooks said.

"It wasn't, it wasn't. Make them say it wasn't, Ma," Little Becky cried.

"Hush," said Becky. "Hush, hush, hush."

"Wasn't," Little Becky breathed.

"You know, most East Germans have never in their lives seen a fresh orange," Harvey declared.

"Whoa," marveled Brooks and Rollins.

"Oh, come on," Becky said. "You swoon when I suggest you eat an orange."

"We'd eat them if there weren't any," Rollins allowed, injured. Their mother was being such a bear while everybody else in the *world* was being pleasant for a change.

"And Glover, you should be taking notes for your class," Becky said.

"Huh?" Glover asked.

"Write something down," Becky told him.

"No pen," Glover said.

"Alden, give him a pen," Becky said.

"But dear, I'm using my pen," Alden said.

"I have an extra pencil," Andy offered.

"Paper," Glover said.

"Paper too?" Becky asked.

"Need . . ." Glover said.

"Paper?" Andy offered.

Andy had been quietly sitting on the far side of the little parlor beside the radiator cover on a side chair he'd carried in from the dining room. When Betsy entered and uncertainly stood blinking at the television which was, at the moment, aroar with live actual sounds from Berlin, Andy bade her take his chair and he fetched another for himself from the dining room which he set down beside her. There was no other place. Side by side they sat. They opened notebooks across their knees. Their elbows collided as they wrote—Andy was left-handed, one of those awkward anomalies, but interesting about him. Betsy worried when Andy recorded an observation and she did not as his elbow jogged hers to write as well, if, in fact, they were studying the same scene.

Andy reported Harvey's assertion that Mikhail Gorbachev was actually one of ours, a Western agent planted ultradeep way back in the fifties which had been the brilliant and patient ploy of then Vice President Nixon, done with Ike's full and enthusiastic support, of course.

Betsy uncertainly spelled Volkskammer, the People's Chamber (oh, Volks like the car) which was the single-chamber Parliament the Easterners had while the other Germany was governed by a Bundestag and a Bundesrat, or two chambers. Betsy wasn't sure what Bundes was supposed to mean. She would have to find out. Tom Brokaw just assumed everyone knew, or maybe he didn't know either, but he was good at acting as if he did.

Arthur, who had been stretching his brain to come up with humorous insights on the news, for he was sometimes billed as a Top Topical Comic (these placards were prewritten) ventured this thought, "After a few days of pricing BMWs and Leica cameras, the East Germans will wall themselves back in again."

"Do you think so?" Harvey asked. "Can't see that happening. Just not human nature."

Phoebe, her head at rest on Arthur's skinny chest, smiled up at him and committed the line to memory although she wondered whether the joke might not be funnier if Arthur said the East Germans had priced lederhosen and cuckoo clocks and gone home. Such tourist fodder was easier to laugh at than expensive cars and cameras which were viewed by most people as objects of desire rather than ridicule.

Alden looked up from his desk and said that happy, singing, and massing Germans were not necessarily a heartwarming sight. "I hope the Soviets stay strong enough to breathe down their necks for a while, at least," he said.

"Well, they aren't strong enough, otherwise they'd be churning up Poland with their tanks," Harvey said. "In fact, try another channel, Becky—the Ruskies may be attacking on ABC."

"Oh, but don't you think Russia is just starting to see how much nicer it is to be a popular country?" Betsy asked.

Glover thought he must be hallucinating and reds didn't normally make him hallucinate; they just helped keep him agreeably down. He leaned forward, leather boots crunching, so he could stare in amazed challenge at Betsy until she noticed he was staring at her in amazed challenge and would spare them any more of her comments. But Betsy was intent, now, upon the television screen where a background piece on the Marshall Plan was airing. She was unsure whether she was supposed to know about this because obviously the Marshall Plan was History and not a Current Event—the news footage ran in black and white. Nevertheless, she paid attention. One could want to know about a subject just for the sake of knowing as Andy had pointed out to her when he interviewed her rather extensively one recent afternoon about local dating and intergender interpersonal relations and she had reminded him that she was as much a stranger to the mores of the place as he. Still, it seemed, Andy had to ask.

"That section of the Wall is going to fall down on top of somebody," Ginger remarked with a lack of alarm as live coverage resumed. After all, she was thousands of miles distant from the action. Betsy said, "Oh my," and Brooks and Rollins roused from their dreamy contemplation of the bitten-off threads accumulating on Glover's head (*when* would thread-head Glover figure it *out?*). They rolled onto their sides and watched the TV with every hope of becoming eyewitnesses. Little Becky took advantage of another outburst of cheering (as that section of wall fell) to open her Hershey Bar with tiny mouse snips of her fingernail along the outer wrappings.

"I remember when that Wall went up," said Lily, rather severely.

"Well, it wasn't so tremendously long ago," Harvey said. "I have tweed jackets that are older. British tailoring. Though," he added thoughtfully, "I'm sure the East Germans also wear jackets just as old, and pants, and ties, still, they wouldn't have boughten theirs on Bond Street."

Commercials interrupted again, for Mazda, Kentucky Fried Chicken, Your Friends at the First National Bank of Boston, and a promo for a future episode of the wordy weekly melodrama *thirtysomething*. Becky pressed the mute button.

Alden said, "Betsy, you don't think the United States is popular, do you? You don't think the rest of the world likes us? Haven't you ever been to, to France?"

"The main problem with us is, we're so set on being liked," Harvey said. "That's our error. We should be instilling healthy respect and fear. I tell you, the minute the Russians started to worry about having smiles on their faces on the six o'clock news, I said to myself, the Party's over. (Ha, there's a line for you, Arthur.) But no, being *nice* doesn't work for nation-states."

"That's only because you men run all the countries," Ginger said, "and everything else that catches your fancy in between."

"But my dear, the hand that rocks the cradle is the hand that rules the world," Harvey allowed gallantly.

"So some snarky man alleged," Ginger replied. "But tonight I'm not going to argue with you. Tonight I'm on all of personkind's side. I'm even happy for that man there lassoed around a lamppost who looks exactly like Jerry Falwell's fatter and even more unpleasantly inclined brother."

Everyone peered at the television but no one would give Ginger the satisfaction of agreeing she was right about the resemblance. She would only be encouraged to make more of these disadvantageous comparisons possibly involving one's own appearance and some other villain in the news.

Alden completed the Fairweathers' bill. He nipped the several pages with the embosser and he moved before the fire. He leaned over the screen and browned and age-spotted the sheets of paper against the heat of the flames. He displayed his effort to Becky who skewered her needle through the lapel of her blouse and tugged off her silver thimble and said, "Now that that's out of your system, make out a sensible account, although, frankly I just wish you'd have nothing more to do with those awful people. They're not worth your bothering about." And Alden understood then that Becky hadn't been angry at *him* all evening long. She had been angry on his behalf. Alden crumpled his handiwork and pitched it into the fire. The owls' eyes glowed a warmer yellow as the paper caught and was consumed. "Yes, forget them," Alden agreed. "Who needs the young Fairweathers? Let's write off the likes of the young Fairweathers," he said, and Becky cocked a slight smile in his direction. So, they were united again against a common foe.

"I think I'll start the cocoa," Betsy said eventually as the clock on the big-parlor mantelpiece faintly tolled half past an hour which she guessed must be a late one here and everywhere else on earth. The Germans were sagging, their cheers were flagging, and the blows of their pickaxes were skidding and slipping. The newsmen kept talking. Becky switched to a local weather report. If tomorrow was going to be a fine day, she would wash everyone's duvet covers and line-dry them.

One by one, the family joined Betsy in the kitchen with second thoughts and recommendations concerning the cocoa—she should add mini-marshmallows, a drop of peppermint extract, a shot of crème de menthe. Little Becky had to prevent anyone else from putting their mouth on her new New Kids mug. Becky tapped three aspirin from the community bottle kept on the countertop and she conscientiously sipped from a cup of grapefruit juice. Andy only wanted a glass of water. He sat on his high stool beside the serving hatch, his notebook pushed out of sight behind a square box of Pilot Crackers. After filling their electric kettle at the faucet, Arthur and Phoebe said good night and disappeared up the stairs to brew mung tea which according to the instructions printed on the side of the bag would leach toxins from their systems as they slept, although Arthur's fading voice was heard objecting that he wasn't sure he didn't rather require disturbing impurities to run quiet riot through his dormant brain for professional comedic purposes.

Harvey reminded Betsy that the recipe on the cocoa tin called for a dash of salt. Betsy didn't think salt was necessary and Uncle Harvey always got carried away. He seized the shaker when her back was turned and the chocolate tasted briny. Glover clumped past the stove where Betsy stood her ground against Harvey's contribution, whisking the mixture to a froth, which went further that way, into all the lined up mugs she had to fill. She took the cocoa's temperature by sticking a finger into the pot.

"Cocoa, Glover?" she offered.

"No," he said. He turned in a tight pivot and stalked across the kitchen floor with rigid precision. He snapped his bedroom door shut behind him, an action as unpleasantly meant but not as blamably rude as a slam.

"His feet are killing him," Becky said. "And I'm not certain he won't need help getting those boots off, or else I'm sure he would already have removed them."

"Brooks, Rollins," Alden said. "Why don't you help your brother."

No, they thought not. They sidled in front of the corkboard, mockingly at first and then more seriously mulling over Little Becky's information and instructions.

"Of course," Harvey was saying, "they won't enjoy many more of those big Olympic wins, the East Germans. They'll have to shut down those factories in the Erzgebirge Mountains where they bred sprinters with marathoners to achieve speed and endurance, which can backfire when you get a slow one who blows up after fifty feet. Those were the ones they sent to Afghanistan. They sent armies of those to Afghanistan, poor buggers."

"We should ask Lily if she wants anything," Becky said, after a pause.

"No, Aunt Lily never wants," Betsy knew.

"Didn't that crème de menthe suggestion register, speaking of things one does want?" Ginger asked as she sniffed the mug Betsy had handed her.

"Hey," Brooks spoke up. "Win a trip to Disney World."

"Disney World sucks," said Rollins.

"Oh. Right," said Brooks.

"Still. *Disney* World," Rollins allowed.

Little Becky realized then that had she won $10,000, she might have bought an airline ticket and flown off to Berlin where she could have laughed and yelled and jumped around and rejoiced and stayed out way late, so way late that the day got early again—she'd never done that before. Except, of course, her mother would never have let her go out and run around and rejoice beneath the Wall. Her mother would send her up to bed in her hotel room at the usual absurd hour with wax plugs stuck in her ears so she wouldn't be kept awake by all the noisy rejoicing. This realization lent some perspective to losing all that money. And $10,000 was not really so very much, Little Becky decided. Not even $10,000 would have been enough to solve the very least of her problems no matter how hard she tried to spend it on a car she couldn't drive or on a stupid trip she would not be allowed to enjoy. No, if Manfred in the Morning thought he was so great, he should have kept on moving the decimal point and adding zeroes to his Big Deal Dollar total. Little Becky was still willing to believe that $100,000 might do the trick, at least in her own situation.

"Red Letter Day, anyway," Harvey said, raising his cocoa mug toward the wall calendar. "Ought to circle the date and next year we'll fly the flag."

"In Women's Chorus after quite a lively discussion we voted to observe the events of the moment in our own private and quiet and respectful ways," Becky remarked to Lily who had come into the kitchen to remove a package of suet from the freezer to thaw overnight on the drainboard for the next morning's bird-feeding chores.

"I suspect Women's Chorus is wise to be thoughtful about the collapse of the Soviet Bloc," Lily said, for if her own family was any guide to go by, unfettered liberty and a world of choices presented a not unmixed basket of blessings to those to whom the prize had fallen by design or desire or default. This dogged pursuit of happiness, Lily reflected, could lead one on such a merry chase.

Chapter Four ❧ A Hill Holiday

L ILY'S SEVENTY-FIVE-YEAR-OLD Christmas cactus broke out in blossoms early that December as it had not bloomed for the past twenty years, and Lily wasn't sure she was entirely happy about the unusual profusion of the lush and showing-off flowers so brightly and tropically outshining and crowding out the Boston Fern and a spotty-leafed philodendron on the big-parlor windowsill. Some evenings she had to draw the curtains early against this further evidence of yet another change in the very ecology of her house.

The family had come to hear all about the plant's remarkable reawakening from Penny Nicholls, who knew its history, the afternoon she dropped by to remind Harvey of the Senior Village Youth Gift Grab Wrap-A-Ree party and to tell him he had to provide a present for a ten-year-old boy who liked dinosaurs, for she had taken the liberty of drawing a particularly pitiful case history from Mack MacNally's tartan cap at the Organizing Committee Meeting.

"There now, you see, even the Christmas cactus is happy that your house has come alive again," Penny told Lily.

"Oh?" asked Lily distantly. Penny had charged into the big parlor on her own, ignoring Lily's automatic and symbolic indication of the way to the kitchen which Penny knew perfectly well for herself. Penny had flung off the toreador's broad cape she fancied herself in nowadays, which soared and settled like a great bat upon the coatrack, and she revealed herself decked out in a lime-green sweatshirt with the message WORLD'S #1 GRANDMA spelled out in glitter glue across the front. This sweatshirt bloused over what Ginger later explained to Lily were leggings and not a pair of badly shrunk long johns as Lily had feared they must be, poor Penny, blithely prancing off to committee meetings and unscheduled social calls half-dressed in her regrettably grey underpinnings.

Lily drifted toward the windowsill and snapped the dry and papery spent blossoms from the Christmas cactus and she pulled off several more blooms that weren't entirely dry and papery and spent.

"It's blooming from all our breathing and talking so much and raising the nitrogen content in the air," Harvey happily argued back. He and Penny were a sparring and contradicting old pair. "There's nothing heartwarming here, it's science," he contended.

"Nonsense," Penny insisted. "Plants know. Mother Nature is very wonderful." She impulsively linked arms with Ginger who had wandered downstairs and effected an entrance, alerted by the sound of tires crunching over the driveway gravel. Ginger had sprayed Nuits de Printemps in her hair and thrown a cashmere shawl over her crumpled sweats before descending—solely, it turned out, for Mrs. Nicholls's benefit. How it continued to pain Ginger that her bedroom failed to overlook the driveway. She wondered if she could rig some sort of bull's-eye mirror device so she could see around the corner of the house. They had those mirrors installed all along the Amalfi Drive. Still, she and Louis had witnessed the aftermaths of some awful crashes when they were last there, a few years back so perhaps they really weren't that much help.

"And your poor Aunt Lily won't be left on her lonesome ownsome, wearing a red paper hat and eating a warmed-up bowl of cream of potato Soup-For-One *this* Christmas," Penny told Ginger.

"Soup-For-One, oh no," Ginger virtuously agreed. "We won't let Lily go through that sad sort of Christmas again. We'll make it an absolutely marvelous day for her." Evidently Ginger had forgotten she had vowed to boycott the holidays altogether this year. The day after Thanksgiving, reacting to the slablike bulk of the *Boston Globe* as it sat upon the kitchen table massive with advertisements for luxury furs and luxury household appliances and luxury holiday tours, Ginger had, as she waited for the coffee to reperk, delivered a scathing speech against compulsory joy and phony familialness. Alden had challenged her to say phony familialness five times fast, Lily recalled, and surprisingly,

Brooks and Rollins, who happened to be present, possessed the nimblest tongues.

"Of course, Meals on Wheels comes round with a hot turkey dinner on the twenty-fourth," Penny was explaining, "but that just isn't the same as having it on the big day itself, unless you stick the plate in the fridge and microwave it on the twenty-fifth bearing in mind to remove the cranberry sauce first, you don't want that hot. And a lot of them don't even have microwaves."

"Absolutely not," Ginger said. "Charity shouldn't be personally convenient for the giver, should it? I mean to say, it doesn't really count as charity if you're not awfully bothered and put out by your efforts." She smiled at Lily and held out her hand lovingly. Lily deposited the crumpled remains of spent blossoms in her palm and Ginger's smile wavered as she stared at the slight debris, working out what it must be.

Lily thought but did not say that Penny could only have come up with details like the red paper hat and the cream of potato soup from some solitary Christmas Day of her own. Penny had never been known to look very far beyond the end of her own nose, although her nose, to give her her due, was a nice long one. But Lily hoped for Penny's sake her holidays would be livelier now that she was the belle of Senior Village and had snared Harvey, of all people, as her beau.

"Becky has found a recipe for wassail punch in one of her women's magazines," Ginger said.

"Has she? I don't think wassail cup is wassail cup unless you wassail for it," Penny said. "It's wassail only in context."

"Really? I'll have to mention that to Becky," Ginger replied. "She ought to know. She's the musical one."

"How about whining for wine?" Harvey offered, indicating, if one knew the house, the vicinity of the dining room liquor cupboard.

"Please, please, please," Penny grinned, and whimpered.

"Actually, I mean Scotch," Harvey said.

"Well, don't scotch on the Scotch, neither," Penny said pertly.

Lily found herself wondering whether the mystery of the never-blooming plant had its solution somewhere in Becky's habit of watering the roots up to a point and then placing the pot in a dark closet and subsequently returning it to the windowsill in a carefully timed transfer ascertained by consulting *The Complete Guide to Household Plants*, which, as far as Lily was concerned, was not playing entirely fair to encourage the windowsill plants to behave in unusual ways which might be interpreted by some people as being propitious.

"So," Penny said, settling back for a good long visit. "Half a tot, Harvey, I'm driving the Senior Van to Shop 'Til You Drop at the Freedomway Mall, twenty percent off selected items for all over-sixty-fives, Lily."

"I don't know that I care to shop until I drop, Penny," Lily said.

"Well, a lot of them do," Penny said. "But tell me, what are your plans for the holidays so we can coordinate our doings," she added.

"You're as bad as that young Andy fellow," Harvey said. "All his questions. I told him I was going to paint myself green and climb the Congo's steeple for my Christmas. He didn't buy it, but he wrote something down anyway. 'Spect even fresh answers mean a lot in his so-called discipline."

ALDEN AND BECKY LABORED outside by the barn beneath an unsolid coffee-junket-colored sky. It was trying to snow. Big, messy sample batch flakes spattered against the barnboards, adhering and dissolving and deepening the stain of the bleached red paint. Alden raked away the mat of wet and blackened leaves rising and pressing against the bottom tiers of his woodpile. Becky tugged at the wiry, curlicuing stalk of a vine that had coiled itself around and about the logs as she meditated upon the practical uses of such a vine. There was so much of it and it resisted her tugs so determinedly. This is a very well made vine, Becky thought proprietarily.

For Alden had quite unexpectedly taken her up on one of her business ideas. That morning over their breakfast of split and broiled cranberry nut muffins she had mentioned, quite out of the blue, "What if we tied up pretty and portable bundles of attractive, specially selected logs with plaid ribbons and bows and sold them in New York at exquisite little shops to the Christmas crowds? Think of logical linkages one associates with an evening by the fire—reading, needlework, after-dinner drinks and cigars. We could ask our old wine merchant to take some.

And we could call it, oh, boutique firewood. *We* would have fallen for boutique firewood."

"Of course, all this wood will be too green actually to burn," Alden allowed now as he surveyed his woodpile. He scraped away a last layer of leaves. From the corner of his eye he saw a fringed and rippling shape detach itself from a shard of bark and scuttle away. He peered and prodded with a tine of his rake and satisfied himself that a shard of bark had not come spontaneously alive.

"If we charge enough, no one will want to burn their wood," Becky assured him. "They'll keep their bundles for show arranged on their polished brass andirons or in their polished copper buckets, the same way no one ever uses their best guest bathroom soap, not even the guests do."

"Well, all right. There's the woodpile. You choose what you think the assortment should be. You have the eye for design," Alden said.

Becky considered. "We'll want pine, of course, for the scent, and oak because the bark is so textural, and that nice white paper birch because it's so New Englandy. And you didn't chop down anything really rare, did you? People would like it if they could point to, oh, say, a piece of old Yankee shipbuilder's mahogany in their copper buckets."

Alden said he didn't think mahogany was very New Englandy, being a tropical hardwood, but he had taken down a dead, leaning hawthorn from the end of Lily's terrace.

"Hawthorn? That's very New Englandy sounding," said Becky.

"Dickens would be more Christmassy," Alden remarked.

"Now you're making fun," said Becky.

"If you save that vine you've been tangling with," Alden said, "we can bind up the bundles with lengths of that. The tartan ribbon will only serve for show." He wore a wide smear of leaf mold across his cheek, he had caught a splinter in his thumb, and he faced hard hours of chopping the logs down to a more portable size; nevertheless, this was better than sitting around all day and thinking too much and tasting old tooth fillings with the tip of his tongue.

"I only wish this were grapevine," Becky said, pulling and straightening and neatening a springing, curling heap. "Grapevine is the really more desirable vine."

"We'll just call it country vine," Alden said. "Anything country has cachet in the city."

"Yes, we always fell for the country label," Becky remembered. "Though there's country and there's country. I have to say Provençal country has the edge at the moment, but that can't be helped. Then again, Provençal country tends to evoke summertime and lavender and briny olives and natural stone swimming pools, doesn't it?" She heard the yearning in her voice and she fell silent.

"It's only that logs have such a rolling-about quality," Alden said. "We're going to need tartan ribbon *and* vine both to contain the bundles." The rolling-about quality became evident as Alden upset some critical balance with a prod of his rake and the pile collapsed. Loosed logs chased Alden and Becky as they backstepped out of harm's way.

"Look, there's all the pretty white paper birch at the bottom of the stack. Getting dirty," Becky said.

"Yes, I guess the birch would be on the bottom," Alden recalled. "My first project was cleaning up Lily's birch grove after our moving van mowed into it."

Becky crouched and flicked at a log with her glove. The pale bark was bruised. "It's too bad we didn't think of this sooner. I'll go get the whisk broom and try to give them a good brush," she said.

"I'll shift some wood into the barn for you," Alden called after her. "It's only getting wetter out here."

For a better snow was falling. The field, with its stubble of frost-shorn grasses and weeds was whitening patchily in a pattern of filled-in low spots and uncovered risen knolls. There was a picture wherever you looked, Alden thought, and he was well satisfied with his surroundings and with his project, believing that some aspect of the immemorial rightness of the scene, the swirling snow and old red barnboards and whitening field and darker fringe of the barrier forest, would communicate itself through their Country Boutique Salon Log Selection, as if the special genius of the place might yet be immured in the wood.

A few days later Alden and Becky, and Ginger as well, sat around the kitchen table, squares of paper set before them. They were stacks of thick, grey, rough-textured, handmade paper Becky had found at

Towne Artisans, a new shop in the old Oddfellows Building, offering for sale pottery shapes and wool-knitted shapes and shapes executed across canvases in acrylics, watercolors, and oils. Becky had wandered the shop's several aisles puzzling over all the shapes, not liking to ask, What is this? The artisans themselves staffed the premises and one never knew about artisanic sensibilities. But she had found the sort of paper she wanted there, several boxes of a rustic, honest, naive, and expensive paper which conveyed just the air she was after for the hand-lettered labels they planned to affix to every parcel of Select North Country Hearth Warmers. (They had changed the name. The family had voted by a show of hands at supper, market research, Alden said. Andy scribbled a note in the serving hatch but they'd all become used to the rush of his pen across 3 × 5 cards—Ginger had long since hardened them to the scrape of a pen across a 3 × 5 card.)

Now, Ginger's pen skidded over a lump in her square of paper where she had encountered a shred of calico, recognizable as calico (this was handmade rag paper). *Hand sawn*, she wrote, by *Tim Burr*. Oh, the second *r* resembled an *n*. That bump of calico.

"Tim Burr," she pronounced firmly at the lettering. She creased the paper in half and reached and spun the lazy Susan and plucked the lobster pick from between the saltshaker and the pepper mill and she punctured the upper left corner of the folded label. She spun the lazy Susan again and helped herself to a ball of bristly twine and the pinking shears. She snipped a bit of twine from the ball, an awkward endeavor. The twine fell between the shear's loosely enmeshing teeth. Ginger had to pull the twine back and forth across the scissors' blade. Then, she threaded the piece of twine through the lobster-picked hole, another task not easily accomplished—the hole was small, the end of the twine thick and fraying. She expelled a satisfied breath and added the label to her pile. She had completed seventeen.

"How many did you say that you needed, of the tags?" she asked.

"Two hundred," said Alden.

"So many?" Ginger complained even though she had offered to help when Becky mentioned she and Alden were going to have to be creative and invent a cast of woodcutters to populate their mythical North

Country timberland—like Saul Onion, Alden had said, only not exactly like Saul Onion. Saul Onion wasn't a very good example, it was only an example.

Hand sawn, Becky wrote, by *North Wood*. She rotated the lazy Susan. Bottles, jars, the spoon jar, cruets, clinked and rattled past. They clinked and rattled past her twice.

"The paper picker?" Becky asked. "The lobster thing paper puncher picker?" She was tired.

"Oh. Sorry," said Ginger and tossed it to her.

Hand sawn, Ginger wrote, by *Hew Asher*.

"Hew Asher," she said aloud. "His mother was Acadian, I think."

"Was she," said Becky.

"What if I put, *Sawn* by *Coney Pines?*" Alden asked. He flicked shreds of paper pulp from the point of his pen nib.

"Oh no, he sounds like someone's accountant," Ginger said.

"Yes, I'm afraid I can picture your Coney Pines," Becky agreed. "I think he'd saw one log halfway through and then have to sit down."

"*I* can picture Hew Asher," Ginger said, "with his Acadian blood. He's tall as an oak and as strong as an elk and his black hair flares back along his beautiful head in a wave. He keeps slicking back his black hair with his long, pitchy fingers, for his long hair falls into his ice-blue eyes as he bends to lift precious wild morels from the forest floor which he then sautés with secret herbs and essences known only to him and the wild wolves." She subsided into her thoughts. All of her labels would read, *Hand Sawn* by *Hew Asher*.

And Becky could picture North Wood, who, she knew, was a far finer man than Ginger's Hew. North's hair, his height, his heritage did not concern her. Her North was a man of qualities. North was a stalwart. One could turn to North, one could run to North, one could cling to North, and one would always know where one stood, oh, *true* North.

"I hope they're all as susceptible as Ginger in New York," Alden spoke to Becky. He nodded toward his dreaming sister and raised amused eyebrows.

"Don't make fun," said Becky. "You are in no position to make fun of anyone, frankly, Alden."

. . .

AT FOUR-THIRTY the following morning, Spaz eased his Loadstar up to the barn door, and he and Gee commenced heaving log bundles into the truck bed. They were halfway down the heap by the time Alden ventured outside, rubbing his eyes and pulling on his work gloves. Spaz's truck was rigged with a battery of daybright lights fixed above the cab. Spaz kept his own hours.

Alden protested the heaving—tartan bows were untying, tartan ribbons were straggling. He more carefully carried and arranged individual Olde North Country Holiday Hearth Warmers (a further improvement on appellation—Becky said they'd hit every buzzword, except buzz) as Gee and Spaz energetically outpaced him and Alden was obliged to match their efforts. He was paying Gee and Spaz for the day, he was paying for gas, he was thinking of where on earth to take the pair for lunch, but local honor required him to work harder than his crew. He had hired them so he was better than them, the figuring ran, although Alden guessed this was just a wily ploy on local labor's part. Still, Alden knew, if the need were to arise during the day for one of them to fall upon a live grenade, it would have to be he who made the supreme sacrifice. His bewildered Becky would only be offered a tongue-tied account of the tragedy by the abashed Weedens but then, Becky might not prove as inconsolable as he would wish her to be. She had been short with him again last night, and she had slept resolutely through his pre-dawnbreak departure. He had been considerate, of course. Nevertheless, the sound of a considerately pulled open sock drawer, while not loud, is lengthy. Becky ought, Alden thought, to have lifted her head from her pillow and mentioned, Good Luck.

"Z'it?" Gee was at his elbow, asking.

"What?" Alden asked.

"Z'it?"

Oh, is this it?

"Yes," Alden said.

They climbed into the truck. Spaz had left the motor rumbling and the heater churning. The cab's interior sweltered like Calcutta. Somehow, Alden was maneuvered into the middle position as he had meant not to be. He sat on a hump. Gee leaned into him, unselfconscious as a hound dog, and fell asleep, his nose and chin buried in the collars of his several plaid shirts, flannel, wool on top. A clutch of plaid ribbons spilled from his uppermost breast pocket which Gee had scooped from the barn floor and assumed had sprung loose from his ensemble like foliage. Spaz may have slumbered as well. His head lolled above his scarf (Princeton's colors, but surely not) and on the far side of Worcester he tried to downshift the knob of Alden's knee. But the truck held the road and was pointed the right way. Alden watched the road. Spaz perked up and followed Alden's direction as city traffic and city signs and the city itself appeared through breaks in the clouds. Spaz was not very familiar with New York, never having been there before in his life, he explained. He had promised his mother he would never go there and he would have to be mindful to remember not to tell her what he'd been up to today.

The local linkages had been established. They were to make deliveries at the Aldens' former wine merchant, a tobacconist (fine cigars, humidors, packs of the wide world's cigarettes, those Italian wax matches called *fiammiferi*), at the floral designer they had liked and who remembered them and who had wondered what had become of the Lowes, and at Artefacts, Inc., a fine arts and antiques establishment where Alden and Becky were also known and had often browsed in the past. All of the shop owners had agreed to handle the Hearth Warmers after Becky had explained her idea so persuasively over the telephone. Indeed, they were all looking forward—

"The street where we lived," Alden told Gee and Spaz as he fell back along old routes through the old neighborhood. There were wreaths on doors and trees in lobbies and strings of lights switched on and bright against the grey day. Their old building had a new doorman out front who looked shifty—his hair was combed to cover a spreading bald spot. But Alden's perspective had altered, sitting high above the curve of a strong truck fender. He felt not unlike a conqueror returning in a captured tank. Pedestrians thought twice, other traffic wasn't so sure at the approach of the juddering, mud-splattered Loadstar. Spaz had clapped on a leather helmet hat when he spotted his first business sign not written in God's Own English. Gee gawped out the window, staring and staring through his lashless eyes. Alden hadn't noticed, back in Towne, the unguarded lashlessness of Gee's eyes.

"Park along here, Spaz," Alden said. "Any old where will do."

Alden chatted his way through the slight paperwork he and Becky had generated, businesslike, as Gee and Spaz toted bundles. Shop assistants retied bows, twitched the labels round, read them, and begrudged a smile. They stacked, just inside doorways, attractive displays. One could almost sniff the pine, or a pine-ish savor which would turn pinier in the steam heat. Alden was told how well he looked, how relaxed, how unencumbered by whatever it was that had formerly encumbered him. He was handed cash at which he glanced only briefly. It seemed too complicated to sort and count cash which looked so unlikely, anyway, and which stretched the slim lines of his billfold when inserted. He bought two interesting cases of odd-lot bottles at the wine merchant, and a box of cigars for Harvey for Christmas at the tobacconist. At the floral designer, he tendered the baby present for the Incan orphan who had just arrived from Peru—Becky had searched everywhere for a stuffed alpaca Alpaca with a beautiful face. Alden admired Artefacts' lately acquired Pennsylvania Chippendale chest, very like the one Lily had had carted up to her bedroom although Lily's piece retained its original hardware. Alden glanced out Artefacts' door. Gee and Spaz squatted by the curb smoking the Turkish cigarettes they had bought at the tobacconist, pooling their funds. He could tell Gee and Spaz thought the cigarettes tasted strange—they held the tips a half-inch from their puckered lips as they pulled the blue smoke into their lungs. They hated Turkish cigarettes. This proved it.

"Lunch?" Alden offered when they were settled again in the truck. "I feel we've earned our lunch. There's a Cajun place not too far from here," he ventured, where, perhaps, his companions would be taken for the men who had delivered the gator steaks and lingered on to dine and thus inspire only interested and even respectful comment from the other patrons.

But Gee and Spaz had brought tuna and onion sandwiches and a six-pack. Alden ducked into a deli. They ate in the truck. Alden offered garlic dill pickles which were accepted. They didn't sit too well on Gee's unaccustomed stomach.

"Anything you fellows care to see in the city before we head back to the sticks?" Alden asked. This was the men's first visit, after all, and Alden was in no particular hurry to return to Towne. Indeed, a short stop at his old office was not unimaginable—if not this time, then next time he might drop in. This time, he'd drive by and test how much he minded, just driving by.

"We can see the decorations on Fifth Avenue. Or I have my membership card to the Metropolitan on me," Alden said. "I think I can still get you onto the floor of the Stock Exchange, that's an experience not open to all. Or there's always a U.N. tour."

Gee nudged Spaz. Spaz elbowed Gee. They were sitting side by side. Alden had won the window seat when he returned from his deli run. Gee had attempted to switch, but Alden wouldn't hear of Gee dislodging himself.

"We'd like to see," said Spaz, "the place where King Kong died."

"All right," said Alden. He considered. "Turn left here," he said.

And, as Alden told Becky later (who was speaking to him and fascinated by his account of the day and pleased because she had found two bottles of a favorite Beaujolais in one of the odd-lot cartons), when they got to 34th Street, Alden's best guess where impact had occurred, and as Alden pointed to a spot on the sidewalk and pronounced, Here, Gee and Spaz had leaned forward and peered upward through the windshield as if they believed the great beast was yet to be viewed mid-fall, midflight, mid-destiny, caught at the last instant before the sky lost its hold and the outlines of earth grew huge. Alden told Becky he had been touched by this beyond any reasonable explanation for it.

ANDY TOOK OFF for Florida in the middle of the month. He was used to observing an academic calendar and he had not visited his mother for more than a year. Last Christmas he'd spent with Renata which his mother had minded, some girl preferred to her. This year she would continue to resent his neglect of the previous year and begin to blame him in advance for his absence the following year, predicting he would forsake her once again. If Andy could be counted on for anything, it was that he could not be counted on. His mother was going to have a splendid holiday.

Betsy returned from babysitting late. Mrs. Snowdon had taken the wrong exit on her way home from the Mall, where she had hopelessly roamed the stores with her long, amended list and her Visa card. Betsy had noticed right away the Alaska-shaped oil slick at the top of the driveway bowl where Andy's car was always parked at that hour of the evening. It was suppertime and Andy was supposed to be stationed at the serving hatch charting the dynamics of the family's dinner conversation in his marble-boarded notebook. The oil slick stretched, blackly glistening, signaling some stock-footage message of a hasty decampment by the light of the carriage lamp that had been switched on against her late return by Phoebe who kept an eye out for Betsy. No one else seemed to think of her, these clouded nights when darkness fell so early and Phoebe could not help but remember the opportunistic haunts and ghoulies she had so deeply believed in all through her rural and solitary mountain girlhood. She had known a girl who disappeared forever, just going out to the shed.

"Aunt Lily? Aunt Lily?" Betsy asked before she dropped her coat and her bookbag at the foot of the back stairs. "Where's Andy's car? Where's Andy?"

"Delaware? By now," Lily supposed, which was not the information Betsy sought but Lily was contributing her own expert knowledge. Lily herself had twice driven down to Florida with maps cluttering the passenger seat and a compass affixed to the dashboard, its needle unreassuringly fidgeting beneath a clear plastic dome. Nevertheless, she had discovered Florida easily enough. One went southwest and then traveled south some more through all the Civil War states. Lily had rather enjoyed the drive, and staying at Quality Inns and eating continental breakfasts while reading the foreign news from Georgia. She had not enjoyed herself at Olive and Frank's tangerine-orange-painted bungalow that sat at the edge of the flat and pallid and not very oceany smelling Gulf of Mexico. She had grown weary of having to agree, yes, it was very remarkable to be able to sit outside on a February afternoon wearing nothing but a cotton sweater, which, apparently, had sounded indecent to no one but herself, wearing nothing but a cotton sweater. Florida, Lily felt, had a coarsening effect upon displaced northern old people. She would never forget the object Olive had made in her Neighborhood Association crafts class—a billed cap devised from flattened and pierced Budweiser beer cans, perforated along the edges and cobbled together with thick orange-yarn crochet stitches. Olive had given this hat to Lily to wear outside in the worst of the sun but her head was too round to carry it, thank goodness, for politeness would otherwise have mandated a public appearance somewhere in the beer can hat had it fit.

"I mean, Aunt Lily," Betsy was standing before her patiently waiting for Lily to snap out of her reverie, "where has Andy gone?"

"Home to Florida, he said," Lily told Betsy.

"He has a home? In Florida?" Betsy asked.

"He has a mother there, evidently," Lily said.

"He does? A mother? We haven't asked him very much about himself, have we?" Betsy said. "I mean, we're so busy talking about ourselves all the time, we haven't been very thoughtful about him. I can't even begin to picture what Andy's mother could be like, can you?"

Based upon her Florida experiences, Lily said, she probably could.

"Oh yes," Lily added, "Andy would like someone to catalogue the Christmas cards that come. He's made a list of attributes to look for." She fished a sheet of paper from her sweater pocket and handed it to Betsy.

"Overtly religious," Betsy read, "nonreligious, New Age religious—Mummy gets those—Santa-centered, nature-centered, nostalgia-centered. List symbols, images, yes, okay, I see what he's after. It's interesting, because I've already noticed that Uncle Harvey receives cards that all say they're remembering his sad loss at this happy time of year, and Uncle Alden's say, our positive thoughts are with you at this happy time of year, and Mummy's are all, our concerned thoughts are with you. I think Andy will be interested in all the commiserating cards, don't you, Aunt Lily?"

"They are certainly a phenomenon," Lily agreed.

. . .

AND ANDY DROVE down to Florida in a day and a half with his radio switched on loud. After Maryland, he turned to his tape collection because of the high Country and Christian content crowding the airwaves. Big Confederate-flagged trucks bore down upon his VW which shuddered in their backdraft. The earth reddened where ruts had been cut by plow or Caterpillar, and the air softened. The cold and damp no longer bit but, rather, insinuated itself through the flannel of his shirt. He had pulled off his gloves and struggled from his confining parka when he spotted his first goblet-silhouetted magnolia tree, a tradition from other trips south. The girls behind the counters of the off-interstate Hardee's became more cordial very late at night and very early in the morning as they filled his silver thermos with coffee and asked him where he'd come from and how far he was going, growing thoughtful when he told them he was headed from Boston to Palm Beach which seemed to describe to those homegrown and grounded girls the farthest limits of an unknown world.

Andy shot down Rte. 95 to the turnoff to Jupiter, actually, where his mother had bought a subsiding little house within sound of the ocean and sight of the water's reflected glimmers and projected moods playing off her salmon-pink-painted patio walls. His mother was out reading to the blind as she had warned him she might be when he had called from Jacksonville to let her know he had made it to Jacksonville. Andy had had to wrest the duplicate front door key from Mrs. Lloyd who lived next door to his mother behind the Spanish hacienda-style portcullis. The warder-like Mrs. Lloyd had made Andy prove who he was before surrendering the key to him. She had never met Andy for he had not come home even once during the sixteen months Mrs. Lloyd had lived beside his dear mother, she reminded him.

"Aren't there any pictures of me on a table?" Andy asked. "Graduation pictures? I'm always graduating from somewhere. Don't you recognize me from a picture?"

Mrs. Lloyd countered he may have disguised himself as the son of the house, who had struck her, from his pictures, as more of a type than an individual, a point Andy had to concede; he was such a product of his environments.

So Andy answered sharp questions about family names and birth-dates, and it seemed that his own and his mother's account of her birth year did not tally. This marked a victory for Mrs. Lloyd, bettering a bad son on her own, fortified doorstep. When Andy mentioned his road weariness as the reason for his error—that of failing to remember his mother's preferred year of birth—Mrs. Lloyd told him he should have Planned Better than to arrive unequal to a test. Andy decided he approved of the Hill method of keeping the spare key beneath an over-turned geranium pot on the back porch, if, indeed, the door had been locked in the first place. Miss Hill had a cryptic saying, One need not lock for everything, and Andy had yet to unlock the meaning of that.

TODAY IS SATURDAY, Dec. 16, 1989 (a notice board hanging beside the elevator door in the foyer read)

You reside at Havenhurst Adult Care Facility, Rte. 63, Towne, Mass., USA Our President is Mr. George Herbert Walker Bush.

Happy Birthdays This Month To: Dec. 3 Bessy Wesson 89 years young
Dec. 16 Sarah Angell 78 years young
Dec. 26 Nana Doucette 100 years young
Welcome to the Century Club Nana!

Field Trip Sign-Up: Monday, Dec. 18, 1989. We are all invited to Towne Senior Village for a Pancake Supper and Christmas Card Swap. If your wheelchair bound and planning to attend, contact Mrs. Russo.

Our Next Holiday: Christmas, Monday, Dec. 25, 1989

Today's Weather Will Be: Cold and Windy! Bundle up if you plan to go outside!

Today's Lunch Menu: Individual Chicken Pot Pies, Creamedy Mashed potatoes, Baked Winter squash,

Individual Custard Fruit Cups, or Individual Diet Tray.

Today's Activity: Towne Women's Chorus will perform
their "Holidays Are Made of Memories
Like These" musical program in the Residents' Lounge at 2:30 P.M.

The residents and their visitors had assembled on folding chairs in
the Residents' Lounge. They faced a shallow stage erected at the drafty
northern end of the overlong room. The stage was empty, as yet, but the
general feeling prevailed that the space ought to be watched. An upright
piano had been rolled to the foot of the stage and someone, carried away
with her bedecking and adorning, had wired a holly garland along the
length of the keyboard. Rosalie Chubb, however, said she would be able
to play once she became used to the sensation of plunging her hands
into a thicket. There had been rival decorating gangs at work at Havenhurst, Becky concluded as she stood at the back of the room, sizing up
the house. Two trees, a real specimen and a silvery, shimmery fake, were
set in opposite corners and several window ledges supported several
styles of manger scenes—plastic, papier-mâché, porcelain baby Jesuses
lay upon hay and burlap and satin cushions in their separate cradles,
lying there prematurely, Becky noted, for in Hill households, the baby
Jesus did not make his appearance until Christmas Day. He waited in
a designated Heaven set upon a high bookshelf until the morning of
the 25th when he was ceremoniously floated down to earth after one
of the children remembered to ask, Hey, where's— Andy had quizzed
Becky about family rituals before he took off for Florida and she had
neglected to mention that one. Brooks and Rollins always supplied dive-
bombing fighter jet sound effects to accompany the Messiah's descent
(after someone recalled on which high bookshelf he was languishing).
Then, hushed and forbidden, they produced the sounds silently as Little
Becky shrieked and pelted them with foam packing peanuts. She sulked
after she was scolded for defending the Lord and she began to re-
wrap her presents to return to her evil brothers and her horrible parents.
This was also a tradition, Becky remembered as she made her careful

way through the audience of white heads and bags of knitting set upon the floor—the folding chairs had been arranged without reference to a central aisle—and she could only think, we are all such veterans of Christmas.

The members of Women's Chorus had to step over an abundance of potted poinsettias to achieve the stage above which white pine swags were suspended only as high as elderly and afflicted arms could stretch. The swags and paper chains and reindeer cutouts drooped and tangled with women choristers' earrings and hairstyles. Cynthia Peck, who was young and susceptible, swatted and giggled.

It is nice to hear young laughter, several Havenhurst ladies remarked. Old laughter could be so wheezy and cut off abruptly.

Anna Webster huffed into a pitch pipe and Rosalie Chubb searched for and sounded an approximate note on the piano. Becky, from her vantage point on the raised stage, gazed round rather curiously for this was the establishment that was trying so hard to recruit Lily, although Lily had said she hadn't heard from them lately. Surely this was no place for Lily, with its hectoring message board and evidence of factions and hard-held opinions over Christmas trees and crèches, and Becky spied oxygen tanks stacked in a corner next to a fire extinguisher, unwisely so, she thought, for the wrong cylinder could easily be snatched for the wrong emergency.

> *"When Christ was born of Mary free,*
> *In Bethlehem, that fair citie,*
> *Angels sang there with mirth and glee*
> *'In excelsis gloria,' "* Becky sang.

The residents of Havenhurst sang along as best they could and their visitors tried not to mind the waveriness and inaccuracies of the old voices trilling at their sides, for the visitors were quite sure a Sing-Along wasn't intended; Women's Chorus had not asked them to feel free to join in. But the residents had been subjected to so much in the way of participatory entertainment—to mass jazzercising, to an experiment in past life regression when they counted backward from 100 and then glanced quickly down at their feet which, for a fleeting instant, were supposed to appear to them shod in the style of a previous life, in Egyptian sandals, Pictish leather wraps, Edwardian buttoned boots, or, dismayingly, as brutishly bare and mud-scoured with long yellow toenails—that they, the residents, jumped in before they could be singled out and compelled to come forward to verify, for example, that the magician's assistant had truly disappeared from the Chinese cabinet into which she had just been jammed for, of course, one could not be sure what other tricks a magician might have up his sleeve.

Women's Chorus, unused to being sung back at, sang forth a little louder.

> *"The foxes found rest, and the birds had their nest,*
> *In the shade of the forest tree;*
> *But thy couch was the sod, O thou son of God,*
> *In the desert of Galilee.*
> *Oh come to my heart, Lord Jesus!*
> *There is room in my heart for thee,"* Becky sang.

She had become aware of a man in the audience who was trying mightily not to smile. His smile, the smile he was fighting, flashed off and on with the glee of the wicked, Becky decided. It was not a smile signaling tender memories and sweet sorrows recalled as his old mother or granny or whoever she was, atilt beside his elbow, wandered in song along a theretofore unexplored route toward and roundabout but never quite attaining "O Little Town of Bethlehem." The man, who wore a short leather jacket with a mouton collar, an old jacket—the leather was jointed with cracked white lines—was not the sort of man Becky approved of. Motorcycles, she thought repressively. Nevertheless, she detected dash there.

The man murmured into the old woman's ear. She cupped her ear. He whispered again and removed himself to the far end of the lounge where a closed door bore a sign, SMOKERS' ROOM. He nudged the door ajar and lit a cigarette and held the cigarette in his right hand behind the door. He ducked his head inside the room to inhale, then he straightened and forgetfully exhaled above the audience. An attentive niece coughed warningly on behalf of a cherished aunt too frail to cough for herself.

But in fact, Becky was prepared to be grateful for the presence of the so easily amused man for, most unexpectedly, Arthur was slated to appear next. Naomi Liebenthal, Women's Chorus Outreach Chairperson, had caught his comedy act one night at the Imperial Wok, and maybe it was all the umbrella drinks she'd consumed, but Arthur had tickled her funnybone and she had asked him to help plump out the program after the Brazen Bellringers, popular local favorites, had a scheduling conflict.

> *"And idol forms shall perish,*
> *And error shall decay,*
> *And Christ shall wield his scepter,*
> *Our Lord and God for aye, "* Becky sang and bowed.

Women's Chorus departed the stage and members sat where they could find space among the folding chairs for they had been invited to stay on after the performance to chat and mingle and they were going to be served little cakes or something.

Arthur ambled onstage as if he'd come in to sweep up. His lanky, oversized extinct bird looks were arresting. Rough red plumage sprouted wildly from his head. His legs were long stalks with articulated knees visible through the holes in his deplorable jeans. He observed the audience with a glittering eye turned sideways, a rapidly blinking and uncomprehending eye which seemed to signal Arthur's worldview—he was a distracted being, always out of his element, striving to make sense with what brain he possessed, a brain he had to jump-start manually upon occasion as he chopped the back of his head with the heel of his hand. He began to describe a childhood Christmas when his parents told him they had bought him a puppy, but the puppy, it turned out, was a very special dog who worked undercover for the FBI and was, at present, living incognito with an organized crime family. But, Arthur said, he had been allowed to meet the puppy in the park encountered on walks, in his various guises—as an Irish setter named Troy, as a Welsh corgi named Missie, as a sheltie named Scoop. They were all Arthur's puppy, who had stolen away from his spying and reporting duties at the crime family's compound, to frolic for a few happy minutes with his *real* little boy.

"Oh, my dear," the softhearted Anna Webster breathed at Becky.

Becky was only grateful Arthur wasn't making spirited public fun of her or Alden or the children. She raised her eyebrows and shrugged at Anna.

The residents were grateful Arthur wasn't telling jokes about dentures or elder sex and they emitted little sighing syllables at intervals. The visitors, who by then were trying not to glance at their watches, tended to applaud Arthur's punch lines as an alternative to laughing at them for laughter was difficult to come up with convincingly. The man who had been smoking and upon whom Becky was counting to enjoy Arthur heartily and, she hoped, infectiously, had wandered forward. He sat on the piano bench, an arm settled, with a discordant plunk, among the holly leaves, and he studied Arthur, soberly, silently. Becky hoped Arthur hadn't noticed the leather-jacketed man's near scowl of concentration as Arthur soldiered on, observing that all the bank robbers and bunco artists and murderesses who had been put away for thirty years at the conclusions of old *Dragnet* episodes must all have been released from prison by now. They were all out, they were all out and *old*, Arthur charged as he stared accusingly at the straggling rows of white heads. "Is Mayhem Mary here?" he wanted to know.

"We have a Mary May*hew*," someone spoke up and was shushed.

ON THE DAY BEFORE Christmas, Alden dragged back to the house the eight-foot-high ideally conical and densely branched tree he had hunted down out in the woods and felled with a sharp ax and bundled in burlap for the rough haul home. He had wandered widely through Lily's woods. Nature unaided did not produce very presentable fir trees and he may even have strayed off Lily's property during his long search. He discovered his perfect tree up on a ridge which he would have sworn was still Lily's land but for some bright yellow surveyor's tape and neon slashes of paint marking a boundary. He took the tree anyway for, obviously, someone was planning to build up there. He didn't mention the surveying activity to Lily, in part because he forgot, in part because he knew she would mind this encroachment along her border. Lily could make the North Koreans look casual about missteps over a line.

Becky sought Lily in her bedroom where Lily was wrapping presents. The wrapping was proceeding slowly because Lily hadn't been able to locate her Scotch tape dispenser which had thoroughly disappeared. Lily had her suspicions the dispenser was mixed up somehow in the muddle on Ginger's unmade bed, Ginger's gala Christmas headquarters, all shiny catalogues and splitting shopping bags and trailing paper—Ginger was doing her best on the budget Betsy was holding her to. But the mere idea of requiring Ginger to search among her scattered effects made the blue vein beneath Lily's parchment-thin forehead skin throb. So, at present, Lily was using her Elmer's Glue (which the reliable Becky had dependably returned after making her lamp repairs) to secure her wrapping. This was proving to be time-consuming for she had to press a firm thumb back and forth along the seams until they stuck. She sat on the edge of her bed running her thumb over the end of a box of Rose Geranium Soap. She lifted the package to her nose and sniffed. An earthy, sweet smell emanated through the wrappings and Betsy would guess what she was getting but that couldn't be helped. Then again, Betsy ought not to be rummaging among her gifts and, to be fair, it was unlikely she would. Betsy was being rather wan about the holidays.

Lily had not picked up gift tags. It was complicated enough to have to buy a special bolt of wrapping paper featuring Santa's round and red and puffy heart-patient's face, selected for the children's sake. She wrote directly on the package with a felt-tip marker—To Betsy from her Aunt Lily. Merry Christmas, she added as an afterthought. She used old yarn for ribbon. Lily did not want for old yarn.

"Oh, excuse me," Becky said, opening Lily's door a crack for Lily had answered *Yes* to her knock although it may have been a *Yes?* requiring further explanation through the door before she was granted admittance but, really, she had only come to ask a simple question and she didn't see the need for having to ask Lily twice, to ask whether she might ask. On rare occasions, Becky rebelled.

"Am I interrupting?" she asked, coming into the room. She stepped upon layers of rugs and sat—she had her choice of chairs—on the nearer wing chair. Such a cozy lair. Her elbow bumped the library book on an adjacent table, which Lily would rather have been reading than getting on with her present-wrapping. Becky averted her eyes from the yet-to-be-wrapped gifts piled upon Lily's bed, nevertheless she had seen enough to satisfy her curiosity. They had not exchanged presents with Lily in the past—they had exchanged cards and Becky had always included the latest family lineup picture from their most recent vacation. But this year was different, and Becky hoped they would all do neither too much nor too little. Belatedly, Lily drew an afghan up and over two Random House Dictionaries, several bottles of Vita Bath Oil, a buffalo plaid scarf snaking out of a narrow box from Jordan Marsh. Nothing to be concerned about there, Becky thought, most items under twenty-five dollars but not too far under.

"I'm afraid we need a tree stand," Becky explained, "because ours is too small. We only ever had those spindly little tubercular trees you get in the city but Alden has gone out in the woods and found a real giant for us this year, so I don't suppose we could borrow your tree stand?"

But Lily said she had long since donated her stand to the All Saints' White Elephant Table when she had given up her holiday decorating except for the front door wreath, to which she was beholdened by the Animal Rescue League. She was indelibly on their delivery list. They continued to assume year after year that she still required a 14-inch balsam round with a red bow and a bayberry spray, which wreath would remain affixed to her front door through the rest of the winter until it blew off of its own accord in a stiff March wind, and shreds of the once-red ribbon would reappear entwined among the twigs and grasses of the robins' nests in May, so Lily really didn't mind being stuck on the Animal Rescue League's list.

"I hope you don't care if we're a bit festive," Becky said. "We're a cheerful bunch, deep down under," she supposed.

"And Harvey can be awfully happy too," Lily agreed. Last night in the kitchen he'd seized her and waltzed her round the table as he sang, "Be jubilant my feet." He'd steered her into the handle of the cellar door and overnight she had formed a great purple bruise which sat too high on her hip for remonstration purposes.

Becky next routed Glover from his off-kitchen bedroom where he'd been sleeping the afternoon away although he was not aware he'd been asleep. He thought he'd been reading *Alone,* filched from Lily's bookshelves, but for the past hour he'd been dreaming his own version of an Antarctic marooning. The hatch to his burrowed hutch had clanged shut while he was out feeding the penguins and there he stood in his stocking feet and a turtleneck pullover, banging unvailingly at the door as the six-month night descended.

"You were having a bad dream," his mother informed him coolly and he was too shaken to argue.

"Anyway, get up. I need you to run some errands," Becky said. She handed him a piece of paper upon which she had roughly traced round the bottom of the tree trunk as Alden held the tree erect. TREE STAND TO FIT THIS TREE REQUIRED, she had written.

"Try the Ben Franklin Store," she told Glover. "Do you know which store that is? It says Ben Franklin on the sign. And here's a list of a few things I need at the IGA, spelled I-G-A on the sign." She held the car keys over her head as she extracted a promise from Glover that he would drive responsibly and come right home. Glover thought of reminding his mother how old he was and how tall and that he wasn't completely stupid but he didn't want to supply her with an opening to start nagging him about his college applications. (Next fall, there you'll be, left outside in the cold and knocking at the gates, his father kept saying.)

Brooks and Rollins flung themselves into the backseat of the old Volvo as Glover was about to drive off and he suffered their presences because he was still recovering from the effect of having been so very alone.

Then, even though her mother had told her not to, Little Becky again disturbed Lily in her room. Lily answered, "Just a minute," to the loose-knuckled knocking at her door and Little Becky waited for what she took to be a minute. She spoke directly into the doorjamb. "Aunt Lily, please, please, please," she tediously, strenuously begged.

"Just a minute," Lily repeated, but now Little Becky's red-hot ear pressed against the door detected interesting rustles and crackles of shopping bags and packages being hidden away in bureau drawers—

they scraped open and shut—and inside the blanket chest—the lid thumped.

The door opened at last and Little Becky slumped like a rag doll into the room, her greedy button eyes darting everywhere, but Lily had been thorough in her desire not to satisfy the importunate child's curiosity, hardly a Christmassy sentiment on Lily's part, but there it was.

"We need mornaments," Little Becky blurted. "Because the tree Dad got is so way huge."

"You need what? I don't know what you mean," said Lily.

"More ornaments," Little Becky pronounced. "Please, please, please." The scratchy needle of Little Becky's voice was caught in the groove of her neediness.

"But you must have your own ornaments," Lily said. "They must have come from your own home along with that stand that didn't fit your father's tree. I'm sure you have very pretty things from New York." Lily supposed she meant they had sophisticated decorations and not pretty ones, since they'd originated in New York where it sounded to Lily nothing had ever been simple.

"Please. No we don't have nice ornaments. I'm sick of them. *Every* Christmas, and there aren't enough and I want to see yours, please."

"I don't like to enter Andy's room," Lily temporized, but she knew she had lost when she stopped saying no and began giving reasons why not.

"They're in Andy's room? But he's not here so we can go look," Little Becky insisted. "You can go into someone's room in an emergency when they're not there."

"Emergency?" Lily questioned.

Betsy sat on her bedroom's skimpy rag rug critically reading *Sonnets from the Portuguese* in a small brown book with yellowed, brittle pages she had found on top of the bathroom hamper. She was mentally amending all the "thee"s and "thou"s to "you"s and "your"s because thee and thou sounded so antique and insincere. Did Elizabeth address Robert as "thee" in daily life? Betsy thought not, although who could say for sure about those two? She meticulously consumed an apple, starting at the upper left corner and biting in sequence all around and down as she read, "Go from me. Yet I feel that I shall stand Henceforward in *your* shadow," and, as she read, she became aware of voices and footfalls emanating from Andy's room across the hall, toward which her awareness seemed to maintain an address. She marked her place in her book with the yanked-off apple stem and, setting her apple and her book upon her desk, she prepared to interfere on the absent Andy's behalf.

Little Becky was jouncing on the bedspread, a natural-colored coverlet in a pattern called Abigail Adams which had lost half its fringe in the clothes dryer and would cost a fortune now from a catalogue, so the fringe situation was a real pity. The blue-wool-clad flank of Aunt Lily extended from the closet, the deep dark closet angled beneath the rise of the attic stairs, a cavelike space piled with cardboard boxes shoved far back into the recess. Colder air seeped into the room. All of Lily's closets provided cold storage. Her interior walls were unusually thick, Andy said. He'd made interior and exterior measurements of the house and could chart the discrepancies.

"Aunt Lily?" Betsy asked concernedly. Aunt Lily shouldn't be down on her hands and knees like that, and Little Becky shouldn't jump on the mattress. "Stop that, you'll break Andy's bed," she instructed Little Becky in an impatient aside.

"Aunt Lily," Little Becky objected, jumping more strenuously in protest so that a strained inner slat of dry old wood snapped in two. Little Becky suddenly stood up to her thick ankles in sunken bedding.

"Now look what you've done," said Betsy.

"I didn't," Little Becky protested. "Mean to," she clarified. She hopped to the floor and sagged against Andy's bureau. "Aunt Lily," she complained in general injury.

"Is that Betsy I hear out there?" Lily asked. "Can you help me with this, Betsy?"

"Yes, of course," Betsy said. She peered inside the closet.

"Can you catch ahold of the bottom box marked Newer Old Curtains while I lift up the top one?" Lily asked.

"Curtains?" Betsy asked, easing in beside Lily. The arm of one of Andy's jackets, the greeny-brown Harris tweed jacket with leather buttons and leather arm patches he had worn all fall on his daily constitutional walks in the woods, brushed against her cheek rubbing extrascratchily from the burrs Andy had picked up on his travels—Lily's woods, Andy had noted, were unimproved. So Andy had left behind clothes. Betsy had not known until that moment how uncertain she had been that he was coming back. She could, of course, have scouted his room and his closet on her own but it was better this way, to let providence inform her at a well-chosen interval, as a gift in this season of gifts.

"Gently," Lily cautioned as Betsy seized the box with a surge of energy.

"They're ornaments," Little Becky spoke up repressively.

"Well, the box says curtains," Betsy answered, pulling the square carton into the center of the room, rucking up Andy's rag rug and straightening it with her foot.

"Aunt Lily is getting me ornaments," Little Becky said.

"Yes. I understand that now," Betsy said.

"I took down the newer curtains and rehung the old old curtains which I realized looked nice again," Lily remembered. "There. See. I wrote ornaments on the other side of the box. I'm sure I must have thought at the time the curtains would cushion the ornaments, that's what I must have been thinking." She gripped the edge of Andy's bureau top and hauled herself up, shutting the closet door behind her with a push of her heel. Her hip twinged and she wished she hadn't seen, among the other piled, stowed-away boxes, the one labeled Olive (Dresses). Through a gap in the top flap she had glimpsed stripes, the intense mauve and shiny almond stripes of Olive's last best dress worn to Olive's last best occasion, a dinner out that she hadn't been able to eat. The horizontal stripes of the dress were meant to make her appear wider, Olive's word. *I don't want anyone to guess,* she had said. She had always relished secrets, no matter, it seemed, what the secret was. That had been Olive's last year, the last year which she had lived out at Lily's looked after by Lily and the Visiting Nurse, and the last year Lily had bothered with Christmas, and the year Lily had taken against her new curtains because every succeeding morning she had drawn them back to gaze upon sadder and sadder days. The tale of that whole long terrible year was told in the juxtaposition of boxes pushed to the back of the cold-aired closet where they were meant to stay forever unreferred to. Although were Andy present, he might have scribbled a note querying the significance of the particularities of the box constructions, and even have asked Lily what her thoughts were upon the subject.

THE BOYS RETURNED from the village where they had completed their Christmas shopping at the Ben Franklin Store, the True Value, the Rexall, and Lydia Spofford Antiques. Marilyn Rathbone, who lived above her shop, opened to the boys' knocks and pleas and found them several very nice pieces of Sandwich glass for their mother. Marilyn said to especially wish their Aunt Lily a very Merry Christmas. The boys promised and promptly forgot their promise. Last, at the IGA in the Gourmet Aisle, they came across flat cans of smoked clams and smoked herring in horseradish sauce which seemed to have Uncle Harvey's name on them.

"But didn't you remember my brown sugar?" Becky asked as the boys descended upon her in the kitchen, shedding coats, prying off boots, and glancing inside and exchanging a clutch of paper bags rather worse for wear. A very large tree stand slid from one bag and wheeled across the sloping kitchen floor.

Becky slid a sheet of gingerbread men from the oven—Hot, she warned the boys as they snatched—and she fumbled raisins from a big, sticky-sided box and pressed them into the soft torsos for buttons. She was not clever and she did not rise to gingerbread men's faces. An early private effort had produced a colony of staring, despairing accident victims whom she had straightaway thrown to the grackles.

"Brown sugar?" the boys asked, mystified, and duly got Becky's goat. They bleated laughter as she pulled off her apron and grabbed her purse and prepared to set out with flour on her face. Glover plunked a carton of brown sugar down on the counter, dark brown, and she'd asked specifically for light. Well, even Julia Child didn't seem to think there was much difference but Glover wouldn't know that.

Alden had caught their voices and he came and hustled the boys into the big parlor where the tall fir tree was leaning against the wall, one long straying branch lifting up the skirt of the camelback sofa, which gave the tree a raffish personality and instantly disposed the boys in its favor.

"Hey," said Brooks, or Rollins. "Cool tree."

Alden told the boys to remove the heavy table from the window recess. Brooks stepped on the bullion fringe of the skirt as Rollins lifted. The cloth slid and all the family portraits fell flat on their faces as if they'd been mown down by machine-gun fire.

"Cool," said Glover.

"Where'll we put the table, Dad?" asked Rollins.

"What?" asked Alden.

"Where'll we put the table, Dad?" asked Brooks.

"What?" asked Alden. He stepped one way, then the other, determining where he could drive nails least visibly into the crown molding to secure his guy wires. The boys lugged the table this way and that, stepping back and forth with him until they grew weary and set the table down before the glass-fronted bookcase so that no one would be able to get to the Francis Parkman or Washington Irving or J. Fenimore Cooper for the next week or two should the need arise.

Alden told Rollins to crouch on the floor and hold the new tree stand steady and he and Brooks lifted the tree and lowered it into the stand's clamping mechanism. Glover lay on the sofa and watched them.

"Are we straight?" Alden asked Glover.

"Huh?" Glover asked.

"Is the tree straight?"

"Straight?"

"The tree?"

"The tree?"

BALANCING A TRICKY TRAY on her hip, supporting a platter of gingerbread men, chocolate and vanilla pinwheels, cinnamon macaroons, Nero's ears, pecan wreaths, vanille batons, and florentines, an unsteady pitcher of eggnog, and Lily's best cut-glass punch cups from the back of the china cupboard, Becky paused by the door of the little parlor where the boys were sprawled before the TV watching a basketball game.

"Snacks. A lovely holiday cookie assortment," she said. "For everyone who helps to decorate the tree."

"Ma-ha," they objected, because that didn't sound fair, the part about having to help.

Little Becky happily, fussily affixed bisque angels and crystal snow-drops to the branches of the tree. Wearing Lily's old felt and appliqué tree skirt as a cape—Cold, she complained, although she looked over-heated and scarlet—Little Becky massively flitted between the tree and the picture-frame table where she had stacked the pictures in a heap— Mt. Greylock, Alden called the mound—and where she had set up a Christmas Village of miniature houses and shops and a church and a mirror pond overlooked by Mt. Greylock topped now by cotton tuft snowdrifts. Aunt Lily had said the components of the Christmas Village could be Little Becky's own to keep, forever and ever. At any rate, Aunt Lily had said, Have it, then, when Little Becky yanked the first of the darling little cottages up by its chimney from the bottom of the orna-ment box, exclaiming with an eye watching her Great Aunt, I wish, how I wish, this could be mine.

"Aunt Lily?" Little Becky asked. "Does the church go beside the mir-ror pond or does the little red schoolhouse go there?"

"Whichever you decide," Lily said. She sat in the big parlor with her library book maintaining a presence because she couldn't always remove herself to the quiet and calm of her own room. But she was not partici-pating, because then she might seem to be interfering in the family's preparations.

"I'll put the pond in between them so they can share," Little Becky announced magnanimously. She was going to be nice to everyone as she had resolved always to be should the day ever come when she was put in charge.

Betsy sat cross-legged by the fire, patiently attaching hanging hooks to the ornaments that had lost theirs or needed tangled thread loops to be replaced as Little Becky bowled the unsatisfactory ornaments to her across the carpet. It seemed treacherous to Betsy to do very much more to decorate a house that wasn't really home but she hoped that con-tributing in a behind-the-scenes capacity allowed her to pull her own weight without betraying her father, who had called last week to tell her he had made plans to go skiing in Utah with old and reliable friends who never spoke of Ginger and who never forgot to exclude her from their drink orders ("*Three* white wines, please."). Betsy knew it would be unpleasant for the rest of the family not to seem to be enjoying herself, while it would feel wrong in her heart to enjoy herself truly. This was not a difficult trick to pull off, and she need not even pull the trick off very well, for no one in the household paid enough attention to her to notice the difference between a perfunctory performance and a sincere one. But if this were a real Christmas Eve at home, Betsy would wear red tights and weave a silver ribbon through her braid. She would have sprayed all the household mirrors with borders of fake frost, and recorded a few lines of "Joy to the World" on the telephone answering machine.

She picked up a spun-glass candy cane which sounded broken inside when she shook it. Little Becky hovered above her, staring down at the perfect part in her perfect cousin's perfect hair. She thumped onto her knees. Her Christmas cape shed sequins and beads and cotton batting shreds of snow. She thrust a demanding hand in Betsy's face and wriggled fingers which smelled of cookie chocolate and old ornament dust. Betsy was letting her down badly in the ornament hook reattachment department, she wanted Betsy to know.

Alden sidestepped through the French door. He had hooked it open with his finger and closed it with his chin as he carried an armful of firewood. He stuffed the basket beside the hearth with split logs and he wondered how the North Country Boutique Hearthwarmers were faring in the bedecked drawing rooms of Manhattan. His imagination lingered over a tray of cocktails and he made his selections from a levitating assortment of hors d'oeuvres and he heard himself utter a telling remark as well-coiffed heads bent nearer to catch his every pronouncement. He sighed and helped himself to a stack of gingerbread men and tried a little cup of the eggnog, the Golden kind from Hood's, which he thought he and Becky had agreed was almost too rich. He told Little Becky the tree was shaping up very nicely although he wasn't looking at the tree, but staring so intently into the fire he had made that the bright flames burned a black hole into the center of his sight. Little Becky girdled the tree with a length of maroon cording she had found in a bowl, lacing the cord from branch to branch.

"Look," she said. "Look."

Ginger sat at the top of the stairs listening to them, then she sat on the landing halfway down the stairs watching them below. She waited for

someone to remember her and come in search of her to coax her to lend
her expertise and her gaiety to the scene, then, she descended, at last, on
her own. She wore an ancestral pair of flannel pajamas and a down vest
and slipper socks. She entered the big parlor and shivered.

"Big ornaments on the lower branches and little ones on the top," she
remarked generally.

"What?" asked Little Becky spinning round. Her cape flared.

Ginger lowered herself onto the sofa, stretched out long, and propped
herself on an elbow and shook out the latest *New Yorker* she had carried
downstairs scrolled under her arm. She coiled a hand up and behind her
head, having sought a soft pillow to no avail, her languid hand delving
beneath the sofa where she seemed to believe pillows were being kept
from her.

"What?" asked Little Becky again. The cape gave her courage.

"Nothing, darling," Becky said. These little flare-ups were exacerbated by the holidays when everyone expected to feel happy all the time
but somehow didn't, so they contrived to make themselves even more
wretched just to show whomever it was they blamed. Becky had read an
article in *Family Circle* on family flare-ups.

"Oh, you're here, Lily," Ginger said, just noticing her aunt. Lily
turned a page of her library book in reply.

"Fetch me one of those eggnogs, would you Betsy," Ginger said. "Is
that nutmeg grated all over the top? Well, try to get me some from
underneath."

"Yes, Mummy." Betsy rose and approached the pitcher of eggnog
consideringly.

Arthur strode in, flashing his usual big expectant grin. Phoebe, a step
behind, wore ornament earrings showing two Currier and Ives scenes,
Sleighing to Grandmother's House and *Carving the Goose,* which everyone
at the hospital had admired excessively. They appreciated a little effort,
down at the hospital at this time of year.

"Do please have some goodies," Becky said, steering them toward
the cookie platter. The sweets weren't moving very fast since she had
forbidden the boys and cut off Little Becky who had been overdoing.

Phoebe admired a florentine and Arthur, examining a pinwheel
cookie, remarked that chocolate wasn't the opposite of vanilla. The true

opposite of chocolate was strawberry, and the real opposite of vanilla was vinegar.

"That so?" asked Alden. "Is there a chart like one of those color wheels at the paint store?"

"Hey? No, it's like, you know, the opposite of turkey is cotton candy," Arthur clarified.

"Ah, I see," said Alden. He glanced significantly at Little Becky who thought he was making a face at her and she rushed to her Christmas Village and prayed to become Thumbelina so she could live all by herself in the Holly Cottage beside the Wishing Well within convenient wishing distance. She petitioned fiercely that she might shrink and the townspeople figures spring to life and that she and they and the village all be transported far far away from the picture-frame table for otherwise her parents would just pluck her tiny protesting form from the skating pond and place her in a rinsed-out instant-coffee jar and race her to a doctor or, more likely in this case, to a scientist.

"Surely the opposite of cotton candy is roast beef," Ginger spoke up.

"Do you think so?" asked Phoebe. "I think the opposite of roast beef is tossed salad."

Lily turned another page in her library book and Harvey, who had announced at breakfast that he was setting off on a major shopping expedition (though no one had become too worked up over his statement) returned, unencumbered by bundles other than a brown paper bag bulging with something he was pleased to consult at intervals. He sang, "The heck with the halls and the boughs of holly" as he unwound his scarf and drew off his suede gloves finger by finger, carefully, for the cashmere lining was detaching. He swerved into the big parlor, called by the colored lights and chattering voices. He hugged his brown paper bag and he jogged Betsy's elbow as she poured eggnog, drop by inspected drop, into a cut-glass cup.

"I don't know what all this holiday anguish is about. I finished my shopping in five minutes in one stop," he boasted. "And none of you will guess what I've bought all of you. Well, I'll tell you all one thing, one hint. You're all receiving the same thing."

"Guess," Harvey commanded after a moment during which Arthur further mentioned that the opposite of butterscotch had to be deviled ham.

"Oh, we want to be surprised," Becky said. "Have a treat. Join the tree-trimming party." She neatened the ranks of the vanille batons and passed the platter of cookies beneath his nose.

"No thank you, dear," Harvey said. "I can't eat another bite. I've just had panettone at Betty Florio's and an almond-filled coffee cake at Mary Swenson's, and Penny Nicholls made one of those looks-like-a-Christmas-tree-shape-with-green-frosting cakes, and I have Sue Pace's Napoleon secretly in my pocket because I was uncomfortable by the time I reached her unit, she's on the second floor, and I didn't want to mention Betty or Mary or Penny to her, though they'll compare notes later on in the Game Room—they can't miss their bridge, not even on Christmas Eve." Harvey had lately taken to thinking out loud. "I'm offering the Napoleon now." He reached for his cardigan pocket.

"Oh dear," said Becky. "I'm not having much luck with *my* baking."

"Boys," Alden called. "Come try some of your mother's delicious baking."

"Can't," Brooks, or Rollins, bellowed back. "Ma said we can't eat if we don't help."

"Yes, I did say that actually," Becky admitted.

"Hark at them," Harvey said. "They'd rather go hungry than make an effort."

"They have graham crackers and salsa under the afghan," Little Becky reported.

"Just come and apply a little tinsel, boys. Or at least hang up your personal baby name silver ornaments. Make a symbolic effort," Alden called.

"Ma-ha, it's *my* tree. They'll wreck it, Aunt Lily," Little Becky appealed.

Lily shut her library book and closed her eyes, feigning sleep, watching them through her eyelashes. At her age, it could not be construed as unforgivably rude to drift off within the family circle. Indeed, in her youth, the children would have been hushed and instructed to tiptoe away and finish the decorating after the old people had their rest. Holiday celebrations had often been suspended for elderly naps as baseball games are suspended for rain. People were disappointed but they understood.

"It's a family tree, so to speak," Becky said. "Everyone who wants to can take part pleasantly."

"Betsy, my sweet," Ginger said, glooming into the cup of eggnog Betsy had just handed her. "I'm afraid I must not have made myself clear about my nutmeg issue."

When the front doorbell jangled they all stared at one another and wondered who could be calling because no one was expecting a visitor. They speculated who it could not possibly be—not Arthur's parents who surely weren't mad enough to forsake Fiji (where they had last been heard from) for Towne in winter, and Harvey had covered all his widows on his cake-and-coffee crawl through Senior Village. Becky's brother and his wife, who lived outside of Boulder, had already sent a card and a big Swiss Colony Fruit and Cheese and Salami Pyramid so their duty was done. "A girl for Glover?" Alden asked. "Nah," said Glover, he'd taken care of all the girls. Lily opened her eyes and said her friends knew better than to intrude upon a family evening.

"Shall I go see?" Betsy asked reasonably, and she picked a zigzag route, avoiding displaced furniture and the reclining figures of Arthur and Phoebe laughing all out of proportion as they bit the heads off gingerbread men, and she sidestepped the boys who had tumbled into the big parlor and were now pelting one another with angel hair, attempting to stick angel hair on one another's heads so they could point and squeal *You're an angel* in high-pitched voices.

In the front hall, it occurred to Betsy that, of course, her father had canceled his Utah ski trip and flown, instead, to Boston to be with her and Ginger. He must have realized how very wrong it was to permit the estrangement to drag on for one day longer, and, finding himself at the airport, he simply took one plane rather than another. He'd have his downhill skis with him, and he'd be wearing his peaked Tibetan cap with the hangdog leather earflaps that Ginger so disliked and said made Louis look like Deputy Dawg. Betsy would have to snatch the cap from her father's head before her mother spotted it and said something she didn't really mean. This critical reunion was going to have to be carried off flawlessly. Her parents were going to have to realize they loved one another all over again in a heartbeat before each had time to seize and defend another fixed position. And Betsy, who had convinced herself that her father stood on the other side of the front door and that if she handled the next few minutes properly by the end of the week she would be back in Kansas calling all her friends and saying, "Hi, it's me. I'm back, yes, really," threw open the wide door and beamed her greatest smile upon Mr. Oscarsson who was just raising a fist to knock because, thus far, tugging on the dead-looking doorbell pull had not roused anyone.

"Betsy," Oscar uttered accusingly, for as he had envisioned this scene Ginger was supposed to come to the door and melt into his arms and they would wander off together to a private dinner because Ginger doted on dinners at little recherché hideaways. Oscar had not thought the word *recherché* in his imaginings but that was what he intended for Ginger's sake.

Betsy was so shocked she forgot to stop smiling.

"Is your mother to home?" Oscar asked and he stepped into the hallway, for the early evening pressed rawly cold and the gunmetal-grey sky had been spitting projectiles at him and he didn't think Betsy was going to remember her manners anytime soon and invite him inside. He flopped his overfull garment bag on the deacon's bench as faux-brass buckles scraped across polished wood. He looked around with open curiosity, not at the moment searching for Ginger (Betsy's presence assured hers) but taking in the rise of the staircase and the rich variety of the scattered carpets upon which, to give him credit, he did not step but stepped around in his big wet traveling overshoes.

Betsy retreated a backward lurch to each of Oscar's forward steps, and then she turned and ran up the stairs clinging to the banister and leaning into the curve of the staircase so that she seemed to spiral up and up through the ceiling as if being borne away by a cyclone. Oscar thought that Betsy was being awfully hard on such an old house. Such clapboarding as he had been able to see by the light of a carriage lamp struck him as blistering and warping and here inside his nose detected the smell of dry rot as a musty note below the interesting aroma of spicy-buttery baking.

He had been left to discover Ginger on his own. He followed the sound of variously droning, complaining, and murmuring voices into the big parlor. Ginger spied him first for she too had thought of Louis and been on guard. She sat up as if stung, tipping her undrinkable eggnog onto her down vest and into her lap.

"Oscar," she gasped, and she daubed at the eggnog with her *New Yorker*, the pages of which were too glossy to be absorbent.

Becky threw Ginger a tangle of angel hair to mop herself with and she told Little Becky to go to her room and advised the boys to return to their televised basketball game.

"Game sucks," Brooks said.

"Game's over," Rollins said. "By now."

"Why do I have to go to my room?" Little Becky demanded. She passionately grasped a cardboard-and-glitter reindeer silhouette.

"Just for a while, go upstairs. It's nothing *you've* done," Becky said.

Ginger decided now was not the time to work herself up to an outburst over Becky's unnecessarily dire emphasis—nothing *you've* done—for, more urgently, she had to invent a graceful introduction to explain Oscar.

"Alden?" Becky asked helplessly, but Alden was staring at Oscar attempting to construct a banishing speech for his sister's seducer who, in the flesh, seemed only ruddy and genial and very, very ordinary. Alden quelled a sense of disappointment in the still attractive and undeniably worldly and quite intelligent when she wasn't being foolish Ginger, who, once having made up her mind to do wrong surely could have done better for herself.

"Hey," Arthur spoke up pleasantly.

"Hey," echoed Phoebe less certainly. She had paid more attention than Arthur had to the household gossip, being sensitive to the local line on paramours, which was a fluctuating one.

Harvey seemed to think Oscar was the UPS man working overtime and he pulled out his wallet and counted several singles to tip him with, all the while remarking what an excellent outfit UPS was. He had been an early fan and investor.

"Aunt Lily," Ginger announced firmly, leading Oscar to Lily's chairside. "This is Oscar Oscarsson, a friend of ours from Kansas." A friend of the family, Oscar was—Ginger could think on her feet.

Lily opened her eyes and asked, "Is Louis parking the car, then?" for in her experience of Ginger's husband, he had always been off parking a car or running out to pick up an out-of-town newspaper or fetch a gallon of ice cream after determining a consensus as to the flavor though once he'd asked them all to vote secretly on folded scraps of paper which he collected and then bought a pint of every flavor requested, quite a breathtaking gesture, Lily had thought at the time, and she had enjoyed her Frozen Pudding which never was the winning flavor in a dessert democracy. Then again, Louis might be viewed as having tried too hard. Perhaps that had been the problem with Louis.

"Louis?" Oscar muttered at Ginger, who hushed him.

"No, no, Aunt Lily, Louis wasn't able to come out. Oscar happened to find himself in the area," Ginger said airily now.

"Is his wife parking the car, then?" Lily asked.

"No, Oscar doesn't have a wife, Auntie," Ginger explained. "He is a lonely bachelor."

"I say," Alden spoke up, as Becky prodded him. "I mean to say."

"I see," sighed Lily with nothing more to ask for she had become inured to people showing up and moving into her house for no good reason even when they clogged her ears with their reasons. "I don't suppose Andy will mind if we put Mr., Mr., your guest, in his room for a day or two at most?" Lily craftily mentioned a time frame. "Do you think Andy would mind? Betsy?" Lily asked, for Betsy seemed to be the person to consult for a reading on Andy's likely thoughts since she was doing that Christmas card assessment work for him, but the girl had vanished. She must already be putting fresh sheets on Andy's bed, Lily decided.

"Perfect Auntie," Ginger said sweetly, although Oscar didn't feel he was too keen on having to share with this Andy fellow, whoever he was. This doubling up of the bedroom facilities was going to interfere with certain plans he had formulated for later that night, certain daring plans, Oscar realized now that he had seen what a houseful of Hills he would have to contend with.

"Oscar, you must want to freshen up," Ginger added. "I'll show you the way."

Oscar, who seemed not to know where to put his big calloused hands although they kept gravitating to the vicinity of Ginger's waist, said yes, he could do with some freshening up, and Ginger took him away before he could begin to describe how very unfresh he felt after his long day's exertions just getting here.

"So that was Ginger's fancy man," declared Harvey, snapping his fingers a beat behind.

"He doesn't look very fancy to me," Little Becky argued back.

AFTER A SIMPLE SUPPER (tomato soup, tuna sandwiches, celery sticks, and the Swiss Colony Pyramid opened and on offer to pep up the menu) Oscar had volunteered to put the dishes in the dishwasher. He heard himself offering to buy Miss Hill a dishwasher when she told him she did not possess one.

Miss Hill had said, "No, thank you. That won't be necessary," and Oscar was relieved for by then he had become carried away trying to make himself agreeable. He had brought a clattering stack of soup plates into the kitchen. Receiving them, Miss Hill had winced—at the stacking and at the clattering, for they were using the Spode that evening. Ginger had quietly come down the back stairs and reset the table, Becky having only rated the occasion as one worthy of the ovenproof Pfaltzgraff although her choice was a reflection of the meal already planned and not a judgment of Oscar. Still, if the matter were ever to be argued, Ginger might well ask why Becky hadn't rated Oscar worthy of an emergency boeuf bourguignon from the freezer chest, and she could have thrown together one of her Caesar salads and hurried a batch of popovers into the oven and *then* set the table with the Spode instead of the Pfaltzgraff, to which Becky's reply would have been, I didn't want to confuse the poor man with extra forks and the finger bowls. As it was, tomato soup and tuna on Spode had confused the Hills.

Not necessary? Oscar wondered what the old woman had meant when she told him his impulsively offered gift was not necessary? Not necessary because the family was prepared to like him for himself, or not necessary because nothing he could do would ever make him acceptable to them? Or was *not necessary* just a favorite formula hereabouts, for he noticed the kitchen also lacked a garbage disposal, an automatic ice-maker in the refrigerator door, and a trash compactor, which were not particularly necessary but were handy to have, nevertheless. It occurred to Oscar that a high road was being taken all around and about him. When Miss Hill turned her back to him, rinsing dishes by hand at her kitchen sink, he read the cork notice board hanging on the wall as if searching for further clues—REMEMBER! Today's KROC Christmas Winning Word is JOLLY HOLLY . . . BARK LIKE A REINDEER when MUS-98 calls between one and three p.m., it is for to win a NEW SNOWMOBILE! Oscar pictured the entire Hill family hightailing their way up and over the high road in an absurdly overloaded snowmobile.

Throughout supper, Oscar had felt their narrowed and similar eyes watching him, then flickering away as he turned to attempt a pleasant word. He had plucked a fine red pomegranate from the epergne—they called the towering fruit-piled contraption in the center of the table an epergne—and he had caused all of the plums and apples and tangerines and sprigs of fir to slump and slide onto the tablecloth. The family, with their narrowed and similar eyes, had watched the pomegranates roll to a stop against the feet of their water glasses and the tangerines thud into the celery dish and the apples drop over the edge of the table, and they had just nudged the pomegranates away as they picked up their water glasses and reached beneath the tangerines for celery sticks with a lack of reaction which Oscar suspected was less polite than resigned—his feelings were not being spared, rather, they were not being incited any further. And then he had managed to alienate Ginger's brother by referring to Alden's projected raspberry plantation as a kitchen garden, and he had dismissed soft fruits as being too temperamental a crop to be seriously considered by anyone rooted in rural reality. Then, when Alden had asked, "What about specializing in designer greens—escarole, and endive, and varietal lettuces?" Oscar had asked, "What are those when they're at home?" After which, responding to Mr. Harvey Hill's establishment air, to the way he had snorted at the news contained in his evening paper and wore a tie and jacket at home, at ease in his lounger chair, Oscar had asked Ginger's distinguished uncle whether he was privileged to know any Kennedys and whether he could recommend any likely watering holes where Oscar could view them respectfully from a distance during his time in Massachusetts. Oscar pried his sandwich apart and picked out the chopped gherkins as Harvey sputtered and thrashed a wand of celery.

"Hold your breath and count to ten, sir," Oscar advised, but even Little Becky appreciated that Oscar's assumption of hiccups was a grave misdiagnosis. Uncle Harvey wasn't hiccuping. He was going mental with fury.

Ginger had been no help to him although at first she seemed to have decided to rise to the challenge of launching Oscar. She had changed into her long black velvet skirt and an ice-blue quilted satin jacket and her crystal jewelry with the tricky clasps—dressed to preside and persuade. Yes, her initial impulse had been to apply every effort but as she was making her entrance into the dining room (delayed by an encounter with Betsy outside the bathroom door that had left her quivering at the girl's intransigence) she had noticed how Oscar's brown-shirted back spread wider than the back of Lily's William and Mary style dining room side chair in which he was already sitting and musing, as if his decision mattered, over foil-wrapped gift pyramid selection wedges of Muenster and Colby and Cheddar cheeses. Stuffed crescents of Oscar's brown shirt obtruded between and beyond the vertical rails and turned supports of the chair and Ginger, when she consulted her feelings about this, experienced no stab of compassion for the large awkward man perched on the too fragile chair so very far from his prairie home on Christmas Eve. The thought came to Ginger then, that Oscar might not do, that he might not do after all.

"Does Betsy know dinner is served?" Lily had asked her.

"Oh, yes, Betsy," Ginger recalled. "She's going to babysit at the Snowdons'."

"Tonight? But that's a shame, having to go out tonight of all nights," Becky said.

"She says they want her to stay over and help out during the day tomorrow as well," Ginger announced calmly.

"But that's not right," Becky said.

"Apparently Martha Stewart suggested some such hiring-a-helper scheme in one of her books. Betsy says she's going to fold discarded wrapping paper and untangle ribbons and help out with a new pet turtle and prepare their breakfasts while the Snowdon family enjoys being a family together," Ginger explained.

"Smart gal, that Martha Stewart," Harvey said. "Pretty gal, too. Know people who know her, in Westport. No flies on her. Well, there wouldn't be, would there, in Westport. They spray. They spray something that interferes with the flies' reproductive cycles, though I think I'd rather be killed outright if I had to make a choice."

"Gal with some funny ideas about hired help, anyway," Alden said. "How can you let Betsy go out to work on Christmas Eve, Ginger?"

"Oh, but Betsy's heart is set," Ginger said.

BETSY LEFT HER SAMSONITE overnight case at the top of the stairs. Mr. Snowdon would be coming for her on his way back from the International Pet Village where they had been holding the turtle Mrs. Snowdon had reserved. Mr. Snowdon hoped the turtle would come with operating instructions—turtles lived in such a variety of habitats, in deserts, in swamps, in Borneo, and he had no idea which sort of turtle his wife had liked the looks of in the tank. Mr. Snowdon had mentioned all this when Betsy called to say she thought she could come over to help out after all. He had not asked Betsy why she had changed her mind. He had asked Betsy whether she knew what turtles ate. Ought he to pick up hamburger, acanthus leaves, slugs?

Betsy listened down the stairwell for the family's whereabouts. They had mustered in the dining room. Their chairs scraped, their cutlery clipped, their voices spoke back and forth, Oscar's inquiring tones followed by variously quelling replies and silences until Oscar inquired again about something else. They would keep at that game for hours, Betsy knew, dishing it out and dining on indefinitely.

She walked softly, swiftly, across the upper hall and entered Andy's room. Oscar had left the bedside lamp burning—how thoughtless of Aunt Lily's expensive and delicate electricity—and he had dumped his garment bag across Andy's floor, the zipper yanked apart, a tangle of shirt arms punching their way out into the air. Betsy sniffed Oscar's alcoholic aftershave. She knew its synthetic musk undertones well—she had detected the scent before on late afternoons at home when her mother was nowhere to be found and then, suddenly, the musk note, a heavy sigh, the click of a bottle against a glass signaled her mother was present again.

Betsy had to steel herself to begin to search among Oscar's terrible belongings. She knelt reluctantly on the floor beside his asprawl garment bag. She stood abruptly. Oscar wouldn't have packed a photograph of himself, would he?

She wondered hopelessly whether some other emblem of Oscar would serve as well, a strand of his hair, perhaps? She moved to the bureau top. She passed over his ticking wristwatch, his return American Airlines ticket envelope, a stub of breath gum, a furl of Kleenex lifted from the box in the bathroom, his ancient bent toothbrush, an open penknife. Oscar's hairbrush lay among the folds of the mussed bureau scarf. Impaled on its bristles were clumps of his rust-colored hair. Betsy spotted his wallet as well. Of course—she snatched it and fumbled through its private contents, dismissing his blood donor's card, a plastic-covered 23rd Psalm, his Visa, Shell, and Discover cards. There—she came upon a square of overlit face, his blunt chin thrust forward, his rusty hair tufted behind his ears in a last-ditch effort to smarten up.

But Betsy's hand hesitated. Could she bring herself to take his driver's license, which seemed to her to mark an impropitious affront to the issuing state of Kansas? She must remain on excellent and honorable terms with Kansas. Nothing must sully her eventual, longed-for return there.

What else was there that might be of use? She flurried the Kleenex, she shook the American Airlines envelope, and a snapshot of her mother slid onto the bureau top. Ginger stood beside the butterfly bush outside the dining room window at home. Ginger was shading her eyes and pointing at the buddleia, which was the true subject of the photo. Ginger's right leg was a blur, already on its way out of the picture.

Betsy's heart hardened. She stared at the photograph, which was such a very wrong family photograph for Oscar to possess, for Oscar to have borne across the country and carried over the threshold of the faraway house to which Ginger had fled, and for Oscar to be holding in abeyance as documentary evidence to produce while asserting his rights should the need arise. Unforgivable, was Betsy's verdict.

So a charged Betsy lifted Oscar's license from his wallet and because she meant business, she helped herself to a clump of his rusty hair even if a hair specimen were to tip the balance and worsen the spell. She didn't care.

Spell, the article said, and not a curse, according to the two-inch square of filler item she had clipped from the *Midwest Shoppers' News and Job Mart* that had been tucked under the wiper blades of her mother's car in a parking lot one autumn day two years ago. The brief article described an obeah rite performed to make someone disappear forever from one's life. Two years ago, when Oscar had not even been a storm cloud on the horizon, Betsy had clipped and saved the small square of newsprint at the bottom of the old Mozart chocolate box that contained other intriguing oddments—found feathers, a silver dollar from the year she was born, Apache arrowheads. The clipping had rubbed and rustled among the oddments and its last lines had crumbled away to dust and grit. Betsy could not recall what the last lines cautioned or counseled but she responded to the very mysteriousness of the appearance—and incipient disappearance—of the message, which could only have been ordained.

She flew lightly down the back stairs, skipping the next-but-one step from the bottom that twanged underfoot when stepped upon. The kitchen was clear. They were still engaged in the dining room. At the moment (she heard through the serving hatch) they were trying to decide whether the gift-box salami had turned funny in transit, which should keep them occupied, particularly if the salami really was funny. They would have to work out how funny and then compose a suitable thank you note to Hap and Rosemary out in Colorado without letting on how disappointing the Gift Pyramid had been. Harvey thought they should be told the truth. Becky said no, she would rather not know if she were them. Oscar, whose business it was not, said he would report directly to the Swiss Colony and complain and maybe get a free replacement assortment in apology. Oh no, that wouldn't be right, said Harvey.

Betsy opened the cupboard above the stove and reached high for the large red box of kosher salt that was always kept there because no one had had any use for kosher salt for years. She rapidly descended the cellar stairs. She twisted on the hanging lightbulb otherwise left loose in its socket, the light fixture suspended just where anyone coming down the stairs into the black cellar would walk right into it and so locate it. Betsy rubbed her forehead, not hurt but alerted by the thwack and rebounding thwack. The cellar, dimly alight now, was full of the large rumbling furnace and elephant-grey furnace pipes seeping warmth and condensation. Some window screens were stacked, empty paint cans were piled, and a washer and dryer sat on a platform in the driest corner. The cellar was a two-hundred-year-old hole in the ground.

There was a lower-ceilinged chamber leading off the cellar proper, dirt-floored and entered through an opening covered by a canvas flap. Here they swept the water that overflowed from the washing machine and it was not a place where anyone was inclined to linger. Indeed, the cellar annex was the only corner of the house where one might leave some private piece of hocus-pocus undisturbed, as prescribed.

If all this weren't so unpleasant, the rite probably wouldn't work, Betsy was still enough of a Protestant to remind herself as she crouched and duckwalked under the flap. (She had to protect her pale corduroy knees from the dirt and damp.) Earlier in the evening, she had made some preparations, stashing a candle and a book of matches behind the flap. She lit the candle. The article hadn't called for candlelight but it seemed appropriately occult and atmospheric; besides, there was no other source of light. She had also stowed the long cardboard tube in which the calendar she had bought her mother had come (Chateaux of the Loire 1990) and which was resealable at either end with plastic inserts. She dropped Oscar's license into the tube and shook down the strands of his hair and she pried up the pouring spout of the box of salt and tilted it over the tube. She shook the salt box. She rapped its bottom. Nothing emerged. She hit the box harder and hurt her hand. The ancient salt had fused into a brick. She raised her candle and cast about for a cudgel. She spied a discarded awl, its wooden handle cracked and splintering. She ripped the cardboard covering from the block of salt and began to strike and strike with the awl. Chunks flew off the block. She gathered and stuffed the pieces and bits down the tube until the tube was filled to the top. She slammed on the plastic insert and then, as the rite dictated, she had to set the salt-covered photograph of Oscar in a place where it would never, ever, be disturbed.

She had already decided upon the spot where she would stow her fetish. The stone foundation wall met the joists of the floor above, forming a shelf unseeable in the dark and barely visible by the shadowy leaps and falls of uneasy candlelight. As she set the tube upon the ledge, it seemed to leap of its own accord from her hand into a space behind the wall where it wedged, unreachable and presumably secure forever. If she ever had second thoughts, she could never now retrieve the charm.

So, the deed was irrevocable, as if the spell were already working, taking itself out of her hands snatched by unseen hands. And Betsy was having second thoughts about the hair which, for all she knew, upped the ante curse-wise (no, not curse, she'd cast a *spell*). She supposed she ought to make her wishes entirely clear, that she only wanted Mr. Oscarsson to disappear from their lives absolutely and for all time although of course she didn't mean any harm, any real harm, to come to him. He wasn't supposed to die. In fact, she hoped he wouldn't die for the next year or two at least. Otherwise, she would have to feel responsible. Knowing herself, Betsy would feel obliged to confess and to atone which would interfere with her plans for her further education if she had to drop out of school and join some sort of youth service brigade and live in the inner city and scrape gang graffiti from municipal walls until her own slate was declared relatively clean again.

Perhaps, Betsy thought, she should pray, or petition, for the specific result she desired from the spell. She knelt upon pieces of the torn-off salt box. Cold damp seeped through to her pale, corduroy knees. She didn't want the odd little obeah god, whom she assumed she had summoned, rattling around in her thoughts, some alien demi-devilish imp prying and suggesting inappropriately in her inner ear, so she spoke aloud, "I would appreciate it if you could arrange for this man, for Mr. Oscarsson, to leave us alone. To just go off and live his own life and let us be, just as if he'd never been. Thank you very much. And with thy spirit, Amen," she added like the good Episcopalian that she was.

BETSY, PINKER IN THE FACE than usual, was sitting on the deacon's bench in the front hall alert and erect, her ankles crossed beside her neat little overnight bag, much like a young governess fresh out of the orphanage in an English novel waiting, just waiting, for the next chapter to begin, when Mr. Snowdon came to the door. No one else heard him arrive for he had left his noisy sports car halfway down the driveway because of the ruts and rocks and icy patches he didn't dare take on with his low undercarriage. He was in a hurry, however. He wasn't sure how long the turtle would last in the cold for it seemed a particularly luckless turtle to him. It carried the aura of the last turtle left in the tank after all the more desirable turtles, the glamour turtles, had been selected by pet seekers with more on the ball than his wife.

The front door swung open at his knock in a silently gliding manner that struck him as being rather enchanted. He sighed inwardly and yearned toward the Hills' dining room where voices were rising and falling. He smelled spicy baking and fresh-cut fir boughs and hardwood fires. He wondered if Miss Hill would be offended if he made an offer on the amazing famille rose punch bowl sitting, at considerable risk from passing elbows, on a tipsy bamboo table and, at that moment, he suffered an insight into his own great thirst for antiques. He could stuff his reproduction Federalist-style house on Governor Bradford Circle with all of Miss Hill's vases and bowls and tables and lowboys and his house would never smell of spicy baking and his dining room would never resound with a vigorous and far-reaching discussion swinging—he listened—from the pyramids to the Swiss.

Betsy lifted on her parka and knotted a challis scarf over her head and around her shoulders.

"Are you really sure you want to leave all this?" Mr. Snowdon asked. He gestured toward the holly and ivy twined with silvery ribbons threaded through the balustrade all the way up to the staircase landing.

"Yes," said Betsy shortly.

"Well, bye," she called, not very loudly, but her mother must have been listening all the while on the mother/daughter frequency.

"Bye darling," she called back. "Have a wonderful time."

"Yes. I will," Betsy answered bleakly. She glanced worriedly at the floor. She peered as if she were seeing through the floor before shaking off a thought.

"She'll have a wonderful time," Ginger had informed everyone around the table. "She has such independent urges these days, I can only be mindful not to clip her wings."

So that's how it's going to be, thought Lily, thought Harvey, thought Becky, thought Alden. We're going to pretend that everything is just fine. Nevertheless, nothing could be decided and resolved and made right tonight, and Ginger's version of events was one they were willing to accept.

" 'Spect Santy Claus will find Betsy anywhere," Harvey said lightly.

OSCAR REMAINED ON his best behavior, as did Ginger. She scarcely knew him or herself, for that matter, as they met once again beneath Lily's complicated roof where, in their variant guises, they were not really taking to one another to be perfectly frank.

For Ginger did not shy from frankness. Her frankness was one of the traits she admired about herself, her willingness to face inconvenient truths, preferably about other people, of course; still, it could be invigorating to be hoist on one's own petard. (Ginger mistakenly took this to be a nautical term involving sails and rigging and she pictured herself bravely breasting the azure ocean waves like a magnificent carved figurehead.) So, with a surge of honest energy, she almost eagerly admitted to herself that she had never cared for Oscar's clothes, his double-knit Sansabelt slacks, his Ban-lon shirts banded with wide and bright horizontal stripes. He possessed a sports jacket with shoulder pads so thrusting and shelf-like he could keep potted cyclamens on them, she had always privately thought; she may even have mentioned this possibility to Oscar playfully. Perhaps Oscar's regrettable dress sense was why she had always been in such a hurry to remove his clothes, Ginger mused, enlightened.

Oh, how human she was proving to be after all, so fallibly, funnily human.

Ginger hid her smile behind her hand. The evening had become one of those awkward evenings when they all sat with nothing much to say and were reduced to asking, *Why are you smiling? What, was I smiling? Well, I can't really say. Oh, I thought perhaps something was funny. I'd like to hear if it's something funny that we can all appreciate.*

Ginger tucked her legs beneath an afghan as she lay upon the sofa in the big parlor where they had adjourned at Lily's suggestion after the supper dishes had been put away. Lily had supposed they should make a point of enjoying the Christmas decorations since they had gone to the bother of putting them up and they had all, Ginger and Alden, the boys, the Beckys, Arthur, Phoebe, Lily, Harvey, and Oscar, drifted in and sat, arranged on chairs and the rugs, consciously watching the tree as if they expected it to perform for them. Little Becky gloomed above her Christmas Village, which was now failing to beguile her. She had half hoped interesting developments would occur on their own up and down the pebble-grey linoleum strip lane of the village's Main Street, but the inhabitants lolled where she had set them down in tableaux which failed to evolve.

Oscar, for his part, was slowly coming to the conclusion that he had never really cared for Ginger's exacting and pronouncing conversation. For Ginger was, at present, whimsically yet obstinately instructing Little Becky to rehang certain ornaments, declaring that the reindeer didn't like being next to the Three Bears—he was afraid they would eat him—and the Sugarplum Fairy didn't care to share a branch with a Santa's Elf because elves were antagonistic to fairies.

"How do you know?" Little Becky demanded warily as if she was afraid her aunt really might possess some highly unlikely inside information.

"Oh, that's common knowledge in pixie circles," Ginger said.

It suddenly became clear to Oscar why he had always been in such a rush to silence Ginger's questions and avowals with deep and serious and otherwise-expressing kisses. It was a pity he could not indulge in preemptive lovemaking at the moment but he was buoyed by this useful insight into his Ginger strategy. Theretofore, he had just been winging his responses instinctively but now he was in possession of a sound and comprehensible reason. He was reminded how correct he had been to plant winter rye a season before the Department of Agriculture issued an advisory advocating that very rotation. He had been guided by the same sensibility then, by men's intuition, he had men's intuition, that's what he had.

Alden, sitting back in the doily-draped wing chair, remarked that pixie circles sounded like a breakfast cereal, and Becky speculated what they'd be like—pink and white and round, of course, but how could one reproduce the essence of the flavor of dew?

"You just make them real sweet and tell people that's how dew tastes," Glover said roughly. If anyone put up with a stupider family, he didn't want to hear about it. He snorted when his father remarked what a shrewd observation he had made about the gullibility of consumers. Sure I'm shrewd, Glover thought. Who wouldn't be shrewd, in this crowd?

LATER, AFTER ALDEN and Becky and Little Becky and Phoebe and Lily returned from the midnight service at All Saints' and Lily nudged down the thermostat and they splashed through their quick wash-ups in the bathroom and called back and forth, Good night and Merry Christmas (for by now it was Christmas), and padded down the hall or up the attic stairs to bed, Ginger completed her own eventful, creaking, crooked walk across the wide, dark hallway. She cracked open Oscar's bedroom door as the hinges lamented, inch by inch. She entered and traversed the room, stumbling against Oscar's flung-down garment bag. Really, he ought to have made sure her way was clear but he was hopeless. She had to think of everything. But she put that thought aside for she wasn't really thinking at the moment. She lifted an edge of woolen blanket and slid into bed beside Oscar. He rolled over in his massive, grumbling sleepiness and awoke at once.

"Rotten mattress," he muttered thickly. "Won't do my back any good. I'll have to wear the brace again after tonight. Honey."

"I have only come to talk to you," Ginger said, "in quiet private."

"Of course you have," Oscar said. "Quiet private." He leaned contentedly into the idea of quiet private.

They lay entwined, recalling all the other times they had lain entwined like this upon the flatter beds they had known in Kansas. Ginger had kept count of their afternoons together. Oscar had kept the complimentary coffee packets their hotel chain of choice provided. Ginger could not have brought a packet home without having to tell the tale of how she had come by it and to remember her tale, which she would have spun in too much detail as she kept talking to keep Louis from getting a word in.

"Why did you come here?" Ginger asked, prepared even now, despite herself, to be convinced by a striking reply.

"Well, you know, I figured it out that you'd run away so's I'd run along after you," Oscar told her.

"No," said Ginger, slowly. "I don't think that's what I wanted." For she had not run away. Every step of the way here had been a struggle onward. Every instinct she possessed pressed to drag her back. A word, the merest word might have stopped her.

"Still, I guess you needed time to yourself, and now you've had six months to think on things," Oscar allowed.

"Yes, it has been six months. So why did you take six months to come after me if you thought you were supposed to come running?" Ginger asked.

"I had to figure out what you wanted," Oscar said. "You are not very easy to read. You're like a mystery, or a thriller, or a romantic book."

"Now you're just concocting justifications, first for not coming and then for coming," Ginger charged. "You have no idea why you're here."

"There wasn't any concocting," Oscar said. "I'm not some clever concoctor. No, my course of action just came to me. I realized what I was meant to do. My course was there to be realized once I wised up enough to see it."

"Like the discovery of gravity?" Ginger suggested. "Which was really only a recognition of a fact, not a discovery."

"What? Yes, like gravity, just like gravity, so don't fight gravity," Oscar spoke through her tumbled hair, across her shuttered eyes, into her tender mouth.

"But my entire life has become a crusade against gravity," Ginger protested, not very coherently. Nevertheless, she ticked a mental note to remember her avowal for her book. She would write a chapter protesting all this falling, all this falling for and falling into and falling from, for where did that ever leave one but finally, fallen down?

"Honey?" Oscar asked eventually. "When will your divorce be final? Because we've got to stop meeting like this." He chuckled and his big chest rumbled and the bedsprings rasped unrhythmically beneath his heaving weight. "We have got to make plans," Oscar said.

Ginger's eyes flew apart and snapped shut again. He felt the rapid up and down scratch of her lashes against his sheltering arm. She feigned sleep although not convincingly. Her breaths were spaced raggedly and she lay rigid within his embrace, so unlike her usual uncoiled and unguarded languor when, it seemed to Oscar, Ginger melted and melded into the mattress and metamorphosed into a kind of upholstered bolster of a woman against whom he reposed in perfect peace. Now, as she seemed poised to spring from his side, he held her all the harder and Ginger fell limp and still as a trapped thing, not quiet but latent. Oscar had always thought of this luxuriating stretch of time lying beside Ginger as *afterward*, the calm spell that followed the near clash of their coming together, and before the rumpled rush of their parting when Ginger cried, *No, no, no,* at the time told on Oscar's watch face and she cursed the evil, evil man who had invented pantyhose.

Afterward, the word itself had become so strongly and particularly identified with lying beside Ginger in this not unhappy yet not unshadowed dream state that Oscar had found himself burning turkey-wattle red and stammering his reply when a buddy, spying him at the Farmers' Federation Annual Meeting, had hollered across the conference room, Let's us get together for a beer, *afterwards.* Then, the simple act of having a beer had turned treacherous. The presence of a pale skin-pink curving sofa in the hotel lobby had flustered Oscar. He had not been able to speak of threatened wheat subsidy cuts intelligently. He had stared into the grain of the wood of the bar counter and flinched when a pretty voice placed an order for a Pink Lady and a ginger ale. No, Oscar was no good at all at suppressing an inconvenient conscience and evidently the universe, or at least the local universe in the vicinity of Kansas City, had been informed of his sins and was not about to let him forget, even for the duration of a casual Red Rock and a fistful of the kind of corn chips he liked, that he was indeed a fallen individual.

But when she had first approached him—and she had approached him—Ginger had spoken fluently, promising him that nothing of what they contemplated would be wrong if neither of them believed they were doing wrong, a construction he had accepted without poking and prodding the foundation for weak points. He would not have bought a portable silo with less soul-searching. They were caught in the final throes of Ginger's husband's failing campaign for the State Senate. Oscar, a party workhorse, dispatched volunteers and canvassers down at the dispirited headquarters, volunteers and canvassers who, at that late, lost hour seldom showed up to be sent out on hopeless forays among the unsympathetic electorate. Oscar had had time on his hands. Ginger sat on the edge of his desk and launched I LIKE LOUIS buttons into the air like tiddly-winks. She wore an off-the-shoulder scarlet gown. She and Louis had attended a Meet the Candidate Night at the Elks' Lodge. Ginger had been ill-advised in her choice of costume, for the event featured a pig roast and a square dance. (But she'd known that, of course she'd known.)

As she had sat on Oscar's desk, her scarlet lips had moved convincingly, speaking round words of persuasion, her sparkly-lidded eyes had locked his eyes in a soul-to-soul searching stare, and they had agreed upon an hour and a place to meet again. Louis, who was being interviewed for a weekly paper handed out free at grocery stores, waved at Ginger from across the room. Louis had winked and shrugged and tapped his watch and subsequently been labeled as unresponsive and arrogant and bored and cold in the ensuing article written by an obvious admirer of his opponent.

Ginger had read aloud from this unflattering profile of Louis on the occasion of her second rendezvous with Oscar. She had read him a rather lengthy excerpt from *The Second Sex* during their initial tryst, and Oscar had observed that Ginger was using up disproportionate blocks of their unabundant time together on all this reading. Ginger had flared at that. Oscar explained himself further, "But I only want to be with you, honey. All these other folks make us seem like such a crowd." The folksiness of his *folks*. Ginger marveled at what an authentic specimen she had landed for herself and she flexed as Oscar worked to mollify her. She had declared herself placated, after a while, and she left her self-reference books at home where she took out her reading-aloud impulses on Louis. She quizzed him on the contents of selected passages and she was able to accuse him of never listening, of being unresponsive and arrogant and bored and cold, as he failed her set tests.

As Oscar rehearsed the story of their affair, he admitted his involvement with Ginger marked quite the most alarming event of his life. But, he allowed, it was not necessarily a bad thing to be alarmed. He had been known to plunk down his five dollars for a movie that looked like a roller coaster ride in the previews. He maintained that a flush of fear scoured dangerous plaque from his heart valves. (His own dad had dropped dead at fifty of a stroke.) Ginger had taken him out of himself. He used to fritter away his after-hours, feet up on the couch, a bowl of Corn Chex balanced on his stomach, tilted toward his chin. He consulted the TV between catnaps. The shape of his evenings did not change with the advent of Ginger. He distractedly consulted the TV between catnaps (and sometimes dreamed confusedly, incompletely, that the blond one of *Cagney and Lacey* was his girlfriend) but he waited now for Ginger to call him. She had promised to call every night, even if she was only able to whisper, *Can't talk. 'Night*. Indeed, so brief were her messages that he found his chief consolation was the ringing, at last, of the telephone at the wolf or the witching hour. He had taken to dropping his pencil into his pants cuff or his sandwich onto his Week-At-A-Glance Planner page when his business telephone jangled, although neither of the girls in his office ever guessed he was waging an illicit and energetic romance. They decided between themselves his trouble must be gambling debts because his only acknowledged susceptibility was for the football pools. Well, Mr. Oscarsson could well afford a little hobby, his office girls agreed.

And now he had gone so far as to ask Ginger to marry him for, Oscar supposed, that was what had just happened here. Logically, to inquire after the progress of her divorce and to allude to the irregularity of their present position and to insist that they had plans to consider—the human mind would naturally move along marriage lines, and Ginger's mind had never been known not to leap onto any outgoing train of thought and ride it hard until the track ran out on the great salt plains. Mention the price per pound he was getting for his milk-fed veal, and Ginger would arrive at the sore subject of her own weight. Oscar could not have begun to trace the route she took to get there. Nevertheless, he only knew no allusion was ever lost on her and so he knew his question had been recognized for what it was and Ginger, being Ginger, had thoroughly considered his offer and handed him his answer which he, less natively astute than she but intensively tutored over the past months, knew he would discover if he applied himself to the problem she had posed him as her reply.

Besides, he had not asked her very elegantly. He had not tendered the sort of written-out-in-advance and practiced-before-the-mirror proposal a woman could share—probe, parse—with her woman friends. The defining moment could not be reenacted in remembrance at anniversary dinners without causing public scandal. No, he would have to try her again. He knew he could do better. Come to think of it, he had put the critical question with far more grace in the past, three times before kneeling at the feet of two different women, neither of whom, however, had been able to grant him the supreme compliment of ceding him her hand in marriage. Nevertheless, they had assured him how lovely it had been to be asked the way he had asked.

LILY HAD GIVEN Alden the warm scarf and Becky a pair of sharp, well-balanced scissors.

"Just what we needed," Alden said, lying on the big parlor sofa, his hands folded over his uncomfortably full stomach, taking time out in the lull of midafternoon Christmas Day, to marvel anew at a world in which one widowed lady had baked a Devil's Food cake for Harvey while a second lady had risen to Angel Food. Alden had just partaken of a slice of each with a glass of milk, almost reverently sampling as if he were reinventing Holy Communion, but nothing very sublime had come of his experiment except a new taste for the cakes in conjunction.

"Lily gave us things we were always borrowing from her," Becky said, glancing up from the cookbook Ginger had chosen for her, *Chicken Again?—How to Make the Old Stand-By Stand Out!*, and which she had inscribed, *Hopefully these ideas will be helpful*. Helpfully these ideas will be hopeful, Becky had amended the message.

"Then we should have borrowed better stuff," Brooks or Rollins said. They had received dictionaries in which they had looked up jackanapes, one of Uncle Harvey's usual words for them which had turned out to mean more or less what they thought it did.

Brooks and Rollins, rather pleased with themselves, had given everyone videos which they had reproduced from rental tapes using the
household's two VCRs. They had selected, with much thought and discussion, appropriate titles—*The Longest Day* for Uncle Harvey, *Little
Women* for Little Becky, *Bananas* for Arthur and Phoebe—and they had
composed and printed very professionally on their desktop publishing
system slick and descriptive labels. Alden said his bootleg copy of *Network* looked uncannily professionally done which he'd meant nicely if
not a bit worriedly.

Oscar had given Ginger a DeLuxe Heating Pad. The box it came in
was of a size and shape suitable for a silk blouse or a cashmere sweater.
Ginger, sitting cross-legged beside the tree, delving and taking it upon
herself to distribute all the gifts, had exclaimed when she saw her own
name inscribed upon the tag. There were so many gifts for Alden's children, and Lily was also doing very well for herself, while Ginger had
been quietly sliding Betsy's presents beneath the bullion fringe of the
picture frame table's long skirt.

"What can this be for me?" Ginger had asked, fingers crossed for
cashmere, as she pulled off the pretty, professionally tied ribbons and
wrapping. "From *Oscar,*" she announced.

"Oh," she uttered on a falling note.

All eyes veered from Ginger and regarded Oscar.

"Well, you wrote me how cold your bed seemed these days," Oscar
explained, proud of himself for having taken her hint.

Becky had been obliged to speak suddenly into the silence. "Who's
for French toast?" she asked, rising and heading for the kitchen before
she had opened her big present from Alden—jewels in a small box. She
had an idea they would be sapphires. The other day Alden had mentioned how the waters of Caneel Bay had been a particularly sapphire-y
blue. Becky thought not. She would have said they were aquamarine but
she didn't disagree with him for Alden was laying the groundwork for
sapphires and not aquamarines. Becky understood that.

Now, dull and dulled by midafternoon ennui, Brooks and Rollins lay
on their stomachs in front of a snapping and flaring fire. They propped
themselves on their elbows and listlessly reached up and into the famille
rose punch bowl brought into the big parlor and set upon a low ottoman.

They withdrew small, printed-on squares of cardboard and, employing the blunt edges of some sterling butter knives they had pocketed at Christmas dinner for this purpose, scraped a flat metallic coating from the surfaces of the cardboard squares. Metallic shreds adhered to their palms, their shirt cuffs, and fell onto the scuffed Kirman carpet.

"No," said Brooks.

"No good," said Rollins.

They grunted and tossed the cardboard squares over the top of the fire screen where a small heap of scrapped squares had settled on the hearth bricks.

For Harvey had given the family two old shoeboxes full of Massachusetts State Lottery Scratch Tickets. Alden said Harvey must have bought five hundred dollars worth at the package store on the Salem Road. Becky had been horrified as the boys and Little Becky snatched handsful of the things and understood at once how to play, but Alden had predicted the children would learn a valuable lesson on the non-winnability of lotteries and other games of chance.

Brooks and Rollins rolled onto their backs, very disenchanted. The cat, curved against the contours of the wood basket's interior, ignored them as they beckoned her, guessing correctly that the bored boys wanted to initiate a session of corner the cat.

"Hand hurts," Brooks complained.

"Hurt my hand," Rollins confirmed. "All that—"

"Scratching," Brooks agreed.

"You see," Alden told Becky.

"What?" Becky asked, not looking up from a recipe for Chicken Piquant, an apricot-and-chili-sauced entrée. She was wondering if she could sneak some frozen broccoli florettes into the sauce. "See what?"

"See, the boys are going off gambling," Alden said.

"But Little Becky has won fifty dollars so far. I've had to ban her," Becky said. "That's quite enough for her to have won."

"Huh," said Alden. "Fifty dollars for Little B.? How annoying."

Ginger wandered into the big parlor. (Oscar had been napping since he'd limped away from the dinner table and groaned his way up the stairs to his room where one could only imagine him lying near death atop his bedspread with his shoes on and his belt unbuckled.) Ginger frowned at Alden and Becky, so smugly together, and she stepped over Brooks and Rollins. She selected a scratch ticket from the bowl. She seemed to believe she was picking a good one. The first few she touched did not feel "right." She rasped away the metallic coating with her sharp thumbnail.

"I've got two leprechaun faces showing," she said. "Do I win? What do I win? Nothing? Why is this supposed to be fun? I'm not having fun, I only have these scratchy granules stuck under my thumbnail."

The telephone rang then. Ginger bustled into the hall and was about to pick up when a thought occurred to her—Louis might very well be calling Betsy and Ginger did not want to have to explain why Betsy was not there. The telephone rang on and Lily reluctantly appeared at the dining room doorway. She had been separating the sky pieces from the masonry pieces of her new Great Wall of China jigsaw puzzle at the dining room table, assisted by Little Becky who was specializing in the Wall's sightseers, all of whom seemed to have black hair and to wear dark blue pajama suits and were as undifferentiated as the sky itself, the reconstruction of which Little Becky had craftily, she thought, eschewed.

Lily reached past Ginger who was pinned in place beneath the weight of her heavy conscience.

"Well?" Lily spoke severely into the receiver.

"One moment," she said, and she asked at large, "Glover?"

"Glover?" A cry was taken up.

Glover stumbled from the little parlor. He was following the siege of the Vatican Mission in Panama City on TV, where that dire-looking General Noriega had been holed up since the invasion of a few days earlier. The army, our army, was blasting the Mission from all sides with pounding loud rock music to drive out Noriega who Uncle Harvey said was a dedicated opera buff and whose ears must be bleeding by now. Cool, Glover had said, it was real cool of the army to, like, bother the enemy. Glover could get behind that kind of strategy. And since he seemed so interested in military matters, Uncle Harvey had told him a few interesting official secrets left over from D-Day—the secret password had been a phrase no German tongue could pronounce. Very cool.

"Yeah?" Glover spoke into the phone. "Missy? Yeah? Merry. . . . Right."

He listened to a gabbling voice. He sighed. Lily withdrew.

"Your present?" Glover asked. "Look, I already gave you what you wanted."

He listened. He chuckled.

"No, I already gave you what you wanted," he repeated.

He listened. He preened. He leaned into the wall.

"So, I gotta give it to you all over again?"

"God," Ginger remarked, and she shuddered and drifted back to the big parlor. She dropped into a wing chair and began to read through the household's Christmas cards, all collected in a red painted basket labeled Santa's Mailbag. Harvey had received dozens of big stiff printed cards from corporations, politicians, foundations, and charities. She wondered how Betsy, in her cataloguing of the cards for Andy, had characterized those. Andy had sent a postcard from Florida—a fat retired Santa in a Speedo—asking them to calculate, as well, the ratio of religious to secular decorations in the house, if they'd be so kind, although so many of the decorations were ambiguously borderline—candles, angel-cat ornaments, holly, which was sacred to Druids.

"We didn't receive a card from William this year," Alden observed as Ginger pushed away the card basket. "I hope he isn't being peevish."

"Yes, we did, one came. I put it—somewhere," Becky said.

William's card this year had been an exquisite stand-up affair that opened into an intricately precise Notre Dame Cathedral with flying buttresses, the Rose Window, all of the gargoyles. But the envelope had been addressed to Becky alone and on the blank space, on the *place* in front of the cathedral, William had written in his exquisite hand, *If you let me, I will lay all of Paris at your feet.* Becky had thrust the thing in her handkerchief drawer at once and having in effect hidden it, she was stuck with that course. To produce the card now would seem revelatory, if only of her first impulse not to share William's joke, his foolish joke. Surely, William had meant the message as a joke, and she didn't feel like sharing William's joke.

William's card—put somewhere? Ginger was momentarily alert to the hesitation in Becky's answer, but then her shoulders sagged. This was merely Becky, after all, who had misplaced a piece of correspondence in the midst of this correspondence-flooded season.

Becky stood and stretched. Her new sapphire tennis bracelet slid up her arm and she said she really ought to pre-spot the damask tablecloth and the vast damask dinner napkins with Shout and throw them in the washing machine before the squash and cranberry and coffee stains could set in permanently.

"Let me do that. You rest," Alden offered from the sofa.

Becky waited a minute. Alden reached down and cast about the floor for his new moccasin slippers. He encountered, instead, his new book, *A Bright Shining Lie,* which he lifted and opened and began to read. Becky left him to it.

So the day droned on and sank to its lowest ebb. The boys were watching *It's a Wonderful Life* on the little-parlor TV, too enervated to jeer, too torpid to channel hop among the frequent commercials running on more pointlessly than ever, offering objects already purchased and found under the tree. The others were reading on their beds or asleep in chairs. Ginger had visited the turkey carcass in the refrigerator and left a legbone sitting in a saucer atop the mirror pond in Little Becky's Christmas Village to make it look as if the villagers had lately killed and eaten a mastodon. Little Becky had hovered so pesteringly in the vicinity of her village and had accused Ginger, whenever Ginger passed by, of walking too heavily and causing the tiny pine trees to topple and the tinier people to fall flat over backwards. Ginger had pointed out that all the tiny people toppled backwards because they wore such weighty knapsacks. They were, Ginger supposed, Norwegians. No, insisted Little Becky, her village was in *Vermont.*

A CAR NOSED UP the driveway, cresting the frozen waves of the driveway ruts. Babe Palmer, riding shotgun, said, "It ought not to be allowed."

Goody said, Oh well, and almost hit a fence post, but Penny Nicholls spoke up from the backseat, asking, "Allowed by whom? Because as far as I'm aware, Lily doesn't have to answer to a Towne Driveway Oversight Committee, at least not yet, but give them time to think of it down at Town Hall."

Penny had put in a long day at the Palmer house ever since Goody had collected her at 9 a.m. from Senior Village, after Babe, who had dutifully called her second cousin Bell in Connecticut to wish them all the benefits of the season, learned that Penny had not gone down to spend the holidays with the Connecticut branch of the family after all, although Penny had quoted the Amtrak schedule to Babe, even inventing a change of trains in Providence where one might pick up a cup of quahog chowder at the station canteen. Babe ought to have questioned that station canteen detail—they didn't have station canteens these days.

But Bell's attitude was so harum-scarum and Babe's ministrations were so chilly, and Penny had hoped she had outmaneuvered all those who felt it was their duty to keep her spirits up over the holidays. They were going to dine on two crown roasts of pork in the Senior Village Common Room, and potluck yams and oyster stew and champagne punch and ambrosia—half the residents had schemed not to have to visit family—and even though Penny had firmly told Babe no, no thank you, really dear, you're too kind but no, Babe had sent Goody over to collect her. Penny had appreciated that Goody's life would be a confirmed hell were he to return alone. Goody had realized that as well but he had manfully not alluded to his coming martyrdom even in a spirit of half-jest and half-appeal, and so, suddenly liking him for that, Penny had capitulated. She foil-wrapped six cider doughnuts as a hostess present for Babe and left the other eighteen with Mack MacNally to contribute when the time came for the Senior Feast.

Babe had prepared a canned ham with canned pineapple rings and a rice with raisins pudding which they ate at quarter past twelve, and if Penny's husband, Buster Nicholls, hadn't died five years earlier they would have been able to play bridge until midnight. Now, all there seemed for them to do was, regretfully, not play bridge. Penny, who had grabbed her knitting bag as she was being escorted out her door by Goody, withdrew into industry and finished the mittens, an Aran Island pattern worked in a natural, waxy wool, she had not had time to complete for Harvey's present. He knew he was getting them. She had shown him the wool and the pattern when he dropped by with her gift, Scotch that came in such an interesting triangular-shaped bottle she looked forward to having the use of after Harvey had drained the Scotch out on his frequent social calls. Harvey had been understanding. "Now, now," he said, "I know you have far better ways to occupy your time than to knit exclusively for me, so I'm very touched and grateful, my dear, or shall be when you've got them done." What a charming man.

It seemed only fair to deliver Harvey's gift on Christmas Day since he'd been such a brick. Displaying the mittens, Penny said, "Let's drop in on the Hills right now, why don't we?"

"Oh, but it's so pleasant here," Babe said, and she stuck a silk pillow behind her back in demonstration of the comfort and fine appointments of her residence.

"We'll swing by on the way home then," Penny said as she consulted the clock on the mantelpiece. "My word, is that the time? I've taken up far too much of your delightful hospitality. Goody, you won't mind a little side trip before dropping me off?"

"No. Not at all," Goody said, glancing at Babe.

"But it's a family day," Babe pointed out repressively.

"Oh, families," Penny remarked feelingly.

To which Babe had felt like answering, Yes, families, right back at her even more feelingly but she couldn't without conceding the point, nor could she stay home to sulk because that would leave Penny and Goody free to visit the Hills for as long as they liked, or at least until Babe called to inquire whether her husband and her late mother's cousin had met with a fatal accident en route, or were they just being discourteously delinquent? She announced she would ride along for the fresh air, but she remained in the car when they arrived. She kept her seat belt fastened and shook her head when Goody opened her door. He shut the door, and in his care not to be accused of slamming, he left the door loosely ajar. He kept the key in the ignition so Babe couldn't say later that she hadn't been able to turn on the heater or listen to the radio, for she was convinced World War III most likely would begin on a National Holiday when the Army and Navy were drunk, and now the key caused a warning wail to commence, notifying that the door was ill-latched. Babe endured the electronic doo-wop of monition as Goody took Penny's elbow and guided her across the Hills' choppy brown lawn, both stepping in a happy hurry. Penny clutched Harvey's mittens in her mittened hand. Neither she nor Goody had assured Babe they wouldn't be long. Indeed, Penny's parting words had been, "Suit yourself," cheerfully stated by one who intended to suit herself.

Babe tugged the door securely shut and twisted sideways in the car seat. Goody had parked so that she was aimed at a view of wintry meadow and she required a view of the house, which had lately lost half its shutters. The wreath on the front door hung askew with its ribbon untying. Babe almost expected to see the roof and walls bulge upward and outward, there was such a crowd in residence and the Hills were not small or quiet people. Babe's imagination could be engaged by such grotesqueries. She sometimes saw the faces of the damned among the crumpled coffee filters and orange peels when she glanced down into her kitchen wastebasket. Which reminded her, she'd been meaning to have her eyes checked. She peered, she squinted through the windshield as a weird figure approached, swathed in a dark cloak, wearing a mask, wielding long, thin sticks, and making a halting, lurching progress. Babe rolled down her window and hallooed.

Little Becky slithered to a stop beside the car.

"Couldn't you wait for snow?" Babe asked. "Is it good for skis to walk on frozen ground?"

Little Becky, who suspected she was being criticized, blurted defensively, "My Dad *said* I could. He told me to. Go out. Anyway, there was snow. Before. It melted."

"Alden said," Babe nodded as if that confirmed some opinion she held of Alden. "So, you're the daughter. You were pointed out to me one day at the IGA. You were eating potato chips from a bag I very much doubt you had yet to purchase."

"Huh?" Little Becky asked. She stood still and leaned on her poles, then she skidded and thudded against the side of the Palmer car as the long tips of her skis slid beneath the undercarriage. Babe stared at toggle buttons and a heaving chest flattened against the window glass. She eased herself out the driver's side door and dealt with the situation.

As they were sitting on the stone wall catching their breaths, it occurred to Babe to ask the child what she had wanted to know all along. "Has your Uncle Louis come for the holidays?" she inquired.

"What?" Little Becky asked, shifting uneasily. Such coldness seeped from the stones. She drooped. The entire day had been so no-Christmas, inside and out. She couldn't believe it. In New York she would have been at her second showing of the opening day of a big new blockbuster movie. She would have stood in an unraveling, roistering line for an hour, and then another hour. Fun.

"Your Aunt Ginger's husband, your Uncle Louis, was he able to join you all for a few days?" Babe clarified.

"No. But Mr. Oscarsson came," Little Becky said.

"Mr. Oscarsson? Who's Mr. Oscarsson?" Babe asked.

"He's, I think he's Aunt Ginger's . . ." Little Becky stopped and gazed in rapt puzzlement at the distant toes of her new skis. If this were an episode of *Knott's Landing* she could have rattled on indefinitely about intrigues and infidelities, but she could not quite connect the dots of TV drama with that slow, rumbling Mr. Oscarsson in his wide shirts and her caustic aunt who went through a roll of Tums every two days.

"Aunt Ginger's what?" Babe asked. "Oh, I see," she said as Little Becky stood abruptly and trudged off on her skis, tilting and tipping over frozen tuffets, jamming the points of her poles against the iron earth, insisting over her shoulder, "*I* don't know."

"Well, I certainly can't miss this." Babe spoke aloud to herself, a practice she routinely deplored in others.

None of the Hills had realized Babe was waiting outside in the car. No one missed her at all, except Lily who had looked, perhaps preventively, to ascertain that Babe was not lurking on the front step unknotting her scarf and prying off her storm boots before springing herself on them all. Oscar, having rambled downstairs after his long, disorienting nap, attempted too aggressively to remove Penny's flaring toreador's cape and confiscate her spare pair of mittens. He had yet to locate the appropriate pitch for his friendly overtures in this house. As Oscar advanced, Penny hunched into her cape and scooted into the big parlor where she sat upon the sofa as if the sofa were Safe in a rough-and-tumble game of tag.

"Who was that?" she asked Lily.

"These?" asked Lily. "Try one, they're very good," she said, offering Penny a box of Mint Melt-Aways that had come in someone's stocking.

Alden asked Goody what he'd like to drink and Goody couldn't say, so Alden suggested the Merlot he'd found in the odd lot case of wine he'd bought in New York, and he and Goody sat back and discussed the circumstances of Alden's field trip back to the city.

Becky headed for the kitchen and warmed the plum pudding and hard sauce in the microwave. She set the old Coalport plates and dessert forks and teaspoons on the tray of the tea wagon. She doused the plum pudding with brandy and, turning the sliced and eaten side toward herself, she pushed the laden tea wagon across the dining room and, pausing at the big-parlor doorsill, she ignited the pudding with a wooden match. The boys raised the volume of the little-parlor TV, for Penny's exclamations at the appearance of the flaming pudding had such a carrying-on, whooping quality. Harvey had received his present and he'd immediately slipped the mittens onto his hands declaring he'd keep them on until spring. He kept them on as Becky passed around plates of pudding and Penny bade him to sit beside her as she balanced their plates upon her knees and fed him dainty forkfuls as he clasped his mittened hands.

Ginger had crouched at the top of the stairs listening to the initial greetings being exchanged below. Then she had flown to her bedroom and slipped off her crumpled slacks and jersey. She pulled on her green satin hostess knickerbockers and a white-and-silver-shot angora tunic which made her look, in her treacherous full-length mirror, like a dandelion clock about to scatter to the winds. She scanned her closet, and chairbacks and floor, and she struggled into an old standby navy-blue wool sheath and stuck on, sticking herself, a gold circle pin, which dim ensemble made her appear even more maiden-auntly than Lily (who, most unexpectedly, was wearing the sweatshirt Arthur and Phoebe had given her, apple green and appliquéd with poinsettia leaves by a co-worker of Phoebe's and offered for sale at the back of the hospital cafeteria from mid-November on). Oh, you are so fat, Ginger accused the swollen image in her mirror. She rattled through her closet again and pulled out a cocktail dress, a black number with chiffon sleeves and a lace overlay. The jeweled sash wouldn't meet around her waist, so she tied it twice round her forehead, lifting her hair like a cloud above her face. *Not* fat, but bosomy, she told herself as she once again consulted her mirror and rather liked what she saw there now. Bosomy was *good*.

Ginger and Babe almost collided in the front hall beneath the Italian papier-mâché angel hanging by the string Little Becky had lassoed up and over the etched-glass hanging light fixture. Babe had quietly let herself in after she had knocked, not very loudly because she was bound to catch them all unaware, enjoying themselves in candid congregation, but Ginger's yelp of "Babe!" as their back-to-back collision was just averted, lost Babe her planned advantage of surprise.

Ginger recovered her composure, gratifyingly aware of how very much more attractive she was than Babe with her sparse haircut and grey skirt and grey twin set and grey teeth and grey skin. Ginger linked arms with Babe and drew her across the doorway of the big parlor where she halted to allow everyone time to notice them properly. Heads had already been turned by Ginger's warning (it seemed) utterance, and eyes blinked the apparition in the doorway into focus. As Alden said later, the sight of the two women standing side by side had the unnerving effect upon one of watching two movies at once, one filmed in vivid Technicolor and the other captured in shades of black and white.

"Aren't you cold?" Lily asked Ginger, noting her niece's expanse of plump and pinkening skin. "Haven't you a sweater?" she asked.

"Oh, come look at the tree," Ginger offered expansively, pulling Babe across the room. Ginger's extravagantly high heels gored floorboards and pocked carpet pile. Babe's crepe soles thumped alongside.

"Yes, just look at that tree," Babe said with practiced tonelessness.

Ginger unhooked her arm from Babe's as she reached to wind the spring of a trilling mechanical bird sitting upon a branch. Ginger felt the need for music—madder music and stronger wine, she was about to cry for. She had spotted the opened bottle and she was keen to catch up with the others.

"A nuthatch with a robin's song," Lily told Penny as the tin bird whirrily chirped. The error had always bothered her. She always had to explain that the ornament manufacturers had installed the wrong mechanism.

"A nuthatch with a robin's song," Lily said to Oscar, who did not at all understand what she was going on about.

"So are you bragging or complaining, honey?" he asked Lily jollily.

BETSY RETURNED CHRISTMAS night. Mr. Snowdon drove her as far up the driveway as the ice and ruts allowed, and she assured him she could safely walk the rest of the way on her own across Lily's sloping lawns. The house was well in view, a lamp burning behind every frost-traced window, and Mr. Snowdon had the restless children with him in the car for Mrs. Snowdon had not wished to be left alone with them in their overstimulated states after too much sugar and too much holiday. Mrs. Snowdon had regarded Betsy's abrupt request to be driven back to the River Road as an abandonment of her duties before the children had splashed through their Betsy-supervised baths and been persuaded into their pajamas and then climbed into their beds at Betsy's special request to be read their current story, *Charlotte's Web*, by Betsy, who rose to character voices and permitted close study of the illustrations and patiently answered questions about the bathing habits of spiders because, the little Snowdons said, there were often spiders to be found in their bathtubs.

Mr. Snowdon had promised the children he'd drive them home past the house on Conant Street where a spotlit Santa stood on the rooftop waving and emitting recorded greetings. He hoped the newly formed Conant Street Neighborhood Association had not yet succeeded in pulling the plug on the display.

Jennica, Alexianna, and Jonathan-Michael, huddled in the backseat, would not say good-bye and thank you to Betsy.

"Okay, then," Betsy said, for she had long ago learned to be immune to most manifestations of temperament and she much preferred the cold shoulder to the hot confrontation. At home, she had always been able to finish her homework in peace and watch what she liked on television when her mother silently and distantly brooded over how she'd been wronged.

Mr. Snowdon passed her a check at which she did not look before folding it into her parka pocket. They had all behaved as if Betsy were just helping out from the goodness of her heart as an auxiliary member of the family who could also be sent to the kitchen to make the pancakes and be asked to vacuum packing material and pine needles from the rugs. Betsy had also kept the turtle with her in the guest room for the children had been frightened by the turtle's reptilian head questing from its shell and they had been even more disturbed by the head's withdrawal within the otherwise dead-looking carapace, knowing that the snaky face was just inside.

Betsy turned and walked away quickly without waiting to watch Mr. Snowdon safely back down the dangerous driveway and to call out a helpful "Be careful" should he start to fishtail and slither into the swamp which never quite froze because decomposing marshmallows and skunk cabbage heated the water. Aunt Becky said there could be an alternative energy business there if one could only harness the weeds, but Betsy didn't suppose Mr. Snowdon would want to hear about Aunt Becky's science project when he was up to his knees in brown water and the kids were screaming.

Betsy's Samsonite bag bumped against the back of her leg with every step. She jumped in and out of the glare of the widely swinging beams of the Snowdon car's headlights for she wished her return to the house to be unheralded—and now that she was nearly there, deferred. Betsy thumped down her suitcase and sat upon its flat top, hugging her thin, frozen knees with her down-fattened arms and breathing into the upturned collar of her jacket, which warmed her. Her breath smelled sharply of the candy cane shards she had tucked under her tongue. Her hot, sharp, steady breath—my Life Force, Betsy suddenly, unaccountably thought. She had not realized someone of her age and in her situation could independently possess such a power within. She wasn't sure she wanted any part of a Life Force.

For she was free now to think about her obeah experiment. How satisfying as it had been to perform the rite, when, for the first time in her utterly orderly and standard-issue existence she had experienced the pull of the primitive. It had been so very convenient not to consider Mr. Oscarsson's wishes and feelings. It had been so very freeing not to have to care what became of him, when the responsibility had been taken from her hands, when the spell had fallen, or been pushed or snatched, irretrievably behind the stone foundation, when she had opened a door and invited an accommodating devil inside. But she had been naïve to think a devil would be hers to command. She did not suppose any summoned demon would go away quietly, would perform only as requested and then wash his hands and screw the cap back on the Ron Rico Rum bottle and turn off the lights. No, once on the premises, he would want to stick around and take advantage, just like one of the family.

Betsy envisioned him, the wiry little imp with a wide, white smile, dressed in an unbuttoned Hawaiian shirt and wrinkled clam-diggers and an unraveling straw hat. Uncle Harvey would look up and start to give him thunder, but, Betsy knew, the angry imp would strike Uncle Harvey dumb and bind him round and round with the curtain pulls and cinch him tightly in his armchair in the little parlor facing the TV turned perpetually to the *CBS Evening News*. And as for the rest of them, excepting Aunts Lily and Becky who would avert their eyes and retire to their rooms with, respectively, a library book and the mending, at the first hint of an unearthly presence, Betsy feared that the rest of them would smilingly welcome the stranger. *What a delightful accent . . . what a persuasive argument spoken by that lilting, engaging voice. . . .* They would nod agreeably along with his insinuating cadences just as readily as they tapped their toes to *Evening at Pops.* Betsy could see them cheerfully, willingly, being led one by one back through that newly opened door, forsaking the 40-watt lightbulbs and muted shades of Aunt Lily's house for the bright lights and utter blackness of the Otherworld.

She had brought ruin upon her family on Christmas Day and evermore they would be as cursed as one of those ancient Greek families, one of those closed, misery-muddled Greek families locked together throughout eternity on the side of a vase, fated always to stare balefully at one another across the dinner table set with bitter herbs and brackish water, with nothing nice ever served to pep up the supper menu.

Yes, and that was all she needed, Betsy leaned into her knees and sighed, to be doomed to remain forever at Aunt Lily's house, trapped by her guilt and her conscience, condemned always to mop up the mess she'd made as the result of one small and inexpert and not very deeply meant bit of Voodoo business. It didn't seem fair that, just at the moment she had discovered her Life Force, circumstances were gathering to quash it.

Betsy heaved herself to her feet and trailed around to the back door and entered, her heart absurdly apace. New skis, she noted dully, stacked on the glass-enclosed porch. She wondered if she had gotten anything good—she'd been left out of the present opening at the Snowdons'.

"Oh, there you are," Alden said, mildly smiling at her as he stirred the two-quart copper-bottomed pot on the stovetop. "Join the party. I'm mulling cider. Can I include you in a cup? We missed you today, it wasn't so bad," he added.

"What? Oh, no," Betsy said. "Thank you."

She dropped her suitcase in the middle of the linoleum and shrugged off her parka and draped it over a chairback from which it slid. Alden did not comment and picked up after her as she passed into the hallway. She stood outside the big-parlor door and watched them.

Her mother and Mr. Palmer relaxed in front of the Christmas tree, as at ease with one another as the older couple in a Lifestyle Supplement advertisement for anniversary diamonds. Ginger toed a pile of unopened gifts further beneath the picture frame table's fringed cloth covering, and she said she wanted to show Goody the presents she had received. She leaned over in the lowest-cut dress she had brought from home to search among her little stash of treasures. "Here," she said, straightening, taking hold of Goody's instantly offered arm.

"Do you like this?" she asked. She uncapped a small crystal bottle and depressed a nozzle with a red-tipped finger. "Ombre Rose," she pronounced at him.

They leaned into the mist she had sprayed between them, eyes closed and lashed shut as they breathed in unison drafts of the same scented air.

"Yes," said Goody, "I do like that."

"But then," said Ginger, again leaning over and rustling among her gifts, "there's also my new Passion."

Mr. Oscarsson sat at the less atilt end of the long, big-parlor sofa with Mrs. Palmer at his side, and they were having quite a conversation. Babe asked intense and interested questions and Oscar, who believed he had found a friend here at last (for he counted Ginger as someone other than a friend to him), was delighted to discuss at length everything he could think of worth mentioning about himself. He had no idea, of course, just what he was laying bare before Babe in all candor, if not innocence. Nor would Babe appreciate just what she had learned until she carried the information home as she would carry home her portion of plum pudding twisted in a napkin to enjoy tomorrow when, she said, she would have found her appetite again. She would reheat the plum pudding in a bubbling double boiler and spoon on the hard sauce and she would rehash her talk with Oscar. Then, bearing in mind the difficulty she faced and the end she sought, she would sample the pudding in small, considering bites and say to herself, Too much ginger, there is far too much Ginger in all of this.

Ginger conducted Goody across the room as he began to sneeze in the scented air. Babe waved a white hankie at him from the sofa, though not as a sign of some surrender—rather, she was semaphoring that she had brought a blister pack of his Dristan tablets along in her purse.

Ginger and Goody stood, now, the anniversary and diamond couple, before the fire which had been burning all day. The mantelpiece swag of laurel and holly was browning and curling, holly berries detached and dropped. Ginger leaned over the rose famille bowl and her red-tipped fingers felt among the tickets until they touched one and then another that felt "right." She extracted a try for her and a try for Goody. Babe and Oscar could not be tempted when Ginger remembered to offer.

"You folks?" she asked, over a chiffon shoulder.

"How?" asked Goody, holding out his square of pasteboard, unsure how to play, but Ginger was expert by now. She scratched away at the metallic coating with the point of her high heel. As she leaned to remove and to refit her shoe, Goody instantly offered his arm.

"You've won," Ginger cried. "You've won a free ticket. Look, everyone, Goody's won a free ticket. You have a free ticket to win another ticket, another chance. You see, you have another chance," she informed Goody.

Betsy turned away from them all then and she started up the winding stairs. She almost had to smile, although she bit back the smile, for the scene she had just witnessed, quite a performance, to be sure, but only the usual and the practiced one, had struck her tonight as a mere divertissement which could only be regarded with relief and not a little gratitude that there had been nothing worse going on.

THE DAY AFTER CHRISTMAS, Oscar was gone. He might as well have been swept up and bundled away with the crushed boxes and tangled packing material as, on Tuesday morning he was noticed not to be underfoot at breakfast requiring something hot and hearty to tide him over until his hot and hearty lunch. Becky had already heated his Grape Nuts in the heavy iron frying pan, intermittently seizing the pan by the handle and giving the Grape Nuts a rattle so they wouldn't burn black across the bottom, when Ginger, she-bearish in a new plush bathrobe, her present from Lily, padded into the kitchen. She shot her usual flinch of grudging greeting at the family presences propped around the table or standing with their backs against the countertops and cupboards, raising or lowering cereal spoons and coffee cups and wedges of toast on which jam glistened, to or from their smudged and unreplying mouths.

"Just coffee," Ginger said faintly, bravely, and she heaved herself into the chair next to Harvey who, being rather an expert on women in the morning, shifted, anticipating expansive gestures. He preventively slid his bowl of canned mandarin orange segments in juice out of the range of her elbow, and he raised a barrier of newsprint between them.

The boys smirked and Little Becky flushed scarlet and Betsy suffered inside as they waited for Oscar to enter the kitchen, trailing Ginger by the three discreet minutes they had scheduled to elapse as the decent interval between their carefully separate appearances. Yesterday morning, Oscar had timed the three decorous minutes on his big blunt base-metal watch face. He strode through the door, his lips silently prompting, Three ... two ... one ...

So, where was he? Rollins poked Brooks who snorted and swallowed the wrong way. A gout of milk spewed from his nose.

"Ma-ha," Little Becky yelped. "Brooks got nose milk on my doughnut."

"Don't be disgusting," Becky told Brooks, or Little Becky. She shook the pan of Grape Nuts and plucked a Kleenex from her sweater sleeve for Brooks and she cracked and began to remove the shell from the top of Alden's soft-boiled egg which was sitting cradled atop a ceramic egg cup, a yellow, big-eyed chick that was older than Alden. Becky sheared off the top of the exposed white and set the egg cap upon a saucer.

"Thanks," said Alden. He prodded a knob of soft butter into the center of his perfectly timed egg with his spoon tip and lightly tapped on salt, pepper, and a bit more salt. He refit the cap of white and sat back, reading the rear wall of Harvey's newspaper barricade, as he waited for the butter to melt and meld into the yolk.

Becky lifted a spatula and, catching Ginger's eye, pointed inquiringly to the frying pan. Ginger shook her head. Really? Becky's expression asked. Ginger nodded. Becky switched off the burner beneath the frying pan and poured a tall glass of orange juice back into the carton and rehooked a new coffee mug to the new coffee mug tree. She glanced again at Ginger who was managing to look frail and flushed and belligerent at once, as if she had just taken it upon herself to clean the entire house from bottom to top.

Lily came into the kitchen last, greeting the family briskly. She correctly corrected Brooks, "Hush, please, Brooks," as he singsonged *Nose milk, nose milk,* into Little Becky's crimson ear. Lily was sharp that morning, telling Brooks apart from Rollins. Always an early awakener if not, these days, an early riser, Lily had overheard through her bedroom door and overlooked from her bedroom window (forsaking her warm bed to do so) the particulars of Oscar's leave-taking from Ginger.

"Have you got everything?" Ginger's voice had asked.

"I'll call if I left anything," Oscar answered.

"No, no, be sure now," Ginger's voice insisted, and then Ginger's eager footsteps and Oscar's slower ones, weighed by his garment bag and carry-on clutch, retreated and moved outside.

Lily observed the brief study of an unfurled road map; Ginger's impatient finger traced the directest route to the highway. She leaned into Oscar and bestowed a quick kiss. Oscar's arm detained her and they shared a less quick kiss. Ginger pulled away. Oscar hauled her back. Ginger broke free and to soften her action—she had pushed him away ungently—she pointed to the sky and playfully motioned, Fly, fly, he mustn't miss his plane. No, he had time. Oscar dismissed the overreaching sky with a wave. Ginger, outside in just her robe, shivered. Cold, she indicated, and she submitted to a long, last embrace as Oscar said whatever it was he needed to say to her and she let him kiss her again because she felt so sorry for him, of course. Oscar quit her, at last, with a grin and assurances. Ginger would have to sit down and write him one final, difficult, explanatory letter which would catch him by surprise, or not.

Lily had slipped into Andy's room and removed all signs of Oscar's habitation, the several *National Geographic*s (May, June, July 1962) he had asked to borrow from the stack in the back hall, and the water glass he required by his bedside for he had said he often awoke in the middle of the night coughing and he needed to sip; Lily sniffed, bourbon. She found nothing sensational slipped behind the headboard or forgotten in the night table drawer for which she was thankful, because if Ginger thought Lily hadn't known what she and Oscar were up to, if Ginger thought she was the only Hill who had brought a lover here and sat blandly across from him at the dinner table maintaining he was a colleague from work or a friend of the family or just someone very keen upon attending the Towne Apple or Strawberry or Snowflake Festival, then, Lily supposed, I have successfully averted my eyes and closed my ears and held my tongue.

She unmade the bed. She did not want the chore to fall to Betsy; that would not be appropriate. She freed the four corners of the bottom sheet and bundled the sheets, blankets, bedspread, and pillows, mistakenly, and crammed the lot inside the bathroom hamper. She spent several minutes trying to close the lid, succeeding at last by catching an edge of the lid beneath the curving lip of the old bathtub. Someone else would bump the hamper lid free and ajar again, but then that would be their problem.

Now, Lily looked almost fondly upon Ginger, for Oscar, who had been her guest, had demonstrated rare good grace to limit the duration of his visit to thirty-nine hours, Lily calculated. She moved around the kitchen table and lightly tapped Ginger's hunched shoulder and she said with satisfaction, "That's that," as if she assumed Ginger was as satisfied as she to have just seen the last of Oscar.

"That's that," Ginger calmly agreed.

Alden lifted amazed, inquiring eyebrows at Becky who, standing over the big shiny toaster poised to rescue Alden's English muffin from the maw of the veteran apparatus at the critical instant it allowed between golden brownness and charred black, was no less amazed by Ginger's composure in the face of Lily's remark.

Lily lifted her personal cup and saucer (very old, Limoges, a flowered pattern) from the high cupboard above the stove, heretofore concealed behind a box of Kosher salt which had just lately vanished and kept safe and separate from all the other clustering, chipping, casually rinsed cups and saucers and mugs, and she poured herself coffee, draining the pot. She selected a plain doughnut from the box on the countertop. Becky offered to dredge the doughnut through cinnamon sugar and pop it in the microwave for twenty seconds which sounded fine to Lily. She sat at the end of the table catty-cornered from Glover who was separating the raisins from the bran flakes in his cereal bowl and arranging them on opposing sides as if he meant for them to wage a naval war for supremacy of the Milky White Sea.

Ginger stood then, vitally and woundedly rising to her swaying height, and clutched her robe and several shawls of paisley challis and fringed wool about herself as if they alone loved her now. Lily had swanned in and stolen the last of the coffee to which she had already laid verbal claim and was about to do something about once she had gathered her forces and pulled herself together after enacting that harrowing farewell scene. And why hadn't Becky poured her a cup of coffee instead of whisking away Oscar's intended orange juice as if the sight of the forlorn glass would make Ginger weep? Really, though, it was too bad of Lily. That warm cinnamon doughnut looked good, but Lily's was probably the last of those as well.

Ginger snatched the empty pot from the stove and knocked the grounds into the sink as Becky had asked her not to do so often she had given up asking. Splashing water and spilling coffee beans which rolled and scattered, she crushed beans in the little electric grinder that was a new gift from the young Aldens, and she reassembled the components of the pot, jamming them together as they resisted reassemblage. It was an ancient, tarnished pot with a dented basket. The young Aldens ought to have given Lily one of those Mr. Coffee machines for Christmas, Ginger thought as she slammed the pot onto the back burner and, frowning at a spot on the far wall, she grimly waited for the first coffee-smelling burble to rise in the glass bulb on the lid top.

So that's it. Alden quirked understanding eyebrows at Becky. Ginger was going to be high-minded about the exit of Oscar and take the low road concerning coffee.

Betsy alone continued to think of Oscar. She kept track of his estimated whereabouts throughout the day, telling herself *now* he's on the plane, he's in the air, he's eating his snack and hoping there's seconds, he's holding his breath—they're landing, he's collecting his bags, he's found his car in the long-term parking lot, he's driving down the highway, *now* he's passing the Mall, he's stopping at the long light and he's pondering the time and temperature and prime lending rate digitally flashing on the sign of the First Deposit Bank on the corner, he's driving across town beneath the lampposts decorated for Christmas, he's passing the courthouse and going round the traffic circle, he's driving out of town into the countryside, and now he's slowing down at the end of the street where we used to live before he came along and spoiled everything. He's glancing down the street out of habit to see whether Daddy's car is sitting in the driveway, whether Mummy's car is there, whether he can stop and visit Mummy only, of course, nobody at all is home now. It occurred to Betsy then, as she thought of the uninhabited house, of the rooms where no one sat, of the emptied closets, idled kitchen, neglected gardens, and the lamps on timer switches pretending to themselves their services were still necessary, that it was Mr. Oscarsson who had unloosed the far stronger and more devastating charm against them all long before she had attempted to work her own feeble and belated conjuration on him.

LATER THAT AFTERNOON, as Little Becky lurked in the little parlor within range of the kitchen where there were such interesting and diminishing leftovers upon which she essayed frequent, secret raids, the kitchen wall phone rang.

"I'll get, I'll get it," Little Becky cried against the trill of the telephone and she dashed on her lead feet skidding along the rugs and chattering the sherry glasses set out that hospitable time of year on the sideboard in the dining room. "I've got it," she yelled as she snatched the receiver before the third ring erupted which was against Aunt Lily's rules, or if not rules, for Lily didn't have rules as such, but she did express preferences and one of her preferences was that the telephone be allowed to ring several times—six, seven, eight, nine, or ten times—before being answered, lest one seem too eager. But Little Becky had never really known an uneager waking moment.

"W-I-L-D plays the hits for me, Alf in the Afternoon makes my day, Arf, arf, arf, KWOW gets my seal of approval," Little Becky rattled off the day's winning responses. She also knew that KROC's Artist of the Day was Poison and Magic Martin's Cash Pot currently held fifty-seven Big Deal dollars, although the amount was subject to change at any moment when he spun the Winning Wheel. She monitored that situation, twenty minutes past every hour when Magic Martin had to *say.*

"Huh? What? Oh." Little Becky's shoulders sagged. "Yes, I'll get him." She held the receiver against her chest. The telephone cord was a very long one and stretched as Little Becky wandered over to the back stairs. Her new Christmas jeans scraped, inner thigh upon inner thigh, and they had stained her skin purple just above her knee where she had slopped a cranberry juice cocktail. The stiff new material creaked as she scaled several steps, as far as the cord allowed.

"Arthur," she called. "Arthur-er. For you."

She acknowledged his faint answer and trailed the telephone cord across the room. She tangled with a tall kitchen chairback, yanked the cord free, and flung open the refrigerator door. She scrabbled turkey shreds from the keel of the carcass and swigged the last half-inch of eggnog (sourish, so she swallowed fast) from the carton and scooped up a quivery handful of Cherry Jell-O and pineapple salad which she held up to the light before swallowing down. Arthur took the sticky receiver from her and absentmindedly raked gummy fingers through his hair as he listened far more than he spoke, which didn't suit Little Becky who stared at him inquiringly and impatiently over the rim of a can of Pepsi Free.

"Give Arthur space, sweet pea," Becky reminded Little Becky as she came into the kitchen to wonder about supper, turkey noodly soup from scratch, she thought, if she started now. She had an onion, she had a carrot, she had noodles. Would anyone mind encountering escarole in turkey soup? She had all that escarole. But Becky paused and she stared at Arthur whose face was signaling every joyful feeling known to man. Arthur's awry and wayward features formed a readable sequence of reactions to the speaker at the other end of the line—Am I hearing right?—of daring to believe, of astonishment at the import of what he was daring to believe, and at last, a suffusion of calm and radiant jubilation marked him and he briefly became as beautiful as one of Leonardo's angels in his exaltation. Believe it or not, Becky would say later, as she retold the tale, he looked like the angel in the *Madonna of the Rocks* with his high forehead and invisible eyebrows and the golden red fluff of his pageboy. That's what being handed heaven can do for you, Becky supposed.

"Pen, pen, pen," Arthur was whispering urgently and Little Becky grabbed a Sharpwriter from the spoon mug which was turning into a general catch-all, spoons, pens, chopsticks, interesting twigs.

Arthur scribbled across Lily's yellow kitchen wall, unapologetically, exuberantly scrawling, Continental Airlines, 8.30 a.m., Wednesday a.m., LIMO will meet ME.

"Hey," Little Becky objected, "he's writing on . . ."

"Hush," Becky snapped. "What is it?" she asked Arthur as Arthur rang off, but Arthur was summoning Phoebe, calling, "Phoebe, Phoebe, Phoebe," up the back stairs as she hurried down still clutching her new counted cross-stitch project, which she had just begun on the day off she had been given because she had agreed to work at the hospital on New Year's Day.

"They want me in L.A.," Arthur announced. "I have to go there."

"Want you? But what have you done?" Phoebe asked worriedly even as she resolved—one could see her mentally bracing and composing herself—to stand by him, regardless.

"What have I done?" Arthur asked. "What have I done is to land myself a featured role in a sure to be picked up weekly comedy series on, Jesus, what did the guy say, which network was it? Anyway, it was one I'd heard of. Well, I'll fill in all that when I get there. Who am I to have an opinion on which network, at this point? But the guy said, the guy said, they're topnotch all the way. They're sending a limo. To the airport. To meet me." He tapped the wall where the word LIMO was written which made everything real and true.

"Who's this guy?" asked Phoebe.

"Yes, who is this person?" asked Becky.

"The guy on the phone," Little Becky explained, sidling over to Arthur's side. *TV,* after all.

"I didn't entirely catch his name. Edward something or maybe something Edwards, but you know where he's from, you know where he saw me perform? *Here.* He caught my act at that gig I did at the old people's home two weeks ago which just goes to show you, exposure is everything because you never know where somebody important's going to be," Arthur told them.

"Oh, for goodness sake," Becky declared. "I was there too, with Women's Chorus. Oh dear, no one discovered me."

"Right, with the Chorus ladies, you were there. So you know how great I was that day," Arthur said. "And Edward Something, or Something Edwards, was the guy in a leather jacket visiting his old aunt, he's all she has left in this world, he said, otherwise he wouldn't have been caught dead there."

"He sounds kind," Phoebe said.

"He was the man who smoked," Becky recalled. "Yes, he was very interested in you, Arthur. I could tell from the way he studied you."

"I'll say he was interested," Arthur brayed.

"Well, what rare good luck," Becky added.

"You make your own luck in this world," Arthur informed her gravely, and Becky hoped that Arthur, after a full thirty seconds in the limelight, wasn't becoming sententious as so many entertainment types seemed to be these days on talk shows, endorsing political candidates and naggingly promoting trash recycling, as if any of them ever carried out the rubbish unless they were enrolled in some sort of court-ordered program.

"How long will you be gone?" Phoebe asked.

"Forever, I hope," Arthur brayed again.

"Ma-ha," Little Becky protested, because it wasn't fair for Arthur to go away forever just when he was no longer going to be an embarrassing connection, somebody to pretend not to know when he said Hi to her in passing at the Freedomway Mall as he did one time when she was having an accidental but actual conversation with Missy DeStefano about the outfits in the Empire Store's windows and what kind of dresses Glover liked—on *girls*, that is, not to wear *himself*.

"I'm so happy for you," Phoebe said feelingly but ambiguously, for she may, to susceptible ears, have spoken *you* with the faintest, plaintive emphasis. Arthur's ears, his protuberant, inherently comedic ears, picked up on the softly sounded note of doubt.

"You know I'll send for you, Phoebe," he promised. "As soon as I'm set."

"Oh yes, not until you're set," Phoebe agreed. "And in the meanwhile, it's only sensible for me to keep on working and all, otherwise . . . Do you think I can stay on here? Will Miss Hill mind?"

"Of course you'll stay here with us, we wouldn't have it any other way," Becky said. She tugged at Little Becky's sweatshirt sleeve. "Come, let's give Arthur and Phoebe privacy to discuss their wonderful news."

"What wonderful news?" Ginger wanted to know. "I could use some wonderful news for a change," she observed as she rummaged through the cookie tin, thoughts of which had drawn her to the kitchen, although she possessed, as well, an instinct for the epicenter.

"It's a hoax. It has to be a hoax," she informed Arthur after he explained. "Those horrible boys disguising their voices were having him on," she spoke confidentially to Becky as Little Becky took advantage and palmed from the open cookie tin the last five vanille batons Ginger had had her eye on before she was sidetracked by having to set everybody else straight.

A SECOND CALL followed that day, for Alden from Roger Arsenault, his New York wine merchant who had accepted a consignment of Olde North Country Hearth Warmers (or whatever they'd ended up calling the things). Roger was as angry with Alden as the boutique firewood customers had been with him, customers who had sat up late and awakened early so keen were they to describe the complete nonsuccess of their Yuletide Hearth Warmer experience to Roger.

"Calm down," Alden counseled Roger.

Little Becky, folded over a chairback and anxious for her father to get off the line because Television might need to talk to Arthur again, listened impatiently, thumping and rocking the chair legs.

"Vermin?" Alden asked. "What manner of vermin?

"Ah," Alden understood. "Those little creatures sound like centipedes. And I'm familiar with the glossy, hard-backed beetles. They woke up, did they?

"Though no," Alden said, "that hasn't been our experience, but of course we burn our wood. We bring it in from outside and burn—

"Yes, well," Alden supposed, "they must have been hibernating under the bark and then been reactivated by the warmth of indoors. Nature is very wise, but she can be snookered.

"I don't think they'll survive long," Alden told Roger. "I'm sure there's nothing for them to eat and besides, they'll come tentacle to tentacle with the resident roaches—

"Cavalier?" Alden asked. "Look, if a few stray insects is all it takes to ruin a family's Christmas then I wouldn't care to be any of them should a real problem ever crop up.

"That's my last word? That's my last word," Alden laughed. "Sue me? Sue me." He pulled out his empty pants pocket lining and winked at Little Becky.

"Back to the old drawing board," he remarked to her, as he clicked down the receiver. "Don't mention this to your mother. The Hearth Warmers were her idea and she's never understood that just having an idea is the least of starting any new undertaking."

"Don't tell Ma?" asked Little Becky. "You mean, don't tell Ma?" she questioned. She had had no idea that they did not always have to tell her mother everything.

Chapter Five

The Hills and Love

W E CAUGHT COLDS all winter long, or perhaps it was the same
cold we never quite shed. We were always stuffy," Lily told
Andy. "The colds seemed to regroup between periods of relative dor-
mancy and we were always giving one another handkerchiefs as gifts, I
remember. We matched our hankies to our outfits on dressy occasions.
White hankies, they'd be, but the border lace or embroidery could
match, or contrast. My sister, Olive, was, at one time, a great believer in
contrasts. Red and blue, yellow and blue, orange and blue, whereas I
preferred blue and blue, though I might have tinkered with the shade."

"Ah," Andy answered as Lily broke off to give him time to record
her observations, as he had taught her to do over the course of their
interviews these past several months. Andy looked down at his empty
notebook page. He blew upon his chill-stiffened fingers, which evidence
of discomfort Lily failed to notice or chose not to see. They sat at opposite ends of the hard-cushioned big-parlor sofa, Lily upright with her
usual excellent posture, the invisible steel rod rising an imaginary inch
behind her backbone. Andy, skewed, faced her, one knee drawn up onto
the cushion, one arm slung along the sofa's curving camelback. His
notebook skidded from his aslant knee and splattered 3×5 cards onto
the rug. He hesitated for the several seconds he needed to remember
that Lily wouldn't dive to retrieve his notebook and cards to spare him
the strain and effort and inconvenience of reaching for them himself.
He had yet to recover fully from his visit home.

Andy, you're so drawn and tired and you can't deceive me, if you
hadn't sat outside so foolishly yesterday and turned neon in the sun,
you'd still be pale as cream, his mother had accused him. She had run to
serial accusations as she sectioned his morning grapefruit and banished

the early-rising parakeets racketing in the hibiscus bush outside the kitchenette window.

Andy had been relieved to quit Florida but it was not necessarily an unalloyed joy to be back among the Hills. For Andy had had time to think, driving a thousand miles of eventless interstate highway back to Towne. He didn't know how scholars of the past had been able to come up with their ideas, their insights, their inspirations, without the benefit of the transporting, freeing, revelatory rhythms of a solo cross-country drive with the radio tuned loud and unheard. However, on this latest trip north, the unrolling ribbon of excellent road surface had unaccountably failed to carry his thoughts along. As he passed from state to state, from shabby old Georgia to swamped South Carolina on toward New Jersey traffic, he remained stuck. What, ultimately, was he to make of the Hills? His thesis was going absolutely nowhere. He decided he must best blame William who had sent him to them with every treacherous reassurance that these people would be the making of him. Why had he believed William? Why hadn't he asked more critical questions at that off-kilter Mexican lunch? Now Andy recalled, his several weak queries had been brushed aside as briskly as William might flick lint from his sleeve because, Andy realized in a flash of clarity, William had had something hidden up that sleeve from which he had successfully diverted Andy's attention by snapping his fingers and making Andy blink away from his own reasonable wish to see more clearly what was to come.

Colds, Andy wrote in his retrieved notebook. *Frequent white hankies, atavistic significance of?* Colds, he knew, were not caught from being cold but from viruses. Still, did the Hills, believing otherwise, contrive to catch peculiarly original, psychogenic, foul-weather-generated, winter-woebegotten colds? Could he ask them to sneeze onto sterile slide plates? Professor Janacek doted on hard datum.

The front door banged shut and Andy started. ("Ginger's home from that new lawyer she's trying," Lily said.) His notebook shot from his knee to the floor and a sheet of notepaper was ejected from its pages. He sprang to retrieve his half-written, biweekly letter to William before Lily could see what he had had to say, so far.

Dear Uncle William [it read], I've been back in Towne for two days, having left Florida on New Year's Day. I went to bed on the Eve itself, early and alone. What does that bode for the nineties?

I missed the great scandal over Christmas when Mrs. Tuckerman's lonely lover showed up and was summarily routed. I wish I'd been here although I have the feeling I would have watched events from behind raised fingers as at one of those movies reviewers refer to as being too intense for some young viewers. Mrs. Lowe was my informant on this episode. My first night back we sat up late together over an excellent Cabernet she said Alden wouldn't appreciate (and I did my best to!). He had just snored her loose from her slumbers and then the smell of the pine pitch indelibly lodged in his hair prevented her return to the arms of Morpheus. The "interview" turned confidential under the influence of the hour and the wine and Becky expressed more sympathy and understanding of her sister-in-law's unhappiness than I would have expected from such an estimable wife and mother.

IN THE MIDDLE OF February an airmail envelope as blue and unsubstantial as a swatch of foreign sky and addressed to Rebecca Lowe had arrived and been set down by an incurious Lily upon the piecrust table along with the rest of the day's post. There were the usual bills, some personal correspondence, and an assortment of catalogues and flyers and appeals, for the Hills were regarded as likely prospects or at least had declared an interest when filling in postcards and sending away for additional information on paddle-wheel steamer trips down the Amazon and John Deere tractors and Vita-Life Vitamin Therapy and how to Be All You Can Be in the Army. This last brochure had been sent to Glover and must have represented someone's idea of a joke, although as Alden was to point out when he happened upon and studied the Army's pitch, the military's handsomely photographed promise of foreign travel and access to shiny and expensive machinery and life-affirming ten-mile morning health sprints silhouetted against a golden sunrise might well be viewed as attractive by those who yearned after the Amazon, a tractor, the vigor of Youth.

"Nothing for you," Lily had answered Ginger (the Vita-Life price list was for Harvey) when Ginger called down from the top of the stairs to ask, and to let Lily know that an eye was being kept upon her— Ginger had once come upon her aunt stoking a fire with the crumpled pages of a brand new Tiffany catalogue, Lily having taken it upon herself to assume Ginger had no means to buy herself jewels and so no reason to look only to regret.

Becky, who had popped her head through the little-parlor door and quirked an inquiring eyebrow, gathered that Lily was informing her, Nothing for you. However, Lily's view of the little-parlor door was blocked by the overcrowded coatrack and she had not noticed Becky. Becky, trying not to feel too unfairly snapped at (for Lily had been firm with Ginger), returned to her task of correcting all the misprinted lyrics in the Women's Chorus Valentine Program Songbook—*I love you turly, You've lost that loving reeling, Sweet creams be yours, dear.* Well, Becky had sniffed pot smoke in the air at the printer's shop when she stopped by to pick up the order—somehow, she'd been put in charge of the Songbooks—although she hadn't selected the printer, who was Anna Webster's nephew and always got the job because no one had the heart to tell Anna what her nephew was famous for.

It was Little Becky who spotted the blue airmail envelope later that afternoon when she came home from school and, as was her habit, wandered through the ground-floor rooms. She rooted round the kitchen. She flicked the little-parlor TV on and off. She patted chair cushions. She picked up and examined magazines. She stared into the pictures on the walls. She always made certain that the details hadn't shifted or changed during the day while she was off at school, for nothing had seemed real to her since she'd been whisked away to Towne, to Aunt Lily's cold, old house, and been told, This is home now.

Little Becky gurgled down a Diet Pepsi. She scattered Oreo crumbs and she thought her sparse thoughts. She couldn't decide whether to pull the thread that dangled from the end of her pullover jersey sleeve because what if the entire cuff came free and swirled around her wrist like a cloth bracelet? This had happened to her before.

The square of sky-blue envelope caught her eye. How pretty—Little Becky reached for the letter and, amazingly, beheld her own name written across its front. The thin paper rustled beneath her fingertip as she

traced R . . . E . . . B . . . . Airmail, she noticed, which meant her letter
had come from away. Who did she know who was far away? Were the
New Kids touring the World? How faithless of her not to know but the
unfanned flame had been flickering of late. They had not written back,
unless they had written back now.

But who else might she know from—Little Becky peered at the post-
mark against which a snowflake, an icicle drip, a rain plop had splattered, blurring and slurring away the foreign-inked words, stupid,
no-good, disappearing foreign ink. Oh, don't let the whole mysterious
message dissolve and fade away like skywriting in the wind above a professional baseball game, Little Becky silently, hectoringly prayed.

She carried off the letter, ducking into the chilly and unfrequented
big parlor. She flung herself upon the hard and slippery sofa and automatically reached above her head and helped herself to a fused clump of
peppermint drops from the domed jar that sat upon the Sheraton sewing table. She carefully lifted and resettled the jar top, silently, silently,
because somebody was always listening and criticizing, although her
father said no, it wasn't that they listened, it was just that they were
always having to hear.

Little Becky crunched the candy pieces. An old metal filling twinged
and a droplet of minted drool trickled from the corner of her mouth
which she swiped away as she worried open the envelope. She attacked
the flap, scrabbled, tore, and extracted the single, closely written page.
She eagerly sought the closing.

I am, believe me, ever your devoted, William.

Oh, well, look, if Mr. Baskett meant to write to her mother, he should
have put Mrs. Alden Lowe on the envelope. That was the true etiquette
of the situation because a married lady was her husband's name even
when her husband was dead. Aunt Lily had said so when she was writing
her Christmas cards to all her widow friends and the custom was respectful, not creepy, Aunt Lily had said. Actually, Aunt Lily had only sternly
answered back, Respectful, when Little Becky yelped, Creepy. Aunt
Lily didn't use many ordinary words.

Nor, apparently, did Mr. Baskett. Little Becky could not easily read
his affectedly Cyrillic hand. Her lazy eyes wallowed across the spate of
curlicuing words.

Carissima Rebecca, the salutation murmured, but romance languages or any romantic language at all remained a cipher to Little Becky. She did not linger over Mr. Baskett's roundabout construction, "*. . . and so, if I am not to come for you, write and tell me no. But since it has always been impossible for you ever to tell me yes, except for one time, except for one time, I shall make this easy for you. I have always heard the secret assent in your silences. Say nothing and I shall come for you, at last.*"

The peppermints had melted into a craggy lunarscape shape which Little Becky's tongue explored, urgently seeking some commodious sheltering cavern there, as she began to realize that her mother would not be pleased at having her private letter ripped into and read, or, at any rate, sort of read. Little Becky considered a few more of the elaborately written words and it had occurred to her, then, that this was not exactly an appropriate (to use one of Aunt Lily's peculiar words) letter for her mother to receive, for a married lady wasn't supposed to be called, Little Becky peered, . . . *my most beloved paragon.* Surely that was very wrong for Mr. Baskett to to have written and for her mother to be told. Her father certainly would mind. No one was supposed to love a married lady.

The last of the sharp candy shards had dissolved, filling the cavities in Little Becky's head with icy, decisive air, the cool minted astringency causing her to think very clearly for once. She acted in a flash, shoving the letter and the envelope beneath the sofa cushion, jamming the pieces further, deeper into the crease of the sofa frame where they would never, ever be found.

THE PILGRIM FATHERS HAD initially contemplated advancing the Gospel of the Kingdom of Christ along Guiana's gentle, sunny shore but ultimately they had rejected that option, and for all the other reasons they professed for not voyaging there, Ginger read between the lines and determined they had feared the fortunate climate and nature's easy bounty would prove too pleasant and corrupting and distracting from their Higher Purposes. Ginger sat at her desk delving into *The Bradford History.* She had wanted to discover who had washed the dishes after the first Thanksgiving but William Bradford remained mute on that point.

He was, however, very good at describing the diseases and plagues that beset the colonists and the poor, susceptible Indeans, and it seemed that certain settlers had begun behaving badly right off the bat which she found reassuring. Lily was always implying that standards had been markedly higher once upon a time.

Ginger leaned on her elbows and gazed beyond her ice-flecked window with its rattling sash and cracked lower pane which would never be replaced because the glass was original glass—wavy and bubbled and green-tinted. Outside it had been and would be endlessly winter. Oh, she deplored the Pilgrims for having been so pigheadedly puritanical as she viewed a frozen earth with crusts of shattery ice tracing over all the ruts and sunken footprints. A sour lemon sun was pendent in the low, taupe sky. A ragged grackle shivered on a bare, buoyant branch and then, abruptly, launched itself as, below, the back door banged twice and bumped shut. Becky, with Alden's parka slung over her shoulders, dashed across the dooryard and snatched the solid bedsheets pegged to the clothesline. She hurried inside with the stiff and awkward shapes of the sheets flapping like wings beneath her arms. The grackle swooped back onto its branch and reperched with an aggrieved yet respectful glimmer in its flat, glossy eye, focused now upon the eruptive back door.

It has fallen in love with her, Ginger snorted to herself. She knew that look.

Ginger turned her head away from the window. She studied her reflection in the scarf- and bead-draped mirror that hung above her cluttered bureau top. She looked flattened, she decided, as if she'd been rolled over by events too oppressive for even the bravest heart to bear. She shuddered and she reached about in her wild hair with pale fingertips, piling, rearranging, reconstructing her crowning glory. She would be Carly Simon, she would be Charlotte Corday, she would be the Flavian Woman such as she had seen her in the Capitoline Museum. This last representation required careful crimping and most of her concentration, as she built up the crest of curls to an impressive height above her noble brow, but with the small portion of her mind that was uninvolved with her hair Ginger thought about the evening to come, taking her speculations about events to come in tiny sips like bitter coffee, or nibbling at them as at scorched macaroons, or paring away, cell by cell, as at the very old corn on her biggest toe.

Well.

Babe Palmer had called one day last week out of the sheer and deep royal blue and she had asked Ginger to come to dinner to meet her unmarried cousin Earl. Babe had been that bald about her plan. He was a single man, an unattached bachelor, that is, he was an only Earl. Ginger had meant to say No, of course. She had intended to say No, of course not, but astonishingly what she had uttered aloud was a Yes. Hearing her own familiar voice betray her, Ginger had stared down upon the receiver, as appalled as when she had dropped her large, loose-fitting topaz ring down a whirling garbage disposal, as irrevocably, as carelessly let slip as that Yes.

Nevertheless, Ginger truly believed there were no accidents. She prided herself on her strict intellectual honesty in holding on to that tenet even when to do so was personally inconvenient to herself. She supposed, now, she had said yes because in fact she wanted to go to Babe's dinner party. She wanted to experience the inside of Babe's house, which she was sure smelled of Glade air freshener in the least-selling scent. Ginger did not doubt that all of Babe's chairs stood with their backs to the walls.

She lowered her arms and waggled her needle-and-pin-stuck hands until the blood flowed back into them, plumping the veins. After all, the Flavian Woman would have had Greek slaves to dress her hair. Ginger thought she would have been happier, she would have fared far better had she been born into ancient Flavia, wherever that had been. Yes, she would have flourished in Flavia. She would have looked well in a tunic or chiton or whatever flowing garment they had worn. Her shoulders were still good, good shoulders lasted. Ginger resentfully imagined her own good shoulders had been lasting since Flavian times, whenever those had been.

She couldn't decide whether Babe had meant anything by the timing of this dinner party of hers, "We'll expect you on Friday, the sixteenth." February 16th, two days after Valentine's Day, when the candy hearts were being sold at a discount and the hothouse roses were turning brown in all the hot houses.

After a while, after again consulting her mirror, Ginger wondered whether she might not have piled her hair too high, because Earl might not be a particularly tall man. Babe, the compact Babe, could pass without stooping beneath the set of former schoolyard monkey bars perdurably cemented to the grounds of the Senior Village complex. Ginger had observed this one day while she was sitting stuck in Lily's car waiting for a NorCo Fuel oil truck to negotiate a narrow downtown corner. Babe, in her perpetual busy hurry, strode across the Seniors' open space on her stumpy marching legs, taking the shortcut through to the broken-iced round of pond behind the police station where the fat and foolish Canadian geese were wintering over. Babe toted a basket of breadcrusts which she denied to some darting sparrows. She struck out at one—the tiny bird staggered in the air. Ginger had noticed all this as the Norco Fuel oil truck backed down an eighteenth-century lane holding up twentieth-century traffic.

Small-town life. One came across everyone eventually. One observed them and one was observed in turn. Ginger was sure Babe had heard all about those several times Ginger and Goody had met since Christmas down at the YMCA where Goody ran his laps around the indoor track during the winter months, and where Ginger had taken to showing up for the Meditation Hour which convened in a darkened chamber with pallets on the floor and a poster of Rabindranath Tagore thumbtacked to the wall. An aerobics class thumped overhead and the stinging odor of chlorine drifted in from the swimming pool as the water was roiled by amateur divers. Lana Arnetti, the reed-thin and otherworldly instructress, advised her Meditators to learn to lean into stress instead of fighting against it, which worked for Ginger until the radio in the crafts class down in the basement began to broadcast that song, "You Are the Wind Beneath My Wings," the radio tuned up extra loud because this was everyone's favorite song of the moment. It was, however, a song Ginger had come particularly to despise and she hated it even more since she had identified it on a 3×5 card as the rallying ballad of all the passive-aggressive females who had discovered their very own anthem, one which they needn't sing for themselves but compelled their victims to sing to them as they simpered and bravely denied themselves fulfilling careers and necessary dental procedures and the uncollapsed portion of a favorite dessert. Sometimes, Ginger simply couldn't stand women even though she herself was one.

Then, as the song chafed along, Ginger did not meditate, sitting cross-legged on her padded pallet. Rather, she concentrated her separate thoughts darkly, because if anyone was expecting her to become the wind beneath their wings, they could jolly well look ahead to a fiery crash, no survivors. Nevertheless, she emerged from the dim chamber in a cooler and calmer state than the discharged aerobicizers who milled, sweating like sliced and salted raw eggplants. Ginger sailed serenely through them toward the Veri-Fine Fruit Juice machine where Goody was bound to be bumped into, post-jog. He would be searching his running shorts' several small pockets for the quarters he was sure he hadn't forgotten to bring. Ginger never pointed out to him that his quarters had jounced from his shallow pockets and fallen onto the running track and been snatched by the small boys, truant from Gym-Boree!, who routinely patrolled the track for lost change. Because then Babe would stitch Velcro tabs across Goody's pocket openings and so deprive Ginger of her opportunity to produce her own quarters, eventually, from the bottom of her capacious satchel. She fished for quarters (*so* disorganized, she helplessly explained) as Goody, a bit muzzy from dehydration, for his running seemed to make him ill rather than healthy, automatically accepted the pale silky scarf, the Passion-scented lace-edged hankie, her current paperback reading (*Women Who Love Too Much,* etc.), which Ginger handed over to him in a wifely, burdening manner.

Directly across from the drinks machine was an old leather sofa into which one could subside. Ginger sank onto a cushion. Today, she was wearing her dream togs, a powder-blue leotard, Fair Isle leg-warmers, an Incan poncho, a kind of romantically mystic Celtic–pre-Columbian look intended and achieved. Goody slotted three quarters, and three quarters more, into the Veri-Fine coin box and collected an Apple Juice for himself and a Cran-Apple for Ginger which, he remembered from week to week, was her tipple.

"Sit here next to me," Ginger commanded and Goody instantly obeyed, falling into the sofa's springless depths.

He drank deeply, at the mercy of his thirst. Ginger sprawled confiningly beside him, her foot positioned to hook his ankle, a hand poised to clutch his arm should he make a run for it—after all, he was a runner. She sipped sparingly and began to chat ongoingly as if Goody knew all about her daily concerns, the common thread of all that linked them easily taken up.

She confided that meditation lowered her blood pressure even as her search for a righteous divorce lawyer kept raising her numbers. She recalled the day he had driven her to Boston to interview yet another dud lawyer, but how kind Goody was to assist her in her quest. She spoke of her afternoon spent wrestling with her book's "Sexual Imagery in Housecleaning Products" chapter. A mop's significance was obvious to all, but what about a Handi-Wipe? Iconographically, what was that all about? Goody said he was afraid he could not say, as Ginger shushed him. Listen, she ordered. The crafts class radio, the wailing radio, was broadcasting "Tie a Yellow Ribbon 'Round the Old Oak Tree." She despised that song, Ginger said. You wouldn't catch her tying any stupid yellow ribbons around anything. She'd get a restraining order and nail a mammoth KEEP OUT, GO AWAY sign to a tree so there wouldn't be any question. The man in the song had been in prison, for God's sake. Oh, but who was she to condemn another woman? A woman could be very foolish about a man, she promised Goody.

Goody had made his move as Ginger gestured expansively, shaking her fist and motioning a kick with her foot. He heaved himself from the deep sofa's grip. Warm leather released reluctantly and lover-like along the backs of his bare legs.

"The time," he stated generally. He deposited his empty juice bottle into the clear-glass recycling bin and stepped into his buckle-up galoshes and pulled on his overcoat. Covered, except for a glimpse of red knees, he turned to catch Ginger's last remark.

"I'll be seeing you," she said. "Soon," she smiled.

"Oh yes, soon," Goody said honorably for he owed her seventy-five cents for his apple juice and several more seventy-five cents from the times before. "Soon," he stressed, conscious of the debt.

" 'Til then, then," Ginger added for the benefit of assorted overhearers in line at the Veri-Fine machine who were only too willing to believe they had witnessed one rendezvous and dared to hope they possessed secret knowledge that there was going to be yet another tryst. Still, as Ginger told herself tolerantly, those other women had evil minds and if Babe, duly reported to with a word picture painted in red and purple hues, chose to think the worst of her husband then that only reflected rather poorly upon their marriage, did it not? Besides, when she and Louis had started to have their problems, when the whispering had sizzled and hissed all around and about them, there had been good reason, had there not?

If Goody would not jump, he might have to be pushed.

Nevertheless, if Ginger had meant for Babe to worry, she had not intended that she act. But here they were, she'd goaded Babe into action, although hers seemed a very elementary response, a very direct and unsubtle tactic launched to steer Ginger away from Goody and on toward Earl. Unless Babe was being very clever, though how and in what manner her guile might manifest itself Ginger had yet to fathom. She examined the proposed dinner party from every angle and sharp refracting point which her own abilities as a deviser recommended to her. There had to be a jagged rock, unseen but now not to be unexpected, against which Babe meant for all of Ginger's hopes to be dashed.

HARVEY PARKED PENNY NICHOLLS in the big parlor to wait while he packed his overnight bag. He tracked Becky down in the kitchen, interrupting her at the ironing board to ask if Penny might be kept occupied by a cup of tea and perhaps some delicious treat which Becky could always be counted upon to produce so graciously and so spontaneously. Becky said yes, and tried not to smile at the transparency of Harvey's charm offensive, and Harvey, knowing he'd been found out, tried not to smile back.

As the kettle came to the boil, Becky set a pretty old decoupage tray with china cups and saucers, silver spoons from the spoon jar, and the Wedgwood sugar and creamer. There was a box of Mystic Mints in the freezer and Becky arranged a dozen on a pretty painted fruit plate, formerly one of a set and now the only one remaining. Poor thing, Becky thought, dwelling sadly upon the plate's aloneness rather than celebrating its survival.

Presently, Ginger wandered into the kitchen to rummage through the refrigerator, having decided after the spell in front of her mirror to give herself a last-minute yogurt and avocado facial before her evening out. Trying to be helpful, Becky told her they only had pineapple cottage cheese and broccoli, which Ginger didn't think would do the trick.

"My skin gets so murky looking at this time of year," she complained. "I need the sun. I'm one of those sun-deprived people. It's a syndrome, you know. I need brightness and radiance to surround me so that I too can shine as I'm meant to shine."

"Uh huh," Becky said. She was ironing some small linen napkins to place on Penny's tray because they were so much nicer than paper ones.

"Who's here?" Ginger asked as she noticed the properly set tray. Old chipped mugs and the milk carton would do for a mere family snack. She helped herself to a Mystic Mint. It had been her idea to freeze them; they were best that way.

"This is for Penny Nicholls. She and Harvey are driving down to Connecticut to his house to dismantle his chandelier because he doesn't want to sell it with the house, not that he's about to sell that house anytime soon in this economy Alden says, but Harvey's got some sort of fixation about his chandelier, although it's a magnificent piece. We saw one very like it at Winterthur, actually," Becky said. "Harvey's is finer, Alden and I thought."

"You say Penny Nicholls's here? I'll carry in the tray. I want a word with her, and I'll have a cup of tea too," Ginger said and she drifted from the kitchen without the tray which was so typical that Becky could only sigh and replenish the plate of Mystic Mints.

Left to amuse herself, Penny prowled round the chilly parlor. She was reminded of her own lost parlor as she shut her eyes and breathed in deeply of the well-managed mustiness that marked the air of long-lived-in dwellings. Indeed, she felt herself back in her own lost house when she opened her eyes to the gloomy and sinuous pattern of the paper on the wall, and the shaggy Boston fern and small tree of a jade plant resident on the windowsill, and the heavily hanging curtains from which one might raise flurrying cloudlets of dust and spores if one flicked against the fabric with a fingernail. There would be a set of the works of Francis Parkman taking up a shelf of the glass-front bookcase—yes, there it was, just as it should be. Penny loved her life at Senior Village, but sometimes she wished she could go home, if only for the weekend.

Lily's antiques were as unfashionable as Penny's own, at least Penny had been told they were unfashionable by the dealers who had invited themselves over to make grudging offers on her mahogany sideboard and filigreed dictionary stand and a drum table almost identical to the one in the big parlor's corner, although Lily's table was not marred by the moisture rings of too many glasses set down on the wood during the cocktail hours the Nichollses had always enjoyed. Not that Lily's table's better condition would count in her favor.

"What do you take me for?" Penny had asked, spurning all offers, and she had made arrangements to place everything that didn't fit into her new condo's reduced-size rooms into storage at a superior sort of climate-controlled warehouse place reassuringly visible to her whenever she drove past it on Rte. 128. She planned to point out the facility to Harvey if they went that way. Perhaps she'd invite him to stop and they could gain admittance to the warehouse and lounge on her Duncan Phyfe sofa, angled into a 12' × 18' cubicle, and pretend to watch the *Sid Caesar Show* on her old black-and-white Magnavox TV. Perhaps she'd find a forgotten bottle of sherry in the sideboard and they could set their drinks down on the faux tole-ware TV trays she'd won with Green Stamps back when Green Stamps had been earnestly collected and pasted into booklets.

But they probably wouldn't drive past her furniture. Harvey had boasted of knowing some speedy and secret passage to Hartford when he invited her to come along on his chandelier-dismantling expedition, saying he needed her expertise and good advice and they would be gone overnight. Penny could not imagine what his secret route might be. Not very logically, she wondered if he'd solved the space-time continuum when he worked for Aetna—he'd had a very big job there, she knew.

Still, life had not ceased to be interesting, Penny reflected, and she credited her own get-up-and-go for keeping it so. After all, she'd been campaigning vigorously on her own behalf as a veteran of the moving wars for months now to win this invitation to the splendid mansion in Connecticut. She had packed two boutique boxes of Kleenex for the individual wrapping of each chandelier prism which she would produce at the necessary moment, and also brown paper and a red Magic Marker because you really couldn't count on your old brain to remember what every misshapen package contained even as you told yourself you would. Harvey would say, Bless you, old girl, which would be very gratifying. Tape, she had brought tape as well.

Ginger invaded Penny's pleasant musings. She exclaimed at Penny and professed to be happy to see her, although Penny couldn't imagine why. Strictly speaking, Ginger had never been someone whom she had known all that well, but she was someone of whom she had heard rather a great deal. Indeed, Ginger had been very much mentioned over the years. Olive, at the end, lingering upstairs in Lily's quietest bedroom, had more or less predicted the failure of her difficult daughter's marriage, and if she'd been off by seventeen years or so, Olive would have said that Ginger was the stubbornest girl who had ever drawn breath. Olive would have said that Ginger had stayed married just to thwart her mother's doomy presagings. Still, Penny had always rather wondered whether Ginger hadn't had her reasons for being the way she, reportedly, was, for Olive had never been Penny's favorite person. Even as a girl, Olive had minded other people's business for them. Penny could well imagine Olive bristling and chewing the insides of her lips, and the tip of her nose alternately pinching and flaring at the prospect of Penny's overnight trip away with Harvey and so, for the time being, Penny decided she was on Ginger's side. And what an exotic-looking woman she'd grown up to be. What fascinating, elaborately arranged hair she had which sprouted from her head like some sort of complicated botanical root system illustration in an ancient herbal encyclopedia temporarily on display at the library opened to a special page.

By the time Becky backed through the big-parlor door carrying an overloaded tray, china cups clinking and the teapot dribbling down its spout as it would always do, Ginger and Penny were sitting side by side on the sofa and Penny was catching and patting Ginger's gesturing hands as Ginger expressed herself at length.

"And then when I told Louis I didn't think I loved him anymore, he said, well, just so long as I didn't love him any less that was all right with him," Ginger was saying. "What do you do with such a man?"

"He's an attorney, dear, isn't he?" Penny asked. "They often tend to retreat into semantics when they're emotionally moved. They're trained that way so they can plead for mass murderers without thinking too hard about what they're actually doing."

"Yes, but Louis is a tax attorney," Ginger said.

"Taxes you say? But taxes are very visceral. Taxes cut one to the quick. Death and taxes, for heaven's sake," Penny said. "Besides, what did you say to Louis? You said you said to him you didn't think you loved him anymore. Because if you said you didn't *think* you loved him, you were making allowances for second thoughts. You weren't really sure, were you? And even if you didn't say so at the time to Louis, you said so just now to me so at some point the possibility of having second thoughts has occurred to you," Penny concluded. She enjoyed fixing broken things. She enjoyed rubbing up against a nub.

"I don't know. I don't know what I said," Ginger replied. "Isn't that fascinating? My last confrontation with Louis really is rather a blank to me." She subsided into thought.

Becky let the teacups rattle on their saucers as she put down the tray and began to pour. She had set a cup for herself, and Harvey's capacious Souvenir of Capri mug and several more cups for anyone else who might show up to sip and chat. The clip of china on china tended to draw out the family as a shallow pool of beer left outside overnight in a jar top will attract slugs in the garden, although the point of that exercise is to drown the pests.

Penny said, How lovely, dear, to Becky, and Ginger murmured, Yes, lovely, how perfectly lovely. She wished Becky would go away because Becky had already heard the story of the final days of Ginger's marriage and Becky had a way of withholding comment which was very marked.

"Of course I buried my own late husband relatively early," Penny said, to which Becky and Ginger responded with more murmurs although Becky's were heartfelt while Ginger, for a second or two, not very sensibly wondered if by citing his relatively early burial, Penny had meant she had had Buster interred before he had entirely passed on.

"Yes, he was taken by surprise," Penny said. "I didn't have a chance to anticipate and work out how I was going to feel. I was numb, I was wild, I was—everything," she recalled.

"Death is definitely neater than divorce, emotionally speaking," Ginger agreed. "When they die, oh, you're terrifically grief-stricken but at least death isn't ambiguous and inconclusive and, oh, you know, like you left your oldest pair of slippers in some hotel room and even though they're not worth pursuing, you do wonder about them sometimes. Is the chambermaid wearing them and enjoying them? You know where they are when someone dies. You don't ask yourself, where are their slippered feet idling tonight?"

"Well, as I said, you do have to bury them," Penny said. "Although the gang at Senior Village is more and more opting for cremation now in their prearrangements, which strikes me as being too strong a response. I don't want to rise up as just a puff of smoke on Judgment Day. That would be very limiting, I should think, to come back as just a puff of smoke and a handful of gritty ash."

"Do you wish Louis were dead?" Becky challenged Ginger.

"I didn't say that. I'd be very sad. I suppose I'd be shattered . . ."

"It's never a very easy time," Penny remarked soothingly and she asked for another cup of delicious tea which Becky poured with a consciously steadied hand, explaining it wasn't any special sort of tea, really, just the IGA's own brand but which one might well think was Earl Grey if one didn't know.

Penny, who had believed she'd been served a special company brew and had wondered whether Harvey hadn't stayed Becky's hand as she reached for the everyday tea and revealed that this was going to be a momentous day for Penny and himself, was let down, but she didn't let on.

"Well," Ginger began again, brightly. "I'll be dining with some of your family this evening, Penny. Babe asked me, and Goody of course, and her cousin Earl will be there. Do you know about Earl?"

"Of course I know about Earl. They don't keep him hidden under a rock. He's my cousin Janet's boy. He'd be Babe's second cousin, or some degree of cousin removed-ness. They're not particularly close but they're of an age." Penny seemed to think that sufficiently explained Earl.

Ginger, however, sought more specific information. She needed to prepare. The evening ahead required a fine strategy of her own. Should she dress up or dress down for Earl, or immerse herself in golfing statistics to fabricate a common interest? Had he fallen serially in love with a long strand of women, all of whom, or none of whom, conformed to a pattern which she, Ginger, should contrive to emulate or to break? She meant to sparkle at this Earl tonight, if only for the pleasure of seeing her brilliance reflected in Goody's admiring eye as grey little Babe squinted at them all from her corner.

"Babe didn't mention, what does Earl do?" Ginger was forced to ask.

"What *is* Earl doing nowadays?" Penny wondered, in turn. "He was an air-traffic controller originally, but he got caught up in all that strike business. Well, he knew better. I told him so at the time that President Reagan meant what he said. Then Earl was very keen to go to Seminary. Remorse, I thought, and nothing came of that although he's still very involved in the Congregational Youth Fellowship—they're the Congregational branch of the family. Now he's trying his hand at a franchise he's bought into. He goes out to people's houses and assesses their security situation and then he installs an alarm system for them. He's notified when there's an intruder. I know he wears a beeper on him because it beeped last Thanksgiving when I was there with them and Babe nearly dropped her squash-and-peanut casserole hot out of the oven, and I wished she had dropped it, frankly, squash and peanuts don't work. I'm not sure the recipe didn't say pecans. Of course, Babe is wound too tight. But exactly what Earl thinks he can do once he's been beeped about a burglar, I'm not sure, other than memorize an intruder's features for the Ident-A-Kit technician. I suppose Earl is capable of that much, noticing misspelled tattoos or whether or not someone has a beard. Although if I were a burglar, I'd wear a false beard when I was working. Ask him tonight, ask Earl, what if it's a false beard? Are there methods of detecting false beards by how it's hooked over the ears? There's some conversation for you, Ginger, if the talk slows down. Ask him, do the hairs of a false beard melt and frazzle like rayon if you hold a match to them? But how do you get a burglar to let you hold a match to his face? Offer him a cigarette? Not that anyone smokes these days very much, but I sense the burglary class smokes if anyone does."

Becky smiled privately into her teacup but Ginger spotted the crinkles encasing her eyes and the plumping of her cheeks and the pinkening of her skin and a slight convulsion of her shoulders.

"He sounds extremely enterprising," Ginger said, bound to take Earl's side but all the while aware of how absurd one had to make oneself over the men in one's life, even over the men only potentially in one's life. But she quashed that thought at once; otherwise, one could hardly carry on and she was determined to carry on. What else could one do, but carry on?

"I don't know, Earl's always seemed more of a lost soul to me," Penny said. "And speaking of lost souls, where's Harvey? We should be on our way before dark. It'll be dark before you know it." She stood and ambled into the hall and yoo-hooed up the stairs, "Harvey Hill, you're keeping a lady waiting."

BETSY LEFT SCHOOL late that afternoon after staying behind for a scheduled hour of computer time. The machine responded to the gentle pressure of her finger taps, or so Mr. Prentice, watching over her shoulder, told her. Betsy very much doubted an insensible machine could be said to like her particularly and she hoped Mr. Prentice was not going to become a complete problem before she finished her extra-credit statistics project in which she was developing a program to tell Aunt Lily on which day of the week her birthday was going to fall up to the year 2100. Ginger had said that any idiot savant could figure out as much by counting on his fingers and nose. Ginger was peeved Betsy hadn't chosen her birthday but Betsy knew better than to inform her mother she was going to turn fifty on a Tuesday because her mother would find a way to blame Betsy not only for the Tuesday but for the fifty as well. Mr. Prentice had told Betsy that carrying her program as far as the year 2100 was overkill, or, possibly, underkill. Betsy hadn't laughed for she knew better than to encourage Mr. Prentice by laughing at his jokes. Besides, she had grown rather fond of her great-aunt and she hadn't wanted to set any very logical limit to Lily's reasonable life expectancy. Were she being reasonable, Betsy need only consult Uncle Alden's ten-year desk planner calendar. The whole idea, which was admittedly not much of an idea, had come of browsing through her Book of Common Prayer which listed three centuries of Easter Sunday dates. In 2011, Easter would fall as late as it possibly could, on April 24, when Betsy would be thirty-eight years old and she hoped in a position to afford a really nice spring outfit although she supposed there would be no point in deciding upon the outfit now because styles would be different then and perhaps she too would no longer be the same and so set upon buying everything in blue.

Besides, Betsy only wished to keep busy, too busy to receive other unwelcome thoughts which, nevertheless, clustered and pressed behind her eyes demanding admittance to the well-defended fastness that was her mind. But Betsy had continued to view a hundred versions of Mr. Oscarsson's accursed death in fluid and sliding images which got in somehow, because—Betsy shook her head and touched the Delete key—because, after all, she had invited them. So she had suffered visions of Mr. Oscarsson dead, suddenly in his sleep, suddenly by traffic accident, suddenly of a storm that surged off the plains raging only over him, tossing him, tearing him, perforating him with lightning strikes. Though now, it seemed, Mr. Oscarsson had up and married one of his office girls. A friend from Kansas had just sent Betsy a newspaper clipping annotated with the comforting comment, Too weird, huh?, and a sharp arrow indicating the photo of the bride (big hair, tiny face, glasses). Betsy was buoyed by this news. Married, she was quite certain, Mr. Oscarsson would be a much harder target to hit. The clinging body of his newly beloved would keep any demi-divine projectile from getting too clear a shot at Oscar. Betsy had not told her mother. Someone else could bravely, or brazenly, inform Ginger, and by the quality of Ginger's silence on the subject, Betsy would know when this occurred.

Well-wrapped in her great-grandmother's Persian lamb coat and a jersey felt turban from which she had removed a glittering jewel, Betsy stood above the broad and shallow steps that terraced down to the rank of late buses rumbling and fuming at curbside and spottily filling with students who had run to catch a bus which seemed about to depart without them. Betsy, who had noticed her idling bus was driverless, chose to stand in the open air, kept very warm within her Hill inheritance of sturdy and oversized outerwear.

She tilted her face toward a silvery disk set low in the sky. Was that the last of the sun or an early moon? She remained in place, entertaining a few not very original thoughts about how one could not be sure about much of anything on, or apparently, off this earth until, through the thick pelt and heavy satin lining of her sleeve she became aware of pressure upon her upper arm and of a voice, not from around Towne, speaking her name.

"Bes-ty. Bes-ty."

She shrugged away the touch as she turned toward the voice. The components of a face wavily assembled—Betsy's eyes were blurred from gazing into the sun, or moon. She saw a round, bristle-topped head, the creased arcs of eyes, ruddy mounds of grin-stretched cheeks, all balanced atop the inverted triangle of a Vandyke-style beard. The beard struck her as rather wispily recent and, mentally, she removed it. Of course.

"I am Stefan from last summer on the train trip eastward ho!," he announced fluently, as if he was used to inserting an explanation like a surname into the blank stares that so often greeted him. *I am Stefan who you must have known would be persistent when you met me on that long sad train ride across the American continent.*

"But what are you doing here?" Betsy could only ask.

Stefan had been to a denim store sometime during the past months. Perhaps he fancied he had assimilated but he stood out like a stoat in the Arctic snow. Betsy wished some great winged predator would swoop from the sky and carry him off. Wafers of faces were witnessing their encounter from every other school bus window.

"Are you not amazed?" Stefan demanded to know. "Because you neglected to give me your address, we neither none of us had writing pencils or papers at the last, that day, I remember. Still, your most pleasant mother revealed your final destination to me as I asked again, But where may I find you? Towne, she said, the town of Towne, population 1900, my later research revealed. Why, I told to myself, so small a place. I had only to travel there and ask of you around."

"You asked about me? Where? Who?" Betsy asked.

"Yes, I asked of you at the little everything store, at the coffee and doughnut and cheese-smelted sandwich counter. Try the school, they all said, and instructed me to here, this place. School," Stefan said.

The buses were rolling off. Betsy watched them go, helpless as she nodded along with the tale of Stefan's efforts to find her. Stefan, after all, was a guest in her country. She supposed she was obliged to be courteous although she could not forget how he had licked her hand last summer. She could still summon the flick of his snakey tongue across her palm and even now she sometimes found herself locked in the bathroom scrubbing the spot with an old wooden nailbrush. On this wintry day, however, Betsy was wearing the heavy, fur-lined leather gloves her father had sent her for Christmas which she had marked, as per his instructions, in the Saks catalogue as a pair she liked.

"But why aren't you in Rhode Island? Aren't you supposed to be in Rhode Island?" Betsy asked.

"Yes, but my host family handed me a spare car and a road map and three hundred dollars for my expensives and compelled me to seize the opportunity of my vacation week to seek more of America. Go, go, they said, and don't return to us until ten P.M. Sunday night after the *Masterpiece Theatre* presentation is over," Stefan said.

"That was very thoughtful of them," Betsy said.

Stefan aimed a look at her and saw she was sincere.

"But three hundred dollars and one week does not take me far in this vast land, I discovered, so I came up to Boston only and have immersed in its history and sights while staying with acquaintances on the floor at B.U. Today, I scheduled to drive to the north. At Marblehead Harbor, for example, I stood and surveyed the area of ocean surface where during the War of 1812 the mortally wounded Captain Lawrence, commander of the American frigate *Chesapeake,* spoke his final words, 'Don't give up the ship.' And as I need not to tell you, the ship was then boarded and taken by the British enemy, so the famous American phrase of defiance is an ironic motto which I did not appreciate before my vacation travels and extensive guidebook consultations."

"Oh my," said Betsy. "Yes. Of course. The *Chesapeake.*"

They were walking, skittering across a patch of ice. Stefan clasped the vicinity of Betsy's fur-clad elbow as they stepped over low snowbanks set like a series of hurdles across the nearly empty parking lot. They made their way toward Stefan's car, a boxy Gremlin with a plastic daisy wired to its antenna by a former au pair of Stefan's host family who had never been able to remember where she'd left the car when she went to the Mall.

"Where shall we go first?" Stefan asked, opening the passenger door.

Betsy slid inside and Stefan carefully tucked the folds of her long, generous coat around her legs. *These* were his continental manners. "For I am the tourist and you are my tour guide," he said.

"It will be dark soon," Betsy said, "and we won't be able to see. Besides, there's nothing to see."

"There is always something of interest to admire. A proud new Post Office, the house where the murder was," Stefan suggested.

"What murder?" asked Betsy, alarmed.

"There is always a murder house in small-town America," Stefan assured her.

Betsy supposed this was almost true but she wasn't about to admit as much to Stefan. Instead, she proposed, "We'll drive up to the top of Prospect Street where you can see nearly to the ocean. Harriet Beecher Stowe recommended the view once. She said, 'Oh, what a pleasant prospect.' There's an historical marker telling all about why Prospect Street is called Prospect Street."

"An historical marker!" Stefan marveled.

As they drove along, Betsy pointed out Senior Village, and the giant chestnut tree, impressive even without its leaves, presiding over the green which, no, was not green now, Betsy had to concede, but was a green nonetheless. Betsy showed Stefan the house that had burned and the old house with the high cupola where a strobe-lit witch's silhouette had flown round and round and round last Halloween night. Stefan peered and veered and Betsy refrained from further travelogue after Stefan drove over an edge of Anna Webster's lawn when Betsy said, "Mrs. Webster lives there, she's nice."

They did not linger on the crest of Prospect Street. The Scenic Overlook hadn't been plowed out which was just as well for the Overlook was a spot where couples went to be alone, Betsy suddenly recalled having heard and she wondered whether Stefan had any way of knowing that as well for he seemed to possess an extraordinarily informational guidebook.

"If it weren't getting dark and cloudy and if the trees hadn't grown so tall, then you could almost see the ocean. Of course, the land was all in fields when Harriet Beecher Stowe visited, Aunt Lily said," Betsy mentioned on the unviewable view's behalf.

"Who is Aunt Lily?" Stefan asked.

"Where I live now, with Aunt Lily," Betsy said.

"But Aunt Lily will wonder where we are. We must go to her at once. I look forward to meeting Aunt Lily and your charming mother again also," Stefan said.

Betsy had intended to ask, to insist if need be, that Stefan drop her off in the village where she could find a ride home with someone who lived out the River Road way. She would provide Stefan with clearly written instructions back to the highway, and remember to slide her glove back on quickly (which she would have had to remove to write the directions on a torn-off notebook page) before he could bow over her hand and secretly lick her palm good-bye as all the late-afternoon coffee drinkers, who would have been watching strange Stefan, bearded and denimed and declaiming in the long mirror behind the microwave and the frappe machine, marveled at witnessing such an Old World leave-taking. Betsy, for her part, would say good-bye and farewell firmly and finally. But all of that seemed too complicated even to envision and far too complicated to carry off and so Betsy told Stefan, "Oh, all right, we'll go home. Drive over the bridge and hang a right." The remainder of the journey was spent in tiresome discussion of the meaning and the origin and the application of the idiom she had just employed.

BECKY RETURNED TO the kitchen to brew a second pot of tea and she found Harvey in there, pressing a pair of pajamas at her ironing board, a burgundy tattersal-plaid cotton Brooks Brothers pair, new and evidently saved for an occasion and just unwrapped and unpinned and shaken out. He was making a fair job of the ironing so Becky didn't offer to take over. Besides, a certain delicacy prevented her as she experienced an unbidden vision of Harvey and Penny, dressed in their sensible nightclothes, heading off to bed happily hand in hand, puffing a bit as they ascended the grand staircase of Harvey's Connecticut house for they'd be in rather a hurry.

Harvey steamed a stiff crease down the front of his pajama legs. He was an exceptionally well-groomed old gentleman. He pulled more common pins from the pajamas' folds and stuck them into the ironing board's padded cover, thriftily saving them.

"Are you gals entertaining Penny?" Harvey asked. "I heard her yelping now. Don't tease her too hard and tire her out for me."

Harvey had put together a bag of groceries for his trip, packing a loaf of rye bread, a half carton of brown eggs, six Delicious apples, and a jar of instant coffee. He had placed a hammer and a pair of pliers for chandelier dismantling purposes on top of the egg carton. Becky reorganized the bag, putting the hammer and pliers on the bottom.

Camping out in a shuttered, echoing, empty house, would seem like an adventure, dare she think it would be a romantic one, with the right person beside you, of course. For a heartbeat, the right person remained an unidentifiably shadowy presence in her imaginings of such a scene. Becky shook off the thought.

"Will you be all right for food?" she asked Harvey, reverting to her usual practicality.

"The sideboard is full of Chinese menus," Harvey said, "and there's a cabinet full of liquor unless the caretaker's been tippling but he probably won't have gone for the Laphroiag, it's an acquired taste. Then again, he may have been keen to establish one. Anyway, there's cans in the pantry—soup."

"I'll give you a few tea bags too, Penny likes our brand, and take the rest of the Mystic Mints and a tub of your yogurt margarine, no one else likes it, just you, and this nice plum jam. I'm putting some dishwashing liquid in an old pickle jar and twenty aspirins tied in a clean hankie. You shouldn't need any more than twenty aspirins. You shouldn't take more in just two days," Becky told him.

"Thank you," Harvey said. Becky was an inveterate arranger and it was always his policy to let women be efficient on his behalf.

The back door bumped open and shut. Icy air fluttered the curtains and set the wall calendar asway and Phoebe came in, home from the hospital. She was wrapped in her plaid greatcoat and a fun fur bonnet with grosgrain ribbons that tied under her chin. She had slipped off her wet storm boots in the back hall and she padded along on her long stockinged feet until she recovered her fun fur slippers which she'd left to bake all day beneath the kitchen radiator. She scuffed into them and unbuttoned her coat.

"Any calls come for me?" she asked as she always asked. She checked the cork message board, reading the spate of messages, most executed in Little Becky's sprawling, excitable hand.

The QKC Super Jackpot is $300. The MLX secret word for today is Rockabilly. If WEBI calls *guess* Door Number 12. Glover—call Missy. Alden—Gee Weeden called in re a used truck—what's this about a used truck? Remember, Always answer "What's love got to do with it?" for the WPOP Ansa-Thon Prize! Pleeze! Glover—call Missy twice.

"Maybe Arthur will call later. He knows your hours," Becky pointed out. "Why don't you have a cup of tea? Penny Nicholls and Ginger are in the big parlor," she added. This may or may not have been stated as a caution, but Phoebe took it as such.

She was tired of fielding questions about Arthur and his progress in California. Hollywood, everyone enthused, but it wasn't Hollywood where Arthur was—it was some sort of bungalowed, strip-malled suburb, Arthur said, quite unenchanted. The view from his hotel room window was of a commercial laundry and a freeway off-ramp.

Phoebe had not heard from Arthur in four days, and so her news of him was the same old news. They, the producers, were going to perm Arthur's hair to even wilder curls and tangles, and they were going to redden the red. They want me to glow in the dark, Phoebe, Arthur had told her. Phoebe couldn't picture that. Would she be able to tell him in a crowd were they suddenly thrown into a crowd, together yet apart?

Arthur had only five lines to speak in the first episode of the sitcom but he had been given pages of physical comedy to perform including a full four-minute sequence when, for reasons integral to the plot, he was to be dangled upside down outside a skyscraper window as "Mavis" and "Brock," the series' battling lovers, argued back and forth about a vital and misdirected postcard which, in fact, had found its way into "R.T." 's back pocket and which was to be produced by him at the very last moment as he was being hauled in through a skyscraper window only to be snatched from his fingers by the wind and last seen soaring and cartwheeling above the rooftops of the "City." They, the producers, had not yet decided where the city was to be located. They were leaning toward the Pacific Northwest because the Pacific Northwest was the opposite of the popular but perhaps overdue to wane in popularity Northeast. But Chicago was testing well too, Arthur said, and they were going to have to make a decision soon so they, the producers, could shade subsequent episodes with local color.

All of this was rather a lot for Phoebe to have to explain to the too-frequent questions put to her when she only knew that she missed Arthur more than reason should allow. She wondered what he was doing, hour after hour. She tracked his days as each hour occurred for him three hours after they had occurred for her. She ate lunch while he was having breakfast. When she had survived another morning without him, he had yet to face his own early hours alone, although per-haps he did not feel as alone as she, as he greeted hours that Phoebe had already met.

"I gather the boy is kept busy," Harvey said. He was lining up his pajama sleeves to press a crisp crease along their length. He ironed like a man, slowly, fussily, singeing the tips of his fingers with jets of steam, and always expelling a surprised syllable when this happened.

"Yes, yes he is," Phoebe said. "Last time he called he told me that every night they make him go out to clubs and parties and such because he has to meet people and make himself known. He's creating an interest."

Harvey might have said something about that but he refrained.

"Of course Arthur has to make the rounds," Becky said. "He's embarking on a very difficult career. And I'm sure Arthur will call now that he knows you're home. He's probably tried to call and not gotten through because the phone has been so busy." She motioned toward the message board.

"I have call-waiting at the hospital," Phoebe said.

"We're not call-waiting people," Harvey said. "Call-hold-on-while-I-answer-my-other-call because they might be more important than you, I call it."

"Well, anyway," Phoebe said, lingering by the back stairs. "I've brought home the next to the newest Ruth Rendell from the library to read. I won't be wanting any supper, I don't think. I'll just nibble if I feel like anything later. I think I'm coming down with a bug. I think a bug must explain for how I feel." Her rabbity look was more pronounced that evening, with her pinkening nose and quivering lips that didn't quite cover her large, square teeth.

Caught in the headlights, Becky thought.

"I'll have to brain that boy," Harvey said before Phoebe had quite climbed the stairs.

Becky hushed him, touching a finger to her lips.

"Why shush at me?" Harvey asked. "I'm on that girl's side. The boy brought her here and then abandoned her. I'm surprised her people haven't hunted him down and horsewhipped him. I understand they're countryfolk. They should own a horsewhip or a shotgun or a hulk of a brother with ham fists who administers down-home justice."

"Surely Phoebe hasn't been abandoned," Becky protested.

"You're right. You have to marry them first before you can abandon them," Harvey said. "What we have here is more a case of having been mislaid."

WILLIAM BASKETT WORE a long loden coat and a cashmere scarf so soft and fine that its silky length could be drawn through any wedding ring volunteered for demonstration purposes. He wore a homburg hat whose stiff shape did not quite conform to the contours of his impressive skull. The hat sat precariously, although it looked secure enough to admiring observers, which contrariety William took as an admonitory echo of several larger concerns he bore, and he wore the hat as it was so he would never cease to be aware, whenever he ventured from his flat or office or local coffeehouse or concert hall or art cinema or intriguing new picture gallery, that life itself must be approached as a balancing act. For, otherwise, he would have returned to his haberdasher as often as need be to have the matter of the hat put right, the uniqueness of his cranium honored, and accommodated, just as the jut of his stomach and the slope of his shoulders had been so satisfactorily tailored to over the years.

It would have been a revelation to walk a mile in William's bespoke shoes although he would never have permitted that. Nor did anyone ever borrow his fountain pen lest they bend its 18K gold nib to their will. His Nib's nib, ran the mutter round the outer office where there was so often a scurry for a sharpened pencil or a working ballpoint pen, for William ran a very tight ship. He was sometimes observed in the evenings ruffling blamefully through the embassy wastebaskets gathering carelessly tossed paper for the recycling bins whose appearance had been his brainchild although no one had theretofore taken William for a particular friend of the earth.

William was someone whom it was, no doubt, very pleasant to be and a life's work to be with, or so Becky had come to believe over the years during his infrequent trips to New York. Then, bracing for his visit, she had turned the apartment over to a team of professional cleaners while she checked into Elizabeth Arden for the day, and phoned through her slim file of music circle friends to scare up tickets to something tremendous. She harried a caterer, she nagged Alden about the wines, she sent the children out to the movies and urged them not to hurry home. And Becky often thought of William when sorry domestic lapses occurred, when recipes collapsed, or her last pair of stockings laddered, or her camera shutter jammed, when the children bleated, when Alden was terminated, I'm so glad William isn't here to witness this, Becky would think. At least he has been spared this, whatever else she had been unable to spare him.

I'm so glad William isn't here, Becky was thinking at that very moment as she picked up the refilled teapot by its Duco Cement-repaired handle which elected that inning to detach from the pot proper.

William, rattling along in his discount rental car, recalled the way to Towne from the terrible journey twenty years earlier. The memory was seared into his soul, the occasion of his formative tragedy. He swerved off the highway and beetled on through the self-consciously quaint village which seemed to have receded even further into the eighteenth century as the twentieth rolled cynically on. They had buried the powerlines and enacted statutes to keep the signage all crooked and bygone and illegible. He raced toward the road that curved to the bank of the narrow river flowing blackly beneath a crust of ice. Houses, never there before, flashed past his eyes as just so many vulgar holiday pavilions erected across a sacred battleground. He saw a tall (taller, now) stand of hemlocks, and the rusted (near rusted through, now) vault of a mailbox. He slowed and approached. He knew the place. This was the place. He had homed here like Odysseus, that other long wanderer. William had traveled across the Northern Hemisphere in the dead of winter, been delayed fifteen hours in Frankfurt am Main, endured standby status from London immured in Coach, and missed the first available flight from New York after mishearing a squawking P.A. announcement pitched in no language known to man.

This had been such an unlikely setting for the great drama of his life, William reflected, as he slithered up the sloping, S-curve driveway in his nonperformance car. Twenty years earlier this had been a sun-splashed fastness of arbors and blossoms and fragrant and mockingly lonely walks. Indeed, he had been serenaded by a mockingbird whose rolling call had been identified by Miss Hill, the maiden aunt, whom he had encountered also wandering alone through a further field. Now, he fancied the grounds had been sunk in drear wintriness since his last departure, waiting, bleak and blasted, for him to return to reclaim his beloved and to right the great wrong that had occurred in the orchard beneath a canopy of apple-heavy boughs as a hundred evil and implicated guests watched and smiled and approved.

As he parked, William spied Andy's shabby car which he remembered from the ride to the airport last summer after his highly satisfactory interview with the young man, who had, after all, come through as hoped and desired these past months with a sequence of reports on Becky's state, her state of affairs, her state of mind, and dare one say, her state of grace. Andy was a fan of the excellent Mrs. Lowe and for that good opinion William was almost inclined to forgive his nephew's habit of interlarding his long letters abroad with copious copy about himself.

William struggled to break free of his rental car capsule, neglecting to unhitch his seat belt which he was unaccustomed to but had been sworn to use lest his—extortionary—rental car insurance be invalidated by noncompliance. Mother Hen America, William had spoken through gritted teeth and his resentment reared anew as, tethered to a Chevy, he lost his forward momentum. Still, it wouldn't hurt to hang fire, he told himself, before commencing the storming of this particular castle, to cling to the last illusionary minutes before the reality of action intruded. William stretched and breathed deeply of the local air, a cold and characterless draft. Bandit-eyed chickadees fidgeted above a feeder of seed, a snow shovel leaned against a tree trunk, a fieldstone pathway was domed with clear ice. The house was missing half its shutters and the clapboards needed paint. Sand had been flung at the granite front step. William knew he would remember every detail down to the day of his death—the chickadees' immaculate feathering, the bent haft of the shovel, the pockmarks in the ice, the blistered paint, the crunch of sand underfoot, the deep interior silences of the house which only darkened as he pressed the effectless bell with a pigskin thumb.

HALFWAY UP THE STAIRS, Lily had to turn around and pad back down again, all the while firmly holding on to her eyeglasses which had been the object of her search through the lower rooms. Her aim had been to find her glasses and to avoid the visitor who showed no sign of quitting the big parlor anytime soon, not that Lily held anything against Penny Nicholls to whom she was prepared to be most cordial were she to take Harvey off her hands. Nevertheless, Penny was not to be encouraged to think of Lily as a fellow sister and to feel free to move into the house with her excessively slip-covered Nicholls family furniture and begin to divvy up the pantry shelves, mentally or otherwise, so there would be room for labeled and expiration-dated jars of the Nicholls family recipe cauliflower florets and ridged coins of carrots preserved in dilly brine.

Luckily, Lily's spectacles had not been forgotten, after all, in the big parlor where Penny had been left to languish. Lily had only half-formulated an unlikely plan to extricate them from beneath Penny's thrusting nose by means of the telescoping fruit-picker arm fetched from the barn, aided, perhaps, by a diversionary setting-off of the kitchen oven timer. Not necessary. Lily had left her eyeglasses in the little parlor beneath her overturned library book, both summarily abandoned when she beat her retreat at the sounds of Harvey's and Penny's voices cheerfully arguing the relative merits of salting or sanding the front step. Harvey and Penny both supported salt. They argued at Lily in absentia, for Lily was the big sand apologist, Harvey said. Lily, he said, thought she was some kind of ecologist, and Harvey and Penny knew where they stood in relation to that breed—although if Lily fancied herself such an advocate for the Green Revolution, she had let herself be persuaded away from her principles easily enough last fall, seduced by the easy lure of forbidden leaf-burning to facilitate the clearing of her lawns.

"Seduced! Lily!" the lively Penny had blurted.

"Ha," barked Harvey.

Small wonder Lily had forgotten her eyeglasses.

And now someone was determinedly knocking upon the front door and apparently no one in the household but Lily, halfway up the stairs, was capable of answering a knock upon a door. Not that anyone ever comes to see me, Lily thought, not without satisfaction. The few people she cared to know would never take it upon themselves to "feel free." The kettle shrilled from the kitchen and Ginger was broadcasting one of her aggrieved speeches from the big parlor and Penny chimed in with her two cents worth. All this visiting, Lily thought, as she often thought these days.

The front door, slumped out of true on fatigued and ancient hinges, wouldn't budge. Lily, needing her two hands to twist the knob and jiggle the latch, slid her glasses into her cardigan pocket (impressing on her memory, *glasses* in *cardigan* pocket) and she hauled the door open. She frowned at the jamb. She fumbled in her cardigan pocket for her glasses and slipped them onto her nose. She peered at the mortise and reamed it with her fingertip as if it were a waxy ear canal and then she raised her eyes and regarded William as if he too struck her as being not quite all that he should be.

William, fist raised to pound the door, stepped back.

"Yes?" asked Lily repressively. Her lenses fogged over white and opaque in the variant airs.

William, unaccountably startled by this quite natural effect, could not find his voice.

A circling and searching influx of chilly draft drew Becky from the kitchen. She tutted, as she came, at someone's carelessness. Could no one else in the household but she shut a door? Someone ought to invent a domestic electric eye system for doors in houses full of impossible adolescents and distracted pre-divorcées, another excellent business opportunity just begging for the right entrepreneurial spirit to come along and exploit it. Why can't Alden? she thought.

William advanced as Becky approached. She was wearing lime-green wide-wale corduroy trousers, a red-and-white-heart-printed turtleneck jersey, an oversized Black Watch plaid flannel shirt, a pair of Alden's slipper socks, and a yellow gingham check apron with a ripe tomato appliqué stitched to its pocket. She'd just gone in for a short, practical haircut from Doris the night driver's niece, who had just started Beauty School. Becky's nose and forehead shone from the effort of mopping up after the mishap with the teapot and she had a Band-Aid plastered on her chin after a recent tumble on the ice. She had wrenched her neck in the fall and she held her head awry. Nevertheless, her smile of welcome was brilliant and William's answering smile was triumphant. Lily heard Becky's identifying cry of William.

William. Lily had been led to believe that he lived far away from Towne deep in Eastern Europe where he was so necessary and important that the grateful locals had named a tongue-and-rhubarb sandwich after him—unless that had just been one of Alden's sayings, she grasped now.

"Only a flying visit," William was saying. "I'm not really here. Events press, but I was in the vicinity." He had prepared this speech to deliver at once before a witness to establish that none of this had been devised.

"What a surprise," Becky exclaimed. "Oh Lily, I'm so surprised. Imagine, William here. Andy will be surprised. Well, I confess myself very surprised, William."

William felt it was perhaps unsubtle of Becky to feign surprise by continuing to insist how surprised she was; however, their audience of Lily, the spinster-ornithologist, probably needed to be beaten over the head. And Becky was wise to establish that William must have come to visit Andy. He had, William congratulated himself, played the Andy card perfectly.

"Yes, a word with Andy," William said. "Has he been behaving himself?"

"Yes," Lily spoke up. "Yes, he has."

"Splendid," said William, gazing at Becky.

"You'll stay for dinner?" Becky asked. "You can stay for dinner? Lily, won't it be lovely if William can stay for dinner?"

"For dinner," Lily said.

"Yes, I shall look forward to dining with you this evening," William said. "Just let me settle myself. I noticed something called the By-Way Motor Hotel just beside the Interstate. A large neon-lit sign welcoming Big Rig Truckers had just been switched on, it caught my eye. I may be wise to arrange accommodations now, before the big riggers converge."

"Very wise," Lily said.

"Don't be silly, William," Becky told him. "You can't stay at that place. They just had a murder there."

"They only had a shooting," Lily said. "The man hasn't actually died."

"Not died, no," Becky said. "But he's still in the hospital. Phoebe said Dr. Dunlop said he hasn't seen a stomach wound like that since Vietnam."

"At any rate, the man brought his troubles on himself. He and some married woman from Swampscott were having an inappropriate meeting." Lily's voice dropped to a whisper. She would say no more in front of the fastidious Mr. Baskett.

"Well, a love nest is the last place for William to be found," Becky declared.

"Pray don't let me be any trouble to you," William said, smarting a bit at Becky's assertion. But what did it matter where he perched for the trice he intended to be in town, for he and Becky would so soon be going away. He required only a convenient springboard, a hot bath, a stiff drink, and time alone with Becky to make plans.

"William really can't stay there," Becky appealed to Lily. "What will he think of us?"

And Lily supposed since Harvey's room would be empty for the night, there was nothing to do but place William in there. Lily brightened at the thought of Harvey's resentment of a stranger's head cradled upon his personal eiderdown pillows and of a stranger's alien wardrobe suspended from his jealously guarded wooden coat hangers, and she looked forward almost with enjoyment to the prospect of Harvey's rout of a too tarrisome William, should William tarry. With a slight nod and a brief glance up the stairway, Lily indicated to Becky that she might invite William to stay with them.

William accepted at once. A well-packed and theretofore undeclared grip was carried in from the front step, and Lily received William's top-coat after he had removed it with some difficulty. He was a bulky man wearing a heavy suit and his arms moved like the unarticulated limbs of a presentation doll. There were no spindles free, so Lily buttoned the coat in place around the mass of everyone else's outerwear already adhering to the coatrack, and she swung his scarf around the collar and balanced his beautiful hat upon the coatrack's finial, all in a quite inno-cent attempt to keep William's accoutrements of such obvious quality from slithering and sliding to the floor as had been known to happen with the lesser garments of, dare she say, lesser guests, for this William seemed such a finger-snapping rajah. There was, she intuited, a side to him she would rather not be shown, although her plumped and jaunty William-totem was held by successive and startled passers-by to be revelation enough of his true nature.

HARVEY AND PENNY took off in a happy commotion of false starts. They effected a quick return to search for Harvey's cholesterol-lowering prescription among the clutter of bottles and cruets on the lazy Susan and they received a peppering of last-minute advice which had belatedly occurred to Lily after they had taken off the first time. She regarded their reappearance as an opportunity.

"Mind you don't go falling off any stepladders when you're bother-ing your chandelier," Lily warned Harvey. She didn't care to have Har-vey carried back to Towne on a stretcher to live out his life motionless except for his tongue in her best front bedroom.

She followed Harvey and Penny out to the car.

"Run back inside," Penny said. "You're shivering in just your sweater."

"Don't stand on the top step of the stepladder." Lily ignored Penny, expanding on her theme.

"Why'd they put a step there, then?" asked Harvey provocatively. He slammed the trunk shut and had to open it again because the shoulder strap of Penny's overnight bag was dragging outside over the bumper.

"You ought to hire a lad," advised Lily, "to climb ladders."

"A likely lad," trilled Penny from the broad front seat of Harvey's mid-luxury car. She shed her storm coat and unzipped her storm boots and slipped a Sinatra cassette into the dashboard stereo player. She placed an opened but unsampled Whitman's Sampler on the console and she reached over and competently adjusted the lumbar support on the driver's seat side.

Lily saw that Harvey had placed himself in highly capable hands. Penny would know what to do in the event of a ladder accident or electrical mishap or unlucky tread upon the shower soap to minimize the damage to Harvey's creaky old frame. She would stabilize his back upon a plank and dial 911.

"I just rated a smile from Lily," marveled Penny to Harvey as they again drove off, gliding around the driveway bend, and taking the big bump slowly.

"Don't bet on it," Harvey said. "I suspect she just had gas."

AS HE AND BETSY ROUNDED the driveway curve and the house rose before them, Stefan began to look forward to his tour. It had been his experience that Americans longed to lead visitors round their dwelling places to display their treasures, to recount remodeling dramas, and to bid them to guess what the yearly heating bill amounted to. Stefan always hazarded, Twenty thousand dollars?, which he had learned was a jaw-dropping estimate. Twenty thousand dollars! Well no, not quite.

Betsy had spotted at once the strange car parked beside Andy's Bug. An Avis rental sticker blinked in and out of focus as Stefan's headlights swooped.

"Stop," she commanded Stefan and she leaped from the car and bolted up the walk and disappeared into the house.

"Dad?" she called up the front stairs, into the big parlor, down the hallway. "Daddy?"

"No, dear," Becky's voice answered from the big parlor. "It's our friend Mr. Baskett who's here. Come say hello."

Stefan had trailed after Betsy, collecting her bookbag, her turban, her scarf, which she had dropped as she ran. He meant to display them if anyone challenged him at the front door, but Betsy herself met him there and weakly let him pass. She steered him past the big parlor from which voices carried and she deposited him in the little parlor.

"I'll make you a sandwich for the road," she said. "That is, a sandwich for you to eat in your car on your way back to Boston," she clarified. "Not a sandwich to feed to the road or anything," she said, to cut off Stefan's next question.

"Yes, make it one for my baby and one more for the road," Stefan said. "Hiccup," he embellished. "American drinking songs are so different from the robust drinking songs of my country. Yours are so regretting. I wrote a term paper on the subject."

"Is bologna okay? A bologna sandwich?" Betsy asked. "With German mustard?"

"What terrible reception," Stefan remarked, as he lowered himself into Harvey's lounge chair and clicked on the television with the remote. "Which is CNN? I am a junkie for up-to-the-minute information. The world is unraveling and I must keep abreast. Besides, I am Dutch not German mustard, remember, and I have decided I shall dine you out tonight after coming all this way. No, no, it is my pleasure, my insistence. But first, may I see the house tour? As soon as this episode of *Lost in Space* is over. It is new to me, this episode, this new peril the Robinsons find themselves in on a distant, unknown planet."

"No, we can't do that," Betsy said.

"No we can't do what?" asked Stefan.

"A house tour isn't possible. This is a home, not some attraction."

"After our delicious dinner, we'll see," said Stefan. "And I must pay my regards to your lovely mother."

"No. My mother is going out for the evening. She mustn't be disturbed while she's getting ready."

"Then I must impress myself upon your aunt, just after this exciting episode is concluded."

"Aunt Lily really doesn't meet people."

"Oh, is she an eremite then?"

"I, I don't think so."

William had briefly called upon Andy in his room. He had ruffled 3 × 5 cards, deprecated Andy's computer software, inquired in the most general way after the progress of his thesis, and had been quite unmoved by Andy's confession, not easily pled, that his work was not going well. William gave his best, which was not, perhaps, quite good enough, to Andy's mother who worshiped William and which William permitted. Andy listened helplessly through his door to William's retreating footfalls, and, suddenly needing fresher air and stronger diversions, he wandered downstairs. Instinct, he believed, drew him toward the little parlor and to Betsy.

"If your aunt is an eremite—" came the accented accusation.

"Please stop saying that," replied Betsy wearily. "Aunt Lily isn't—"

"You don't know what an eremite is. You think it is sexual perversity," said Stefan, delighted. "Americans always think three-syllable words they don't understand is sexual perversity."

"Have you seen my *Testermann on Civitas*?" Andy interrupted, entering.

"Your Testermann on civitas?" Stefan was enchanted.

"It's a book," Andy informed him quellingly. "About the evolution of the nation-state."

"Oh, Andy," Betsy said. "This is Stefan from the train last summer when Mummy and I came here last summer. He's tracked me down. And Stefan, this is Andy, who is our, who is a—" she explained in a rush and then stumbled.

"Researcher," supplied Andy. "I'm the researcher in residence."

"My Rhode Island host family employs a physical trainer. He arrives in a specially equipped van," Stefan said, "and requires three forty-five-minute all-aerobic workouts a week. He wears Spandex, even in the snow."

"Well, Miss Hill would never stand for a personal trainer," Andy said.

"She wouldn't hop, skip, or jump for a personal trainer," added Betsy.

Andy stared at her and then he laughed and Betsy, who had never been known before to giggle, giggled.

"It wasn't really funny," Betsy said.

"No, but it was funny for *you*," Andy pointed out.

"You know, I often think of things to say but I never get the chance, somehow," Betsy told him.

Andy nodded. He had charted the flow of family conversation, and the two most junior status females, i.e., Betsy and Little Becky, were next to the least verbal after Glover, although his silences were not situational, they were willed.

"Uh huh, uh huh, uh huh," said Stefan impatiently. "But we were just deciding what we were going to eat and where we are going to eat it. Betsy and I are going out together," he notified Andy. "Tonight. Out. I and Betsy."

"What do you say if I come too? I'm at loose ends tonight," Andy said. "If that's all right with you, Betsy?"

"Please. Come. Please come," said Betsy.

Stefan, muttering his thoughts in his native tongue, levered himself out of Harvey's lounger and ungraciously inquired of Andy, "Can you snap on it, then. I am in starvation. Since breakfast I have had nothing, which was only dry Weetabix smuggled from the B.U. cafeteria in a pixie cup."

"Let's ask Phoebe too," Betsy suggested. "She's been stuck at home lately."

"Good idea, but let's shake a leg before Stefan here perishes," Andy said.

The mention of the shaking of a leg mollified Stefan, who did not want to ask but who began to hope there might be mixed dancing later.

BABE PALMER WAS neither a natural nor an easy hostess and she would not have proposed this evening or this guest list on the mere premise of promoting a pleasant time among friends. Oh, sometimes she would marshal her forces when hospitality was owed, when certain social debts had accrued, and then she could measure her reciprocal efforts against what must be repaid—a pie for a pie, her basic calculations ran.

All afternoon as she marched through her preparations, Babe had spoken aloud to the onions she was chopping, to the dust mop she was pushing, to the wax candles whose bases she was whittling away at until they fit into her old oak barley-twist holders.

If they're expecting hot skewered appetizers, they've come to the wrong house, if they're working up a thirst for fine French wine they can just stop at a bar on their way home, if Ginger Hill Lowe Whatever-She-Calls-Herself-Now expects me to hand over my husband without a murmur and gratify all those so-called friends of mine who called to warn me of tender moments observed at the Y . . .

Babe seized a pair of poultry shears and bustled outside to snip an upright branch of juniper from the foundation plantings. She jammed the branch into a water-filled tumbler and she clipped on a dozen or more orphan earrings, rhinestone, plastic cameos, fake pearls, which she had gathered from her jewelry box. She owned more single earrings than pairs. Her earlobes were near-vestigial tucks and she lost her earrings routinely. They slid from her little lobes and fell down her neckline and worked their ways to the floor and tramply feet unnoticed—or if not unnoticed and not unfelt, then not decently retrievable en intimate route.

Babe placed the tumbler on a raffia mat set upon the center of the dining room table between the candlesticks—her centerpiece. What an economical effect, what an economical effect from every angle of the dining room. She decided to submit her idea, her Evergreen Everlost Earring Table Topper, to the Ask Heloise column in care of the *Towne Crier,* where the feature appeared, and win the cash prize for the Hint of the Week, not to mention achieving the glory.

Anything in trousers, Ginger will go for, because that man I met at Christmas at Lily's was nothing to write home about or to leave home over. I do believe Ginger will chase any stick that's thrown across her path and I will throw Earl her way. Earl will do for Ginger and if Earl is smitten (he never meets women, he is primed to be smitten) he is big enough and insistent enough at least to hinder Ginger in her dead set at Goody. I shall throw Earl and Ginger at each other.

This, Babe reckoned, could be accomplished any number of ways, perhaps by a sharp tug of one end of the Welcome mat as the pair of them mounted her steep front steps.

. . .

ALDEN HAD ADMITTED Earl to the house. Earl offered a hand to Alden and then turned to the William totem arranged on the coatrack. Earl blinked and stepped back and back until he bumped the deacon's bench and he sat heavily at the further, more shadowed end, hunched inside his duffle coat.

"Ginger is. Ginger is," Alden told Earl, deciding not to say Ginger was, as yet, arraying herself and might still be a while. No doubt Ginger would resent Alden's letting slip that Ginger did not arise from her bed every morning already primed for the day, much as Athena had stepped full-blown in her womanly wisdom and beauty from the brow of Zeus. Ginger had once favorably mentioned this emergence of Athena, and Alden had received her remark as self-referential.

He offered the not entirely at ease Earl a drink. "What's your pleasure?" he asked.

"A beer?" Earl guessed, as one of Lily's students might always have asked, George Washington? in answer to every question on an ill-prepared-for American history quiz.

Alden had already suffered a previous awkward encounter with William whom he'd run into outside the bathroom door as William emerged pink-tinted and sweet-smelling after sluicing away the dust of his international travels. Alden, a striped towel slung over his shoulder, had yet to curry the wood chips from his hair and swipe the dirt from his face—he'd been out all day cutting up a wide old maple that had fallen across a driveway down on Lancelot Lane during a wind squall. The weather was strange that winter, everyone was saying. "Good for business," Alden heard himself maintaining.

Actually, all William had said to Alden was, "Hard luck, all that business last year." William was redolent of lavender soap and Hungary Water, and in a hurry to retreat to his room for he was dripping onto the shabby oblong of the upper-hall Bokhara carpet. William had been handed one of Lily's oldest and least absorbent towels—this was the day before laundry day and the better towels were swelling the hamper lid—and Alden hadn't been given the chance to reply to the challenge of William's condolences that he had not merely experienced hard luck,

Rather, he had been swept up and cast aside by a tidal wave of politics and policy and events roaring down Wall Street at one cataclysmic moment in time. The weather had been weird all over, Alden would have said, and very bad for business.

Every bathroom surface was glazed with condensation and there was no hot water left in the tank and William had left a drift of crescent-shaped shards of pared-off horn-hard yellowed toenails across the bathtub bottom. Alden had shuddered through a cold splash and, buttoning on a clean plaid flannel shirt, had thumped down the stairs to admit Ginger's newest potential suitor who, according to unwritten family law, Alden now had to keep an eye on lest he wander off-limits or run away—Alden wasn't sure what long-ago offense had occasioned the law. Perhaps the family had just come to believe that a courting male might suddenly turn feral, and so bore watching.

When Ginger at last materialized at the curve of the stairway, she looked very splendid indeed, as if she were about to depart for some televised arts and entertainment awards show with every expectation of carrying home a glittering orb.

"Why, you look beautiful," Alden told Ginger, because Earl could only stare. Alden watched Ginger decide whether to berate him for seeming surprised that she could easily become extremely beautiful when she felt like it, or whether to laugh delightedly and to tolerantly remark, "Oh, Alden."

She chose the latter course, and thus far on this rare evening out, Earl was not able to believe his luck.

BECKY AND WILLIAM WERE in the big parlor sipping gritty and sourish sherry from the very old balustroid wineglasses with air tears in the knops. William was so taken with his glass he hardly minded the sherry as he held the glass up to the lamplight and ran his finger round the rim and traced down the curve of the stem. Nor did he realize that it was just Cheez Whiz that Becky had spread across a small Limoges plateful of Saltines. He nibbled and speculated, "Some local cheesemaker's version of a vivid yellow Camembert?"

Becky, experiencing an odd and old surge of self-possession, did not explain about Cheez Whiz, and how this wasn't even real Cheez Whiz but Value Masters' lesser store-brand substance, Cheez Whip. Instead, she smiled and asked, "Isn't it an interesting attempt?"

William was such an innocent, really, despite, or perhaps because of all his years abroad. Oh, but she was fond of him. What beautiful socks he wore. They were soft and intricate Argyles.

"What time did Gee call about the truck?" Alden eventually joined them in the big parlor, wanting to know. After seeing Ginger so successfully off, he had checked the kitchen message board.

"That was around noon. Gee said he'd be home anytime after six and just to swing by if you're interested and he'll take you to his cousin who is in actual possession of the vehicle," Becky said. "But don't call him. There's some complicated reason why he's unreachable by phone after six. I think it upsets his hens and then they don't lay, and my question is, are his hens resident in Gee's house or is Gee resident in the hens' house? But how was your day, by the way? Mine has turned out delightfully. William, here, imagine." She reached for Alden's arm. "And I didn't know we were in the market for a truck, actually."

"Gee said all that to you?" Alden asked. He leaned over the back of her chair and he kissed the top of her head. She felt overheated to him through her chopped-off hair.

"I'm not sure how I elicited so much information from his mumblings. It was almost a telepathic process," Becky said. "Gee is part of our local color," she told William. "He's a Yankee bachelor man. Lily taught him in school. He brought mayonnaise sandwiches for lunch and he had to sit in the front row because he had a lazy eye. Well, Lily made sure he learned to read and write, all right, and Gee has certainly been a friend to Alden."

William glanced at Alden, and Alden, aware of the glance, became knowledgeable about trucks. He mentioned tonnage and haulage and was prepared to become specific about gears.

"Boys," Becky interrupted him to call out. She heard the hisses of their snapped-open pop-top cans of Pepsi and the clump of their boots as they returned from wherever they had loitered and lurked away the late winter afternoon.

"*The A-Team*'s on," Brooks, or Rollins, hollered back.

"Come here, please. I want you to say hello to someone," Becky answered.

"Hello," they bellowed back. "Hello. Hello."

"Alden," Becky said.

"Boys," Alden commanded sharply.

"But *The A-Team*'s on," Brooks bleated. "Except someone else's here watching sucky *Lost in Space*. We don't watch *Lost in Space*. It's sucky. Who is this guy? Hey, who are you, guy?"

"*The A-Team*'s on in six minutes," Rollins warned the interloper, and he and Brooks and Glover trailed into the big parlor and arranged themselves in a slouching row. They slugged from their cans of Pepsi, heads tilted back, pouring the drink down in a way they had developed to bypass the effort and delay of having to swallow. Evidently they were running a race which Glover won. He slammed his empty can down upon the picture frame table. Several ancestresses fell flat on their by now permanently affronted faces as Becky, Alden, and William stared, disconcerted yet impressed. Alden wasn't sure the boys couldn't drown themselves, pouring liquids down their gullets like that as had several prominent rock band drummers in the late sixties. He recalled having been saddened and appalled at the time.

"You remember Mr. Baskett," Becky said.

William conventionally remarked that the boys had grown since he'd last seen them. They seemed now to form a wall of boys, a wall of boys who had stood between Becky and him for far too long. But she could no longer hide behind them. Surely, she could no longer regard them as children who required her hands to wipe their snotty noses and peel the pith from their orange segments or whatever services maternal women hankered to provide their broods. But these boys, who were falling upon the plate of Camembert and biscuits (like locusts, he thought informedly; he had viewed UNESCO film of a recent plague on the African subcontinent), these boys were of the age where they ought to be striking out for the wilderness or going off to hunt and gather among the local virgin population for mates, or, most properly, striving archetypally and representationally to kill their father and assume his lost position in the tribe. William would like to see that. He'd like to foster that. But Becky needn't linger for the last act.

William thought of asking the boys what they intended to do with their lives, which was what one asked one's friends' children. They would answer lawyer or arbitrageur, or glassblower if they attended a very progressive school. But Alden, who sensed that William was about to ask something of the sort and who didn't want to give his boys any further opening to grieve their mother (for their usual answer to the usual question was that they aspired to be roadies for the Boss only their sucky parents wouldn't sign the papers) spoke up.

"There's a truck available, boys, an old Loadstar, not a pickup but a real truck, one of the big ones," Alden said.

"Cool, Dad," said Glover unexpectedly.

"Cool," echoed Brooks and Rollins.

"Do you think so?" Alden asked. "Are you really interested? Then come with me to have a look at it. I'd value your input."

A wary look overcast Glover's face until he realized his father was goofing on Mr. Baskett, bothery Mr. Baskett sitting there tipping and tilting his sherry glass so that it twinkled and sparked which seemed to enchant Mr. Baskett, the twinkling and the sparking. Mr. Baskett wouldn't know a Loadstar truck if one hit him, and picturing this event cheered Glover. All of his life, at least all of his life that he could remember since he had discovered his hands and feet and, spontaneously, Newton's Third Law, he had been told not to damage Mr. Baskett's paint and not to swing from his lintel posts, whatever they were. If Glover had known what they were he would have bounced off them like a tetherball. His parents seemed to have believed Mr. Baskett was a God, watching over every fleck of paint that fell, instead of a fat old guy who had lucked onto a real sweet rent-control deal and then struck a shady pact with his parents and it was people like them, like his parents and Mr. Baskett, thought Glover virtuously, who caused homelessness in America.

"But not tonight? You're not going to look at this truck contraption thing tonight? Because I'd hoped we'd all go out to dinner and thoroughly enjoy having William here with us," Becky said.

"Sure, Dad," Glover said. "I want to come with you."

"Us too," said Rollins. "We're going with Dad."

"With Dad," affirmed Brooks.

"All right, all the menfolk go with me. The Hill menfolk inspect a truck," Alden said, as if such an unlikely picture required an explanatory caption.

"But does this have to be tonight?" asked Becky.

"This is a sought-after truck," Alden said. "Gee's got me first crack. If I can get there first, I'm first."

"What does that mean? And have we discussed a truck?" asked Becky.

"We're discussing the truck right now," Alden pointed out.

"This is not really discussing. This is—springing," Becky said.

"I shall take the ladies out to dinner," William stepped in to offer. Privately, he blessed the rustic Gee and his nitwit arrangements.

"Do that," Alden said to William. "You can squire the ladies. Have yourselves a ball. The boys and I'll just grab a bite to eat on the road. At a truck stop," he added, inspired.

ANDY, BETSY, PHOEBE, and Stefan drove down to the Casa di Napoli in the overloaded Bug. They grabbed the last booth beside the beverage cooler, near the kitchen door. Betsy sat beside Andy and across the table from Phoebe and from Stefan who had been finessed out of Betsy range. They had sent him off bearing the bundle of their coats to hang from the curved hooks that resembled a row of crones' noses and chins lining the drafty outer doorway, a task he had performed in a conscientious manner, gratified he'd been handed the opportunity to touch and to trace the rich whorls and coils of Betsy's old fur coat's pelt.

But now Stefan leaned sulkily against the high wooden back of the booth and fidgeted with the macramé tassel of a plant hanger suspended too low over the table. Brown philodendron leaves dropped into the sugar bowl, rustling among the blue and pink packets of sugar substitutes. Phoebe brushed his hand and said, "Don't."

Arthur had been so funny here one night, she recalled. He had stood on a makeshift stage in the aglare light of a temporary spot in front of the panoramic fresco of the crumbling Parthenon in its prime, a depiction which seemed to suggest the temple had been built as a romantic ruin to attract the ancient and sentimental tourist trade. Arthur had ragged on fast food that night. He had maintained that the consumption of fast food led to a faster metabolism resulting in premature aging and the shriveling and shrinking away of flesh and form until you turned into one of the scrabbling cockroaches forever damned to haunt fast-food joints. That's who cockroaches were, former fast-food freaks, Arthur had said, as he stomped his heavy boot on the floor. The audience had flinched, then tittered, then warily regarded a cold french fry, a calzone, their date for the evening.

Phoebe was finding it hard to remain in serious mourning for her life with Arthur, not that every memory was a funny one, though there was a high foolishness quotient which colored every recollection. As she hid in her attic room night after night curled around her pillow and braced against every fresh wave of sorrow accompanying each succeeding thought of Arthur, she was not consoled by a further understanding that much of the foolishness had been her own.

Andy flirted gently with Calliope, the heavily pregnant waitress and daughter-in-law of the hardworking family who owned the Casa di Napoli. Calliope, whose aproned-over stomach jutted, professed herself surprised that Andy had shown up tonight with so many friends that he required a booth instead of his usual single swivel stool at the end of the counter. Andy asked, mock hopefully, if Calliope was jealous. Yes, she admitted, yes, of course.

"You'll want the ziti," Calliope told Andy. "And a salad. There's Sam Adams on tap tonight."

"I also. For me the same," Stefan swiftly bid.

"Betsy?" Andy asked.

"I'd like a slice of plain cheese pizza and a diet Coke, please."

"Have more than that," Calliope advised, smiling down at Andy. "She needs more than that. She's a thin one."

"Okay, two slices, please," Betsy said.

Calliope was already acting motherly and she was scarcely beyond girlhood herself, Betsy observed. Calliope must just recently have come from her stony, Old World village, having left behind her own hovering, black-shawled, ululating crone of a mother who ripped out the stitches of Calliope's trousseau linens and made Calliope sew them all over again until they were perfect. Betsy had been reading too many romance novels at the Snowdons' which was all they had on their bookshelves except for Mr. Snowdon's hundreds of Civil War books, and Betsy had come to appreciate that marriage and motherhood was the time-tested and traditional method for fleeing a place and a parent, according to all the expert authoresses who could never not see their ways clear to a thoroughly happy ending.

"This one," Stefan spoke up, jabbing Phoebe in her side, "is the real pole bean."

"Beanpole," Betsy and Andy corrected him.

"I mean, the word is beanpole," Betsy amended. "Not that Phoebe is one. I don't mean you are, Phoebe."

"That's all right," Phoebe said. "I've always been skinny. Arthur never minded. I'll have a salad, house dressing on the side, and garlic bread. Why not garlic bread? A big basket of very garlicky bread, please," she told Calliope.

Calliope swayed slightly. "All set then?" she asked faintly, and wandered off toward the kitchen, rubbing the small of her back.

"She ought to be lying down," Phoebe said. "I'll bet I'll be admitting her to the hospital before the week is out. I'll keep 12-A open for her. It's the best room. It's got a view of the woods and it's right across from the nursery so she'll get her baby first and keep it 'til last at feeding time."

"She and George are in the middle of buying a house," Andy said. "It's a race whether the baby will be here before they can pass papers and paint the smallest bedroom blue. Their game plan is very tight."

"Their game plan," Phoebe marveled, rather sadly. "Other people do have them, don't they?"

"My host American father played football for the Yankees," Stefan announced impressively.

LILY STOOD AT the kitchen sink washing teacups and listening to the wall phone ring. It had rung seven times and nobody else could be bothered to answer. Lily had almost decided to break down and buy an answering machine but she knew she would not be able to abide the sound of her own voice advising callers to leave their brief messages after the beep, although perhaps she could substitute the word *tone* for beep, would she mind less the sound of her own voice advising callers to wait for the tone? The wall phone emitted an eighth trill, a ninth. Whoever they were, they were determined to have their say which did not endear them to Lily.

"Hello," she said.

"Who?" she asked.

She listened. She licked her thumb and massaged a smudge from the refrigerator door.

"Very well," she said. "You want me to know there has been a strange man in a strange car sighted on the block. Although I don't live on a block. I live on a road. Besides, I'm not a member of your Neighborhood Watch, you said?"

She listened. She gazed at the ceiling and wondered how it too had become so smudged. Cook smoke? She would have to fetch a ladder when no one was about to order her off ladders and give all the paint a good scrub with lemon ammonia and soda water shaken in a jar.

"Very well," she said. "If I see the car which I shan't since I can't see the road from my house I'm to—what? Watch the car, is that your mandate? No? I'm to call you? But I don't call people after dark in the evening. It alarms them needlessly."

"Anything important?" Becky asked, gliding into the kitchen as Lily rang off. Becky held a locket to her throat, the ends of a gold chain draped over her black silk shoulders. She turned and bent her knees—she was wearing her highest heels tonight—as Lily tried to latch the clasp. She fumbled. This was one of her bad hand days.

"That was a Neighborhood Watch captain, I believe she characterized herself. She lives in the Bermudian pink house on Galahad Avenue behind all that zebra grass. I must remember, zebra grass, so I never let anyone give me some at a plant swap, I suspect it starts small. We got into the Bermudian pink and the zebra grass to identify herself further, because I'd never heard of her or her organization."

"I'm afraid I joined the Watch one afternoon. Some woman came to the door with her little pamphlet and it's difficult to say no to looking out for one's neighbor when a specimen neighbor is standing right there in front of you with supporting literature on offer," Becky explained.

Lily thought then of Miss Maude Fido, an old-timer of some re-nown who had lived alone over on the Mill End Road. Maude had let the house across the field from her burn to the ground even though she had spied the first devil licks of flame spiking up through the eaves. She had had to up herself and all her bits and pieces and resettle, bent over her bits of sewing, in her back room so she would not be obliged to know further. She had not, Maude plainly owned to the out-of-town insurance adjustor, wished to interfere. Even the Smithsons, scratching a borrowed rake through the warm grey ashes of their home and re-covering two fused christening mugs and a dutch oven roaster pan, had acknowledged that they had always known Miss Fido to make a reli-gion of keeping herself to herself. Maude had been cracked, to be sure, but not perhaps unimaginably cracked for those days, whereas these days all notions of discretion and reserve had lurched to the opposite extreme. Lily bristled at the earful of information just relayed to her over the telephone and evidently required of her to act upon. But Andy might be able to make sense of the sea change in the response reflexes of one's too-noticing, or not-noticing-enough neighbors, Lily thought.

"Never mind about the locket," Becky said. "Here's William. Wil-liam, can you try?" She turned and held the two ends of the clasp behind her head.

"Of course."

William stepped behind her. He lifted a few short strands of hair and caressed her hands as he took up the ends of the chain. He leaned and breathed deeply of her nape, inhaling and holding on to his precious breaths to savor the pure scent of her neck, a clear scent, he determined, and sharpish, and sunny, which made him dream, just there on his feet, of his Becky dressed in her summer cottons and at rest in his arms at his fond and stern bidding after exerting herself in some lovingly unneces-sary activity on his behalf. He did not know the scent he cherished was that of an enzymatic spot-removal product with which Becky had pre-emptively scrubbed a tea-tray napkin smudged by Ginger's dark shade of lipstick, and which substance had residually coated her fingers (for not washing easily away was the substance's great quality) as Becky reached up and absently rubbed her wrenched neck muscles. But had he

known, William might, at some very low moment to come, have struck
out and endeavored to buy a bottle of the stuff.

"There," said William as the clasp finally clicked and the slight
weight of her locket slid across her silken dress front. "Linked at last,"
he murmured.

Becky edged away from him and busied herself selectively transfer-
ring contents of her everyday satchel bag into her small beaded evening
clutch which she would carry tonight as an emblem of occasion. Little
Becky, who had just trampled down the back stairs, draped herself over
a chairback to demonstrate how terribly terribly taxed she was by all this
going-out activity.

Just now, Little Becky hadn't been able to close the back zipper of her
only surviving best dinner dress, a blue wool princess line with long
white cuffed sleeves and a white piqué Pilgrim collar and no pockets.
Awful.

"We'll sew you in," her mother had said ruthlessly, when Little
Becky, spinning and spinning in her bedroom, pulling at the prevented
zipper, had wailed for aid. Her mother had charged into her room wearing her black lace slip, her breasts and her stomach rounded plumply
against the thin material.

"You'll just have to wear your old school blazer over the stitches. It
still fits, doesn't it?"

Yes, it had been bought to see her through.

"But what if there's an emergency and I'm stuck in my dress and I
can't get out?" Little Becky thought to ask as her mother plied an impatient needle and thread.

"Just what sort of emergency do you foresee that you'll have to hurry
out of your dress?" Becky asked her back, sounding amused and not at
all like her usual concerned and worried self who was supposed to be
engaged by discussions of possible problematic ifs.

And now her mother was stuffing a compact and a lipstick and keys
into that beady shiny way-too-small little bag and there wouldn't be
room for Little Becky's book, a dog-eared paperback copy of *Cujo*, for
this outing promised to be so wall-kickingly boring Little Becky had
planned ahead. She jammed the book into her blazer pocket and she
heard stitches tearing, which stitches she didn't know but figured she'd

find out and it wouldn't be good. She ducked into the back hall and privately lifted up her dress skirt and jammed her paperback book under the too tight waistband of her half slip. The book seemed secure enough there. She jumped up and down experimentally and the book didn't budge but a jar of the last mustard picalilli her great-grandmother ever made hopped from its place of honor on the home-canning shelf and landed softly on the pile of used newspapers, so that was all right.

"Is there a Neighborhood Watch alert, Lily?" Becky asked. "Why don't you come with us. You'll be all on your own otherwise if there's a prowler or someone about."

"It's just some overreaction to a strange car. Cars have a right to be on a road," Lily said open-mindedly. "Even if the driver is black."

"Oh dear, was it because of the driver that they're watching? Perhaps you misheard, perhaps the car is black," Becky said.

"Both. Both are black which I understand only enhanced their concern," Lily said.

"Well, we'll quietly resign from the Watch tomorrow," Becky said.

William had donned his loden coat, retrieved from its odd presentation on the coatrack (*not* to think about, he told himself). He had drawn on his pigskin gloves and knotted his scarf and he was tapping the brim of his lovely hat so that Becky would take the hint, but she dithered. She opened the refrigerator door.

"Here's the rest of the rice pilaf and there's leftover fried chicken in a bowl for your supper, Lily. You can microwave them, hit power eight, three minutes, then see. Oh, who put the milk carton back in empty? It's so annoying, I never know when we're out. Has everyone made a note of the missing child before I toss it?" She held up the carton. "Erika Martinez, age five, missing from Monterey, California since 1985. Those poor people."

What a wonderful woman, thought William. She cares for everyone and he wanted her to care only for him. This was exquisitely, endlessly, his sorrow. He was a starving man banished from the banquet, a traveler expiring of thirst and denied the way to the oasis. He wondered how long he would have to live on the sweetness of the scent of the nape of Becky's neck and he prayed he wouldn't have to find out. Then, as he lingered in Miss Hill's overheated and overbright kitchen, he realized he was being given a rare glimpse of a laboratory for life. He saw brown eggs in a bowl. He smelled sour yeast. A stockpot burbled on the stove top. There was fruit in a bowl. Here, where Becky presided and prevailed, nourishment at last seemed achievable. He resolved to speak before the night was over, and henceforth she would preside and prevail solely for him.

"But my good coat won't fit over my blazer and dress and everything," Little Becky complained. "And it's cold out and I'll freeze to death. I shouldn't have to freeze to death. I'll just stay home with Aunt Lily."

"There's a muskrat coat upstairs in my closet you can have," Lily unexpectedly offered. Any further delay of the departure of the dining-out party would overlap the peremptory returns of earlier leave-takers. "I'm sure the coat will fit you."

"Muskrat? Fur? Really? For me? To have have? For forever and forever to keep?" Little Becky asked to make sure for certain. Her button eyes gleamed.

"Yes," Lily said. "Yes, yes."

"Let's think about this," Becky said as Little Becky pounded up the back stairs.

"But how very mature you look," William had told Little Becky as she bounded back into the kitchen enveloped by the coat, triumphantly twirling and hugging herself with her sleeves. "Why, you look entirely grown up," William had said. "You look like a young lady ready to take on the world all on her own."

IF SHE WERE WORTH her salt she'd fetch the stepladder from the barn and scrub that kitchen ceiling, Lily told herself, but just the thought of venturing out into the bitter night air and disentangling the six-foot ladder from the clutches of leaf rakes and paint tarps and cracked flower-pots containing powder-dry dirt and dead geranium stalks wearied her. Instead, she brewed tea in the pot she liked less—the pot she liked more required mending again. She spread the last of the Cheez Whip on saltines and she quartered an unpeeled apple for nutritional balance and she carried a tray into the little parlor. She turned off the television left prattling witlessly on to itself and she sat in Harvey's marvelous (although she'd never admit as much to him) chair, her tray balanced on her lap, her feet and calves levered up to a revelatory level of comfort and repose. She stirred her tea rather noisily because she was alone. Silent stirring was the rule, of course, when others were about. One dipped one's spoon and limply swished, never satisfactorily dissolving the sugar which settled as sediment at the bottom of the cup. Only when one was alone could one stir away to one's complete satisfaction, when the sound of spoon bumping against china offended no one's sensibilities but one's own, and then the click, click had sounded like the ring of freedom to Lily's ears. Tea sipped in solitude not only tasted sweeter, in fact it was, she told herself, taking an appreciative sip as she ruffled through pieces of the morning paper she had not yet had a chance to look at.

Harvey, whose paper this was, had drawn devil horns and serpent fangs on President Gorbachev's face, just as he had formerly drawn devil horns and serpent fangs and ragged scars and elf's ears and crossed eyes on the faces of Cordell Hull and William O. Douglas and Eleanor Roosevelt when he came upon their pictures in the newspapers of the past. Some habits never changed. Poor Naomi had once confided how embarrassed she was to donate twine-tied bundles of the *Hartford Courant* to the Boy Scouts' paper drives with photos of Abe Ribicoff and Lowell Weicker and Judge Sirica recast as pirates and dunces. But, Lily thought, Penny Nicholls wouldn't care what the Boy Scouts thought. Penny would keep Harvey supplied with sharpened crayons and tape his best efforts to the refrigerator door.

Penny Nicholls certainly knew what men wanted, Lily decided, and Lily wondered, now, what her sister Olive would have made of Penny going off with Harvey to spend the night alone with him in his big empty house. No better than she should be, Olive would have said, which would have been saying a lot, the way Olive expressed herself. She had searingly whispered when she discussed improprieties, and improprieties had seemed to obsess, or perhaps, sustain her at the end. She had slowly turned her head one way and the other, prying the bedroom shadows as if some listening stranger had filtered in through the half inch of open window. Olive was momentarily expecting Death

himself and she wished to appear as a worthy old soul to him. Of course
she was bucking for heaven. Lily had had to bend down to hear, nearly
laying her own cheek upon the hot and flattened pillow to catch Olive's
condemnatory remarks. Lily had been breathed upon with shallow
medicine-tainted huffs. Olive had had nothing good to say about the
mysterious things men and women got up to together. And yet, Lily
thought, and yet—

How rare it was to sit in such solitude and think her own thoughts.
Lily drank her tea and crunched crackers ignoring the crumbs that settled on her lap. She set her cup down upon the dropleaf table at her
elbow without a saucer underneath it and it occurred to her that her
natural state must be one of slothfulness. Then again, if being careless
of cracker crumbs on the night before vacuuming day and forgetting the
saucer was her idea of kicking over the traces, she must be a remarkably
undissolute old person and at the moment she was feeling an uncommonly unsophisticated one as well.

Carryings-on had been another of Olive's muffled and sibilant
accusations, although Lily had always unaccountably thought of carou-
sels when Olive made the charge. Carryings-on on a carousel—Lily's
mind's eye, averting itself from Olive's dolors, had supplied the unlikely
picture where one couldn't carry on with very much before toppling off
the prancing, gold-plumed, silver-white horse. It was fortunate Olive
had never been any sort of a mind reader. She would have wondered
about Lily of whom she had always been so sure.

Nevertheless, Lily didn't doubt that carryings-on of the Olive-
censured variety had been occurring beneath her roof for some time
now, and today there had been particular flare-ups in several quarters—
Harvey's virtual elopement with the no-better-than-she-should-be-but-
very-good-for-Harvey Penny Nicholls, that foreign boy turning up in
obvious pursuit of Betsy, Ginger's transformation into a glamorous
creature who could not possibly have emerged from such a messy
bedroom all for the sake of dinner with Babe Palmer's spare cousin
although Ginger's dress-up efforts were for Goody Palmer's sake—
even Lily appreciated that. And not that it was any of Lily's business,
but William Baskett's behavior toward Becky in the kitchen just now
had not been at all appropriate.

Lily had watched him clearly reflected in the deep black and mirror-like door of the microwave oven as he nuzzled and caressed the back of Becky's neck. Lily had not meant to watch, but as flickeringly captured in the square of oven door, the scene had taken on such a televised air that she had viewed it irresistibly as if it were a performance being enacted for her to observe—William's lingering hands, the yearning of his body length bent over Becky like a Frenchman sheltering his baguette from the rain as Lily had thought at the time, for William seemed so hungry. But it was Becky's face that Lily had most noticed. Becky had been startled, at first, and then an unreadable languor stole over her and she accepted William's attentions. They stayed as they were, worshipper and object, until Little Becky blundered into the kitchen arguing to the air against having to go out with the grown-ups and only then had Becky broken away from William and become flustered and as usual and herself again.

Well, at least Lily had made sure the girl accompanied her mother and Mr. Baskett although a very major piece of bribery had been necessary to achieve that end. Lily could not imagine a more discouraging presence than that of the large and unhappy girl seated between Becky and William at the table, scowling over her menu and snuffing out the candles with exaggerated gusting sighs and bolting down her expensive dinner in her zeal to be reunited with the coat of her dreams. If Lily knew anything at all, she knew what it took to dishearten a suitor, for all of her experiences had run that way; being unaware of lipstick on one's teeth, too earnestly botanizing on strolls *à deux* through a spring meadow, appearing too tall in high heels and too stolid in low ones, wearing dresses the colors of stains on a tablecloth—cranberry or mustard or grape. *Were you a hit tonight, Lily, or do you remain a Miss?* Ardor was dampened easily, or had been in her case, where the attractions were so slight to begin with, and she had given up trying altogether one Saturday evening, one long-ago winter.

They had all had colds of course, as she had tried to describe to Andy how less than well they had often been. Her parents were sealed in their bedroom sharing the vaporizer steam. Olive had a sick cold but she was going out for the evening despite a low, persistent fever. She had gargled with salt water and was slowly preparing herself, powdering her red nose, rouging her pale cheeks, masking the sharp smell of Vick's with Arpège. Olive could not not go out on Saturday night. If word ever got round that she had stayed home on a Saturday night she would be finished, she said, though Lily never saw how word would get round if one stayed quietly in one's room and did not show oneself, alone and unaccompanied, in some public place. One could always stay home with a good book and to that end, Lily had gone down to the big parlor to find herself a book, a heavy, dusty, worthwhile volume of the Francis Parkman (*A Half Century of Conflict* had come first to her fingertips). Because even then, even as her few chances had been reluctantly reclassified as missed chances, Lily could still not quite not believe that somehow, Someone might still seek her out even in the very heart of her remote and well-defended home and she did not want to be discovered reading a work of mere fiction.

She had selected her book and switched off the floor lamp because the Hills never left lamps burning in unoccupied rooms but she lingered on in the gloom. Her own cold was on the wane. She was draining and, at the moment, working up to a sneeze. Her inner nose pricked, pressure was building. She snatched her handkerchief from her cardigan sleeve and stationed it below her chin. A sneeze ought not to be suppressed but should be contained.

She had turned her back to the empty room in automatic deference to the possibility of Someone standing there. She stood still and expectant as the sneeze welled. She sniffed cautiously, encouragingly, and she didn't hear the crick of the opening parlor door hinges, nor was she aware of the swift tap and pad of footsteps hurrying toward her across the floor and rug and floor and rug.

Harvey had answered the front doorbell. "I heard her coughing in the parlor," he must have said motioning the caller on his way. Harvey's younger-brother mind was fixated on the box kite he was constructing in an attic workshop he had contrived.

So Lily had been seized and kissed in the big parlor. A confident hand had gripped her shoulder and an insinuating hand circled her waist and a dark round of face bore down upon her face searching expertly for her mouth and Lily had responded. "And here you are," she had thought. Then, as abruptly, the face flinched apart from hers, the hands pushed away her waist, her shoulder, and a voice spoke, amused and unfazed, declaring, "But you're the wrong one." And Lily had felt the wrong one ever since. Everyone professed to remember their first kiss. Lily never volunteered that she had known for certain when she'd been given her last one.

Olive had only ever gone out with that man twice. Lily remembered his name and who he was and what he did and what had become of him, all quite unremarkable. He'd been no one, really, nobody in fact. Olive, in order never to stay home on a Saturday night, had handed herself over to some very ordinary young men and last summer, fifty years on, Olive's only daughter had shown herself all around Towne wearing a raggedy-hemmed and fading-away T-shirt printed with the words YOU HAVE TO KISS A LOT OF FROGS BEFORE YOU FIND YOUR PRINCE.

HANNAH'S OCCUPIED AN ANCIENT Federalist house set on the edge of a dormant mixed–fruit tree orchard located in a far corner of Towne. The restaurant had earned a starred entry in *The Undiscovered New England Guide: Back Roads and Byways Off the Beaten Path*. "Savor Old-Timey surroundings flavored with up-to-the-minute presentations of the freshest local ingredients." The *Guide* further suggested a walk through the West Towne Village Cemetery where some Revolutionary War dead lay beneath lichened and leaning headstones oddly carved with leering angels and horned lambs—a gently penitent option that often appealed to the too-well-fed who faced a longish drive home.

Becky described all this to William who absently allowed, "Oh, yes?" for now that he had Becky by his side, wrested from that donjon where he had found her, he could not chat banally. He could only treasure each shared breath of air he took. He could only grieve for the Band-Aid on her chin and the rigidity in her neck from her terrible tumble on an icy step. He wished only to remain encapsulated within the heated and smoothly running Alden family station wagon and drive through the long winter night to the very edge of all they knew of earth where they could launch themselves into the unknown, sans Little Becky who sat in the backseat breathing loudly through her nose.

Becky was driving because she was familiar with the way.

"Is anyone coming at us from the left?" Becky asked Little Becky at a dark crossroads. "I can't turn my head to look."

"Huh?" asked Little Becky. "What? your left or my left?"

"They're the same lefts," Becky said.

"No, I'm facing sidewise with my feet on the seat because Dad's big saw is all on the floor so your left is my backwards, and anyways, nobody's ever coming all this way out here," Little Becky answered. She had privately declared a moratorium on any further cooperation that night, especially now that she had her coat.

Becky supposed she was all right to proceed. She inched into the crossroad and tooted on her horn and flashed her blinkers. William, roused from his reveries, rather fervently offered to be her eyes, if only she would allow him, but Becky briskly but not unkindly informed him she only needed a reliable lookout until the spasm in her neck relaxed its grip.

Then, Little Becky who knew she was being unfairly condemned (*not* reliable) because she had explained about the big saw and how left was backwards, indignantly yelped, "Look out!" giving her mother and Mr. Baskett both temporary heart attacks. Her mother braked severely and Mr. Baskett, who had not fastened his seat belt, lurched toward the windshield hitting his eyebrows on the lowered visor. Good.

But they arrived in one piece, as Becky said, and were shown to the table she had requested in the niche beside the breakfront crammed with Flow Blueware because if she were ever going to collect anything seriously that's what she'd collect, Becky also said. Little Becky might have mentioned conversationally but did not that she had recently begun to collect the silvery inner wrappings of stick gum because she had seen in a magazine where you flatten them out and pound them together and cover the headboard of your bed all over and it looked like outer space if you painted your walls black—and that was going to be a battle, black paint, they'd never let her get away with black paint.

Becky glanced at the menu and she smiled at William in her whole-hearted way. She had known what she wanted at once, lobster quenelles in a Pernod sauce. Her eye had gone right to them. She set down her menu. A perfect choice, William agreed, and lay his menu tenderly atop hers. Becky's smile swerved a bit.

"Darling?" Becky asked.

Oh. She was speaking to Little Becky.

"Huh?" Little Becky asked.

"What do you feel like?"

"What?"

"What do you want to order? To eat?"

"To order to eat?"

William was knowledgeable about wine for several minutes as the waiter waited. William posed a few sharp questions and settled for something. Becky smiled her assent at the vineyard and the year William pronounced, and she smiled at the waiter as well.

Then, twisting and straining, Little Becky reached up and under the snowy tablecloth and her skirt and she extracted her paperback. She rose, a bookworm place marker dropped to the floor which the waiter retrieved and returned to her as she wandered off to read her horror book by the wide and welcoming and fully involved fire in the main dining room. She perched out of the way upon a very sturdy fender.

"Let her stay there," William said as Becky wondered how to fetch Little Becky back without causing a scene and, in fact, some of their fellow diners-out were regarding the deeply reading girl as if she were one of the charming features of the place along with the dried artemeisia hanging from the ceiling beams and the soft New Age music welling up from behind pots of forced narcissi.

"Alden says if this place was any quainter all the waiters would have catarrh, and small pox scars, just like in the good old days."

But William hadn't flown across seven time zones (he yawned irresistibly) to hear what else Alden had said. Becky's letters had been reporting what Alden had to say for the past twenty years. After several pages of Becky's account of the latest event or situation or disaster with the children or the car or the plumbing, the figure of Alden always waded in. Sometimes, he literally waded in, as the time during a Key West winter vacation when the boys had secretly constructed a raft from chaise longues and empty Evian bottles so they could defect to Cuba where, they had heard, the beaches were better and everyone there was too busy being poor to hog all the tennis courts. On that occasion, standing up to his knees in the Straits of Florida, frowning upon the flotilla of bedraggled boys returning under escort, Alden had delivered one of his deft summing-up pronouncements which was, as usual so apropos, so very neat ("Even Castro doesn't deserve you"), that Alden had then strolled away as if the case were closed, and it was Becky who had to propitiate the Coast Guard and the resort management and the appalled bystanders. Becky's role in these dramas was always parenthetically described—I found some buckets, I spoke to the police, I searched high and low and located some fabric that almost matched.

What a remarkable woman.

"Who?" asked Becky, gazing around the dining room. "Who's remarkable?" she wanted to know. She was prepared to admire anyone who was noteworthy and perhaps learn something useful about a dress sense or an eyebrow arch.

"Did I speak aloud?" William asked, astonished. "I thought I was musing to myself. No, I think I have always thought that you are a remarkable woman, Rebecca."

"Well, thank you, William, but actually I'm not at all remarkable. I'm really not very much of anything except, perhaps, capable. I think I've turned out pretty capable. Lately, I've surprised myself, how I can manage to manage."

"No, no, no," William corrected her almost irritably. "You are remarkable. You are magnificent. You are the paragon of all women, your voice, your smile, your spirit, your soul. It has always been and always will be you as far as I'm concerned."

"Oh no. Oh dear. It can't be me. And I thought you'd gotten over all that, that time when I forgot myself." Becky dropped her voice. He had made her conscious of her voice.

"I shall never get over all that, as you call it," William said. "Because it was all to me, it was everything."

Becky shifted uneasily. "Oh dear," she could only say again.

"But, as you said at the time, if only the flowers hadn't been arranged," William almost accused her.

"No, I believe I said, if only the hors d'oeuvres hadn't been ordered, that's what I said. But it's more romantic for you to remember I said the flowers had been picked and not that the chicken salad had been made, and the rector was booked, and people were flying in from Denver.

You've cast everything in a very falsely romantic light because you never had time to grow tired of me. Had we limped along to some sorry conclusion, you would have been quite relieved and then you would have moved gratefully on. You're not still pining, you just think you are. Oh, I'm so vexed with you, William. You're using me as an excuse not to marry some perfectly lovely woman somewhere out there in the wide world who is searching and alone because there really aren't enough good men to go around. No one should have two men to herself, I won't have it," Becky said, and she suddenly thought well of Harvey who kept filling his vacancies.

"So, you've come to know all about limping toward a sorry conclusion, have you?" William asked. He had listened selectively.

The first courses were wafted onto the table. Little Becky returned and devoured savory bundles of spinach-wrapped, herb-spiked wild mushrooms poached in cider and napped with a reduction cream sauce. Then she wandered off to play with the owners' (Hannah herself, who cooked, and David who saw to everything else) agreeable little baby whose nightly appearance on an Afghani tribal folk art rug beside the bar was another feature of the place.

"That looked good," Becky said, swiping up some of the sauce from Little Becky's plate with a crust of Hannah's excellent bread. "Oh, have some," she offered for she felt she had to offer William something.

William and Becky's quenelles had been very successful as well but he had consumed them perfunctorily while endeavoring to exchange significant looks with Becky over Little Becky's head. Now, waving away the bread plate, he told Becky, "I remember everything exactly as it happened. You agreed to meet me in Castine. Wherever I am, wherever I go in the world, I find myself on the map relative to one tiny and tremendous point in Maine. I know the miles from anywhere on earth. Test me, ask me, from Warsaw, Kinshasa, Mexico City."

"I thought you had invited me there to take my mind off the wedding frenzy, which was all getting to be a bit much. Ginger's bridesmaid dress didn't fit, we'd just found out, and Alden's mother, who was not a warm woman, only made me miss my own mother more. But that's no excuse. I knew better than to agree to meet you, but they all urged me to go. I remember I thought at the time, how they trust me. And then I thought, oh, they just want me out of the way so they can talk about me. And after a while, after I imagined what they were saying, I made up my mind to prove all their assumptions were wrong. And that's why I was so reckless. If the drive up had been less long I'd have arrived in a far more sensible state of mind."

"You were so lovely with recklessness. You are so lovely," William said simply. "And if you hadn't wanted me to come, if you hadn't wanted to see me this time, you should have told me so."

"But I had no idea . . ."

"I sent a letter. I explained."

"A letter? I received no letter."

"No? No letter? Damn the postal service. I had to use regular channels."

Their entrées were served. Little Becky thumped back to her place and tore through winter squash raviolis with a sharp cheddar and port wine sauce nested on a bed of braised winter greens. Becky concentrated very hard on her pheasant with Calvados and apples. She supposed Lily would be sorry to hear she had eaten pheasant.

"Stay and chat politely," Becky told her as Little Becky scraped back her chair.

"No. I have to," Little Becky insisted. "I have to *go,*" she whispered urgently and she escaped to the ladies' room where she perched upon a padded stool before a mirrored recess. She sniffed at and sampled the countertop offerings of hand lotions and essential oils, deciding to discover which was her best one. She scented her fingertips, the backs of her hands, her palms, her wrists, her forearms, and her knees until she ran out of patches of skin to anoint and she decreed moss rose her very favorite. She moved the moss rose bottle to the front of the clutter of containers. First. After which, the mirrored alcove afforded her a variety of novel views of herself all at once, the front, the sides, the back, and the top of her head. Every angle smiled and nodded and attended only to her and she knew she was among friends. How wonderful it would be, to be among friends, she thought.

"You must choose," William sternly prompted Becky for she was not saying all that he had imagined she would say when he had planned this moment.

"Choose?" Becky asked. "But I have chosen, not that there ever was a question. Or, if there was, briefly, a question you must believe me that the answer just wasn't you."

"Yes, yes, I humbly acceded to your wishes then. But now I know you have come to regret your decision," William said.

"Have I? Have I? Wherever did you get that impression?" Becky asked.

"I have had eyes in your house, and ears. I know what's been happening. I know that Alden has fallen by the wayside and he's dragging you down with him and that you are near the end of your rope," William said.

"Eyes in the house? Ears? Do you mean Andy? Andy has been reporting to you? But I liked Andy," Becky protested. "I have confided in Andy. How could Andy?"

"Andy didn't fully appreciate all that he was telling me. But a naïve informant is the truest one, I have found," William said. "So, now that you know what I know, I am asking you to freely choose. Choose now. Choose again. Choose differently."

"Now? Choose now? Why must I choose now? I really don't think you're quite yourself at the moment, and you will thank me later when you understand how very hard I'm trying not to let you say what you seem to want to insist upon saying. Oh, I blame myself for living in your apartment all these years, but how could I have told Alden why we couldn't possibly accept such favorable terms? It's just too unkind of you too, William. You've been pulling my strings for twenty years. But I won't let you upset our friendship at this point," Becky said. "Let's just say it's a lovely surprise to see you, I can't imagine what happened to your letter, and I suppose if I were foolish enough to believe you, I would be flattered, but I'm totally unconvinced. And now I'm going to enjoy the rest of the evening."

"I'm enjoying the evening," she informed the waiter who approached with another bottle of wine.

"Madam," he said.

"If we saw more of you," Becky told William, "things would be on a much more even keel."

"Well, you won't be seeing any more of me at all," William said with bitter satisfaction. "Not unless you come away with me, and come away with me now. I shall never again return to the United States."

"Don't be like that, so dramatic. You'll be retiring before too long. Your apartment is empty and waiting for you. Alden and I always talked about the time you'd come home for good and run for Congress, or governor. You have the résumé and the manner. In fact, we're going to help. Alden already has some slogans planned." She paused. She recalled they had not been very serious slogans. "And you'll be surprised at life in the States these days. Even the little Towne IGA bakes its own croissants. They're a bit doughy, but . . ."

William hushed her. "Listen to me," he said. "Don't try to persuade me of anything. Let me talk. Let me explain. Something has happened. It was a risk for me to come here at all but I knew you wouldn't come to me. Not again, not as you agreed to come once before."

"Are you ill?" Becky asked. "You aren't ill, are you? If you're ill, if there's anything I can do, that we can all do, if you're ill?"

"It's not an illness. Not that, no. It's something that's happened. It's something I've done," William said.

"But whatever can you have done?" Becky asked. "I can't begin to guess. You must be mistaken."

William seized her hand. She dropped her fork into the sugar bowl. William cleared his throat. He could not quite meet her eye. "Recent events," he began, "recent events abroad have made my position in certain circles rather equivocal in that there is a whole new ball game, as they say, out there."

"Whatever are you talking about?" Becky wondered. "Recent events have been wonderful, although they weren't very attractive to the Ceauşescus last Christmas. I don't think it's ever all right to line people up against walls and shoot them no matter what they've done. They looked so crumpled lying there, especially on Christmas. Alden said they should at least have waited till Boxing Day to clean up details like that."

"And they may be very unattractive to me," William said, wincing at what Alden had had to say for himself yet again.

"Don't be absurd. You're an American diplomat. You have all those tall strong Marines at your beck and call," Becky said.

"No, I may have all those tall strong Marines at my door, Rebecca. I may have all those tall strong Marines at my throat."

"Oh, I see," said Becky. "I'm afraid I do see. But whatever can you have done?" She had learned, over the years, to ask this question quite calmly of her boys. They were lulled into giving her more honest accounts of themselves.

"I backed the loser, as they say."

"But the losers were—oh, William, I should have thought you had more sense. Those people were so grey, they were so dour, and forgive me for pointing this out, but quite a few of them were actually quite evil. I mean to say, I list a bit to the left myself, although please don't tell Alden I said so, but really, William."

"This is not easily explained," William said. "I can explain to you, but you must be instructed as gradually as I myself came to see the true facts and assimilated them and, yes, acted upon them. And that's why I've come so suddenly and so necessarily to beg you, if I must, to go away with me. Come now, and come on faith."

"Go where?" Becky asked, unwisely, she knew, but she had always loved travel. She missed traveling most of all the privileges of her former life just lately lost. And Alden, she realized now, wore best when she could regard him in the context of a fresh view. He was an excellent husband when waving happily from a point on a jetty while making particular arrangements with the locals.

"Your passport is current? You can use your own passport for the time being. And you'll need warm clothes. That is, warm weather clothes, just enough to start. We'll buy what you need once we're settled. I'll buy you new white dresses. I always see you in white."

"Oh no. I can never wear white. I look so pale in white."

"Then whatever shade dresses you wish. Lemon-y yellow, shell-y pink." He strove to guess the color that would convince her. "May sky blue. The beginning of green green of Japanese tea splashed upon a damask cloth."

Becky seemed, for a moment, to will him to discover the shade that tinged the shadows of her most hidden dreams. But he would have to name the color for her to know it.

"Red?" William blundered on.

"No," Becky said. "I'm not going anywhere with you. And I suggest you turn yourself in and take your medicine. We'll stand by you. We can't approve, but we'll be there, Alden and I. Harvey won't be sympathetic, of course, and I'm not sure you'd really want Ginger in your corner, holding press conferences—though I doubt any of this is as serious as you pretend. Perhaps you're not quite as important as you think you are," she suggested gently. How Alden had minded learning that lesson rather too late in his life to bounce back very effectively from the shock of having been dropped.

"Don't decide now. I realize it's too much to take in. I'm not going away until tomorrow, though it will have to be tomorrow, because I've misdirected my potential pursuers but not indefinitely," William said. "Yes, what is it?" he asked.

The waiter wished to recite the dessert menu. Becky only wanted coffee because she was going to lie awake all night anyway but William, whose appetite had returned after he unburdened himself, regretted having underappreciated his previous courses and he allowed himself to be tempted by a dacquoise.

"Where's Little B.?" Becky asked. Little Becky liked dacquoise and she never had them nowadays. "Have we lost Little B.?"

Hannah had fetched Little Becky from the powder room and invited her into the winding-down kitchen (for the hour was late) where Little Becky test-tasted a contemplated dessert offering, a praline ice cream ball dusted with crushed Almond Roca, doused with Frangelico, and set alight. Little Becky expertly rolled flavors on her tongue. She didn't want to be rude to Hannah who hadn't yelled at her for hogging the ladies' room and knocking over the bottle of Sandalwood essence ("Mmmm," Hannah had breathed in and only smiled). Nevertheless, the ice cream invention needed a countertaste to undercut the sweetness.

"Crème fraîche?" Little Becky asked tentatively. "You know, like in a plop on the plate?"

"Yes, exactly right," agreed Hannah. "A sophisticated choice," she added as she prepared a revised portion to keep Little Becky busy in the kitchen as the girl's mother continued in her obviously consequential talk with the not unattractive man (he was heavyset, but as an owner-chef Hannah warmed to the established appetite) who was certainly not the plaid-shirted and mildly smiling and rather distrait husband. The Lowes had been in the restaurant a few times and they were the sort of discerning and delighted patrons who left a pleasant aftertaste. But even amiable people had their complications and Hannah was convinced there was a story being told at the table in the alcove which the mother did, and the daughter did not, need to hear.

"Would you like to work here this summer?" Hannah asked Little Becky, then. "Mainly I'd want you as junior waitstaff, filling water glasses and busing, but I'll need you in the kitchen sometimes. You can peel vegetables to start and pick up a few tricks along the way."

"Can I?" cried Little Becky. "Yes, yes, I want to work here. This *summer*."

LILY PICKED UP the kitchen wall phone on the eleventh ring and warily she asked, "Yes?"

"I want Phoebe, Aunt Lily," Arthur's voice, all the way from California, insisted.

"But Phoebe isn't here," Lily said.

"Not there? Has she gone away? She said she wouldn't go away," Arthur's voice cried across the country.

"She's out for the evening, Arthur. She's out for the evening with a party of young people," Lily told him.

"A party of young people?" Arthur mulled over that one. A cinematic scene unreeled in his mind of laughing girls and laughing boys, of Phoebe, laughing. They were decked out in long, home-knit scarves and great pompoms of mittens and striped stocking caps erect on their heads, and they motored through the countryside in a wood-paneled station wagon convertible beneath an orange and spherical and rather too low-hanging moon. How odd that the moon was so orange, for the rest of Arthur's mind movie played in a black-and-white world of rich shadows and bright clarity. Sure, if anyone deserved a good time, it was Phoebe.

"Well, listen, Aunt Lily," Arthur said. "Will you please tell Phoebe to

call me when she comes in. It's real important, it's of paramount impor-
tance that she does. Anytime she gets in, tell her. Here's the number
where I am, write it down, where I am. Please."

"I have it," Lily said. "Phoebe will get your message."

"Urgently. Tell her to call urgently," Arthur said.

"But Arthur," Lily offered. "If there's a problem, can I be of help?"

"No, it's not really a problem, or it is a problem, actually, that Phoebe
isn't there, or here. That's what I want. I want Phoebe to be *there* so I
can tell her she's got to come *here*. Do you see why it's so urgent, Aunt
Lily?" Arthur asked.

Yes, Lily said she saw.

"YOU ARE STARTING to look good to me," Stefan accused Phoebe, and
Phoebe capably avoided his threatened kiss. She shifted slightly and he
pitched sideways and lay flat along the Casa di Napoli booth's bench
seat unsure as a bowled-over beetle which way was up. He awaited assistance and when none came, he began to nestle against the sticky plasti-
cized Casa di Napoli menu that Phoebe had placed between Stefan and
her leg.

"Either Stefan doesn't have much of a head or he's had a head start,"
Andy observed.

"I thought that wine-y smell was some sort of awful European aftershave he was wearing," Betsy said.

"But he's bearded," Phoebe pointed out.

"Then he must have been drinking all day," Betsy said. "And he
shouldn't have been drinking at all. He must be underage. He's in
America for high school. I don't think Calliope should have served him,
actually."

"Probably not," Andy said. "But the Henry Kissinger diction and
the Leon Trotsky goatee make him come across as wisenheimerish beyond his years. Oh, just belt him if he's bothering you, Phoebe," Andy
advised.

"We really ought to be going, anyway," Phoebe said, glancing at her
watch. The time was half past seven on the West Coast where they were

dismantling the day and just beginning to imagine night. Arthur might, she thought unavailingly, Arthur might—

Stefan scrabbled at the menu. "Phooby," he muttered thickly. "Phooby? Are you there? Knock, knock, who's there? Phooby?"

"We can't just leave him here," Betsy said. "I mean, we can't, can we? Calliope will get in trouble. But he's not very manageable under the best of circumstances. What shall we do with him?"

"Arthur says that when people get like this when he's performing, he just agrees with everything they say very firmly," Phoebe recalled.

ANDY AND PHOEBE STEERED Stefan along the icy walk and maneuvered him into the house. He seemed to know where he was and he veered toward the dining room and the cluster of heavy, semifilled decanters gleaming on the sideboard. But Andy and Phoebe hauled him toward the stairs and hoisted him up step by step, clumping and bumping him along to Andy's room as imperfectly smothered outbursts of oaths and exclamations escaped from them all. Betsy had been charged with locating and distracting Lily whom she found in the little parlor dozing on Harvey's extended recliner with a library book on her lap and Agnes coiled at her feet. A 40-watt bulb cast an Old Masterish light. The fire sputtered. The owls' eyes were dimmed but remained alive.

"Aunt Lily?" Betsy asked. "Are you asleep? Don't wake up," she advised, belatedly whispering.

But, rousing now, Lily straightened the chair, toed away the cat, and opened her book.

"Betsy?" she asked.

"Only me," Betsy said, "telling you we're, you know, all home now."

"All right. No, wait," Lily said slowly recalling. There was a reason she had sat up. She had something to tell someone. "I need a word with . . ." she paused.

"Oh, I know. I'm so sorry about the noise," Betsy launched into an explanation. "Dinner disagreed with Stefan at the pizza place. He's— sick, but we'll simmer down. He'll have to spend the night. He can't drive because he's so—sick."

"Fetch him a basin, then," Lily said, changing tack momentarily.

"A basin. I will," Betsy said and bolted for the door, grateful that Lily chose to respond practically and had not asked to be told the details.

"No, wait," Lily said. "First tell Phoebe that Arthur called and she is to call him back tonight no matter the time. I wrote the number down in the kitchen. She's to call him, he's waiting for her to call. Tell her to call."

"Really? Arthur called? What did he want? Did he say? I hope it's good news," Betsy said. "Did it sound good? Do you think it's good news, Aunt Lily? I'll tell her right away."

"Yes, I think it's very good news for Phoebe," Lily said. "But first fetch the basin."

"Right. First I'll fetch the basin," Betsy said.

STEFAN LAY HEAVILY ASLEEP upon Andy's bed and he was likely to remain so until morning. A chipped porcelain bowl sat on the pillow beside his head and Andy had flung a blanket over him to blot out the sight of so much indulgence in denim, in alcohol, in abuse of hospitality. Andy did not draw the window shade, thinking ahead to the dazzling spike of earliest sunlight that would seek out and irradiate Stefan at dawn, and he pitched Stefan's not easily removed cowboy boots (snakeskin, stiletto-heeled, sour-sock-smelling) onto the floor between the bed and the window where, Andy hoped, Stefan would stumble over them as he blindly and madly dashed to yank the shade down. Andy eyed the shade. He snapped it fully up and wound the pull cord twice around the curtain rod as he felt himself becoming the star player in a future Hill family instructional anecdote on the perils of being self-invited, foreign, drunk, and a chaser of young Hill women.

Carrying his robe and pajama bottoms and the first book that came to hand (*Philology and Function*, Third Edition) he wandered down into the kitchen where Betsy enthused, more demonstrably happy than Phoebe, about Arthur's sudden call. For Phoebe had phoned Arthur. She had been calm, even solemn, as she listened to his plans for her. She had suffered greatly for weeks now and she carried herself carefully as if she were just emerging from a serious illness. But, better than most,

Phoebe knew how little time the modern world allowed for recovery from even the most perilous procedure and she did not doubt she would arise quite restored in the morning prepared to pack her belongings, resign from her position at the hospital, catch a plane. Still, she didn't feel up to sitting in the kitchen until all hours to talk and talk about the rest of her life as Betsy had been prepared to do. "Oh, Phoebe," Betsy said. "Oh, Phoebe." Carrying a mug of Mung tea so she would not dream, Phoebe disappeared up the back stairs and it was then that Betsy turned to Andy and declared herself to be in love with love.

MUCH LATER AS Earl was driving Ginger home, a vivid light on the dashboard blinked and a two-way radio chattered an address. Earl cranked down his window and, reaching with his long arm, affixed a magnetized, cone-shaped glowing and whirling object to the roof of his car. NORTHEAST SECURITY EMERGENCY . . . NORTHEAST SECURITY EMERGENCY highlighted lettering insisted as he flew over the back roads. Snowbank tumuli, shuttered residences, the thick trunks and twisting arms of trees, the loaf shapes of mailboxes, were interestingly, urgently streaked with alarm-alarm orange illumination. Earl monitored a police scanner, all the while communicating with his own headquarters in a number-larded language that defeated Ginger's perfectly natural desire to listen in on the details of the unfolding upset.

Her presence in the passenger seat "interfered" as a charged Earl had irritably observed, and Ginger was required to press one foot against the radio console and to place one hand on the ceiling light fixture to clear the static of which she very much doubted she was the cause. Her personal aura was remarkably light. She knew. She had had her aura charted and it was pure silver, a Gifted One had told her. Nevertheless, she awkwardly perched as she had been bidden, acting as a kind of twisted metal coat hanger antenna and she withheld comment although she permitted several long sighs to seethe through her clamped teeth. The windshield began to cloud. Earl swiped a see-through swath with an impatient palm.

Of course the evening had not gone well. There was no point dwelling on the evening. At the very beginning, stowing her into his car, Earl had closed the door on the sweeping skirt of her grandmother's beautiful golden-hued mink coat. The hem had dragged through the slush and grime and motor oil all the way from the River Road to Main Street where the Palmers lived in Babe's parents' old place and about which Ginger had been frankly curious—some lovely old mill-work was visible through the uncurtained and alight windows late at night as one happened to drive by and chanced to glance that way, raised panels, dentil molding, a bowfronted corner cupboard—Ginger had not had a very good view—also, a pilastered mantel, a Queen Anne gilt-wood wall mirror, age spotted but still serviceable, and a longcase clock that ran fast.

The worst of the damage to her coat had been revealed in the Palmers' foyer as outer garments were surrendered. Ginger had been obliged to be perfectly charming about the damage, about the frazzled and tar-blackened and shredding golden pelt and satin lining as Babe stood by the door twisting Ginger's faux Hermès scarf like a garotte and smiling a malign and expectant little smile.

Earl started in on blaming the deep darkness at the top of Miss Hill's driveway, otherwise he would have seen the overspill of coat—besides, personal security concerns dictated a hundred-foot zone of incandescence around the perimeters of all residential abodes, so Miss Hill was in dangerous error if not actual default—there wasn't a law, yet. Babe was of the opinion that Ginger herself should have kept better track of the netherward billowings of her exuberant garment. Goody, who had received the coat and had sympathetically draped it over the banister rail, knelt and examined the harm done and wondered whether Spot Off would help. Babe had stiffened. She was beginning to ask herself whether women's hems weren't one of those areas men ought not to have opinions about. A hem, she thought wildly, could be construed as a gateway. Ginger would have been extremely interested in this insight had Babe spoken of it aloud, but Babe was bound by then to herd every-one into the dining room. The longcase clock seemed to think it was five after six and the odor of overcooking drifted from the kitchen quarters, of tired onions, of a too-brown crust.

"Get up, Goody," Babe said, and Goody got up from his knees.

"I'm not sure about the Spot Off," Ginger said. "But I do seem to recall a lovely old Armenian gentleman in Peabody who always saw to furs. Oh, wait, was he rugs?"

Then Babe recounted her big fight with Briter-Ways Cleansers over the All Saints' surplices as she seated everyone. The dining room air was chilly. Ginger wished she had her coat. Oh, her coat.

Goody allowed he wasn't at all knowledgeable about such subjects, but couldn't Ginger cut off the damaged part and shorten her coat?

Babe told Goody to say grace. He repeated a standard one. They all uttered Amen.

Ginger asked Babe if she had bought her unusual centerpiece at the Citizens with Special Needs Sheltered Workshop Shop which was enjoying a small vogue with the recent emergence of outsider art as a collectible commodity.

"What's outsider art?" asked Earl. "Lawn ornaments?"

Ginger explained.

"No," said Babe. "I didn't buy the centerpiece there."

"Did you take the skin off my piece of chicken?" Goody asked Babe, which revived the sore question of the coat, this further mention of skins.

"Yes, you may eat that piece of chicken as I have given it to you," Babe said.

"I mean to say, minks get mussy in their real life," Earl spoke up. "The little critters swim, don't they, they frolic in the muck, that is before they're stunned and electrocuted."

"I think mine is the equivalent of roadkill mink," Ginger said.

"Is Kraft's Pepper Ranch Salad Dressing Lite the salad dressing I can eat?" Goody asked.

"Yes," Babe said.

"Is it the salad dressing that I like?" Goody inquired.

("Don't move," Earl's voice broke into Ginger's thoughts, for Ginger had been agitatedly twitching and Earl's radio emitted frizzles and blurts.)

Then Ginger had told Goody, in answer to his question, she really couldn't say what her cholesterol count was. Goody said she really ought to know and Ginger said, oh, she liked to be surprised.

"What, by the first heart attack?" suggested Babe.

"Oh, my heart," answered Ginger, as if that organ was always giving her trouble of some sort.

Earl was inspired to describe the finer points of a timely home security checkup and outlined his prescriptive solution to the average home owner's average home's risks and liabilities, but he could not be drawn out on the details of a recent burglary and house trashing in Towne.

"I heard they poured a box of Tide in the Jacuzzi and left the motor running and the water on," Ginger had probed. "Come on, you can tell us. It's not as if you're a real policeman who swore an oath."

Earl had delivered a speech on the coming privatization of all public services. Someday we will select and contract our own firefighters, for example, with a choice of water or foam extinguishings, or even, he explained, a giant vacuumizing unit which would suck the air itself out from under a fire, effectively smothering it.

"I can't picture that at all. Where would one plug such a unit in? I mean to say, one always has to plug in the vacuum first which is not always easy to do at Lily's house," Ginger said, not that she'd done much vacuuming lately but she had observed Betsy on her hands and knees searching along the baseboards behind heavy furniture for any available outlet.

"Babe," Goody asked, sotto voce, "may I have a second dinner roll if I only have three-quarters of a dessert?"

That she had ever failed to see Goody clearly, Ginger understood then. She had been very mistaken. Time played such variations on memory. Time took its toll on youth and promise. Time trivialized, time tarnished, time tampered. Nevertheless, Ginger reminded herself, time could also temper and improve and enrich some others among us. Ginger flexed on her own behalf. Time, she concluded, ultimately told the truth.

"Tell me, do you still recite the 'Desiderata'?" Ginger asked Goody.

"Yes," Babe spoke up defiantly. "He certainly does."

"Oh dear," Ginger murmured tolerantly.

No, no version of Goody was going to ride to her rescue, not unless Babe ordered him to go forth, and reknotted his tie and reminded him to carry his umbrella before he departed—and then she would peremptorily summon him back because he'd forgotten to place a good-bye peck upon her dry, freckled cheek. The Palmers conducted that sort of marriage. Babe's wedding portrait still hung on the living room wall, an unstylish artifact from the early seventies. Babe had not been a pretty bride but she had been a resolute one. The band of her princess veil sat low and straight across her brow.

("Ess, two, one, six, over," Earl replied to his headquarters. "Ess, two, one, six, over, damn it," he barked, which fierceness, Ginger was sure, was only an act on his part. He was not attempting to impress her by this point in the evening, however. He was just trying to show her.)

They had played cards after dinner. No one had told Ginger there would be bridge. She thought one was supposed to be warned in advance if there was going to be bridge. She would have to write to Miss Manners for the last word, and she composed her letter in her mind, *Dear Maîtresse, Is not the considerate hostess obliged to issue a minatory statement?*

They sat around a too-small card table. Their knees milled and brushed and bumped. Ginger took no joy in the contact. She drew in her elbows and locked her knees. Earl picked up Ginger's coffee cup and drank from it.

"Too sweet," he sputtered, clipping cup against saucer.

Ginger arched an eyebrow. "Surely not," she said.

The Palmers, partnered, spatted, and Earl was impatient with Ginger who could only vaguely play. She consulted a scrawled-upon crib sheet which she amended as fresh situations arose during the course of play.

"Are we playing for money?" Ginger asked. "No. Ah, we're playing for glory."

Glory. The Palmers and Earl arranged their hands uneasily.

Ginger wondered why she hadn't stayed home tonight of all nights and concentrated on charming William. She could have played another contest with him, far more successfully—And have you read?, And have you been to?, And do you know?, And don't you think? She would have made certain that any little game advanced with William ended in a big, satisfactory tie. Dear William, he must know so few people in the States, these days. Such a pity he had to make do with Becky as his dinner companion. One could not imagine such an unbracing evening. One would have liked to have been the flower in the vase upon their table, a tall, stately, sympathetically nodding purple iris, she thought, whose lovely petals William touched with a tender finger.

Hurry, Ginger thought now. Hurry, she thought as Earl drove doggedly on. Perhaps there would be time to sit up with William and chat and get to know him—whom, in truth, she didn't really know at all but seemed to know all about, Becky so frequently mentioned his likes. How handy to know a man's likes for plainsong and Siena and naval histories told from the nonvictors' perspectives.

Then Earl pulled to an abrupt and maddening stop alongside a Towne police cruiser parked at the end of a driveway off Modred Lane.

"Stay here," he ordered Ginger as he got out to confer with an officer who was only, after all, Eddie Eddy. Ginger used to know his sister. She peered through the windshield and waved. Betty was the sister's name, inevitably, pronounced Beddy. Earl waved back at Ginger to stop waving.

When Earl returned to the car, he removed the wobbling and exclaiming Northeast Security Emergency cone and tossed it into the backseat.

"So?" Ginger asked. "What is it? What did Eddie say? What's going on?"

"False alarm," Earl said. He reached across her ankle and snapped off his scanner. "Nothing's going on. There is no emergency here tonight." He failed to meet her unconvinced stare.

"Then why is Eddie standing there?" Ginger asked. "Why is he standing in the middle of the road in the middle of the night? What were you two talking about if there was nothing to talk about? I can't believe you. Clearly, there's not nothing going on."

"Well, I told you."

"Well, I don't believe you."

"Well then."

ALDEN AND THE BOYS rose early the next morning and shuffled to their attic bedroom windows to gaze down upon the driveway bowl. They had all dreamed about the truck in rushes of rumble and motion and surreal and rolling-about cargoes of faces from the past (Alden) and shipments of bootleg videos (the boys). They thumped down to the kitchen and Alden plugged in the coffeepot and they moved outside to picnic on hot coffee and jelly sticks. Glover and Alden sat high in the truck cab on sprung seats of tough and tobacco-smelling leather. Brooks and Rollins lounged in the capacious bed upon rearrangements of the several massive studded spare tires that did not fit the Loadstar but which might be bartered for some that could be used. There was a communicating window at the rear of the cab which slid open and shut and they passed the doughnut box back and forth among themselves. The bed of the truck was open to the elements but could be enclosed by erecting iron arches and tying on a tarp. Very Okie, Alden had said.

They warmed their hands around their coffee mugs and were quiet together in the manner of cowboys or miners or some such species of hollow-eyed workingmen who bore honest grime under their fingernails and knuckles. And they had "passed," as Alden put it, last night at the Towne Line Diner, where they stopped for dinner. They had sat at the counter hunched in their parkas. They ordered chili and burgers all the way after they overheard them being ordered by the regular patrons and which turned out to be burgers with every option piled on. They carried on a conversation with the waitress whose boyfriend drove a real big rig too, she told them. She had noticed as they pulled into the lot in the Loadstar. Her ears perked right up at the grumbly purr of a real big engine braking and winding down.

"And yet all powered by such a little key," Alden had marveled, displaying the key newly attached to his key ring. Well, they had "passed" up until that point.

Admittedly, the truck was less lovely by daylight, for they had only viewed it by moonlight and the darting passes of a failing flashlight beam. The truck's surface showed, now, abraded and dented and no longer milk white but white-ish, a kind of neglected tooth color. Still, the look was less a used than a veteran one as Alden optimistically said. It was too bad they couldn't go out on the road again until the paperwork could be completed at the Registry on Monday morning. The drive home last night from Gee's cousin Gum Chew's used car and what-have-you lot had not been entirely legal. Gum, who was keen to complete the sale, had wired a loose license plate to the rear bumper, an

expired vanity plate that spelled out KIKKBUT which Alden had supposed was somebody's name (it looked Finnish?) until the boys began
to pronounce it.

Lily had been up and about since dawn filling the birdfeeders and
breaking the ice that had glassed over the terrace flagstones. She didn't
want any broken necks to add to her burdens, an adamant invalid supine
on a sofa and requiring hourly snack trays and fresh magazines and
physical therapy. She chipped away with a garden edger and kept her
back turned to the driveway where she had noted something very like a
truck was parked and she had sensibly decided not to know anything
more about it.

But here was Alden at her elbow, bidding her to admire the object.

"So very large," she remarked after they had walked around the truck
twice. "So large one would almost think such a vehicle ought to be
immobile." Alden and the boys received her comment as an eccentric
yet an interested one.

Alden sent Brooks and Rollins inside to fetch a mug of coffee for Lily
and before she knew what she was about, Alden was hoisting her up
into the cab which put her in mind of boarding an elephant. She had
always rather wanted to ride an elephant, floating serenely, regally
high in a canopied howdah. Nor would she have minded riding atop a
camel in the shade of the Great Pyramids, she reflected, and she realized she could almost understand Alden's enthusiasm for alternative
transportation.

"And what are your plans for this?" Lily asked.

"Aside from my own uses, lugging wood for the wood business when
the wood business gets going," Alden said, "I'm going to hire myself
out as a general carrier. When you think of the times you've said to
yourself, if only I had a truck. Well, here's the truck for toting lumber
home from the lumberyard or, say, from an auction where you can't bid
on a really terrific armoire because there's no good way of getting it
home. I can linger on the outskirts of estate sales, availably. I'm going to
target the small-load, short-distance market. That's what you have to do
these days. You have to identify and target a niche. Then, who knows,
maybe I'll build up to a fleet of trucks. First, though, we'll have to come
up with a name for the company."

"A La Cart?" Lily suggested.

"Yes," said Alden, delighted. "A La Cart, ad hoc, *après*-auction haulage a specialty. Although it will hurt Becky's feelings that we've come up with a company name and motto and an entire business without her input. Still, she'll have some ideas we haven't even thought of, I'm sure, and we'll let her decide our corporate color scheme because I'm thinking now, we ought to paint the truck eye-catchingly."

BETSY AND ANDY AWOKE early as well. Betsy's narrow bed could scarcely contain them. They noticed this now as they had not noticed last night. They lay, at present unfolding and coming to, aware of sharp knees and angled elbows jutting, no longer silken skinned entwining limbs simply, intricately, inevitably fitting together. When they found their voices and thought to speak (last night all language had been banished) they agreed they did not wish to be discovered in Betsy's room. Although, Betsy said, the sky wouldn't fall if they were, but it would be an unkindness to saddle the family with yet another subject not to be discussed at the breakfast table. Breakfasts were already such Quaker meetings.

Nevertheless, Andy was reluctant to leave her side. The bed made such a warm burrow. Huffs of a draft nudged the suspended ceiling light and rustled the pages of a letter scattered across the bureau top. Icy air touched his ventured and retracted foot. He returned to Betsy and murmured into her shoulder. His larynx thrummed against her upper arm. He was saying something about being so happy here, here he was happy. Betsy, gratified, curled against him. No, she could not quite curl against him. She unlaced her captive hands from Andy's grasp and she reached and fumbled above her head. She could not raise her head. A lock of her secretly wild hair, eagerly unbound by Andy, had wound round a headboard spindle sometime during the night. She tried to recall how that had happened.

"Just cut me loose," Betsy said. "There's scissors at my desk. In the drawer."

"I won't cut off your hair," Andy said. "Never. Never your lovely hair. I'll free you."

"All right, all right," Betsy said. "But hurry. They're all getting up. I hear footsteps clomping. I hear water in the pipes."

Andy was painstaking. Betsy didn't flash in anger. They knew a significant challenge was being met and matched as Andy pulled at and uncoiled a hundred pale, polished strands. Betsy bore each tug and pinch of her scalp in silence. Threads of hair, not quite hopelessly entangled, released and spiraled free. Not long, Andy promised, not long, he promised again. There.

He massaged and kissed her poor, wrenched neck and Betsy swiftly braided her hair out of further harm's way. A plait rose upright from her nape, as soft and asway as an aigrette.

"You are exquisite. You are perfect," Andy said, charmed by all her graceful motions.

"Perfect," Betsy uttered faintly.

How daunting to be told she was perfect. How perilous to be valued for her perfection. Would Andy never overlook an error on her part? For she was, she knew, far less good than she appeared to be. Every step she took these days was one calculated to make her mother's course show even worse. Betsy shone for the blackest of reasons against the darkest of designs. She wished she could tell Andy, of all people, how her worthy acts stood tall only in opposition, but she would never respect him if he said he understood.

Besides, she supposed Andy was not citing her inner worth, such as it was. He was responding to her physical beauty, for which she could claim even less credit. One simply was, or was not, beautiful, and she could not quite work out how not to be so. Could she wear glasses, grow fat, convince a surgeon to sever some crucial nerve and freeze her face into a glowering mask? But what if she changed her mind? She very well might, for she had observed how very much the favored ones cared when they began to lose their looks—how they haunted all mirrors, at first, not quite sure, and then hunted down less clear and more forgiving mirrors, and, at last, shrouded every mirrored surface with scarves and lingerie. No, good looks mattered even if you pretended not to notice how smiles and chairs and advantages were especially offered to you when you came into a room. Betsy saw, then, that her life might be very pleasant indeed, if she just let nature take its course. Cloaks would be spread across puddles, the gates to secret gardens would swing open at her approach, and as she entered, ripe plums would drop into her lap. And I shall let them, she resolved now.

Andy felt Betsy fall limp, resistless. Her slight weight became a dead weight in his arms, disconcertingly so, and he wondered whether he had taken on more than he intended, although, admittedly, his intentions had been well-defined last night, but not definitive. He had not meant anything so concrete as this. He slowly slid his arms from beneath her.

"I must be brave," he stated. He flung back blankets and stood and shrugged on his robe. He listened at the door—voices called, a radio sang, water and heat shuddered through pipes—and after sketching a sort of blessing in the icy air, he left her.

Betsy settled back among replumped pillows. She stretched her legs and sought the hollow where the mattress was still warm from Andy. She touched her lips reminiscently and decided that her favorite place of all was a bed after a lover had departed. Although that might change in the future when she had access to bigger beds, so it was nothing to worry about, this strong yen to be by herself again. Her mother, Betsy supposed, would have taken ten years at the psychiatrist to figure out that one, ten years of twice a week coming home with red-rimmed eyes and restorative jars and sample vials from the Elizabeth Arden counter. But those would be such enjoyable years for Ginger, being able to talk about herself, being able to talk about sex and herself, and rounding off her big emotional day with shopping. Oh, her mother . . .

Betsy listened through her wall toward the bathroom. It was occupied. She reached, there was always a book within reach in her little room, and she scooped a small brown volume with yellow brittle pages from her windowsill. She would sample E.B.B. as fatidic commentator on her situation. Betsy opened at random and read where her eye happened first. "I never gave a lock of hair away / To a man, dearest, except this to you—" Which was too spooky for words.

THE EVENTS OF the previous evening had left William not unhopeful. After twenty years of hanging fire, it was only to be expected that the match was, necessarily, a dampened one. The affair required sustained and gentle warmth and insistently whispering breaths to coax a spark, for just a spark was all he knew he needed after twenty years of such drought, after twenty years' accumulation of crumpled letters and desiccated floral tributes, after twenty arid years during which he had burned and Becky had been bled nearly dry by her ridiculous family's incessant claims and demands.

William sat on the edge of Harvey's high and firm and wide widower's bed and he returned the gazes of Harvey's three lost wives as he pulled up his socks, a calf-high, camel-colored lamb's-wool pair. He was not unencouraged. He would not be discouraged. He felt as if he had just passed seven mitigating hours, dreaming usefully, in a shrine to robust matrimonial prospects. Harvey's handkerchief drawer, where William had routinely routed, held a cache of sentimental artifacts— theater programs, swizzle sticks from happy hours, several snowy and lacy lawn hankies far daintier than Harvey's own well-ironed linen square, monogrammed with three vertical lines intersected by a horizontal bar. Were these seized or tendered tokens, William wondered. Such prizes, the few prizes, had been seized, in his experience. He himself possessed a golden button that had fallen from the cuff of Becky's blazer during a New York visit in 1974, a No. 2 Pentech pencil she had clenched between her teeth as she worried over an *International Herald Tribune* crossword puzzle in 1986, and the paper doily that bore the cream scone she had enjoyed when he coaxed her off to Newport, two summers ago. He kept his treasures in an accordion-fold compartment of his briefcase. He seldom consulted them but he knew they were there, which had almost been enough until now.

Let me succeed. William paused before the triptych frame and made a formal request of the Three Graces as he called the wives, for he couldn't remember their names, if he had ever learned them. But they smiled upon him, the old girls as Harvey himself called them, as they could always be counted upon to smile sweetly no matter what scheme was being laid before them, for they had been posed and photographed and retouched to a high standard of female complicity. They regarded William understandingly as he slid open Harvey's handkerchief drawer and slipped a swizzle stick molded like the Venus de Milo at its nonbusiness end into his jacket pocket. For luck, he told the gallery of kind lost ladies.

William firmed his shoulders—his shape was such that they did not square—as he ventured from Harvey's room, taking his first steps forward into his uncertain future, and he tangled with a bundle of unfolded laundry misplaced on the upper hall floor, one of Alden's flannel shirtsleeves snagging round his ankle.

Becky was waiting for him in Lily's yellow-walled and cinnamon-smelling kitchen. She was alone as William had meant to find her and as Becky had contrived to be found for there was so much not to be said and she was determined to demonstrate to William that the non-saying was going to begin now.

She had guarded a final jelly stick for William. She had refused Alden a third cup of coffee to carry out to the truck to place on the broad dashboard as he labored to repair the broken latch of the glove compartment hatch. William mistook Becky's efforts to ensure him his breakfast as a solicitous one. In fact, Becky was bound not to coddle eggs or butter crustless toast angles or press juice from fresh grapefruits for William. Nor was she prepared to brew him a new pot of Hawaiian Kona coffee of which a few hoarded ounces of beans remained. She did not explain all this to William as he thanked her for the last doughnut, slightly crushed and lightly weeping sap onto a dusted-off Delft plate (her sole concession to his sensibilities). She hardened her heart. She did not reach for a sprouting shallot and the omelet pan.

"I'll keep you company with a cup of tea," she said as she sat across the table from him, for as well as being secretly firm with him, she had resolved to behave openly and naturally in William's company to persuade him that she had utterly forgotten how he had forgotten himself the night before. But she was finding that when the time came to play Becky as usual, she gave a shaky performance. She could think of nothing noncommittal to say—the personal, world politics, foreign travel, last night's dinner entrée choices, where William would find himself tomorrow, were all too fraught with meaning to mention, and yet, those were the subjects that loomed. How long have you loved me?, have you always loved me?, why do you love me?, what will it take to make you cease to love me?, were the questions she had pondered as she lay awake beneath the blanketing blackness hunched away from the slowly breathing weight of Alden. Where would we go?, how would we live?, have you faith enough for both of us to take on the wrath of the decrying world?, she had importuned the darkness that William had summoned and which he inhabited, his image impressed against the lid of Becky's clenched-shut eye. By faint first light she had begun to glimpse as well the tentative outlines of a picture of herself. She was walking freely across a sunny public space. A piazza? A park? A loosely woven basket swung from her arm. She could not quite see what the basket carried. Fruit, she guessed because of the basket's shape, some sweet and fragrant fruit native to the land of the piazza or the sunny park, and just gathered that day at the cusp of its goodness.

Betsy could only smile at William across the kitchen table because, she seemed to recall, she often smiled. She was a pleasant woman. Everybody said so.

William rotated the lazy Susan with a prodding finger. A long-necked bottle of tarragon vinegar, a stout and sticky jug of unsulphured molasses, a cylindrical jar of seedless raspberry jam, all clinking and trembling together, impeded his view and when her face was revealed, so clearly, so dearly smiling upon him, his hand flew to his heart and he cried out, "Oh Becky. Oh my love. Oh my darling dear one."

It occurred to Becky that human beings often sounded least sincere when they were being most fervent. Poor William, on the wrong side of forty, fat as a friar, and unaware of the slick of lemony jelly plopped onto his chin, was behaving like a swain of twenty, and yet she believed him. There had been the ring of truth in his resonating cry. She had felt its reverberative roll just as on a long-ago vacation in Italy she had felt the pulse of proclaiming cathedral bells through the soles of her feet and irresistibly been drawn inside to kneel at the side altar of a church of the wrong denomination.

Out in the driveway bowl, Alden's absurd truck roared, briefly alive. The very house shuddered, the oval-faced spoons in the spoon jar chattered back and forth, and diesel fumes whiffed through the unsolidly fitting window above the sink. The wide old floorboards and patchy linoleum trembled now through the soles of Becky's shoes, those susceptible soles, and in the roar and the shudder and the smell of fuel, she could only imagine a jumbo jet taking off and that she herself was aboard being lifted up and borne away. She braced herself. She had never been a brave airline passenger. To tell the truth, she carried a Valium and Vermouth cocktail in a pocket flask, but she had always enjoyed wherever she went once she got there, once she recovered from her imposed fogginess and her ankles unswelled. Oh yes, she was ready to take off, but not in Alden's impossible truck. She was not going anywhere, locked inside its battered cab.

"I forgot your cream," Becky said, jumping up and unlocking her gaze from William's. "Although actually, it's not cream, it's only Pream, and it's not even real Pream, it's a Pream substitute. Alden says it's sort of a Sean Connery, Roger Moore, Timothy Dalton progression, speaking coffee-creamer-wise," she explained as she transferred a few powdery spoonsful from the big jar into a little pottery bowl. "Or would that be the opposite of a progression? A regression, Alden must have meant, or a devolving, or backsliding, or losing of ground . . ." her voice trailed off.

As she set the bowl upon the table before him, William reached and seized her arm and turned her hand over and kissed the pale, tender underside where her skin stretched softest and her veins fluttered blue and close to the surface beneath his murmury rain of kisses. How clever of William to discover, no, how clever of William to rediscover the back of her wrist after all these years.

"You mustn't," she said, dreamily.

"Yes. I must," he insisted.

"But someone is coming," she said, suddenly alert.

"What? Who's there?" William called. Recklessly, he looked for Alden, he hoped for Alden, an Alden who would be incensed, although far more likely, Alden, encountering his wife and his friend linked in mid-romantic gesture, would lean against a kitchen counter, cross his arms, and deliver one of his remarks. William would have to create passions enough for all of them.

"Show yourself," William demanded. He rose, his chest impressively puffed, his chin outthrust.

A face peered, then, round the doorpost. The face was not known to Becky or to William, a pale and bearded and young yet oddly aged face suffering from something. Greyed, pebbly eyes blinked at them in slow painful motion and a red and swollen mouth worked itself uselessly

before words formed and emerged, a slurred string of foreignly muttered words uttered in the cadence of a challenge.

William released Becky's wrist and he fell back into his chair. His
hand flailed, knocking against his coffee mug. A wave of coffee welled
and spilled. He exclaimed aloud, a general oath.

"You there," the stranger rasped thickly. "Be . . . you . . . silent."

William flushed. His cheeks mottled the colors of the remnants of a
deep, old bruise and he gasped after unrecoverable breaths.

William wouldn't be used to rude international teenagers, Becky supposed, although obviously this particular sorry specimen was less ill-
mannered than very, very hungover which was not, of course, any
excuse for him. Rather, Becky considered this a deeper indictment.

"Who are you?" she asked sternly. "What are you doing here?"

"Besty," Stefan mewled, after he recovered a thought.

"Betsy," Becky set him straight.

"Yes. Betsy," Stefan clarified. "I want . . . Betsy," he stated.

"Well, she isn't here," Becky informed him.

"Is not here?" Stefan slowly echoed, unconvinced. He peered toward
an ajar cabinet door as if Betsy might be crouched within, concealed
from him. He regarded suspiciously the wastebasket and having fixed
his point, in his shaky opinion, he retreated through the dining room
door.

"What an unpleasant boy. I'm surprised at Betsy for encouraging
him," Becky said. "Although to be fair, Betsy really doesn't have to
encourage anyone. Boys just follow her home. Men are foolish too. Some
of those babysitting-job fathers, driving her home. I've sometimes worried . . . But William, are you all right?" she asked. "William?"

For William had not recovered from his shock. His respiration ran
ragged and once again his hand struggled above his heart. Becky sat
beside him and sopped at the coffee he had sloshed onto the table surface
with the several Kleenexes plucked from her sweater sleeve.

"There," she said decisively. "No harm done."

They sat side by side as William's panic subsided and Becky retreated
into thoughts of her own. She had, for almost a minute, almost made up
her mind to go away with William as he had asked. For a moment their
elopement had seemed possible; to run away had become her profound-

est desire, indeed, her very departure already seemed a fait accompli. For even though she had not known where they were to flee, she had felt herself to be there already, ensconced in whatever warm patch of far-away refuge where he and she would yet be welcomed. An impending life had flashed before her eyes. She would be well looked after. She would be appreciated, and appreciative, dining out, enjoying conversations, having the insides of her wrists kissed while sitting by the sea sipping a local wine, she and William enisled together, untouchable as long as they remained out of touch. Yes, she had told herself, yes, she had made a choice, but she had not been able to tell William above the rumble and roar of Alden's insupportable truck in which Alden, she wryly supposed now, had idled to her rescue.

"I thought he'd come for me," William said when he could speak. "From Bonn or Warsaw, that they'd found me. I didn't think they'd find me. So soon."

"Yes, I gathered all that," Becky said. "It must not be very comfortable being you at present," she observed. "Being panicked by a foreign exchange student."

"As I told you, I shouldn't be here. It's only because of you that I risked . . ."

"No one asked you to come."

"And there's no time for games . . ."

"I am not engaging in games."

"They are frankly becoming tiresome, your professions of scruples."

"Yes, I'm afraid scruples are very tiresome," Becky agreed. She could go so far as to agree with him on that.

AWAY DOWN IN the village, the bells in the Congregational steeple tolled the noon hour, twelve thin and trailing notes seeking out the Hills and the Hill visitors, who consulted their watches and the household clocks, which confirmed within a minute or two how the day had half gone while they had accomplished very little and had much still to do. Reminded, then, they made their moves.

Becky emerged from her attic bedroom stepping briskly and with naturally high color spotting her cheeks. She marched bravely down the attic steps and passed by William's hopelessly ajar door. She descended the main stairs, her head held high, and turned toward the kitchen where she seized her grocery shopping list and expandable coupon portfolio from the kitchen desk drawer.

Little Becky waylaid her mother in the pantry, crowding her against the leaning twenty-pound bag of Maine potatoes kept, and going a bit punkish, in a corner.

"Can I come?" Little Becky asked. "I want to come to the grocery store. I'm coming." She dogged her mother as Becky opened a cupboard door and rattled a box of cornflakes and hefted a carton of dates and shook a cylinder of cornmeal. She did not amend her list. She would rely on her memory, which she preferred, at present, to stock with incidentals.

"Because I really want to come," Little Becky nattered. "I have to come."

The new issue of *Tiger Beat* with a big, promised Bon Jovi article and pictures was due out that very day, and if it wasn't on the magazine rack at the IGA, she was going to ask, because that only meant they hadn't restocked the magazine rack. And if not, she was going to seek out whoever was in charge of the IGA and make them. Oh, she hoped she would be fierce enough to fight for Bon Jovi when the time came.

She jammed her hand through the detaching sleeve lining of her amazing new muskrat coat, the wearing of which her mother seemed about to mention but didn't. Heels incompletely inserted into her snow boots, one fuzzy red mitten lost and not found, Little Becky pursued her mother, continuing to plead.

"Oh, all right, come," Becky said absently. "I don't care."

Good, it was always good when her mother said she didn't care, because she didn't approve of *Tiger Beat* (too teen-y) and Bon Jovi (too pretty). It was excellent her mother didn't care because Little Becky had long since figured out that with her parents caring about always meant caring against.

PHOEBE HAD ALREADY CALLED her supervisor at the hospital and resigned her position with far too many apologies. Mrs. Ludwig, whom

Phoebe appreciated she could now allow herself to dislike, had managed to convey at once that Phoebe was letting the side down badly, nevertheless, Mrs. Ludwig informed Phoebe, she could easily be replaced. The weekend admissions clerk had been asking for more hours. She had a new horse to support. She was horse mad, that one. She would marry a horse if she could.

"So, that's all right then," Phoebe said, after a pause.

"All right for some," Mrs. Ludwig answered back.

Now Phoebe had to decide what to pack and what to leave behind. A suitcase lay open across her mattress and a row of cartons salvaged from the Lowes' moving day last fall stood against the board wall of her small attic chamber. She clattered her work suits from the closet and shook them free of their hangers, her pink-and-black Chanel-look houndstooth check, her turquoise peplum style that she wore on Monday mornings because it was a cheerful color, her camel-hair outfit with chocolate braid running around a raised collar and flared cuffs which she knew was noticeably stylish for Towne but which might not be quite the thing in California.

Phoebe pitched the hangers into a box labeled, in Becky's hand, BATTERED WORTHLESS TIN CANDLESTICKS, to mislead the New York thieves who she knew would have been tempted by her sterling candelabrum had they but known. Phoebe folded her suits into her case. She wished she had sheets of rustling tissue paper to tuck between her garments for she had read that tissue-paper layering was the mark of truly superior packing and she very much wanted to report to her new life in Los Angeles as a person who would not be embarrassed, indeed, as someone who would be gratified, were the locks of her suitcase to spring open and its contents scattered and offered across the Arrivals concourse of LAX.

Oh, how she wanted her life to begin.

Arthur had told her to bring his bristling Jokes and Ideas files. She lifted them from their box and fitted them inside a carry-on bag. ("Don't check them through," Arthur had said. "People are interested.") She placed their yogurt-making machine inside the just-emptied Jokes and Ideas files box and pushed the box into a corner and then she sat down upon the mattress, her head in her hands.

"We're going places, Phoebe," Arthur had crowed over the telephone last night, but did it really feel that way to her? She hoped all this activity would not turn out to be mere displacement, because she had liked her job at the hospital. She liked this quiet corner of the world. She had been keeping an eye on the apartment-for-rent ads in the *Towne Crier,* lately. She even liked Arthur's people; they were coming round, she thought. Miss Hill had sat up till all hours last night to make sure she got her message to go to California, and Phoebe knew in her heart that hadn't been because Miss Lily was keen to see the last of her.

But if she and Arthur were going to end up, in a few months' time, back where they had started out, if they were going to come slinking back to Towne with their tails between their legs, forever after bound to rail, boringly indignant, against the excesses and insufficiencies and evils of California, Phoebe would just as soon not put herself through all these unsettling, in-between motions. Perhaps she and Arthur ought to have allowed their life to begin here, now, wherever they found themselves.

Still, it was very wrong of her to permit such doubts to accompany her packing, for those darkening doubts would secret themselves in the folds of her poly-silk blouses and slip among the knife-edge creases of her skirts and when she arrived in California she would shake those doubts loose and free to fly away and flourish in the spiritually unstable air of the place and make mischief all around and about Arthur. They would crouch down, one atop the other, and trip and tumble him from whatever fragile foothold he had found there.

Oh, don't think, Phoebe thought firmly.

Arthur told her to leave the cat behind. He seemed to feel his Aunt Lily had taken to the creature, and he had instructed Phoebe to sell the Jeep. Alden had offered to handle that detail for he fancied himself an automotive deal maker. He said he'd speak to Gum. (Who?) And she really had to get down to the hospital to clean out her desk and post a farewell message on the interoffice net and reserve the corner room on the Neonatal floor for Calliope which she might as well do now for the day was slipping away—noon, the bells tolled. She would finish her packing at the last minute when there wouldn't be time to linger too long over her doubts and decisions—these shoes?, this scarf?, was

Arthur really good enough? Besides, Arthur had told her not to bring anything except his files and her toothbrush and her retainer. He meant for her to buy everything new. The women in L.A. dressed different, he'd said. Her flight was booked for Sunday evening.

Phoebe ran down the attic stairs, the back stairs, the cellar stairs. The washing machine, which Phoebe had started earlier with her week's washing, churned and clumped and expelled the usual soapy wash of water through its flapping lid as it spun madly through the rinse cycle. Phoebe picked up the push broom and swished the little flood through the low doorway into the dirt-floored ell which was a mess of mud now, so much soapy water had been spilled of late. Miss Hill said there must be something wrong with the washing machine but she was keeping an eye on the situation. Miss Hill tended to believe that household appliances were sometimes capable of recovering on their own from whatever ailed them if no one made a fuss.

LILY COLLECTED HER library books from her bedroom nightstand, from the little-parlor trestle table, from a kitchen windowsill, and she made an attempt in Harvey's bedroom, for Harvey was light-fingered where her library books were concerned. She pushed open the door without knocking—it stood ajar—and she was startled by the presence of William, to whom, if she had not forgotten, she had not given any thought. William was not aware of Lily's brief intrusion as he leaned before Harvey's bureau, his hands grasping the bureau top's marble edge. He was facing the photographs of Harvey's lost wives, with his eyes shut and his lips moving (the mirror revealed him). The book Lily sought, an early Miss Read from Lily's reread list, lay splayed across the bureau top. Mr. Baskett quite obviously ought not to be disturbed. Indeed, in kindness, he ought not to be spied upon, such a funny pear-shaped man wearing wide-bottomed trousers and hardworking suspenders, seen at unfair disadvantage when not quite fully dressed for William was ever careful to present a particular view of himself to the world, and this was a distinctly private, even a prayerful moment for him. Perhaps, Lily speculated, he had contracted some fierce strain of religion in one of those Brueghel-canvas countries he frequented, where, she imagined, Sundays would pass slowly for a man without the clamor of a family or gutters to clean. Well, whatever strong notion gripped him, at least he had not made a nuisance of himself. And his travel bag was packed and set by the door, so that was all right.

Lily withdrew. The library would fine her three cents a day until Miss Read was returned, but that couldn't be helped, even though the late return would mark a blot on her record. She always brought her books back on time unless a blizzard interfered, in which case a reasonable period of amnesty was announced in the paper.

Ginger's bat's ears detected the zippering-up of Lily's storm coat. She flew down the stairway and encountered Lily by the coatrack, where Lily had been slowed by her search for her crocheted beret that had somehow slid down the sleeve of Harvey's old ulster overcoat, which he never wore but wouldn't donate to Goodwill. It was still too good for the likes of them.

"Lily, Lily, I need a ride to the village," Ginger pressed.

"I shan't be long," Lily said warily.

"Nor shall I," Ginger said airily, as she folded herself into Betsy's Persian lamb coat since her own coat, forlornly drooping from a spindle, was so damaged. She lowered a fuchsia triangle of chiffon scarf over her head and tied the ends loosely under her chin. She slid on a pair of very large and very dark glasses and plumped a cashmere scarf up and over the lower half of her face and swirled a chenille shawl around her shoulders, achieving, a glance in the glass of the front hall secretary desk assured her, her invisible-woman look.

"I'm not going to linger," Lily said.

"Nor am I," Ginger said, but she chose to be mysterious about her errand because it was such an inglorious one. She only meant to pick up some senna seeds at the Rexall.

BETSY AND ANDY COULD FIND no corner of the house in which to be fully alone. They were assailed by noise and buffeted by personalities. They felt tender to the touch. They needed to talk, endlessly and urgently. They wanted only to remain silent and together. Kisses welled. Their arms tended and withdrew.

They agreed to attempt to read. Andy had to get through *The Myth of Culture and Community*. Betsy had been assigned *Twelfth Night*. They sat, arranged at opposite ends of the big-parlor sofa. Betsy gazed at Andy and Andy underlined passages at random. A bar of sunlight found its way through a gap in the heavy, ill-drawn curtain and lay flat across the sofa cushions, linking them—Andy's denim knee and Betsy's corduroy lap. The sun bar burned between them like a fuse alight all its length.

One of Uncle Harvey's show tunes, one of the show tunes he sang on his night to wash the supper dishes, kept running through Betsy's head . . . "Sweetheart, they're suspecting things, people will say we're in . . ." No, Betsy didn't care to be happened upon exchanging show tunes or the like with Andy. She couldn't bear to have her private life endlessly commented upon by the family chorus.

"Let's get out of here," she said.

"All right," said Andy. "Where to?"

"I don't know. Anywhere at all."

"All right, we can go there."

STEFAN, WHO HAD GONE to ground on the little-parlor sofa, tentatively raised his pounding head as the noon bells cruelly struck. When he did not swoon dead away, he attempted to sit upright, and having sat up, carefully but not unsuccessfully, he endeavored to stand. He tottered as he gained his feet, but that was the very early American pine flooring of the room gone atilt, not he. The ceiling plane swooped, but that also was an architectural effect.

There's nothing more for me here, Stefan thought practically. Betsy was not a jolly girl, or if she was a jolly girl, she was being jolly with that other fellow from last night who, nevertheless, was such a sourputz to meet. Stefan shook his head, cautiously. This Towne was a confusing place.

THE DAY WAS RAW and gusts of snow sputtered down from the greyness above. Alden and the boys crowded into the truck cab. They had dragged the old plow blade from its barn stall and they had spent the last hour battering and banging the blade onto a mechanism attached to the front of the truck. Interior levers, stiffly manipulable after they oiled them, raised or lowered the blade and they were pretty sure there had to be some way to steer the blade to the left or the right, for otherwise they would only keep plowing themselves smack into snow mounds of their own making. Alden predicted they would figure it out as they went along.

Everyone quit the house at once. Car doors thudded, engines drummed on, exhaust fumes smoked and mixed, and they moved off down the driveway in a procession. At the bottom of the hill, Lily and Ginger turned right on the River Road, headed for the village. Stefan went right as specified by Betsy's explicit directions back to the highway, and Andy and Betsy took the left to get away from Stefan. Phoebe veered left, on her way to the hospital, and Becky and Little Becky were just behind her on their way to a cash machine. William desolately bore right, compelled to pass through Towne Village one final time for one fixing and memorial look. Alden and the boys, last in line, swerved suddenly into the woods where the remains of a loggers' ancient road angled back up through the trees. They lowered the plow blade and cut through the dense, compacted snow. So far so good. The disturbed snow did not mound but flew to either side.

The aerial surveillance plane observed the truck as it unexpectedly took off cross country and the spotter radioed for one of the pursuit cars to return to Alpha Base (Lily's place). Alden and the boys were easily overtaken. The plow had struck a great gnarled stump they had forgotten had been dragged into the middle of the old track to discourage the occasional incursions of off-road vehicles.

Alden had slammed into the steering wheel when the truck crashed and he was wondering if this was what it felt like to break one's sternum. "All right boys?" he asked between breaths. "Everyone okay?"

The top of Glover's head had thudded off the unpadded roof of the truck's cab. "No," he said. "I'm not all right."

Brooks bled from his mouth into the palm of his glove. "Rollins," he said. "Rollins, look at my tongue. I think it's been bit off."

But Rollins, who was sitting wedged in the well behind the driver's seat, had wrenched his back and he couldn't twist round to see. Instead, he observed that if Brooks had lost his tongue, he wouldn't be able to talk, like the guy in *Fists of Flame III* who had been de-tongued by Ninjas and thereafter communicated by mental telepathy and a voiceover narration of his deepest thoughts.

"Huh? Ninjas?" asked Glover, drifting in and out through hazy pain. "Oh Jesus," he said, "where?"

The pursuit truck, bucking over the ruts, pulled up behind them and two agents displaying drawn guns emerged and approached the stalled truck. They yanked open the doors, shouting so excitedly and inarticulately that Alden and the boys couldn't comprehend the precise nature of how they had offended, but they had come recently enough from New York that they did not demand or even wish to know further. They tumbled from the truck, demonstrations of their various injuries deferred for the moment except for Brooks's unstanchable bleeding. The gun-waving strangers lined them up alongside the truck bed and, slipping on rubber gloves, searched Alden and the boys who all carried in their back pockets Swiss Army knives which were confiscated. The four identical knives, the Mountaineer Edition, each engraved in flowing script with a name and a date, commemorated the day three years earlier when Alden and his boys had climbed Mt. Evans. They were going to want to get those knives back.

"Who are you people?" Alden asked. The detail of the protective gloves pulled on had clued him that this might be an official inquiry. "Procedurally, aren't you required to identify yourselves? Boys, make a note. We were ambushed by gun-bearing individuals on our own property who did not clearly and reassuringly identify themselves to us. Not, of course, that we don't wish to cooperate freely and openly to get to the bottom of this misunderstanding. But afterward, we'll review and assess this incident calmly." Alden asked himself, as he spoke, what the boys had done now.

"Yeah," said the boys. "Yeah, Dad, we will."

"You there," said one of the agents, not unkindly pointing to Brooks. "Pick up some snow and put it on your lip. But do it slow."

"S'not by s'lip. S'tongue," Brooks said.

"It's not his lip, it's his tongue," Rollins said.

"This isn't about our temporary and admittedly irregular truck registration?" Alden suddenly thought to mention.

TEARS, UNSTOPPABLE TEARS, blurred William's eyes. As he blinked and swiped them from his cheeks where they slipped and stung, he misread a rustic road sign and turned down Galahad Lane which presently ended in the bulb of a cul-de-sac. Uncertainly, hoping for a road, he nosed down the Larkins' wide, hot-topped driveway which curled through woods and ended before their hidden house. The Larkins were away in Florida, for they could never abide Towne in February. Had they been in residence, their beagle mix JoJo would have flown from his watching post on the breezeway and bitten William's tires and held him at bay in his car until Phil or Phyllis distracted JoJo with a Milkbone biscuit tossed onto the garden shed roof.

Although William knew nothing of the Larkins or their habits, he understood at once that the premises were deserted. A weather-battered brown-paper-wrapped and twine-tied parcel sat on the front doorstep where a delivery must have left it some days before when the regular UPS driver, who never lingered long because of JoJo's violence, had just flung the package and fled.

Careless of someone, thought William as he so often had had reason to think and to be grateful for. He parked beside a three-car garage, backing in beneath a canopy of romantically overhanging cone-laden larch boughs that put him in mind of his late holiday haunts in the Harz Mountains. He intended to pull himself together before going any further. He would chew a Diazepam and consult a local map and put Becky out of his mind, not of course forever, but for the next few weeks when he would have to keep his wits about him. One compartmentalized, one prioritized.

Slowly, a racket loudened, a mechanical rumble and rat-a-tat whirring filled his ears. He peered upward through his windshield and watched a low-flying helicopter with military markings skim over the treetops. The chopper was obviously searching, methodically, thoroughly, and he did not doubt it was searching for him. Villains would not run that thick and fast on the ground hereabouts.

Well, they couldn't see him. He might as well be sitting tight in some shadowy glade in Europe, although soon enough the authorities would search reported-to-be-empty residences. A known threat could be rendered a non-threat however, William reminded himself.

William let himself out of his car. He tried a garage door. It lifted. Good, there was no need for tiresome and telltale breaking and entering. A large and reliable Buick sat in the garage's middle bay. Its door was unlocked as well, but it was too much to expect the key to be in the ignition. Never mind. William searched a nearby tool bench where he found a hammer and a pair of rubber-handled pliers. He returned to the Buick and fitted himself in behind the wheel and cracked a portion of the steering column with the hammer and, reaching down, grinning and holding his breath, he scraped two plastic-covered wires down to the metal and twisted them together with the pliers. He had done this before, in theory. He heard a sputter. Oh, yes. His foot sought and depressed a gas pedal and he eased the car out into the driveway leaving it to run. He started his rental car and backed it neatly over the oil patch that had pooled beneath the long-parked Buick. He retrieved his grip from the trunk and wrenching the license plate from the back bumper, he tossed it into the trunk. He moved from tire to tire and twisted open the valves. Air escaped with expiring sighs and the tires sagged. Last, he unlatched and lifted the hood and convincingly, he thought, he laid an oily rag and a screwdriver fetched from the workbench left hopelessly on top of the radiator.

As he more calmly drove through Towne Village, circling twice round the snow-shrouded green, William decided to make his way to Newark Airport, fly to Seattle, and follow an out-of-season tourist-y trail to Victoria and beyond.

STEFAN GOT AWAY as well. He drove fast as a rabbit. He failed to observe stop signs. He passed slower traffic on double yellow lines. He popped in an ancient Blind Faith cassette and turned the player on so loud his car trembled and thudded as he bore down upon and overtook sedately traveling family sedans. Stefan was honked at, shouted after, and his bad example was brought up that night round several supper tables. Even so, the official car chasing him might have caught him had the decision not been made to recover the overflowing litter bag Stefan suddenly flung out through his cranked-down window when an old banana peel began to smell.

But everyone else had been stopped and driven back to the house by uncommunicative operatives. They were met at their own front door and escorted into the little parlor. They were not permitted to remove their coats and boots and scarves and hats. Ice and snow flecks melted from their outer garments onto the floorboards and carpets and upholstery in coins of shine and dark. Had the room been warmer, they might have steamed. They were refused a fire, however, lest they make a pyre of incriminating documents.

"I believe they want to preserve our persons as possible crime scenes," Alden supposed aloud. He had had a not uncordial chat with the man in charge. "This is all merely procedural."

"But it's not you, it's not us they want, surely," Andy said. "Any of us," he stressed. Andy was sure he would have known of some outstanding Hill family crime.

"No, not us. I've divined as much as that they want William," Alden said. "William, of all people, has done something. Evidently, he's been spying for the other side all the while he was wearing his American diplomat's hat."

"William," Ginger exclaimed. "Where is William?" she asked Becky. Becky shook her head.

"They seem to think we may have orchestrated his escape," Alden said.

"We couldn't orchestrate 'Happy Birthday,'" Ginger said sourly.

Glover snorted, then clutched his brow. He swayed and tipped onto the sofa.

"My arresting officer said I was being detained for my own safety and convenience," Phoebe said. "He's from Tennessee. I asked him. I could just place his voice."

"Oh, you had a nice one," Betsy said. "Ours, Andy's and mine, was like a robot."

"Ma's and mine's looked like Bill Cosby," Little Becky said. "But he wasn't funny at all."

"Hush," Becky said. "They may be monitoring our conversation."

"Cool," said Brooks, or Rollins.

"We need a lawyer," Ginger said. "What a shame Louis isn't here. What a shame Daddy isn't here," she said to Betsy. "How I wish Daddy were here."

"No, we're in some lawyerless limbo. I inquired first thing. We've fallen through a crack," Alden said.

Lily stood in the doorway and watched the comings and goings of the strangers in her house between the shoulders of two junior appearing agents installed as guards just outside the little-parlor door. Hot steel had entered Lily's soul. The white wire whorls of her hair crackled with electricity when she pulled off her crocheted hat and jammed it in her storm coat pocket. She turned. Her angry eyes flashed and met Alden's own, which fell before her stare. She said, "If Harvey were here, he would annihilate these people."

"Harvey!" exclaimed Ginger. "I only hope Dan Rather doesn't get ahold of this story. Harvey would die, either that or he'd kill someone. He'd probably prefer to kill somebody."

"Perhaps we should give Harvey a call," Alden allowed. "I don't doubt he could make a few calls of his own and straighten this out."

"Can't you call someone, Alden?" Becky asked. "Can't *you* make a few calls of your own?"

"I don't know. Shoot. The name that leaps to mind is William," Alden said. "I've always thought he'd be our point man, should the roof ever cave in."

"No outside calls at all permitted at present, sir," said one of the agents stationed outside the door.

"If you break that vase," Lily's voice carried across the set of broad, blocking shoulders, "if you break that vase, I'll write to President Bush. I assume he's your superior—oh, it's that Mr. Sessions, I shall write to him then. You, yes, you there, I'm talking to you. There's nothing inside that vase you're holding upside down. I don't hide things inside vases. Oh, right, very well, yes, I hide dead insects inside vases. I can't watch this."

"Maybe they'll let me call Captain Raven if I ask them," Glover spoke up.

"Yeah, we'll activate the bat signal," Rollins sniggered. Brooks punched him.

"No, I mean Captain Raven. He's in the Army. He's a real Army guy. He's my recruiting officer," Glover said. He rolled onto his elbow.

"Your what?" asked Becky.

"What I just said," Glover informed her. "And I'll tell you this, if Mr. Baskett screws my chances with the Army, I'm gonna be mega-pissed."

"Alden," Becky appealed helplessly.

"You're not joining any Army," Alden said. "Just get on the waiting list at a half-decent college and I'll make a few calls. That'll be the time to make a few calls."

"Yes, I am too joining the Army. I'm eighteen in six weeks," Glover said.

"Yes, well, when we're all released from federal custody I'll have a word with this Captain Raven," Alden said. "Have you signed anything?"

"Captain Raven?" asked Ginger. "That can't be his name. Whose army is it? Las Vegas's?"

"Now is not the time to spring bombshells," Becky said. "Another bombshell," she amended. "And no arguments. No more arguments."

"It's all educational now, in the Army. I put down for computers and airborne and I tested high for languages," Glover muttered. Brooks and Rollins, who didn't know what to think, sat on the rug and played listless gin rummy with sticky old Bicycle cards. Brooks's mouth began to bleed again. He swiped his tongue on his sleeve, and picked off lint.

Andy wondered if he were not swimming in particularly deep waters, since William was his uncle. He tried to quantify the degree of consanguinity—a second marriage complicated his calculations yet halved, he felt, his liability, William's and his common grume diluted. He supposed he should be taking notes on the Hills' reactions to this invasion of their home. The prevailing instinct seemed to be to call someone, which was not unreasonable. Andy himself wanted to place an urgent call, to his university, to his department head. Then again, he could just hear Professor Janacek's heavy voice, full sigh, inquiring, What now, Mr. Happening? What next? Smoke signals, semaphores, church bells, tocsins, jungle drums, proclaimers on horseback—humankind had long since made arrangements to express, loudly, their alarm. He and the Hills only reflected that tradition, Andy supposed.

Oh, but his heart yearned toward Betsy. He did not want to end up aged and loveless and alone and under indictment like his uncle. They had contrived to sit side by side upon the bench ottoman and Ginger had lowered herself onto the bench, as well, crowding Betsy and Andy together. Betsy leaned lightly into Andy. He allowed his arm to wrap as lightly around her shoulders. Ginger didn't notice as she chattered on, "I knew something was afoot last night. Earl and I were stopped by the police (well, just Eddie Eddy) and Earl must have learned what was going on, in his semiofficial capacity. No wonder he looked at me so strangely. No wonder the evening ended so abruptly. He won't call again, I'll tell you that."

Brooks and Rollins conferred quietly over the configurations of their card game. "They're looking everywhere in the house, these guys, the Feds," Rollins said to Brooks. "They'll be looking in our closet."

"Do you think they're gonna notice?"

"Oh yeah, they're gonna notice."

They were summoned individually for their private interviews in the big parlor. Becky was asked for first.

"Oh my," she said, rising, smoothing her coat skirt, rezipping her storm boots. She kissed Alden formally upon his offered cheek.

"Ma," bleated Little Becky who was beginning to think this was sort of like the French Revolution, which she had heard about in school last fall because Mrs. Roseby her history teacher said this was the French Revolution's birthday and the events in Paris and Versailles of 1789 carried Special Meaning Today which all of us must heed in 1989, although Little Becky had not particularly harkened to this Meaning as outlined in class. Now, of course, she wished she had.

Cadmus Stewart, the man in charge, with whom Alden believed he had formed a slight rapport earlier, could not have been more reassuring. He bade Becky remove her bulky outer garments as he apologized for the zealous strictures imposed by several of his younger associates. He invited Becky to regret yet to understand their youthful zealotry along with him. Becky's coat and boots and purse were whisked away, to be examined. She asked, for her feet were cold and her unshod state struck her as undignified and thus disadvantageous, "My shoes?" A comfortable pair, described by her, was fetched from the large collection of family shoes left in the front hall during boot season.

But Becky was not persuaded that Mr. Stewart was entirely on her side, for by then Becky had realized that she occupied a side of her own unsuspected by all. She had been thinking of what she would say, and not say, to defend her hidden position.

"My husband's aunt," she said austerely, "is an elderly lady. My husband has bruised his sternum, my eldest son has bumped his head, and my youngest boy has bitten his tongue."

Mr. Stewart said he quite understood and asked her to call him Cadmus.

The picture frame table had been cleared. The pictures were arranged in a staring, glaring gallery along the top of the glass-fronted bookcase. A psychological tactic, Becky thought warily, making her sit eye to eye across from Great-Aunt Julia, who had been a famously good American. She had always sat with her back to the ocean because some among the ocean's waves may have washed upon foreign shores. Aunt Julia had possessed and studied large, unscrolling oceanographic charts from which she had made her calculations. If Becky had to confess to anything, perhaps she would confess to Aunt Julia, who was only a relation by marriage. The picture frame table now bore folders, plastic envelopes, piles of papers. How swiftly, how dauntingly, the small army of searchers had assembled documents. Cadmus and Becky sat at the table. He tossed a gold-tone automatic pencil onto the maroon cloth covering as if surrendering his recording role. A dust puff mushroomed. He indicated the spot on his chin that corresponded to the Band-Aided patch on Becky's own.

"Has someone, did someone?" he asked gently.

"Did someone, has someone what?" Becky asked.

"Do that? To you?"

"Of course not, what a suggestion. Is that how your mind has been trained to work?" she asked interestedly. "No, I fell on the ice. We had a slight thaw the other day which glazed everything over after the refreeze."

Cadmus bowed his head and he lifted the tabs securing a manila paper envelope. He shook out a sky-blue envelope and several shapes of golden and fluttering foil. He slid the sky-blue envelope across the table to Becky. She saw that the letter was addressed to her and she withdrew the single sheet of paper within and began to read as Cadmus smoothed the table's cloth top which had ruched beneath his fingertip as he propelled the envelope.

"Oh dear," Becky said, tenting her hands above the single sheet of paper. Irresistibly, she glanced down and reread words between her loosely laced fingers. "But I never saw this. How did you come by it?"

"It was found stuffed under a sofa cushion."

"Under a sofa cushion alongside those candy wrappers? I see." A plausible sequence of events occurred to her.

"So, you do apprehend why I might have not unreasonably posited. . . ?" Cadmus indicated the spot on his chin that corresponded to the Band-Aided patch on Becky's own.

"Well," Becky said. She hoped Cadmus would continue to speak in this manner. The effort of decoding took most of the sting from the message. "I was unaware of any letter."

"But it's been opened. Was it misdirected?"

"Oh, my daughter who is also called Rebecca must have opened it in error and then thought I would mind. Such an unexceptional letter from an old family friend," Becky heard her own voice asserting.

Cadmus's eyebrows thought not.

"For example," Becky felt compelled to explain, "his use of 'carissima' is a *pun*. My maiden name was *Car*lisle." She hoped she didn't look too pleased with herself as she came up with that construction, and Cadmus seemed to credit her ingenuity if not her attribution.

"Besides, has it lately become a crime to receive such a silly letter?" Becky asked reasonably. Indeed, for one of the not so very many improper letters of her life to have been impounded by the federal authorities seemed harsh.

"No, no, of course not," Cadmus assured her. "But it is our belief, based upon the evidence of the letter, that you are someone in whom Mr. Baskett may have confided."

"Confided?"

"No?"

"And what exactly is there for William to confide?" Becky asked cautiously. "What has he—what do you imagine he's involved with?"

Cadmus told her more or less what William had told her last night.

"Oh, do you think?" Becky asked. "Really, I mean, do you think?" Becky decided that as the tired mother of four adolescents, she had learned very well how to emit meandering and vaporous pronouncements.

"And if we only knew how to find William, he would have the opportunity to explain himself," Cadmus said.

"But he was here. He's been here since yesterday afternoon. You should have talked to him then. I know you had agents in the area. The Neighborhood Watch reported seeing the man who detained my daughter and me. And how is it that you managed to round up the rest of us and not William, the very one you sought? I must say, I'm not terribly impressed."

"So, you've no idea where Mr. Baskett was headed from here?" Cadmus asked.

"No, William didn't say. Honestly not," she added, which she realized was an error—to highlight when she was being forthcoming. Besides, she supposed she could point Cadmus in a direction if she wanted to. A warm place, William had told her, they were to flee to a warm place, he and she together. Hot, or cold, Becky could have advised Cadmus as his hand hovered over a map of the world. But she had the feeling that once she started to confess to William's declaration of his enduring love and revealed his ambition to run away with her for forever after, she would find herself insisting and arguing and defending the extreme unlikeliness of such an avowal and such a desire on William's part.

Becky was released into the kitchen, which had been searched and cleared, Cadmus said. Someone, Becky saw, had pried the sifter top from the can of Ajax and combed through the contents with a silver dessert fork. She wondered what they thought they were looking for and just how they figured the mystery object could have been secreted inside a sealed cylinder. It occurred to her, then, that some among the swarming agents were not necessarily masterminds. Well, they didn't need to be rocket scientists to dismantle suspects' sink traps, did they? William would mind very much if he ever learned that the Varsity team had not been sent on the chase. She could picture him whiling away the watches of his exile penning edgy letters of complaint to those whom it ought to have concerned.

Mr. Cadmus Stewart had no idea who he was dealing with.

Perhaps poor Cadmus would like a cup of tea. Becky put the kettle on. She hoped he didn't take lemon because she was out of lemons, though whose fault was it that she'd been intercepted en route to the IGA intending to pick up six lemons for eighty-nine cents? Witness her shopping list, which they had confiscated. And what about supper tonight? She propped up the lid of the freezer. Its contents had been wrenched free of the ice shield that habitually gripped them and been prodded and replaced. Oh, all that lasagna from last fall, she'd forgotten. She didn't like to break into the freezer stores, but then again, if today didn't count as a freezer-stores emergency situation, whatever would? And was she obliged to offer the search party a meal? How could she manage? Even Lily didn't have chairs enough to seat a second-string swarm. A buffet might work, she decided, if they'd allow her into the dining room to iron a tablecloth and count out plates. She would have to see where the household stood in the liquor department. Most of the young men, and the young women too, looked like beer drinkers. Out-of-Towne Spirits delivered in Towne if one paid by credit card over the telephone. The town of Towne was dry (Hannah's had jumped through hoops to win a variance to serve liquor) so one had to maneuver around that not very convenient fact. Becky sighed, and she would not have been able to say whether she was relieved or not to find her unusual day so swiftly reverted to form.

THE FAMILY READILY TOOK to being questioned closely about their recent activities. Andy and his percontatorial ways had inured them to answering unusual questions, and these official queries were very much more to the point than Andy's most recent request to name their five most favorite nineteenth-century political novels in reverse order of preference. The family grasped that they stood accused, but knowing themselves to be entirely innocent, it seemed to them in their innocence that there could be no wrong answer, whatever the question might be. They were, in fact, keen to give their accounts, and no one would look at them askance for having no particular thoughts on the works of the late Lord Beaconsfield.

Ginger liked the looks of Cadmus Stewart. She knew at once that she could believe in him, for this was going to be her new touchstone, belief in a man. She had just settled on this tenet as she languished in the little parlor and reviewed how very close she had come to captivating William and entwining her fate so direly with his. This Cadmus had been sent from the State Department. Ginger had overheard two female agents as they discussed him, each attempting to claim the greater acquaintance with him, although neither knew him very well, Ginger could tell from the way they vamped. So, he had been sent from State, which was quite her favorite Department, Ginger maintained to herself now, its offices furnished with antique treasures and rugs and portraits pinched from the Smithsonian's collections and staffed by alternately donnish and dashing personnel. For one met the world at large with one's most gracious face turned outward. Ginger appreciated how that worked, as nations nodded each to each.

Cadmus was one of those dark-headed and keen-featured and hooded-eyed American men who seem to carry a drop of golden eagle blood in their veins, Ginger fancied. He had loosened his tie and shed his jacket. He did not wear a wedding ring, nor, for that matter, did Ginger. She guessed his hair was grown just long enough to wear scooped in a spikey tail on the weekends when he played some energetic and not to be readily guessed-at sport—archery, snooker, hurling—Ginger wasn't sure which diversion she would wish upon him, whichever enjoyed the best après atmosphere and surroundings, she decided.

She surrendered her fur coat to a functionary who was not prepared to receive such a weight. The coat spun and fainted onto the floorboards and Cadmus and Ginger both exclaimed.

"La," said Ginger, which was to be her new, all-purpose interjectory syllable, she instantly resolved. It struck such a Collette-ish note.

"La." Cadmus tasted the word that had just been on her tongue, it seemed to Ginger. They sat across from one another at the cleared-off picture frame table.

"How," Ginger asked sincerely, "can I help? Because I'm very anxious to help."

"Just a few odds and ends," Cadmus said. He shook an item from an envelope onto the tabletop. "They found this," he said.

"My checkbook? Where? Where was it?" Ginger wanted to know. "I can never lay my hands on . . ."

"The checkbook was discovered wedged on a ledge behind a metal plaque screwed into a wall in the upper hallway, which struck its discoverer as a strange and not accidental place for it to be concealed," Cadmus said. "Can you think of a reason?"

"Oh yes, my daughter hides the checkbook from me from time to time. She's so budget-minded." Ginger waved away budgets and reached for the checkbook.

"And we have noted regular deposits of three thousand dollars on the first of every month. We wondered, what is the source of those regular payments?"

"What?" Ginger asked. "What regular payments? To me? By whom?"

"If you could just explain so we can rule out . . ."

"Well," Ginger reflected. "My husband, my daughter's father, must have been sending money all along and they didn't tell me because they knew I'd rip up anything that came from him and send the shreds back to him by registered mail. Mark you, this is a tactic on his part. He means to establish a stipend, a pitiful stipend and argue that my unwitting acceptance constitutes an agreement I'll be forced to live with."

"I see," said Cadmus, not unsympathetically. "All of that is easily verifiable. But then, there was the further question of your disguise."

"My disguise?" Ginger asked, utterly confused. She craned and consulted the bull's-eye mirror hanging from the far wall. Her forefinger irresistibly tugged the pad of flesh beneath her jaw.

"Your appearance when your vehicle was stopped and you were detained was remarked upon. How wrapped and concealed you were beneath a hat, scarves, very dark glasses," Cadmus said.

"That is my style. La, what do you think, that William pays me three thousand dollars a month to drive through Towne incognito?" Ginger inquired. "To what end. I mean, what could *I* personally do to undermine the system on my little own?" she asked, as if genuinely seeking information.

"The theory strains credulity," Cadmus agreed, "but I'm bound to rule out all impossibilities and absurdities as presented."

"We'll be here all night, with this family," Ginger promised, smoothly she thought.

"Nearly through," Cadmus promised back. He opened a small notebook and turned to a marked page. "Certain writings were found in your bedroom, a quantity of pages, which drew attention . . ."

"My book?" Ginger asked. "You have been reading my book, the book I'm writing?" she asked alertly.

"Ah, it's a book, then?" Cadmus penciled a clarification upon the notebook page. "At any rate, the bulk of the manuscript has been speed-read and, let's see, are there further questions?" He consulted the notebook. "No, it says here the contents are of no interest. Whatsoever."

"Of no interest whatsoever?" Ginger asked him faintly and leaned back in her chair. "Oh," she spoke. "Oh," she repeated. She said it again, "Oh."

Then Cadmus routinely asked, "Have you overheard any significant telephone calls, been asked to deliver a package and if so, where is the package and to whom is it addressed? Did you observe Mr. Baskett in the act of shredding, burning, flushing, or concealing documents? Have you yourself been contacted by a representative of a foreign power or subversive organization on Mr. Baskett's behalf? Can you think of anything to say, any information however slight or peripheral which may exist in support of or refutation of any issue under discussion here?"

"No," said Ginger, "and may I have my checkbook?"

"Not at present, no," said Cadmus.

LITTLE BECKY CRIED too hard at the flourishing of the sky-blue envelope for Cadmus to make any sense of her answers. Becky rushed in from the kitchen wiping floury hands on her apron front and she accused him, "How could you make her cry?"

Little Becky gulped back a sob. "I didn't, I didn't—" she said.

"I know, I know, of course not," soothed her mother.

"Mean to," finished Little Becky.

CADMUS LISTENED COURTEOUSLY as Andy traced his precise consanguineous linkage to William. Whatever the relationship was, a second marriage had halved the cognate connection, Andy wished to make clear. But Cadmus happened to know, having read the transcripts of the surveillance tapes, that Baskett did not think very highly of his young relative's abilities and would never have trusted or relied upon him in the matter at hand.

BETSY WELCOMED the opportunity to discuss Stefan with an official representative of the U.S. government. Stefan, whose last name had never been offered, which was in itself highly suspicious, had harassed her on the train from Kansas and then he had hunted her down here and bothered her all over again. Wasn't there some sort of law restricting interstate alien hounding of citizens?, Betsy asked.

"Because I'm going to register to vote this June 14," Betsy said. "Which is my eighteenth birthday as well as Flag Day. I guess I'll have to go down to the Towne Town Hall, but I wish I could register at home, in Kansas. Towne still uses those paper ballots. Uncle Harvey says all the Democrat vote counters are issued secret eraser rings by the DNC. The stones are not sardonyx, they're Rubber-Rites . . ."

Cadmus brought her back to the subject of William.

"Well, you know, I *heard* Mr. Baskett's voice, but I never actually set eyes on him. This is, you will find, a house of doors and missed opportunities . . ."

Cadmus slid the checkbook across the tabletop.

"Oh darn. Has my mother been shown that checkbook? What did she say? Did she go all pale and quiet and disappointed? I have to hide it, otherwise she'll run out and buy a whole new wardrobe to fit her when she loses forty pounds, or she'll send a big flashy check to the Red Cross whenever she sees a picture of a dog stranded on a flooded rooftop. I suppose you had to tell her about my father's deposits? I wish you'd consulted me first. I wish you hadn't found my hiding place. You must be better than Mummy because, believe me, she's looked. But I know what your clue was. The crosshairs of the screws that keep the plaque on have gone shiny from being worked so often by the screwdriver. I'd noticed that myself and I was going to try to dullen them again with soap or something. Now I'll have to find another spot she can't find. But that was the best hiding place in the entire house," Betsy assured Cadmus.

Cadmus was rather overwhelmed by the pretty and emphatic girl who had preferred not to sit but stood in slight silhouette before the French door's fading light. She posed in first position, her neat head tilting toward him. As she veered from topic to topic, sent off on such expressive tangents by his least query, she changed her position. She stood on pointe, she sketched a constrained pas glissé, and Cadmus missed the brief flit of concern that darkened her face as, straining on her toes, she obliquely viewed the collection of artifacts spread across the picture frame table searching for a second item extracted from another place of concealment, less concerned by the necessity of owning to her small experiment in the grey arts than by the prospect of any redounding unmaking of her mischief.

"So," said Betsy, suddenly sunnier, "I'm sure you'll catch up with Mr. Baskett very soon. I can see nothing gets past you," she assured Cadmus.

"THEN HE WANTED to know where I slept last night since we dumped Stefan on my bed, where I'd found to sleep," Andy told Betsy. They sat on the first landing of the main stairway, a spot that seemed to commit them to being neither here nor there in the midst of the fray. They fell silent and drew up their legs as paired agents plodded up and down the stairs.

"He asked you that? And what did you tell him?" Betsy asked.

"I said I slept on the sofa there in the big parlor. I said that because I was staring right at it, finding it difficult to meet Cadmus's candid gaze at that moment," Andy said.

"But that sofa's so uncomfortable. It's like sitting on someone's skinny lap when you were little," Betsy objected.

"That's more or less what Cadmus pointed out and then I must have looked shifty because he suddenly wanted to know if I'd heard William prowling around downstairs last night, why I don't know, hiding something, maybe. I didn't answer very well. I said I slept through that part, when William wandered, which I don't know that he did, if he did, I was so profoundly asleep at the time," Andy said.

"With your head on that itchy blue roses needlepoint pillow? Under that mothbally afghan?" Betsy asked. "With the mantel clock tocking and bonging?"

"I know, I know, I'm not any good at dissembling," Andy admitted. "But didn't Cadmus ask you about your whereabouts last night?"

"No, no, I deflected his attention utterly elsewhere," Betsy said. "I did not give him the chance."

PHOEBE DID NOT DISAGREE with Cadmus that it might indeed appear rather odd to the preternaturally suspicious-minded that on today of all days she had quit her job on a moment's notice and commenced to pack her bags and abruptly announced she was taking off for California. But, Phoebe explained, Arthur had called, he had called for her to come, he had called for her to come at once. And furthermore, Phoebe said, in her experience when events happened, they tended to happen all at once. Didn't Cadmus believe in synchronicity? Because here they had all been trundling along for months now, dreary as dirt, and waiting, just waiting for the next big thing to begin.

"One year at home," Phoebe remembered, "everyone grew purple cleomes by their mailboxes, right out of the blue. One year, cleomes nowhere and the next everywhere. We marveled at the fact."

"Perhaps your local nurseryman had stocked cleomes?" Cadmus asked.

"No, there wasn't such a person thereabouts," Phoebe said.

"Seeds blown in on the wind?" Cadmus suggested. "A recommendation by an admired local gardener? Free samples? A rural route beautification project sponsored by the Post Office?"

"You see how hard you want to understand?" Phoebe asked. "And I'm here to tell you, there's nothing to explain, there's only your own good sense to recognize what's been handed you and to take it."

GLOVER FOUND HIMSELF strangely serene over the prospect of a thorough search of the house by a swarm of law enforcement professionals. He had, just lately, crushed his last dozen reds down to grit and dust beneath the bowl of a silver soup spoon, and he had fed the powder to the big plants on the big-parlor windowsill, digging it into their soil with the silver spoon. He had performed this ceremony on the day he decided the Army was for him, when he had sworn an oath to himself that he would, from that day forward, repudiate all dangerous living, even if it meant taking his family straight up and cold.

Cadmus had said he did not think Glover's future career in the military would be compromised by his parents' friend's activities, and he wished Glover well and he gave him his card which bore a splendid seal.

THEN BROOKS AND ROLLINS were read the riot act concerning the illegal reproduction and sale of copyrighted video material (Vide the FBI warning). Brooks nudged Rollins who was on the verge of protesting the confiscation of all their current stock. Their present inventory was low. This raid upon their enterprise could have been worse. They hung their heads in the accepted manifestation of shame too heavy to bear.

"Sir," said Rollins.

"Sir," said Brooks.

"Yes?" asked Cadmus.

Rollins and Brooks rocked from foot to foot. "Sir?" they asked, startled into unison.

Cadmus smiled. "Nothing sir," he said, "just sir, sir?"

Nevertheless, Cadmus advised them, the fine quality of their technical work had been admired and of particular note was the high standard they had achieved in their packaging—the well-selected stills extracted from film footage, the evocative typography, the pithy capsule reviews produced on a desktop publishing system they had modified for their needs. The cross-referenced client list that helped them target their marketing efforts—they knew their Horror fans, their Action devotees—also reflected an advanced aptitude for commerce.

"If only," Cadmus said, "you two could try to apply your many gifts less illicitly. By that I mean technology is changing and advancing so rapidly there are untold areas which are not yet regulated. If I were a pirate, if I were a pirate, which I'm not, I'd steer toward those fresh waters, that's what I'd do."

"Cool," said Brooks, or Rollins.

CADMUS AND ALDEN WALKED back and forth outside across the terrace stones. Cadmus smoked a pipe. A premium-tobacco haze swirled sweetly from a briar bowl. The day was greying down toward a night which promised to be a dark one. The local moon, the faraway stars, had failed to appear, Alden noticed as he looked for them between the tangled ramifications of the treetops.

The search of the house was winding down as well. Lights were winking out in successive windows marking the course of a last, considering walk-through from the third floor, to the second, to the first. Square incident cases that earlier had been carried into the house were now being carried out and hefted into the backs of several panel trucks. The agents, distinctly off-duty, removed their FBI team jackets and assumed their own, equally uniform, parkas. They all handled cigarettes. They produced them, offered them, flared matches, and lit them out in the open air. No one whom Alden knew smoked any longer. His circle had been scared clean by early-morning coughing jags and unsettling incidents of breathlessness on the squash court. Now, Alden had to wonder if these federal employees enjoyed access to some hush-hush government method of circumventing the awful printed warning on the side of the pack. For he had never, until that very day, truly apprehended the Centimanian reach and grasp and gathered fist of the U.S. government. Theretofore, he had believed that all those processed and graded functionaries laboring inside all those photogenic Washington buildings lining the parade routes toiled there to serve him. Some of them had, from time to time, written and enacted and implemented certain banking and securities legislation about which he had had reason to feel strongly. He rather enjoyed the quadrennial spectacle of electioneering. On the sole occasion the IRS tried to pick a bone with him, his cubicled auditor had slid a copy of his résumé across the desk to Alden beneath the cover of the Lowes' disputed 1981 federal tax return and Alden had made sure that the résumé found its way into the proper hands at his firm. The ex-IRS man had done very well there: indeed he had outlasted Alden's own tenure. Perhaps Alden could write a screenplay about him. *All About Steve*, he'd call it. Perhaps he'd pitch the idea to young Arthur out there in Hollywood.

Yes, the universe had lurched out of true. Tonight the moon, the stars, shone above other domains. The smallest of worms had turned. Strangers, not his divorcing adult sister, were ransacking his sock drawer. He was not free to go. If he were to walk—slithering, sliding in his haste—down the icy driveway ruts, he would be ordered to come back, and Alden was struck by how very strong was his impulse to walk away from all this, nearly as strong as had been his compulsion last year to make his swift and total getaway from the accumulating miseries of New York.

He traveled back and forth across the terrace stones twice to Cadmus's single passage. All this running away, Alden thought. He stopped in his tracks and Cadmus, unmindful in a swirl of smoke, head down, walked into him. They strolled on, in tandem.

"What doesn't make sense to me," Alden spoke, "is why William ever came here if you people were so hot on his heels. Of course, he may not have known you were so near. It would be very like William to overestimate his position. But now, here's a thought, had William long ago stashed necessary documents, say, a false passport or visas, in the New York apartment on one of his visits, inside a sofa cushion or taped to the bottom of a guest room bureau drawer? Which we moved quite unknowingly from New York to Towne, forcing him to come here. There's a theory. He came to retrieve, not to leave something."

"That's one theory," Cadmus agreed.

"And Becky would not have told you, but William has always been sweet on her. Although I can't see William jeopardizing his own well-being on the strength of staging some sentimental farewell. At any rate, she got an excellent dinner from him. He threw caution to the wind where the wine was concerned, Becky said. She was a little flushed herself when she came home," Alden said. "Becky has a palate."

"Nobody is looking for Mr. Baskett at the local diner," Cadmus agreed.

"And as it's William you want, I can't fathom how he managed to get away. I would never have called him an action figure. I've seen him stymied by a door latch," Alden said.

"The Williams of the world tend to have that kind of luck. I think it's their general experience of the regular rules being suspended for them which tips the balance in cases like this in the first place. If you always seem to win, you're more apt to play the game," Cadmus said.

"Until you lose," Alden remarked.

"I do have to clear up one question with you," Cadmus said. "A number of bankbooks, stock certificates, bonds, and statements were discovered hidden in a desk drawer up in the attic. The combined balance was very large."

"I wouldn't characterize those items as having been hidden. Kept private, certainly, but not hidden," Alden objected.

"Additional assets were found rolled inside an empty presentation Glenfiddich tin, and, for example, a not unsizable dividend check from Coca-Cola fell from between the pages of a bedside book on forestry management," Cadmus said.

"Marking my place. Look, I can't be bothered running to the bank with every little check. I let them accumulate," Alden said.

"I have to ask. Can you account for the origin of such—resources?" Cadmus asked.

"The terms of my severance from my late employer were favorable," Alden said.

"But the general impression, locally, has been that you were quite hard up," Cadmus said.

"Was that the impression? Have you been wandering around gathering impressions? Perhaps I meant to give that impression. I don't know.

I've been in such a state," Alden said. "Becky has been a brick," he declared.

"You know, my brother went through a similar experience," Cadmus said. "He was with Merrill Lynch and then, rather suddenly, he wasn't."

"What was his name?" asked Alden. "Did I know him?"

"Paisley Stewart. Paz?" said Cadmus.

"Of course, Paz. That was very wrong, what happened to him. What's he up to nowadays?"

"At first he retreated to his lodge in Montana. He was divorced by then. Well, that was part of his trouble. He tried to set himself up as a professional fly tier which absorbed him for a while. Then he started writing poetry about the river. That's when I went to see him and we agreed, he was ready to take up his place in the world again. In the meantime, an excellent opportunity had arisen in Bangkok through a combination of private enterprise and U.S. aid, an airline servicing some new tourist areas, and it's really taken off, as they say. As they also say, there was Paz one day tying flies and the next, he's . . ."

Alden smiled. "Bangkok," he repeated, consideringly. Lately, he realized, he had rather overlooked the rest of the great world.

"He's remarried, a brilliant woman from Myanmar. She's an economist," Cadmus mentioned.

"Good for Paz," said Alden.

"I can't offer you Asia," Cadmus said. "Actually, I'm not offering you anything, at the moment, but I can suggest, I can recommend, I'm in a position to notice and to suggest and to recommend."

Alden nodded in the dark, and uttered a note of assent.

"We have to think about the future," Cadmus said. "We have to take up the slack. There seems to be more future now than there formerly was. We have to decide what we're going to do about all those places and people who previously didn't figure, as far as we were concerned."

"We do have our work cut out for us," Alden agreed.

LILY MARKED HER PLACE in the library book she had been reading with a brown leaf twitched from the philodendron plant on the window-sill and stiffly, for she had been tensely sitting for hours now, she made her way from the little parlor. No one prevented her. The unpleasant young sentries had decamped on their own volition. They had observed Lily, alone, and left her to herself.

Lily frowned at the state of the front hall. The old Kazak runner had been taken up and put down again but in reversed position. The fraying edge was supposed to lie beneath the deacon's bench out of further harm's way, which any thoughtful person ought to have noticed and respected. The wide front door had been left flapping open, and from down in the cellar Lily could hear the furnace tremendously thumping, straining to heat half of North America. She would have to call the oil company to come out a week early to fill the tank and it was going to be inconvenient to pay them within ten days to qualify for her 2 percent early bird discount, a valued customer perquisite, because she had intended, that very afternoon, to write her big half-yearly household insurance check. Lily did not really have any money worries but she did have certain money arrangements which she did not believe she had to explain to anyone.

Family voices chattered from the kitchen, a precinct to be avoided, and there was activity in the dining room. She caught the snowy flourish of an unfurling tablecloth through the ajar door. Lily turned and no one prevented her from climbing the staircase. Betsy and Andy, met on the first landing, knew better than to attempt to say anything consoling, and Lily set her hand atop the round of Betsy's head as she passed, though not as if she had mistaken Betsy's head for a newel post finial. Lily was consoling Betsy.

In her bedroom, Lily's yoyo afghan had been refolded over the back of the wrong chair. On her bureau top, her silver-backed mirror lay with the reflecting side facing the ceiling which was, of course, bad luck. Agnes, who was not allowed on her bed, lay across the spread shedding the silvery needles of fur which spiked into the weave of its pattern and at which Lily plucked, some nights, as compulsively as an Alzheimer's patient worrying a coverlet. When she sat down heavily in her rocking chair, the cushion hit the small of her back at just the wrong spot. She practiced, then, what she was going to say when she had her say. Someone had handled all the Hydrox cookies she kept for her own consumption inside an old shortbread tin. She would not care for them now.

"Yes," she answered the eventual knock at her door.

Cadmus hesitated, and entered, announcing himself.

A single light burned dimly on the bedside table. The room seemed a shadowy warehouse, rug lapping over rug, stuffed chairs standing arm to arm, pictures (he peered) hanging from pictures. A more solid shadow arose and stalked across the bedclothes. The shadow leaped at him and thudded down an insolent inch from the tips of his shoes.

Miss Hill's pale hand floated out of the gloom and indicated a low hassock opposite her own rocking chair. Cadmus sat, more or less at Miss Hill's knee. He had been told she had taught grade school and he guessed she had not lost her touch.

He balanced his briefcase across his own knee. He asked, "May I?" and reached up and switched on a floor lamp. He unlatched his case and withdrew papers and arranged them. Miss Hill possessed the gift of stillness. Lamp glare glinted from her glasses lenses so he could not look her in the eye, not that he wished to. Miss Hill was not going to like what he had to tell her.

"I have," he said, "one or two matters to discuss with you."

Lily's white head inclined once, and she retrieved her current knitting exercise from the project bag slung from the arm of her chair. Positioned, her needles clicked along a beige sleeve, as it appeared to be, a not very well knit beige sleeve at which Lily did not look as she tweaked at yarn and gently waved the wands of her needles.

"There was a reason," Cadmus began, "that bells went off when Mr. Baskett wrote to your address and proposed his visit here, Miss Hill. Miss Hill, are you aware that you have an FBI file?"

"I?" asked Lily. "Certainly not." She was a Republican, even though she got awfully mad at them sometimes. She smiled thinly at Cadmus as if she meant to be as polite as possible, under the circumstances, about his attempted joke, but, truly, this had been a very long day for everyone.

"Did you once write to a Mr. Avalon at the Restport Retirement Home? Did you mention you owned weapons and subscribed to certain reactionary political theories and did you threaten him with a view to impressing those opinions upon him and the people in his care?" Cadmus asked, as he consulted a sheet of paper.

"For heaven's sake," Lily said.

"This Mr. Avalon, who is responsible for the safety and well-being of a number of elderly people residing at his facility was alarmed enough by the import of your letter to forward it to the Massachusetts Department of Social Services who, as a matter of policy, redirected the letter to the FBI and their domestic terrorism division, which processed the information. Your name was new to them. Local inquiries turned up nothing very irregular, nor could any links be forged between you and any known organization. But your case was noted and placed on a tertiary watch status and, in their view, this vigilance paid off when another subject under a more pressing course of surveillance, the suspect William Baskett, established contact with your address and that is, as I said, when the bells went off," Cadmus explained.

Lily had dropped her knitting. A hand had sought her running heart, a hand had caught the first rise of the sharp cry that broke across her lips as Cadmus revealed local inquiries had been made. *Who* had been approached by official strangers in Towne alluding mysteriously-maladroitly to the not-to-be-specified offense about which the consulted and intrigued mind could only posit crime after crime? Whose glance must Lily not care to meet from now on? To whom must she express off-putting unenlightenment should anyone be so unkind as to mention, and would she have to maintain a 3 × 5 card file to keep track of the stories she'd spun? Must she evermore turn, as old acquaintances hailed her a shade too eagerly on Front Street, and enact fascination with the overpriced mechanical banks and nested teacups ranged in Lydia Spofford's bow window? Then, would Marilyn Rathbone inveigle her onto the premises and "get" to the wounded Lily at last? Oh, what would people think, official inquiries being made in the village, and Hill family heirlooms going unquietly on sale for all to see as they stepped from the Post Office to Peddocks'?

"It is my opinion," Cadmus told Lily, "that you were not responsible for the contents of the letter. Having spent time with your family . . ."

"Well, my family," Lily forgot herself so far as to let fall then.

Chapter Six   # The Hills Take Wing

MISS HILL? Are you there?"
Lily was sitting at the kitchen table scoring the sides of nasturtium seeds with the point of a lobster pick. She gathered and dropped the nicked seeds into a pedestal-footed cut-glass dessert bowl half full of warm water spiked with a quarter teaspoon of her homemade plant food mixture which was known in her gardening circle as Stand Back! Stand Back! or you'd be knocked flat as your rose mallow and catmint and white dittany leaped from the earth and unloosed their leaves like boxers throwing punches, Lily's gardening circle said. Or a formula for a bomb, the FBI had tried to allege when they discovered her recipe, containing ammonia and Epsom salts and saltpeter, written for the sake of permanence in black paint across a board nailed above her potting bench. That charge had surfaced in the official report of the not-entire Incident for several interviews had had to be censored and, anyway, in the end, the Boston Bureau of the FBI had preferred to keep news of their botched raid quiet. The version that filtered out onto Main Street had sounded so unlikely people couldn't believe it however much some of them would have liked to, and based upon what they'd heard, there were even those who went out of their way not to wave at Eddie Eddy the next time they drove past him out on traffic detail.

Egged on by Penny Nicholls, who had returned from the chandelier-dismantling expedition full of pep and feeling empowered, Harvey, who was mad he'd missed all the uproar, traveled down to Washington and demanded to read the official record. Afterward, he met a Congressman pal for martinis at the Watergate (still a frisson at the mention, Watergate) and his pal had offered to ask a question on the House floor, to wit, why should an elderly and keenly patriotic veteran of the Second World War receive an utterly gratuitous documentary rebuke by a bureaucratic so-and-so laboring in his airless cubicle for the simple act of sketching a mustachio and fez and snarl of ragged chest hairs upon a newspaper photograph of Lloyd M. Bentsen, motivated to do so by the near-medical necessity of letting off steam? Not to speak of the complete non-necessity for that same hive-headed bureaucrat to insert further fresh remarks about the Hill family's apparent addiction to gambling after the litter of many hundreds of last Christmas's losing lottery scratch tickets had been uncovered stuffed inside an old shortbread tin for want of a better disposition of the things.

"And then they made a lot of other fresh remarks about young Arthur's comedy files but I informed them it was his patriotic duty in 1988 to come up with Dukakis jokes and even they had to concede that point."

"Oh Harvey, can't you just let it drop?" Lily asked him, but Harvey told her he had returned from Washington all fired up to research and to write his own report on the report.

"And do you have to keep your chandelier in that tremendous box in the middle of the dining room? I'm going to throw a sheet over it and use it as a sideboard," Lily had said.

"Miss Hill? Are you there?"

Lily heard Andy's call, his second call, but she did not reply because answering voices carried around corners and echoed off ceilings and seekers-after could become as misdirected as scientific maze mice by a not very helpfully offered, "I'm here." It did not occur to Lily to let Andy know, "I'm in the kitchen." One did not carry on conversations from room to room.

Lily slit the top of a third packet of nasturtium seeds and spilled the contents onto the tabletop. Seeds scattered. Deftly, she chased and corraled them with a licked fingertip.

"Miss Hill?" the voice more faintly inquired. Andy's search had moved upstairs.

Lily was not often to be found in the kitchen. The kitchen had long since become Becky's province, but Becky was now so busy elsewhere that Ginger had prepared dinner twice in the past week. First she had produced a tremendously effortful Thai banquet flavored with Nam Poc and lemongrass which she had gone out of her way to procure somewhere, and then she had created an ambitious coulibiac of salmon so substantial she had to convey it to the table on the dusted-off Thanksgiving turkey platter with branches of parsley obscuring the holiday motif. At the moment, Ginger had a flock of frozen quail thawing on the countertop, a sight—their drooping heads, their lifeless eyes staring through huge, translucent lids—that struck Lily as sad but interesting. Ginger claimed to know a way of preparing quail that was simple but devastating and, Lily had to admit to herself, she was looking forward to supper.

"Ah, Miss Hill, there you are." Andy had come down the back stairs. He bore a bouquet twisted in florists' wrapping in one hand and a square brown box tied with red-and-white-striped bakery string dangling from the other. The box held twenty-four mocha cakes packed in two tiers, one atop the other. He had been concerned about the bottom layer losing its jam dollops to the underside of the upper layer. He had asked for two separate boxes and been refused but reassured that this was how mocha cakes were always packed and no one else had ever raised the issue. But little cakes and bright flowers were not usual purchases for Andy. He had asked the florist how long the flowers would survive, in transit, out of water.

"Survive?" the florist had questioned him back. "It's no longer a matter of them surviving."

"Here you are, Miss Hill," Andy said. He held out the wrapped bundle.

"These aren't your jonquils," he added.

Lily's reaching hand stopped short.

"I mean, I didn't pick these flowers from your yard"—where jonquils nodded by the hundreds across the field and which he had not noticed before, for his mind had been trained on other matters. Indeed, only this morning had he risen from his desk and driven down to the village to the Stationery Stop to buy a binder to hold his completed thesis, and on happy impulse he had visited Blossom Thyme and Sweet Surrender and finally, spontaneously, Lydia Spofford Antiques as well. Downtown Towne ran, these days, to shoppes, and the meandering brick sidewalks tilted passers-by toward and then slid them on through the charming, renovated door fronts. Andy knew he would not miss

Towne when he went away, but he would never cease to marvel at the place.

"These jonquils came from a shop. I saw them in the window and I wanted to say thank you to you and to celebrate," Andy said.

"Yes, I appreciated at once these are a different kind," Lily said. "I don't really have kinds of jonquils. Mine are just the plain ones." She received the flowers. She tore free the paper and plunged the bunch upside down and then snapped them erect. This seemed to startle and revive the petals. "I'll find them a vase," said Lily.

Andy set his cake box on the countertop a distance away from some sparrows lying on their narrow backs in a sad puddle of their own melt. Sparrow juice they'll call it, he thought as he trailed Lily into the dining room. Had Miss Hill heard what he'd just said? Why are you thanking me?, she ought to have asked. What are we celebrating?, she ought to have wanted to know.

Lily had lowered herself to her knees to rummage through the crowded shelf of the cupboard underneath the china closet. She pulled out a pale yellow pitcher with daffodils molded in relief upon its side which had been pushed away to the back of the shelf since its last appearance last spring. Andy crouched beside Lily.

"This has always been the jonquil vase," Lily said, "but I can see this vase is too tall for your flowers, still, that can't be helped. You can't make stems longer. Well, actually you can. There's a heavy, clear glass disk punched with holes which you place in the bottom of a vase or bowl, they fit better in bowls, and you angle individual stems into individual holes and it boosts the flowers and holds them in place. They're called frogs, those glass disks, I suppose because they sit in the water so stilly, just as frogs do."

She paused to allow Andy to jot a note on a card outlining her etymological theorizing, but Andy seemed not to have appreciated her effort.

"This lusterware jug will do," Lily said. "There," she said, working the rounded base free and up and over a cluster of milk-glass bud vases, just cheap things bought in bulk for the guests' tables at someone's wedding reception years ago and, of course, held on to.

Lily was short of breath from reaching and talking all at once. Andy helped her to her feet, a hand cupping each elbow.

"Oh, I left the vase I wanted on the rug." Lily gazed down at the distant floor and Andy stooped and recovered it for her.

They returned to the kitchen. Andy sat at the table and spun the lazy Susan and wondered what on earth Lily was doing to those peculiar seeds which looked like shrunken walnuts. He sorted loose seeds according to size as Lily filled the vase with water and dropped in an aspirin tablet from the large aspirin bottle kept so availably on the countertop. She slit the ends of each jonquil stem with a steak knife so the stalks could more deeply drink.

"I bought mocha cakes as well," Andy said. "A Hill family favorite."

"Supper will be an occasion. Ginger is preparing quail."

"Is that what those are?" Andy asked. He supposed Harvey would have the family calling all the limp little birds Dan by the time they were nibbling at the slender drumsticks.

"But you said you meant to celebrate," Lily recalled. "Have we overlooked your birthday?"

"No, that was back in January."

"Then we did forget. I wish you'd told us. We would have . . ." But Lily didn't suppose it mattered, going into what they might have done for Andy on his day.

"I've finished my thesis, Miss Hill," Andy said. "I've just been out buying a binder."

"A binder," Lily repeated, for so many pages they required a containment system. She believed him.

"And so you see, here we are. I shall always be grateful for your cooperation and your kindness. I have to return to campus for a few days, and I have strong hopes of being given a fellowship and a teaching post." Andy had rehearsed a kind of summing-up speech in the car driving back to the house after performing his several significant errands. But he had been distracted from his work of mental composition as his car rounded the driveway curve and he beheld the bright and abobble heads of the jonquils which he wasn't convinced hadn't rared up and charged into aggressive bloom during the hour he was away. Thus, his valedictory remarks were not as polished as he had intended them to be. He had wished to make a gift of acknowledging Lily's gift to him.

Lily attended to Andy's description of his newly minted future as she bent over the flowers which, indeed, were arranging themselves. Jonquils are naturally upright and dignified entities; each just turned away from each. The effect was pleasing from every angle. Lily would be able to place the pitcher, cushioned upon a circlet of doily, at the center of a round table, on the dining room table, she thought, and she would say to all at supper tonight, These came from Andy, in celebration.

LATER THAT AFTERNOON, Lily walked down to the road to collect the mail from the box. The day was warm and she left her cardigan hanging from the hammock hook pounded into the trunk of the most massive of the copper beeches. This spring was unexceptional. A typically late, wet snow at which everyone nevertheless professed to be amazed had felled tree limbs and caused power outages. The river rose with the thaw and lapped over the River Road. Harvey's car had stalled out in a flooded low point and he stood like a radiant ornament upon his hood until a D.P.W. truck came along making waves and saved him, or saved his new Birkenstock sandals. If not for concern for them, he would have waded out on his own. But he had enjoyed the rescue episode and the impromptu tow and he gave the D.P.W. crew the bottle of Bombay gin which had been rolling around in his trunk thudding against his golf clubs every time he made a U-turn.

Lily's first purple crocus had pushed through the lawn on St. Patrick's Day. Birds, weaving their nests, availed themselves of her Christmas wreath ribbon and the yarn scraps and dryer lint clumps Lily spiked onto branches of privet hedge. The Larkins returned from the South and discovered their car had been exchanged for a lesser model so all that William Baskett business was briefly resurrected and hushed up again. On the nineteenth of April, as she did every year, Lily pulled on her rubber boots and tramped through the woods to the further swamp to find the first polliwogs, which were never not there, on the nineteenth, freshly hatched into the bell-clear water. They were so very small Lily had to crouch down upon the wet leaf mold resting her knees upon her opened hands. She looked and looked until she saw them, as black and as definite as commas on a contract.

The Ben Franklin store started stocking flats of seedlings out front on a board bench a month too early but Lily always fell for a few six-packs, not able to resist the petunia colors and the pansies' expressions. Then, overnight, her field was adrift with nodding daffodils. The lilacs would flower next, and then it would be the irises' turn. Lily had begun to work in her garden, kneeling on a square of newspaper and digging with a trowel in her perennial bed, turning up the seeds of weeds that needed only five seconds of sunlight to germinate, she had read. It was foolish of her, Lily knew, but now and then she allowed a trowelful of earth to sit in the sun as she slowly counted to five.

The trees were leafing out on schedule. Lily walked down her driveway beneath the fresh pale shade they were beginning to cast. Blackflies swirled around her head and sipped from the corners of her eyes. She skirted the deep driveway puddle which carried shards of sky and brightness and shades of green on its breeze-brushed surface. She walked through tender underbrush and startled a striped snake which unwound itself and rippled away. Try as she might, Lily could never wholly love a snake.

As she gained the road, a loaded flatbed truck from the lumberyard thundered past her, followed by a rig of churning cement. Lily fell back against her mailbox post buffeted by the after draft as she was put in mind of an invading army. And the big trucks always drove too fast for the River Road. Turtles were often crossing the pavement at this time of year, "calling" upon one another, as Lily had explained to Little Becky, who was, of course, old enough to be told the facts and, anyway, had immediately apprehended them on her own. The child had improved since Becky and Alden allowed her to work on Friday nights and Saturdays at Hannah's peeling Jerusalem artichokes and filling water carafes.

Lily wrenched open her rusted mailbox flap. She winnowed away a cloud of blackflies with her handful of catalogues and envelopes. Perhaps, thinking of improvements, she would buy a new mailbox. Hers had lost its red flag to the plow last winter and now, if she wished to leave a letter out for Linda the mailman to pick up as Linda was happy to do, Lily had to loop a notifying red rag around the latch. This could turn into a production should she forget the rag and have to return to the house to fetch it.

So many catalogues. Lily tucked them under her arm. She shuffled through letters—the Army for Glover, his university for Andy, her father for Betsy, foreign stamps for Alden. Oh good, the property tax bill had come at last. The town was so late with them this year that Lily had stopped by the Towne Offices to ask if her notice had been lost. Necessary paperwork had been known to fall into a well formed between the Treasurer's table and the Assessor's file cabinet. The Towne School Budget had gone missing for a week once, in 1962, and the teachers had chipped in and bought Rollie French who was Head of Selectmen then a millefleurs paperweight. But he took it with him when he retired from public life and so the Towne Town Hall paperwork was vulnerable once again to an open window or a heedless elbow. Lily had explained all this to Doreen Wilder, the Town Clerk, whom Lily had taught in second grade, a pleasant child. Doreen had apologized for Lily's having to come in and ask for her property tax bill. Doreen had been as nervous as if she were owning to a tardy homework assignment.

"Yes, your notice will be late. I'm so sorry, Miss Hill," Doreen said. "I'm very very sorry."

"I'm in no hurry to pay taxes," Lily said, smiling and rising to a little joke which Doreen had failed to appreciate but then, her former students could never quite accept that Lily might be human. Lily was used to grown adults with children of their own stopping short and standing up straighter and becoming mindful of their manners when she encountered them again out in the world at large. And yet, Lily always made a point of mentioning a positive memory of them—penmanship, musicality, a dodge-em game won, but to some it seemed she was holding them up against their former selves and finding them wanting because they had not written books in their perfect penmanship, they had not played their clarinet in a symphony orchestra.

Which was not necessarily a bad state of affairs, Lily told herself as she strolled up the driveway, sliding a finger against the sealed Towne envelope flap (she was curious as to the exact amount due) because, frankly, she no longer wished to be bothered and she had been so very much bothered of late. But all that might be about to change. The family seemed to have noticed it was spring again. They had looked up from their books and their reveries and viewed the greening countryside and flowering fields. They remembered that flowers had been arranged in a vase placed upon their bureau tops the evening they arrived, asking Lily if she would mind if they stayed for a while. Now, they were murmuring among themselves, Why, this is where we came in. They were looking for their coats and their purses. They were sliding about their feet, searching for their shoes.

Lily skirted the deep puddle and rounded the driveway curve and looked almost fondly upon her house. She would definitely hire a young man this summer to paint the shutters and the trim and possibly the barn, which was the sort of structure commonly said to be held together solely by its paint. She sat, then, upon the flat-topped granite boulder the glacier had thoughtfully dropped in a corner of the lawn at the end of the last Ice Age, and she extracted an oblong of thin paper from the envelope she had worried open.

Lily snatched off her eyeglasses and put them back on. She gazed up at the sky. Her eyes blurred and teared at the blank blue brightness, and, unseeingly, she stared at the slip of paper she clutched in her hand. Numbers swirled, forming and unforming, writhing and unreeling in mythical amounts pried from some dark and haunted book of worst reckonings and mystic numbers discovered and abandoned by Druids.

"Bad news?" Harvey's voice asked. "Had yourself a shock?"

Lily's color concerned him. She was pale as a poison mushroom cap and her posture had failed her—she was all hunched over in her misery as Harvey later told Penny, who said she really couldn't picture that.

Harvey set down his hedgeclippers and he had to pull the empty envelope from Lily's constricted fingers. He peered inside. Empty. Bah, he crumpled the envelope and threw it to the ground. He tugged at the thin paper slip Lily clung to. It tore in two. Harvey scowled at his half and he slowly eased the other half free. He fit the two pieces together and uttered a sound, a bitter laughing bark of fury and revelation. Oh, he knew what those brigands down in the village were up to.

"Lily," he brushed back a white cotton curl and spoke into her ear. "Lily, we won't let them get away with this. But you can't sit on a rock until the sun's gone down. Your bottom will get neuralgia from the cold."

And Lily pulled herself together for, otherwise, Harvey's comments would grow louder and ruder and he would draw a crowd. He would call on his new pocket telephone and summon a crowd just as he had summoned the D.P.W. to pluck him from his flooded car that day.

"What happened?" Lily asked Harvey. "When was the property reassessed at two and a half million dollars? It was three hundred and two thousand which was excessive enough, I thought."

"Well," said Harvey, frowning at some very small print. "They've put you down as having nineteen house lots—"

"But I don't," Lily waved her hand. "Do you see nineteen house lots, Harvey?"

"Something must have changed. Before, you were assessed as agricultural land, now, out of the blue, you're nineteen potential house lots. I thought we were landlocked here. I thought you weren't buildable anywhere. There's the railroad right-of-way on the north border, and you abut the state forest to the east, and the county owns the strip all along the River Road in case they need to widen it."

"Which they never will now since they put the highway exit ramp someplace else," Lily recalled.

"And Bing Fassner owns that little piece between you and the new development." Harvey snapped his fingers. "That's what happened. They must of whacked a road to Bing's land and written him up big for house lots. He must have been forced to sell. He never had beans to make soup with."

"He should have told me, he should have warned me," Lily said.

"Suspect he felt too bad about it," Harvey said. "But we'll have to find out who they are, who the developer is."

"Why? What does it matter?" Lily asked.

"Least we can do is cold shoulder them in the village," Harvey said. "Cross Front Street and look like we've smelled something should our paths threaten to cross."

"Small comfort, that. Then you'd be on the wrong side of Front Street," Lily said. "I mean, you're usually on your way to Peddocks' for coffee."

"That wasn't my point. My point was, they, whoever they are, must have shot a road through Bing's land straight to the edge of yours.

Because you're the big fish they're really after. They'll come to you, Lily. You're going to be courted," Harvey said. "Lily, you're going to receive an offer."

"But I don't want an offer," Lily said. "I want to be as I was. I managed, just well enough, as I was, but I can't manage that." She indicated the halves of the bill in Harvey's hand. "Not two and a half million dollars at the current tax rate, or at any rate."

"I probably can . . ." Harvey started to say.

Lily silenced him with a look.

"But I shouldn't have to," Harvey began again, "I can try to think of a way out of this."

"Do that, Harvey," Lily said. "Do that."

BETSY TOUCHED THE CHAIN around her neck and smiled across the dining room table at Andy. Alden and Becky, wearing pinstripe suits and polished shoes, slipped into their chairs and said they were sorry they were late but the traffic on Rte. 1 had been awful.

"How lovely," Becky said to mollify Ginger who, costumed as cook, her sleeves rolled up, a bandanna covering her excessively coiling and springing hair, bore down upon the dining room table leveling a sloshing platter at them all.

"What are those?" Brooks asked.

"They have heads," Rollins observed, not unfavorably.

"Do we get to eat the heads?" Glover asked.

"I know those. We serve those all the time at the restaurant," Little Becky said. "We sauté them, wrapped in grape leaves with grapes and shallots and port. They're excellent," she assured Ginger. "*Caille,* we call them," she informed her brothers, coming up with the name.

Andy, who had consented to join the family tonight because he no longer functioned as observer here, blinked several times when Little Becky named the main course.

"Always a treat," Penny Nicholls remarked generally. Penny was often at the house now. She and Harvey were refinishing the upright piano they had acquired on impulse at Gum Chew's place as part of the deal they'd struck when they returned Alden's hardly used used truck (Alden suddenly being too busy to negotiate on his own behalf). They had run the piano back to the house in the first and last run of the Loadstar and the strong boys had been enlisted to heft the piano from the truck bed to the barn where, as Harvey now remarked, he and Penny were about to commence having lessons with a pretty gal from Wenham who'd come to the house.

"Out in the barn," Harvey said, "where we won't bother anybody but the owls. Their nestlings are big enough to fend for themselves. I just saw one strangling a mouseling in its talons."

"Did you know baby horned owls are hatched a month ahead of other baby birds and small mammals so they'll be just big enough to prey upon the newer babies as they emerge later in the spring, Aunt Lily says," Betsy spoke up. She shook her head sorrowfully as the platter of quail floated by.

"Is this true, Lily?" Penny asked almost accusingly.

"What excellent parents," Ginger declared on behalf of the owls for Ginger knew herself to be an excellent parent as well. Betsy had heard in the affirmative from Wellesley College although Wellesley no longer seemed to be Betsy's heart's desire. She had been slow about filling in forms. She'd been not very interested in the roommate match-up questionnaire—musical preferences, carnivore or vegetarian, early bird or vampire? You answer the questions, Betsy told Ginger, you can like my roommate for me. "Because," Ginger said, "you have to give your child the best possible start in life."

"Yes, Mummy," Betsy was compelled to say before Ginger would unlock her eyes from Betsy's.

"Do we eat the quail's legs, Ma?" Brooks asked. "Right down to the feet?"

"Eat what's edible, boys," Becky said.

"There's a man in Japan who eats bicycles," Rollins said.

Alden judged the time had come to speak up on his own behalf. "We're official," he said. "We're signed and sealed and it's a done deal. Becky and I and Little Becky, as well, are headed for Czechoslovakia. We had our final meeting with the representatives from the World

Bank. I'm going to head a fledgling Bond department . . ." Cadmus had put the word out in appropriate channels. "And Becky has talked herself into her own position developing a prototype small business loan and development program aimed at the distaff side. She impressed them with her vision. Actually, I think they're only taking me on to get Becky."

"Why, Becky," Penny exclaimed. "Alden, too," she marveled. "But Becky," she exclaimed again.

"Czechoslovakia?" Little Becky asked. "I don't want to go there," she automatically objected.

"But we're going to live in a castle, dear," Becky said. "We've signed a lease."

"What about us?" Brooks asked. "We're not going to sucky Czechoslovakia. We'd rather go to . . ."

"The moon," Rollins supplied extravagantly.

"No, Czechoslovakia won't have you," Alden said. "You two are being sent to Uncle Hap in Colorado. During the week you'll be resident at the Range School, and Hap and Rosemary will take you on at the ranch on weekends. He needs a couple of extra hands."

"Isn't that a military school, Dad? Do we have to wear uniforms?" Brooks asked.

"Yes, we made certain. Stiff, starchy, itchy, proper uniforms."

"And then we have to do ranch stuff on Saturdays?" Brooks asked.

"Yes, and Uncle Hap will take you orienteering on Sundays," Alden said. "That's his new hobby, getting lost in the woods on Sundays."

"Cool," Glover said.

"What kind of castle?" Little Becky asked.

"I've seen a picture. It's stone and grey and there's a great front door studded with nailheads and we'll be in the city but on our own parkland with neighboring castles. Perhaps we'll have a neighboring prince, imagine, your very own age. Oh, you'll think you've stepped into a *My Bookhouse* illustration," Becky said.

"And nobody will know me," Little Becky said.

"They'll get to know you, dear," Becky said.

"Will they? Will they have to?" Little Becky asked.

"And there will be ample room for all of you to visit," Becky offered.

"We'll be there," Penny assured her. "Harvey and I plan to travel. We have a touch of the old wanderlust."

"I might sign on with your outfit myself," Harvey said to Alden. "I don't want to live in a castle, though. I may have just gotten rid of a drafty old pile. The Land Pirate says the real estate slump is over. Cross your fingers the inspection goes full steam ahead. But I can be your ear to the ground at this end. But no, you couldn't make me live in a castle again."

"You know, I think you're onto something, Harvey," Alden said. "In fact there are people you ought to see before they return to Prague. I'll set up a meeting."

"So, it sounds like it will be just you and me from now on, Lily," Ginger observed forlornly.

Lily counted the heads around the table. She placed going-away hats on them all—cowboy hats on Brooks and Rollins, caps and gowns on Betsy and Andy. Glover wore a smart General MacArthur cap, and Alden and the Beckys received Tyrolean hats, the closest Lily could come to a style from the part of the world they were bound for. Penny and Harvey sported travelers' topees. Ginger, who Lily suspected would also think of somewhere else to go, would find herself something stylish. Only Lily remained bareheaded. She could not come up with an emblematic hat for herself—her knit beret, her plastic rain hood, the felt cloche she maintained for church. For where was she to end up after her house was sold out from under her? She would not move to Florida where they wore billed caps composed of flattened Budweiser cans perforated and stitched into shape with orange yarn half-hitch loops.

"Lily?" Alden was asking her. "Lily, why the long face? You're not going to be sorry to see us go? Surely, you'll breathe a sigh of relief when you've got your own life back again?"

And then, although she had thought the matter was going to remain private between them, Harvey explained about the shocking reassessment. Penny, his prior confidante, whooped her analysis of the situation.

"But how absurd," Becky said. She stood and walked to Lily's place and hugged her.

Brooks and Rollins thought it was way cool Aunt Lily was so thumping rich until Glover enlightened them—not rich but owing.

"But I like it here," Little Becky said. "Even if I can't be here, I want here to be here."

"Yes, well we all feel like that, but other people have other ideas," Alden said.

"If only Louis were here," Ginger said. "Because taxes are his passion. He could get to the bottom of all this in an instant, I'm sure, the way his mind seizes on a tax problem. What a pity we can't consult Louis. If only he were here."

"But Daddy is going to come," Betsy spoke up. "Daddy has promised to come and he can help Aunt Lily while he's here, because—we weren't going to say yet, but Andy, can I tell them? Yes? Andy and I are going to be married. Look, I have a ring." She pulled a chain up from her T-shirt front. She unlatched the chain's clasp and slid free a ring. She slid it round her finger. "Look, an amethyst, an old old amethyst from Lydia Spofford's in a Tiffany box."

The ring was important. Andy hadn't known he and Betsy were meant to be married until the stone in its old gold setting glimmered at him from a bowfront display window on Front Street. He had placed his bouquet of jonquils and his carton of cakes and the bag containing his binder upon the wicker settee put out for sale on the sidewalk. He had been steered inside the shoppe as if by an unseen hand gently urging him on, perhaps the very ghost hand on which the ring had once been worn, which was why, Andy said, Betsy had to say yes.

"For a young lady?" Marilyn had asked Andy as he held the stone up to the light.

"For *the* young lady," Andy had said.

All eyes, the alike family eyes, moved from the very sweet ring to Ginger.

"Splendid," remarked Ginger. She sounded as if she had just been unhooked from an acid drip. Her mind cast backward for clues—how they had left the house apart and returned together, how often they had been come upon in the big parlor earnestly conferring, Betsy's recent cooling toward Wellesley, hushed footfalls heard late at night. Ginger added two and two together and she came up with those two. She pushed her chair back from the table as if she needed space to think. She hoisted her sleeves and straightened her bandanna, pulling it lower across her brow, searching all the while for the emotion she truly felt. Because what she felt was going to be her boon companion with whom she would be in constant consultation at least until all this getting married nonsense blew over.

"You're very young, dear," Becky reminded Betsy. "You're really very, very young. Even older people don't always know their own minds."

Ginger gazed at Becky. "Well, you know, the last U.S. census I read included a statistic for widows under the age of fifteen which, naturally, presumes even earlier marriages."

"Mummy," Betsy cried, starting on a hopeful and concluding on a hopeless note. "Andy is not going to die. I mean, not not ever but not soon, he isn't going to die."

"Oh, I've no doubt he's fit enough," Ginger drawled.

"Get up, Rollins," Harvey said. "You there, Andy boy, sit next to the girl."

"Huh?" Rollins asked.

"Sir?" Andy asked.

"Move."

The exchange was accomplished. Rollins rose and carried his dinner plate and milk glass and cutlery around to Andy's chair. Andy forgot his place setting, which was handed round to him. He slung his arm around Betsy's slight shoulders and he kissed her ring finger.

"That's nice," Penny said. She was relishing her supper although she really couldn't eat her quail because it still seemed to have a personality. She had hidden her portion beneath her potatoes dauphine which was a pity—she could have done justice to the potatoes dauphine. No, the aspect of supper Penny was relishing was all the news, except for Lily's problem, of course.

Becky spoke again. "I know it's none of my business, but Betsy, you must consider very carefully, and it's not solely a question of your youth."

Little Becky emitted a squeak, a pinched and escaping utterance of the general shrieking despair her mother's boresome interference engendered, for a newborn ambition had begun to form deep within Little Becky. This ambition had begun to burn as vitally as some strange and self-generating organ fired into existence in a theretofore unoccupied cavity below her last rib. Little Becky truly and only desired to become Betsy's bridesmaid. And then, when Little Becky met all the new people in Czechoslovakia, she would do so as a girl who had been a bridesmaid.

Ginger addressed Becky. "But as you very well know, the mean age for the onset of the human female's menses has dropped . . . for heaven's sake," Ginger interrupted herself. She leaned forward, her voice confidentially lowered, "Darling Betsy, if it's a *baby,* that happens all the time. It's appalling how easily it happens, but you don't have to go through with, with this marriage charade. You don't want to be a plump little bride holding an enormous, cascading bouquet of stephanotis in front of your stomach. Those bouquets might as well be casket sprays, to mourn the death of all of life's other possibilities you are forsaking."

"Perhaps we should all excuse ourselves," Alden said.

"No, stay. Andy bought a special dessert, especially," Betsy said. "And there isn't any baby," she hissed at Ginger.

"I swear not," said Andy.

"Oh, good," said Ginger. "I was prepared to be magnificent. I'd even have offered to raise the child as my own, but what would Daddy have said? What will Daddy say?"

"Daddy says fine. He says, go ahead. We called him."

"You called Daddy? First? Before coming to me? He blames me. Did he say he blames me?" Ginger asked.

"No, Daddy said fine, and who was he to tell me what to do with my life and I reminded him, you're my father, that's who you are," Betsy said.

"He's bitter," Ginger said.

"No, he's happy. He's very surprised but he's happy if I'm happy and I'm happy, Mummy, at last," Betsy said.

"When?" Lily asked. "When will the wedding be?"

"Soon?" guessed Betsy. "Later in June, early in July?"

"In summer," said Lily. Later in June or early in July there would be old roses for the altar and for the tables and she had dessert plates and punch cups enough for sixty guests if they wanted tea sandwiches and bowls of strawberries. Oh, but the cake lady Lily had always relied on had died. Who could make the cake? And late in June or early in July they could be outside. They could pitch a marquee in the field against the threat of rain although a marquee would be damp and dark in the rain and dim and roasting with all those trapped hornets bumping and batting against the roof if the day turned up sunny. Lily was not a fan of marquees. She'd rather trust in the weather but she knew the final decision was up to Betsy and Andy. However, if they wanted her advice, she could provide worthwhile counsel, having been through this sort of thing so very often, not as a direct participant, of course, but as a worker bee, so to speak. Notions of a particularly nice present for that nice girl Betsy were beginning to occur to Lily, assembling in a crystalline form belling like a goblet yet lit from within, a lamp, perhaps. Betsy ought to cherish something old and something Hill. And this very well might be our last occasion here, Lily thought. It would have to serve.

"Aunt Lily," Little Becky's voice loudly entreated, breaking off Lily's further thoughts. "Aunt Lily, say they can, say Betsy and Andy can."

"It's what we want," Betsy also appealed to Lily.

"Then get on with your plans," Harvey said. "Is there any coffee?" he asked Becky. He hadn't quite cottoned onto the change in the catering situation.

"There's French Roast from the Coffee Bazaar. I've ground my own beans and filtered them with spring water," said Ginger, rising. "Coffee all around?" she asked the table at large. "With top cream and raw sugar cubes."

"Spring water? We have our own private well water. What's she need to run out to buy commercial spring water for? For the pretty label?" Alden wondered. "We have wonderful water here."

"I know, honey," Penny said. "I can't get enough of the stuff."

"Lily," Becky said. "Please promise you'll come visit us in Prague. What about for Christmas? Think about next Christmas."

Lily smiled and did not say she had not yet finished thinking about last Christmas.

"I'm going to quiz your father on taxes myself," Harvey was saying to Betsy. "Because I'm going to have a capital gains issue when my house sells and my tax man has lost his acumen. Oh, he clings to his form like an old circus lion will roar at a whip but I ask you, where are his teeth? In a glass on the nightstand."

"Daddy will," Betsy promised vaguely. "Be happy to."

"And have you told your mother, Andy?" Becky asked.

"Oh yes. We called her as well, after we called Mr. Tuckerman, and she's wondering whether to send Uncle William an invitation since he obviously can't come, as if she even knew where to send it, so that's hardly an issue at the moment," Andy said.

"Perhaps you can send an announcement later," Becky suggested, and she realized that here, now, was a new link to William just forged. She would speak of him, from time to time, as her niece's by marriage uncle by marriage.

"But when are we going to Czechoslovakia because I have to tell Hannah, she really counts on me, she said so," Little Becky asked Alden who told her they would be leaving soon—they would just stay for the wedding and then they too must be off.

Brooks and Rollins were reminding themselves that Uncle Hap in Colorado was really kind of cool. He had his own ranch and his own cattle brand, which, admittedly, was only an H and a smiley face, but still, the brand sizzled when it hit the cow's flank.

"You're going to get away with it," Glover remarked across the table to Betsy.

"That's what I was thinking," Betsy answered, because Uncle Harvey had wanted his coffee and her mother had jumped up to show what a superior hostess she was to Aunt Becky and the subject had changed and the date of the big Czechoslovakia decampment was now pending on the wedding date and Uncle Harvey was counting on her father to come and straighten out his tax problem, and Aunt Lily too would need her father's help although Mrs. Nicholls was assuring Aunt Lily they would all get to the bottom of the outrageous tax reassessment because half of Senior Village had been forced to sell their homes and it was time to make a stand. And even Little Becky was smiling and looking forward to being the center of positive attention as a member of the wedding party. She would get to wear a new long dress and serious makeup and a veil.

ANDY HAD TO RETURN to campus for a spell to tie up loose ends and to ride the wave of the splash he had made for as far as it would take him from the place that had launched him. Betsy saw him off. She walked alongside the Bug as Andy chugged down the driveway lane, her arm lightly laid upon the sill of Andy's cranked-down window. Everything seemed to remind her of marching down an aisle. Even now, she practiced her sedate pacing, measuring her steps against the turn of the tires which demonstrated the fluidity to which she aspired. She was not going to be one of those brides who lolloped, whose veil jounced and flapped, who arrived at the altar rail six bars ahead of the concluding note of the organ voluntary. Such an awkward pause ensued, and the last days had made one long awkward pause between her announcement and the event which was still some weeks away.

"Good luck, Andy," Betsy said, on the verge of the River Road.

"I'll call you tonight."

"Okay."

They were not an excitable couple. The family did not have to forsake comfortable chairs and prime TV programs to give the young couple privacy. The pair had gotten over the swimmy and swoony stage of the initial enchantment rather swiftly. Having made sure of one another, they turned to making sure of the details.

"I have your lunch," Betsy added, her practical last word as she passed a paper bag through his open window. She had given him a white American cheese sandwich and red grapes as Andy found out beyond Sturbridge when he recognized he was hungry. A mayonnaise-coated lettuce leaf dropped from his loosely constructed sandwich onto his pants leg, and when he turned his brown paper lunch bag upside down to shake out a napkin, a single silver-wrapped Hershey's kiss fell into his lap.

Betsy, he reminded himself, was very, very young.

When he arrived later that afternoon, Andy knew he no longer fit on campus. As he strolled across the shaded and shadowed quadrangles, leafy branches of the surviving campus elms brushed the top of his head and the rise of his cheek (he was smiling). They had not done so, ever, in the past but now even the trees were telling him he had outgrown the place, gracefully and fondly expressing farewell with their cool and textured touch.

Andy did not run into anyone he knew. Faces were familiar but only as types—as if the campus had been recast while he was away, Andy thought.

He found Professor Janacek by chance in his tower office. The professor greeted Andy warmly and denied (although Andy had not accused) that he had been caught napping. Indeed, the professor said, he had been leaning back in his—endowed—swivel chair, eyes closed and hands clasped over his stomach recalling the salient features of Andy's most admirable thesis.

"Yes, I was thinking about you and 'The Penny Under the Rug,' " Professor Janacek said. "I think I shall let you get away with that title. I shall allow you to be evocative just this once and for the last time because I am pleased with you. Your work," he drew a breath and pronounced, "your work is the kind of work careers are based upon. That is, the kind of career I expect you expect to have. Mind you, you don't have a book yet, but you have an article, Andy. I have made calls on your behalf. You are being mentioned. I am seeing to it that you are being mentioned."

"Sir," Andy said, bowing his head as if for a knighting, and his eyes gazed up at the little Braque swirl suspended behind Professor Janacek's head. The Braque, which had always been there, had since been joined by a small Brancusi object. Andy didn't know what one was supposed to call these tiny, but precious, efforts, nevertheless, Andy rather thought he'd like to invest in Art for his own eventual office. He wondered how one got in on the ground floor of acquiring the next generation of Braque or Brancusi, something affordable and not large, something easily portable as he made his own way up from the ground floor. That is, as he and Betsy made their way. For a moment the thought flickered across his consciousness that Betsy was yet another prize acquired early and perspicaciously. He had intended to draw out old Janacek on the subject of Art, but, Andy decided, perhaps he would trust to his own eye and instinct. Then again, the Professor would enjoy being asked.

"Sir," Andy said. "I'm thinking of buying a small picture, as a wedding present to myself."

"AND THEN PROFESSOR JANACEK and Andy went out to eat, actually, I think they went out to drink. Professor Janacek is very excited about 'The Penny Under the Rug' which is all about the aftereffects of an FBI raid on an enclosed community, meaning us. Because Andy said Professor Janacek said that as one totalitarian society dies another one may be rising. That's us, I mean, that's America, which may be changing. Because with our external enemies all gone now, we, as members of the human species will create internal enemies, because societies need adversaries to help to define what their society is, or as is more often the case, to define what their society is not all about."

Betsy had just gotten off the kitchen telephone with Andy. Harvey had been listening in on her half of the conversation while he stood over a saucepan of cocoa warming on the stove top. Now, Betsy was filling him in on Andy's portion of their talk which somehow only seemed polite. Harvey listened and flicked the salt shaker over the saucepan before Betsy could prevent him.

"Janacek?" Harvey asked. "What is it with this family and Czechs?"

"And Andy is going to speak at a seminar on closed circuit TV, to a gathering of five hundred students located in three different states. Professor Janacek says Andy has carved out a niche, and besides being a teacher, Andy might possibly also have a sideline in consulting or being an expert witness at trials and such, you know, like when the government shoots innocent citizens when they are only exercising their constitutional rights or even when the government shoots not so innocent citizens when they're violating somebody else's constitutional rights. Because you can't go around killing people, even unpleasant people, at least not without a trial, even if you are the government," Betsy said.

"Especially if you're the U.S. government. Noblesse oblige and all that. We lead the world by our fine example," Harvey agreed. He dipped a fingertip into the saucepan and winced. Too hot. He added a splash of milk and a pinch of cocoa and poured his drink into his Foxy Grampa mug, a gag gift from Penny. "And just what did Andy conclude are the aftereffects of an FBI raid on an enclosed community such as ours?" Harvey asked. "I am curious, what are our symptoms?"

"Well, the potential symptoms are insomnia," Betsy said. "And anger, depression, loss of self-esteem, a feeling of powerlessness, a need for solitude, a need for companionship, and also very interestingly in certain cases there is identification with and capitulation to the intervening authority figure."

"Sorry I missed it," Harvey said tartly. "With that list, Andy'll be in on the kill at the civil trial when they're assessing the damages to a pack of mud-matted, high-smelling militiamen routed from their boondocks stronghold. Remind me to tell Andy where to start buying his suits. He'll want to come across as a corporate and not an academic hired gun. Juries won't pay out nearly so much on the say-so of leather elbow patches and tweeds you could scour this pot with." Harvey held up the scorched saucepan.

"Andy says he's applying for a grant to study a rural Christian survivalist community whose leader is in prison, and he'll have to buy a camouflage suit and a feedstore cap to blend in, he said," Betsy said.

"Well, your Uncle Alden won't be needing his Towne Co-Op cap very much longer," Harvey pointed out. "Andy can wear that if he really thinks he wants to spend his time with the likes of wilderness Christians. But when's the lad coming home?"

"He'll be back next week."

"WE ARE DROWNING in tulle," Ginger reported over the telephone. She had been burning up the wires between Towne and Kansas. The latest telephone bill, Scotch-taped to the refrigerator door, showed rows of Area Code 316 calls—ninety-seven minutes, one hundred and eighteen minutes, two hundred minutes—which Lily said she was going to question. The telephone company's adding machine must have overheated and began chattering out zeroes by the time it arrived at page five of the

Hills' formidable May AT&T bill. This June's bill was going to be an eyeful.

Ginger had established her gala wedding headquarters in the front hall. She shoved a kneehole desk beneath the stair rise and she wrestled a sturdy-armed captain's chair from the dining room. She presided there by the hour, working the telephone and consulting her stack of *Bride's Magazine* and *Modern Bride* and *Traditional Bride* and *Young Bride* and *Metropolitan Bride* and the *World of Brides.* She scrawled notes to herself—*There is a man in Reading who rents a horse-drawn and delightful carriage for the ride to and from the church. He bought the Cinderella Pumpkin Coach from Storyland's bankruptcy sale. Ask if the pumpkin is still orange and if so, can it be painted a mid-ripening gourd green instead to match our color scheme???* Becky picked up one such note and read it. Darker writing bled through from the other side. She turned over the sheet of paper and read, *Men base all of their assumptions about women upon one woman, whereas women don't base all of their assumptions about men upon one man.*

Oh, Ginger was recycling manuscript pages.

Ginger pushed pins into Lily's soft old plaster walls securing fabric swatches alongside pictures torn from magazines of table settings and honeymoon situations and samples of engraved invitations (which were not under any circumstances to be printed by Anna Webster's nephew, hadn't anyone heard about that young man and his habits?). The coatrack bore several mother-of-the-bride hats Ginger needed to study and to think about. She was creating her ensemble from the top down. My hat, as she explained to anyone who would still listen, will matter.

But it was not possible not to overhear Ginger's verbalizations. Her carrying voice sounded in every corner of the house. Her words welled up the stairs, resonated in the kitchen, and visited the parlors as she put tough questions about layer slippage and marzipan digestibility to cake designers. She la-la-tummed the music she meant to have for the agents of string quartets. She reacted to caterers' proposals with cries and happy little moans as she collected menus and estimates. "And now I must consult with my daughter," Ginger always explained before she rang off. But Betsy seemed to have ideas of her own which, nevertheless, she failed to impart to her mother. Ginger's aim now, was to hit upon Betsy's wishes by this scattershot method.

Ginger was at her very best when on the line with her old Kansas friends. She dialed. She identified herself. She held the exclaiming receiver extra inches from her ear. She waited until an eager and expectant silence fell into which she dropped her bombshell.

"Yes, my little Betsy. Though of course she's no longer so little."

Ginger ignored any tentative attempts to question her concerning the tiresome old business that had caused her to go away the previous summer. Instead, she delivered a happy and constructive speech.

She presented herself as a Henry James–style mother who had led a lovely daughter East, to the Old World, and guided her toward a brilliant marriage to a distinguished scholar of the human condition. Her real friends let her get away with that. Her other friends reminded her that the Gilded Age was over and said they were pretty sure there weren't many happy endings to be found in Henry James although, admittedly, it could be hard to get through to the end with him but you felt you knew what was coming.

And Ginger had been told half a dozen times that Oscar had up and married one of his office girls, which she had known all along, she said. She had practically ordered him to settle down with someone uncontroversial and get on with his life.

"You must come to the wedding," Ginger would say after the pause. "We're counting on your coming. Don't say no just yet. You must come."

It would have made so much more sense to hold the wedding in Kansas, but Betsy was indifferent now and Ginger was adamant. Kansas was coming to her, Ginger said. Lily hoped Ginger understood there wasn't room for half of Kansas to stay at the house, however, she had heard that the By-Way Motor Hotel had quieted down since they lost their liquor license after last winter's near-fatal shooting. The Eastern Star was going to hold their annual meeting in the hotel's Heritage Room now that the Congo basement was off-limits because they'd just found out they had asbestos ceiling tiles, so that was a positive endorsement.

Betsy let Ginger know the wedding date, which proved to mark to the year and a day their flight from home. Ginger suspected Betsy had rigged that fairy-tale timing but in truth, Betsy had jumped at the first available Saturday on Mr. Penworthy's July calendar. Marriage came into season as surely as the lilacs and the apple blossoms, Mr. Penworthy had said, studying the entries in his datebook, his fingers tapping his private opinion of the inked-in matches-to-be. His remark had worried Betsy. Did he think she and Andy were just being susceptible to some sweetness in the air? She and Andy were required to meet with him in the rectory study for serious talks about marriage. Andy and Mr. Penworthy argued theoretically and happily over the origins of the leviratic law one week, and the decline of hetaerism among the ancient Hellenes the next. For her part, Betsy was quite certain she knew what she was getting herself into. Mrs. Penworthy, who said hello when Betsy and Andy entered and good-bye when they left, seemed tired but content although one day she took Betsy aside and told her that when she was eighteen she had wanted to marry Lindsey Buckingham.

Somehow, it was decided the reception was to be held outside in the field, which would have to be mown. Gee Weeden knew a man who would oblige for the hay. Lily said there would be roses, masses of Constance Spry tumbling along the wall on the far side of the meadow (and which might a year hence be torn up by their roots to make way for a hangar-sized house with a five-car garage). Mrs. Snowdon unexpectedly offered to write the invitations. She revealed that she used to create beautiful calligraphy menus and *cartes de place* for official affairs when she and Mr. Snowdon lived in Philadelphia and were first making their way in the world. Hannah offered to cook for the reception. She had started out as a caterer and she liked to keep her hand in, she said.

One afternoon Betsy slipped away on her own and bought a dress at the vintage clothing shop where Ginevra Platt-Willey had said she always shopped for costumes. Betsy found a white lawn shirt dress with a tucked and pleated bodice and a long, bell-shaped skirt. Betsy brought the dress home in an authentic Balenciaga box. Ginger loved the box and she hated the dress.

"Darling, it's so draggly. And there's that rust stain on the skirt. Oh, God, if it is rust," she said.

"They said at the shop I could pin a sprig of ferns and a flower or two over the spot. It's only a little spot. You have to be looking to criticize to even find it," said Betsy. "Maybe I'll pin ferns and flowers all over the dress."

"You'll look like some sort of retro hippie wanna-be," Ginger said. "And please don't tell me you're planning to wear a circlet of flowers in your hair with ribbon streamers flowing down your back. Oh, Betsy, don't. I have a line on some precious and old Alençon lace if you're really after a vintage look. And at least let me hem that dress. You'll step out the bottom, it's so long. You'll fall flat on your face and you'll crush your bouquet and then I won't be able to have it dried and saved for you to keep forever in a presentation case. I have a brochure. The effect is charming."

"No, Mummy," Betsy said. "I won't let you hem my dress. You'll do something on purpose to ruin it and then you'll try to tell me your hand went into an uncontrollable spasm and your scissors ran amok . . ."

"If you're trying to hurt my feelings, you're succeeding splendidly," Ginger told her.

"I'm not trying to hurt your feelings. I'm just not trying *not* to anymore, and if you have noticed a difference lately, Mummy, that's what you've noticed," Betsy said.

Alden, who happened to overhear the exchange, told Becky he was beginning to wonder if Andy knew what he was letting himself in for. Perhaps the apple didn't fall very far from the tree, after all.

IN THE MIDST OF these other considerations, Lily heard one day from a representative of TowneVest Corporation and she agreed to receive a Miss Tina Angler the following afternoon for a little chat, as the representative characterized the proposed meeting.

"A very little chat," Lily restated firmly.

Harvey, when consulted, advised that the brief interview take place outside on the terrace. Otherwise, this Miss Angler would craftily ask to use the lavatory and take advantage of Lily's old ears and naïvely trusting nature to prowl and poke in every corner of the house on her way to and from the facilities, ferreting for information to use against Lily in any entirely mythical negotiations to come. For instance, Miss Angler would find the mineral-encrusted buckets stationed at the ready beneath the usual roof leaks, which buckets of course might be gathered and hidden in anticipation of such a presumptuous house crawl, but then they'd have to hustle and realign the pails within the ringed ridges they'd made in the rugs before the next downpour threatened and likely they'd forget. They all had so much else on their minds at the moment which was why the buckets had been left out in the first place after the last storm.

"But she can still ask to visit the lav, even when she's outside, and I'd be obliged to let her in," Lily had said. "It would be unpleasant not to."

"No. Give her nothing to drink, if Miss Angler is so disposed to piddle like a puppy," Harvey said. "Keep her strictly outside with nothing on offer even though it's the sherry hour you've committed us to seeing her. Oh yes, I'll be there. You want me there, don't you?"

Lily said she believed she did.

When Miss Angler arrived and approached Harvey and Lily who stuck to the terrace stones as if to a beachhead, she handed Lily a business card at which Lily glanced. Oh dear, Tina was a Teena, which Lily would rather not have known, although Miss Angler's parents were the ones to blame. The last year she taught school, Lily had had a Hidey in class. Lily had known then, the time had come for her to retreat into private life.

"Are you with us, Lily?" Harvey had to ask her.

There were twenty-eight chairs scattered across the terrace. All of the wicker, wrought iron, Adirondack, metal tubing, and plastic-mesh-webbing chaises and chairs had been dragged from the barn and were being hosed down and air-cured and patched up, after a fashion, anticipating the crowd that would drop by after the wedding service.

"You folks must like to sit a lot," observed Miss Angler when told to sit anywhere. She opted for something high-backed in rattan.

Neither Lily nor Harvey explained there was to be a celebration, and they remained standing. Harvey paced, and Lily plucked spent blossoms from the petunias planted in one of the terrace urns.

"Such a big old place," Miss Angler said, rearing back her head and staring up at the side facade of the house. "You must just rattle around in there."

"Such an odd phrase, rattling around," Harvey said, considering it.

"Why is the term usually applied to old people living in large houses? Are you referencing our old bones, Miss Angler? Are you anticipating the not too distant future when I and my sister will be naught but skeleton and skull?"

"Like seeds in a husk," Lily spoke up. "We're not really old skeletons. Miss Angler thinks we're like dried-up seeds in a husk."

"There, now we've rattled Miss Angler," Harvey warned Lily. "Nice pink plump Miss Angler."

After a pause, and after a question put by Harvey, Miss Angler would not name the persons operating behind TowneVest Corp. They wished to remain in the background. In any event, Miss Angler said, you will not know them.

"I have a wide acquaintance," Harvey said.

"What are, what would their plans be?" Lily asked, if only to confirm whether she had pictured the worst.

"We intend to establish a community of luxury homes, each nestled on its own manageable-sized section of grounds because these overly large properties," Miss Angler waved toward the horizon, "are so impractical in these busy times, fooling with gardens and suchlike."

Lily frowned.

"People desire estate-lettes nowadays?" Harvey suggested.

"Yes, yes they do," Miss Angler agreed. "And this planned, gated community of luxury estate-lettes," Harvey was awarded a little smile of acknowledgment, "will be called, in your family's honor, Hillcrest Farms."

Which Lily didn't think sounded quite right. "Isn't that the name of a breakfast sausage company?" she asked.

"You're thinking of Hillshire Farms, Lily," Harvey came up with the name after a moment during which they all considered.

"That's it, Hillshire. But the names are uncomfortably close," Lily said.

"Yes, it summons up a miasma of greasy fat frying hanging over the place. I mean, there would be an odor. The man will ask you where to deliver your mulch and you won't like to say," Harvey said. "No, your idea sounds unacceptable," he told Miss Angler. "We can't let folks new to Towne come to the awful realization after the fact what they've boughten themselves in for."

Miss Angler, who had only been cozying up to the old folks—she had yet to mention the proposed Lily Lane, though no doubt the old woman would object that that sounded too much like one of Superman's girl-friends if given the chance—decided the time had come to get to the point.

"But surely you'll want to hear the range of a possible offer," she said. "I am authorized today, not to offer, but to begin to raise the range of a possibly forthcoming offer."

"Oh, I don't think that sounds very meaningful to us, do you, Lily?" Harvey said. "If you're not really authorized, and our old ears might mishear you. We could all end up in court."

Lily said she'd just as soon avoid a big trial.

"Pretty enough gal," Harvey remarked before Miss Angler was quite out of range, "only it makes you suspect their big guns must be pretty small caliber if she's their opening salvo."

But Lily didn't think there would need to be all that much of a battle to defeat her, in the end.

"JUST WAIT UNTIL Daddy gets here," had become Ginger's dire prom-ise to Betsy for the last weeks even as Betsy held her ground and Gin-ger retreated. No, said Betsy, to the videographer-cum-director who would "stage" the wedding, "act" by precious "act," and, Yes, said Betsy, Ginevra Platt-Willey was too going to sing "You Are the Wind Beneath My Wings" before the vows, and Ginger could wear her mother-of-pearl, mother-of-the-bride commemorative earplugs if she did not wish to hear.

Louis, hurried along at the very end by a suddenly clear notion of a practical tack he could at last take, had caught an earlier and more direct flight from Wichita and he arrived ahead of schedule at Logan. His rental vehicle was waiting for him at the curb. He had requested a van, for he was sure he would be required to fetch and to carry in the coming days and, indeed, he had decided it would be best under the circumstances to be able to absent himself from the house on useful, wedding-generated errands. There would be cases of wine and masses of flowers and Andy Happening's flying-in-from-Florida mother to be collected. Louis, thus far unconsulted on the details, could only imagine the most basic components of the celebration to come but he did not doubt Ginger would greet him at the door waving an annotated and important To-Do list, one which he would pretend to read while Ginger affected to point out the most drastically imperative errands for him to attend to first. Their shoulders would bump, their hands would touch across a scrawled word or two of wedding bother, he would lace a mutually steadying arm around her waist, for they would both be uncertain. Louis could only imagine the most basic components of a reconciliation.

Pretty countryside, he thought as he turned off the highway, variously green, hilly, rocky, cultivated, quaint. Sitting uncommonly high in the van's boosted driver's seat, he enjoyed an expanded view. The local rocks had been arranged into walls, gardens bloomed in soft, coordinating colors, specimen trees timed to flower in sequence were flowering in sequence. Within the village limits, he remembered having been told, the utility lines had been buried so that movie companies might set up and film historical dramas among Towne's historical roads and residences, as dirt was dumped and raked over pavement and satellite dishes were wreathed in foliage. No film company had come as yet to take advantage, but Louis guessed Towne entertained dramas enough of its own in the meanwhile. He himself was on his way to take up his part in what he hoped would be the final scene or two of his wife's latest, and he hoped last, theatrics.

Louis had not been back to Towne since he attended the funeral of his mother-in-law. On that occasion, he recalled, he had been sent to meet a train to collect some cousins, and later he had been asked to run out to fetch ice cream. He had jumped at those opportunities to absent himself from the house on that visit as well. Hills in mourning had been snappish and brusque with one another. They had quarreled over the time the cousins' train was due in at Hamilton station, and they could not agree upon the precise year in which some pointlessly significant badminton tournament had occurred. No one mentioned the dead, departed one. It was as if Olive had somehow discredited herself and embarrassed the rest of them by dying just a bit too sadly and too soon upstairs in one of Lily's bedrooms while the fiction had been maintained all along that she was just there visiting while her place in Florida was being painted. Too sadly and too soon, not unlike his daughter's precipitous marriage, Louis thought.

Landmarks Betsy had mentioned when reminding him of the route through Towne were appearing—the flat, greeny-black meandering river, a mailbox painted like the original American flag, the pine tree that tilted and dropped needles over the road that collected like a rough carpet there. Betsy had said she would tie a balloon to Lily's forsaken-looking mailbox and there one was, a silver bright Mylar globe plumped with helium, tethered and revolving in the slight breeze rising off the river. WELCOME, it read. WELCOME, it read.

But he had arrived before the time he told them to expect him and there was no one about to receive him. He called several names, Ginger? Betsy? Miss Lily? Ginger?, and he let himself in through the front door. He set his two snapped-shut suitcases down at the foot of the gracefully ascending staircase and he wandered through the lower rooms, which, though not very familiar to him, nevertheless struck him as not being in their usual states. Preparations were in evidence everywhere. Piles of net fabric, a cluster of white bud vases, rolls of ribbons, pieces of fabric were left lying about in arrangements which obviously ought not to be disturbed. In the larger of the sitting rooms a tabletop was beginning to be heaped with opened and unopened wedding gifts. Louis leaned and looked at tags—the table wobbled beneath his weight, one shorter leg imperfectly propped by a little brown bound volume too slight to be anything but poetry.

LILY WAS OUT in the barn sanding ancient bird droppings from the top of the old cedar picnic table that was going to hold the best cut-crystal bowl and punch cups at the reception. The table would, of course, be covered with a cloth—with linen or damask or perhaps with fresh young pink-and-white gingham check if they bought the fabric and cut and hemmed it in time—but it wouldn't be very nice to know what lay just underneath the covering. And what if the wind flapped up a corner of the tablecloth and revealed the bird spots and spatters beneath? At an everyday picnic, Lily would anchor the four corners of a tablecloth with rocks but that was too casual a solution for a wedding. Still, they could collect the rocks beforehand and wrap them in pink gingham check (if they were going to go with the gingham check) and tie them with pink grosgrain ribbon. Only then, the guests might mistake the scattered parcels for favors, and open them with every expectation of finding Jordan Almonds and Buttermints and a matchbook embossed with the day's date and the entwining initials A&B. (The effect was charming, Ginger said.)

Lily was using an electric sander. She held on tight as the shuddering apparatus skidded over the board planks kicking up the cedar scent long dormant in the wood, which pleased her. At that moment, she began to feel less anxious about the wedding. If the preparations brought about such a residual benefit, perhaps Betsy would be all right in her choice and her decision. Lily switched off her screeching sander and bent and placed her nose against a friction-heated and fragrant board. Louis, who had been standing behind her for several minutes waiting for the noise to abate, stepped forward.

"Louis," Lily exclaimed. "Louis is here," she called to someone.

Ginger's Uncle Harvey stood up from behind what appeared to be a battered old piano centered on a square of tarp placed in a shadowy apse of the barn.

"Well, Louis," Harvey said, setting down a polishing cloth and a can of paste wax. "Just the man I want to see."

"Ginger," Lily spoke up, not without alarm. "Ginger is having a fitting for her wedding-day dress. She isn't here."

"And Betsy?" Louis asked.

"Betsy? Betsy was going to be here. And I suppose you'll be wanting to meet Andy. But they aren't here. You're early, aren't you?" Lily said.

"Yes."

"Because I was planning to give you all lunch, you and Ginger and Betsy and Andy, out on the terrace," Lily said. She had made a tuna salad. She had washed a lettuce. She had hidden strawberries beneath an overturned colander so with luck no one had found and eaten them. She had asked Harvey's advice on wine, not for something that went with tuna salad and strawberries, but for a wine that had placating qualities; she required a wine of well-being. She understood that certain vintages had high opinions of their good effects upon the persons who consumed them. Harvey had recommended not a particular label but had counseled providing a copious amount.

"You can still feed the troops, Lily," Harvey said. "But first, since you're here early and at loose ends, Louis, I want to pick your brain. Are you wearing shoes?" he asked.

Louis glanced down at his feet. "Yes?" he said.

"Because Lily and I had best take you out into the woods to see for yourself," Harvey said.

So Louis found himself trailing Lily and Harvey across the field and into the early-summer woods. He was not averse to stretching his legs after his day spent in the air and on the road. And, he supposed, as he kept pace behind the swiftly moving old people, avoiding the slaps of overgrowing branches and squelching along the edge of a Lost World swamp of slime and leaping life, he would have been rather disappointed had the family eccentricity not manifested itself. The Hills, and née Hills, could behave quite plausibly, even graciously, to outsiders, and he had not been certain whether he would be met again as a stranger or a friend. This easy abduction of himself and the forced march seemed an endorsement.

The bugs were fierce. Filmy flies sipped from his tearing eyes. Mosquitoes drilled for his life's blood. His back twitched with crawling sensations—sweat, he assured himself as he swiped his forehead. The old ones were spry, however, and they had grabbed protective mesh hoods from a hook before starting out. (They had looked, not very sincerely, for a spare hood for Louis.) Harvey trotted and Lily tramped stoutly as they squabbled back and forth—something about angles and offers. Louis could not hear them well. He had fallen behind on the barely discernible path they were following which put him in mind of a sinister sketch across the landscape laid down by smugglers or partisan guerrillas preparing for a final assault upon a provincial capital.

"Louis?"

He heard his name called and he battered through a last thicket of tightly branched little fir trees which impeded his passage as determinedly as reporters at a society arraignment (in Louis's real-life experience).

"We've lost Louis," Harvey was saying, not without a smack of satisfaction at having outpaced the younger but heavier man. "No, no, no, here he is, he's come the wrong way round."

"He's been badly scratched," Lily remarked worriedly. She was thinking of some formal picture sittings Ginger had scheduled. Ginger would mind if Louis had to be turned this way and that to find a presentable side, particularly if that side did not align with the perfect pose of herself Ginger had discovered in the front hall mirror and around which she meant to organize the wedding party when the time came to sort themselves out before the camera.

"I'm all right, Miss Lily," Louis assured her, mistaking the reason for her concern. "Some astringent pitch has settled in the wounds," he said, indicating his cheek. "Probably an old Indian cure, pitch in a wound," he hazarded, looking toward Harvey as if for confirmation. Harvey harrumphed in protest. Who was Louis calling an old Indian?

Then Lily and Harvey rolled up their mesh hoods and took off their eyeglasses and rubbed the lenses unimprovingly with untucked corners of their shirttails, all the while expectantly regarding Louis who returned their diminished gazes and attempted to divine what they required of him.

"Well?" demanded Harvey. "And what do you make of *this*?" he wanted to know. He swept his eyeglasses panoramically as if even they had to have a look.

"Oh, is someone building up here on the ridge?" Louis asked, noticing now that trees had been toppled and the forest floor gouged and scored by the tracks of an earthmover. "Nice spot for a house," Louis said. "I suspect if you cut down those tall hemlocks in the way you'd have a grand view back down to the village."

ALDEN AND BECKY RETURNED from their Czech lessons in Cambridge with an émigré and retired vocal coach who now taught the spoken word to select students who came recommended by sources who had also come recommended. They were learning how to order in restaurants and how to buy concert tickets and which seats to request and which to refuse with contempt at Smetana Hall. They made efforts to pronounce the names of everyday household objects—chair, door, lamp, book, fireplace poker, piano bench, metronome. Madame Um (the effort to pronounce her name had ended) assured them that most of the up-and-coming Czechs they would encounter would speak English, and the old ones gargled on in German (Alden said) but it was well taken when foreigners made an attempt. It occurred to Alden and Becky that Madame Um, ensconced in her Bohemian lair on Craigie Circle, failed to understand—the Czechs were going to be the foreigners in Czecho-slovakia in the days to come when even the most monoglot of Ameri-cans would know themselves to be at home in almost any corner of the world, and welcome to it.

They had come upon the younger boys hopping and mincing their way barefoot up the driveway. They had been swimming in the river. They carried wrung-out T-shirts which they snapped at one another. Their hair snaked across their faces in skinny queues.

"Louis is here?" Alden asked them, tossing his not very dogeared Czech grammar down upon the piecrust table and indicating the suit-cases set at the foot of the stairway.

"*We* don't know," Brooks said.

"Carry your Uncle Louis's bags up to, up to where? Where should they put Louis's bags?" Alden asked Becky.

"I have no idea," Becky said, "and we ought not to interfere. Let Louis and Ginger work out where he's going to sleep. Boys, put the bags down. Leave them. Yes, I know Dad said to help but some help isn't helping."

Brooks and Rollins dropped the bags and stalked off. They were heard laughing excessively behind the little-parlor door.

LATER, LOUIS QUIETLY CARRIED his own suitcases up to Ginger's room, which she had gone so far as to tidy. She had piled her reference books in a neat pillar in one corner and collected manuscript pages in a cardboard box and undraped beads and scarves from the mirror and gathered all the wine bottles and glasses and cake plates and apple cores and sandwich crusts from her mantel. She had folded almost all of her clothes away in the bureau and hung them up in the closet. She had left a drawer empty and three wooden hangers clear for Louis. There were the last of the peonies in a vase on the mantel. She had changed the sheets and found a foam rubber pillow in the blanket chest—down and feathers provided insufficient support for Louis's large, thoughtful head. She had even vacuumed. She had clogged Lily's Hoover with dust clumps and paper clips and cotton puffs. She had nearly lost her temper and Lily had come upon her muttering and ramming a curtain rod up the hose. Lily had shown Ginger how to reverse the vacuum's motor and aim the hose out an open window to shoot the blockage material into the air—which soared most satisfyingly like a shot across the bows.

"I think the main culprit was one of Alden's socks," Ginger had said. "I can see it there snagged on a lilac."

That first evening, Ginger and Louis drove off to dine alone at Hannah's where Little Becky waited on them even though the best table in the quiet niche beside the beehive oven wasn't her usual station. She brought them extra bread in their basket, and herb butter. She explained the evening's specials very thoroughly. She fetched Hannah herself whenever their wineglasses needed to be refilled. She drizzled generous citrus sauce on their scallops ceviche. She lingered and told Uncle Louis how nice Andy Happening was, and how nice Aunt Lily was, and how cousin Arthur was going to be on television, in a comedy show. Phoebe was nice too. It was too bad Uncle Louis hadn't been able to come to visit when Phoebe and Arthur were still living at the house. And did Uncle Louis want to know who else was nice? Well, Mrs. Nicholls was turning out to be pretty nice too.

Then Hannah called Little Becky into the kitchen to scoop tea-flavored sorbet onto minted shortbread disks, but Little Becky had watched when the swinging door swung open into the dining room, and she got to see Uncle Louis giving Aunt Ginger diamond earrings in a box. Ginger had put them on and gauged the effect in Uncle Louis's eyes and then taken them off and put them back in the box. Maybe she was saving them for the wedding, so everyone should act big surprised when Aunt Ginger showed up wearing her huge new diamond earrings, that was Little Becky's advice. Yes, Aunt Ginger had liked her new earrings so much she had cried, good crying, not like the other kind, Little Becky said.

Louis and Betsy drove off to lunch at Hannah's the following day.

Little Becky wasn't scheduled to work, so no impressionistic account of glimpses and snatches of their attitudes and conversation was available, not that anyone imagined there would be fireworks or waterworks. Father and daughter shared a balanced temperament. Louis's mien was judicious and Betsy, having observed parent and parent from her cradle onward had long ago chosen equanimity as her own measure too, which was a large part of Ginger's problem, in Alden's opinion. With his sister's born talent for harrowing and faction, her little family in its grey unrufflability must have retreated to its dovecote below the shadowfall of her circling hawk all those years they lived together on the brink of the featureless prairie where the doves held every advantage. They could always see a hawk coming from a very long way off.

"Daddy still says all right to my marrying you even after he's met you," Betsy told Andy after her return. She had brought home half of her wild mushroom duxelle en croute with sauce béarnaise wrapped in a twist of tinfoil. She had found Andy outside reposing on a terrace chaise longue reading *Hawaii,* which he'd unambitiously extracted from Lily's bookshelves. He had sampled a page or two, then closed his eyes and reflected, not uncomplacently, how well arranged this wedding business was. All that was required of the groom was to stand by availably, or even just to lie about with a book, enough at hand to allow the various women called in to assist with the preparations to be able to get a good look at him. Why, he's quite handsome, the women had whispered at Betsy, as if that were important or, even, true. Perhaps it did matter, because Betsy was so beautiful and he was not yet powerful or wealthy, so that left only his looks to justify her decision. The women, Andy told himself, didn't want to send a rising star player to a minor league team.

"Daddy still says?" Andy opened his eyes and smiled at Betsy. The sun lifted a halo from her golden hair and a marvelous butterfly had alighted upon her shoulder and was flexing its meticulously drawn and colored-in wings. Betsy was a Disney Botticelli, Andy decided. Yes, she was going to be perfect in California where he had just landed a teaching post.

"And what if Daddy still hadn't said all right even after he'd met me?" Andy asked, dropping his book and accepting the foil-wrapped packet and a coin silver spoon with a deep, round bowl. He had not had lunch. He had rather counted on Betsy's appetite being unequal to her portion.

"Well," Betsy considered. She sat on the edge of his chaise and swiped a lock of hair from his brow (he was under orders from Ginger to have a haircut forty-eight hours before the ceremony so he would be at his best), "I would never have selected someone who wouldn't be all right so it was perfectly safe to let Daddy have his say. Isn't that mushroom thing delicious? We're having them at the reception in finger size with dipping sauce instead of a sauced sauce."

And later that afternoon, Louis and Andy returned to Hannah's for a drink. The three stools along the short length of the old barnboard bar top were taken up by two tourist couples—the less prosperous husband who wore the lesser wristwatch and was not the one driving the Lexus stood and reached between the wives, who were obviously sisters, to pick up and put down his glass. The visitors enthused over the local stone walls which they seemed to believe were a naturally occurring phenomenon. The barman, who knew Louis by now and who was going to tend bar at the reception, suggested Louis and Andy retreat to the garden where they could talk in quiet. Andy wondered how the barman knew Louis intended to talk to him although he himself did not doubt he was about to receive a major talking-to. Perhaps their relative bearings had suggested as much, even to the chattering tourists whose eyes followed Louis's and Andy's slow retreat through the side door and down the scented geranium-edged path to the private, tended corner.

As it was, Louis listened rather more than he spoke. Andy had been shaken into fluency. But when Louis did have his say, whatever he had had to say had resonated with Andy. As Harvey observed, drinks with Louis had sobered young Andy. Alden revealed that Andy had subsequently come to him and asked for advice on long-range financial planning. He sought a name on the West Coast to consult as soon as he and Betsy were settled. Alden recommended an old school friend, Dexter, his name was.

"And Ginger vacuumed her bedroom," Becky said. "I am beginning to look upon Louis as a White Knight."

"Louis?" asked Harvey. "Don't think you'd find armor to fit him."

"I don't know. Louis might as well be wearing a suit of armor a foot thick," Alden said, thinking of Ginger. "Or he's got a rhinoceros hide for skin."

"Oh no. Louis is tremendously sensitive. He must be a man of great understanding," Becky said. "And just because he's a tad overweight doesn't mean he can't be very deep and full of sincere feelings for Ginger despite everything, and, and be very romantic and unrealistic about her, for that matter."

"Can't see it myself," Harvey said. "Of course," he nodded politely to Becky who had become very pale and was striking matches off a matchbook embossed with a July date and the entwining initials A and B, as she set alight dandelion clocks—they were having this conversation as they stood about on the lawn—"of course," Harvey said, "I'm not a gal so I never know why all you gals consent to take us fellows on." He winked at Alden who was wondering why Becky so vehemently defended the sensibilities of fat men. Alden patted his own stomach to see whether he had put on weight that Becky had noticed and he had not.

Presently, as well, Louis asked Lily if she would mind if he found a team to paint the house trim and put the shutters back up before the wedding day. Yes, Lily agreed, the house would show up shabbily in the wedding photos if immediate steps weren't taken—and Harvey seemed to have forgotten that he had come home to Towne with the declared intention of painting the shutters. For the house could look rather fine when in good repair, and Lily showed Louis how well the house had taken a picture in past wedding photos, a stack of old photo albums having been dug out from under the far eaves as the family had become testily reminiscent recalling (and comparing and contrasting) past celebrations. Hadn't the outfit that Olive had worn when Harvey married Amy made her look like a hunchback gargoyle? At any rate, Olive had always turned to Paris for inspiration so she could be said to have succeeded in her long-ago ambition on that long-ago day.

Louis sat upon the big-parlor sofa, albums splayed across his lap. He turned over leaves and remarked how the shrubbery had grown. The photos had been mounted on pages of black, semi-corrugated paper that gouged off in particles beneath his fingernails no matter how careful he tried to be. Ginger, Ginger, Ginger, Lily quietly pointed out his wife at every age, always, for the camera, smiling.

Well, Louis had continued, after a pause, if Lily didn't mind he had already hired the painters. The Rector of All Saints', whom Louis had made a point of meeting and speaking to, had recommended a family of hardworking Cambodians the local church community was sponsoring. There would be seven Samrins coming over from Lawrence in the morning. They wouldn't need transportation. They had recently bought their own truck, but if Lily could provide the drop cloths and the rags, that would be appreciated. The Rev. Penworthy had indicated the Samrins could not be persuaded to convert even their most ragged clothing into rags.

"And Penworthy warned me, don't touch any of them on the head," Louis said. "Their heads are sacred to them, apparently, but aside from that we should just be natural."

"We'd better tell Harvey," Lily supposed. "If he's really pleased with the job they're doing he might try to pet one."

SO THE PAINTING GOT under way at once and the Hills awoke to the mingled chirrups of birdsong and Khmer outside their bedroom windows as the Samrins began work at six-thirty. They worked so long and so hard that Lily had to slow them down with cold drinks and molasses cookies carried out to the terrace during the heat of the day. She motioned them down off ladders, she insisted they finish all the molasses cookies. And as Becky packed boxes bound for Czechoslovakia and crates destined for a storage facility off Rte. 128 that Penny Nicholls had recommended, she set aside shirts and jackets and a set of Corian cookware and a not too wobbly floor lamp and a stack of old Golden Books for the little ones, which the Samrins were happy to receive and not embarrassed as Becky had hoped they would not be. Harvey said Samrin was a good old Cambodian name and he learned the family had been manufacturers of bicycle parts with a factory outside Phnom Penh. He offered all the broken bicycles in the barn to Mr. Samrin, Sr., who said he could get them in good working order again and sell them. He said he would split the profits fifty-fifty with Mr. Hill. He and Harvey shook hands on the deal.

The Samrins, for their part, were touched by the closeness and the unity of the extended Hill clan, who seemed to survive by farming—they possessed a few fruit trees and a vegetable patch and a field of grain which was, at the moment, being harvested. After a technician came and tuned and toned an old piano being stored in the barn, the Samrins speculated that the Hills supplemented their smallholding with a sideline in festival entertainment as Harvey and Penny practiced scales and chords and sang show tunes out in the open air. It was evident, as well, that the Hills were preparing for a feast day. The young girls were being fitted for traditional costumes. The older women assembled dishes and draperies and flowers. Gift offerings, more of which arrived daily, were being displayed on a long table in the principal room of the large dwelling as a measure of the regard in which the family was held.

And, evidently, the oldest son was about to be conscripted into the American military. An officer wearing crisp summer khakis met with the young man and his parents in an attic sitting room (as Hun Samrin scraped and caulked an attic window ledge during the course of the interview). The captain spoke at length, the son uttered syllables of assent, the father asked stern questions, the mother daubed her eyes with a white handkerchief, but in the end, papers were fanned across a desktop and signed. Mrs. Lowe endured a consoling embrace from the American captain. Feelings were high and not uncomplicated. The father chucked the son's shoulder and he shook hands with the captain. Later, a date of departure was circled on the heavily marked July calendar page thumbtacked to the back of a kitchen door. Someone highlighted the designated day with a flourish of red and blue stars. The same hand had drawn bells and ribbons around the square of another notable day to come.

"MUNG SAMRIN CAN WEAR all of Great-Aunt Sarah's lovely old calfskin pumps, they have the same tiny feet," Ginger told Louis. "And Mung fits Aunt Sarah's tiny karakul coat and her tiny karakul hat which perches like a beanie on my head, but it falls down over Mung's little ears so she'll be warm next winter. Last winter she only had a raincoat to wear. Those poor people, imagine, having to flee your home by the dark of the moon with nothing but the clothes on your back and a bundle in your hands. I could weep for them, I could honestly weep."

Louis did not remind Ginger that she too had fled her home with only an impulsively and incompletely packed suitcase. The events did not compare. Nevertheless, he cast an anxious eye. Had the parallel occurred to Ginger? But no, she lay quietly, unconcernedly beside him. He was reminded of something else as well.

"Miss Lily's tax assessment problem," he mentioned. "I've looked into it."

"Oh good," Ginger said. "I know Lily's been so worried but she hasn't wanted to press you about it."

"I'm going to advise her to retain an attorney. She needs someone from Massachusetts. It's involved, there's a lot going on there," Louis said.

"But Lily doesn't believe in lawyers," Ginger said.

Louis did not remind Ginger that attorneys were not chimeras to be believed in or not. At present, however, he would not risk any disagreement with Ginger. Even a disagreement by proxy, challenging Lily's quaint prejudice, would be as unwise as exposing an invalid to an open window.

"Because you see, darling, Lily is not asking you as a lawyer. She is asking you as someone she knows who knows about the law," Ginger explained.

They were lying side by side on Ginger's pillow-heaped bed. Ginger sat semi-upright. She was folding starch-stiffened napkins into decorative shapes following the instructions in the *Bride's Magazine* propped against her knee and opened to the article on setting a Magical Memorable Table to Marvel At. She had made the fan shape. She was attempting the swan shape. Louis, who had brought work from Kansas, set aside a folder of papers which slithered off the slippery pink coverlet and scattered its contents across the rug. Such a soft mattress, so many piled pillows. He tried to raise himself on his elbow and subsided up to his chin among silky sheets and softly spun summerweight blankets.

"Does this look like a swan to you?" Ginger asked. She held up the napkin, narrowed at both ends and puffed and pulled in the middle.

"Yes," Louis said.

"It does, doesn't it? The wing-y part is cleverly done, but I think I prefer the fan. Which do you think you prefer?" Ginger asked.

"The fan."

"But don't you like the swan? Doesn't it look like a swan? Aren't swans bridal? Wagnerian and bridal?"

"Yes."

"But you prefer the fan?"

"I prefer the fan."

"So do I," said Ginger. "They're simpler to make and anyway, I can just picture the family mistaking the swans for ducks and then the reception will degenerate into an ornithological discussion. They'll drag out the Roger Tory Peterson and poor Betsy will be ceremoniously cutting the cake and they'll all be bent over the waterfowl chapter. No, I'll make fans. They can't mistake a fan."

"Then we agree," Louis said.

"Yes we do, don't we, we do agree," Ginger said. "I'm so glad we agree." She regarded him, rather sharply, but Louis had received her assertion calmly. He rolled onto his side and groped over the edge of the bed, scrabbling for his scattered papers. He reordered them on the mound of his stomach and began to read, instantly immersed in a drone of words and figures. Ginger resisted her great desire to prod him with a pointed fingertip to demonstrate (to whom?, to the invisible watching presence perched on her shoulder?) that Louis was insensible to feelings, insensible to her. But the watching presence did not goad her now into confrontation with Louis. Rather, it counseled acceptance of Louis and the way he was.

Ginger shook out the swan shape and attempted a second fan which was not as successful as the first because the starch had been folded from the fabric when she creased and molded the swan. Recognizing this, Ginger did not lose her temper. She cast aside the crumpled napkin and ruffled through her *Bride's Magazine* to the pictorial essay on Mother of the Bride Beauty Makeovers where she discovered there was nothing to instruct her and much to deplore, which cheered her.

"Whose footsteps do I hear?" Ginger asked, because Betsy and Andy had gone out for the afternoon and evening—a picnic on the beach, a walk on the moonlit beach—and she was listening for their return so she could see for herself whether Andy had reported for his haircut. Armande, the Towne Barber, never made appointments, customers just caught him when his pole was spinning, but Ginger had made him write down Andy's name and a time on a business card which she conveyed to Andy. Then all of this out-of-the-blue romp-on-the-beach business had arisen so Ginger's arrangements were threatened.

"Betsy?" Ginger called. "Andy?"

The footsteps faltered, then resumed. Ancient floorboards creaked, beneath the lightest and most reluctant of treads.

"Come here, I want a word," Ginger ordered.

Lily did not like being summoned in this way. She was relieved, of course, that Ginger's life's upsets seemed to be righting themselves, nevertheless, Lily should think such a last-minute rescue (Ginger had always required saving from herself) ought to have made Ginger humble, not high-handed. And Louis had come on like a mandarin for the past week, conferring his blessings over expensive dinners and arranging to have her house painted behind her back and now the paint was flying on so fast she was sure it wouldn't stick. Perhaps the two, Ginger and Louis, could only suit one another after all.

Lily shoved her bottle of Mylanta and her spoon into her quilted summer bathrobe's deep pocket and she unlatched Ginger's bedroom door. Nor did Lily particularly wish to visit, so late at night, a bedroom where, as she tried not to imagine, a marital reconciliation had been taking place. But Kings and Queens of old had received guests in their bedchambers. Ginger may have been proceeding along those lines, for they would all be served up the fruits of Ginger's past months of reading and research for years to come and, Lily recalled, Ginger had spoken admiringly of what she had learned about court etiquette.

Ginger was sitting austerely and judgmentally against her headboard. She had swept her pillows to the floor. Louis was sunk among blankets and more pillows but he heaved himself upright with a great effort (a lower back problem there, Lily diagnosed, caused by the weight he carried and exacerbated by Ginger's marshmallow mattress).

"Lily!" Ginger said. "I thought you were, never mind, I want to talk to you too, or at any rate, Louis does. Louis, tell her, tell Lily what—

well, you haven't told me either, tell us both what you think. There won't be time after tomorrow. Andy's family is descending on us tomorrow."

Which made sense to hear Louis out now, so Lily sat on a straight-backed chair just inside the door.

"If it were up to me," Louis began, "which it isn't, I've told Ginger you have to retain a more local attorney, but were I working on your behalf, I would challenge the reassessment on the grounds that the new road joining Sir Galahad Lane to your property is not yet paved. There are no utilities brought in and planning permission has not been applied for. I checked. And I happen to know there were perk tests on the adjoining land to yours and they didn't pass and they, whoever they are behind TowneVest, are praying for a dry summer so they can test again and possibly squeak by. But *your* land perked."

"How do you know that?" Lily asked.

"Because the Samrins were hired last fall to dig the holes and haul the buckets of water up to the test sites and they were told to keep the whole matter under their hats. I was discussing American idioms with old Mr. Samrin and he asked about that particular expression." Louis looked pleased with himself. "We were chatting in French."

"Isn't Louis brilliant?" Ginger marveled. "Louis, you're brilliant," she marveled again.

"And I suddenly found myself becoming very interested in what Samrin had to say. He doesn't know who hired them for the work, but Penworthy set up the job."

"In all innocence," Lily supposed. "Harvey ought to hear this too. He was just down in the kitchen peeling himself an orange. Harvey?" she called. "Come here. Bring your orange with you."

Harvey was brought up to speed as he sat at the end of the bed propped against the footboard eating sliced and sugared orange rounds from a bowl. He thoughtfully flicked seeds back into the bowl as he listened.

"Tell me," Ginger said, "wasn't Louis brilliant to discover all that. You can't keep anything from Louis," she enthused, as Louis thought but did not say that Ginger had not always been so pleased with his talent for finding things out.

"Good man," Harvey agreed. "So, you think Lily's new assessment was, at the very least, precipitous. Obviously it was an effort to force Lily to sell. Old maiden lady, not very sharp, scared into a panic, on a fixed income, running around waving her hands in the air, carrying on, moaning and groaning woe is me, woe is me. Because the land those pirates have already bought has proved worthless to them. Lily is the ultimate target."

"All right, Louis," Lily said. "I'll consult my lawyer."

"Is he here in Towne?" Louis asked. "Because I think I'd go out of town for this because you can't know who's in whose pocket."

"Oh, intrigue," exclaimed Ginger.

"Alden knows a lawyer," Lily said. "There's someone clever in Boston, isn't there, Ginger? Didn't you once . . ."

"I can't recall," Ginger said levelly. "You'll have to ask Alden."

"But eventually, if TowneVest is determined, they'll make the improvements and you probably will be liable for that assessment. In which case, if I were you, I'd look to see if you could get away with selling just one building lot to block further encroachment along the new road," Louis said. "You'll gain yourself a little nest egg. You can take a trip or buy a new car or remodel the bathroom and install a new water heater. You'd have to be sure of your buyer though. You'd have to know they weren't going to turn around and resell to TowneVest. And you'll have to look at the plot plans and anticipate every way TowneVest can get at you with an access road and gerrymander the lot you sell to guard against that."

"You see, Louis has thought of everything," Ginger said warmly. "Why don't *we* buy the land, Louis? *We* could build a getaway weekend cottage. Betsy and Andy would adore it too."

"But we're in Wichita and they'll be in Santa Barbara," Louis pointed out. "Weekends would be impractical."

"No, I'll build the house," Harvey spoke up. "Been meaning to set myself up some other place around about. Can't sponge on Lily forever. Too many stairs here, anyway. And I won't even wait for their road. I'll turn my back on their road. I'll plant a hedge between me and their road. Lily, what's that thorny fast-growing hedge with the deep red berries that squash flat and in tandem with the thorn scratches indelibly tattoo interlopers with proof positive of their trespass? I'll get some of those, and I'll knock my own driveway off of Lily's driveway and we'll visit back and forth through the woods on golf carts. I'll buy us a couple of golf carts, you can have one of your own, Lily. You'll have to deed me a right-of-way."

"Yes, I could do that," Lily allowed.

"And I have to confess up front that I won't be living there alone. Penny will be there too, I'm planning to marry her," Harvey said. "I've always found it better to marry than to . . ."

"Does Penny know about this?" Ginger cried. "Because *I* didn't know. Have you even asked her?"

"No, not yet, so don't you go mentioning it. I want to tell her first. I want to see the expression on her face when she finds out. In fact, what time is it? Maybe I'll go see her now." He tilted his bowl and drank off the sweetened orange juice, sieving discarded seeds between his teeth.

"No, Harvey," Ginger said. "You can't show up out of the blue at this hour. She'll have curlers in her hair and night creme on her face, not expressions of joy or shock or stunned disbelief. Won't she, Lily?"

Privately, Lily didn't think Penny would be cocooned in nightly restoratives. Penny wore a short crop haircut and her skin was ridged and rutted beneath the bright makeup she always had slapped on down to her chin but no further. Even Lily had noticed the contrast with the pale skin on Penny's neck. But perhaps Penny intended to signal that she was still making an effort.

"And you certainly can't go driving excitedly around Towne in just your pajamas and robe and slippers, Harvey," Ginger said. "You'll wind up in the *Crier*'s Police Notes column. No, do as I say, Harvey. Take Penny out to Hannah's tomorrow night and give her a beautiful ring. I don't care how old she is, she'll want a diamond, won't she, Louis?"

But Louis was drafting a few notes for his River Road/TowneVest file, for it was clear to him that he was going to end up maintaining a file on Miss Lily and her future activities.

"ARE WE REALLY GOING to go through with this wedding?" Betsy asked Andy.

"Yes. I've been counting the days until," Andy said, "and I'm counting on all the days after."

They were almost alone on the long sweep of ocean beach. The sun had quietly disappeared several hours past, not picturesquely flaring, then dropping, doused, into the water as occurred off the edge of California where the sunsets were arranged better, Andy said. Betsy, whose point of reference would always be centered in Kansas, did not particularly root for either coast, but Andy was already an advocate of the western one.

They sat beneath a blanket and dug their feet into the warmish sand and shared a last bottle of warmish wine cooler. Betsy shrugged the scratchy plaid stadium blanket from her shoulders where a sunburn was just newly akindle. Andy had warned her the sun was even stronger in California. Betsy guessed she would have to be more careful there. She would wear a hat and sunglasses and white cotton mitts and scarves and wraps and only emerge into the out-of-doors covered like a High Islam lady in Arabia, she supposed. And indeed, she regarded her safe and fond marriage to come as purdah of a sort. Assured of love, she would not be distracted by the search or by the other searchers. This afternoon, lying next to Andy on their shared blanket, she had observed some classmates—or classmates until their graduation a few weeks before— at serious play on the sand, having noisy fun of a sort chasing one another and allowing, or not, a soft-landing tackle and capture. I am well out of that, Betsy thought.

"One might even say California is essentially an emerging nation," Andy said. He spoke toward what he hoped were not Betsy's second thoughts. He had, he wished to remind her, offered her his entire world and she had wholeheartedly accepted.

"Maybe we'll see Arthur and Phoebe sometime, and some of their new friends," Betsy said. "Just think who their new friends might be."

"I imagine we'll be hobnobbing," Andy agreed.

Betsy tilted forward and rummaged inside her beach satchel for a tube of aloe lotion. Her fingers bumped the clamshell she had found lying half in, half out of the water, half buried in the sand. The lower part of a shell, bleached and washed brilliantly white, a full four inches across, had caught her eye as it lay imperfectly concealed. She had plans for the shell. She was going to paint, in pale watercolors, Andy's name and her own and the day's date inside the shell, along with blue double u's for waves and the silvery grey V of a faraway gull wheeling out of view, and then she would keep the shell forever, set down upon successive bureau tops in succeeding houses (they were going to do very well for themselves, Andy promised) to hold her hairpins and elastics and found buttons and the rings tugged from her fingers before she worked in her garden or kneaded sticky bread dough.

First, though, her immediate aim was to race through her B.A. in two-and-a-half years and then charge straight into law school (she could do all of that at the university where Andy was going to teach), and she was not certain when the gardening and baking would fit into her schedule for the next five years or so. But she had been exposed daily to issues of bridal magazines left bristling with annotated markers upon the foot of her bed all of which contained an article or two detailing how one was supposed to set about housekeeping, and she had just been given an electric pizzelle maker by Andy's mother's Bridge Club so she was not surprised these conventional and homely ideals floated to the surface of her thoughts.

"My mother and that lot are coming tomorrow," Andy mentioned. "If it's not tomorrow already. It feels like tomorrow."

Of course, Betsy was thinking of nothing but the future. She moved through the present days as one who had already been through them. Even her sunburn, even as it flashed hot, discoloring and marking her knees, her nose, her ears, was just the sunburn she had had on her wedding day, the one that had made her so pink and freckled and peeling for the wedding pictures, the sunburn that had caused her mother, in her last act as the mother of an unmarried daughter still at home, to cry out and carry on because Betsy had sat out in the sun too long solely to sabotage the work of the sensitive and expensive photographer whom Ginger had convinced to consent to practice his art at their modest affair. Betsy scarcely felt the burn and when the tube of aloe failed to come immediately to hand, she gave up searching among her paperback and Andy's thick book, her flip-flops, Andy's car keys, Andy's wallet, their crumpled wax-paper sandwich wrappers. She swaddled, instead, the clamshell in smoothed-out wax paper for safer keeping, for she meant the painted and shellacked shell to contain for all time her resolve and her reasons and her hopes of the day.

"I hope your mother likes me," Betsy said. "Not to excess or anything. I don't expect that, but enough so we can talk on the phone without creepiness until you pick up the extension."

"That's not unreasonable," Andy said. He would recommend this standard to his mother, as well. He would represent it as his own idea, and he would mention the desired avoidance of awkwardness between his mother and his wife.

"We'll screen calls anyway," Betsy said. "They'll all expect us to be out in the good weather and all. Because I'm going to predict my mother will be calling us a lot."

LOUIS AND ANDY DROVE the rental van in to Logan to meet Lee Happening and the members of her party, her sister Antonia, and Antonia's daughter Pet, and Pet's husband Patrick. Mrs. Happening embraced Andy, then released and peered at him intently for he had squirmed like an impostor within her arms. She dispatched him to retrieve her two large new Ventura tapestry-patterned suitcases, readily identifiable by the black ribbon rosettes knotted to their handles. Pet sent Patrick after him. Mrs. Happening sought and leaned upon her sister's tensed and offered arm, and the pair made their way toward a sliding exit door and the fully described and easily spotted and illegally parked van for which Antonia, who seemed less wan than her sister, had been handed the only key. As the sisters walked slowly away, Mrs. Happening's ankles crossed as if she were balanced on ill-fitting ice skates, and Louis wondered if the woman drank. He resolved, then, never to trust her alone with the someday grandchildren. He and Ginger would have to trump any proposed Florida winter school vacation with a far more dazzling Caribbean one, which would make waves in the extended family, of course, but somehow Louis didn't forecast clear sailing in the Lee Happening zone even though they had not yet even been adequately introduced. Each had only more or less deduced who the other must be among all the others milling on the crowded airport concourse. Their wary looks might be said to have met first. But it further occurred to

Louis that he and Ginger might very well wrest enjoyment of a sort from their dealings with Lee over the years to come, those same years which lately had yawned rather darkly before him, however assuredly, however single-mindedly, his reclamation of Ginger and the resumption of their lives together had seemed to have been accomplished. The annual necessity of devising ever more dazzling getaways with the eventual grandchildren, Ginger would rise to that, concocting great fun for the little ones and thinking up great fun against Lee Happening.

Louis had reserved all of the rooms at the Olde Towne Academy Bed and Breakfast Inn to accommodate the out-of-town guests. Andy only pointed to the complicated roofline of Lily's house just rising above the summer-lush treetops as they drove on past along the River Road. The Samrins were making a final push to complete the exterior painting and a professional cleaning crew was at work inside scrubbing and polishing their way from room to room. Gee had shown up in a borrowed bulldozer to commence busting a road through to Harvey and Penny's building site, for Harvey and Penny (who had been asked and who had said yes) were that keen to get cracking on their project. They were forgoing the fussy formalities of land surveys and plot plans and blueprints. The Pilgrim Fathers hadn't waited for a Planning Committee to pronounce permission granted, Harvey said, and where would the Pilgrim Fathers have been had *they* waited for a planning committee to pronounce, he wanted to know.

"Cohasset?" suggested Ginger, which everyone knew was a much better address than Plymouth.

Lily had spoken up above the swell of contending family voices and the chatter of Samrins from window to window and the hums and thumps of the cleaners and the growl of the laboring dozer as Louis and Andy were leaving for the airport. She had advised waiting for a calmer moment for the Hills and the Happenings to come face to face lest Andy's family receive an impression. She did not characterize the impression they would receive as being the wrong one. She only hoped to schedule an optimum time for the encounter, in the foyer of All Saints', perhaps, as they were all being hushed and hurried along by the ushers who had just been given the high sign from the altar.

"But give your mother our best regards," Lily called over her shoulder as she set off across the field to ask Gee if he was sure he knew what he was supposed to be doing.

"Ma'll understand," Andy assured Lily, and of course, as the van took the curves of the River Road and drove on through a field of young corn which was just beginning to look like corn, Mrs. Happening could not help but feel farmed out.

"I THOUGHT THAT went well, considering," Alden said to Lily as they drove from the church ahead of the lingering pack, back to the house where there was nothing much left to be done but in Lily's experience, arrangements had a way of becoming undone. The tables, set with cloths and crockery and flowers out in the orchard, could be tipped over by a nosing-about deer. Hannah, who was cooking on site, might short a fuse when she plugged her powerful and professional crepe maker into the overloaded kitchen outlet and start a smoldering fire down in the corner of the cellar where empty and half-empty paint cans had been stacked out of sight until the next Toxic Disposal Day at the dump. The house itself might be wreathed with flames at that very moment, although the fire whistle hadn't blared during the service. Lily had been listening with only one ear tuned to the familiar prayers and music and promises.

"One wedding ceremony down," Alden expanded, "and sixty years of wedded bliss to go. Perhaps they're being wise to give themselves so much time together."

"So far so good," Lily agreed.

Alden glanced at Lily. She had bought a new navy-blue suit for the wedding which Becky said actually looked rather smart on her, and Lily had even consented to have the hem raised two inches which had made all the difference. Lily's new hat, a pale blue swan's-down Queen Motherly toque, floated serenely on her head. Her gloves presented immaculately white even though she'd indulged herself in some weeding of the churchyard's shade garden while waiting for Betsy and Louis to arrive. Lily had steadied herself with a hand placed on the bronze Jesus' jutting hip and energetically pulled long strands of bindweed out from among the hostas growing round his plinth as she remarked to Lee Happening that had it been up to her Jesus wouldn't be standing around up to his knees in greenery. Jesus had wandered through the desert and Lily had suggested at the time that cactus be planted instead but she had been overruled. Lee, who liked to think she was a gardener and who liked to think she knew her Bible, had seemed to like Lily. Alden decided he felt confident he and Becky could leave for Czechoslovakia with easy consciences. Lily seemed equal to the task of looking after herself when she was on her own again. Perhaps the past year had served as a sort of rest cure for her as the family shouldered her various burdens and now she was ready to take them up again on her own.

"I was going to shut Agnes in my bedroom so she wouldn't leap onto the cake," Lily said. "I hope she hasn't leaped onto the cake."

For somebody had to think of everything while the rest of the family bumped from the windowpanes to the walls like moths whose eyes were turned to brighter lights. That very morning, Lily had been obliged to drive down to the Do-Nut Hole to fetch Danish pastries and blueberry muffins for breakfast. They had all bounded down to the kitchen in their bathrobes, having just showered or while waiting for the shower to fall free, expecting on that day of all days for an extra effort to have been made. Glover said he'd like a mushroom omelette and hash browns and Harvey told him he'd have to wait until he was in the Army to be pampered like that. Little Becky had only wanted an apple. She needed to lose a final pound before ten o'clock to achieve her ideal bridesmaid weight goal which she had written in red grease pencil on the side of the refrigerator above her Aunt Ginger's scale.

"Is that Andy's car by the side of the road?" Alden asked, slowing. "Is that them standing above the river?"

"Yes," said Lily. "But drive on, let them be." They obviously wanted to be on their own. They seemed to be throwing stem after stem pulled from Betsy's bouquet into the water. Ginger was going to mind when she found out about that.

"I thought they were in a big hurry to get home for their party," Alden said.

For after the ceremony, Betsy and Andy had flown down the aisle,

Betsy's veil buoyant and aswirl and catching Andy's back and wrapping them together in a departing blur. The organ blurted. Ginevra Platt-Willey's beautiful voice began to sing. Mr. Penworthy stood startled at the altar rail. He had planned to speak a few parting words of his own after the Blessing. He was fond of this young couple.

Professor Janacek, Andy's best man, who had driven down from Maine *(Vacationland)* for the day, had taken up the chase. Jennica and Alexianna Snowdon, the overdressed and overwhelmed flower girls, circlets of Queen of Denmark roses slipping over their eyes, trotted after him. He had scooped them up and carried them, and Little Becky, laughing with relief because she hadn't dropped Betsy's bouquet or stepped on her hem, raced to catch up with the rest of the wedding party. Alden and Lily slipped out the side door as the congregation sat quietly on listening to Ginevra, the Hill side smiling and nodding at the Happening side now that they were all vaguely related. The Happening side rustled through their strange hymnals to satisfy themselves just how many more verses of "The voice that breathed o'er Eden" there were to go, which was a song they had always heard of but never heard sung.

"And now we know why," Pat whispered to Pet.

"THERE IS NO POINT in organizing a reception line. We might as well attempt to herd cats," Ginger said to Louis.

"They all seem to be enjoying themselves in their own ways," Louis said tolerantly. They linked arms. Ginger's cartwheel hat silkily brushed his cheek.

The wedding guests had scattered—across the terrace, the lawns, the upper field—and Harvey and Penny were leading a happy band into the woods to admire the future home of the future Mr. and Mrs. Harvey Hill. Among the band were several intrigued Kansans; some of Harvey's very amused grandchildren; Louis's brother, who looked like Louis; Mr. and, surprisingly, Mrs. Snowdon, not heretofore recognized as being very much of a walker; and the Rev. Penworthy who liked Nature and who was thinking up a sermon based upon the Evening

Prayer Psalter for the Fifth Sunday after Trinity, "The earth is the Lord's and all that therein is." He twisted his ankle in a root hole.

Green gingham cloth-covered tables were placed between the rows of low-boughed apple trees and distributed around a white fluted column bearing an enormous arrangement of twelve dozen white roses and white stock and lady's mantle and trailing ivy. Hannah's servers moved among the tables carrying trays. Six rose-and-ivy-entwined arbors described a grassy circle meant to contain further ceremony—the cake cutting, the bouquet flinging, the last speech Louis had been assigned to deliver from his heart—if, indeed, Betsy and Andy could be located at the critical moment. They had pelted off after the expedition slogging up to the building site, although at least Ginger didn't have to fret that mud and brambles would ruin Betsy's dress. Betsy had won the dress argument which had flickered until the previous afternoon when the seamstress whom Ginger had kept standing by declared that time was up for even the most basic of alterations to be made to any other dress.

"We ought not just to stand here," Ginger said, steering Louis away from the long board bar set up inside the barn door where Hannah's barman was arranging bottles. "People will think we're keeping an eye on."

"Well, I am keeping an eye on but only to make sure that everyone gets what they want," Louis said.

They strolled down to thank Brooks and Rollins who had been parking cars on the lower lawn and who lingered by the cars as if to make certain they stayed parked. The boys wore navy-blue blazers, pink shirts, red ties, khaki trousers, and loafers, which was how they had once dressed every day for school and which reassumed and respectable appearance, they realized, would provide better cover when, after Louis and Ginger stopped checking up on them, they took off in Louis's brother's Jaguar, driven all the way from Chicago and about to be driven by Brooks and Rollins just as far as the River Road bridge and possibly around and about the rolling corners of the Camelot Estates subdivision and maybe on down to the village, where they entertained hopes of being observed by the local weird kids as they wheeled past the weird kids' Towne Common hangout on the beaten-down grass between the Civil War cannon and the bandstand, hooting and tooting for several crowning circuits.

"We really ought to seek out Lee Happening and be lovely to her," Ginger said.

"I believe I noticed Becky being lovely to her in the herb garden," Louis said.

"Then we can be lovely later."

"LAVENDER, HYSSOP, ASSORTED BASILS, mint, rosemary in the clay pots, garlic, sweet marjoram, rose geranium, lemon geranium, cinnamon geranium; that's all pennyroyal, which as you can see, spreads."

Becky and Lee Happening and Antonia moved among spikes and clumps and masses of leafage and flowerings, making their ways over flat stones set down in the ground without particular reference to the human tread. Becky indicated and named the plants she knew. Antonia crouched and pinched and sniffed and Lee stood in a patch of sunheated southernwood which wanted to make her sneeze. Her teeth sawed back and forth and her hands flapped off-fendingly.

The sisters had engineered this stroll with Becky, for Andy had told them it was Becky with whom William had seemed to have enjoyed a deep and old and unusual friendship.

They had a rapport, Andy had said. You'd almost think there was something between them, he'd added, if you didn't know better, because, bottom line, Becky's a saint although not in an odious way. She's completely unaware she's a saint.

Lee and Antonia had resolved to have a close chat with this inspirational and informational person, although talking over the events of the day later that evening, gratefully lounging back at the Olde Towne Academy Inn, they dismissed Andy's absurd attraction theory; foolish Andy was seeing stars everywhere.

For they had known right away that Becky was simply a very nice woman. They had taken to Becky as they had not taken to Betsy's breezy and unpenitent mother who had finally called on them at the inn the previous evening and promptly purchased the Mission-style reading lamp on Pet and Pat's bedroom night table (many of Academy House's antiques were discreetly for sale at prices that looked as if they were being quoted in lire on small folded-over cards tucked inside the drawers of highboys and between the fretwork of folding screens), leaving poor Pat, who was a forensic psychiatrist, unable to review a pressing case file.

"Shallots, calendula, thyme, God bless you. I have a hankie here, somewhere, up my sleeve," Becky said.

"Oh no, it's far too pretty. Well, thank you," Lee said.

Then, speaking at once, Lee and Antonia began to describe to Becky the William they had known, who was nothing at all like the William he had become. They projected and soul-searched and wept a little, sharing the hankie between them. They apologized on William's behalf for all the trouble and heartache and inconvenience he had caused. They wished to apologize to the world, but the excellent Becky seemed the next best thing.

Becky played with a sprig of lemon geranium and murmured soothingly indistinct syllables. Her instinct, when William's half-sisters (as they had identified themselves to her) approached her so purposefully, had been to retreat to Lily's herbs to avail them all of the plants' palliative, curative, and even Lethean qualities. She held a wand of lavender toward the sisters and felt an utter fraud, but safely so. She would credit William with this—if he had known which official secrets to spill, he had also known which private ones to keep.

She let Lee and Antonia say all that they had to say twice over, for in Becky's experience, emotional people needed to state and then to restate their troubles, and then she reminded them, "But if not for William, Betsy and Andy would never have met."

"Well, there is that," Lee supposed she was obliged to concede.

"Andy's earthly happiness assured," Antonia added rather wildly, "and yet William can't even know. We can't tell him. We have no idea where he is."

"We worry so," said Lee. "If we only knew."

"Perhaps it's better not to know," suggested Becky. For what good was it for them to know about William's view of the Khalij Surt through the louvered windows of his honey-colored villa and of his daily drive to the Souk for the English papers which came a week late, and of how he dreamed only of the day when Becky would join him? His servants, necessarily cautious of strangers, had been taught her image should William be out when she came to him at last. William had been writing Becky long, petitioning letters, sent to her through an intermediary.

"If we were only sure he's at least all right," Lee said. "If he's even alive."

"Oh yes, he's alive all right or our phones wouldn't still be tapped," Antónia said. "Of course our phones are tapped. Don't you hear those hollow pop pop pops every time when you first pick up?"

"I think that's Alden waving at me from the field," Becky said. "I'd better go see what he wants now."

"NOT WAVING BUT swatting," Alden explained to Professor Janacek. The upper field was alive with filmy green flies.

"Ah," said Professor Janacek, who did not catch the reference, although Ginevra Platt-Willey had laughed and Ginger, of course, and Mrs. Penworthy, and Pet and Pat, and Lana Arnetti from the Y, as well. It occurred to Alden that he was going to miss being surrounded by congenial people who caught his meanings. He doubted his remarks would ever be appreciated in Czech. Madame Um had struck him on the head with a scrolled libretto (*Prodana Nevesta*) as they took their last leave of her.

Alden hoped they weren't all such sticklers in Prague, but he didn't mind this Janacek fellow, who had driven down from Maine in his seersucker suit with a tall red-headed young American girlfriend beside him in the front seat. She wore her resort wear—a halter top, sarong skirt, and a floppy straw hat—to the wedding, but she was so good-looking no one noticed, or if they noticed, they only felt themselves to be frumps. As Becky had pointed out, everyone else was dressed as if Talbots had exploded.

Janacek was a well of information about Prague, or at least, the Prague he had known and had left in 1968. He scrawled names and addresses in the margins of his wedding leaflet as he cited people whom Alden and Becky would come to love, of shops they would soon adore, of cafés and bakeries and hidden squares and the very corners where the bounteous and brutal history of his native land had happened. He spoke of museums and architecture and the quality of the light in the late afternoons as one stood upon the Charles Bridge and dreamed of better days to come.

"Or as is the case now, you can stand there and hum a few bars of 'Happy Days Are Here Again'," said Alden.

"You will love my country," promised the Professor who, after all, as the sponsor of Andy's thesis knew he was in a strong position to make authoritative statements about Hill partialities and private assumptions about Hill susceptibilities.

He asked Alden, then, if he would mind delivering a Sony Trinitron VCR to his elderly aunt who lived in Mariánské Lázně, a charming destination in its own right—there was a spa, walking, golf—which Alden and his family would enjoy. The Professor had brought the VCR with him in the trunk of his car, still sealed in its box. It was to be an eightieth-birthday present for his aunt, an unmarried lady, a former schoolteacher and the heart of the scattered Janacek clan. She spoke better English than the English and she would be enchanted to have the Lowes stay with her indefinitely, the Professor enthused. And since Alden would be staying a while in Mariánské Lázně, would Alden mind picking up a few regional delicacies to send back to America? Janacek produced a list. He yearned for a very specific flavor of fruit syrup, for a certain cough pastille, and shaving soap, tinned traditional biscuits, a bottle of the very fountain-pen ink with which he had written his first, youthful tract. Janacek handed Alden a check, as well, drawn on his bank in Prague where certain funds languished, useless to him in the West and hostage to Byzantine and restrictive regulations which, it was his hope, Alden would be in a position to sort out and do away with in his soon to be assumed position as the savior of the Czech banking and investment system.

Alden said he'd see what he could do and he intercepted Becky beside the privet hedge. He attempted to pass the list and the check on to her.

"Oh, Alden," she said. "It's easy enough to tell a person no. You just have to be firm."

She walked up to the Professor to inquire whether the outlet plugs in his native land were standard or variable, and did he recommend any particular universal adapter, which she would really rather purchase in the States because, well, frankly, because she did not doubt they would be much more reliable.

GEORGE AND CALLIOPE, taking the afternoon off from the Casa di Napoli, had brought their baby in a soft woven basket with carrying handles. They set the basket down beneath the shade of the big maple and arranged lawn chairs in a drift around the sleeping child. The baby was a good baby, everyone said. It awoke and smiled and raised its stellate hands to the faces that peered over the side of the basket. Nearly everyone came for a look at the nearly new baby. The young Snowdons and the young Penworthys loitered and teased to play Mothers and Husbands and House with the real baby—the youngest Penworthy had grown too big to heft and lug and shut in a salvaged Produit de Bordeaux box—until Lily sent them off to the barn to fetch the old badminton set. She said they had better play with that, instead, out in the just-mown field.

Glover wanted to talk to George, who had been in the service. His company colors hung behind the cash register at the Casa di Napoli. George had enjoyed his stint, and he enjoyed talking to Glover whom he advised, if he wished to advance in the Army, never to hesitate to display his initiative while being ever mindful not to step out of line.

Glover considered George's words. He applied them to his just recently acquired apprehension that time could take its *time* unwinding the tangled messages he received and failed, frustratingly, to understand at the very moment. Glover guessed George's advice would make good and eventual sense when he was in uniform and under orders. In the past, Glover had resisted, he had resented, being told what he didn't already know, and he recognized now the great flaw inherent in that construction. Soon, he would be called upon to take apart and put together again an M-16 with his eyes blindfolded. Captain Raven had cited this as an instance of what Glover could expect during his first weeks at Basic, and Glover meant to pay attention when that demonstration was going on lest he slide the firing clip on backwards and shoot himself in the eye on his very first go at target practice. Yes, he could see for himself that he had no idea.

"Hey baby, listen to your parents," Glover told the sleeping child who awoke and blew a froth of sour, milky bubbles.

"Oh, you," said Calliope, swiping away the froth with a cloth.

They discussed the situation in Kuwait, guessing what would happen and what ought to happen until Ginevra approached, carrying a bottle of wine and four goblets held elegantly upside down, her fingers laced around their stems. She announced she did not believe in war but Glover told her today's Army was an Army of Peacekeepers. Ginevra declared she would write to Glover at his Army address to make sure he kept his word.

"All right," Glover allowed. He wrote the particulars on the slip of paper supplied by Calliope with George's automatic pencil.

Ginevra sat back in an Adirondack chair and lifted her wineglass toward a beam of sun—the wine and all that had only been accessories. She was going to be attending Berklee in the fall and then she was going to connect with a roistering bar band and become a righteous girl singer, at least for a while. She thought what a pity it was that Glover would be leaving Towne in just three days. He was such a challenge. She wished, at once, to save him and to serve him, such an unexpected warrior. She wondered why Missy De Stefano hadn't been invited to the wedding because she'd run into Missy at the Freedomway Mall and Missy had been bragging about the dress she'd bought for the big day.

Glover, who was racing George to the bottom of the bottle Ginevra had brought, reflected how lucky it was he wasn't due at Camp until Tuesday afternoon now that he knew Ginevra so well.

"Write even when I don't write back," he told her.

"Should I let him get away with that?" Ginevra asked Calliope.

"Yes," said Calliope. "His letters won't be all so interesting anyway, but you will be amazed at what you have to say for yourself."

GINGER HAD TO FABRICATE a dinner gong. Hannah's helpers had said, We're ready, but the guests and the wedding party had all vanished into the Childe Hassam summer landscape—oh, they had drawn a perfect day.

Ginger had been certain there was a household dinner gong. Her mind's ear echoed with the mellow summonings of years' past. But Lily, hunted down and quizzed as to the dinner gong's whereabouts, impatiently told her no, one summer there had just been a child's xylophone struck with the three signature notes of the NBC peacock call until the joke wore thin. Lily was short with Ginger, for she had been interrupted in the middle of negotiations with Hannah who, impressed by Lily's green thumb and extensive gardens and sunny prospects, had asked her if she would consider supplying her restaurant with some very specific herbs and produce which Hannah required. Hannah would provide seeds from Provence and Hunan province and Oaxaca state which Lily could plant in the quantities Hannah needed. And indeed, Lily might wish to sell any surplus by the side of the road, down at the end of her driveway, Hannah suggested. Yes, Lily said, perhaps she might. Perhaps she would speak to Harvey's contractor about building a little stand in the clearing beside the mailbox. She wondered what she would dare to charge for a bunch of tarragon.

Ginger found a sheet of tin left over from an old attempt to mend the gutters and she selected the black croquet mallet from the croquet cart. She directed Louis to hold the sheet of tin loosely and away from himself and she two-handedly swung the mallet. Her silky sleeves fluttered and flew with effort. She was happily unaware she had caught a smudge of green shutter paint on one pale sleeve.

"Herding cats would be easier," she complained. "I'd just call them to their saucers by whirring the electric can opener." But it was Louis's belief that Ginger was energized and not enraged by her grievance.

"There. At last, I'm getting their attention," Ginger declared, entirely satisfied.

Professor Janacek's beautiful girlfriend, who was a Theater Arts major, turned her porcelain figurine head toward the peals and booms and rumbles Ginger was raising and she spoke, " 'If by your art, my dearest father, you have put the wild waters in this roar, allay them,' " and she was prepared to go on but the Professor hushed her, for now was not the time to resurrect her Miranda although, certainly, they had both basked in her triumph in the part.

And the expedition of discovery was now trailing back from the inspection of the building site, its members scrawled upon by barbed branches, welted and bloodied by bug bites. Ripped stockings clung to mud-smeared legs. Pants legs were stained and ringed to the level of misstep in the swamp, hats were wilted and damaged, neckties tossed loose round collars. Several Kansans had picked lolling and expiring bunches of Lily's lady's slippers as they really ought not to have done, but everyone chattered excitedly at once about Harvey and Penny's wonderful house-to-be which was going to have windows for walls and one central and enormous bedroom should they decide to become invalids someday and vacuum-sealed drawers and cupboards in the kitchen so their cornflakes and saltines would not go soft during the worst of the August weather. Harvey and Penny were thinking of everything.

"Daddy?" The young Penworthys, who were losing badly at badminton to the young Snowdons, flung their rackets at the Snowdons' leaping-about knees and swarmed their father, which marked the correct reception of the hero of the expedition. For the Reverend had been able to recall without consulting his daybook who had hired the Samrins to dig holes and carry water along Lily's ridge last fall: Royall Beswick, the Towne Assessor himself. Penny had whooped and demonstrated at the news. First thing Monday morning, she vowed, she was going to initiate the next American Revolution down at the Towne Town Hall. Harvey had to prevent Penny from hieing off back to Senior Village to thrash out a press release and to begin to paint protest signs at the common room's community easel.

"Ginger's organized some sort of la-di-dah bean feed and she'll come whacking at us with that mallet if we don't tie on the feedsack," he said. "Anyway, that cooker gal from the place we like's dishing it out."

"BETSY AND ANDY are leaving."

"So soon?"

"Look at them, so young."

"She's so terribly young."

"Is that her going-away outfit? Boxer shorts and that faded sunflower T-shirt. Andy looks nice, though, very serious."

"Well, she's so young."

"How I wish his father could have been . . . I even wish William . . ."

"They're hoping to make it to Stockbridge by dark."

"Whose car is that?"

"Oh, Louis bought them . . . he took one look at the VW."

"Stockbridge? I assume they're staying at the Red Lion? They'll enjoy that. We always do."

"But what's the name of that wonderful inn in Lenox?"

"They're not going to Lenox, they're going to Stockbridge."

"Is that the new bigger Civic?"

"Why does it matter if they get to Stockbridge after dark?"

"I suspect that's just their excuse."

"You want to do something tonight, Ginevra?"

"All right, Glover."

"Okay."

"And then Betsy and Andy are driving across country to California. They're going to stop at Williamsburg, New Orleans, the Grand Canyon, Mt. Rushmore, and Yosemite."

"The Grand Canyon!"

"Can't picture their route. Sounds roundabout. Hey kids, are you certain about your route? I say, hey kids, did you ask Triple A about a Trip-Tik?"

"Damn, we forgot to spray 'Just Married' across their back window. And who was in charge of collecting old shoes?"

"Betsy swore us not to."

"Where's your brother? If he's stowed away in their trunk . . ."

"I'm here, Dad. I didn't."

"Well, don't."

"There's no room in their trunk. It's all stuffed with stuff."

"They do have a lot of stuff."

"They're driving to California to live, you know."

"Come on, Ginevra. This is all over here."

"No wait, I want to see."

"Wave. Wave good-bye to Betsy and her husband. Yes, I know you'll miss Betsy. I'm going to miss Betsy too. I don't know what I'll do without my Betsy," Mrs. Snowdon said to the young Snowdons.

Betsy and Andy nearly forgot to acknowledge the farewells, so intent were they upon unfolding a road map with a mind to remembering the trick of refolding it neatly between referrals, but Little Becky, in her last act as bridesmaid, approached their idling car to prompt the pair.

"You guys," she said, and indicated with a stern sweep of her eyes toward the well-wishers assembled at the top of the driveway and ranged across the lawns.

The wedding guests had parted around the figure of Ginger, maintaining a respectful buffer against any final manifestation of high feelings on her part. Even Louis had withdrawn from his station by her elbow, electing to watch carefully the left rear tire of the new Civic which looked a little low to him. But Ginger remained remarkably calm as her only daughter and—Ginger would have to get used to calling him—her son-in-law prepared to drive away, to drive straight on through to their futures, to drive all the way to the end of the known map where they would discover that their new continent stretched on for a hundred million more uncharted miles beyond. If Betsy and Andy believed their crisply stowed map was going to guide them past all the wrong turns and missed exits and deeply regretted bypasses, they were very much mistaken. A small smile crimped Ginger's lips and a farseeing haze softened her eyes. Becky, who knew someone really ought to stand in support of Ginger at this critical moment, accepted that it must fall to her to do the decent thing, and she moved to Ginger's side.

"Everything went splendidly," Becky declared in her most positive voice.

"Do you think so?" murmured Ginger.

For Ginger was reviewing the day's small disasters—that outrageous dash down the aisle, Betsy's lost bouquet for which Ginger had searched everywhere, the septuagenarian couple's usurpation of the young couple's thunder. Half the champagne toasts had been raised to Harvey and Penny and their ridiculous house. And then Betsy had failed to put on the proper traveling costume Ginger had lovingly, as a last act, laid out upon her bed, the sky-blue linen suit and a lace camisole blouse which now would never be worn unless Little Becky could possibly wriggle into them if she stuck to her diet. Ginger was also convinced that every official photograph would depict a blur, a back, a blank. Betsy and Andy had been too distracted to pose. The expensive artist-photographer had complained of them.

But Ginger was not convinced there wouldn't be another occasion, someday, the one which she would then regard as the real wedding. She had learned a great deal from this initial outing which could be put to good use for the next one. She would insist upon being given more time to plan, and of course she would be back on her own turf, in Kansas, at home, and she would know exactly whom to call.

Ginger stood, removed from the gathering, thinking her own thoughts. She glanced at the unreservedly happy faces of all the others as Lily moved from guest to guest shedding feathers from her hat and hugging a ten-pound bag of Northeast Songbird Mixture to her chest and bidding everyone to scoop up handsful of flax and millet and sunflower seeds to throw after Betsy and Andy. What a grand idea, they were all saying, far better to throw seed than to toss rice or confetti or stones, for one of the Happening side claimed to have been to a wedding where colored aquarium pebbles had been cast at the newlyweds. ("What were they, adulterers?" Alden asked Louis and then wished he hadn't.) Becky reached down into the sack of seed and only perfunctorily discharged her portion as Ginger palmed and flicked away a small amount which fell upon her open-toed Joan and David mother-of-the-very-young-bride shoes.

Something about the quality of Becky's farewell wave struck Ginger as well. Becky's upraised hand moved deliberately up and down in a vaguely window-washing motion as if she too were trying to see her way clear and beyond a clouded pane to a happy enough ending for the just-married couple, and perhaps for all the married couples.

"They haven't a clue what they're in for," Ginger suddenly confided to Becky.

"No, they don't," Becky agreed wholeheartedly. Ginger braced for Becky's further conventional comment of cozy sympathy and easy optimism, but Becky, instead, plucked at her sleeve for the hankie which was not to be found there. Ginger offered her own which she had not needed, and she stopped thinking about herself and Louis, she stopped thinking about Betsy and Andy, and she wondered, finally and for the first time, about Becky and Alden. She and Becky might have been better friends that past year, she realized. They might have helped one another. They might have trusted one another. They might have talked. But all that might-have-been would remain unresolved in the past. Everything was, so surprisingly, turning out for the best all around and Ginger no longer needed to run the risk of attempting such an alliance.

LILY PASSED THROUGH the front hall, cleared at last of the boxes and crates around which she had for the past few weeks been obliged to pick her way, banging her better hip against sharp corners and, once, becoming turned around entirely in the dark on her way to the kitchen late at night when she was sure she had left the oven on, for she had awakened and smelled a mist of electricity. The little parlor had been completely cut off for several days by a tower of trunks. They had all had to scramble over the little-parlor windowsill the night Arthur's television show was aired—a sneak summer preview, his network announced in the spirit, it seemed, of their unusual means of ingress to watch Arthur's carryings-on. They were quite fascinated by his performance. They had not been entirely certain what it was Arthur did—what talent, in fact, he possessed and for which he was being paid ten thousand dollars per episode as Harvey had made it his business to find out. They all wondered where it could have come from, Arthur's flair, for he had made them laugh. He was quite the best feature of *Barry's World!*, even though Arthur only received fourth billing. They all wondered if the more famous Barry minded being left in the dust by Arthur's brilliant star quality. The family had sat on in the little parlor after the closing credits rolled, recalling past examples of Hill theatricality and wit, remembering a cousin who could dance on her toes, an aunt who could be persuaded to recite "Annabel Lee," and Alden demonstrated a gift for mimicry. He could do the time Uncle Harvey had instructed the boys on how to kill mosquitoes. Which had not been the worst way to pass one of their final evenings together, Lily decided, pleasantly enough.

Just yesterday, the last of the parcels had been called for and carted off by the international movers who, after all, had turned out to be Americans hired by the State Department and not louche, cheroot-puffing, vase-shattering Frenchmen as Lily had feared they might be. She had had her Larousse dictionary standing by, splayed open to all the words for Careful. Soon, the Lowes' Calphalon pots and pans and their angle-poise reading lamps and twelve-packs of Scott tissue would be crossing the choppy Atlantic. Just as the Empire desk and the Windsor chairs and the gilt rosewood mirror Ginger had always loved and which Lily had said might as well be hers now, had been carried off a week before by another band of movers and were rolling west in the back of a fast pantechnicon van, on toward the prairie. The Sèvres service had flown back to Wichita on Ginger's lap. She had even been allowed to hold on to the box during takeoff and landing after the flight attendant had been shown just what the box held.

The people were gone as well. They had departed in fits and starts, in mishaps of fogbound flights and broken landing gears that held them up, or down, hindered by spuming radiators and traffic jams on the interstate, panicked by eleventh-hour losses of tickets and passports and vital addresses written on lost scraps of paper in disappearing ink. Glover had been forgotten entirely by the Army van bound for Basic Training. He had sat on his suitcase by the side of the River Road for an hour and a half, brushing away green flies and the offers of rides at least as far as the village, for word had gotten round that one of the Lowe boys was off to join the Army, although just how the Army planned to keep itself and its soldiers occupied in this brave new world of peace and concord, opinion was divided. At last, it made sense for Glover to drive himself down to New Jersey in the family Volvo which, other-wise, was just going to be left sitting at the top of Lily's driveway.

Even Harvey and Penny had taken off on a tour of their children's summer places. A strike at the cement mixers' local was holding up work on the foundation of their house and rather than fret beside the excava-tion hole as it filled with cinquefoil and maple sprouts, they visited Osterville, Squam Lake, and Vinalhaven. They wanted everyone to get to know one another before the projected autumn, or autumnish, wed-ding date, and familiarization came about rather quickly in close summer quarters over the succession of cloudy late-summer days they seemed to have brought with them.

"We were having a beautiful summer until you came," several daughters-in-law spoke before they thought, and Penny whooped and Harvey hark-harked as the daughters-in-law tripped over their tongues attempting to restate their welcomes. Penny and Harvey were not comfortable old people, nor had they ever been congenial middle-aged people, and from what their children could surmise, they were just as glad they hadn't had to deal with their parents in their youths.

Now, Lily wandered out to the terrace where she had her choice among the collection of chaise longues which were not set down as randomly as first appeared across the terrace stones. The chairs had been pulled by their last occupants into or out of a shadow or the sun, away from or closer to an ongoing conversation according to a preference. Nevertheless, the effect of such a tangle of chairs was that of the aftermath of a smashup, as if the terrace had run hard against the rocks. Lily's chosen chaise, the one she could manage to get out of once she had gotten into it, placed her feet in the midday sun and left her head well within the shade cast by the kitchen ell, and she also commanded a clear view down the driveway as far as the jog it took to skirt the swamp, for she had found she still could not not keep a wary eye trained upon that avenue of approach. She hoped quiet time on her own would restore her capacity to sit and to be unable to say precisely what she had been contemplating if challenged to do so. She hoped not to be challenged to do so.

But at the moment, Lily had letters to write, for the family had all very promptly written to her once they'd arrived in their new situations. Well, they were demonstrating their excellent Hill manners, even the boys, of whom she would not have guessed such a civilized streak. Perhaps Glover was under orders in the Army, and Brooks and Rollins at the Range School as well, to practice their penmanship. Lily settled back, positioning the writing board she had fetched from the invalid's supply cupboard. (For Ginger had returned the writing board at the last, and the thermometer and the eyecup and the icebag.) Lily fished the fat packet of correspondence from the pocket of her divided skirt—they all seemed to have had a great deal to say for themselves. They described strange new landscapes (Brooks, on his dormitory cubicle), and deep culture shocks (Betsy, in California), and odd items found on the dinner menu (Glover, on the enlisted men's mess), and how warm and welcoming the natives were (Ginger, back in Kansas), and how very much at home they felt (Becky, in Czechoslovakia). Becky and Alden and Little Becky had quickly become accustomed to castle life, once they had learned bowls of soup cooled to insipidity on the journey from the kitchen quarters to the banquet hall, so they switched to a covered tureen. They had found they could keep the wall tapestries from flapping in the interior breezes by weighting their hems with ancient shot borrowed from coffers in the armaments chamber.

Lily pulled a sheet of Durable Bond into place and she clicked down the point of her pen and she began to write.

She asked Becky if they had made sure that the ancient shot wasn't live lest it spark against ancient stone walls and detonate during a dinner party, for she guessed the local people would still be jumpy after their Revolution even though it had been such a civilized one. Lily told Ginger she had no idea whether there was a readership clamoring for a roman à clef about a town like Towne, for she, Lily, did not read current fiction because of the Language. Lily agreed with Betsy that California sounded a very odd place, but Betsy herself would be odd if she didn't think California was odd, so that was all right. Lily complimented Arthur on his recent television performance because it only seemed correct to acknowledge such a conspicuous event in a great-nephew's life; besides, it was a Hill tenet to say nothing at all if one had nothing nice to say, and therefore her silence could well be so construed by young Arthur. She wrote a brief note to Glover telling him to tuck into the shoebox of stacked and Saran-wrapped Congo Bars she had baked for him, and she wrote a second note to Brooks and Rollins to say she hoped they enjoyed the shoebox of stacked and Saran-wrapped Congo Bars she had baked for them with second thoughts in the event they discovered she had baked for their older brother and not for them, should, in this flurry of letter writing, Congo Bars ever be mentioned.

Lily addressed envelopes with the strange new addresses Ginger had copied in all their precise, fussing detail on 3 × 5 cards one very organized afternoon and left upon their bureau tops. Though the family would not, of course, keep up with all this keeping in touch. Lily's own letters to them also included an account of the resurfacing of the Salem Road with an application of hot tar and sand which had caused a traffic tie-up when the second shift of the furniture-polish factory let out and a woman driver had fainted from the mix of tar fumes and car fumes and the heavy banana-oil odor that was vented twice a day from the factory's air ducts, which news would probably not invite or inspire swift responses, for the stricken woman was no one they knew, although they would all have been interested and gratified had the victim, instead, been Babe Palmer. Still, this failure to engage her correspondents was not accomplished by design. Lily rather enjoyed receiving a letter among her usual bills and circulars. She certainly preferred a letter to a mistimed telephone call, for the family, when far away as they were all far away now, were not at all adept at calculating the difference in hours between their time zones and her own—even when earlier, holding and rotating apples plucked from the epergne, they attempted to work out which way it was the globe turned and whether they should add or subtract a three or a six or a twelve from the local time told on their wristwatch faces. Lily wondered why this was so. They ought to have had a clearer idea of where they stood, these people who were so convinced the world revolved around them. They had all been expensively educated. She had been shown the canceled checks.

But Harvey, who still had his wits about him regardless, had taken to calling Lily promptly every morning at nine-thirty for the past week he had been away to inquire after the status of the cementers' work stoppage. Lily, for her part, was under instructions to call the Local's Strike Update Hotline number Harvey had pinned to the kitchen message board. Every morning at nine, Lily listened to the latest recorded report on the status of negotiations, and then she was told a little-known fact from This Day in Labor History. Lily guessed the Communications Officer possessed a special-interest calendar. She planned to buy herself the Gardener's Year Illustrated calendar next January when Little Becky's paean to her last, most favorite pop group swaying on the back of the cellar door finally expired. Lily was looking forward to 1991.

Harvey had been chatty that morning. He and Penny were currently up at Squam Lake where the weather was grey and their mattresses were musty and he complained he had yet to see hide nor hair of one of the vaunted loons, for, apparently, some movie had been filmed at the lake featuring the loons. Lily didn't know. She wasn't a moviegoer because of the Language. She reminded Harvey he had never been much of a bird-watcher. Harvey agreed, he had never been a lawn ornament.

"But," Lily asked, "haven't you heard a loon? Hearing them is the point."

"No," Harvey said. "They're all Nichollses here. It's all cannonballs and Geronimo yells off the end of the dock."

"Oh," said Lily.

"And Bucky Nicholls came right out with it last night, no beating around the bush. He asked how Penny and I were, how'd he put it, how were we going to arrange our assets, and I could read on his face he was trying to figure out which of us, Penny or me, was going to be the longest laster. Because at that moment Penny was choking on a rancid cashew from a can she'd found under the boathouse. I'm setting the scene here. There was his old mother gasping and clutching her throat and Bucky suddenly wanted to know about her portfolio instead of getting her a glass of ice water."

"I'm sure you and Penny are being sensible," Lily said.

"Yes. We're telling both sides there will be no need to take sides," Harvey said.

"Well," said Lily. "Good. The funerals will be pleasant occasions then."

"Not that either of us is going anywhere soon," Harvey said sharply. "We've switched to Butter Buds and we've been walking a mile a day out to the main road to buy corn and tomatoes and a couple of cider doughnuts. So that's our plan; after we've built the house, we're not going anywhere except to Anguilla next February since we've paid a deposit down."

Lily had said she would have to look up Anguilla in the atlas.

She squared the short stack of envelopes she had addressed and slid them into the pocket of her divided skirt. She would run down to the P.O. later, and stop by Harris Desmaris's office on the off-chance he was in and wasn't too busy on a winding-down late-summer afternoon for a chat about her investments and her insurance and the state of Harvey's clear title to his building site and to mention some ideas about her will.

Not that she was about to go anywhere, either. Secretly, and therefore advantageously, Lily would vie with Harvey. She would walk two miles a day and not eat cider doughnuts while she was about it. Nevertheless, Lily could foresee a day in twenty years' time or so when she would finally wear out and die, after a week or two in bed, from nothing very specific but something very final. She might even linger for a month if she was waiting for the outcome of a particularly interesting court trial or if she was wrapped up in the imminent landing of the first Americans on Mars. She'd like to see that. She had questions about Mars—she was sure they had water there. But Harris had been after her for a long time about making out a will. He had told her horror tales of the mischief wrought by intestate individuals to which Lily had listened, properly deploring the inconvenience to the living even as she privately decided her real rooting interest lay with the recalcitrant dead, who had also probably not planned on going anywhere.

In the meanwhile, Lily had trusted that the right decision about the disposition of her earthly share would be arrived at in its own way and in its own time. How this was to come about, she did not know and would not speculate. She had told herself that she must just leave a "door" open and the solution would drift in like a dragonfly. For in Lily's experience, dragonflies so seldom ventured into a dwelling that the apparition of one surely would mean something.

And then that morning on the telephone with Harvey, she had at last seen her dragonfly. Harvey had been rattling on as usual about his various fads and affairs and Lily had nodded along as she gazed through the kitchen doorway into the shadowy and blessedly emptied front hall, liking the way the slant of the sun through the pier-glass windows squared off and apportioned bright passages of rug and the grained wood of floorboards, and refracted up the wall highlighting the spidering cracks in the original plaster, which in Lily's opinion appeared as elegantly etched as if by frost on a window pane. Her gaze had settled, then, upon the coatrack, which had regained its original spare outline. Her own white cotton summer sweater drooped from a peg next to the belled collar she had bought for Agnes and which Agnes did not care to wear. And left behind on another spindle was the straw hat Betsy had been wearing out in the sun. The hat had once belonged to Lily and Harvey's

Uncle Harvey but Betsy had made it her own by knotting a leaf-patterned scarf around the brim and sticking a cameo pin in the crown. Alongside the hat hung the jacket Little Becky had forgotten, at the very end, to pack, her shiny sateen jacket vividly appliquéd with the New Kids' 1988 World Tour logo across the back, and which she had taken to wearing turned inside out after she realized she no longer loved the New Kids quite so much as she used to. But the jacket's lining proved to be a pretty paisley print in its own right so that was all right. The hat and the jacket were waiting on the coatrack as if the girls were about to sweep into the hall and snatch their things and scatter outside into the garden, into the woods, down the driveway, away on an errand, off to see friends. That was when Lily knew.

In twenty years or so, the girls would be the right ages. Women in their thirties were energetic. They would climb high ladders and knock hornets' nests from the eaves. They would be keen to scrub the bathroom tiles and reorganize the linen cupboard. They would work out between them what to do about the house. Little Becky would be sentimental and Betsy very practical and the right choices would be made. Little Becky would always be eager to please and Betsy always reluctant to take advantage.

Alden and Becky would be touched for Little Becky's sake that she had been so favored, and Ginger would be furious at having been slighted herself, but she would carry on as if the house were somehow her own, and Betsy would let her, up to a point. Oh, Lily could see them all as they thronged round the driveway curve. She even saw the ones who did not yet exist, Little Becky's someday husband and their children, Betsy's yellow-haired daughter—and the boys' pleasant wives and attractive families, as well. The young cousins would play inexpert croquet outside on the lawn as the adults met in the big parlor to discuss serious matters, keeping their voices soft, forgetting Lily was no longer lying ill upstairs. And their voices would remain soft when they remembered Lily was no longer lying ill upstairs.

No, Lily did not doubt they would return, just as they had all gone away before, as time and time again she had stood on the terrace dressed in her best and waved and wished them well as they married well. She had said good-bye to her brother and her sister and her nephews and nieces as they flew from the house in their two by twos, striding hand in hand, side by side, two by two, as if issuing from the Ark itself.

And then the tale had been turned around. How like me to get things all backward, Lily thought as she lay half in the sun and half in the shade, too content to stir. Her pen dropped from her flexing fingers onto the terrace stones and rolled out of reach.

No, Lily reconsidered. How very like the family to skew events around into their usual muddles and dramas as they came rolling back home. They arrived alone now, or in numbers, shrugging off their coats, peeling off their boots, requiring a single freshly made-up bed or half a dozen beds in the attic, wanting to know, *Is my room just as I left it?* Saying, *Remember I was working on that thousand-piece puzzle, it was the* Birth of Venus. *I'd finished her feet and the clamshell and two of those tender Renaissance trees. You say it's been dismantled? By whom? You needed the dining room table? What time is supper then? What are we having for supper? Oh.*

Daily life on the Ark, however had the Noahs borne it, that yearlong drift in searching circles afloat above their ruined world as the lambs and goats and she-bears and tigers and workhorses and owls and swans and geese among them contended for the best cabin and a preeminent chair upon the deck, all the while scanning the lowering skies, bent against the gales, complaining of the rain, glossed by lightning snaps, watching the far horizon for the first hint of land, for the greening crest of the highest hilltop to appear which they recognized at once and reclaimed as their own. Then they packed up their bags and shrugged on their coats and uttered their thanks and were gone.